The Book of Life

ALSO BY DEBORAH HARKNESS

A Discovery of Witches

Shadow of Night

DEBORAH HARKNESS

The Book of Life

VIKING

VIKING

Published by the Penguin Group

Penguin Group (USA) LLC

375 Hudson Street

New York, New York 10014

USA | Canada | UK | Ireland | Australia | New Zealand | India | South Africa | China

penguin.com

A Penguin Random House Company

First published by Viking Penguin, a member of Penguin Group (USA) LLC, 2014

LIBRARY OF CONGRESS CATALOGING-IN-PUBLICATION DATA

Harkness, Deborah E.

The book of life : a novel / Deborah Harkness.

pages cm.—(All souls trilogy; 3)

ISBN 978-0-670-02559-6

Export edition ISBN 978-0-525-42722-3

1. Witches—Fiction. 2. Women historians—Fiction. 3. Vampires—Fiction. 4. Science and magic—Fiction. 5. Time travel—Fiction. I. Title.

PS3608.A7436B66 2014

813'.6—dc23   2014004495

Printed in the United States of America

5 7 9 10 8 6

Set in Adobe Garamond Pro

Designed by Francesca Belanger

For Karen, who knows why

It is not the strongest of the species that survives,

nor the most intelligent that survives. It is the one

that is most adaptable to change.

—PHILIPPE DE CLERMONT,
OFTEN ATTRIBUTED TO CHARLES DARWIN

Sol in Cancer

The signe of the Crabbe pertains to houses, lands,
treasures, and whatever is hidden. It is the fourth
house of the Zodiak. It signifies death and
the end of thinges.

—Anonymous English Commonplace Book, c. 1590,
Gonçalves MS 4890, f. 8^r

1

Ghosts didn't have much substance. All they were composed of was memories and heart. Atop one of Sept-Tours' round towers, Emily Mather pressed a diaphanous hand against the spot in the center of her chest that even now was heavy with dread.

Does it ever get easier? Her voice, like the rest of her, was almost imperceptible. *The watching? The waiting? The knowing?*

Not that I've noticed, Philippe de Clermont replied shortly. He was perched nearby, studying his own transparent fingers. Of all the things Philippe disliked about being dead—the inability to touch his wife, Ysabeau; his lack of smell or taste; the fact that he had no muscles for a good sparring match—invisibility topped the list. It was a constant reminder of how inconsequential he had become.

Emily's face fell, and Philippe silently cursed himself. Since she'd died, the witch had been his constant companion, cutting his loneliness in two. What was he thinking, barking at her as if she were a servant?

Perhaps it will be easier when they don't need us anymore, Philippe said in a gentler tone. He might be the more experienced ghost, but it was Emily who understood the metaphysics of their situation. What the witch had told him went against everything Philippe believed about the afterworld. He thought the living saw the dead *because* they needed something from them: assistance, forgiveness, retribution. Emily insisted these were nothing more than human myths, and it was only when the living moved on and let go that the dead could appear to them.

This information made Ysabeau's failure to notice him somewhat easier to bear, but not much.

"I can't wait to see Em's reaction. She's going to be so surprised." Diana's warm alto floated up to the battlements.

Diana and Matthew, Emily and Philippe said in unison, peering down to the cobbled courtyard that surrounded the château.

There, Philippe said, pointing at the drive. Even dead, he had vampire sight that was sharper than any human's. He was also still handsomer than any man had a right to be, with his broad shoulders and devilish grin. He turned the latter on Emily, who couldn't help grinning back. *They are a fine couple, are they not? Look how much my son has changed.*

Vampires weren't supposed to be altered by the passing of time, and therefore Emily expected to see the same black hair, so dark it glinted blue; the same mutable gray-green eyes, cool and remote as a winter sea; the same pale skin and wide mouth. There were a few subtle differences, though, as Philippe suggested. Matthew's hair was shorter, and he had a beard that made him look even more dangerous, like a pirate. She gasped.

Is Matthew . . . bigger?

He is. I fattened him up when he and Diana were here in 1590. Books were making him soft. Matthew needed to fight more and read less. Philippe had always contended there was such a thing as too much education. Matthew was living proof of it.

Diana looks different, too. More like her mother, with that long, coppery hair, Em said, acknowledging the most obvious change in her niece.

Diana stumbled on a cobblestone, and Matthew's hand shot out to steady her. Once, Emily had seen Matthew's incessant hovering as a sign of vampire overprotectiveness. Now, with the perspicacity of a ghost, she realized that this tendency stemmed from his preternatural awareness of every change in Diana's expression, every shift of mood, every sign of fatigue or hunger. Today, however, Matthew's concern seemed even more focused and acute.

It's not just Diana's hair that has changed. Philippe's face had a look of wonder. *Diana is with child—Matthew's child.*

Emily examined her niece more carefully, using the enhanced grasp of truth that death afforded. Philippe was right—in part. *You mean "with children." Diana is having twins.*

Twins, Philippe said in an awed voice. He looked away, distracted by the appearance of his wife. *Look, here are Ysabeau and Sarah with Sophie and Margaret.*

What will happen now, Philippe? Emily asked, her heart growing heavier with anticipation.

Endings. Beginnings, Philippe said with deliberate vagueness. *Change.*
Diana has never liked change, Emily said.
That is because Diana is afraid of what she must become, Philippe replied.

Marcus Whitmore had faced horrors aplenty since the night in 1781 when Matthew de Clermont made him a vampire. None had prepared him for today's ordeal: telling Diana Bishop that her beloved aunt, Emily Mather, was dead.

Marcus had received the phone call from Ysabeau while he and Nathaniel Wilson were watching the television news in the family library. Sophie, Nathaniel's wife, and their baby, Margaret, were dozing on a nearby sofa.

"The temple," Ysabeau had said breathlessly, her tone frantic. "Come. At once."

Marcus had obeyed his grandmother without question, only taking time to shout for his cousin, Gallowglass, and his Aunt Verin on his way out the door.

The summer half-light of evening had lightened further as he approached the clearing at the top of the mountain, brightened by the otherworldly power that Marcus glimpsed through the trees. His hair stood at attention at the magic in the air.

Then he scented the presence of a vampire, Gerbert of Aurillac. And someone else—a witch.

A light, purposeful step sounded down the stone corridor, drawing Marcus out of the past and back into the present. The heavy door opened, creaking as it always did.

"Hello, sweetheart." Marcus turned from the view of the Auvergne countryside and drew a deep breath. Phoebe Taylor's scent reminded him of the thicket of lilac bushes that had grown outside the red-painted door of his family's farm. Delicate and resolute, the fragrance had symbolized the hope of spring after a long Massachusetts winter and conjured up his long-dead mother's understanding smile. Now it only made Marcus think of the petite, iron-willed woman before him.

"Everything will be all right." Phoebe reached up and straightened his collar, her olive eyes full of concern. Marcus had taken to wearing more formal clothes than concert T-shirts around the same time he'd started to sign his letters Marcus de Clermont instead of Marcus Whitmore—the name she'd first known him by, before he had told her about vampires, fifteen-hundred-year-old fathers, French castles full of forbidding relatives, and a witch named Diana Bishop. It was, in Marcus's opinion, nothing short of miraculous that Phoebe had remained at his side.

"No. It won't." He caught one of her hands and planted a kiss on the palm. Phoebe didn't know Matthew. "Stay here with Nathaniel and the rest of them. Please."

"For the final time, Marcus Whitmore, I will be standing beside you when you greet your father and his wife. I don't believe we need discuss it further." Phoebe held out her hand. "Shall we?"

Marcus put his hand in Phoebe's, but instead of following her out the door as she expected, he tugged her toward him. Phoebe came to rest against his chest, one hand clasped in his and the other pressed to his heart. She looked at him with surprise.

"Very well. But if you come down with me, Phoebe, there are conditions. First, you are with me or with Ysabeau at all times."

Phoebe opened her mouth to protest, but Marcus's serious look silenced her.

"Second, if I tell you to leave the room, you will do so. No delay. No questions. Go straight to Fernando. He'll be in the chapel or the kitchen." Marcus searched her face and saw a wary acceptance. "Third, do not, under any circumstances, get within arm's reach of my father. Agreed?"

Phoebe nodded. Like any good diplomat, she was prepared to follow Marcus's rules—for now. But if Marcus's father was the monster some in the house seemed to think he was, Phoebe would do what she must.

Fernando Gonçalves poured beaten eggs into the hot skillet, blanketing the browned potatoes already in the pan. His tortilla española was one of the few dishes Sarah Bishop would eat, and today of all days the widow needed sustenance.

Gallowglass sat at the kitchen table, picking drops of wax out of a crack in the ancient boards. With his collar-length blond hair and muscular build, he looked like a morose bear. Tattoos snaked around his forearms and biceps in bright swirls of color. Their subject matter revealed whatever was on Gallowglass's mind at the moment, for a tattoo lasted only a few months on a vampire. Right now he seemed to be thinking about his roots, for his arms were covered with Celtic knotwork, runes, and fabulous beasts drawn from Norse and Gaelic myths and legends.

"Stop worrying." Fernando's voice was as warm and cultured as sherry aged in oak barrels.

Gallowglass looked up for a moment, then returned his attention to the wax.

"No one will prevent Matthew from doing what he must, Gallowglass. Avenging Emily's death is a matter of honor." Fernando turned off the heat and joined Gallowglass at the table, bare feet moving silently across the flagstone floors. As he walked, he rolled down the sleeves of his white shirt. It was pristine, in spite of the hours he'd spent in the kitchen that day. He tucked the shirt into the waistband of his jeans and ran his fingers through his dark, wavy hair.

"Marcus is going to try to take the blame, you know," Gallowglass said. "But Emily's death wasn't the boy's fault."

The scene on the mountain had been oddly peaceful, considering the circumstances. Gallowglass had arrived at the temple a few moments after Marcus. There had been nothing but silence and the sight of Emily Mather kneeling inside a circle marked out with pale rocks. The witch Peter Knox had been with her, his hands on her head and a look of anticipation—even hunger—on his face. Gerbert of Aurillac, the de Clermonts' nearest vampire neighbor, was looking on with interest.

"Emily!" Sarah's anguished cry had torn through the silence with such force that even Gerbert stepped back.

Startled, Knox released Emily. She crumpled to the ground, unconscious. Sarah beat the other witch back with a single, powerful spell that sent Knox flying across the clearing.

"No, Marcus didn't kill her," Fernando said, drawing Gallowglass's attention. "But his negligence—"

"Inexperience," Gallowglass interjected.

"Negligence," Fernando repeated, "did play a role in the tragedy. Marcus knows that and accepts responsibility for it."

"Marcus didn't ask to be in charge," Gallowglass grumbled.

"No. I nominated him for the position, and Matthew agreed it was the right decision." Fernando pressed Gallowglass's shoulder briefly and returned to the stove.

"Is that why you came? Because you felt guilty about refusing to lead the brotherhood when Matthew asked for your help?" No one had been more surprised than Gallowglass when Fernando turned up at Sept-Tours. Fernando had avoided the place ever since Gallowglass's father, Hugh de Clermont, died in the fourteenth century.

"I am here because Matthew was there for me after the French king executed Hugh. I was alone in all the world then, except for my grief." Fernando's tone was harsh. "And I refused to lead the Knights of Lazarus because I am not a de Clermont."

"You were Father's mate!" Gallowglass protested. "You are as much a de Clermont as Ysabeau or her children!"

Fernando carefully shut the oven door. "I *am* Hugh's mate," he said, his back still turned. "Your father will never be past tense to me."

"Sorry, Fernando," Gallowglass said, stricken. Though Hugh had been dead for nearly seven centuries, Fernando had never recovered from the loss. Gallowglass doubted he ever would.

"As for my being a de Clermont," Fernando continued, still staring at the wall over the stove, "Philippe disagreed."

Gallowglass resumed his nervous picking at the wax. Fernando poured two glasses of red wine and carried them to the table.

"Here," he said, thrusting one at Gallowglass. "You'll need your strength today, too."

Marthe bustled into the kitchen. Ysabeau's housekeeper ruled over this part of the château and was not pleased to see intruders in it. After giving Fernando and Gallowglass sour looks, she sniffed and wrested the oven door open.

"That is my best pan!" she said accusingly.

"I know. That's why I'm using it," Fernando replied, taking a sip of wine.

"You do not belong in the kitchen, Dom Fernando. Go upstairs. Take Gallowglass with you." Marthe took a packet of tea and a teapot from the shelf by the sink. Then she noticed the towel-wrapped pot sitting on a tray next to cups, saucers, milk, and sugar. Her frown deepened.

"What is wrong with my being here?" Fernando demanded.

"You are not a servant," Marthe said. She picked the lid off the top of the pot and sniffed suspiciously at its contents.

"It's Diana's favorite. You told me what she liked, remember?" Fernando smiled sadly. "And everyone in this house serves the de Clermonts, Marthe. The only difference is that you, Alain, and Victoire are paid handsomely to do so. The rest of us are expected to be grateful for the privilege."

"With good reason. Other *manjasang* dream of being part of this family. See that you remember that in future—and the lemon, Dom Fernando," Marthe said, placing emphasis on his lordly title. She picked up the tea tray. "By the way, your eggs are burning."

Fernando leaped up to rescue them.

"As for you," Marthe said, fixing her black eyes on Gallowglass, "you did not tell us everything you should have about Matthew and his wife."

Gallowglass looked down into his wine with a guilty expression.

"*Madame* your grandmother will deal with you later." On that bone-chilling note, Marthe stalked out of the room.

"What have you done now?" asked Fernando, putting his tortilla—which was not ruined, *Alhamdulillah*—on the stove. Long experience had taught him that whatever the mess, Gallowglass had made it with good intentions and complete disregard for possible disaster.

"Weeell," Gallowglass said, drawing out the vowels as only a Scot could, "I might have left one or two things out of the tale."

"Like what?" Fernando said, catching a whiff of catastrophe among the kitchen's homely scents.

"Like the fact that Auntie is pregnant—and by none other than Matthew. And the fact that Granddad adopted her as a daughter. Lord, his blood vow was deafening." Gallowglass looked reflective. "Do you think we'll still be able to hear it?"

Fernando stood, openmouthed and silent.

"Don't look at me that way. It didn't seem right to share the news about the babe. Women can be funny about such things. And Philippe told Auntie Verin about the blood vow before he died in 1945, and she never said a word either!" Gallowglass said defensively.

A concussion tore the air, as if a silent bomb had been detonated. Something green and fiery streaked past the kitchen window.

"What the hell was that?" Fernando flung the door open and shielded his eyes against the bright sunlight.

"One pissed-off witch, I imagine." Gallowglass's tone was glum. "Sarah must have told Diana and Matthew the news about Emily."

"Not the explosion. That!" Fernando pointed to Saint-Lucien's bell tower, which was being circled by a winged, two-legged, fire-breathing creature. Gallowglass rose for a better look.

"That's Corra. She goes where Auntie goes," Gallowglass said matter-of-factly.

"But that's a *dragon*." Fernando turned wild eyes on his stepson.

"Bah! That's no dragon. Can't you see she's only got two legs? Corra is a firedrake." Gallowglass twisted his arm to show off a tattoo of a winged creature that strongly resembled the airborne beast. "Like this. I might have left out one or two details, but I did warn everybody that Auntie Diana wasn't going to be the same witch she was before."

"It's true, honey. Em is dead." The stress of telling Diana and Matthew was clearly too much for her. Sarah could have sworn that she saw a dragon. Fernando was right. She needed to cut back on the whiskey.

"I don't believe you." Diana's voice was high and sharp with panic. She searched Ysabeau's grand salon as though she expected to find Emily hiding behind one of the ornate settees.

"Emily's not here, Diana." Matthew's hushed voice was infused with regret and tenderness as he stepped before her. "She's gone."

"No." Diana tried to push past him and continue her search, but Matthew drew her into his arms.

"I'm so sorry, Sarah," Matthew said, holding Diana tight to his body.

"Don't say you're sorry!" Diana cried, struggling to free herself from the vampire's unbreakable hold. She pounded on Matthew's shoulder with her fist. "Em isn't dead! This is a nightmare. Wake me up, Matthew—please! I want to wake up and find we're still in 1591."

"This isn't a nightmare," Sarah said. The long weeks had convinced her that Em's death was horribly real.

"Then I took a wrong turn—or tied a bad knot in the timewalking spell. This can't be where we were supposed to end up!" Diana was shaking from head to toe with grief and shock. "Em promised she would never leave without saying good-bye."

"Em didn't have time to say good-bye—to anyone. But that doesn't mean she didn't love you." Sarah reminded herself of this a hundred times a day.

"Diana should sit," Marcus said, pulling a chair closer to Sarah. In many ways Matthew's son looked like the same twenty-something surfer who had walked into the Bishop house last October. His leather cord, with its strange assortment of objects gathered over the centuries, was still tangled in the blond hair at the nape of his neck. The Converse sneakers he loved remained on his feet. The guarded, sad look in his eyes was new, however.

Sarah was grateful for the presence of Marcus and Ysabeau, but the person she really wanted at her side at this moment was Fernando. He'd been her rock during this ordeal.

"Thank you, Marcus," Matthew said, settling Diana in the seat. Phoebe tried to press a glass of water into Diana's hand. When Diana just stared at it blankly, Matthew took it and placed it on a nearby table.

All eyes alighted on Sarah.

Sarah was no good at this kind of thing. Diana was the historian in the family. She would know where to start and how to string the confusing events into a coherent story with a beginning, a middle, and an end, and perhaps even a plausible explanation of why Emily had died.

"There's no easy way to tell you this," Diana's aunt began.

"You don't have to tell us anything," Matthew said, his eyes filled with compassion and sympathy. "The explanations can wait."

"No. You both need to know." Sarah reached for the glass of whiskey that usually sat at her side, but there was nothing there. She looked to Marcus in mute appeal.

"Emily died up at the old temple," Marcus said, taking up the role of storyteller.

"The temple dedicated to the goddess?" Diana whispered, her brow creasing with the effort to concentrate.

"Yes," Sarah croaked, coughing to dislodge the lump in her throat. "Emily was spending more and more time up there."

"Was she alone?" Matthew's expression was no longer warm and understanding, and his tone was frosty.

Silence descended again, this one heavy and awkward.

"Emily wouldn't let anyone go with her," Sarah said, steeling herself to be honest. Diana was a witch, too, and would know if she strayed from the truth. "Marcus tried to convince her to take someone with her, but Emily refused."

"Why did she want to be alone?" Diana said, picking up on Sarah's own uneasiness. "What was going on, Sarah?"

"Since January, Em had been turning to the higher magics for guidance." Sarah looked away from Diana's shocked face. "She was having terrible premonitions of death and disaster and thought they might help her figure out why."

"But Em always said higher magics were too dark for witches to handle safely," Diana said, her voice rising again. "She said any witch who thought she was immune to their dangers would find out the hard way just how powerful they were."

"She spoke from experience," Sarah said. "They can be addictive. Emily didn't want you to know she'd felt their lure, honey. She hadn't touched a scrying stone or tried to summon a spirit for decades."

"Summon spirits?" Matthew's eyes narrowed into slits. With his dark beard, he looked truly terrifying.

"I think she was trying to reach Rebecca. If I'd realized how far she'd gone in her attempts, I would have tried harder to stop her." Sarah's eyes brimmed with tears. "Peter Knox must have sensed the power Emily was working with, and the higher magics have always fascinated him. Once he found her—"

"Knox?" Matthew spoke softly, but the hairs on the back of Sarah's neck rose in warning.

"When we found Em, Knox and Gerbert were there, too," Marcus explained, looking miserable at the admission. "She'd suffered a heart attack. Emily must have been under enormous stress trying to resist whatever Knox was doing. She was barely conscious. I tried to revive her. So did Sarah. But there was nothing either of us could do."

"Why were Gerbert and Knox here? And what in the world did Knox hope to gain from killing Em?" Diana cried.

"I don't think Knox was trying to kill her, honey," Sarah replied. "Knox was reading Emily's thoughts, or trying his best to. Her last words were, 'I know the secret of Ashmole 782, and you will never possess it.'"

"Ashmole 782?" Diana looked stunned. "Are you sure?"

"Positive." Sarah wished her niece had never found that damned manuscript in the Bodleian Library. It was the cause of most of their present problems.

"Knox insisted that the de Clermonts had missing pages from Diana's manuscript and knew its secrets," Ysabeau chimed in. "Verin and I told Knox he was mistaken, but the only thing that distracted him from the subject was the baby. Margaret."

"Nathaniel and Sophie followed us to the temple. Margaret was with them," Marcus explained in answer to Matthew's astonished stare. "Before Emily fell unconscious, Knox saw Margaret and demanded to know how two daemons had given birth to a baby witch. Knox invoked the covenant. He threatened to take Margaret to the Congregation pending investigation into what he called 'serious breaches' of law. While we were trying to revive Emily and get the baby to safety, Gerbert and Knox slipped away."

Until recently Sarah had always seen the Congregation and the covenant as necessary evils. It was not easy for the three otherworldly species—daemons, vampires, and witches—to live among humans. All had been targets of human fear and violence at some point in history, and creatures had long ago agreed to a covenant to minimize the risk of their world's coming to human attention. It limited fraternization between species as well as any participation in human religion or politics. The nine-member Congregation enforced the covenant and made sure that creatures abided by its terms. Now that Diana and Matthew were home, the Congregation could go to hell and take their covenant with them as far as Sarah was concerned.

Diana's head swung around, and a look of disbelief passed over her face.

"Gallowglass?" she breathed as the salon filled with the scent of the sea.

"Welcome home, Auntie." Gallowglass stepped forward, his golden beard gleaming where the sunlight struck it. Diana stared at him in astonishment before a sob broke free.

"There, there." Gallowglass lifted her into a bear hug. "It's been some time since the sight of me brought a woman to tears. Besides, it really should be me weeping at our reunion. As far as you're concerned, it's been only a few days since we spoke. By my reckoning it's been centuries."

Something numinous flickered around the edges of Diana's body, like a candle slowly catching light. Sarah blinked. She really was going to have to lay off the booze.

Matthew and his nephew exchanged glances. Matthew's expression grew even more concerned as Diana's tears increased and the glow surrounding her intensified.

"Let Matthew take you upstairs." Gallowglass reached into a pocket and pulled out a crumpled yellow bandanna. He offered this to Diana, carefully shielding her from view.

"Is she all right?" Sarah asked.

"Just a wee bit tired," Gallowglass said as he and Matthew hustled Diana off toward Matthew's remote tower rooms.

Once Diana and Matthew were gone, Sarah's fragile composure cracked, and she began to weep. Reliving the events of Em's death was a daily occurrence, but having to do so with Diana was even more painful. Fernando appeared, his expression concerned.

"It's all right, Sarah. Let it out," Fernando murmured, drawing her close.

"Where were you when I needed you?" Sarah demanded as her weeping turned to sobs.

"I'm here now," Fernando said, rocking her gently. "And Diana and Matthew are safely home."

"I can't stop shaking." Diana's teeth were chattering, and her limbs were jerking as if pulled by invisible strings. Gallowglass pressed his lips together, standing back while Matthew wrapped a blanket tight around his wife.

"That's the shock, *mon coeur*," Matthew murmured, pressing a kiss to her cheek. It wasn't just the death of Emily but the memories of the earlier, traumatic loss of her parents that were causing her distress. He rubbed her arms, the blanket moving against her flesh. "Can you get some wine, Gallowglass?"

"I shouldn't. The babies . . ." Diana began. Her expression turned wild and her tears returned. "They'll never know Em. Our children will grow up not knowing Em."

"Here." Gallowglass thrust a silver flask in Matthew's direction. His uncle looked at him gratefully.

"Even better," Matthew said, pulling the stopper free. "Just a sip, Diana. It won't hurt the twins, and it will help calm you. I'll have Marthe bring up some black tea with plenty of sugar."

"I'm going to kill Peter Knox," Diana said fiercely after she'd taken a sip of whiskey. The light around her grew brighter.

"Not today you're not," Matthew said firmly, handing the flask back to Gallowglass.

"Has Auntie's *glaem* been this bright since you returned?" Gallowglass hadn't seen Diana Bishop since 1591, but he didn't recall it being this noticeable.

"Yes. She's been wearing a disguising spell. The shock must have knocked it out of place," Matthew said, lowering her onto the sofa. "Diana wanted Emily and Sarah to enjoy the fact that they were going to be grandmothers before they started asking questions about her increased power."

Gallowglass bit back an oath.

"Better?" Matthew asked, drawing Diana's fingers to his lips.

Diana nodded. Her teeth were still chattering, Gallowglass noted. It made him ache to think about the effort it must be taking for her to control herself.

"I am so sorry about Emily," Matthew said, cupping her face between his hands.

"Is it our fault? Did we stay in the past too long, like Dad said?" Diana spoke so softly it was hard for even Gallowglass to hear.

"Of course not," Gallowglass replied, his voice brusque. "Peter Knox did this. Nobody else is to blame."

"Let's not worry about who's to blame," Matthew said, but his eyes were angry.

Gallowglass gave him a nod of understanding. Matthew would have plenty to say about Knox and Gerbert—later. Right now he was concerned with his wife.

"Emily would want you to focus on taking care of yourself and Sarah. That's enough for now." Matthew brushed back the coppery strands that were stuck to Diana's cheeks by the salt from her tears.

"I should go back downstairs," Diana said, drawing Gallowglass's bright yellow bandanna to her eyes. "Sarah needs me."

"Let's stay up here a bit longer. Wait for Marthe to bring the tea," Matthew said, sitting down next to her. Diana slumped against him, her breath hiccupping in and out as she tried to hold back the tears.

"I'll leave you two," Gallowglass said gruffly.

Matthew nodded in silent thanks.

"Thank you, Gallowglass," Diana said, holding out the bandanna.

"Keep it," he said, turning for the stairs.

"We're alone. You don't have to be strong now," Matthew murmured to Diana as Gallowglass descended the twisting staircase.

Gallowglass left Matthew and Diana twined together in an unbreakable knot, their faces twisted with pain and sorrow, each giving the other the comfort they could not find for themselves.

I should never have summoned you here. I should have found another way to get my answers. Emily turned to face her closest friend. *You should be with Stephen.*

I'd rather be here with my daughter than anywhere else, Rebecca Bishop said. *Stephen understands.* She turned back to the sight of Diana and Matthew, still locked in their sorrowful embrace.

Do not fear. Matthew will take care of her, Philippe said. He was still trying to figure out Rebecca Bishop—she was an unusually challenging creature, and as skilled at keeping secrets as any vampire.

They'll take care of each other, Rebecca said, her hand over her heart, *just as I knew they would.*

2

Matthew raced down the curving stone staircase that wound between his tower rooms at Sept-Tours and the main floor of the château. He avoided the slippery spot on the thirtieth tread and the rough patch on the seventeenth where Baldwin's sword had bashed the edge during one of their arguments.

Matthew had built the tower addition as his private refuge, a place apart from the relentless busyness that always surrounded Philippe and Ysabeau. Vampire families were large and noisy, with two or more bloodlines coming uncomfortably together and trying to live as one happy pack. This seldom happened with predators, even those who walked on two legs and lived in fine houses. As a result, Matthew's tower was designed primarily for defense. It had no doors to muffle a vampire's stealthy approach and no way out except for the way you came in. His careful arrangements spoke volumes about his relationships with his brothers and sisters.

Tonight his tower's isolation seemed confining, a far cry from the busy life he and Diana had created in Elizabethan London, surrounded by family and friends. Matthew's job as a spy for the queen had been challenging but rewarding. From his former seat on the Congregation, he had managed to save a few witches from hanging. Diana had begun the lifelong process of growing into her powers as a witch. They'd even taken in two orphaned children and given them a chance at a better future. Their life in the sixteenth century had not always been easy, but their days had been filled with love and the sense of hope that followed Diana wherever she went. Here at Sept-Tours, they seemed surrounded on all sides by death and de Clermonts.

The combination made Matthew restless, and the anger he kept so carefully in check whenever Diana was near him was dangerously close to the surface. Blood rage—the sickness that Matthew had inherited from Ysabeau when she'd made him—could take over a vampire's mind and body quickly, leaving no room for reason or control. In an effort to keep the blood rage in check, Matthew had reluctantly agreed to leave Diana in Ysabeau's care while he walked around the castle grounds with his dogs, Fallon and Hector, trying to clear his head.

Gallowglass was crooning a sea chantey in the château's great hall. For reasons Matthew couldn't fathom, every other verse was punctuated by expletives and ultimatums. After a moment of indecision, Matthew's curiosity won out.

"Fucking firedrake." Gallowglass had one of the pikes down from the cache of weapons by the entrance and was waving it slowly in the air. " *'Farewell and adieu to you, ladies of Spain.'* Get your arse down here, or Granny will poach you in white wine and feed you to the dogs. *'For we've received orders for to sail for old England.'* What are you thinking, flying around the house like a demented parakeet? *'And we may never see you fair ladies again.'*"

"What the hell are you doing?" Matthew demanded.

Gallowglass turned wide blue eyes on Matthew. The younger man was wearing a black T-shirt adorned with a skull and crossbones. Something had slashed the back, rending it from left shoulder to right hip. The holes in his nephew's jeans looked to be the result of wear, not war, and his hair was shaggy even by Gallowglassian standards. Ysabeau had taken to calling him "Sir Vagabond," but this had done little to improve his grooming.

"Trying to catch your wife's wee beastie." Gallowglass made a sudden upward thrust with the pike. There was a shriek of surprise, followed by a hail of pale green scales that shattered like isinglass when they hit the floor. The blond hair on Gallowglass's forearms shimmered with their iridescent green dust. He sneezed.

Corra, Diana's familiar, was clinging to the minstrels' gallery with her talons, chattering madly and clacking her tongue. She waved hello to Matthew with her barbed tail, piercing a priceless tapestry depicting a unicorn in a garden. Matthew winced.

"I had her cornered in the chapel, up by the altar, but Corra is a cunning lass," Gallowglass said with a touch of pride. "She was hiding atop Granddad's tomb, her wings spread wide. I mistook her for an effigy. Now look at her. Up in the rafters, vainglorious as the devil and twice as much trouble. Why, she's put her tail through one of Ysabeau's favorite draperies. Granny is going to have a stroke."

"If Corra is anything like her mistress, cornering her won't end well," Matthew said mildly. "Try reasoning with her instead."

"Oh, aye. That works very well with Auntie Diana." Gallowglass sniffed. "Whatever possessed you to let Corra out of your sight?"

"The more active the firedrake is, the calmer Diana seems," Matthew said.

"Perhaps, but Corra is hell on the decor. She broke one of Granny's Sèvres vases this afternoon."

"So long as it wasn't one of the blue ones with the lion heads that Philippe gave her, I shouldn't worry." Matthew groaned when he saw Gallowglass's expression. *"Merde."*

"That was Alain's response, too." Gallowglass leaned on his pike.

"Ysabeau will have to make do with one less piece of pottery," Matthew said. "Corra may be a nuisance, but Diana is sleeping soundly for the first time since we came home."

"Oh, well, that's all right, then. Just tell Ysabeau that Corra's clumsiness is good for the grandbabies. Granny will hand over her vases as sacrificial offerings. Meanwhile I'll try to keep the flying termagant entertained so Auntie can sleep."

"How are you going to do that?" Matthew asked with skepticism.

"Sing to her, of course." Gallowglass looked up. Corra cooed at his renewed attention, stretching her wings a bit farther so that they caught the light from the torches stuck into brackets along the walls. Taking this as an encouraging sign, Gallowglass drew a deep breath and began another booming ballad.

"My head turns round, I'm in a flame, / I love like any dragon. / Say would you know my mistress's name?"

Corra clacked her teeth in approval. Gallowglass grinned and began to move the pike like a metronome. He waggled his eyebrows at Matthew before singing his next lines.

> *"I sent her trinkets without end,*
> *Gems, pearls, to make her civil,*
> *Till having nothing more to send,*
> *I sent her—to the devil."*

"Good luck," Matthew murmured, sincerely hoping that Corra didn't understand the lyrics.

Matthew scanned the nearby rooms, cataloging their occupants. Hamish was in the family library doing paperwork, based on the sound of pen scratching against paper and the faint scent of lavender and peppermint he detected. Matthew hesitated for a moment, then pushed the door open.

"Time for an old friend?" he asked.

"I was beginning to think you were avoiding me." Hamish Osborne put down his pen and loosened his tie, which was covered in a summery floral print most men wouldn't have had the courage to wear. Even in the French countryside, Hamish was dressed as if for a meeting with members of Parliament in a navy pin-striped suit with a lavender shirt. It made him look like a dapper throwback to Edwardian days.

Matthew knew that the daemon was trying to provoke an argument. He and Hamish had been friends for decades, ever since the two of them were at Oxford. Their friendship was based on mutual respect and had been kept strong because of their compatible, razor-sharp intellects. Between Hamish and Matthew, even simple exchanges could be as complicated and strategic as a chess game between two masters. But it was too soon in their conversation to let Hamish put him at a disadvantage.

"How is Diana?" Hamish had noted Matthew's deliberate refusal to take the bait.

"As well as can be expected."

"I would have asked her myself, of course, but your nephew told me to go away." Hamish picked up a wineglass and took a sip. "Wine?"

"Did it come from my cellar or Baldwin's?" Matthew's seemingly innocuous question served as a subtle reminder that now that he and Diana were back, Hamish might have to choose between Matthew and the rest of the de Clermonts.

"It's claret." Hamish swirled the contents in the glass while he waited for Matthew's reaction. "Expensive. Old. Fine."

Matthew's lip curled. "Thank you, no. I've never had the same fondness for the stuff as most of my family." He'd rather fill the fountains in the garden with Baldwin's store of precious Bordeaux than drink it.

"What's the story with the dragon?" A muscle in Hamish's jaws twitched, whether from amusement or anger, Matthew couldn't tell. "Gallowglass says Diana brought it back as a souvenir, but nobody believes him."

"She belongs to Diana," Matthew said. "You'll have to ask her."

"You've got everybody at Sept-Tours quaking in their boots, you know." With this abrupt change of topic, Hamish approached. "The rest of them haven't realized yet that the most terrified person in the château is *you*."

"And how is William?" Matthew could make a dizzying change in subject as effectively as any daemon.

"Sweet William has planted his affections elsewhere." Hamish's mouth twisted, and he turned away, his obvious distress bringing their game to an unexpected close.

"I'm so sorry, Hamish." Matthew had thought the relationship would last. "William loved you."

"Not enough." Hamish shrugged but couldn't hide the pain in his eyes. "You'll have to pin your romantic hopes on Marcus and Phoebe, I'm afraid."

"I've barely spoken to the girl," Matthew said. He sighed and poured himself a glass of Baldwin's claret. "What can you tell me about her?"

"Young Miss Taylor works at one of the auction houses in London— Sotheby's or Christie's. I never can keep them straight," Hamish said, sinking into a leather armchair in front of the cold fireplace. "Marcus met her when he was picking up something for Ysabeau. I think it's serious."

"It is." Matthew took his wine and prowled along the bookshelves that lined the walls. "Marcus's scent is all over her. He's mated."

"I suspected as much." Hamish sipped and watched his friend's restless movements. "Nobody has said anything, of course. Your family really could teach MI6 a thing or two about secrets."

"Ysabeau should have stopped it. Phoebe is too young for a relationship with a vampire," Matthew said. "She can't be more than twenty-two, yet Marcus has entangled her in an irrevocable bond."

"Oh, yes, forbidding Marcus to fall in love would have gone down a treat," Hamish said, his Scots burr increasing with his amusement. "Marcus is just as pigheaded as you are when it comes to love, it turns out."

"Maybe if he'd been thinking about his job as the leader of the Knights of Lazarus—"

"Stop right there, Matt, before you say something so unfair I might never forgive you for it." Hamish's voice lashed at him. "You know how difficult it is to be the brotherhood's grand master. Marcus was expected to fill some pretty big shoes—and vampire or not, he isn't much older than Phoebe."

The Knights of Lazarus had been founded during the Crusades, a chivalric order established to protect vampire interests in a world that was increasingly dominated by humans. Philippe de Clermont, Ysabeau's mate, had been the first grand master. But he was a legendary figure, not just among vampires but among other creatures as well. It was an impossible task for any man to live up to the standard he'd set.

"I know, but to fall in love—" Matthew protested, his anger mounting.

"Marcus has done a brilliant job, no buts about it," Hamish interrupted. "He's recruited new members and overseen every financial detail of our operations. He demanded that the Congregation punish Knox for his actions here in May and has formally requested the covenant be revoked. Nobody could have done more. Not even you."

"Punishing Knox doesn't begin to address what happened. He and Gerbert violated my home. Knox murdered a woman who was like a mother to my wife." Matthew gulped down his wine in an effort to drown his anger.

"Emily had a heart attack," Hamish cautioned. "Marcus said there's no way to know the cause."

"I know enough," Matthew said with sudden fury, hurling his empty glass across the room. It smashed against the edge of one of the bookshelves, sending shards of glass into the thick carpet. Hamish's eyes widened. "Our children will never have the chance to know Emily now. And Gerbert, who's been on intimate terms with this family for centuries, stood by and watched Knox do it, knowing that Diana was my mate."

"Everyone in the house said you wouldn't let Congregation justice take its course. I didn't believe them." Hamish didn't like the changes he was seeing in his friend. It was as though being in the sixteenth century had ripped the scab off some old, forgotten wound.

"I should have dealt with Gerbert and Knox after they helped Satu Järvinen kidnap Diana and held her at La Pierre. If I had, Emily would still be alive." Matthew's shoulders stiffened with remorse. "But Baldwin forbade it. He said the Congregation had enough trouble on its hands."

"You mean the vampire murders?" Hamish asked.

"Yes. He said if I challenged Gerbert and Knox, I would only make matters worse." News of these murders—with the severed arteries, the absence of blood evidence, the almost animalistic attacks on human bodies—had been in newspapers from London to Moscow. Every story had focused on the murderer's strange method of killing and had threatened to expose vampires to human notice.

"I won't make the mistake of remaining silent again," Matthew continued. "The Knights of Lazarus and the de Clermonts might not be able to protect my wife and her family, but I certainly can."

"You're not a killer, Matt," Hamish insisted. "Don't let your anger blind you."

When Matthew turned black eyes to him, Hamish blanched. Though he knew that Matthew was a few steps closer to the animal kingdom than most creatures who walked on two legs, Hamish had never seen him look quite so wolflike and dangerous.

"Are you sure, Hamish?" Matthew's obsidian eyes blinked, and he turned and stalked from the room.

Following the distinctive licorice-root scent of Marcus Whitmore, mixed tonight with the heady aroma of lilacs, Matthew was easily able to track his son to the family apartments on the second floor of the château. His conscience pricked at the thought of what Marcus might have overheard during this heated exchange, given his son's keen vampire hearing. Matthew pressed his lips together when his nose led him to a door just off the stairs, and he tamped down the flicker of anger that accompanied his realization that Marcus was using Philippe's old office.

Matthew knocked and pushed at the heavy slab of wood without waiting for a response. With the exception of the shiny silver laptop on the desk where the blotter used to be, the room looked exactly as it had on the day Philippe de Clermont died in 1945. The same Bakelite telephone was on a table by the window. Stacks of thin envelopes and curling, yellowed paper stood at the ready for Philippe to write to one of his many correspondents. Tacked to the wall was an old map of Europe, which Philippe had used to track the positions of Hitler's army.

Matthew closed his eyes against the sudden, sharp pain. What Philippe had *not* foreseen was that he would fall into the Nazis' hands. One of the unexpected gifts of their timewalk had been the chance to see Philippe again and be reconciled with him. The price Matthew had to pay was the renewed sense of loss as he once more faced a world without Philippe de Clermont in it.

When Matthew's eyes opened again, he was confronted with the furious face of Phoebe Taylor. It took only a fraction of a second for Marcus to angle his body between Matthew and the warmblooded woman. Matthew was gratified to see that his son hadn't lost all his wits when he took a mate, though if Matthew had wanted to harm Phoebe, the girl would already be dead.

"Marcus." Matthew briefly acknowledged his son before looking beyond him. Phoebe was not Marcus's usual type at all. He had always preferred redheads. "There was no time for a proper introduction when we first met. I'm Matthew Clairmont. Marcus's father."

"I know who you are." Phoebe's proper British accent was the one common to public schools, country houses, and decaying aristocratic families. Marcus, the family's democratic idealist, had fallen for a blueblood.

"Welcome to the family, Miss Taylor." Matthew bowed to hide his smile.

"Phoebe, please." Phoebe stepped around Marcus in a blink, her right hand extended. Matthew ignored it. "In most polite circles, Professor Clairmont, this is where you would take my hand and shake it." Phoebe's expression was more than a little annoyed, her hand still outstretched.

"You're surrounded by vampires. Whatever made you think you would find civilization here?" Matthew studied her with unblinking eyes. Uncomfortable, Phoebe looked away. "You may think my greeting unnecessarily formal, Phoebe, but no vampire touches another's mate—or even his betrothed—without permission." He glanced down at the large emerald on the third finger of her left hand. Marcus had won the stone in a card game in Paris centuries ago. Then and now it was worth a small fortune.

"Oh. Marcus didn't tell me that," Phoebe said with a frown.

"No, but I did give you a few simple rules. Perhaps it's time to review them," Marcus murmured to his fiancée. "We'll rehearse our wedding vows while we're at it."

"Why? You still won't find the word 'obey' in them," Phoebe said crisply.

Before the argument could get off the ground, Matthew coughed again.

"I came to apologize for my outburst in the library," Matthew said. "I am too quick to anger at the moment. Forgive me for my temper."

It was more than temper, but Marcus—like Hamish—didn't know that.

"What outburst?" Phoebe frowned.

"It was nothing," Marcus responded, though his expression suggested otherwise.

"I was also wondering if you would be willing to examine Diana? As you no doubt know, she is carrying twins. I believe she's in the beginning of her second trimester, but we've been out of reach of proper medical care, and I'd like to be sure." Matthew's proffered olive branch, like Phoebe's hand, remained in the air for several long moments before it was acknowledged.

"Of c-course," Marcus stammered. "Thank you for trusting Diana to my care. I won't let you down. And Hamish is right," he added. "Even if I'd performed an autopsy on Emily—which Sarah didn't want—there would have been no way to determine if she was killed by magic or by natural causes. We may never know."

Matthew didn't bother to argue. He would find out the precise role that Knox had played in Emily's death, for the answer would determine how quickly Matthew killed him and how much the witch suffered first.

"Phoebe, it has been a pleasure," Matthew said instead.

"Likewise." The girl lied politely and convincingly. She would be a useful addition to the de Clermont pack.

"Come to Diana in the morning, Marcus. We'll be expecting you." With a final smile and another shallow bow to the fascinating Phoebe Taylor, Matthew left the room.

Matthew's nocturnal prowl around Sept-Tours had not lessened his restlessness or his anger. If anything, the cracks in his control had widened. Frustrated, he took a route back to his rooms that passed by the château's keep and the chapel. Memorials to most of the departed de Clermonts were there—Philippe; Louisa; her twin brother, Louis; Godfrey; Hugh—as well as some of their children and beloved friends and servants.

"Good morning, Matthew." The scent of saffron and bitter orange filled the air.

Fernando. After a long pause, Matthew forced himself to turn.

Usually the chapel's ancient wooden door was closed, as only Matthew spent time there. Tonight it stood open in welcome, and the figure of a man was silhouetted against the warm candlelight inside.

"I hoped I might see you." Fernando swept his arm wide in invitation.

Fernando watched as his brother-in-law made his way toward him, searching his features for the warning signs that Matthew was in trouble:

the enlargement of his pupils, the ripple in his shoulders reminiscent of a wolf's hackles, a roughness deep in his throat.

"Do I pass inspection?" Matthew asked, unable to keep the defensive note from his tone.

"You'll do." Fernando closed the door firmly behind them. "Barely."

Matthew ran his fingers lightly along Philippe's massive sarcophagus in the center of the chapel and moved restlessly around the chamber while Fernando's deep brown eyes followed him.

"Congratulations on your marriage, Matthew," Fernando said. "Though I haven't met Diana yet, Sarah has told me so many stories about her that I feel we are very old friends."

"I'm sorry, Fernando, it's just—" Matthew began, his expression guilty.

Fernando stopped him with a raised hand. "There is no need for apology."

"Thank you for taking care of Diana's aunt," Matthew said. "I know how difficult it is for you to be here."

"The widow needed somebody to think of her pain first. Just as you did for me when Hugh died," Fernando said simply.

At Sept-Tours everybody from Gallowglass and the gardener to Victoire and Ysabeau referred to Sarah by her status relative to Emily rather than by her name, when she was not in the room. It was a title of respect as well as a constant reminder of Sarah's loss.

"I must ask you, Matthew: Does Diana know about your blood rage?" Fernando kept his voice low. The chapel walls were thick, and not much sound escaped, but it was wise to take precautions.

"Of course she knows." Matthew dropped to his knees in front of a small pile of armor and weapons arranged in one of the chapel's carved niches. The space was big enough to hold a coffin, but Hugh de Clermont had been burned at the stake, leaving no body to bury. Matthew had created a memorial to his favorite brother out of painted wood and metal instead: his shield, his gauntlets, his mail hauberk and coat of plates, his sword, his helm.

"Forgive me for insulting you with the suggestion that you would keep something so important from one you love." Fernando boxed him on the ear. "I'm glad you told your wife, but you deserve a whipping for not telling Marcus or Hamish—or Sarah."

"You're welcome to try." Matthew's response carried a threat that would drive off any other member of his family—but not Fernando.

"You'd like a straightforward punishment, wouldn't you? But you aren't getting off so easy. Not this time." Fernando knelt beside him.

There was a long silence while Fernando waited for Matthew to lower his guard.

"The blood rage. It's gotten worse." Matthew hung his head over his clasped hands in an attitude of prayer.

"Of course it has. You're mated now. What did you expect?"

The chemical and emotional responses that accompanied mating were intense, and even perfectly healthy vampires found it difficult to let their mates out of their sight. On those occasions when being together was impossible, it led to irritation, aggression, anxiety, and, in rare cases, madness. For a vampire with blood rage, both the mating impulse and the effects of separation were heightened.

"I expected to handle it." Matthew's forehead lowered until it was resting on his fingers. "I believed that the love I felt for Diana was stronger than the disease."

"Oh, Matthew. You can be more idealistic than Hugh on even his sunniest days." Fernando sighed and put a comforting hand on Matthew's shoulder.

Fernando always lent comfort and assistance to those who needed it—even when they didn't deserve it. He had sent Matthew to study with the surgeon Albucasis, back when he was trying to overcome the deadly rampages that marked his first centuries as a vampire. It was Fernando who kept Hugh—the brother whom Matthew had worshipped—safe from harm as he made his way from battlefield to book and back to the battlefield again. Without Fernando's care Hugh would have shown up to fight with nothing but a volume of poetry, a dull sword, and one gauntlet. And it was Fernando who told Philippe that ordering Matthew back to Jerusalem would be a terrible mistake. Unfortunately, neither Philippe nor Matthew had listened to him.

"I had to force myself to leave her side tonight." Matthew's eyes darted around the chapel. "I can't sit still, I want to kill something—badly—and even so it was almost impossible for me to venture beyond the sound of her breathing."

Fernando listened in silent sympathy, though he wondered why Matthew sounded surprised. Fernando had to remind himself that newly mated vampires often underestimated how strongly the bond could affect them.

"Right now Diana wants to stay close to Sarah and me. But when the grief over Emily's death has subsided, she's going to want to resume her own life," Matthew said, clearly worried.

"Well, she can't. Not with you standing by her elbow." Fernando never minced words with Matthew. Idealists like him needed plain speech or they lost their way. "If Diana loves you, she'll adapt."

"She won't have to adapt," Matthew said through gritted teeth. "I won't take her freedom—no matter what it costs me. I wasn't with Diana at every moment in the sixteenth century. There's no reason for that to change in the twenty-first."

"You managed your feelings in the past because whenever you weren't at her side, Gallowglass was. Oh, he told me all about your life in London and Prague," Fernando said when Matthew turned a startled face his way. "And if not Gallowglass, Diana was with someone else: Philippe, Davy, another witch, Mary, Henry. Do you honestly think that mobile phones are going to give you a comparable sense of connection and control?"

Matthew still looked angry, the blood rage just beneath the surface, but he looked miserable, too. Fernando thought it was a step in the right direction.

"Ysabeau should have stopped you from getting involved with Diana Bishop as soon as it was clear you were feeling a mating bond," Fernando said sternly. Had Matthew been his child, Fernando would have locked him in a steel tower to prevent it.

"She did stop me." Matthew's expression grew even more miserable. "I wasn't fully mated to Diana until we came to Sept-Tours in 1590. Philippe gave us his blessing."

Fernando's mouth filled with bitterness. "That man's arrogance knew no bounds. No doubt he planned to fix everything when you returned to the present."

"Philippe knew he wouldn't be here," Matthew confessed. Fernando's eyes widened. "I didn't tell him about his death. Philippe figured it out for himself."

Fernando swore a blistering oath. He was sure that Matthew's god would forgive the blasphemy, since it was so richly deserved in this case.

"And did your mating with Diana take place before or after Philippe marked her with his blood vow?" Even after the timewalking, Philippe's blood vow was audible and, according to Verin de Clermont and Gallowglass, still deafening. Happily, Fernando was not a full-blooded de Clermont, so Philippe's bloodsong registered as nothing more than a persistent hum.

"After."

"Of course. Philippe's blood vow ensured her safety. *'Noli me tangere,'*" Fernando said with a shake of his head. "Gallowglass was wasting his time watching Diana so closely."

"*'Touch me not, for Caesar's I am,'*" Matthew echoed softly. "It's true. No vampire meddled with her after that. Except Louisa."

"Louisa was as mad as a March hare to ignore your father's wishes on this," Fernando commented. "I take it that's why Philippe sent Louisa packing to the outer reaches of the known world in 1591." The decision had always seemed abrupt, and Philippe hadn't stirred a finger to avenge her later death. Fernando filed away the information for future consideration.

The door swung open. Sarah's cat, Tabitha, shot into the chapel in a streak of gray fur and feline indignation. Gallowglass followed her, bearing a pack of cigarettes in one hand and a silver flask in the other. Tabitha wound her way around Matthew's legs, begging for his attention.

"Sarah's moggy is nearly as troublesome as Auntie's firedrake." Gallowglass thrust the flask in Matthew's direction. "Have some. It's not blood, but it's none of Granny's French stuff either. What she serves makes fine cologne, but it's no good for anything else."

Matthew refused the offering with a shake of the head. Baldwin's wine was already souring his stomach.

"And you call yourself a vampire," Fernando scolded Gallowglass. "Driven to drink by *um pequeno dragão.*"

"*You* try taming Corra if you think it's so bloody easy." Gallowglass removed a cigarette from his pack and put it to his lips. "Or we can vote on what to do with her."

"Vote?" Matthew said, incredulous. "Since when did we vote in this family?"

"Since Marcus took over the Knights of Lazarus," Gallowglass replied, drawing a silver lighter from his pocket. "We've been choking on democracy since the day you left."

Fernando looked at him pointedly.

"What?" Gallowglass said, swinging the lighter open.

"This is a holy place, Gallowglass. And you know how Marcus feels about smoking when there are warmbloods in the house," Fernando said reprovingly.

"And you can imagine my own thoughts on the matter, with my pregnant wife upstairs." Matthew snatched the cigarette from Gallowglass's mouth.

"This family was more fun when we had fewer medical degrees," Gallowglass said darkly. "I remember the good old days, when we sewed ourselves up if we were wounded in battle and didn't give a tinker's dam about our iron levels and vitamin D."

"Oh, yes." Fernando held up his hand, displaying a ragged scar. "Those days were glorious indeed. And your skills with the needle were legendary, *Bife*."

"I got better," Gallowglass said defensively. "I was never as good as Matthew or Marcus, of course. But we can't all go to university."

"Not so long as Philippe was head of the family," Fernando murmured. "He preferred that his children and grandchildren wield swords rather than ideas. It made you all so much more pliable."

There was a grain of truth in the remark, and an ocean of pain behind it.

"I should get back to Diana." Matthew rocked to his feet and rested his hand on Fernando's shoulder for a brief moment before turning to leave.

"Waiting will not make it any easier to tell Marcus and Hamish about the blood rage, my friend," Fernando warned, stopping him.

"I thought after all these years my secret was safe," Matthew said.

"Secrets, like the dead, do not always stay buried," Fernando said sadly. "Tell them. Soon."

Matthew returned to his tower more agitated than when he'd left.

Ysabeau frowned at the sight of him.

"Thank you for watching Diana, *Maman*," he said, kissing Ysabeau's cheek.

"And you, my son?" Ysabeau put her palm to his cheek, searching as Fernando had for signs of blood rage. "Should I be watching over you instead?"

"I'm fine. Truly," Matthew said.

"Of course," Ysabeau replied. This phrase meant many things in his mother's private lexicon. What it never meant was that she agreed with you. "I will be in my room if you need me."

When the sound of his mother's quiet footfalls had faded, Matthew flung wide the windows and pulled his chair close to the open casement. He drank in the intense summer scents of catchfly and the last of the gillyflowers. The sound of Diana's even breathing upstairs blended into the other night songs that only vampires could hear—the clack of stag beetles locking horns as they competed for females, the loirs' wheezing as they ran across the battlements, the high-pitched squeaks of the death's-head hawkmoth, the scrabbling of pine martens climbing the trees. Based on the grunts and snuffles Matthew heard in the garden, Gallowglass had been no more successful catching the wild boar uprooting Marthe's vegetables than he had been in catching Corra.

Normally Matthew relished this quiet hour equidistant from midnight and dawn when the owls had stopped their hooting and even the most disciplined early risers had not yet peeled back the bedcovers. Tonight not even the familiar scents and sounds of home could work their magic.

Only one thing could.

Matthew climbed the stairs to the tower's top floor. There he looked down at Diana's sleeping form. He smoothed her hair, smiling when his wife instinctively pressed her skull deeper into his waiting hand. Impossible as it was, they fit: vampire and witch, man and woman, husband and wife. The hard fist around his heart loosened a few precious millimeters.

Silently Matthew shucked off his clothes and slid into bed. The sheets were tangled around Diana's legs, and he pulled the linen free, settling it over their bodies. Matthew tucked his knees behind Diana's and drew her hips back into his. He drank in the soft, pleasing scent of her—honey and chamomile and willow sap—and feathered a kiss against her bright hair.

After only a few breaths, Matthew's heart calmed and his restlessness seeped away as Diana provided the peace that was eluding him. Here, within the circle of his arms, was all that he had ever wanted. A wife. Children. A family of his own. He let the powerful rightness that he always felt in Diana's presence sink into his soul.

"Matthew?" Diana asked sleepily.

"I'm here," he murmured against her ear, holding her closer. "Go back to sleep. The sun hasn't risen yet."

Instead Diana turned to face him, burrowing into his neck.

"What is it, *mon coeur?*" Matthew frowned and pulled back to study her expression. Her skin was puffy and red from the crying, and the fine lines around her eyes were deepened by worry and grief. It destroyed him to see her this way. "Tell me," he said gently.

"There's no point. No one can fix it," she said sadly.

Matthew smiled. "At least let me try."

"Can you make time stand still?" Diana whispered after a moment of hesitation. "Just for a little while?"

Matthew was an ancient vampire, not a timewalking witch. But he was also a man, and he knew of one way to achieve this magical feat. His head told him that it was too soon after Emily's death, but his body sent other, more persuasive messages.

He lowered his mouth deliberately, giving Diana time to push him away. Instead she threaded her fingers through his cropped hair, returning his kiss with an intensity that stole his breath.

Her fine linen shift had traveled with them from the past, and though practically transparent, it was still a barrier between their flesh. He lifted the cloth, exposing the soft swell of her belly where his children grew, the curve of her breasts that every day ripened with fertile promise. They had not made love since London, and Matthew noticed the additional tightness of Diana's abdomen—a sign that the babies were continuing to develop—as well as the heightened blood flow to her breasts and her sex.

He took his fill of her with his eyes, his fingers, his mouth. But instead of being sated, his hunger for her only increased. Matthew lowered Diana back onto the bed and trailed kisses down her body until he reached the hidden places only he knew. Her hands tried to press his mouth more firmly against her, and he nipped her thigh in a silent reproach.

Once Diana began to fight his control in earnest, demanding softly that he take her, Matthew turned her in his arms and drew one cool hand down her spine.

"You wanted time to stand still," he reminded her.

"It has," Diana insisted, pressing against him in invitation.

"Then why are you rushing me?" Matthew traced the star-shaped scar between her shoulder blades and the crescent moon that swooped from one side of her ribs to the other. He frowned. There was a shadow on her lower back. It was deep within her skin, a pearly gray outline that looked a bit like a firedrake, its jaws biting into the crescent moon above, the wings covering Diana's rib cage, and a tail that disappeared around her hips.

"Why have you stopped?" Diana pushed her hair out of her eyes and craned her neck over her shoulder. "I want time to stand still—not you."

"There's something on your back." Matthew traced the firedrake's wings.

"You mean something else?" she asked with a nervous laugh. She still worried that her healed wounds were blemishes.

"With your other scars, it reminds me of a painting in Mary Sidney's laboratory, the one of the firedrake capturing the moon in its mouth." He wondered if it would be visible to others or if only his vampire eyes could detect it. "It's beautiful. Another sign of your courage."

"You told me I was reckless," Diana said breathlessly as his mouth descended to the dragon's head.

"You are." Matthew traced the swirling path of the dragon's tail with his lips and tongue. His mouth drifted lower, deeper. "It drives me crazy."

He battened his mouth on her, keeping Diana on the edge of desire, stopping his attentions to whisper an endearment or a promise before resuming, never allowing her to be swept away. She wanted satisfaction and the peace that came with forgetting, but he wanted this moment—filled with safety and intimacy—to last forever. Matthew turned Diana to face him. Her lips were soft and full, her eyes dreamy, as he slid slowly inside her. He continued his gentle movements until the upward tick in his wife's heartbeat told him that her climax was near.

Diana cried his name, weaving a spell that put them in the center of the world.

Afterward they lay twined together in the final rose-tinged moments of darkness before dawn. Diana drew Matthew's head to her breast. He gave her a questioning look, and his wife nodded. Matthew lowered his mouth to the silvery moon over a prominent blue vein.

This was the ancient way for a vampire to know his mate, the sacred moment of communion when thoughts and emotions were exchanged honestly and without judgment. Vampires were secretive creatures, but when a vampire took blood from his mate's heart vein, there was a moment of perfect peace and understanding that quieted the constant, dull need to hunt and possess.

Diana's skin parted underneath his teeth, and Matthew drank in a few precious ounces of her blood. With it came a flood of impressions and feelings: joy mixed with sorrow, delight in being back with friends and family tempered with grief, rage over Emily's death held in check by Diana's concern for him and their children.

"I would have spared you this loss if I could have," Matthew murmured, kissing the mark his mouth left on her skin. He rolled them over so that he was on his back and Diana was draped over his recumbent form. She looked down into his eyes.

"I know. Just don't ever leave me, Matthew. Not without saying goodbye."

"I will never leave you," he promised.

Diana touched her lips to Matthew's forehead. She pressed them into the skin between his eyes. Most warmblooded mates could not share in the vampire's ritual of togetherness, but his wife had found a way around the limitation, as she did with most obstacles in her path. Diana had discovered that when she kissed him just here, she also caught glimpses of his innermost thoughts and the dark places where his fears and secrets hid.

Matthew felt nothing more than a tingle of her power as she gave him her witch's kiss and remained as still as possible, wanting Diana to take her fill of him. He forced himself to relax so that his feelings and thoughts could flow unimpeded.

"Welcome home, *sister*." The unexpected scent of wood fires and saddle leather flooded the room, as Baldwin ripped the sheet from the bed.

Diana let out a startled cry. Matthew tried to pull her naked body behind him, but it was too late. His wife was already in the grip of another.

"I could hear my father's blood vow halfway up the drive. You're pregnant, too." Baldwin de Clermont's face was coldly furious under his fiery hair as his eyes dropped to Diana's rounded belly. He twisted her arm so that he could sniff her wrist. "And only Matthew's scent upon you. Well, well."

Baldwin released Diana, and Matthew caught her.

"Get up. Both of you," Baldwin commanded, his fury evident.

"You have no authority over me, Baldwin!" Diana cried, her eyes narrowing.

She couldn't have calculated a response that would have angered Matthew's brother more. Without warning, Baldwin swooped until his face was inches away. Only the firm pressure of Matthew's hand around Baldwin's throat kept the vampire from getting even closer.

"My father's blood vow says I do, witch." Baldwin stared into Diana's eyes, trying to force her through sheer will to look away. When she did not, Baldwin's eyes flickered. "Your wife lacks manners, Matthew. School her, or I will."

"School me?" Diana's eyes widened. Her fingers splayed, and the wind in the room circled her feet, ready to answer her call. High above, Corra shrieked to let her mistress know she was on the way.

"No magic and no dragon," Matthew murmured against her ear, praying that just this once his wife would obey him. He didn't want Baldwin or anyone else in the family to know how much Diana's abilities had grown while they were in London.

Miraculously, Diana nodded.

"What is the meaning of this?" Ysabeau's frosty voice cracked through the room. "The only excuse for your presence here, Baldwin, is that you have lost your senses."

"Careful, Ysabeau. Your claws are showing." Baldwin stalked toward the stairs. "And you forget: I'm the head of the de Clermont family. I don't need an excuse. Meet me in the family library, Matthew. You, too, Diana."

Baldwin turned to level his strange golden-brown eyes at Matthew.

"Don't keep me waiting."

The de Clermont family library was bathed in a gentle predawn light that made everything in it appear in soft focus: the edges of the books, the strong lines of the wooden bookcases that lined the room, the warm golden and blue hues of the Aubusson rug.

What it could not blunt was my anger.

For three days I had thought that nothing could displace my grief over Emily's death, but three minutes in Baldwin's company had proved me wrong.

"Come in, Diana." Baldwin sat in a thronelike Savonarola chair by the tall windows. His burnished red-gold hair gleamed in the lamplight, its color reminding me of the feathers on Augusta, the eagle that Emperor Rudolf hunted with in Prague. Every inch of Baldwin's muscular frame was taut with anger and banked strength.

I looked around the room. We were not the only ones to have been summoned to Baldwin's impromptu meeting. Waiting by the fireplace was a waif of a young woman with skin the color of skim milk and black, spiky hair. Her eyes were deep gray and enormous, fringed with thick lashes. She sniffed the air as though scenting a storm.

"Verin." Matthew had warned me about Philippe's daughters, who were so terrifying that the family asked him to stop making them. But she didn't look very frightening. Verin's face was smooth and serene, her posture easy, and her eyes sparkled with energy and intelligence. Were it not for her unrelieved black clothing, you might mistake her for an elf.

Then I noticed a knife hilt peeking out from her high-heeled black boots.

"Wölfling," Verin replied. It was a cold greeting for a sister to give her brother, but the look she gave me was even more frigid. "Witch."

"It's Diana," I said, my anger flaring.

"I told you there was no way to mistake it," Verin said, turning to Baldwin without acknowledging my reply.

"Why are you here, Baldwin?" Matthew asked.

"I wasn't aware I needed an invitation to come to my father's house," he replied. "But as it happens, I came from Venice to see Marcus."

The eyes of the two men locked.

"Imagine my surprise at finding you here," Baldwin continued. "Nor did I expect to discover that your *mate* is now my sister. Philippe died in 1945. So how is it that I can feel my father's blood vow? Smell it? Hear it?"

"Someone else can catch you up on the news." Matthew took me by the hand and turned to go back upstairs.

"Neither of you is leaving my sight until I find out how that witch tricked a blood vow from a dead vampire." Baldwin's voice was low with menace.

"It was no trick," I said, indignant.

"Was it necromancy, then? Some foul resurrection spell?" Baldwin asked. "Or did you conjure his spirit and force him to give you his vow?"

"What happened between Philippe and me had nothing to do with my magic and everything to do with his generosity." My own anger burned hotter.

"You make it sound as though you knew him," Baldwin said. "That's impossible."

"Not for a timewalker," I replied.

"Timewalker?" Baldwin was stunned.

"Diana and I have been in the past," Matthew explained. "In 1590, to be exact. We were here at Sept-Tours just before Christmas."

"You saw Philippe?" Baldwin asked.

"We did. Philippe was alone that winter. He sent a coin and ordered me home," Matthew said. The de Clermonts present understood their father's private code: When a command was sent along with one of Philippe's ancient silver coins, the recipient was to obey without question.

"December? That means we have to endure five more months of Philippe's bloodsong," Verin muttered, her fingers pinching the bridge of her nose as though her head ached. I frowned.

"Why five months?" I asked.

"According to our legends, a vampire's blood vow sings for a year and a day. All vampires can hear it, but the song is particularly loud and clear to those who carry Philippe's blood in their veins," Baldwin said.

"Philippe said he wanted there to be no doubt I was a de Clermont," I said, looking up at Matthew. All the vampires who had met me in the sixteenth century must have heard Philippe's bloodsong and known I was not only Matthew's mate but also Philippe de Clermont's daughter. Philippe had been protecting me during every step of our journey through the past.

"No witch will ever be recognized as a de Clermont." Baldwin's voice was flat and final.

"I already am." I held up my left hand so he could see my wedding ring. "Matthew and I are married as well as mated. Your father hosted the ceremony. If Saint-Lucien's parish registers survive, you'll find our wedding took place on the seventh of December, 1590."

"What we will likely find, should we go to the village, is that a single page has been torn out of the priest's book," Verin said under her breath. "*Atta* always covered his tracks."

"Whether you and Matthew are married is of no consequence, for Matthew is not a true de Clermont either," Baldwin said coldly. "He is merely the child of my father's mate."

"That's ridiculous," I protested. "Philippe considered Matthew his son. Matthew calls you brother and Verin sister."

"I am not that whelp's sister. We share no blood, only a name," Verin said. "And thank God for it."

"You will find, Diana, that marriage and mating don't count for much with most of the de Clermonts," said a quiet voice with a marked Spanish or Portuguese accent. It came from the mouth of a stranger standing just inside the door. His dark hair and espresso-colored eyes set off his pale golden skin and light shirt.

"Your presence wasn't requested, Fernando," Baldwin said angrily.

"As you know, I come when I'm needed, not when I'm called." Fernando bowed slightly in my direction. "Fernando Gonçalves. I am very sorry for your loss."

The man's name pricked at my memory. I'd heard it somewhere before.

"You're the man Matthew asked to lead the Knights of Lazarus when he gave up the position of grand master," I said, finally placing him. Fernando Gonçalves was reputed to be one of the brotherhood's most formidable warriors. Judging by the breadth of his shoulders and his overall fitness, I had no doubt this was true.

"He did." Like that of all vampires, Fernando's voice was warm and rich, filling the room with otherworldly sound. "But Hugh de Clermont is my mate. Ever since he died alongside the Templars, I have had little to do with chivalric orders, for even the bravest knights lack the courage to keep their promises." Fernando fixed his dark eyes on Matthew's brother. "Isn't that right, Baldwin?"

"Are you challenging me?" Baldwin said, standing.

"Do I need to?" Fernando smiled. He was shorter than Baldwin, but something told me he would not be easy to best in battle. "I would not have thought you would ignore your father's blood vow, Baldwin."

"We have no idea what Philippe wanted from the witch. He might have been trying to learn more about her power. Or she could have used magic to coerce him," Baldwin said, his chin jutting out at a stubborn angle.

"Don't be daft. Auntie didn't use any magic on Granddad." Gallowglass breezed into the room, as relaxed as if the de Clermonts always met at half past four in the morning to discuss urgent business.

"Now that Gallowglass is here, I'll leave the de Clermonts to their own devices." Fernando nodded to Matthew. "Call if you need me, Matthew."

"We'll be just fine. We're family, after all." Gallowglass blinked innocently at Verin and Baldwin as Fernando departed. "As for what Philippe wanted, it's quite simple, Uncle: He wanted you to formally acknowledge Diana as his daughter. Ask Verin."

"What does he mean?" Baldwin demanded of his sister.

"*Atta* summoned me a few days before he died," Verin said, her voice low and her expression miserable. The word "*Atta*" was unfamiliar, but it was clearly a daughterly endearment. "Philippe was worried that you might ignore his blood vow. He made me swear to acknowledge it, no matter what."

"Philippe's oath was private—something between him and me. It doesn't need to be acknowledged. Not by you or anyone else." I didn't want my memories of Philippe—or that moment—damaged by Baldwin and Verin.

"Nothing is more public than adopting a warmblood into a vampire clan," Verin told me. She looked at Matthew. "Didn't you take the time to teach the witch our vampire customs before you rushed into this forbidden affair?"

"Time was a luxury we didn't have," I replied instead. From the very beginning of our relationship, Ysabeau had warned me that I had a lot to learn about vampires. After this conversation, the topic of blood vows was moving to the head of my research agenda.

"Then let me explain it to you," Verin said, her voice sharper than any schoolmarm's. "Before Philippe's bloodsong fades, one of his full-blooded children must acknowledge it. Unless that happens, you are not truly a de Clermont and no other vampire is obligated to honor you as such."

"Is that all? I don't care about vampire honor. Being Matthew's wife is enough for me." The more I heard about becoming a de Clermont, the less I liked it.

"If that were true, then my father wouldn't have adopted you," Verin observed.

"We will compromise," Baldwin said. "Surely Philippe would be satisfied if, when the witch's children are born, their names are listed among my kin on the de Clermont family pedigree." His words sounded magnanimous, but I was sure there was some darker purpose to them.

"My children are not your kin." Matthew's voice sounded like thunder.

"They are if Diana is a de Clermont as she claims," Baldwin said with a smile.

"Wait. What pedigree?" I needed to back up a step in the argument.

"The Congregation maintains official pedigrees of all vampire families," Baldwin said. "Some no longer observe the tradition. The de Clermonts do. The pedigrees include information about rebirths, deaths, and the names of mates and their offspring."

My hand automatically covered my belly. I wanted the Congregation to remain unaware of my children for as long as possible. Based on the wary look in Matthew's eyes, he felt the same way.

"Maybe your timewalking will be enough to satisfy questions about the blood vow, but only the blackest of magics—or infidelity—can explain this pregnancy," Baldwin said, relishing his brother's discomfort. "The children cannot be yours, Matthew."

"Diana is carrying *my* children," Matthew said, his eyes dangerously dark.

"Impossible," Baldwin stated flatly.

"True," Matthew retorted.

"If so, they'll be the most hated—and the most hunted—children the world has ever known. Creatures will be baying for their blood. And yours," Baldwin said.

I registered Matthew's sudden departure from my side at the same moment that I heard Baldwin's chair break. When the blur of movement ceased, Matthew stood behind his brother with his arm locked around Baldwin's throat, pressing a knife into the skin over his brother's heart.

Verin looked down at her boot in amazement and found nothing but an empty scabbard. She swore.

"You may be head of the family, Baldwin, but never forget that I am its assassin," Matthew growled.

"Assassin?" I tried to hide my confusion as another hidden side of Matthew was brought to light.

Scientist. Vampire. Warrior. Spy. Prince.

Assassin.

Matthew had told me he was a killer—repeatedly—but I had always considered this part and parcel of being a vampire. I knew he'd killed in self-defense, in battle, and to survive. I'd never dreamed that Matthew committed murder at his family's behest.

"Surely you knew this?" Verin asked in a voice tinged with malice, her cold eyes studying me closely. "If Matthew weren't so good at it, one of us would have put him down long ago."

"We all have a role in this family, Verin." Matthew's voice dripped with bitterness. "Does Ernst know yours—how it begins between soft sheets and a man's thighs?"

Verin moved like lightning, her fingers bent into lethal claws as she went for Matthew.

Vampires were fast, but magic was faster.

I pushed Verin against a wall with a blast of witchwind, keeping her away from my husband and Baldwin long enough for Matthew to exact some promise from his brother and release him.

"Thank you, *ma lionne.*" It was Matthew's usual endearment when I'd done something brave—or incredibly stupid. He handed me Verin's knife. "Hold on to this."

Matthew lifted Verin to her feet while Gallowglass moved closer to stand at my elbow.

"Well, well," Verin murmured when she was standing upright again. "I see why *Atta* was drawn to your wife, but I wouldn't have thought you had the stones for such a woman, Matthew."

"Things change," Matthew said shortly.

"Apparently." Verin gave me an appraising look.

"You'll be keeping your promise to Granddad, then?" Gallowglass asked Verin.

"We'll see," she said cautiously. "I have months to decide."

"Time will pass, but nothing will change." Baldwin looked at me with barely concealed loathing. "Recognizing Matthew's wife will have catastrophic consequences, Verin."

"I honored *Atta*'s wishes while he lived," Verin said. "I cannot ignore them now that he is dead."

"We must take comfort from the fact that the Congregation is already looking for Matthew and his mate," Baldwin said. "Who knows? They may both be dead before December."

After giving us a final, contemptuous look, Baldwin stalked from the room. Verin stole an apologetic glance at Gallowglass and trailed after him.

"So . . . that went well," Gallowglass muttered "Are you all right, Auntie? You've gone a bit shiny."

"The witchwind blew my disguising spell out of place." I tried to tug it around me again.

"Given what happened here this morning, I think you'd better keep it on while Baldwin is at home," Gallowglass suggested.

"Baldwin cannot know of Diana's power. I'd appreciate your help with that, Gallowglass. Fernando's, too." Matthew didn't specify what form this assistance would take.

"Of course. I've been watching over Auntie her whole life," Gallowglass said, matter-of-fact. "I'll not be stopping now."

At these words parts of my past that I had never understood slid into place like jagged puzzle pieces. As a child I'd often felt other creatures watching me, their eyes nudging and tingling and freezing my skin. One had been Peter Knox, my father's enemy and the same witch who had come to Sept-Tours looking for Matthew and me only to kill Em. Could another have been this giant bear of a man, whom I now loved like a brother but had not even met until we traveled back to the sixteenth century?

"You were watching me?" My eyes filled, and I blinked back the tears.

"I promised Granddad I'd keep you safe. For Matthew's sake." Gallowglass's blue eyes softened. "And it's a good thing, too. You were a right hellion: climbing trees, running after bicycles in the street, and heading into the forest without a hint as to where you were going. How your parents managed is beyond me."

"Did Daddy know?" I had to ask. My father had met the big Gael in Elizabethan London, when he'd unexpectedly run into Matthew and me on one of his regular timewalks. Even in modern-day Massachusetts, my father would have recognized Gallowglass on sight. The man was unmistakable.

"I did my best not to show myself."

"That's not what I asked, Gallowglass." I was getting better at ferreting out a vampire's half-truths. "Did my father know you were watching over me?"

"I made sure Stephen saw me just before he and your mother left for Africa that last time," Gallowglass confessed, his voice little more than a whisper. "I thought it might help him to know, when the end came, that I was nearby. You were still such a wee thing. Stephen must have been beside himself with worry thinking about how long it would be before you were with Matthew."

Unbeknownst to Matthew or me, the Bishops and the de Clermonts had been working for years, even centuries, to bring us safely together: Philippe, Gallowglass, my father, Emily, my mother.

"Thank you, Gallowglass," Matthew said hoarsely. Like me, he was surprised by the morning's revelations.

"No need, Uncle. I did it gladly." Gallowglass cleared the emotion from his throat and departed.

An awkward silence fell.

"Christ." Matthew raked his fingers through his hair. It was the usual sign he'd been driven to the end of his patience.

"What are we going to do?" I said, still trying to regain my equilibrium after Baldwin's sudden appearance.

A gentle cough announced a new presence in the room and kept Matthew from responding.

"I am sorry to interrupt, *milord*." Alain Le Merle, Philippe de Clermont's onetime squire, stood in the doorway to the library. He was holding an ancient coffer with the initials P.C. picked out on the top in silver studs and a small ledger bound in green buckram. His salt-and-pepper hair and kind expression were the same as when I'd first met him in 1590. Like Matthew and Gallowglass, he was a fixed star in my universe of change.

"What is it, Alain?" Matthew asked.

"I have business with Madame de Clermont," Alain replied.

"Business?" Matthew frowned. "Can it wait?"

"I'm afraid not," Alain said apologetically. "This is a difficult time I know, *milord*, but *Sieur* Philippe was adamant that Madame de Clermont be given her things as soon as possible."

Alain ushered us back up to our tower. What I saw on Matthew's desk drove the events of the past hour completely from my mind and left me breathless.

A small book bound in brown leather.

An embroidered sleeve, threadbare with age.

Priceless jewels—pearls and diamonds and sapphires.

A golden arrowhead on a long chain.

A pair of miniatures, their bright surfaces as fresh as the day they were painted.

Letters, tied with a faded carnation ribbon.

A silver rat trap, tarnish clinging to the fine engraving.

A gilded astronomical instrument fit for an emperor.

A wooden box carved by a wizard out of a branch from a rowan tree.

The collection of objects didn't look like much, but they held enormous significance, for they represented the past eight months of our lives.

I picked up the small book with a trembling hand and flipped it open. Matthew had given it to me soon after we'd arrived at his mansion in Woodstock. In the autumn of 1590, the book's binding had been fresh and the pages creamy. Today the leather was speckled and the paper yellowed with age. In the past I'd tucked the book away on a high shelf in the Old Lodge, but a bookplate inside told me that it was now the property of a library in Seville. The call mark, *"Manuscrito Gonçalves 4890,"* was inked onto the flyleaf. Someone—Gallowglass, no doubt—had removed the first page. Once it had been covered with my tentative attempts to record my name. The blots from that missing leaf had seeped through to the page below, but the list I'd made of the Elizabethan coins in circulation in 1590 was still legible.

I flipped through the rest of the pages, remembering the headache cure I'd attempted to master in a futile attempt to appear a proper Elizabethan housewife. My diary of daily happenings brought back bittersweet memories of our time with the School of Night. I'd dedicated a handful of pages to an overview of the twelve signs of the zodiac, copied down a few more recipes, and scribbled a packing list for our journey to Sept-Tours in the back. I heard the gentle chime as past and present rubbed against each other, and I spotted the blue and amber threads that were barely visible in the corners of the fireplace.

"How did you get this?" I said, focusing on the here and now.

"Master Gallowglass gave it to Dom Fernando long ago. When he arrived at Sept-Tours in May, Dom Fernando asked me to return it to you," Alain explained.

"It's a miracle anything survived. How did you manage to keep all this hidden from me for so many years?" Matthew picked up the silver rat trap. He had teased me when I'd commissioned one of London's most expensive clockmakers to make the mechanism to catch the rats prowling our attics in the Blackfriars. Monsieur Vallin had designed it to resemble a cat, with ears set on the crossbars and a little mouse perched on the fierce feline's nose. Matthew deliberately sprang the mechanism, and the cat's sharp teeth dug into the flesh of his finger.

"We did as we must, *milord*. We waited. We kept silent. We never lost faith that time would bring Madame de Clermont back to us." A sad smile played at the corners of Alain's mouth. "If only *Sieur* Philippe could have lived to see this day."

At the thought of Philippe, my heart skittered. He must have known how badly his children would react to having me as a sister. Why had he put me in such an impossible situation?

"All right, Diana?" Matthew gently laid his hand over mine.

"Yes. Just a bit overwhelmed." I took up the portraits of Matthew and me wearing fine Elizabethan clothing. Nicholas Hilliard had painted them at the Countess of Pembroke's request. She and the Earl of Northumberland had given the tiny likenesses to us as wedding gifts. The two of them had been Matthew's friends at first—along with the other members of the School of Night: Walter Raleigh, George Chapman, Thomas Harriot, and Christopher Marlowe. In time most of them became my friends, too.

"It was Madame Ysabeau who found the miniatures," Alain explained. "She scoured the newspapers every day looking for traces of you—anomalies that stood out from the rest of the day's events. When Madame Ysabeau saw these in an auction notice, she sent Master Marcus to London. It's how he met Mademoiselle Phoebe."

"This sleeve came from your wedding dress." Matthew touched the fragile fabric, tracing the outlines of a cornucopia, the traditional symbol of abundance. "I will never forget the sight of you, coming down the hill to the village with the torches blazing and the children clearing the way through the snow." His smile was full of love and a pleased pride.

"After the wedding many men in the village offered to pay Madame de Clermont court, should you tire of her." Alain chuckled.

"Thank you for keeping all of these memories for me." I looked down at the desk. "It's much too easy to think I somehow imagined everything—that we were never really there in 1590. This makes that time seem real again."

"*Sieur* Philippe thought you might feel that way. Alas, there are two more items that require your attention, Madame de Clermont." Alain held out the ledger. A tied string kept it from being opened, and a blob of wax sealed the knot to the cover.

"What's this?" I frowned and took the ledger. It was far thinner than the ones here in Matthew's study that contained the financial records of the Knights of Lazarus.

"Your accounts, *madame.*"

"I thought Hamish was keeping my finances." He'd left piles of documents for me, all of them awaiting my signature.

"Mr. Osborne took charge of your marriage settlement from *milord.* These are the funds you received from *Sieur* Philippe." Alain's attention lingered for a moment on my forehead, where Philippe had placed his blood to claim me as his daughter.

Curious, I cracked the seal and opened the covers. The little account book had been rebound periodically when more pages were required. The first entries were made on thick sixteenth-century paper and dated from the year 1591. One accounted for the deposit of the dowry that Philippe had provided when I married Matthew: 20,000 Venetian zecchini and 30,000 silver Reichsthaler. Every subsequent investment of that money—such as the roll-over of any interest paid on the funds and the houses and land purchased with the proceeds—was meticulously accounted for in Alain's neat hand. I flipped through to the final pages of the book. The last entry, made on sparkling white bond, was dated 4 July 2010, the day we had arrived back at Sept-Tours. My eyes popped at the amount indicated in the assets column.

"I am sorry it is not more," Alain said hastily, mistaking my reaction for alarm. "I invested your money as I did my own, but the more lucrative, and therefore riskier, opportunities would have required *Sieur* Baldwin's approval, and of course he could not know of your existence."

"It's more than I could ever imagine possessing, Alain." Matthew had settled a substantial amount of property on me when he drew up our marriage agreement, but this was a vast sum. Philippe had wanted me to have financial independence like the rest of the de Clermont women. And as I had learned this morning, my father-in-law, whether dead or alive, got what he wanted. I put the ledger aside. "Thank you."

"It was my pleasure," Alain said with a bow. He drew something from his pocket. "Finally, *Sieur* Philippe instructed me to give you this."

Alain handed me an envelope made from cheap, thin stock. My name was on the front. Though the poor adhesive had long since dried up, the envelope had been sealed with a swirl of black and red waxes. An ancient coin was embedded in it: Philippe's special signal.

"*Sieur* Philippe worked on this letter for over an hour. He made me read it back to him when he finished, to be sure that it captured what he wanted to say."

"When?" Matthew asked hoarsely.

"The day he died." Alain's expression was haunted.

The shaky handwriting belonged to someone too old or infirm to hold a pen properly. It was a vivid reminder of how much Philippe had suffered. I traced my name. When my fingertips reached the final letter, I dragged them across the surface of the envelope, pulling at the letters so that they unraveled. First there was a pool of black on the envelope, and then the ink resolved into the image of a man's face. It was still beautiful, though ravaged with pain and marred by a deep, empty socket where once a tawny eye had shimmered with intelligence and humor.

"You didn't tell me the Nazis had blinded him." I knew that my father-in-law had been tortured, but I had never imagined his captors had inflicted this much damage. I studied the other wounds on Philippe's face. Mercifully, there weren't enough letters in my name to draw a detailed portrait. I touched my father-in-law's cheek gently, and the image dissolved, leaving an ink stain on the envelope. With a flick of my fingers, the stain lifted into a small black tornado. When the whirling stopped, the letters dropped back into their proper place.

"*Sieur* Philippe often spoke with you about his troubles, Madame de Clermont," Alain continued softly, "when the pain was very bad."

"Spoke with her?" Matthew repeated numbly.

"Almost every day," Alain said with a nod. "He would bid me to send everyone from that part of the château, for fear someone would overhear. Madame de Clermont brought *Sieur* Philippe comfort when no one else could."

I turned the envelope over, tracing the raised markings on the ancient silver coin. "Philippe expected his coins to be returned to him. In person. How can I, if he's dead?"

"Perhaps the answer is inside," Matthew suggested.

I slid my finger under the envelope's seal, freeing the coin from the wax. I carefully removed the fragile sheet of paper, which crackled ominously as it was unfolded.

Philippe's faint scent of bay, figs, and rosemary tickled my nose.

Looking down at the paper, I was grateful for my expertise in deciphering difficult handwriting. After a close look, I began to read the letter aloud.

Diana—

> *Do not let the ghosts of the past steal the joy from the future.*
> *Thank you for holding my hand.*
> *You can let go now.*
> *Your father, in blood and vow,*
> > *Philippe*
>
> *P.S. The coin is for the ferryman. Tell Matthew I will see you safe on the other side.*

I choked on the last few words. They echoed in the silent room.

"So Philippe does expect me to return his coin." He would be sitting on the banks of the river Styx waiting for Charon's boat to bring me across. Perhaps Emily waited with him, and my parents, too. I closed my eyes, hoping to block out the painful images.

"What did he mean, '*Thank you for holding my hand*'?" Matthew asked.

"I promised him he wouldn't be alone in the dark times. That I'd be there, with him." My eyes brimmed with tears. "How can I have no memory of doing so?"

"I don't know, my love. But somehow you managed to keep your promise." Matthew leaned down and kissed me. He looked over my shoulder. "And Philippe made sure he got the last word, as usual."

"What do you mean?" I asked, wiping at my cheeks.

"He left written proof that he freely and gladly wanted you for his daughter." Matthew's long white finger touched the page.

"That is why *Sieur* Philippe wanted Madame de Clermont to have these as soon as possible," Alain admitted.

"I don't understand," I said, looking at Matthew.

"Between the jewels, your dowry, and this letter, it will be impossible for any of Philippe's children—or even the Congregation—to suggest he was somehow forced to bestow a blood vow on you," Matthew explained.

"*Sieur* Philippe knew his children well. He often foresaw their future as easily as any witch," Alain said, nodding. "I will leave you to your memories."

"Thank you, Alain." Matthew waited until the sound of Alain's footsteps faded before saying anything more. He looked down at me with concern. "All right, *mon coeur*?"

"Of course," I murmured, staring at the desk. The past was strewn across it, and a clear future was nowhere to be found.

"I'm going upstairs to change. I won't be long," Matthew said, giving me a kiss. "Then we can go down to breakfast."

"Take your time," I said, mustering what I hoped was a genuine smile.

Once Matthew was gone, I reached for the golden arrowhead that Philippe gave me to wear at my wedding. Its weight was comforting, and the metal warmed quickly to my touch. I slipped its chain over my head.

The arrowhead's point nestled between my breasts, its edges too soft and worn to nick my skin.

I felt a squirming sensation in the pocket of my jeans and drew out a clutch of silk ribbons. My weaver's cords had come with me from the past, and unlike the sleeve from my wedding dress or the faded silk that bound my letters, these strands were fresh and shiny. They twined and danced around my wrists and one another like a handful of brightly colored snakes, merging into new colors for a moment before separating into their original strands and hues. The cords snaked up my arms and wormed their way into my hair as if they were looking for something. I pulled them free and tucked the silks away.

I was supposed to be the weaver. But would I ever comprehend the tangled web that Philippe de Clermont had been spinning when he made me his blood-sworn daughter?

Were you ever going to tell me you were the de Clermont family's assassin?" I asked, reaching for the grapefruit juice.

Matthew looked at me in silence across the kitchen table where Marthe had laid out my morning meal. He had sneaked Hector and Fallon inside, and they were following our conversation—and my selection of foods—with interest.

"And Fernando's relationship with your brother Hugh?" I asked. "I was raised by two women. You couldn't possibly have been withholding that piece of information because you thought I might disapprove."

Hector and Fallon looked to Matthew for an answer. When none was forthcoming, the dogs looked back at me.

"Verin seems nice," I said, deliberately trying to provoke him.

"Nice?" Matthew beetled his eyebrows at me.

"Well, except for the fact she was armed with a knife," I admitted mildly, pleased that my strategy had worked.

"Knives," Matthew corrected me. "She had one in her boot, one in her waistband, and one in her bra."

"Was Verin ever a Girl Scout?" It was my turn to lift my brows.

Before Matthew could answer, Gallowglass shot through the kitchen in a streak of blue and black, followed by Fernando. Matthew scrambled to his feet. When the dogs got up to follow, he pointed to the floor and they immediately sat down again.

"Finish your breakfast, then go to the tower," Matthew ordered just before he vanished. "Take the dogs with you. And don't come down until I come and get you."

"What's going on?" I asked Marthe, blinking at the suddenly vacant room.

"Baldwin is home," she replied, as though this were a sufficient answer.

"Marcus," I said, remembering that Baldwin had returned to see Matthew's son. The dogs and I jumped up. "Where is he?"

"Philippe's office." Marthe frowned. "I do not think Matthew wants you there. There may be bloodshed."

"Story of my life." I was looking over my shoulder when I said it and ran smack into Verin as a result. A dignified older gentleman who had a tall, gaunt frame and kind eyes was with her. I tried to get around them. "Excuse me."

"Where do you think you're going?" Verin asked, blocking my way.

"Philippe's office."

"Matthew told you to go to his tower." Verin's eyes narrowed. "He is your mate, and you're supposed to obey him like a proper vampire wife." Her accent was softly Germanic—not quite German, or Austrian, or Swiss, but something that borrowed from all three.

"What a pity for all of you that I'm a witch." I stuck my hand out to the gentleman, who was watching our conversation with thinly veiled amusement. "Diana Bishop."

"Ernst Neumann. I'm Verin's husband." Ernst's accent placed his origins squarely in the neighborhood of Berlin. "Why not let Diana go after him, *Schatz*? That way you can follow. I know how you hate to miss a good argument. I will wait in the salon for the others."

"Good idea, my love. They can hardly fault me if the witch escapes from the kitchen." Verin regarded him with open admiration and gave him a lingering kiss. Though she looked young enough to be his granddaughter, it was obvious that she and Ernst were deeply in love.

"I have them occasionally," he said with a definite twinkle in his eye. "Now, before Diana runs off and you give chase, tell me: Shall I take a knife or a gun with me in case one of your brothers goes on a rampage?"

Verin considered the matter. "I think Marthe's cleaver should be sufficient. It was enough to slow down Gerbert, and his hide is far thicker than Baldwin's—or Matthew's."

"You took a cleaver to Gerbert?" I liked Ernst more and more.

"That would be an exaggeration," Ernst said, turning slightly pink with embarrassment.

"I fear that Phoebe is trying diplomacy," Verin interrupted, turning me around and facing me in the direction of the tussle. "That never works with Baldwin. We must go."

"If Ernst is taking a knife, I'm taking the dogs." I clicked my fingers at

Hector and Fallon and set off at a fast trot, the dogs following near my heels barking and wagging as though we were playing a grand game.

The second-floor landing that led to the family apartments was crowded with concerned onlookers when we arrived: Nathaniel, a round-eyed Sophie with Margaret in her arms, Hamish in a splendid silk paisley bathrobe and only one side of his face shaved, and Sarah, who appeared to have been woken up by the fracas. Ysabeau exuded ennui as if to say this sort of thing happened all the time.

"Everybody in the salon," I said, drawing Sarah in the direction of the stairs. "Ernst will join you there."

"I don't know what set Marcus off," Hamish said, wiping the shaving cream from his chin with a towel. "Baldwin called for him, and it all seemed fine at first. Then they started shouting."

The small room that Philippe used to conduct his business was filled with vampires and testosterone as Matthew, Fernando, and Gallowglass all jostled for the best position. Baldwin sat in a Windsor chair that was tipped back so he could cross his feet on the desk. Marcus leaned on the other side of the desk, his color high. Marcus's mate—for the petite young woman standing nearby was the one I dimly remembered from our first day back, Phoebe Taylor—was trying to referee the dispute between the head of the de Clermont family and the grand master of the Knights of Lazarus.

"This strange household of witches and daemons you've gathered must disband immediately," Baldwin said, trying without success to rein in his temper. His chair dropped to the floor with a bang.

"Sept-Tours belongs to the Knights of Lazarus! I am the grand master, not you. I say what happens here!" Marcus shouted back.

"Leave it, Marcus." Matthew had his son by the elbow.

"If you don't do exactly what I say, there will *be* no Knights of Lazarus!" Baldwin stood, so that the two vampires were nose to nose.

"Stop threatening me, Baldwin," Marcus said. "You aren't my father, and you aren't my master."

"No, but I am the head of this family." Baldwin's fist met the wooden desk with a resounding crash. "You will listen to me, Marcus, or accept the consequences for your disobedience."

"Why can't the two of you sit down and talk about this reasonably?"

Phoebe said, making a rather courageous effort to separate the two vampires.

Baldwin snarled at her in warning, and Marcus lunged for his uncle's throat.

Matthew grabbed Phoebe and pulled her out of the way. She was shaking, though more from anger than fear. Fernando spun Marcus around and pinned his arms to his sides. Gallowglass clamped his hand on Baldwin's shoulder.

"Do not challenge him," Fernando said sharply, when Marcus tried to worm his way free. "Not unless you are prepared to walk out of this house and never return."

After a few long moments, Marcus nodded. Fernando released him but remained close.

"These threats are absurd," Marcus said in a slightly more measured tone. "The Knights of Lazarus and the Congregation have been in bed with each other for years. We oversee their financial affairs, not to mention help them enforce order among the vampires. Surely—"

"Surely the Congregation wouldn't risk de Clermont family retaliation? Wouldn't violate the sanctuary that has always been afforded to Sept-Tours?" Baldwin shook his head. "They already have, Marcus. The Congregation is not playing games this time. They've been looking for a reason to disband the Knights of Lazarus for years."

"They're doing so now because I brought official charges against Knox for Emily's death?" Marcus asked.

"Only in part. It was your insistence on having the covenant set aside that the Congregation couldn't stomach." Baldwin thrust a roll of parchment at Marcus. Three wax seals hung from the bottom, swaying slightly due to the rough treatment. "We considered your request—again. It's been denied. Again."

That one word—"we"—solved a long-standing mystery. Since the covenant had been signed and the Congregation had been formed in the twelfth century, there had always been a de Clermont among the three vampires at the meeting table. Until now I had not known that creature's present identity: Baldwin.

"It was bad enough that a vampire interfered in a dispute between two witches," he continued. "Demanding reparations for Emily Mather's death was foolish, Marcus. But continuing to challenge the covenant was unforgivably naïve."

"What happened?" Matthew asked. He passed Phoebe into my care, though his look suggested he was none too happy to see me.

"Marcus and the other participants in his little rebellion called for an end to the covenant in April. Marcus declared that the Bishop family was under the direct protection of the Knights of Lazarus, thereby involving the brotherhood."

Matthew looked at Marcus sharply. I didn't know whether to kiss Matthew's son for his efforts to protect my family or chide him for his optimism.

"In May . . . well, you know what happened in May," Baldwin said. "Marcus characterized Emily's death as a hostile act undertaken by members of the Congregation intent on provoking open conflict between creatures. He thought that the Congregation might want to reconsider his earlier request to abandon the covenant in exchange for a truce with the Knights of Lazarus."

"It was an entirely reasonable request." Marcus unrolled the document and scanned the lines.

"Reasonable or not, the measure went down: two in favor and seven opposed," Baldwin reported. "Never allow a vote whose outcome you can't predict in advance, Marcus. You should have discovered that unpleasant truth about democracy by now."

"It's not possible. That means only you and Nathaniel's mother voted in favor of my proposal," Marcus said, bewildered. Agatha Wilson, mother to Marcus's friend Nathaniel, was one of the three daemons who were members of the Congregation.

"Another daemon sided with Agatha," Baldwin said coldly.

"You voted against it?" Clearly Marcus had counted on his family's support. Given my few dealings with Baldwin, I could have told him this was unduly hopeful.

"Let me see that," Matthew said, plucking the parchment from Marcus's fingers. His look demanded that Baldwin explain his actions.

"I had no choice," Baldwin told Matthew. "Do you know how much damage your son has done? From now on there will be whispers about how a young upstart from an inferior branch of the de Clermont family tree tried to mount an insurrection against a thousand years of tradition."

"Inferior?" I was aghast at the insult to Ysabeau. My mother-in-law didn't look at all surprised, however. If anything, she looked even more bored, studying her perfectly manicured long nails.

"You go too far, Baldwin," Gallowglass growled. "You weren't here. The rogue members of the Congregation who came here in May and killed Emily—"

"Gerbert and Knox aren't rogue members!" Baldwin said, his voice rising again. "They belong to a two-thirds majority."

"I don't care. Telling witches, vampires, and daemons to keep to themselves no longer makes sense—if it ever did," Marcus insisted, stony-faced. "Abandoning the covenant is the right thing to do."

"Since when has that mattered?" Baldwin sounded tired.

"It says here that Peter Knox has been censured," Matthew said, looking up from the document.

"More than that, Knox was forced to resign. Gerbert and Satu argued that he was provoked to take action against Emily, but the Congregation couldn't deny he played some role in the witch's death." Baldwin reclaimed his seat behind his father's desk. Though a large man, he did not seem of sufficient stature to occupy Philippe's place.

"So Knox did kill my aunt." My anger—and my power—was rising.

"He claims all he was doing was questioning her about Matthew's whereabouts and the location of a Bodleian Library manuscript—which sounded very much like the sacred text we vampires call the Book of Life," said Baldwin. "Knox said Emily became agitated when he discovered that the Wilsons' daughter was a witch but had two daemon parents. He blames her heart attack on stress."

"Emily was healthy as a horse," I retorted.

"And what price will Knox pay for killing a member of my mate's family?" Matthew asked quietly, his hand on my shoulder.

"Knox has been stripped of his seat and banned from ever serving on the Congregation again," Baldwin said. "Marcus got his way on that at least, but I'm not sure we won't regret it in the end." He and Matthew exchanged another long look. I was missing something vital.

"Who will take his place?" Matthew asked.

"It's too soon to say. The witches insist on a Scottish replacement, on the grounds that Knox hadn't finished out his term. Janet Gowdie is obviously too old to serve again, so my money would be on one of the McNivens—Kate, perhaps. Or possibly Jenny Horne," Baldwin replied.

"The Scots produce powerful witches," Gallowglass said somberly, "and the Gowdies, the Hornes, and the McNivens are the most respected families in the north."

"They may not be as easy to handle as Knox. And one thing is clear: The witches are determined to have the Book of Life," Baldwin said.

"They've always wanted it," Matthew said.

"Not like this. Knox found a letter in Prague. He says it provides proof that you either have or once had the book of origins—or the witches' original book of spells, if you prefer his version of the tale," Baldwin explained. "I told the Congregation this was nothing more than a power-hungry wizard's fantasy, but they didn't believe me. They've ordered a full inquiry."

There were many legends about the contents of the ancient book now hidden in Oxford's Bodleian Library under the call number Ashmole Manuscript 782. The witches believed that it contained the first spells ever cast, the vampires that it told the story of how they were first made. Daemons thought the book held secrets about their kind, too. I had possessed the book too briefly to know which, if any, of these stories were true—but Matthew, Gallowglass, and I knew that whatever else the Book of Life contained paled in comparison to the genetic information bound within its covers. For the Book of Life had been fashioned from the remains of once-living creatures: The parchment was made from their skin, the inks contained their blood, the pages were held together with creature hair and binding glue extracted from their bones.

"Knox said the Book of Life was damaged by a daemon named Edward Kelley, who removed three of its pages in sixteenth-century Prague. He claims you know where those pages are, Matthew." Baldwin looked at him with open curiosity. "Is that true?"

"No," Matthew said honestly, meeting Baldwin's eyes.

Like many of Matthew's answers, this was only a partial truth. He did not know the location of two of the missing pages from the Book of Life. But one of them was safely tucked into a locked drawer of his desk.

"Thank God for that," Baldwin said, satisfied with the answer. "I swore on Philippe's soul that such a charge could not be true."

Gallowglass eyed Fernando blandly. Matthew gazed out the window. Ysabeau, who could smell a lie as easily as any witch, narrowed her eyes at me.

"And the Congregation took you at your word?" Matthew asked.

"Not entirely," Baldwin said with reluctance.

"What other assurances did you make, little viper?" Ysabeau asked lazily. "You hiss so prettily, Baldwin, but there's a sting somewhere."

"I promised the Congregation that Marcus and the Knights of Lazarus would continue to uphold the covenant." Baldwin paused. "Then the Congregation selected an impartial delegation—one witch and one vampire—and charged them with inspecting Sept-Tours from top to bottom. They will make sure there are no witches or daemons or even a scrap of paper from the Book of Life within its walls. Gerbert and Satu Järvinen will be here in one week's time."

The silence was deafening.

"How was I to know that Matthew and Diana were here?" Baldwin said. "But it's no matter. The Congregation's delegation will not find a single irregularity during their visit. That means Diana must go, too."

"What else?" Matthew demanded.

"Is abandoning our friends and families not enough?" Marcus asked. Phoebe slid an arm around his waist in a gesture of comfort.

"Your uncle always delivers the good news first, Marcus," Fernando explained. "And if the prospect of a visit with Gerbert is the good news, the bad news must be very bad."

"The Congregation wants insurance." Matthew swore. "Something that will keep the de Clermonts and the Knights of Lazarus on their best behavior."

"Not something. Someone," Baldwin said flatly.

"Who?" I asked.

"Me, of course," Ysabeau said, sounding unconcerned.

"Absolutely not!" Matthew beheld Baldwin in horror.

"I'm afraid so. I offered them Verin first, but they refused," Baldwin said. Verin appeared mildly affronted.

"The Congregation may be small-minded, but they're not complete fools," Ysabeau murmured. "No one could hold Verin hostage for more than twenty-four hours."

"The witches said it had to be someone who could force Matthew out of hiding. Verin wasn't considered sufficient inducement," Baldwin explained.

"The last time I was held against my will, you were my jailer, Baldwin," Ysabeau said in a syrupy voice. "Will you do the honors again?"

"Not this time," Baldwin said. "Knox and Järvinen wanted you held in Venice, where the Congregation could keep an eye on you, but I refused."

"Why Venice?" I knew that Baldwin had come from there, but I couldn't imagine why the Congregation would prefer it to any other location.

"Venice has been the Congregation's headquarters since the fifteenth century, when we were forced out of Constantinople," Matthew explained quickly. "Nothing happens in the city without the Congregation knowing of it. And Venice is home to scores of creatures who have long-standing relationships with the council—including Domenico's brood."

"A repulsive gathering of ingrates and sycophants," Ysabeau murmured with a delicate shudder. "I'm very glad not to be going there. Even without Domenico's clan, Venice is unbearable this time of year. So many tourists. And the mosquitoes are impossible."

The thought of what vampire blood might do to the mosquito population was deeply disturbing.

"Your comfort was not the Congregation's chief concern, Ysabeau." Baldwin gave her a forbidding look.

"Where am I to go, then?" Ysabeau asked.

"After expressing appropriate initial reluctance given his long-standing friendship with the family, Gerbert has generously agreed to keep you at his home. The Congregation could hardly refuse him," Baldwin replied. "That won't pose a problem, will it?"

Ysabeau lifted her shoulders in an expressive Gallic shrug. "Not for me."

"Gerbert cannot be trusted." Matthew turned on his brother with almost as much anger as Marcus had shown. "Christ, Baldwin. He stood by and watched while Knox worked his magic on Emily!"

"I do hope Gerbert has managed to retain his butcher," Ysabeau mused as though her son had not spoken. "Marthe will have to come with me, of course. You will see to it, Baldwin."

"You're not going," Matthew said. "I'll give myself up first."

Before I could protest, Ysabeau spoke. "No, my son. Gerbert and I have done this before, as you know. I will be back in no time—a few months at most."

"Why is this necessary at all?" Marcus said. "Once the Congregation inspects Sept-Tours and finds nothing objectionable, they should leave us alone."

"The Congregation must have a hostage to demonstrate that they are greater than the de Clermonts," Phoebe explained, showing a remarkable grasp of the situation.

"But, *Grand-mère,*" Marcus began, looking stricken, "it should be me, not you. This is my fault."

"I may be your grandmother, but I am not so old and fragile as you think," Ysabeau said with a touch of frostiness. "My blood, inferior though it might be, does not shrink from its duty."

"Surely there's another way," I protested.

"No, Diana," Ysabeau answered. "We all have our roles in this family. Baldwin will bully us. Marcus will look after the brotherhood. Matthew will look after you, and you will look after my grandchildren. As for me, I find that I am invigorated at the prospect of being held for ransom once more."

My mother-in-law's feral smile made me believe her.

Having helped Baldwin and Marcus to reach a fragile state of détente, Matthew and I returned to our rooms on the other side of the château. Matthew switched on the sound system as soon as we'd passed through the doorway, flooding the room with the intricate strains of Bach. The music made it more difficult for the other vampires in the house to overhear our conversations, so Matthew invariably had something playing in the background.

"It's a good thing we know more about Ashmole 782 than Knox does," I said quietly. "Once I retrieve the book from the Bodleian Library, the Congregation will have to stop handing out ultimatums from Venice and start dealing with us directly. Then we can hold Knox accountable for Emily's death."

Matthew studied me silently for a moment, then poured himself some wine and drank it down in one gulp. He offered me water, but I shook my head. The only thing I craved at this hour was tea. Marcus had urged me to avoid caffeine during the pregnancy, however, and herbal blends were a poor substitute.

"What do you know about the Congregation's vampire pedigrees?" I took a seat on the sofa.

"Not much," Matthew replied, pouring another glass of wine. I frowned. There was no chance of a vampire getting intoxicated by drinking wine from a bottle—the only way that one could feel the influence was to consume blood from an inebriated source—but it wasn't usual for him to drink like this.

"Does the Congregation keep witch and daemon genealogies, too?" I asked, hoping to distract him.

"I don't know. The affairs of witches and daemons never concerned me." Matthew moved across the room and stood facing the fireplace.

"Well, it doesn't matter," I said, all business. "Our top priority has to be Ashmole 782. I'll need to go to Oxford as quickly as possible."

"And what will you do then, *ma lionne*?"

"Figure out a way to recall it." I thought for a moment of the conditions my father had woven through the spell that bound the book to the library. "My father made sure that the Book of Life would come to me if I need it. Our present circumstances certainly qualify."

"So the safety of Ashmole 782 is your chief concern," Matthew said with dangerous softness.

"Of course. That and finding its missing pages," I said. "Without them the Book of Life will never reveal its secrets."

When the daemon alchemist Edward Kelley removed three of its pages in sixteenth-century Prague, he had damaged whatever magic had been used in the making of the book. For protection, the text had burrowed into the parchment, creating a magical palimpsest, and the words chased one another through the pages as if looking for the missing letters. It wasn't possible to read what remained.

"After I recover it, you might be able to figure out which creatures are bound into it, perhaps even date it, by analyzing its genetic information in your lab," I continued. Matthew's scientific work focused on issues of species origins and extinction. "When I locate the two missing pages—"

Matthew turned, his face a calm mask. "You mean when *we* recover Ashmole 782 and when *we* locate the other pages."

"Matthew, be reasonable. Nothing would anger the Congregation more than the news that we were seen together at the Bodleian."

His voice got even softer, his face calmer. "You are more than three months pregnant, Diana. Members of the Congregation have already invaded my home and killed your aunt. Peter Knox is desperate to get his hands on Ashmole 782 and knows that you have the power to do it. Somehow he knows about the Book of Life's missing pages, too. You will not be going to the Bodleian Library or anywhere else without me."

"I have to put the Book of Life back together again," I said, my voice rising.

"Then *we* will, Diana. Right now Ashmole 782 is safely in the library. Leave it there and let this business with the Congregation settle down." Matthew was relying—perhaps too much—on the idea that I was the only witch who could release the spell my father had placed on the book.

"How long will that take?"

"Perhaps until after the babies are born," Matthew said.

"That may be six more months," I said, reining in my anger. "So I'm supposed to wait and gestate. And your plan is to twiddle your thumbs and watch the calendar with me?"

"I will do whatever Baldwin commands," Matthew said, drinking the last of his wine.

"You cannot be serious!" I exclaimed. "Why do you put up with his autocratic nonsense?"

"Because a strong head of the family prevents chaos, unnecessary bloodshed, and worse," Matthew explained. "You forget that I was reborn in a very different time, Diana, when most creatures were expected to obey someone else without question—your lord, your priest, your father, your husband. Carrying out Baldwin's orders is not as difficult for me as it will be for you."

"For me? I'm not a vampire," I retorted. "I don't have to listen to him."

"You do if you're a de Clermont." Matthew gripped my elbows. "The Congregation and vampire tradition have left us with precious few options. By the middle of December, you will be a fully fledged member of Baldwin's family. I know Verin, and she would never renege on a promise made to Philippe."

"I don't need Baldwin's help," I said. "I'm a weaver and have power of my own."

"Baldwin mustn't know about that," Matthew said, holding me tighter. "Not yet. And no one can offer you or our children the security that Baldwin and the rest of the de Clermonts can."

"*You* are a de Clermont," I said, jabbing a finger into his chest. "Philippe made that perfectly clear."

"Not in the eyes of other vampires." Matthew took my hand in his. "I may be Philippe de Clermont's kin, but I am not his blood. You are. For that reason alone, I will do whatever Baldwin asks me to do."

"Even kill Knox?"

Matthew looked surprised.

"You're Baldwin's assassin. Knox trespassed on de Clermont land, which is a direct challenge to the family's honor. I assume that makes Knox your problem." I kept my tone matter-of-fact, but it took effort. I knew that Matthew had killed men before, but somehow the word "assassin" made those deaths more disturbing.

"As I said, I'll follow Baldwin's orders." Matthew's gray eyes had taken on a greenish cast and were cold and lifeless.

"I don't care what Baldwin commands. You can't go after a witch, Matthew—certainly not one who was once a member of the Congregation," I said. "It will only make matters worse."

"After what he did to Emily, Knox is already a dead man," Matthew said. He released me and strode to the window.

The threads around him flashed red and black. The fabric of the world wasn't visible to every witch, but as a weaver—a maker of spells, like my father—I could see it plainly.

I joined Matthew at the window. The sun was up now, highlighting the green hills with gold. It looked so pastoral and serene, but I knew that rocks lay below the surface, as hard and forbidding as the man I loved. I slid my arms around Matthew's waist and rested my head against him. This was how he held me when I needed to feel safe.

"You don't have to go after Knox for me," I told him, "or for Baldwin."

"No," he said softly. "I have to do it for Emily."

They'd laid Em to rest within the ruins of the ancient nearby temple consecrated to the goddess. I'd been there before with Philippe, and Matthew had insisted I see the grave shortly after our return so that I would have to face that my aunt was gone—forever. Since then I'd visited it a few times when I needed quiet and some time to think. Matthew had asked me not to go alone. Today Ysabeau was my escort, as I needed time away from my husband, as well as from Baldwin and the troubles that had soured the air at Sept-Tours.

The place was as beautiful as I remembered, with the cypress trees standing like sentinels around broken columns that were barely visible now. Today the ground was not snow-covered, as it had been in December of 1590, but lush and green—except for the rectangular brown slash that marked Em's final resting place. There were hoofprints in the soft earth and a faint depression on the top.

"A white hart has taken to sleeping on the grave," Ysabeau explained, following my glance. "They are very rare."

"A white buck appeared when Philippe and I came here before my wedding to make offerings to the goddess." I'd felt her power then, ebbing and flowing under my feet. I felt it now, but said nothing. Matthew had been adamant that no one must know about my magic.

"Philippe told me he met you," Ysabeau said. "He left a note for me in the binding of one of Godfrey's alchemical books." Through the notes Philippe and Ysabeau had shared the tiny details of everyday life that would otherwise be easily forgotten.

"How you must miss him." I swallowed down the lump that threatened to choke me. "He was extraordinary, Ysabeau."

"Yes," she said softly. "We shall never see another one such as him."

The two of us stood near the grave, silent and reflective.

"What happened this morning will change everything," Ysabeau said. "The Congregation's inquiry will make it more difficult to keep our secrets. And Matthew has more to hide than most of us."

"Like the fact that he's the family's assassin?" I asked.

"Yes," Ysabeau said. "Many vampire families would dearly like to know which member of the de Clermont clan is responsible for the deaths of their loved ones."

"When we were here with Philippe, I thought I'd uncovered most of Matthew's secrets. I know about his attempted suicide. And what he did for his father." It had been the hardest secret for my husband to reveal—that he had helped Philippe to his death.

"With vampires there is no end to them," Ysabeau said. "But secrets are unreliable allies. They allow us to believe we are safe, yet all the while they are destroying us."

I wondered if I was one of the destructive secrets lying at the heart of the de Clermont family. I drew an envelope from my pocket and handed it to Ysabeau. She saw the crabbed handwriting, and her face froze.

"Alain gave me this note. Philippe wrote it on the day he died," I explained. "I'd like you to read it. I think the message was meant for all of us."

Ysabeau's hand trembled as she unfolded the single sheet. She opened it carefully and read the few lines aloud. One of the lines struck me with renewed force: *"Do not let the ghosts of the past rob the future of its joys."*

"Oh, Philippe," she said sadly. Ysabeau handed back the note and reached for my forehead. For one unguarded moment, I saw the woman she had once been: formidable but capable of joy. She stopped, her finger withdrawing.

I caught her hand. She was colder even than her son. I gently set her icy fingers on the skin between my eyebrows, giving her silent permission to examine the place where Philippe de Clermont had marked me. The pressure of Ysabeau's fingers changed infinitesimally while she explored my forehead. When she stepped away, I could see her throat working.

"I do feel . . . something. A presence, some hint of Philippe." Ysabeau's eyes were shining.

"I wish he were here," I confessed. "He would know what to do about this mess: Baldwin, the blood vow, the Congregation, Knox, even Ashmole 782."

"My husband never *did* anything unless it was absolutely necessary," Ysabeau replied.

"But he was always doing something." I thought of how he'd orchestrated our trip to Sept-Tours in 1590, in spite of the weather and Matthew's reluctance.

"Not so. He watched. He waited. Philippe let others take the risks while he gathered their secrets and stored them up for future use. It is why he survived so long," Ysabeau said.

Ysabeau's words reminded me of the job Philippe had given me in 1590, after he made me his blood-sworn daughter: *Think—and stay alive.*

"Remember that, before you rush back to Oxford for your book," Ysabeau continued, dropping her voice to a whisper. "Remember that in the difficult days to come, as the darkest de Clermont family secrets are exposed to the light. Remember that and you will show them all that you are Philippe de Clermont's daughter in more than name."

5

After two days with Baldwin in residence at Sept-Tours, I not only understood why Matthew had built a tower onto the house, I wished he'd located it in another province—if not another country.

Baldwin made it clear that no matter who legally owned the château, Sept-Tours was his home. He presided over every meal. Alain saw him first thing each morning to receive his orders and periodically throughout the day to report on his progress. The mayor of Saint-Lucien came to call and sat in the salon with him, talking about local affairs. Baldwin examined Marthe's provisioning of the household and grudgingly acknowledged it to be outstanding. He also entered rooms without knocking, took Marcus and Matthew to task for slights real and imagined, and needled Ysabeau about everything from the salon decor to the dust in the great hall.

Nathaniel, Sophie, and Margaret were the first lucky creatures to leave the château. They said a tearful good-bye to Marcus and Phoebe and promised to be in touch once they were settled. Baldwin had urged them to go to Australia and put on a show of solidarity with Nathaniel's mother, who was not only a daemon but also a member of the Congregation. Nathaniel had protested at first, arguing that they would be fine back in North Carolina, but cooler heads—Phoebe's in particular—had prevailed.

When questioned later as to why she'd backed Baldwin in this matter, Phoebe explained that Marcus was worried about Margaret's safety and she would not permit Marcus to take on the responsibility for the baby's well-being. Therefore Nathaniel was going to do what Baldwin thought best. Phoebe's expression warned me that if I had a different opinion on the matter, I could keep it to myself.

Even after this initial wave of departures, Sept-Tours felt crowded with Baldwin, Matthew, and Marcus in it—not to mention Verin, Ysabeau, and Gallowglass. Fernando was less obtrusive, spending much of his time with Sarah or Hamish. We all found hideaways where we could retreat for some much-needed peace and quiet. So it was something of a surprise when Ysabeau burst into Matthew's study with an announcement about Marcus's present whereabouts.

"Marcus is in the Round Tower with Sarah," Ysabeau said, two spots of color brightening her usually pale complexion. "Phoebe and Hamish are with them. They've found the old family pedigrees."

I couldn't imagine why this news had Matthew flinging down his pen and leaping from his chair. When Ysabeau caught my curious look, she gave me a sad smile in return.

"Marcus is about to find out one of his father's secrets," Ysabeau explained.

That got me moving, too.

I had never set foot in the Round Tower, which stood opposite Matthew's and was separated from it by the main part of the château. As soon as we reached it, I comprehended why no one had included it on my château tour.

A round metal grate was sunk into the center of the tower floor. A familiar, damp smell of age, death, and despair emanated from the deep hole it covered.

"An oubliette," I said, temporarily frozen by the sight. Matthew heard me and clattered back down the stairs.

"Philippe built it for a prison. He seldom used it." Matthew's forehead creased with worry.

"Go," I said, waving him and the bad memories away. "We'll be right behind you."

The oubliette on the Round Tower's ground floor was a place of forgetting, but the tower's second floor was a place of remembering. It was stuffed with boxes, papers, documents, and artifacts. This must be the de Clermont family archives.

"No wonder Emily spent so much time up here," Sarah said. She was bent over a long, partially unrolled scroll on a battered worktable, Phoebe at her side. Half a dozen more scrolls lay on the table, waiting to be studied. "She was a genealogy nut."

"Hi!" Marcus waved happily from a high catwalk that circled the room and supported still more boxes and stacks. The dire revelations that Ysabeau feared apparently hadn't happened yet. "Hamish was just about to come and get you."

Marcus vaulted over the catwalk railing and landed softly next to Phoebe. With no ladder or staircase in sight, there was no way to get to that level of storage except to climb using the rough stones for handholds and no way to get down except to jump. Vampire security at its finest.

"What are you looking for?" Matthew said with just the right touch of curiosity. Marcus would never suspect that he had been tipped off.

"A way to get Baldwin off our backs, of course," Marcus said. He handed a worn notebook to Hamish. "There you go. Godfrey's notes on vampire law."

Hamish turned the pages, clearly searching for some useful piece of legal information. Godfrey had been the youngest of Philippe's three male children, known for his formidable, devious intellect. A sense of foreboding began to take root.

"And have you found it?" Matthew said, glancing at the scroll.

"Come and see." Marcus beckoned us toward the table.

"You'll love this, Diana," Sarah said, adjusting her reading glasses. "Marcus said it's a de Clermont family tree. It looks really old."

"It is," I said. The genealogy was medieval, with brightly colored likenesses of Philippe and Ysabeau standing in separate square boxes at the top of the page. Their hands were clasped across the space that divided them. Ribbons of color connected them to the roundels below. Each bubble contained a name. Some were familiar to me—Hugh, Baldwin, Godfrey, Matthew, Verin, Freyja, Stasia. Many were not.

"Twelfth century. French. In the style of the workshop at Saint-Sever," Phoebe said, confirming my sense of the age of the work.

"It all started when I complained to Gallowglass about Baldwin's interference. He told me that Philippe was nearly as bad and that when Hugh got fed up, he struck out on his own with Fernando," Marcus explained. "Gallowglass called their family a scion and said sometimes scions were the only way to keep the peace."

The look of suppressed fury on Matthew's face suggested that peace was the last thing Gallowglass was going to enjoy once his uncle found him.

"I remembered reading something about scions back when Grandfather hoped I would turn to law and take on Godfrey's old duties," Marcus said.

"Found it," Hamish said, his finger tapping against the page. "*'Any male with full-blooded children of his own can establish a scion, provided he has the approval of his sire or the head of his clan. The new scion will be considered a branch of the original family, but in all other ways the new scion's sire shall exercise his will and power freely.'* That sounds straightforward enough, but since Godfrey was involved, there must be more to it."

"Forming a scion—a distinct branch of the de Clermont family under your authority—will solve all of our problems!" Marcus said.

"Not all clan leaders welcome scions, Marcus," Matthew warned.

"Once a rebel, always a rebel," Marcus said with a shrug. "You knew that when you made me."

"And Phoebe?" Matthew's brows lifted. "Does your fiancée share your revolutionary sentiments? She might not like the idea of being cast out of Sept-Tours without a penny after all of your assets are seized by your uncle."

"What do you mean?" Marcus said, uneasy.

"Hamish can correct me if I'm wrong, but I believe the next section of Godfrey's book lays out the penalties associated with establishing a scion without your sire's permission," Matthew replied.

"You're my sire," Marcus said, his chin set in stubborn lines.

"Only in the biological sense: I provided you with my blood so you could be reborn a vampire." Matthew rammed his hands through his hair, a sign that his own frustration was mounting. "And you know how I detest the term 'sire' used in that context. I consider myself your father—not your blood donor."

"I'm asking you to be more than that," Marcus said. "Baldwin is wrong about the covenant and wrong about the Congregation. If you establish a scion, we could chart our own path, make our own decisions."

"Is there some problem with you establishing your own scion, Matt?" Hamish asked. "Now that Diana's pregnant, I would think you'd be eager to get out from under Baldwin's thumb."

"It's not as simple as you think," Matthew told him. "And Baldwin may have reservations."

"What's this, Phoebe?" Sarah's finger pointed to a rough patch in the parchment under Matthew's name. She was more interested in the genealogy than the legal complexities.

Phoebe took a closer look. "It's an erasure of some sort. There used to be another roundel there. I can almost make out the name. Beia—oh, it must be Benjamin. They've used common medieval abbreviations and substituted an *i* for a *j*."

"They scratched out the circle but forgot to get rid of the little red line that connects him to Matthew. Based on that, this Benjamin is one of Matthew's children," Sarah said.

The mention of Benjamin's name made my blood run cold. Matthew did have a son of that name. He was a terrifying creature.

Phoebe unrolled another scroll. This genealogy looked ancient, too, though not quite as old as the one we'd all been studying. She frowned.

"This looks to be from a century later." Phoebe put the parchment on the table. "There's no erasure on this one and no mention of a Benjamin either. He just disappears without a trace."

"Who's Benjamin?" asked Marcus, though I couldn't imagine why. Surely he must know the identities of Matthew's other children.

"Benjamin does not exist." Ysabeau's expression was guarded, and she had chosen her words carefully.

My brain tried to process the implications of Marcus's question and Ysabeau's odd response. If Matthew's son didn't know about Benjamin . . .

"Is that why his name is erased?" Phoebe asked. "Did someone make a mistake?"

"Yes, he was a mistake," Matthew said, his voice hollow.

"But Benjamin does exist," I said, meeting Matthew's gray-green eyes. They were shuttered and remote. "I met him in sixteenth-century Prague."

"Is he alive now?" Hamish asked.

"I don't know. I thought he was dead shortly after I made him in the twelfth century," Matthew replied. "Hundreds of years later, Philippe heard of someone who fit Benjamin's description, but he dropped out of sight again before we could be sure. There were rumors of Benjamin in the nineteenth century, but I never saw any proof."

"I don't understand," Marcus said. "Even if he's dead, Benjamin should still appear in the genealogy."

"I disavowed him. So did Philippe." Matthew closed his eyes rather than meet our curious looks. "Just as a creature can be made part of your family with a blood vow, he can be formally cast out to fend for himself without family or the protection of vampire law. You know how important a pedigree is among vampires, Marcus. Not having an acknowledged bloodline is as serious a stain among vampires as being spellbound is for witches."

It was becoming clearer to me why Baldwin might not want me included in the de Clermont family tree as one of Philippe's children.

"So Benjamin *is* dead," Hamish said. "Legally at least."

"And the dead sometimes rise up to haunt us," Ysabeau murmured, earning a dark look from her son.

"I can't imagine what Benjamin did to make you turn away from your own blood, Matthew." Marcus still sounded confused. "I was a holy terror in my early years, and you didn't abandon me."

"Benjamin was one of the German crusaders who marched with Count Emicho's army toward the Holy Land. When they were beaten in Hungary, he joined up with my brother Godfrey's forces," Matthew began. "Benjamin's mother was the daughter of a prominent merchant in the Levant, and he had learned some Hebrew and even Arabic because of the family's business operations. He was a valuable ally—at first."

"So Benjamin was Godfrey's son?" Sarah asked.

"No," Matthew replied. "He was mine. Benjamin began to trade in de Clermont family secrets. He swore he would expose the existence of creatures—not just vampires but witches and daemons—to the humans in Jerusalem. When I discovered his betrayal, I lost control. Philippe dreamed of creating a safe haven for us all in the Holy Land, a place where we could live without fear. Benjamin had the power to crush Philippe's hopes, and I had given him that power."

I knew my husband well enough to imagine the depth of his guilt and remorse.

"Why didn't you kill him?" Marcus demanded.

"Death was too quick. I wanted to punish Benjamin for being a false friend. I wanted him to suffer as we creatures suffered. I made him a vampire so that if he exposed the de Clermonts, he would have to expose himself." Matthew paused. "Then I abandoned him to fend for himself."

"Who taught him how to survive?" Marcus said, his voice hushed.

"Benjamin taught himself. That was part of his punishment." Matthew held his son's gaze. "It became part of mine, too—God's way of making me atone for my sin. Because I abandoned Benjamin, I didn't know that I had given him the same blood rage that was in my own veins. It was years before I found out what a monster Benjamin had become."

"Blood rage?" Marcus looked at his father incredulously. "That's impossible. It turns you into a cold-blooded killer, without reason or compassion. There hasn't been a case of it for nearly two millennia. You told me so yourself."

"I lied." Matthew's voice cracked at the admission.

"You can't have blood rage, Matt," Hamish said. "There was a mention of it in the family papers. Its symptoms include blind fury, the inability to reason, and an overwhelming instinct to kill. You've never shown any sign of the disease."

"I've learned to control it," Matthew said. "Most of the time."

"If the Congregation were to find out, there would be a price on your head. According to what I've read here, other creatures would have carte blanche to destroy you," Hamish observed, clearly concerned.

"Not just me." Matthew's glance flickered over my rounding abdomen. "My children, too."

Sarah's expression was stricken. "The babies . . ."

"And Marcus?" Phoebe's knuckles showed white on the edge of the table though her voice was calm.

"Marcus is only a carrier," Matthew tried to reassure her. "The symptoms manifest immediately."

Phoebe looked relieved.

Matthew looked his son squarely in the eye. "When I made you, I genuinely believed that I was cured. It had been almost a century since I'd had an episode. It was the Age of Reason. In our pride we believed that all sorts of past evils had been eradicated, from smallpox to superstition. Then you went to New Orleans."

"My own children." Marcus looked wild, and then understanding dawned. "You and Juliette Durand came to the city, and they started turning up dead. I thought Juliette killed them. But it was you. You killed them because of their blood rage."

"Your father had no choice," Ysabeau said. "The Congregation knew there was trouble in New Orleans. Philippe ordered Matthew to deal with it before the vampires found out the cause. Had Matthew refused, you all would have died."

"The other vampires on the Congregation were convinced that the old scourge of blood rage had returned," Matthew said. "They wanted to raze the city and burn it out of existence, but I argued that the madness was a result of youth and inexperience, not blood rage. I was supposed to kill them all. I was supposed to kill you, too, Marcus."

Marcus looked surprised. Ysabeau did not.

"Philippe was furious with me, but I destroyed only those who were symptomatic. I killed them quickly, without pain or fear," Matthew said, his voice dead. I hated the secrets he kept and the lies he told to cover them up, but my heart hurt for him nonetheless. "I explained away the rest of my grandchildren's excesses however I could—poverty, inebriation, greed. Then I took responsibility for what happened in New Orleans, resigned my seat on the Congregation, and swore that you would make no more children until you were older and wiser."

"You told me I was a failure—a disgrace to the family." Marcus was hoarse with suppressed emotion.

"I had to make you stop. I didn't know what else to do." Matthew confessed his sins without asking for forgiveness.

"Who else knows your secret, Matthew?" Sarah asked.

"Verin, Baldwin, Stasia, and Freyja. Fernando and Gallowglass. Miriam. Marthe. Alain." Matthew extended his fingers one by one as the names tumbled from his mouth. "So did Hugh, Godfrey, Hancock, Louisa, and Louis."

Marcus looked at his father bitterly. "I want to know everything. From the beginning."

"Matthew cannot tell you the beginning of this tale," Ysabeau said softly. "Only I can."

"No, *Maman,*" Matthew said, shaking his head. "That's not necessary."

"Of course it is," Ysabeau said. "I brought the disease into the family. I am a carrier, like Marcus."

"You?" Sarah looked stunned.

"The disease was in my sire. He believed it was a great blessing for a lamia to carry his blood, for it made you truly terrifying and nearly impossible to kill." The contempt and loathing with which Ysabeau said the word "sire" made me understand why Matthew disliked the term.

"There was constant warfare between vampires then, and any possible advantage was seized. But I was a disappointment," Ysabeau continued. "My maker's blood did not work in me as he had hoped, though the blood rage was strong in his other children. As a punishment—"

Ysabeau stopped and drew a shaky breath.

"As a punishment," she repeated slowly, "I was locked in a cage to provide my brothers and sisters with a source of entertainment, as well as a creature on whom they could practice killing. My sire did not expect me to survive."

Ysabeau touched her fingers to her lips, unable for a moment to go on.

"I lived for a very long time in that tiny, barred prison—filthy, starving, wounded inside and out, unable to die though I longed for it. But the more I fought and the longer I survived, the more interesting I became. My sire— my father—took me against my will, as did my brothers. Everything that was done to me stemmed from a morbid curiosity to see what might finally tame me. But I was fast—and smart. My sire began to think I might be useful to him after all."

"That's not the story Philippe told," Marcus said numbly. "Grandfather said he rescued you from a fortress—that your maker had kidnapped you and made you a vampire against your will because you were so beautiful he couldn't bear to let anyone else have you. Philippe said your sire made you to serve as his wife."

"All of that was the truth—just not the whole truth." Ysabeau met Marcus's eyes squarely. "Philippe did find me in a fortress and rescued me from that terrible place. But I was no beauty then, no matter what romantic stories your grandfather told later. I'd shorn my head with a broken shell that a bird had dropped on the window ledge, so that they couldn't use my hair to hold me down. I still have the scars, though they are hidden now. One of my legs was broken. An arm, too, I think," Ysabeau said vaguely. "Marthe will remember."

No wonder Ysabeau and Marthe had treated me so tenderly after La Pierre. One had been tortured, and the other had put her back together again after the ordeal. But Ysabeau's tale was not yet finished.

"When Philippe and his soldiers came, they were the answer to my prayers," Ysabeau said. "They killed my sire straightaway. Philippe's men demanded all of my sire's children be put to death so that the evil poison in our blood would not spread. One morning they came and took my brothers and sisters away. Philippe kept me behind. He would not let them touch me. Your grandfather lied and said that I had not been infected with my maker's disease—that someone else had made me and I had killed only to survive. There was no one left to dispute it."

Ysabeau looked at her grandson. "It is why Philippe forgave Matthew for not killing you, Marcus, though he had ordered him to do so. Philippe knew what it was to love someone too much to see him perish unjustly."

But Ysabeau's words did not lift the shadows from Marcus's eyes.

"We kept my secret—Philippe and Marthe and I—for centuries. I made many children before we came to France, and I thought that blood rage was a horror we had left behind. My children all lived long lives and never showed a trace of the illness. Then came Matthew . . ." Ysabeau trailed off. A drop of red formed along her lower lid. She blinked away the blood tear before it could fall.

"By the time I made Matthew, my sire was nothing more than a dark legend among vampires. He was held up as an example of what would happen to us if we gave in to our desires for blood and power. Any vampire even suspected of having blood rage was immediately put down, as was his sire and any offspring," Ysabeau said dispassionately. "But I could not kill my child, and I would not let anyone else do so either. It was not Matthew's fault that he was sick."

"It was no one's fault, *Maman*," Matthew said. "It's a genetic disease—one that we still don't understand. Because of Philippe's initial ruthlessness, and all the family has done to hide the truth, the Congregation doesn't know that the sickness is in my veins."

"They may not know for sure," Ysabeau warned, "but some of the Congregation suspect it. There were vampires who believed that your sister's illness was not madness, as we claimed, but blood rage."

"Gerbert," I whispered.

Ysabeau nodded. "Domenico, too."

"Don't borrow trouble," Matthew said, trying to comfort her. "I've sat at the council table while the disease was discussed, and no one had the slightest inkling I was afflicted with it. So long as they believe blood rage is extinct, our secret is safe."

"I'm afraid I have bad news, then. The Congregation fears that blood rage is back," Marcus said.

"What do you mean?" Matthew asked.

"The vampire murders," Marcus explained.

I'd seen the press clippings Matthew had collected back in his Oxford laboratory last year. The mysterious killings were widespread and had taken place over a number of months. Investigators had been stymied, and the murders had captured human attention.

"The killings seemed to stop this winter, but the Congregation is still dealing with the sensational headlines," Marcus continued. "The perpetrator was never caught, so the Congregation is braced for the killings to resume at any moment. Gerbert told me so in April, when I made my initial request that the covenant be repealed."

"No wonder Baldwin is reluctant to acknowledge me as his sister," I said. "With all the attention Philippe's blood vow would bring to the de Clermont family, someone might start asking questions. You might all become murder suspects."

"The Congregation's official pedigree contains no mention of Benjamin. What Phoebe and Marcus have discovered are only family copies," Ysabeau said. "Philippe said there was no need to share Matthew's . . . indiscretion. When Benjamin was made, the Congregation's pedigrees were in Constantinople. We were in faraway Outremer, struggling to hold our territory in the Holy Land. Who would know if we left him out?"

"But surely other vampires in the Crusader colonies knew about Benjamin?" Hamish asked.

"Very few of those vampires survive. Even fewer would dare to question Philippe's official story," Matthew said. Hamish looked skeptical.

"Hamish is right to worry. When Matthew's marriage to Diana becomes common knowledge—not to mention Philippe's blood vow and the existence of the twins—some who have remained silent about my past may not be willing to do so any longer," Ysabeau said.

This time it was Sarah who repeated the name we were all thinking. "Gerbert."

Ysabeau nodded. "Someone will remember Louisa's escapades. And then another vampire may recall what happened among Marcus's children in New Orleans. Gerbert might remind the Congregation that once, long ago, Matthew showed signs of madness, though he seemed to grow out of them. The de Clermonts will be vulnerable as they have never been before."

"And one or both of the twins might have the disease," Hamish said. "A six-month-old killer is a terrifying prospect. No creature would blame the Congregation for taking action."

"Perhaps a witch's blood will somehow prevent the disease from taking root," Ysabeau said.

"Wait." Marcus's face was still as he concentrated. "When exactly was Benjamin made?"

"In the early twelfth century," Matthew replied, frowning. "After the First Crusade."

"And when did the witch in Jerusalem give birth to a vampire baby?"

"What vampire baby?" Matthew's voice echoed through the room like a gunshot.

"The one that Ysabeau told us about in January," Sarah said. "It turns out you and Diana aren't the only special creatures in the world. This has all happened before."

"I've always thought it was nothing more than a rumor spread to turn creatures against one another," Ysabeau said, her voice shaking. "But Philippe believed the tale. And now Diana has come home pregnant. . . ."

"Tell me, *Maman*," Matthew said. "Everything."

"A vampire raped a witch in Jerusalem. She conceived his child," Ysabeau said, the words coming out in a rush. "We never knew who the vampire was. The witch refused to identify him."

Only weavers could carry a vampire's child—not ordinary witches. Goody Alsop had told me as much in London.

"When?" Matthew's tone was hushed.

Ysabeau looked thoughtful. "Just before the Congregation was formed and the covenant was signed."

"Just after I made Benjamin," Matthew said.

"Perhaps Benjamin inherited more than blood rage from you," Hamish said.

"And the child?" Matthew asked.

"Died of starvation," Ysabeau whispered. "The babe refused her mother's breast."

Matthew shot to his feet.

"Many newborns will not take their mother's milk," Ysabeau protested.

"Did the baby drink blood?" Matthew demanded.

"The mother claimed she did." Ysabeau winced when Matthew's fist struck the table. "But Philippe was not sure. By the time he held the child, she was on the brink of death and would not take any nourishment at all."

"Philippe should have told me about this when he met Diana." Matthew pointed an accusatory finger at Ysabeau. "Failing that, *you* should have told me when I first brought her home."

"And if we all did what we should, we would wake to find ourselves in paradise," Ysabeau said, her temper rising.

"Stop it. Both of you. You can't hate your father or Ysabeau for something you've done yourself, Matthew," Sarah observed quietly. "Besides, we have enough problems in the present without worrying about what happened in the past."

Sarah's words immediately lowered the tension in the room.

"What are we going to do?" Marcus asked his father.

Matthew seemed surprised by the question.

"We're a family," Marcus said, "whether the Congregation recognizes us or not, just as you and Diana are husband and wife no matter what those idiots in Venice believe."

"We'll let Baldwin have his way—for now," Matthew replied after thinking for a moment. "I'll take Sarah and Diana to Oxford. If what you say is true, and another vampire—possibly Benjamin—fathered a child on a witch, we need to know how and why some witches and some vampires can reproduce."

"I'll let Miriam know," Marcus said. "She'll be glad to have you back in the lab again. While you're there, you can try to figure out how blood rage works."

"What do you think I've been doing all these years?" Matthew asked softly.

"Your research," I said, thinking of Matthew's study of creature evolution and genetics. "You haven't been looking solely for creature origins.

You've been trying to figure out how blood rage is contracted and how to cure it."

"No matter what else Miriam and I are doing in the lab, we're always hoping to make some discovery that will lead to a cure," Matthew admitted.

"What can I do?" Hamish asked, capturing Matthew's attention.

"You'll have to leave Sept-Tours, too. I need you to study the covenant— whatever you can find out about early Congregation debates, anything that might shed light on what happened in Jerusalem between the end of the First Crusade and the date the covenant became law." Matthew looked about the Round Tower. "It's too bad you can't work here."

"I'll help with that research if you'd like," said Phoebe.

"Surely you'll go back to London," Hamish said.

"I will stay here, with Marcus," Phoebe said, her chin rising. "I'm not a witch or a daemon. There's no Congregation rule that bars me from remaining at Sept-Tours."

"These restrictions are only temporary," Matthew said. "Once the members of the Congregation satisfy themselves that everything is as it should be at Sept-Tours, Gerbert will take Ysabeau to his house in the Cantal. After that drama Baldwin will soon grow bored and return to New York. Then we can all meet back here. Hopefully by then we'll know more and can make a better plan."

Marcus nodded, though he didn't look pleased. "Of course, if you formed a scion . . ."

"Impossible," Matthew said.

"*'Impossible' n'est pas français,*" Ysabeau said, her tone as tart as vinegar. "And it certainly was not a word in your father's vocabulary."

"The only thing that sounds out of the question to me is remaining within Baldwin's clan and under his direct control," Marcus said, nodding at his grandmother.

"After all the secrets that have been exposed today, you still think my name and blood are something you should be proud to possess?" Matthew asked Marcus.

"Rather you than Baldwin," Marcus said, meeting his father's gaze.

"I don't know how you can bear to have me in your presence," Matthew said softly, turning away, "never mind forgive me."

"I haven't forgiven you," Marcus said evenly. "Find the cure for blood rage. Fight to have the covenant repealed, and refuse to support a Congregation that upholds such unjust laws. Form a scion, so that we can live without Baldwin breathing down our necks."

"And then?" Matthew said, a sardonic lift to his eyebrow.

"Then not only will I forgive you, I'll be the first to offer you my allegiance," Marcus said, "not only as my father but as my sire."

6

Most evenings at Sept-Tours, dinner was a slapdash affair. All of us ate when—and what—we liked. But tonight was our last at the château, and Baldwin had commanded the entire family's presence to give thanks that all of the other creatures were gone and to bid Sarah, Matthew, and me adieu.

I had been given the dubious honor of making the arrangements. If Baldwin expected to cow me, he was going to be disappointed. Having provided meals for the inhabitants of Sept-Tours in 1590, I could surely manage it in modern times. I'd sent out invitations to every vampire, witch, and warmblood still in residence and hoped for the best.

At the moment I was regretting my request that everyone dress formally for dinner. I looped Philippe's pearls around my neck to accompany the golden arrow that I'd taken to wearing, but they skimmed the tops of my thighs and were too long to suit trousers. I returned the pearls to the velvet-lined jewelry box that arrived from Ysabeau, along with a sparkling pair of earrings that brushed my jawline and caught the light. I stabbed the posts through the holes in my ears.

"I've never known you to fuss so much over your jewelry." Matthew came out of the bathroom and studied my reflection in the mirror as he slid a pair of gold cuff links through the buttonholes at his wrists. They were emblazoned with the New College crest, a gesture of fealty to me and to one of his many alma maters.

"Matthew! You've shaved." It had been some time since I'd seen him without his Elizabethan beard and mustache. Though Matthew's appearance would be striking no matter the era or its fashions, this was the clean-cut, elegant man I'd fallen in love with last year.

"Since we're going back to Oxford, I thought I might as well look the part of the university don," he said, his fingers moving over his smooth chin. "It's a relief, actually. Beards really do itch like the devil."

"I love having my handsome professor back, in place of my dangerous prince," I said softly.

Matthew shrugged a charcoal-colored jacket made of fine wool over his shoulders and pulled at his pearl gray cuffs, looking adorably self-conscious. His smile was shy but became more appreciative when I stood up.

"You look beautiful," he said with an admiring whistle. "With or without the pearls."

"Victoire is a miracle worker," I said. Victoire, my vampire seamstress and Alain's wife, had made me a midnight blue pair of trousers and a matching silk blouse with an open neckline that skimmed the edges of my shoulders and fell in soft pleats around my hips. The full shirt hid my swelling midriff without making me look like I was wearing a maternity smock.

"You are especially irresistible in blue," Matthew said.

"What a sweet talker you are." I smoothed his lapels and adjusted his collar. It was completely unnecessary—the jacket fit perfectly, and not a stitch was out of place—but the gestures satisfied my proprietary feelings. I lifted onto my toes to kiss him.

Matthew returned my embrace with enthusiasm, threading his fingers through the coppery strands that fell down my back. My answering sigh was soft and satisfied.

"Oh, I like that sound." Matthew deepened the kiss, and when I made a low, throaty hum, he grinned. "I like that one even more."

"After a kiss like that, a woman should be excused if she's late to dinner," I said, my hands sliding between the waistband of his trousers and his neatly tucked shirt.

"Temptress." Matthew nipped softly at my lip before pulling away.

I took a final look in the mirror. Given Matthew's recent attentions, it was a good thing Victoire hadn't curled and twisted my hair into a more elaborate arrangement, since I'd never have been able to set it to rights again. Happily, I was able to tighten the low ponytail and brush a few hairs back into place.

Finally I wove a disguising spell around me. The effect was like pulling sheer curtains over a sunny window. The spell dulled my coloring and softened my features. I had resorted to wearing it in London and had kept doing so when we returned to the present. No one would look at me twice now—except Matthew, who was scowling at the transformation.

"After we get to Oxford, I want you to stop wearing your disguising spell." Matthew crossed his arms. "I hate that thing."

"I can't go around the university shimmering."

"And I can't go around killing people, even though I have blood rage," Matthew said. "We all have our crosses to bear."

"I thought you didn't want anyone to know how much stronger my power is." At this point I was worried that even casual observers would be drawn to me because of it. In another time, when there were more weavers about, I might not have been so conspicuous.

"I still don't want Baldwin to know, or the rest of the de Clermonts. But please tell Sarah as soon as possible," he said. "You shouldn't have to hide your magic at home."

"It's annoying to weave a disguising spell in the morning and then take it off at night only to weave it again the next day. It's easier to just keep it on." That way I'd never be caught off guard by unexpected visitors or eruptions of undisciplined power.

"Our children are going to know who their mother truly is. They are not going to be brought up in the dark as you were." Matthew's tone brooked no argument.

"And is that sauce good for the gander as well as the goose?" I shot back. "Will the twins know their father has blood rage, or will you keep them in the dark like Marcus?"

"It's not the same. Your magic is a gift. Blood rage is a curse."

"It's exactly the same, and you know it." I took his hands in mine. "We've grown used to hiding what we're ashamed of, you and I. It has to end now, before the children are born. And after this latest crisis with the Congregation is resolved, we are going to sit down—as a family—and discuss the scion business." Marcus was right: If forming a scion meant we wouldn't have to obey Baldwin, it was worth considering.

"Forming a scion comes with responsibilities and obligations. You would be expected to behave like a vampire and function as my consort, helping me control the rest of the family." Matthew shook his head. "You aren't suited to that life, and I won't ask it of you."

"You're not asking," I replied. "I'm offering. And Ysabeau will teach me what I need to know."

"Ysabeau will be the first to try to dissuade you. The pressure she was under as Philippe's mate was inconceivable," Matthew said. "When my father called Ysabeau his general, only the humans laughed. Every vampire knew he was telling the gospel truth. Ysabeau forced, flattered, and cajoled us into doing Philippe's bidding. He could run the whole world because Ysabeau managed his family with an iron fist. Her decisions were absolute and her retribution swift. No one crossed her."

"That sounds challenging but not impossible," I replied mildly.

"It's a full-time job, Diana." Matthew's irritation continued to climb. "Are you ready to give up being Professor Bishop in order to be Mrs. Clairmont?"

"Maybe it's escaped your attention, but *I already have.*"

Matthew blinked.

"I haven't advised a student, stood in front of a classroom, read an academic journal, or published an article in more than a year," I continued.

"That's temporary," Matthew said sharply.

"Really?" My eyebrows shot up. "You're ready to sacrifice your fellowship at All Souls in order to be Mr. Mom? Or are we going to hire a nanny to take care of our doubtless exceptionally challenging children while I go back to work?"

Matthew's silence was telling. This issue had clearly never occurred to him. He'd simply assumed I would somehow juggle teaching and child care with no trouble at all. *Typical,* I thought, before plunging on.

"Except for a brief moment when you ran back to Oxford last year thinking you could play knight in shining armor and this moment of nerves, which I forgive you for, we've faced our troubles together. What makes you think that would change?" I demanded.

"These aren't your troubles," Matthew replied.

"When I took you on, they became my troubles. We already share responsibility for our own children—why not yours as well?"

Matthew stared at me in silence for so long that I became concerned he'd been struck dumb.

"Never again," he finally murmured with a shake of his head. "After today I will never make this mistake again."

"The word 'never' is not in our family vocabulary, Matthew." My anger with him boiled over and I dug my fingers into his shoulders. "Ysabeau says 'impossible' isn't French? Well, 'never' is not Bishop-Clairmont. Don't ever use it again. As for mistakes, how dare you—"

Matthew stole my next words with a kiss. I pounded on his shoulders until my strength—and my interest in beating him to a pulp—subsided. He pulled away with a wry smile.

"You must try to allow me to finish my thoughts. Never"—he caught my fist before it made contact with his shoulder—"never again will I make the mistake of underestimating you."

Matthew took advantage of my astonishment to kiss me more thoroughly than before.

"No wonder Philippe always looked so exhausted," he said ruefully when he was through. "It's very fatiguing pretending you're in charge when your wife actually rules the roost."

"Hmph," I said, finding his analysis of the dynamics of our relationship somewhat suspect.

"While I have your attention, let me make myself clear: I want you to tell Sarah about being a weaver and what happened in London." Matthew's tone was stern. "After that, there will be no more disguising spells at home. Agreed?"

"Agreed." I hoped he didn't notice my crossed fingers.

Alain was waiting for us at the bottom of the stairs, wearing his usual look of circumspection and a dark suit.

"Is everything ready?" I asked him.

"Of course," he murmured, handing me the final menu.

My eyes darted over it. "Perfect. The place cards are arranged? The wine was brought up and decanted? And you found the silver cups?"

Alain's mouth twitched. "All of your instructions were followed to the letter, Madame de Clermont."

"There you are. I was beginning to think you two were going to leave me to the lions." Gallowglass's efforts to dress for dinner had yielded only combed hair and something leather in place of his worn denims, though I supposed cowboy boots qualified as formalwear of a sort. He was, alas, still wearing a T-shirt. This particular garment instructed us to KEEP CALM AND HARLEY ON. It also revealed a staggering number of tattoos.

"Sorry about the shirt, Auntie. It is black," Gallowglass apologized, tracking my glances. "Matthew sent over one of his shirts, but it split down the back when I did up the buttons."

"You look very dashing." I searched the hall for signs of our other guests.

I found Corra instead, perched on the statue of a nymph like an oddly shaped hat. She'd spent the whole day flying around Sept-Tours and Saint-Lucien in exchange for promises of good behavior tomorrow while we were traveling.

"What were you two doing up there all this time?" Sarah emerged from the salon and gave Matthew a suspicious once-over. Like Gallowglass, Sarah took a limited view of formalwear. She was wearing a long lavender shirt that extended past her hips and a pair of ankle-length beige trousers. "We thought we were going to have to send up a search party."

"Diana couldn't find her shoes," Matthew said smoothly. He slid an apologetic glance toward Victoire, who was standing by with a tray of drinks. She had, of course, left my shoes next to the bed.

"That doesn't sound like Victoire." Sarah's eyes narrowed.

Corra squawked and chattered her teeth in agreement, blowing her breath through her nose so that a rain of sparks fell down onto the stone floors. Thankfully, there was no rug.

"Honestly, Diana, couldn't you have brought home something from Elizabethan England that wasn't so much trouble?" Sarah looked at Corra with a sour expression.

"Like what? A snow globe?" I asked.

"First I was subjected to witchwater falling from the tower. Now there is a dragon in my hallway. This is what comes of having witches in the family." Ysabeau appeared in a pale silk suit that perfectly matched the color of the Champagne in the glass she took from Victoire. "There are days when I cannot help thinking the Congregation is right to keep us apart."

"Drink, Madame de Clermont?" Victoire turned to me, rescuing me from the need to respond.

"Thank you," I replied. Her tray held not only wine but also glasses filled with ice cubes containing blue borage flowers and mint leaves, topped up with sparkling water.

"Hello, sister." Verin sauntered out of the salon behind Ysabeau wearing knee-high black boots and an exceedingly short, sleeveless black dress that left more than a few inches of her pearly white legs exposed, as well as the tip of the scabbard strapped to her thigh.

Wondering why Verin thought she needed to dine armed, I reached up with nervous fingers and drew the golden arrowhead from where it had fallen inside the neck of my blouse. It felt like a talisman, and it reminded me of Philippe. Ysabeau's cold eyes latched on to it.

"I thought that arrowhead was lost forever," she said quietly.

"Philippe gave it to me on my wedding day." I started to lift the chain from my neck, thinking it must belong to her.

"No. Philippe wanted you to have it, and it was his to bestow." Ysabeau gently closed my fingers around the worn metal. "You must keep this safe, my child. It is very old and not easily replaced."

"Is dinner ready?" Baldwin boomed, arriving at my side with the suddenness of an earthquake and his usual disregard for a warmblood's nervous system.

"It is," Alain whispered in my ear.

"It is," I said brightly, plastering a smile on my face.

Baldwin offered me his arm.

"Let us go in, *Matthieu*," Ysabeau murmured, taking her son by the hand.

"Diana?" Baldwin prompted, his arm still extended.

I stared up at him with loathing, ignored his proffered arm, and marched toward the door behind Matthew and Ysabeau.

"This is an order, not a request. Defy me and I will turn you and Matthew over to the Congregation without a second thought." Baldwin's voice was menacing.

For a few moments, I considered resisting and to hell with the consequences. If I did, Baldwin would win. *Think,* I reminded myself. *And stay alive.* Then I rested my hand atop his rather than taking his elbow like a modern woman. Baldwin's eyes widened slightly.

"Why so surprised, *brother*?" I demanded. "You've been positively feudal since the moment you arrived. If you're determined to play the role of king, we should do it properly."

"Very well, *sister*." Baldwin's fist tightened under my fingers. It was a reminder of his authority, as well as his power.

Baldwin and I entered the dining room as though it were the audience chamber at Greenwich and we were the king and queen of England. Fernando's mouth twitched at the sight, and Baldwin glowered at him in response.

"Does that little cup have blood in it?" Sarah, seemingly oblivious to the tension, bent over and sniffed at Gallowglass's plate.

"I did not know we still had these," Ysabeau said, holding up one of the engraved silver beakers. She gave me a smile as Marcus settled her into the spot to his left while Matthew rounded the table and did the honors for Phoebe, who sat opposite.

"I had Alain and Marthe search for them. Philippe used them at our wedding feast." I fingered the golden arrowhead. Courtly Ernst pulled out my chair. "Please. Everybody sit."

"The table is beautifully arranged, Diana," Phoebe said appreciatively. But she wasn't looking at the crystal, the precious porcelain, or the fine silver. Instead Phoebe was taking careful note of the arrangement of creatures around the gleaming expanse of rosewood.

Mary Sidney had once told me that the order of table precedence at a banquet was no less complex than the arrangement of troops before a battle. I had observed the rules I'd learned in Elizabethan England as strictly as possible while minimizing the risk of outright war.

"Thank you, Phoebe, but it was all Marthe and Victoire's doing. They picked out the china," I said, deliberately misunderstanding her.

Verin and Fernando stared at the plates before them and exchanged a look. Marthe adored the eye-popping Bleu Celeste pattern Ysabeau had commissioned in the eighteenth century, and Victoire's first choice had been an ostentatious gilded service decorated with swans. I couldn't imagine eating off either and had selected dignified black-and-white neoclassical place settings with the de Clermont ouroboros surrounding a crowned letter *C*.

"I believe we are in danger of being civilized," Verin muttered. "And by warmbloods, too."

"Not a moment too soon," Fernando said, picking up his napkin and spreading it on his lap.

"A toast," Matthew said, raising his glass. "To lost loved ones. May their spirits be with us tonight and always."

There were murmurs of agreement and echoes of his first line as glasses were lifted. Sarah dashed a tear from her eye, and Gallowglass took her hand and gave it a gentle kiss. I choked back my own sorrow and gave Gallowglass a grateful smile.

"Another toast to the health of my sister Diana and to Marcus's fiancée—the newest members of my family." Baldwin raised his glass once more.

"Diana and Phoebe," Marcus said, joining in.

Glasses were lifted around the table, although I thought for a moment that Matthew might direct the contents of his at Baldwin. Sarah took a hesitant sip of her sparkling wine and made a face.

"Let's eat," she said, putting the glass down hastily. "Emily hated it when the food got cold, and I don't imagine Marthe will be any more forgiving."

Dinner proceeded seamlessly. There was cold soup for the warmbloods and tiny silver beakers of blood for the vampires. The trout served for the fish course had been swimming along in the nearby river without a care in the world only a few hours before. Roast chicken came next out of deference to Sarah, who couldn't abide the taste of game birds. Some at the table then had venison, though I abstained. At the end of the meal, Marthe and Alain put footed compotes draped with fruit on the table, along with bowls of nuts and platters of cheese.

"What an excellent meal," Ernst said, sitting back in his chair and patting his lean stomach.

There was a gratifying amount of agreement around the room. Despite the rocky start, we'd enjoyed a perfectly pleasant evening as a family. I relaxed into my chair.

"Since we're all here, we have some news to share," Marcus said, smiling across the table at Phoebe. "As you know, Phoebe has agreed to marry me."

"Have you set a date?" Ysabeau asked.

"Not yet. We've decided to do things the old-fashioned way, you see," Marcus replied.

All the de Clermonts in the room turned to Matthew, their faces frozen.

"I'm not sure old-fashioned is an option," Sarah commented drily, "given the fact the two of you are already sharing a room."

"Vampires have different traditions, Sarah," Phoebe explained. "Marcus asked if I would like to be with him for the rest of his life. I said yes."

"Oh," Sarah said with a puzzled frown.

"You can't mean . . ." I trailed off, my eyes on Matthew.

"I've decided to become a vampire." Phoebe's eyes shone with happiness as she looked at her once-and-forever husband. "Marcus insists that I get used to that before we marry, so yes, our engagement may be a bit longer than we'd like."

Phoebe sounded as though she were contemplating minor plastic surgery or a change of hairstyle, rather than a complete biological transformation.

"I don't want her to have any regrets," Marcus said softly, his face split into a wide grin.

"Phoebe will not become a vampire. I forbid it." Matthew's voice was quiet, but it seemed to echo in the crowded room.

"You don't get a vote. This is our decision—Phoebe's and mine," Marcus said. Then he threw down the gauntlet. "And of course Baldwin's. He is head of the family."

Baldwin tented his fingers in front of his face as though considering the question, while Matthew looked at his son in disbelief. Marcus returned his father's stare with a challenging one of his own.

"All I've ever wanted is a traditional marriage, like Grandfather and Ysabeau enjoyed," Marcus said. "When it comes to love, you're the family revolutionary, Matthew. Not me."

"Even if Phoebe were to become a vampire, it could never be traditional. Because of the blood rage, she should never take blood from your heart vein," Matthew said.

"I'm sure Grandfather took Ysabeau's blood." Marcus looked to his grandmother. "Isn't that right?"

"Do you want to take that risk, knowing what we know now about blood-borne diseases?" Matthew said. "If you truly love her, Marcus, don't change her."

Matthew's phone rang, and he reluctantly looked at the display. "It's Miriam," he said, frowning.

"She wouldn't call at this hour unless something important had come up in the lab," Marcus said.

Matthew switched on the phone's speaker so the warmbloods could hear as well as the vampires and answered the call. "Miriam?"

"No, Father. It's your son. Benjamin."

The voice on the other end of the line was both alien and familiar, as the voices in nightmares often were.

Ysabeau rose to her feet, her face the color of snow.

"Where is Miriam?" Matthew demanded.

"I don't know," Benjamin replied, his tone lazy. "Perhaps with someone named Jason. He's called a few times. Or someone named Amira. She called twice. Miriam is your bitch, Father. Perhaps if you snap your fingers, she will come running."

Marcus opened his mouth, and Baldwin hissed a warning that made his nephew's jaws snap shut.

"I'm told there was trouble at Sept-Tours. Something about a witch," Benjamin said.

Matthew refused to take the bait.

"The witch had discovered a de Clermont secret, I understand, but died before she could reveal it. Such a shame." Benjamin made a sound of mocking sympathy. "Was she anything like the one you were holding in thrall in Prague? A fascinating creature."

Matthew swung his head around, automatically checking that I was safe.

"You always said I was the black sheep of the family, but we're more alike than you want to admit," Benjamin continued. "I've even come to share your appreciation for the company of witches."

I felt the change in the air as the rage surged through Matthew's veins. My skin prickled, and a dull throbbing started in my left thumb.

"Nothing you do interests me," Matthew said coldly.

"Not even if it involves the Book of Life?" Benjamin waited for a few moments. "I know you're looking for it. Does it have some relevance to your research? Difficult subject, genetics."

"What do you want?" Matthew asked.

"Your attention." Benjamin laughed.

Matthew fell silent once more.

"You're not often at a loss for words, Matthew," Benjamin said. "Happily, it's your turn to listen. At last I've found a way to destroy you and the rest of the de Clermonts. Neither the Book of Life nor your pathetic vision of science can help you now."

"I'm going to enjoy making a liar out of you," Matthew promised.

"Oh, I don't think so." Benjamin's voice dropped, as though he were imparting a great secret. "You see, I know what the witches discovered all those years ago. Do you?"

Matthew's eyes locked on mine.

"I'll be in touch," Benjamin said. The line went dead.

"Call the lab," I said urgently, thinking only of Miriam.

Matthew's fingers raced to make the call.

"It's about time you phoned, Matthew. Exactly what am I supposed to be looking for in your DNA? Marcus said to look for reproductive markers. What is that supposed to mean?" Miriam sounded sharp, annoyed, and utterly like herself. "Your in-box is overflowing, and I'm due a vacation, by the way."

"Are you safe?" Matthew's voice was hoarse.

"Yes. Why?"

"Do you know where your phone is?" Matthew asked.

"No. I left it somewhere today. A shop, probably. I'm sure whoever has it will call me."

"He called me instead." Matthew swore. "Benjamin has your phone, Miriam."

The line went silent.

"*Your* Benjamin?" Miriam asked, horrified. "I thought he was dead."

"Alas, he's not," Fernando said with real regret.

"Fernando?" His name came out of Miriam's mouth with a whoosh of relief.

"*Sim, Miriam. Tudo bem contigo?*" Fernando asked gently.

"Thank God you're there. Yes, yes, I'm fine." Miriam's voice shook, but she made a valiant effort to control it. "When was the last time anyone heard from Benjamin?"

"Centuries ago," Baldwin said. "And yet Matthew has been home for only a few weeks, and Benjamin has already found a way to contact him."

"That means Benjamin has been watching and waiting for him," Miriam whispered. "Oh, God."

"Was there anything about our research on your phone, Miriam?" Matthew asked. "Stored e-mails? Data?"

"No. You know I delete my e-mails after I read them." She paused. "My address book. Benjamin has your phone numbers now."

"We'll get new ones," Matthew said briskly. "Don't go home. Stay with Amira at the Old Lodge. I don't want either of you alone. Benjamin mentioned Amira by name." Matthew hesitated. "Jason, too."

Miriam sucked in her breath. "Bertrand's son?"

"It's all right, Miriam," Matthew said, trying to be soothing. I was glad she couldn't see the expression in his eyes. "Benjamin noticed he'd called you a few times, that's all."

"Jason's picture is in my photos. Now Benjamin will be able to recognize him!" Miriam said, clearly rattled. "Jason is all that I have left of my mate, Matthew. If anything were to happen to him—"

"I'll make sure Jason is aware of the danger." Matthew looked to Gallowglass, who immediately picked up his phone.

"Jace?" Gallowglass murmured as he left the room, shutting the door softly behind him.

"Why has Benjamin reappeared now?" Miriam asked numbly.

"I don't know." Matthew looked in my direction. "He knew about Emily's death and mentioned our genetics research and the Book of Life."

I could sense some crucial piece in a larger puzzle fall into place.

"Benjamin was in Prague in 1591," I said slowly. "That must be where Benjamin heard about the Book of Life. Emperor Rudolf had it."

Matthew gave me a warning look. When he spoke, his tone had turned brisk. "Don't worry, Miriam. We'll figure out what Benjamin's after, I promise." Matthew urged Miriam to be careful and told her he'd call her once we reached Oxford. After he hung up, the silence was deafening.

Gallowglass slipped back into the room. "Jace hasn't seen anything out of the ordinary, but he promised to be on guard. So. What do we do now?"

"*We?*" Baldwin said, brows arched.

"Benjamin is my responsibility," Matthew said grimly.

"Yes, he is," Baldwin agreed. "It's high time you acknowledged that and dealt with the chaos you've caused, instead of hiding behind Ysabeau's skirts and indulging in these intellectual fantasies about curing blood rage and discovering the secret of life."

"You may have waited too long, Matthew," Verin added. "It would have been easy to destroy Benjamin in Jerusalem after he was first reborn, but it won't be now. Benjamin couldn't have remained hidden for so long without having children and allies around him."

"Matthew will manage somehow. He is the family assassin, isn't he?" Baldwin said mockingly.

"I'll help," Marcus said to Matthew.

"You aren't going anywhere, Marcus. You'll stay here, at my side, and welcome the Congregation's delegation. So will Gallowglass and Verin. We need a show of family solidarity." Baldwin studied Phoebe closely. She returned his look with an indignant one of her own.

"I've considered your wish to become a vampire, Phoebe," Baldwin reported when his inspection of her was complete, "and I'm prepared to support it, irrespective of Matthew's feelings. Marcus's desire for a traditional mate will demonstrate that the de Clermonts still honor the old ways. You will stay here, too."

"If Marcus wishes me to do so, I would be delighted to remain here in Ysabeau's house. Would that be all right, Ysabeau?" Phoebe used courtesy as both a weapon and a crutch, as only the British could.

"Of course," Ysabeau said, sitting down at last. She gathered her composure and smiled weakly at her grandson's fiancée. "You are always welcome, Phoebe."

"Thank you, Ysabeau," Phoebe replied, giving Baldwin a pointed look.

Baldwin turned his attention to me. "All that's left to decide is what to do with Diana."

"My wife—like my son—is my concern," said Matthew.

"You cannot return to Oxford now." Baldwin ignored his brother's interruption. "Benjamin might still be there."

"We'll go to Amsterdam," Matthew said promptly.

"Also out of the question," Baldwin said. "The house is indefensible. If you cannot ensure her safety, Matthew, Diana will stay with my daughter Miyako."

"Diana would hate Hachiōji," Gallowglass stated with conviction.

"Not to mention Miyako," Verin murmured.

"Then Matthew had better do his duty." Baldwin stood. "Quickly." Matthew's brother left the room so fast he seemed to vanish. Verin and Ernst quickly said their good-nights and followed. Once they'd gone, Ysabeau suggested we adjourn to the salon. There was an ancient stereo there and enough Brahms to muffle the lengthiest of conversations.

"What will you do, Matthew?" Ysabeau still looked shattered. "You cannot let Diana go to Japan. Miyako would eat her alive."

"We're going to the Bishop house in Madison," I said. It was hard to know who was most surprised by this revelation we were going to New York: Ysabeau, Matthew, or Sarah.

"I'm not sure that's a good idea," Matthew said cautiously.

"Em discovered something important here at Sept-Tours—something she'd rather die than reveal." I marveled at how calm I sounded.

"What makes you think so?" Matthew asked.

"Sarah said Em had been poking through things in the Round Tower, where all the de Clermont family records are kept. If she knew about the witch's baby in Jerusalem, she would have wanted to know more," I replied.

"Ysabeau told both of us about the baby," Sarah said, looking at Ysabeau for confirmation. "Then we told Marcus. I still don't see why this means we should go to Madison."

"Because whatever it was that Emily discovered drove her to summon up spirits," I said. "Sarah thinks Emily was trying to reach Mom. Maybe Mom knew something, too. If that's true, we might be able to find out more about it in Madison."

"That's a lot of thinks, mights, and maybes, Auntie," Gallowglass said with a frown.

I looked at my husband, who had not responded to my suggestion but was instead staring absently into his wineglass. "What do you think, Matthew?"

"We can go to Madison," he said. "For now."

"I'll go with you," Fernando murmured. "Keep Sarah company." She smiled at him gratefully.

"There's more going on here than meets the eye—and it involves Knox and Gerbert. Knox came to Sept-Tours because of a letter he'd found in Prague that mentioned Ashmole 782." Matthew looked somber. "It can't be a coincidence that Knox's discovery of that letter coincides with Emily's death and Benjamin's reappearance."

"You were in Prague. The Book of Life was in Prague. Benjamin was in Prague. Knox found something in Prague," Fernando said slowly. "You're right, Matthew. That's more than a coincidence. It's a pattern."

"There's something else—something we haven't told you about the Book of Life," Matthew said. "It's written on parchment made from the skins of daemons, vampires, and witches."

Marcus's eyes widened. "That means it contains genetic information."

"That's right," Matthew said. "We can't let it fall into Knox's hands—or, God forbid, Benjamin's."

"Finding the Book of Life and its missing pages still has to be our top priority," I agreed.

"Not only could it tell us about creature origins and evolution, it may help us understand blood rage," Marcus said. "Still, we might not be able to gather any useful genetic information from it."

"The Bishop house returned the page with the chemical wedding to Diana shortly after we came back," Matthew said. The house was known among the area's witches for its magical misbehavior and often took cherished items for safekeeping, only to restore them to their owners at a later date. "If we can get to a lab, we could test it."

"Unfortunately, it isn't easy to talk your way into state-of-the-art genetics laboratories." Marcus shook his head. "And Baldwin is right. You can't go to Oxford."

"Maybe Chris could find you something at Yale. He's a biochemist, too. Would his lab have the right equipment?" My understanding of laboratory practices petered out around 1715.

"I'm not analyzing a page from the Book of Life in a college laboratory," Matthew said. "I'll look for a private laboratory. There must be something I can hire out."

"Ancient DNA is fragile. We'll need more than a single page to work with if we want reliable results," Marcus warned.

"Another reason to get Ashmole 782 out of the Bodleian," I said.

"It's safe where it is, Diana," Matthew assured me.

"For the moment," I replied.

"Aren't there two more loose pages out there in the world?" Marcus said. "We could look for them first."

"Maybe I can help," Phoebe offered.

"Thanks, Phoebe." I'd seen Marcus's mate in research mode in the Round Tower. I'd be happy to have her skills at my disposal.

"And Benjamin?" Ysabeau asked. "Do you know what he meant when he said he had come to share your appreciation for witches, Matthew?"

Matthew shook his head.

My witch's sixth sense told me that finding out the answer to Ysabeau's question might well be the key to everything.

Sol in Leo

She who is born when the sun is in Leo shall be naturally subtle and witty, and desirous of learning. Whatsoever she heareth or seeth if it seems to comprise any difficulty of matter immediately will she desire to know it. The magic sciences will do her great stead. She shall be familiar to and well beloved by princes. Her first child shall be a female, and the second a male. During her life she shall sustain many troubles and perils.

—Anonymous English Commonplace Book, c. 1590, Gonçalves MS 4890, f. 8ᵛ

7

I stood in Sarah's stillroom and stared through the dust on the surface of the window's wavy glass. The whole house needed a good airing. The stiff brass latch on the sash resisted my attempts at first, but the swollen frame finally gave up the fight and the window rocketed upward, quivering with indignation at the rough treatment.

"Deal with it," I said crossly, turning away and surveying the room before me. It was a familiarly strange place, this room where my aunts had spent so much of their time and I so little. Sarah left her usual disorderly ways at the threshold. In here all was neat and tidy, surfaces clear, mason jars lined up on the shelves, and wooden drawers labeled with their contents. CONEFLOWER, FEVERFEW, MILK THISTLE, SKULLCAP, BONESET, YARROW, MOONWORT.

Though the ingredients for Sarah's craft were not arranged alphabetically, I was sure some witchy principle governed their placement, since she was always able to reach instantly for the herb or seed she needed.

Sarah had taken the Bishop grimoire with her to Sept-Tours, but now it was back where it belonged: resting on what remained of an old pulpit that Em had bought in one of Bouckville's antique shops. She and Sarah had sawed off its supporting pillar, and now the lectern sat on the old kitchen table that had come here with the first Bishops at the end of the eighteenth century. One of the table's legs was markedly shorter than the other—nobody knew why—but the unevenness of the floorboards meant that its surface was surprisingly level and solid. As a child I'd thought it was magic. As an adult I knew it was dumb luck.

Various old appliances and a battered electrical-outlet strip were strewn around Sarah's work surface. There was an avocado green slow cooker, a venerable coffeemaker, two coffee grinders, and a blender. These were the tools of the modern witch, though Sarah kept a big black cauldron by the fireplace for old times' sake. My aunts used the slow cooker for making oils and potions, the coffee grinders and blender for preparing incense and pulverizing herbs, and the coffee machine for brewing infusions. In the corner stood a shining white specimen fridge with a red cross on the door, unplugged and unused.

"Maybe Matthew can find something more high-tech for Sarah," I mused aloud. A Bunsen burner. A few alembics, perhaps. Suddenly I longed for Mary Sidney's well-equipped sixteenth-century laboratory. I looked up, half hoping to see the splendid murals of alchemical processes that decorated her walls at Baynard's Castle.

Instead dried herbs and flowers hung from twine strung up between the exposed rafters. I could identify some of them: the swollen pods of nigella, bursting with tiny seeds; prickly topped milk thistle; long-stemmed mullein crowned with the bright yellow flowers that earned them the name of witches' candles; stalks of fennel. Sarah knew every one of them by sight, touch, taste, and smell. With them she cast spells and manufactured charms. The dried plants were gray with dust, but I knew better than to disturb them. Sarah would never forgive me if she came into her stillroom and discovered nothing but stems.

The stillroom had once been the farmhouse's kitchen. One wall was occupied by a huge fireplace complete with a wide hearth and a pair of ovens. Above it was a storage loft accessible by a rickety old ladder. I'd spent many a rainy afternoon there, curled up with a book listening to the rain patter against the roof. Corra was up there now, one eye open in lazy interest.

I sighed and set the dust motes dancing. It was going to take water— and lots of elbow grease—to make this room welcoming again. And if my mother had known something that might help us find the Book of Life, this is where I would find it.

A soft chime sounded. Then another.

Goody Alsop had taught me how to discern the threads that bound the world and pull on them to weave spells that were not in any grimoire. The threads were around me all the time, and when they brushed together, they made a sort of music. I reached out and snagged a few strands on my fingers. Blue and amber—the colors that connected the past to the present and the future. I'd seen them before, but only in corners where unsuspecting creatures wouldn't be caught in time's warp and weft.

Not surprisingly, time was not behaving as it should in the Bishop house. I twisted the blue and amber threads into a knot and tried to push them back where they belonged, but they sprang back, weighting the air with memories and regret. A weaver's knot wouldn't fix what was wrong here.

My body was damp with perspiration, even though all I'd done was displace the dust and dirt from one location to another. I'd forgotten how hot Madison could be at this time of year. Picking up a bucket full of dingy water, I pushed against the stillroom door. It didn't budge.

"Move, Tabitha," I said, nudging the door another inch in hopes of dislodging the cat.

Tabitha yowled. She refused to join me in the stillroom. It was Sarah and Em's domain, and she considered me an invader.

"I'll set Corra on you," I threatened.

Tabitha shifted. One paw stretched forward past the crack, then the other as she slipped away. Sarah's cat had no wish to battle my familiar, but her dignity forbade a hurried retreat.

I pushed open the back door. Outside, a drone of insects and an unrelenting pounding filled the air. I flung the dirty water off the deck, and Tabitha shot outside to join Fernando. He was standing with a foot propped up on a stump we used to split wood, watching Matthew drive fence posts into the field.

"Is he still at it?" I asked, swinging the empty bucket. The pounding had been going on for days: first replacing loose shingles on the roof, then hammering the trellises into place in the garden, and now mending fences.

"Matthew's mind is quieter when he is working with his hands," Fernando said. "Carving stone, fighting with his sword, sailing a boat, writing a poem, doing an experiment—it doesn't really matter."

"He's thinking about Benjamin." If so, it was no wonder Matthew was seeking distractions.

Fernando's cool attention turned to me. "The more Matthew thinks about his son, the more he is taken back to a time when he did not like himself or the choices he made."

"Matthew doesn't often talk about Jerusalem. He showed me his pilgrim's badge and told me about Eleanor." It wasn't a lot, given how much time Matthew must have spent there. And such ancient memories didn't often reveal themselves to my witch's kiss.

"Ah. Fair Eleanor. Her death was another preventable mistake," Fernando said bitterly. "Matthew should never have gone to the Holy Land the first time, never mind the second. The politics and bloodshed were too much for any young vampire to handle, especially one with blood rage. But Philippe needed every weapon at his disposal if he hoped to succeed in Outremer."

Medieval history was not my area of expertise, but the Crusader colonies brought back hazy memories of bloody conflicts and the deadly siege of Jerusalem.

"Philippe dreamed of setting up a *manjasang* kingdom there, but it was not to be. For once in his life, he underestimated the avarice of the warm-bloods, not to mention their religious fanaticism. Philippe should have left Matthew in Córdoba with Hugh and me, for Matthew was no help to him in Jerusalem or Acre or any of the other places his father sent him." Fernando gave the stump a savage kick, dislodging a bit of moss clinging to the old wood. "Blood rage can be an asset, it seems, when what you want is a killer."

"I don't think you liked Philippe," I said softly.

"In time I came to respect him. But like him?" Fernando shook his head. "No."

Recently, I'd experienced twinges of dislike where Philippe was concerned. He had given Matthew the job of family assassin, after all. Sometimes I looked at my husband, standing alone in the lengthening summer shadows or silhouetted against the light from the window, and saw the heaviness of that responsibility weighing on his shoulders.

Matthew fitted a fence post into the ground and looked up. "Do you need something?" he shouted.

"Nope. Just getting some water," I called back.

"Have Fernando help you." Matthew pointed to the empty bucket. He didn't approve of pregnant women doing heavy lifting.

"Of course," I said noncommittally as Matthew went back to his work.

"You have no intention of letting me carry your bucket." Fernando put a hand over his heart in mock dismay. "You wound me. How will I hold up my head in the de Clermont family if you don't allow me to put you on a pedestal as a proper knight would do?"

"If you keep Matthew from renting that steel roller he's been talking about to resurface the driveway, I'll let you wear shining armor for the rest of the summer." I gave Fernando a peck on the cheek and departed.

Feeling restless and uncomfortable in the heat, I abandoned the empty bucket in the kitchen sink and went in search of my aunt. It wasn't hard to find her. Sarah had taken to sitting in my grandmother's rocking chair in the keeping room and staring at the ebonized tree growing out of the fireplace. In coming back to Madison, Sarah was being forced to confront the loss of Emily in an entirely new way. It had left her subdued and remote.

"It's too hot to clean. I'm going into town to run errands. Do you want to come?" I asked.

"No. I'm okay here," Sarah said, rocking back and forth.

"Hannah O'Neil called again. She's invited us to her Lughnasadh potluck." Since our return we'd received a stream of phone calls from members of the Madison coven. Sarah had told the high priestess, Vivian Harrison, that she was perfectly fine and was being well taken care of by family. After that, she refused to talk to anyone.

Sarah ignored my mention of Hannah's invitation and continued to study the tree. "The ghosts are bound to come back eventually, don't you think?"

The house had been remarkably free of spectral visitors since our return. Matthew blamed Corra, but Sarah and I knew better. With Em so recently gone, the rest of the ghosts were staying away so that we didn't pester them with questions about how she was faring.

"Sure," I said, "but it's probably going to be a while."

"The house is so quiet without them. I never saw them like you did, but you could tell they were around." Sarah rocked with more energy, as if this would somehow bring the ghosts closer.

"Have you decided what to do about the Blasted Tree?" It had been waiting for Matthew and me when we returned from 1591, the gnarled black trunk taking up most of the chimney and its roots and branches extending into the room. Though it seemed devoid of life, the tree did occasionally produce strange fruit: car keys, as well as the image of the chemical wedding that had been torn from Ashmole 782. More recently it had offered up a recipe for rhubarb compote circa 1875 and a pair of false eyelashes circa 1973. Fernando and I thought the tree should be removed, the chimney repaired, and the paneling patched and painted. Sarah and Matthew were less convinced.

"I don't know," Sarah said with a sigh. "I'm getting used to it. We can always decorate it for the holidays."

"The snow is going to blow straight through those cracks come winter," I said, picking up my purse.

"What did I teach you about magical objects?" Sarah asked, and I heard a trace of her normal sharpness.

"Don't touch them until you understand them," I intoned in the voice of a six-year-old.

"Cutting down a magically produced tree certainly qualifies as 'touching,' don't you agree?" Sarah motioned Tabitha away from the hearth, where she was sitting staring at the bark. "We need milk. And eggs. And Fernando wants some kind of fancy rice. He promised to make paella."

"Milk. Eggs. Rice. Got it." I gave Sarah one last worried look. "Tell Matthew I won't be long."

The floorboards in the front hall creaked out a brief complaint as I crossed to the door. I paused, my foot glued in place. The Bishop house was not an ordinary home and had a history of making its feelings known on a variety of issues, from who had a right to occupy it to whether or not it approved of the new paint color on the shutters.

But there was no further response from the house. Like the ghosts, it was waiting.

Outside, Sarah's new car was parked by the front door. Her old Honda Civic had met with a mishap during its return from Montreal, where Matthew and I had left it. A de Clermont functionary had been tasked to drive it back to Madison, but the engine had fallen out somewhere between Bouckville and Watertown. To console Sarah, Matthew had presented her with a metallic purple Mini Cooper, complete with white racing stripes edged with black and silver and a personalized license plate that said NEW BROOM. Matthew hoped this witchy message would obviate Sarah's need to put bumper stickers all over the vehicle, but I feared it was only a matter of time before this car looked like the old one.

In case anyone thought Sarah's new car and her lack of slogans meant her paganism was wavering, Matthew purchased a witch antenna ball. She had red hair and was wearing a pointy hat and sunglasses. No matter where Sarah parked, someone stole it. He kept a box of replacements in the mudroom cupboard.

I waited until Matthew was hammering in his next fence post before jumping into Sarah's Mini. I reversed it and sped away from the house. Matthew hadn't gone so far as to forbid me from leaving the farm unaccompanied, and Sarah knew where I was going. Happy to be getting away, I opened the sunroof to catch the July breezes on my way into town.

My first stop was at the post office. Mrs. Hutchinson eyed the tight swell under the hem of my T-shirt with interest but said nothing. The only other people in the post office were two antiques dealers and Smitty, Matthew's new best friend from the hardware store.

"How is that post maul working out for Mr. Clairmont?" Smitty asked, tapping his sheaf of junk mail against the brim of his John Deere hat. "Haven't sold one of them in ages. Most people want post pounders these days."

"Matthew seems quite happy with it." *Most people aren't six-foot-three vampires,* I thought, chucking the sales flyer for the local grocery store and the offers for new tires into the recycling bin.

"You've caught a good one there," Smitty said, eyeing my wedding ring. "And he seems to be getting along with Miz Bishop, too." This last was said in a slightly awed tone.

My mouth twitched. I picked up the stack of catalogs and bills that remained and put them in my bag. "You take care, Smitty."

"Bye, Mrs. Clairmont. Tell Mr. Clairmont to let me know when he decides about that roller for the driveway."

"It's not Mrs. Clairmont. I still use—Oh, never mind," I said, catching Smitty's confused expression. I opened the door and stepped aside to let two children enter. The kids were in hot pursuit of lollipops, which Mrs. Hutchinson kept on the counter. I was almost out the door when I heard Smitty whispering to the postmistress.

"Have you met Mr. Clairmont, Annie? Nice guy. I was beginning to think Diana was going to be a spinster like Miz Bishop, if you know what I mean," Smitty said, giving Mrs. Hutchinson a meaningful wink.

I turned west onto Route 20, through green fields and past old farmsteads that had once provided food to the area's residents. Many of the properties had been subdivided and their land turned to different purposes. There were schools and offices, a granite yard, a yarn shop in a converted barn.

When I pulled in to the parking lot of the supermarket in nearby Hamilton, it was practically deserted. Even when college was in session, it was never more than half full.

I maneuvered Sarah's car into one of the plentiful open spaces near the doors, parking next to one of the vans that people bought when they had children. It had sliding doors to allow for the easy installation of car seats, lots of cup holders, and beige carpets to hide the cereal that got flung on the floor. My future life flashed before my eyes.

Sarah's zippy little car was a welcome reminder that there were other options, though Matthew would probably insist on a Panzer tank once the twins were born. I eyed the silly green witch on the antenna. As I murmured a few words, the wires in the antenna rerouted themselves through the soft foam ball and the witch's hat. No one would be stealing Sarah's mascot on my watch.

"Nice binding spell," a dry voice said from behind me. "I don't believe I know that one."

I whirled around. The woman standing there was fiftyish with shoulder-length hair that had gone prematurely silver and emerald green eyes. A low hum of power surrounded her—not showy, but solid. This was the high priestess of Madison's coven.

"Hello, Mrs. Harrison." The Harrisons were an old Hamilton family. They'd come from Connecticut, and, like the Bishops, the women kept the family name regardless of marriage. Vivian's husband, Roger, had taken the radical step of changing his last name from Barker to Harrison when the two wed, earning him a revered spot in the coven annals for his willingness to honor tradition and a fair amount of ribbing from the other husbands.

"I think you're old enough to call me Vivian, don't you?" Her eyes dropped to my abdomen. "Going shopping?"

"Uh-huh." No witch could lie to a fellow witch. Under the circumstances it was best to keep my responses brief.

"What a coincidence. So am I." Behind Vivian two shopping carts detached themselves from the stack and rolled out of their corral.

"So you're due in January?" she asked once we were inside. I fumbled and nearly dropped the paper bag of apples grown on a nearby farm.

"Only if I carry the babies to full term. I'm expecting twins."

"Twins are a handful," Vivian said ruefully. "Just ask Abby." She waved at a woman holding two cartons of eggs.

"Hi, Diana. I don't think we've met." Abby put one of the cartons in the section of the cart designed for toddlers. She buckled the eggs into place using the flimsy seat belt. "Once the babies are born, you'll have to come up with a different way to keep them from getting broken. I've got some zucchini for you in the car, so don't even think of buying any."

"Does everybody in the county know that I'm pregnant?" I asked. Not to mention what I was shopping for today.

"Only the witches," Abby said. "And anybody who talks to Smitty." A four-year-old boy in a striped shirt and wearing a Spider-Man mask sped by. "John Pratt! Stop chasing your sister!"

"Not to worry. I found Grace in the cookie aisle," said a handsome man in shorts and a gray and maroon Colgate University T-shirt. He was holding a squirming toddler whose face was smeared with chocolate and cookie crumbs. "Hi, Diana. I'm Abby's husband, Caleb Pratt. I teach here." Caleb's voice was easy, but there was a crackle of energy around him. Could he have a touch of elemental magic?

My question highlighted the fine threads that surrounded him, but Vivian distracted me before I could be certain.

"Caleb is a professor in the anthropology department," Vivian said with pride. "He and Abby have been a welcome addition to the community."

"Nice to meet you," I murmured. The whole coven must shop at the Cost Cutter on Thursday.

"Only when we need to talk business," Abby said, reading my mind with ease. So far as I could tell, she had considerably less magical talent than Vivian or Caleb, but there was obviously some power in her blood. "We expected to see Sarah today, but she's avoiding us. Is she okay?"

"Not really." I hesitated. Once the Madison coven had represented everything I wanted to deny about myself and about being a Bishop. But the witches of London had taught me that there was a price to pay for living cut off from other witches. And the simple truth was that Matthew and I couldn't manage on our own. Not after everything that had transpired at Sept-Tours.

"Something you want to say, Diana?" Vivian looked at me shrewdly.

"I think we need your help." The words slipped out easily. My astonishment must have shown, for the three witches all started to laugh.

"Good. That's what we're here for," she said, casting an approving smile at me. "What's the problem?"

"Sarah's stuck," I said bluntly. "And Matthew and I are in trouble."

"I know. My thumbs have been bothering me for days," Caleb said, bouncing Grace on his hip. "At first I thought it was just the vampires."

"It's more than that." My voice was grim. "It involves witches, too. And the Congregation. My mother may have had a premonition about it, but I don't know where to begin searching for more information."

"What does Sarah say?" Vivian asked.

"Not much. She's mourning Emily all over again. Sarah sits by the fireplace, watches the tree growing out of the hearth, and waits for the ghosts to come back."

"And your husband?" Caleb's eyebrows lifted.

"Matthew's replacing fence posts." I pushed a hand through my hair, lifting the damp strands from my neck. If it got any warmer, you'd be able to fry an egg on Sarah's car.

"A classic example of displaced aggression," Caleb said thoughtfully, "as well as a need to establish firm boundaries."

"What kind of magic is that?" I was astonished that he could know so much about Matthew from my few words.

"It's anthropology." Caleb grinned.

"Maybe we should talk about this somewhere else." Vivian smiled warmly at the growing crowd of onlookers in the produce section. The few humans in the store couldn't help noticing the gathering of four otherworldly creatures, and several were openly listening in on our conversation while pretending to judge the ripeness of cantaloupes and watermelons.

"I'll meet you back at Sarah's in twenty minutes," I said, eager to get away.

"The arborio rice is in aisle five," Caleb said helpfully, handing Grace back to Abby. "It's the closest thing to paella rice in Hamilton. If that's not good enough, you can stop by and see Maureen at the health-food store. She'll special-order some Spanish rice for you. Otherwise you'll have to drive to Syracuse."

"Thanks," I said weakly. There would be no stops at the health-food store, which was the local hangout for witches when they weren't at the Cost Cutter. I pushed my cart in the direction of aisle five. "Good idea."

"Don't forget the milk!" Abby called after me.

When I got back home, Matthew and Fernando were standing in the field, deep in conversation. I put the groceries away and found the bucket in the sink where I'd left it. My fingers automatically reached for the tap, ready to twist it open so that the water flowed.

"What the hell is wrong with me?" I muttered, pulling the empty bucket out of the sink. I carried it back to the stillroom and let the door swing shut.

This room had seen some of my greatest humiliations as a witch. Even though I understood that my past difficulties with magic had come about because I was a weaver and spellbound to boot, it was still difficult to leave the memories of failure behind.

But it was time to try.

Placing the bucket on the hearth, I felt for the tide that always flowed through me. Thanks to my father, not only was I a weaver, but my blood was full of water. Crouching next to the pail, I directed my hand into the shape of a spout and focused on my desires.

Clean. Fresh. New.

Within moments my hand looked like metal rather than flesh and water poured from my fingers, hitting the plastic with a dull thud. Once the bucket was full, my hand was just a hand again. I smiled and sat back on my heels, pleased that I'd been able to work magic in the Bishop house. All around me the air sparkled with colored threads. It no longer felt thick and heavy but bright and full of potential. A cool breeze blew through the open window. Maybe I couldn't solve all of our problems with a single knot, but if I wanted to find out what Emily and my mother knew, I had to start somewhere.

"With knot of one, the spell's begun," I whispered, snagging a silver thread and knotting it securely.

Out of the corner of my eye, I glimpsed the full skirts and a brightly embroidered bodice that belonged to my ancestor Bridget Bishop.

Welcome home, granddaughter, said her ghostly voice.

8

Matthew swung the maul and lowered it onto the head of the wooden post. It landed with a satisfying *thwack* that reverberated up his arms, across his shoulders, and down his back. He lifted the maul again.

"I don't believe you need to strike the post a third time," Fernando drawled from behind him. "It should still be standing straight and tall when the next ice age comes."

Matthew rested the business end of the maul on the ground and propped his arms on the shaft. He was not sweaty or winded. He was, however, annoyed at the interruption.

"What is it, Fernando?"

"I heard you speaking to Baldwin last night," he replied.

Matthew picked up the posthole digger without responding.

"I take it he told you to stay here and not to cause any trouble—for now," Fernando continued.

Matthew thrust the two sharp blades into the earth. They descended quite a bit farther into the soil than they would have if a human had been wielding the tool. He gave the implement a twist, withdrew it from the ground, and picked up a wooden post.

"Come, *Mateus.* Fixing Sarah's fence is hardly the most useful way to spend your time."

"The most *useful* way to spend my time would be to find Benjamin and rid the family of the monster once and for all." Matthew held the seven-foot fence post in one hand as easily as though it weighed no more than a pencil and drove the tip into the soft earth. "Instead I'm waiting for Baldwin to give me permission to do what I should have done long ago."

"Hmm." Fernando studied the fence post. "Why don't you go, then? To hell with Baldwin and his dictatorial ways. See to Benjamin. It will be no trouble for me to look after Diana as well as Sarah."

Matthew turned a scathing glance on Fernando. "I am not going to leave my pregnant mate in the middle of nowhere—not even with you."

"So your plan is to stay here, fixing whatever you can find that is broken, until the happy moment when Baldwin rings to authorize you to kill your own child. Then you will drag Diana along to whatever godforsaken hole Benjamin occupies and eviscerate him in front of your wife?" Fernando flung his hands up in disgust. "Don't be absurd."

"Baldwin won't tolerate anything but obedience, Fernando. He made that very clear at Sept-Tours."

Baldwin had dragged the de Clermont men and Fernando out into the night and explained in brutal and detailed terms just what would befall each and every one of them if he detected a whisper of protest or a glimmer of insurrection. Afterward even Gallowglass had looked shaken.

"There was a time when you enjoyed outflanking Baldwin. But since your father died, you have let your brother treat you abominably." Fernando snagged the post maul before Matthew could get his hands on it.

"I couldn't lose Sept-Tours. *Maman* wouldn't have survived it—not after Philippe's death." Matthew's mother had been far from invincible then. She had been as fragile as blown glass. "The château might technically belong to the Knights of Lazarus, but everyone knows that the brotherhood belongs to the de Clermonts. If Baldwin wanted to challenge Philippe's will and claim Sept-Tours, he would have succeeded, and Ysabeau would have been out in the cold."

"Ysabeau seems to have recovered from Philippe's death. What is your excuse now?"

"Now my wife is a de Clermont." Matthew gave Fernando a level look.

"I see." Fernando snorted. "Marriage has turned your mind to mush and bent your spine like a willow twig, my friend."

"I won't do anything to jeopardize her position. She might not yet understand what it means, but you and I both know how important it is to be counted among Philippe's children," Matthew said. "The de Clermont name will protect her from all sorts of threats."

"And for this tenuous toehold in the family, you would sell your soul to that devil?" Fernando was genuinely surprised.

"For Diana's sake?" Matthew turned away. "I would do anything. Pay any price."

"Your love for her borders on obsession." Fernando stood his ground when Matthew whirled back around, his eyes black. "It is not healthy, *Mateus*. Not for you. Nor for her."

"So Sarah's been filling your ears with my shortcomings, has she? Diana's aunts never really did approve of me." Matthew glared at the house. It may have been a trick of the light, but the house appeared to be shaking on its foundations with laughter.

"Now that I see you with their niece, I understand why," Fernando said mildly. "The blood rage has always made you prone to excessive behavior. Being mated has made it worse."

"I have thirty years with her, Fernando. Forty or fifty, if I'm lucky. How many centuries did you share with Hugh?"

"Six," Fernando bit out.

"And was that enough?" Matthew exploded. "Before you judge me for being consumed with my mate's well-being, put yourself in my shoes and imagine how you would have behaved had you known that your time with Hugh would be so brief."

"Loss is loss, Matthew, and a vampire's soul is as fragile as that of any warmblood. Six hundred years or sixty or six—it doesn't matter. When your mate dies, a part of your soul dies with him. Or her," Fernando said gently. "And you will have your children—Marcus as well as the twins—to comfort you."

"How will any of that matter if Diana is not here to share it?" Matthew looked desperate.

"No wonder you were so hard on Marcus and Phoebe," Fernando said with dawning understanding. "Turning Diana into a vampire is your greatest desire—"

"Never," Matthew interrupted, his voice savage.

"And your greatest horror," Fernando finished.

"If she became a vampire, she would no longer be my Diana," Matthew said. "She would be something—someone—else."

"You might love her just the same," Fernando said.

"How could I, when I love Diana for all that she is?" Matthew replied.

Fernando had no answer for this. He could not imagine Hugh as anything but a vampire. It had defined him, given him the unique combination of fierce courage and dreamy idealism that had made Fernando fall in love with him.

"Your children will change Diana. What will happen to your love when they are born?"

"Nothing," Matthew said roughly, snatching at the maul. Fernando tossed the heavy tool easily from one hand to the other to keep it out of his reach.

"That is the blood rage talking. I can hear it in your voice." The maul went sailing through the air at ninety miles an hour and landed in the O'Neils' yard. Fernando grabbed Matthew by the throat. "I am frightened for your children. It pains me to say it—to even think it—but I have seen you kill someone you loved."

"Diana. Is. Not. Eleanor." Matthew ground out the words one at a time.

"No. What you felt for Eleanor is nothing compared to what you feel for Diana. Yet all it took was a casual touch from Baldwin, a mere suggestion that Eleanor might agree with him rather than you, and you were ready to tear them both apart." Fernando searched Matthew's face. "What will you do if Diana sees to the babies' needs before yours?"

"I'm in control now, Fernando."

"Blood rage heightens all the instincts a vampire has until they are as keen as honed steel. Your possessiveness is already dangerous. How can you be sure you will keep it in check?"

"Christ, Fernando. I can't be sure. Is that what you want me to say?" Matthew drove his fingers through his hair.

"I want you to listen to Marcus instead of building fences and seeing to the gutters," Fernando replied.

"Not you, too. It's madness to even think of branching out on my own with Benjamin on the loose and the Congregation up in arms," Matthew snapped.

"I was not talking about forming a scion." Fernando thought Marcus's idea was excellent, but he knew when to keep his own counsel.

"What, then?" Matthew said with a frown.

"Your work. If you were to focus on the blood rage, you might be able to stop whatever plans Benjamin is setting into motion without striking a single blow." Fernando let this sink in before he continued. "Even Gallowglass thinks you should be in a laboratory analyzing that page you have from the Book of Life, and he doesn't understand the first thing about science."

"None of the local colleges have sufficient laboratories for my needs," Matthew said. "I haven't only been buying new downspouts, you see. I've been making inquiries, too. And you're right. Gallowglass has no idea what my research entails."

Nor did Fernando. Not really. But he knew who did.

"Surely Miriam has been doing *something* while you were gone. She's hardly the type to sit around idly. Can you not go over her most recent findings?" Fernando asked.

"I told her they could wait," Matthew said gruffly.

"Even previously gathered data might prove useful, now that you have Diana and the twins to consider." Fernando would use anything—even Diana—to bait this hook if it would get Matthew acting instead of simply reacting. "Perhaps it's not only the blood rage that explains her pregnancy. Perhaps she and the witch in Jerusalem both inherited an ability to conceive a vampire's child."

"It's possible," Matthew said slowly. Then his attention was caught by Sarah's purple Mini Cooper skidding and slipping along on the loose gravel. Matthew's shoulders lowered, and some of the darkness disappeared from his eyes. "I really have to resurface the driveway," he said absently, watching the car's progress.

Diana got out of the car and waved in their direction. Matthew smiled and waved back.

"You have to start thinking again," Fernando retorted.

Matthew's phone rang. "What is it, Miriam?"

"I've been thinking." Miriam never bothered with pleasantries. Not even the recent scare with Benjamin had changed that.

"What a coincidence," Matthew said drily. "Fernando's just been urging me to do the same."

"Do you remember when someone broke in to Diana's rooms last October? We feared at the time that whoever it was might be looking for genetic information about her—hair, nail clippings, bits of skin."

"Of course I remember," Matthew said, wiping his hand over his face.

"You were sure it was Knox and the American witch Gillian Chamberlain. What if *Benjamin* was involved?" Miriam paused. "I have a really bad feeling about all this, Matthew—like I've woken up from a pleasant dream only to discover that a spider has snared me in his web."

"He wasn't in her rooms. I would have caught the scent." Matthew sounded sure, but there was a trace of worry in his voice as well.

"Benjamin is too smart to have gone himself. He would have sent a lackey—or one of his children. As his sire, you can sniff him out, but you know that the scent signature is practically undetectable in grandchildren." Miriam sighed with exasperation. "Benjamin mentioned witches and your genetics research. You don't believe in coincidences, remember?"

Matthew did remember saying something like that once—long before he'd met Diana. He made an involuntary check on the house. It was a combination of instinct and reflex now, this need to protect his wife. Matthew pushed away Fernando's earlier warning about his obsessiveness.

"Have you had a chance to delve further into Diana's DNA?" He had taken the blood samples and cheek swabs last year.

"What do you think I've been doing all this while? Crocheting blankets in case you came home with babies and weeping about your absence? And yes, I know as much about the twins as the rest—which is to say not nearly enough."

Matthew shook his head ruefully. "I've missed you, Miriam."

"Don't. Because the next time I see you, I'm going to bite you so hard you'll have the scar for years." Miriam's voice shook. "You should have killed Benjamin long ago. You knew he was a monster."

"Even monsters can change," Matthew said softly. "Look at me."

"You were never a monster," she said. "That was a lie you told to keep the rest of us away."

Matthew disagreed, but he let the matter drop. "So what did you learn about Diana?"

"I learned that what we think we know about your wife is minuscule compared to what we don't know. Her nuclear DNA is like a labyrinth: If you go wandering in it, you're likely to get lost," Miriam said, referring to Diana's unique genetic fingerprint. "And her mtDNA is equally perplexing."

"Let's put aside the mtDNA for the moment. All that will tell us is what Diana has in common with her female ancestors." Matthew would get back to Diana's mitochondrial DNA later. "I want to understand what makes her unique."

"What's worrying you?" Miriam knew Matthew well enough to hear what he wasn't saying.

"Her ability to conceive my children, for a start." Matthew drew a deep breath. "And Diana picked up a sort of dragon while she was in the sixteenth century. Corra is a firedrake. And her familiar."

"Familiar? I thought that business about witches and familiars was a human myth. No wonder her transmogrification gene is so strange," Miriam muttered. "A firedrake. Just what we need. Wait a minute. Is it on a leash or something? Can we get a blood sample?"

"Perhaps," Matthew said dubiously. "I'm not sure Corra would cooperate for a cheek swab, though."

"I wonder if she and Diana are genetically related. . . ." Miriam trailed off, intrigued by the possibilities.

"Have you found anything in Diana's witch chromosome that leads you to believe it controls fertility?" Matthew asked.

"That's an entirely new request, and you know that scientists usually don't find anything unless they're looking for it," Miriam said tartly. "Give me a few days, and I'll see what I can uncover. There are so many unidentified genes in Diana's witch chromosome that some days I wonder if she *is* a witch." Miriam laughed.

Matthew remained silent. He couldn't very well tell her that Diana was a weaver when not even Sarah knew.

"You're keeping something from me," Miriam said, a note of accusation in her voice.

"Send me a report on whatever else you've managed to identify," he said. "We'll discuss it more in a few days. Take a look at my DNA profile, too. Focus on whatever genes we haven't identified yet, especially if they're near the blood-rage gene. See if anything strikes you."

"Ooo-kay," Miriam said deliberately. "You have a secure Internet connection, right?"

"As secure as Baldwin's money can buy."

"Pretty damn secure, then," she said under her breath. "Talk to you later. And, Matthew?"

"Yes?" he said, frowning.

"I'm still going to bite you for not killing Benjamin when you had a chance."

"You'll have to catch me first."

"That's easy. All I have to do is catch Diana. You'll walk right into my arms then," she said just before she disconnected.

"Miriam's back in top form," Fernando said.

"She always was able to recover from a crisis with amazing speed," Matthew said fondly. "Do you remember when Bertrand—"

An unfamiliar car turned in to the driveway.

Matthew sprinted toward it, Fernando at his heels.

The gray-haired woman driving a dented navy Volvo didn't seem a bit surprised to be confronted by two vampires, one of them exceptionally tall. Instead she rolled down the window.

"You must be Matthew," the woman said. "I'm Vivian Harrison. Diana asked me to stop by and see Sarah. She's worried about the tree in the keeping room."

"What is that scent?" Fernando asked Matthew.

"Bergamot," Matthew replied, his eyes narrowing.

"It's a common scent! Besides, I'm an accountant," Vivian said indignantly, "not just the coven's high priestess. What do you expect me to smell of—fire and brimstone?"

"Vivian?" Sarah stood at the front door and squinted into the sunlight. "Is someone sick?"

Vivian climbed out of the car. "Nobody's sick. I ran into Diana at the store."

"I see you've met Matthew and Fernando," Sarah said.

"I have." Vivian looked the two of them over. "Goddess preserve us from handsome vampires." She started walking toward the house. "Diana said you've got a bit of trouble."

"Nothing we can't handle," Matthew said with a scowl.

"He always says that. Sometimes he's even right." Sarah beckoned to Vivian. "Come inside. Diana's got iced tea made."

"Everything is fine, Ms. Harrison," Matthew said, stalking alongside the witch.

Diana appeared behind Sarah. She looked at Matthew in fury, her hands on her hips.

"Fine?" she demanded. "Peter Knox murdered Em. There's a tree growing out of the fireplace. I'm pregnant with your children. We've been evicted from Sept-Tours. And the Congregation could show up at any minute and force us to separate. Does that sound fine to you, Vivian?"

"The Peter Knox who had a crush on Diana's mother? Isn't he a member of the Congregation?" Vivian asked.

"Not anymore," Matthew replied.

Vivian shook her finger at Sarah. "You told me Em had a heart attack."

"She did," Sarah said defensively. Vivian's lips curled in disgust. "It's the truth! Matthew's son said that was the cause of death."

"You're awfully good at telling the truth and lying at the same time, Sarah." Vivian's tone softened. "Emily was a big part of our community. So are you. We need to know what really happened in France."

"Knowing whether it's Knox's fault or not won't change anything. Emily will still be dead." Sarah's eyes brimmed with tears. She dashed them away. "And I don't want the coven involved. It's too dangerous."

"We're your friends. We're already involved." Vivian rubbed her hands together. "Sunday is Lughnasadh."

"Lughnasadh?" Sarah said suspiciously. "The Madison coven hasn't celebrated Lughnasadh for decades."

"We don't normally have a big celebration, it's true, but this year Hannah O'Neil is pulling out all the stops to welcome you back home. And to give us all a chance to say good-bye to Em."

"But Matthew—Fernando." Sarah dropped her voice. "The covenant."

Vivian shouted with laughter. "Diana's pregnant. It's a little late to worry about breaking the rules. Besides, the coven knows all about Matthew. Fernando, too."

"They do?" Sarah said, startled.

"They do," Diana said firmly. "Smitty has bonded with Matthew over hand tools, and you know what a gossip he can be." The indulgent smile she gave Matthew took some of the sting out of her words.

"We're known as a progressive coven. If we're lucky, maybe Diana will trust us with whatever is wrapped up inside her disguising spell. See you Sunday." With a smile at Matthew and a wave to Fernando, Vivian got into her car and pulled away.

"Vivian Harrison is a bulldozer," Sarah grumbled.

"Observant, too," Matthew said thoughtfully.

"She is." Sarah studied Diana. "Vivian's right. You are wearing a disguising spell—a good one. Who cast it for you?"

"Nobody. I—" Unable to lie, and still unwilling to tell her aunt the truth, Diana snapped her mouth shut. Matthew scowled.

"Fine. Don't tell me." Sarah stomped back to the keeping room. "And I'm not going to that potluck. The whole coven is on some vegetarian kick. There will be nothing to eat but zucchini and Hannah's famously inedible Key lime pudding pie."

"The widow is feeling more herself," Fernando whispered, giving Diana a thumbs-up as he followed Sarah into the house. "Returning to Madison was a good idea."

"You promised you'd tell Sarah you're a weaver once we were settled here at the Bishop house," Matthew said when he and Diana were alone. "Why haven't you?"

"I'm not the only one keeping secrets. And I'm not just talking about the blood-vow business or even the fact that vampires kill other vampires with blood rage. You should have told me that Hugh and Fernando were a couple. And you definitely should have told me that Philippe had been using your illness as a weapon all these years."

"Does Sarah know that Corra is your familiar, not a souvenir? And what about meeting your father in London?" Matthew crossed his arms.

"It wasn't the right moment," Diana said with a sniff.

"Ah, yes, the elusive right moment." Matthew snorted. "It never comes, Diana. Sometimes we just have to throw caution to the wind and trust the people we love."

"I do trust Sarah." Diana bit her lip. She didn't have to finish. Matthew knew that the real problem was she didn't trust herself or her magic. Not completely.

"Take a walk with me," he said, holding out his hand. "We can talk about this later."

"It's too hot," Diana protested, though she still put her hand in his.

"I'll cool you off," he promised with a smile.

Diana looked at him with interest. Matthew's smile broadened.

His wife—his heart, his mate, his life—stepped down off the porch and into his arms. Diana's eyes were the blue and gold of a summer sky, and Matthew wanted nothing more than to fall headlong into their bright depths, not to lose himself but to be found.

9

"N o wonder we don't celebrate Lughnasadh," Sarah muttered, pushing open the front door. "All those awful songs about the end of summer and the coming of winter—not to mention Mary Bassett's tambourine accompaniment."

"The music wasn't *that* bad," I protested. Matthew's grimace indicated that Sarah had a right to complain.

"Do you have more of that temperamental wine, Fernando?" Sarah flicked on the hall lights. "I need a drink. My head is pounding."

"Tempranillo." Fernando tossed the picnic blankets on the hall bench. "Tempranillo. Remember: It's Spanish."

"French, Spanish, whatever—I need some," she said, sounding desperate.

I stood aside so Abby and Caleb could get in the door. John was conked out in Caleb's arms, but Grace was wide awake. She squirmed to get down.

"Let her go, Abby. She can't hurt anything," Sarah said, heading for the kitchen.

Abby put Grace down, and the child toddled straight toward the stairs. Matthew laughed.

"She has the most amazing instincts when it comes to trouble. No stairs, Grace." Abby swooped in and swung Grace up in the air before depositing her back on the floor and pointing her in the direction of the family room.

"Why don't you put John in the keeping room?" I suggested. John had abandoned his Spider-Man mask and was wearing a T-shirt with the superhero on it instead.

"Thanks, Diana." Caleb whistled. "I see what you mean about the tree, Matthew. So it just sprang up out of the hearth?"

"We think some fire and a bit of blood might have been involved," Matthew explained, shaking out one of the blankets and following Caleb. The two had been chatting all evening about everything from academic politics to Matthew's hospital work at the John Radcliffe to the fate of the polar bears. Matthew arranged a blanket on the floor for John, while Caleb ran his fingers over the bark on the Blasted Tree.

This is what Matthew needs, I realized. *Home. Family. Pack.* Without other people to take care of, he retreated to that dark place where his past deeds haunted him. And he was especially prone to brooding now, given Benjamin's recent reappearance.

I needed this, too. Living in the sixteenth century, in households rather than simply in houses, I had grown accustomed to being surrounded by other people. My fear of being discovered had receded, and in its place had grown a wish to belong.

As a result I'd found the coven potluck surprisingly enjoyable. The Madison witches had occupied an intimidating place in my imagination, but tonight the assembled witches were pleasant and, except for my high-school nemeses Cassie and Lydia, welcoming. They were also surprisingly power-less when compared to the witches I'd known in London. One or two of them had some elemental magic at their disposal, but none were as formi-dable as the firewitches or waterwitches of the past. And the Madison witches who *could* work the craft couldn't hold a candle to Sarah.

"Wine, Abby?" Fernando offered her a glass.

"Sure." Abby giggled. "I'm surprised you made it out of the potluck alive, Fernando. I was positive that someone was going to work a bit of love magic on you."

"Fernando shouldn't have encouraged them," I said with mock severity. "There was no need to both bow *and* kiss Betty Eastey's hand."

"Her poor husband is going to hear nothing but 'Fernando this' and 'Fernando that' for days," Abby said with another giggle.

"The ladies will be very disappointed when they discover they are trying to saddle the wrong horse," Fernando replied. "Your friends told me the most charming stories, Diana. Did you know that vampires are really quite cuddly, once we find our true love?"

"Matthew hasn't exactly been transformed into a teddy bear," I said drily.

"Ah, but you didn't know him before." Fernando's smile was wicked.

"Fernando!" Sarah called from the kitchen. "Come help me light this stupid fire. I can't get it to catch."

Why she felt it was necessary to light a fire in this kind of heat was beyond me, but Sarah said Em had always lit a fire on Lughnasadh, and that was that.

"Duty calls," Fernando murmured, giving Abby a little bow. Like Betty Eastey, she blushed.

"We'll go with you." Caleb took Grace by the hand. "Come on, sprout."

Matthew watched the Pratts troop off to the kitchen, a smile playing at the corner of his mouth.

"That will be us soon," I said, slipping my arms around him.

"That's just what I was thinking." Matthew kissed me. "Are you ready to tell your aunt about being a weaver?"

"As soon as the Pratts leave." Every morning I promised to tell Sarah about all that I'd learned from the London coven, but with every passing day it got harder to share my news.

"You don't have to tell her everything all at once," Matthew said, running his hands over my shoulders. "Just tell her you're a weaver so you can stop wearing this shroud."

We joined the others in the kitchen. Sarah's fire was now crackling merrily in the stillroom, adding to the warmth of the summer evening. We sat around the table, comparing notes on the party and gossiping about the latest coven happenings. Then the talk turned to baseball. Caleb was a Red Sox fan, just like my dad.

"What is it about Harvard men and the Red Sox?" I got up to make some tea.

A flicker of white caught my eye. I smiled and put the kettle on the stove, thinking it was one of the house's missing ghosts. Sarah would be so happy if one of them were ready to apparate again.

That was no ghost.

Grace tottered in front of the stillroom fireplace on unsteady, two-year-old legs. "Pretty," she cooed.

"Grace!"

Startled by my cry, Grace turned her head. That was enough to upset her balance, and she tipped toward the fire.

I'd never reach her in time—not with a kitchen island and twenty-five feet between us. I reached into the pocket of my shorts and pulled out my weaver's cords. They snaked through my fingers and twisted around my wrists just as Grace's scream pierced the air.

But there was no time for spells, either. Instead I acted on pure instinct and rooted my feet into the floor. Water was all around us, trickling through deep arteries that crisscrossed the Bishop land. It was within me, too, and in an effort to focus its raw, elemental power I isolated the filaments of blue, green, and silver that highlighted everything in the kitchen and the still-room that was tied to water.

In a quicksilver flash, I directed a bolt of water at the fireplace. A spout of steam erupted, coals hissed, and Grace hit the slurry of ash and water on the hearth with a thud.

"Grace!" Abby ran past me, followed by Caleb.

Matthew drew me into his arms. I was soaked to the skin and shivering. He rubbed my back, trying to restore some warmth.

"Thank God you have so much power over water, Diana," Abby said, holding a tearful Grace.

"Is she okay?" I asked. "She reached out to steady herself, but she was awfully close to the flames."

"Her hand is a little pink," Caleb said, examining her small fingers. "What do you think, Matthew?"

Matthew took Grace's hand.

"Pretty," she said, her lower lip trembling.

"I know," Matthew murmured. "Fire is very pretty. Very hot, too." He blew on her fingers, and she laughed. Fernando handed him a damp cloth and an ice cube.

"'Gain," she commanded, thrusting her hand in Matthew's face.

"Nothing seems to be damaged, and there are no blisters," Matthew said after obeying the tiny tyrant's command to blow on her fingers once more. He wrapped the cloth carefully around her hand and held the ice cube to it. "She should be fine."

"I didn't know you could wield waterbolts." Sarah looked at me sharply. "Are you okay? You look different—shiny."

"I'm fine." I pulled away from Matthew, trying to draw the tattered remains of my disguising spell around me. I searched the floor surrounding the kitchen island, looking for my dropped weaver's cords in case some surreptitious patching was required.

"What did you get all over yourself?" Sarah grabbed my hand and turned it palm up. What I saw made me gasp.

Each finger bore a strip of color down its center. My pinkie was streaked with brown, my ring finger yellow. A vivid blue marked my middle finger, and red blazed down my index finger in an imperious slash. The colored lines joined together on my palm, continuing on to the fleshy mound at its base in a braided, multicolored rope. There the rope met up with a strand of green that wandered down from my thumb—ironic, given the fate of most of my houseplants. The five-colored twist traveled the short distance to my wrist and formed a knot with five crossings—the pentacle.

"My weaver's cords. They're . . . inside me." I looked up at Matthew in disbelief.

But most weavers used nine cords, not five. I turned over my left palm and discovered the missing strands: black on my thumb, white on my pinkie, gold on my ring finger, and silver on my middle finger. The pointer finger bore no color at all. And the colors that twisted down to my left wrist created an ouroboros, a circle with no beginning and no end that looked like a snake with its tail in its mouth. It was the de Clermont family emblem.

"Is Diana . . . shimmering?" Abby asked.

Still staring at my hands, I flexed my fingers. An explosion of colored threads illuminated the air.

"What was that?" Sarah's eyes were round.

"Threads. They bind the worlds and govern magic," I explained.

Corra chose that moment to return from her hunting. She swooped down the stillroom chimney and landed in the damp pile of wood. Coughing and wheezing, she lurched to her feet.

"Is that . . . a dragon?" Caleb asked.

"No, it's a souvenir," Sarah said. "Diana brought it back with her from Elizabethan England."

"Corra's not a souvenir. She's my familiar," I whispered.

Sarah snorted. "Witches don't have familiars."

"Weavers do," I said. Matthew's hand rested on my lower back, lending quiet support. "You'd better call Vivian. I need to tell you something."

"So the dragon—" Vivian began, her hands wrapped tight around a steaming mug of coffee.

"Firedrake," I interrupted.

"So it—"

"She. Corra is a female."

"—is your familiar?" Vivian finished.

"Yes. Corra appeared when I wove my first spell in London."

"Are all familiars dragons . . . er, firedrakes?" Abby shifted her legs on the family-room couch. We were all settled around the television, except for John, who had slept peacefully through the excitement.

"No. My teacher, Goody Alsop, had a fetch—a shadow self. She was inclined toward air, you see, and a weaver's familiar takes shape according to a witch's elemental predisposition." It was probably the longest utterance I'd ever made on the subject of magic. It was also largely unintelligible to any of the witches present, who didn't know a thing about weavers.

"I have an affinity for water as well as fire," I explained, plunging on. "Unlike dragons, firedrakes are as comfortable in the sea as in the flames."

"They're also able to fly," Vivian said. "Firedrakes actually represent a triplicity of elemental power."

Sarah looked at her in astonishment.

Vivian shrugged. "I have a master's degree in medieval literature. Wyverns—or firedrakes, if you prefer—were once common in European mythology and legends."

"But you . . . you're my accountant," Sarah sputtered.

"Do you have any idea how many English majors are accountants?" Vivian asked with raised eyebrows. She returned her attention to me. "Can you fly, Diana?"

"Yes," I admitted reluctantly. Flight was not a common talent among witches. It was showy, and therefore undesirable if you wanted to live quietly among humans.

"Do other weavers shimmer like you?" Abby asked, tilting her head.

"I don't know if there *are* other weavers. There weren't many left, even in the sixteenth century. Goody Alsop was the only one in the British Isles after the Scottish weaver was executed. There was a weaver in Prague. And my father was a weaver, too. It runs in families."

"Stephen Proctor was not a weaver," Sarah said tartly. "He never shimmered and had no familiar. Your father was a perfectly ordinary witch."

"The Proctors haven't produced a really first-rate witch for generations," Vivian said apologetically.

"Most weavers aren't first-rate at anything—not by traditional standards." It was even true at a genetic level, where Matthew's tests had revealed all sorts of contradictory markers in my blood. "That's why I was never any good with the craft. Sarah can teach anybody how to work a spell—but not me. I was a disaster." My laugh was shaky. "Daddy told me I should have let the spells go in one ear and out the other and then make up my own."

"When did Stephen tell you that?" Sarah's voice cracked across the room.

"In London. Daddy was there in 1591, too. I got my timewalking abilities from him, after all." In spite of Matthew's insistence that I didn't have to tell Sarah everything at once, that's how the story was coming out.

"Did you see Rebecca?" Sarah was wide-eyed.

"No. Just Daddy." Like meeting Philippe de Clermont, seeing my own father again had been an unexpected gift on our journey.

"I'll be damned," Sarah murmured.

"He wasn't there long, but for a few days, there were three weavers in London. We were the talk of the town." And not only because my father kept feeding plot points and lines of dialogue to William Shakespeare.

Sarah opened her mouth to fire off another question, but Vivian held her hand up for quiet.

"If weaving runs in families, why are there so few of you?" Vivian asked.

"Because a long time ago, other witches set out to destroy us." My fingers tightened on the towel that Matthew had wrapped around my shoulders.

"Goody Alsop told us that whole families were murdered to ensure that no children carried on the legacy." Matthew's fingers pressed into the tense muscles in my neck. "Those who survived went into hiding. War, disease, and infant mortality would have put considerable stress on those few remaining bloodlines."

"Why eradicate weavers? New spells would be highly desirable in any coven," Caleb asked.

"I'd kill for a spell that would unfreeze my computer when John jams the keys," Abby added. "I've tried everything: the charm for stuck wheels, the spell for broken locks, the blessing for new endeavors. None of them seem to work with these modern electronics."

"Maybe weavers were too powerful and other witches were jealous. Maybe it was just fear. When it comes right down to it, I don't think creatures are any more accepting of difference than humans are. . . ." My words faded into silence.

"New spells." Caleb whistled. "Where do you start?"

"That depends on the weaver. With me it's a question or a desire. I focus on that, and my cords do the rest." I held my hands up. "I guess my fingers will have to do it now."

"Let me see your hands, Diana," Sarah said. I rose and stood before her, palms outstretched.

Sarah looked closely at the colors. Her fingers traced the pentacle-shaped knot with five crossings on my right wrist.

"That's the fifth knot," I explained while Sarah continued her examination. "Weavers use it to cast spells to overcome challenges or heighten experiences."

"The pentacle represents the elements." Sarah tapped my palm where the brown, yellow, blue, and red streaks twined together. "Here are the four colors that traditionally represent earth, air, water, and fire. And the green on your thumb is associated with the goddess—the goddess as mother in particular."

"Your hand is a magical primer, Diana," Vivian observed, "with the four elements, the pentacle, and the goddess all inscribed on it. It's everything a witch needs to work the craft."

"And this must be the tenth knot." Sarah gently released my right hand to take up my left. She studied the loop around the pulse at my wrist. "It looks like the symbol on the flag flying over Sept-Tours."

"It is. Not all weavers can make the tenth knot, even though it looks so simple." I took a deep breath. "It's the knot of creation. And destruction."

Sarah closed my fingers into a fist and folded her own hand around mine. She and Vivian exchanged a worried look.

"Why is one of my fingers missing a color?" I asked, suddenly uneasy.

"Let's talk about that tomorrow," Sarah said. "It's late. And it's been a long evening."

"We should get these kids into bed." Abby climbed to her feet, careful not to disturb her daughter. "Wait until the rest of the coven hears that Diana can make new spells. Cassie and Lydia will have a fit."

"We can't tell the coven," Sarah said firmly. "Not until we figure out what it all means."

"Diana really is awfully shiny," Abby pointed out. "I didn't notice it before, but even the humans are going to see it."

"I was wearing a disguising spell. I can cast another." One glimpse of Matthew's forbidding expression had me hastily adding, "I wouldn't wear it at home, of course."

"Disguising spell or no, the O'Neils are bound to know something is going on," Vivian said.

Caleb looked somber. "We don't have to inform the whole coven, Sarah, but we can't keep everybody in the dark either. We should choose who to tell and what to tell them."

"It will be far harder to explain Diana's pregnancy than it will be to come up with a good reason for her shimmering," Sarah said, stating the obvious. "She's just starting to show, but with twins the pregnancy is going to be impossible to ignore very soon."

"Which is exactly why we need to be completely honest," Abby argued. "Witches can smell a half-truth just as easily as a lie."

"This will be a test of the coven's loyalty and open-mindedness," Caleb said thoughtfully.

"And if we fail this test?" Sarah asked.

"That would divide us forever," he replied.

"Maybe we should leave." I'd experienced what such divisiveness could do firsthand, and I still had nightmares about what had happened in Scotland when witch turned against witch and the Berwick trials began. I didn't want to be responsible for destroying the Madison coven, forcing people to uproot themselves from houses and farms their families had owned for generations.

"Vivian?" Caleb turned to the coven's leader.

"The decision should be left to Sarah," Vivian said.

"Once I would have believed that all this weaving business should be shared. But I've seen witches do terrible things to each other, and I'm not talking solely about Emily." Sarah glanced in my direction but didn't elaborate.

"I can keep Corra indoors—mostly. I can even avoid going into town. But I'm not going to be able to hide my differences forever, no matter how good my disguising spell," I warned the assembled witches.

"I realize that," Vivian said calmly. "But this isn't just a test—it's an opportunity. When witches set out to destroy the weavers those many years ago, we lost more than lives. We lost bloodlines, expertise, knowledge—all because we feared a power we didn't understand. This is our chance to begin again."

"*'For storms will rage and oceans roar,'*" I whispered. "*'When Gabriel stands on sea and shore. / And as he blows his wondrous horn, / Old worlds die and new be born.'*" Were we in the midst of just such a change?

"Where did you learn that?" Sarah's voice was sharp.

"Goody Alsop shared it with me. It was her teacher's prophecy—Mother Ursula."

"I know whose prophecy it is, Diana," Sarah said. "Mother Ursula was a famous cunning woman and a powerful seer."

"She was?" I wondered why Goody Alsop hadn't told me.

"Yes, she was. For a historian you really are appallingly ignorant of witches' lore," Sarah replied. "I'll be damned. You learned how to weave spells from one of Ursula Shipton's apprentices." Sarah's voice held a note of real respect.

"Then we haven't lost everything," Vivian said softly, "so long as we don't lose you."

Abby and Caleb packed their van with chairs, leftovers, and children. I was on the driveway, waving good-bye, when Vivian approached me, a container of potato salad in one hand.

"If you want Sarah to snap out of her funk and stop staring at that tree, tell her more about weaving. Show her how you do it—insofar as you can."

"I'm still not very good at it, Vivian."

"All the more reason to enlist Sarah's help. She may not be a weaver, but Sarah knows more about the architecture of spells than any witch I've ever met. It will give her a purpose, now that Emily is gone." Vivian gave my hand an encouraging squeeze.

"And the coven?"

"Caleb says this is a test," she replied. "Let's see if we can pass it."

Vivian pulled down the driveway, her car's headlights sweeping the old fence. I returned to the house, turned off the lights, and climbed the stairs to my husband.

"Did you lock the front door?" Matthew asked, putting down his book. He was stretched out on the bed, which was barely long enough to contain him.

"I couldn't. It's a dead bolt, and Sarah lost the key." My eyes strayed to the key to our bedroom door, which the house had helpfully supplied on an earlier occasion. The memories of that night pushed my lips up into a smile.

"Dr. Bishop, are you feeling wanton?" Matthew's tone was as seductive as a caress.

"We're married." I shucked off my shoes and reached for the top button on my seersucker shirt. "It's my wifely duty to have carnal desires where you're concerned."

"And it's my husbandly obligation to satisfy them." Matthew moved from the bed to the bureau at the speed of light. He gently replaced my fingers with his own and slid the button through its hole. Then he moved on to the next, and the next. Each inch of revealed flesh earned a kiss, a soft press of teeth. Five buttons later I was shivering slightly in the humid summer air.

"How strange that you're shivering," he murmured, sliding his hands around to release the clasp on my bra. Matthew brushed his lips over the crescent-shaped scar near my heart. "You don't feel cold."

"It's all relative, vampire." I tightened my fingers in his hair, and he chuckled. "Now, are you going to love me, or do you just want to take my temperature?"

Later I held my hand up before me, turning it this way and that in the silver light. The middle and ring fingers on my left hand each bore a colored line, one the shade of a moonbeam and the other as gold as the sun. The vestiges of the other cords had faded slightly, though a pearly knot was still barely visible on the pale flesh of each wrist.

"What do you think it all means?" Matthew asked, his lips moving against my hair while his fingers traced figure eights and circles on my shoulders.

"That you've married the tattooed lady—or someone possessed by aliens." Between the new lives rooting within me, Corra, and now my weaver's cords, I was beginning to feel crowded inside my own skin.

"I was proud of you tonight. You thought of a way to save Grace so quickly."

"I didn't think at all. When Grace screamed, it flipped some switch in me. I was all instinct then." I twisted in his arms. "Is that dragon thing still on my back?"

"Yes. And it's darker than it was before." Matthew's hands slid around my waist, and he turned me back to face him. "Any theories as to why?"

"Not yet." The answer was just out of my reach. I could feel it, waiting for me.

"Perhaps it has something to do with your power. It's stronger now than it's ever been." Matthew carried my wrist to his mouth. He drank in my scent, then pressed his lips to my veins. "You still give off the scent of summer lightning, but now there's also a note like dynamite when the lit fuse first touches the powder."

"I have enough power. I don't want any more," I said, burrowing into Matthew.

But since we'd returned to Madison, a dark desire was stirring in my blood.

Liar, whispered a familiar voice.

My skin prickled as if a thousand witches were looking at me. But it was only one creature who watched me now: *the goddess.*

I stole a glance around the room, but there was no sign of her. If Matthew were to detect the goddess's presence, he'd start asking questions I didn't want to answer. And he might uncover one secret I was still hiding.

"Thank goodness," I said under my breath.

"Did you say something?" Matthew asked.

"No," I lied again, and crept closer to Matthew. "You must be hearing things."

10

I stumbled downstairs the next morning, exhausted from my encounter with witchwater and the vivid dreams that had followed.

"The house was awfully quiet last night." Sarah stood behind the old pulpit with her reading glasses perched on the end of her nose, red hair wild around her face, and the Bishop grimoire open in front of her. The sight would have given Emily's Puritan ancestor, Cotton Mather, fits.

"Really? I didn't notice." I yawned, trailing my fingers through the old wooden dough trough that held fresh-picked lavender. Soon the herbs would be hanging upside down to dry from the twine running between the rafters. A spider was adding to that serviceable web with a silken version of her own.

"You've certainly been busy this morning," I said, changing the subject. The milk-thistle heads were in the sieve, ready to be shaken to free the seeds from their downy surround. Bunches of yellow-flowered rue and button-centered feverfew were tied with string and ready for hanging. Sarah had dragged out her heavy flower press, and there was a tray of long, aromatic leaves waiting to go into it. Bouquets of newly harvested flowers and herbs sat on the counter, their purpose not yet clear.

"There's lots of work to do," Sarah said. "Someone's been tending to the garden while we were gone, but they have their own plots to take care of, and the winter and spring seeds never got into the ground."

Several anonymous "someones" must have been involved, given the size of the witch's garden at the Bishop house. Thinking to help, I reached for a bunch of rue. The scent of it would always remind me of Satu and the horrors that I'd experienced after she took me from the garden at Sept-Tours to La Pierre. Sarah's hand shot out and intercepted mine.

"Pregnant women don't touch rue, Diana. If you want to help me, go to the garden and cut some moonwort. Use that." She pointed to her white-handled knife. The last time I'd held it, I'd used it to open my own vein and save Matthew. Neither of us had forgotten it. Neither of us mentioned it either.

"Moonwort's that plant with the pods on it, right?"

"Purple flowers. Long stalks. Papery-looking flat disks," Sarah instructed with more patience than usual. "Cut the stems down to the base of the plant. We'll separate the flowers from the rest before we hang them up to dry."

Sarah's garden was tucked into a far corner of the orchard where the apple trees thinned out and the cypresses and oaks of the forest didn't yet overshadow the soil. It was surrounded by palisades of fencing made from metal posts, wire mesh, pickets, retooled pallets—if it could be used to keep out rabbits, voles, and skunks, Sarah had used it. For extra security the whole perimeter was smudged twice a year and warded with protection spells.

Inside the enclosure Sarah had re-created a bit of paradise. Some of the garden's wide paths led to shady glens where ferns and other tender plants found shelter in the shadows of the taller trees. Others bisected the raised vegetable beds that were closest to the house, with their trellises and beanpoles. Normally these would be covered with vegetation—sweet peas and snap peas and beans of every description—but they were skeletal this year.

I skirted Sarah's small teaching garden where she instructed the coven's children—and sometimes their parents—on the elemental associations of various flowers, plants, and herbs. Her young charges had put up their own fence, using paint stirrers, willow twigs, and Popsicle sticks to demarcate their sacred space from that of the larger garden. Easy-to-grow plants like elfwort and yarrow helped the children understand the seasonal cycle of birth, growth, decay, and fallowness that guided any witch's work in the craft. A hollow stump served as a container for mint and other invasive plants.

Two apple trees marked the center of the garden, and a hammock spanned the distance between them. It was wide enough to hold both Sarah and Em, and it had been their favorite spot for dreaming and talking late into the warm summer nights.

Beyond the apple trees, I passed through a second gate into the garden of a professional witch. Sarah's garden served the same purpose as one of my libraries: It provided a source of inspiration and refuge, as well as information and the tools to do her job.

I found the three-foot-high stems topped with purple flowers that Sarah wanted. Mindful to leave enough to self-seed for next year, I filled the wicker basket and returned to the house.

There my aunt and I worked in companionable silence. She chopped off the moonwort flowers, which she would use to make a fragrant oil, and returned the stems to me so that I could tie a bit of twine around each one—no bunches here, for fear of damaging the pods—and hang them to dry.

"How will you use the pods?" I asked, knotting the string.

"Protection charms. When school starts in a few weeks, there will be a demand for them. Moonwort pods are especially good for children, since they keep monsters and nightmares away."

Corra, who was napping in the stillroom loft, cocked her eye in Sarah's direction, and smoke billowed from her nose and mouth in a firedrake's harrumph.

"I've got something else in mind for *you*," Sarah said, pointing her knife in the firedrake's direction.

Unconcerned, Corra turned her back. Her tail flopped over the edge of the loft and hung like a pendulum, its spade-shaped tip moving gently to and fro. Ducking past it, I tied another moonwort stem to the rafters, careful not to shake loose any of the papery ovals that clung to it.

"How long will they hang before they're dried?" I asked, returning to the table.

"A week," Sarah said, looking up briefly. "By then we'll be able to rub the skin from the pods. Underneath is a silver disk."

"Like the moon. Like a mirror," I said, nodding in understanding. "Reflecting the nightmare back on itself, so that it won't disturb the child."

Sarah nodded, too, pleased by my insight.

"Some witches scry with moonwort pods," Sarah continued after a few moments. "The witch in Hamilton who taught high-school chemistry told me that alchemists collected May dew on them to use as a base for the elixir of life."

"That would require a lot of moonwort," I said with a laugh, thinking of all the water Mary Sidney and I had used in our experiments. "I think we should stick to the protection charms."

"Okay, then." Sarah smiled. "For kids I put the charms in dream pillows. They're not as spooky as a poppet or a pentacle made of blackberry canes. If you were going to make one, what ingredients would you use for the stuffing?"

I took a deep breath and focused on the question. Dream pillows didn't have to be big, after all—the size of the palm of my hand would do.

The palm of my hand. Ordinarily I would have run my fingers through my weaver's cords, waiting for inspiration—and guidance—to strike. But the cords were inside me now. When I turned my hands and splayed the fingers wide, shimmering knots appeared over the tracery of veins at my wrist and the thumb and pinkie on my right hand gleamed green and brown in the colors of the craft.

Sarah's mason jars glinted in the light from the windows. I moved toward them, running my little finger down the labels until I felt resistance.

"Agrimony." I traveled along the shelf. "Mugwort."

Using it like the pointer on a Ouija board, I tilted my pinkie backward. "Aniseed." Down moved my finger. "Hops." Up it swooped in a diagonal line to the opposite side. "Valerian."

What was that going to smell like? Too pungent?

My thumb tingled.

"A bay leaf, a few pinches of rosemary, and some thyme," I said.

But what if the child woke up anyway and grabbed at the pillow?

"And five dried beans." It was an odd addition, but my weaver's instinct told me they would make all the difference.

"Well, I'll be damned." Sarah pushed her glasses onto her head. She looked at me in astonishment, then grinned. "It's like an old charm your great-grandmother collected, except hers had mullein and vervain in it, too—and no beans."

"I'd put the beans in the pillows first," I said. "They should rattle against one another if you shake it. You can tell the kids the noise will help with the monsters."

"Nice touch," Sarah admitted. "And the moonwort pods—would you powder them or leave them whole?"

"Whole," I replied, "sewn onto the front of the pillow."

But herbs were only the first half of a protection charm. Words were needed to go along with them. And if any other witch was going to be able to use it, those words had to be packed with potential. The London witches had taught me a great deal, but the spells I wrote tended to lie flat on the page, inert on anyone's tongue but mine. Most spells were written in rhyme, which made them easier to remember as well as livelier. But I was no poet, like Matthew or his friends. I hesitated.

"Something wrong?" Sarah said.

"My gramarye sucks," I confessed, lowering my voice.

"If I had the slightest idea what that was, I'd feel sorry for you," Sarah said drily.

"Gramarye is how a weaver puts magic into words. I can construct spells and perform them myself, but without gramarye they won't work for other witches." I pointed to the Bishop grimoire. "Hundreds and hundreds of weavers came up with the words for those spells, and other witches passed them down through the ages. Even now the spells retain their power. I'm lucky if *my* spells remain potent for an hour."

"What's the problem?" Sarah asked.

"I don't see spells in words but in shapes and colors." The underside of my thumb and pinkie were still slightly discolored. "Red ink helped my fire spell. So did arranging the words on the page so that they made a kind of picture."

"Show me," Sarah said, pushing a piece of scrap paper and a charred stick in my direction. "Witch hazel," she explained when I held it up for clarification. "I use it as a pencil when I'm trying to copy a spell for the first time. If something goes wrong, the aftereffects are less . . . er, permanent than with ink." She colored slightly. One of her unruly spells had caused a cyclone in the bathroom. For weeks we found spatters of suntan lotion and shampoo in the oddest places.

I wrote out the spell I'd devised to set things alight, careful not to say the words to myself and thereby work the magic. When I was through, the index finger of my right hand was glowing red.

"This was my first attempt at gramarye," I said, looking at it critically before handing it to Sarah. "A third-grader probably would have done a better job."

Fire
Ignite till
Roaring bright
Extinguishing night

"It's not *that* bad," Sarah said. When I looked crestfallen, she hastily added, "I've seen worse. Spelling out fire with the first letter of every line was clever. But why a triangle?"

"That's the structure of the spell. It's pretty simple, really—just a thrice-crossed knot." It was my turn to study my work. "Funny thing is, the triangle was a symbol many alchemists used for fire."

"A thrice-crossed knot?" Sarah looked over the frames of her glasses. "You're having one of your Yoda moments." This was her way of letting the air out of my vocabulary.

"I'm making it as plain as I can, Sarah. It would be easier to show you what I mean if my cords weren't inside my hands." I held them up and waggled my fingers at her.

Sarah murmured something, and the ball of twine rolled across the table. "Will ordinary string do, Yoda?"

I stopped the ball by saying my own spell to arrest its motion. It was heavy with the power of earth and had a thicket of thrice-crossed knots surrounding it. Sarah twitched in surprise.

"Of course," I said, pleased by my aunt's reaction. After giving the twine a whack with her knife, I picked up a length of string approximately nine inches long. "Every knot has a different number of crossings. You use two of them in your craft—the slipknot and the double slipknot. Those are the two weaver's knots that all witches know. It's when we come to the third knot that things get complicated."

I wasn't sure if kitchen twine was up to showing what I meant, though. Knots made with my weaver's cords were three-dimensional, but given that I was working with ordinary string, I decided to work on the flat. Holding one end of the length in my left hand, I made a loop to the right, pulled the string loosely under one side of the loop and over the other, and joined the ends together. The result was a trefoil-shaped knot that resembled a triangle.

"See, three crossings," I said. "You try."

When I took my hands off the string, it sprang up into a familiar pyramid with the ends properly fused together into an unbreakable knot. Sarah gasped.

"Cool," I said. "Plain old string works just fine."

"You sound just like your father." Sarah poked at the knot with her finger. "There's one of those hidden in every spell?"

"At least one. Really complicated spells might have two or three knots, each one tying into the threads you saw last night in the keeping room—the ones that bind the world." I smiled. "I guess gramarye is a disguising spell of sorts—one that hides magic's inner workings."

"And when you say the words, it reveals them," Sarah said thoughtfully. "Let's give yours a go."

Before I could warn her, Sarah read the words of my spell aloud. The paper burst into flame in her hands. She dropped it on the table, and I doused it with a shower of conjured water.

"I thought that was a spell for lighting a candle—not setting a house on fire!" she exclaimed, looking at the charred mess.

"Sorry. The spell is still pretty new. It will settle down eventually. Gramarye can't hold a spell together forever, so its magic weakens over time. It's why spells stop working," I explained.

"Really? Then you should be able to figure out the relative ages of spells." Sarah's eyes gleamed. She was a great believer in tradition, and the older a piece of magic was, the more she liked it.

"Maybe," I said doubtfully, "but there are other reasons that spells fail. Weavers have different abilities, for one thing. And if words were left out or changed when later witches copied them, that will compromise the magic, too."

But Sarah was already in front of her spell book, leafing through the pages.

"Here, look at this one." She beckoned me toward her. "I always suspected this was the oldest spell in the Bishop grimoire."

"*An exceeding great charm for drawing clean air into any place,*'" I read aloud, "*'one handed down from old Maude Bishop and proven by me, Charity Bishop, in the year 1705.*'" In the margins were notes made by other witches,

including my grandmother, who had later mastered the spell. A caustic an-
notation by Sarah proclaimed, *"utterly worthless."*

"Well?" Sarah demanded.

"It's dated 1705," I pointed out.

"Yes, but its genealogy goes back beyond that. Em never could find out
who Maude Bishop was—a relative of Bridget's from England, perhaps?"
This unfinished genealogical research project provided Sarah her first opportunity to mention Em's name without sorrow. Vivian was right. Sarah
needed me in her stillroom just as much as I needed to be there.

"Perhaps," I said again, trying not to raise unrealistic hopes.

"Do that thing you did with the jars. Read with your fingers," Sarah
said, pushing the pulpit toward me.

I ran my fingertips lightly over the words of the spell. My skin tingled
in recognition as they encountered the ingredients woven into it: the air
blowing around my ring finger, the sensation of liquid coursing under the
nail of my middle finger, and the explosion of scents that clung to my little
finger.

"Hyssop, marjoram, and lots of salt," I said thoughtfully. These were
common ingredients found in every witch's house and garden.

"So why won't it work?" Sarah was staring at my upraised right hand as
though it were an oracle.

"I'm not sure," I admitted. "And you know I could repeat it a thousand
times and it will never work for me." Sarah and her friends in the coven
were going to have to figure out what was wrong with Maude Bishop's spell
themselves. That, or buy a can of air freshener.

"Maybe you can stitch it back together, or weave a patch, or whatever it
is that witches like you do."

Witches like you. Sarah didn't mean to do it, but her words left me feeling uneasy and isolated. Staring down at the page from the grimoire, I wondered if an inability to perform magic on command was one reason that
weavers had been targeted by their communities.

"It doesn't work that way." I folded my hands atop the open book and
pressed my lips together, withdrawing like a crab into its shell.

"You said weaving started with a question. Ask the spell what's wrong,"
Sarah suggested.

I wished I'd never seen Maude Bishop's cleansing spell. Even more, I wished Sarah had never seen it.

"What are you doing?" Sarah pointed to the Bishop grimoire in horror.

Underneath my hands the writing was unspooling from its neat curlicues. Leftover splatters of ink marred the otherwise blank page. Within moments there was no trace of Maude Bishop's spell except for a small, tight blue-and-yellow knot. I stared at it in fascination and had the sudden urge to—

"Don't touch it!" Sarah cried, waking Corra from her slumber. I jumped away from the book, and Sarah swooped down on it, trapping the knot under a mason jar.

We both peered at the UMO—unfamiliar magical object.

"Now what do we do?" I always thought of spells as living, breathing creations. It seemed unkind to keep it contained.

"I'm not sure there's much we *can* do." Sarah took my left hand and flipped it over, revealing a black-stained thumb.

"I got ink on it," I said.

Sarah shook her head. "That's not ink. That's the color of death. You killed the spell."

"What do you mean, killed it?" I snatched my hand away, holding it behind me like a child caught raiding the cookie jar.

"Don't panic," Sarah said. "Rebecca learned to control it. You can, too."

"My mother?" I thought of the long look that Sarah and Vivian had exchanged last night. "You knew something like this might happen."

"Only after I saw your left hand. It bears all the colors of the higher magics, like exorcism and auguries, just as your right hand shows the colors of the craft." Sarah paused. "It bears the colors of the darker magics, too."

"Good thing I'm right-handed." It was an attempt at humor, but the tremor in my voice gave me away.

"You're not right-handed. You're ambidextrous. You only favor your right hand because that horrible first-grade teacher said left-handed children were demonic." Sarah had seen to it that the woman was formally censured. After experiencing her first Halloween in Madison, Miss Somerton had resigned her position.

I wanted to say I wasn't interested in the higher magics either, but nothing came out.

Sarah looked at me sadly. "You can't lie to another witch, Diana. Especially not a whopper like that."

"No dark magic." Emily had died trying to summon and bind a spirit—probably my mother. Peter Knox was interested in the darker aspects of the craft, too. And dark magic was bound up in Ashmole 782 as well—not to mention more than one thumb's worth of death.

"Dark doesn't have to mean evil," Sarah said. "Is the new moon evil?"

I shook my head. "The dark of the moon is a time for new beginnings."

"Owls? Spiders? Bats? Dragons?" Sarah was using her teacher voice.

"No," I admitted.

"No. They are not. Humans made up those stories about the moon and nocturnal creatures because they represent the unknown. It's no coincidence that they also symbolize wisdom. There is nothing more powerful than knowledge. That's why we're so careful when we teach someone dark magic." Sarah took my hand. "Black is the color of the goddess as crone, plus the color of concealment, bad omens, and death."

"And these?" I wiggled the three other fingers.

"Here we have the color of the goddess as maiden and huntress," she said, folding in my silver middle finger. Now I knew why the goddess's voice sounded as it did. "And here is the color of worldly power." She folded in my golden ring finger. "As for your pinkie, white is the color of divination and prophecy. It's also used to break curses and banish unwanted spirits."

"Except for the death, that doesn't sound so terrible."

"Like I said, dark doesn't necessarily mean evil," Sarah said. "Think about worldly power. In beneficent hands it's a force for good. But if someone abuses it for personal gain or to harm others, it can be terribly destructive. The darkness depends on the witch."

"You said Emily wasn't very good at the higher magics. What about Mom?"

"Rebecca excelled at them. She went straight from bell, book, and candle to calling down the moon," Sarah said wistfully.

Some of what I'd witnessed my mother do when I was a child made sense now, like the night she'd conjured wraiths out of a bowl of water. So, too, did Peter Knox's preoccupation with her.

"Rebecca seemed to lose interest in higher magics once she met your father, though. The only subjects that appealed to her then were anthropology and Stephen. And you, of course," Sarah said. "I don't think she worked much higher magic after you were born."

Not where anybody but Dad or I could see, I thought. "Why didn't you tell me?" I said aloud.

"You didn't want anything to do with magic, remember?" Sarah's hazel gaze held mine. "I saved some of Rebecca's things, just in case you ever showed any ability. The house took the rest."

Sarah murmured a spell—an opening spell, based on the threads that suddenly illuminated the room with shades of red, yellow, and green. A cabinet and drawers appeared to the left of the old fireplace, built into the ancient masonry. The room filled with the scent of lily of the valley and something heavy and exotic that stirred sharp, uncomfortable feelings within me: emptiness and yearning, familiarity and dread. Sarah opened a drawer and took out a chunk of something red and resinous.

"Dragon's blood. I can't smell it without thinking of Rebecca." Sarah sniffed it. "The stuff you can get now isn't as good as this, and it costs an absolute fortune. I wanted to sell this and use the proceeds to fix the roof when it collapsed in the blizzard of '93, but Em wouldn't let me."

"What did Mom use it for?" I said around the lump in my throat.

"Rebecca made ink from it. When she used that ink to copy out a charm, the force of it could suck the power out of half the town. There were lots of blackouts in Madison during your mother's teen years." Sarah chuckled. "Her spell book should be here somewhere—unless the house ate it while I was gone. That will tell you more."

"Spell book?" I frowned. "What was wrong with the Bishop grimoire?"

"Most witches who practice the higher, darker magics keep their own grimoire. It's tradition," Sarah said, rummaging around in the cupboard. "Nope. It doesn't seem to be here."

Despite the pang of disappointment that accompanied Sarah's announcement, I was relieved. I already had one mysterious book in my life. I wasn't sure I wanted another—even if it might shed light on why Emily had been trying to summon my mother's spirit at Sept-Tours.

"Oh, no." Sarah backed away from the cupboard, a look of horror on her face.

"Is there a rat?" My experiences in London had conditioned me to believe that they lurked in every dusty corner. I peered into the cupboard's depths but saw only a collection of grimy jars containing herbs and roots and an ancient clock radio. Its brown cord hung down from the shelf like Corra's tail, waving gently in the breeze. I sneezed.

As if on cue, a strange metallic clinking and rolling started in the walls, like coins being fed into a jukebox. The musical grinding that followed, reminiscent of an old record player set to 33 rpm instead of 45 rpm, soon gave way to a recognizable song.

I cocked my head. "Is that . . . Fleetwood Mac?"

"No. Not again!" Sarah looked as if she'd seen a ghost. I glanced around, but the only invisible presence in the room was Stevie Nicks and a Welsh witch named Rhiannon. In the seventies the song had been a coming-out anthem for scores of witches and wizards.

"I guess the house is waking up." Maybe that was what was upsetting Sarah.

Sarah darted to the door and lifted the latch, but it wouldn't budge. She banged on the wooden panels. The music got louder.

"This isn't my favorite Stevie Nicks tune either," I said, trying to calm her, "but it won't last forever. Maybe you'll like the next song better."

"The next song is 'Over My Head.' I know the whole damn album by heart. Your mother listened to it all through her pregnancy. It went on for months. Just when Rebecca seemed to get over her obsession, Fleetwood Mac's next album came out. It was hell." Sarah tore at her hair.

"Really?" I was always hungry for details about my parents. "Fleetwood Mac seems more like Dad's kind of band."

"We have to stop the music." Sarah went to the window, but the sash wouldn't move. She thumped on the frame in frustration.

"Let me try." The harder I pushed, the louder the music got. There was a momentary pause after Stevie Nicks stopped warbling about Rhiannon. A few seconds later, Christine McVie informed us how nice it was to be in over your head. The window remained closed.

"This is a nightmare!" Sarah exploded. She jammed her hands over her ears to block the sound, then raced to the grimoire and flipped through the pages. "Prudence Willard's dog-bite cure. Patience Severance's method for sweetening sour milk." She flipped some more. "Clara Bishop's spell for stopping up a drafty chimney! That might work."

"But it's music, not smoke," I said, peering over Sarah's shoulder at the lines of text.

"Both are carried on the air." Sarah rolled up her sleeves. "If it doesn't do the trick, we'll try something else. Maybe thunder. I'm good with thunder. That might interrupt the energy and drive the sound away."

I started to hum along to the song. It was catchy, in a 1970s kind of way.

"Don't you start." Sarah's eyes were wild. She turned back to the grimoire. "Get me some eyebright, please. And plug in the coffeemaker."

I dutifully went to the ancient outlet strip and shoved the coffeemaker's cord into it. Electricity leaped from the socket in orange and blue arcs. I jumped back.

"You need a surge protector—preferably one bought in the last decade—or you're going to burn the whole house down," I told Sarah.

She kept muttering as she put a paper filter into the swing-out basket in the coffeemaker, followed by an extensive selection of herbs.

Since we were trapped inside the stillroom and Sarah didn't seem to want my help, I might as well work on the words to accompany my antinightmare spell for the children. I went to my mother's cabinet and found some black ink, a quill pen, and a slip of paper.

Matthew knocked on the windowpane. "Are you two all right? I smelled something burning."

"A minor electrical problem!" I shouted, waving my quill pen in the air. Then I remembered that Matthew was a vampire and could hear me perfectly well through stone, brick, wood, and yes, single panes of glass. I lowered my voice. "Nothing to worry about."

"Over My Head" screeched to a halt, and "You Make Loving Fun" began. *Nice choice,* I thought, smiling at Matthew. Who needed a deejay when you had magical radio?

"Oh, God. The house has moved on to their second album," Sarah groaned. "I hate *Rumours.*"

"Where is that music coming from?" Matthew frowned.

"Mom's old clock radio." I pointed with the feather. "She liked Fleetwood Mac." I glanced at my aunt, who was reciting the words to Clara Bishop's spell with her hands clapped over her ears. "Sarah doesn't."

"Ah." Matthew's brow cleared. "I'll leave you to it, then." He pressed his hand against the glass in a silent gesture of farewell.

My heart filled. Loving Matthew wasn't *all* I wanted to do, but he was definitely the only one for me. I wished there wasn't a pane of glass between us so that I could tell him so.

Glass is only sand and fire. One puff of smoke later, a pile of sand lay on the windowsill. I reached through the empty square in the window frame and clasped his hand.

"Thanks for checking on us. It's been an interesting afternoon. I have a lot to tell you."

Matthew blinked at our twined hands.

"You make me very happy, you know."

"I try," he said with a shy grin.

"You succeed. Do you think Fernando could rescue Sarah?" I lowered my voice. "The house has jammed the stillroom doors and windows shut, and she's about to blow. She's going to need a cigarette when she gets out, and a stiff drink."

"Fernando hasn't rescued a woman in distress for some time, but I'm sure he remembers how," Matthew assured me. "Will the house let him?"

"Give it five minutes or until the music stops, whichever comes first." I pulled free and blew him a kiss. It had rather more fire and water than usual, and enough air behind it to land with a decided smack on his cheek.

I returned to the worktable and dipped my mother's quill pen into the ink. It smelled of blackberries and walnuts. Thanks to my experience with Elizabethan writing implements, I was able to write out the charm for Sarah's dream pillows without a single splotch.

Mirror
Shimmers
Monsters Shake
Banish Nightmares
Until We
Wake

I blew on it gently to set the ink. Very respectable, I decided. It was much better than my spell for conjuring fire, and easy enough for children to remember. When the pods were dry and the papery covering rubbed off, I'd write the charm in tiny letters right on their silvery surface.

Eager to show my work to Sarah, I slid down from the stool. One look at her face convinced me to put it off until my aunt had had her whiskey and a smoke. She'd been hoping for decades that I'd show an interest in magic. I could wait another twenty minutes for my grade in Sleeping Charms 101.

A slight tingle behind me alerted me to a ghostly presence a moment before a hug as soft as down settled around my shoulders.

"Nice job, peanut," whispered a familiar voice. *"Excellent taste in music, too."*

When I turned my head, there was nothing except a faint smudge of green, but I didn't need to see my father to know that he was there.

"Thanks, Dad," I said softly.

Matthew took the news about my mother's proficiency with higher magic better than expected. He had long suspected that something existed between the homely work of the craft and the bright spectacles of elemental magic. He was not at all surprised that I, in another mark of in-betweenness, could practice such a magic. What shocked him was that this talent came through my mother's blood.

"I'll have to take a closer look at your mtDNA workup after all," he said, giving one of my mother's inks a sniff.

"Sounds good." It was the first time Matthew had shown any desire to return to his genetic research. Days had gone by without any mention of Oxford, Baldwin, the Book of Life, or blood rage. And while he might have forgotten that there was genetic information bound up in Ashmole 782, I had not. Once we had the manuscript back in our hands, we were going to need his scientific skills to decipher it.

"You're right. There's definitely blood in it, as well as resin and acacia." Matthew swirled the ink around. Acacia, I'd learned this morning, was the source of gum arabic, which made the ink less runny.

"I thought as much. The inks used in Ashmole 782 had blood in them, too. It must be a more common practice than I thought," I said.

"There's some frankincense in it, too." Matthew said, ignoring my mention of the Book of Life.

"Ah. That's what gives it that exotic scent." I rummaged through the remaining bottles, hoping to find something else to catch his biochemical curiosity.

"That and the blood, of course," Matthew said drily.

"If it's my mother's blood, that could shed even more light on my DNA," I remarked. "My talent for higher magic, too."

"Hmm," Matthew said noncommittally.

"What about this one?" I drew the stopper out of a bottle of blue-green liquid, and the scent of a summer garden filled the air.

"That's made from iris," Matthew said. "Remember your search for green ink in London?"

"So this is what Master Platt's fantastically expensive ink looked like!" I laughed.

"Made from roots imported from Florence. Or so he said." Matthew surveyed the table and its blue, red, black, green, purple, and magenta pots of liquid. "It looks like you have enough ink to keep you going for some time."

He was right: I had enough to get me through the next few weeks. And that was as far as I was willing to project, even if my left pinkie *was* throbbing in anticipation of the future.

"This should be plenty, even with all the jobs Sarah has for me," I agreed. Each of the open jars on the table had a small slip of paper underneath with a note in her sprawling handwriting. *"Mosquito bites,"* read one. *"Better cellphone reception,"* read another. Her requests made me feel like a server at a fast-food restaurant. "Thanks for your help."

"Anytime," Matthew said, kissing me good-bye.

Over the next few days, the routines of daily life began to anchor us to the Bishop house and to each other—even without the steadying presence of Em, who had always been the house's center of gravity.

Fernando was a domestic tyrant—far worse than Em ever was—and his changes to Sarah's diet and exercise plan were radical and inflexible. He signed my aunt up for a CSA program that delivered a box of exotic vegetables like kale and chard every week, and he walked the property's fence line with her whenever she tried to sneak a cigarette. Fernando cooked and cleaned and even plumped cushions—all of which had me wondering about his life with Hugh.

"When we didn't have servants—and that was often the case—I kept the house," he explained, hanging up clothes on the line. "If I'd waited for Hugh to do it, we'd have lived in squalor. He didn't pay attention to such mundane matters as clean sheets or whether we had run out of wine. Hugh was either writing poetry or planning a three-month siege. There was no time in his day for domestic chores."

"And Gallowglass?" I asked, handing him a clothespin.

"Gallowglass is worse. Not even the furniture—or lack of it—matters to him. We came home one night to find our house robbed and Gallowglass sleeping on the table like a Viking warrior ready to be sent out to sea." Fernando shook his head. "Besides, I enjoy the work. Keeping house is like preparing weapons for battle. It's repetitive and very soothing." His confession made me feel less guilty about letting him do all the cooking.

Fernando's other domain, aside from the kitchen, was the toolshed. He'd cleared out what was broken, cleaned and sharpened what remained, and bought items he felt were missing, like a scythe. The edges on the rose secateurs were now so keen you could slice a tomato with them. I was reminded of all the wars that had been fought using common household implements and wondered if Fernando were quietly arming us for combat.

Sarah, for her part, grumbled at the new regime but went along with it. When she got cranky—which was often—she took it out on the house. It was still not fully awake, but periodic rumblings of activity reminded us that its self-imposed hibernation was drawing to a close. Most of its energy was directed at Sarah. One morning we woke to find that all the liquor in the house had been dumped down the sink and a makeshift mobile of empty bottles and silverware was attached to the kitchen light fixture. Matthew and I laughed, but as far as Sarah was concerned, this was war. From that moment my aunt and the house were in an all-out battle for supremacy.

The house was winning, thanks to its chief weapon: Fleetwood Mac. Sarah had bashed Mom's old radio to bits two days after we found it during a never-ending concert of "The Chain." The house retaliated by removing all the toilet-paper rolls from the bathroom cabinets and replacing them with a variety of electronic gadgets capable of playing music. It made for a rousing morning alarm.

Nothing deterred the house from playing selections from the band's first two albums—not even Sarah's defenestration of three record players, an eight-track tape machine, and an ancient Dictaphone. The house simply diverted the music through the furnace, the bass notes reverberating in the ductwork while the treble wafted from the heating vents.

With all her ire directed at the house, Sarah was surprisingly patient and gentle with me. We had turned the stillroom inside out looking for Mom's spell book, going so far as to remove all the drawers and shelves from the cabinet. We'd found some surprisingly graphic love letters from the 1820s hidden beneath one drawer's false bottom and a macabre collection of rodent skulls tacked in orderly rows behind a sliding panel at the back of the shelving, but no spell book. The house would present it when it was ready.

When the music and memories of Emily and my parents became too overwhelming, Sarah and I escaped to the garden or the woods. Today my aunt had offered to show me where baneful plants could be found. The moon would be full dark tonight, the beginning of a new cycle of growth. It would be a propitious time for gathering up the materials for higher magic. Matthew followed us like a shadow as we wended our way through the vegetable patch and the teaching garden. When we reached her witch's garden, Sarah kept walking. A giant moonflower vine marked the boundary between the garden and the woods. It sprawled in every direction, obscuring the fence and the gate underneath.

"Allow me, Sarah." Matthew stepped forward to spring the latch. Until now he'd been sauntering behind us, seemingly interested in the flowers. But I knew that bringing up the rear placed him in the perfect defensive position. He stepped through the gate, made sure nothing dangerous lurked there, and pulled the vine away so Sarah and I could pass through into another world.

There were many magical places on the Bishop homestead—oak groves dedicated to the goddess, long avenues between yew trees that were once old roads and still showed the deep ruts of wagons laden with wood and produce for the markets, even the old Bishop graveyard. But this little grove between the garden and the forest was my favorite.

Dappled sunlight broke through its center, moving through the cypress that surrounded the place. In ages past, it might have been called a fairy ring, because the ground was thick with toadstools and mushrooms. As a child I'd been forbidden to pick anything that grew there. Now I understood why: Every plant here was either baneful or associated with the darker aspects of the craft. Two paths intersected in the middle of the grove.

"A crossroads." I froze.

"The crossroads have been here longer than the house. Some say these pathways were made by the Oneida before the English settled here." Sarah beckoned me forward. "Come and look at this plant. Is it deadly nightshade or black nightshade?"

Instead of listening, I was completely mesmerized by the X in the middle of the grove.

There was power there. Knowledge, too. I felt the familiar push and pull of desire and fear as I saw the clearing through the eyes of those who had walked these paths before.

"What is it?" Matthew asked, his instincts warning him that something was wrong.

But other voices, though faint, had captured my attention: my mother and Emily, my father and my grandmother, and others unknown to me. *Wolfsbane,* the voices whispered. *Skullcap. Devil's bit. Adder's tongue. Witch's broom.* Their chant was punctuated with warnings and suggestions, and their litany of spells included plants that featured in fairy tales.

Gather cinquefoil when the moon is full to extend the reach of your power.
Hellebore makes any disguising spell more effective.
Mistletoe will bring you love and many children.
To see the future more clearly, use black henbane.

"Diana?" Sarah straightened, hands on hips.

"Coming," I murmured, dragging my attention away from the faint voices and going obediently to my aunt's side.

Sarah gave me all sorts of instructions about the plants in the grove. Her words went in one ear and out the other, flowing through me in a way that would have made my father proud. My aunt could recite all the common and botanical names for every wildflower, weed, root, and herb as well as their uses, both benign and baneful. But her mastery was born of reading and study. I had learned the limits of book-based knowledge in Mary Sidney's alchemical laboratory, when I was confronted for the first time with the challenges of doing what I'd spent years reading and writing about as a scholar. There I had discovered that being able to cite alchemical texts was nothing when weighed against experience. But my mother and Emily were no longer here to help me. If I was going to walk the dark paths of higher magic, I was going to have to do it alone.

The prospect terrified me.

Just before moonrise Sarah invited me to go back out with her to gather the plants she would need for this month's work.

I begged off, claiming I was too tired to go along. But it was the insistent call of the voices at the crossroads that made me refuse.

"Does your reluctance to go to the woods tonight have something to do with your trip there this afternoon?" Matthew asked.

"Perhaps," I said, staring out the window. "Sarah and Fernando are back."

My aunt was carrying a basket full of greenery. The kitchen screen slammed shut behind her, and then the stillroom door creaked open. A few minutes later, she and Fernando climbed the stairs. Sarah was wheezing less than she had last week. Fernando's health regime was working.

"Come to bed," Matthew said, turning back the covers.

The night was dark, illuminated only by the stars. Soon it would be midnight, the moment between night and day. The voices at the crossroads grew louder.

"I have to go." I pushed past Matthew and headed downstairs.

"*We* have to go," he said, following me. "I won't stop you or interfere. But you are not going to the woods by yourself."

"There's power there, Matthew. Dark power. I could feel it. And it's been calling to me since the sun set!"

He took me by the elbow and propelled me out the front door. He didn't want anyone to hear the rest of this conversation.

"Then answer its call," he snapped. "Say yes or say no, but don't expect me to sit here and wait quietly for you to return."

"And if I say yes?" I demanded.

"We'll face it. Together."

"I don't believe you. You told me before that you don't want me meddling with life and death. That's the kind of power that's waiting for me where the paths cross in the woods. And I want it!" I wrested my elbow from his grip and jabbed a finger in his chest. "I hate myself for wanting it, but I do!"

I turned from the revulsion that I knew would be in his eyes. Matthew turned my face back toward him.

"I've known that the darkness was in you since I found you in the Bodleian, hiding from the other witches on Mabon."

My breath caught. His eyes held mine.

"I felt its allure, and the darkness in me responded to it. Should I loathe myself, then?" Matthew's voice dropped to a barely audible whisper. "Should you?"

"But you said—"

"I said I didn't want you to meddle with life and death, not that you couldn't do so." Matthew took my hands in his. "I've been covered in blood, held a man's future in my hands, decided if a woman's heart would beat again. Something in your own soul dies each time you make the choice for another. I saw what Juliette's death did to you, and Champier's, too."

"I didn't have a choice in those cases. Not really." Champier would have taken all my memories and hurt the people who were trying to help me. Juliette had been trying to kill Matthew—and would have succeeded had I not called on the goddess.

"Yes you did." Matthew pressed a kiss on my knuckles. "You chose death for them, just as you chose life for me, life for Louisa and Kit even though they tried to harm you, life for Jack when you brought him to our house in the Blackfriars instead of leaving him on the street to starve, life for baby Grace when you rescued her from the fire. Whether you realize it or not, you paid a price every time."

I knew the price I'd paid for Matthew's survival, though he did not: My life belonged to the goddess for as long as she saw fit.

"Philippe was the only other creature I've ever known who made life-or-death decisions as quickly and instinctively as you. The price that Philippe paid was terrible loneliness, one that grew over time. Not even Ysabeau could banish it." Matthew rested his forehead against mine. "I don't want that to be your fate."

But my fate was not my own. It was time to tell Matthew so.

"The night I saved you. Do you remember it?" I asked.

Matthew nodded. He didn't like to talk about the night we'd both almost lost our lives.

"The maiden and the crone were there—two aspects of the goddess." My heart was hammering. "We called Ysabeau after you fixed me up, and I told her I'd seen them." I searched his face for signs of understanding, but he still looked bewildered. "I didn't save you, Matthew. The goddess did. I asked her to do it."

His fingers dug into my arm. "Tell me you didn't strike a bargain with her in exchange."

"You were dying, and I didn't have enough power to heal you." I gripped his shirt. "My blood wouldn't have been enough. But the goddess drew the life out of that ancient oak tree so I could feed it to you through my veins."

"And in return?" Matthew's hands tightened, lifting me until my feet were barely touching the ground. "Your gods and goddesses don't grant boons without getting something back. Philippe taught me that."

"I told her to take anyone, anything, so long as she saved you."

Matthew let go abruptly. "Emily?"

"No." I shook my head. "The goddess wanted a life for a life—not a death for a life. She chose mine." My eyes filled with tears at the look of betrayal I saw on his face. "I didn't know her decision until I wove my first spell. I saw her then. The goddess said she still had work for me to do."

"We're going to fix this." Matthew practically dragged me in the direction of the garden gate. Under the dark sky, the moonflowers that covered it were the only signposts to illuminate our way. We reached the crossroads quickly. Matthew pushed me to the center.

"We can't," I protested.

"If you can weave the tenth knot, you can dissolve whatever promise you made to the goddess," he said roughly.

"No!" My stomach clenched, and my chest started to burn. "I can't just wave my hand and make our agreement disappear."

The dead branches of an ancient oak, the one the goddess had sacrificed so that Matthew would live, were barely visible. Under my feet the earth seemed to shift. I looked down and saw that I was straddling the center of the crossroads. The burning sensation in my heart extended down my arms and into my fingers.

"You will not bind your future to some capricious deity. Not for my sake," Matthew said, his voice shaking with fury.

"Don't speak ill of the goddess here," I warned. "I didn't go to your church and mock your god."

"If you won't break your promise to the goddess, then use your magic to summon her." Matthew joined me where the paths converged.

"Get out of the crossroads, Matthew." The wind was swirling around my feet in a magical storm. Corra shrieked through the night sky, trailing fire like a comet. She circled above us, crying out in warning.

"Not until you call her." Matthew's feet remained where they were. "You won't pay for my life with your own."

"It was my choice." My hair was crackling around my face, fiery tendrils writhing against my neck. "I chose you."

"I won't let you."

"It's already done." My heart thudded, and his heart echoed it. "If the goddess wants me to fulfill some purpose of hers, I'll do it—gladly. Because you're mine, and I'm not done with you yet."

My final words were almost identical to those the goddess had once said to me. They rang with power, quieting the wind and silencing Corra's cries. The fire in my veins subsided, the burning sensation becoming a smoldering heat as the connection between Matthew and me tightened, the links that bound us shining and strong.

"You cannot make me regret what I asked the goddess for, or any price I've paid because of it," I said. "Nor will I break my promise to her. Have you thought about what would happen if I did?"

Matthew remained silent, listening.

"Without you I would never have known Philippe or received his blood vow. I wouldn't be carrying your children. I wouldn't have seen my father or known I was a weaver. Don't you understand?" My hands rose to cradle his face. "In saving your life, I saved mine, too."

"What does she want you to do?" Matthew's voice was rough with emotion.

"I don't know. But there's one thing I'm sure of: The goddess needs me alive to do it."

Matthew's hand came to rest on the space between my hips where our children slept.

I felt a soft flutter. Another. I looked at him in alarm.

His hand flexed over my skin, pressing slightly, and there was a stronger flicker of movement in my belly.

"Is something wrong?" I asked.

"Not at all. The babies. They've quickened." Matthew's expression was awed as well as relieved.

We waited together for the next flurry of activity within me. When it came, Matthew and I both laughed, caught up in the unexpected joy. I tilted back my head. The stars seemed brighter, keeping the darkness of the new moon in balance with the light.

The crossroads was silent, and the sharp need I had felt to be out under the dark moon had passed. It was not death that had brought me here, but life. Hand in hand, Matthew and I went back to the house. When I turned on the kitchen light, something unexpected was waiting for me.

"It's a bit soon for someone to leave me a birthday present," I said, eyeing the strangely wrapped parcel. When Matthew moved forward to examine it more closely, I put out a hand and stopped him. "Don't touch it."

He looked at me in confusion.

"It's got enough magical wards on it to repel an army," I explained.

The package was thin and rectangular. An odd assortment of wrapping paper had been patched together to cover it: pink paper with storks, paper covered with primary-colored inchworms forming the shape of the number four, garish Christmas-tree wrapping paper, and silver foil with embossed wedding bells. A bouquet of bright bows covered its surface.

"Where did it come from?" Matthew asked.

"The house, I think." I poked it with my finger. "I recognize some of the wrapping paper from birthdays past."

"Are you sure it's for you?" He looked dubious.

I nodded. The package was definitely for me. Gingerly I picked it up. The bows, all of which had been used before and therefore lacked adhesive, slipped off and rained down on the kitchen island.

"Shall I get Sarah?" Matthew asked.

"No. I've got it covered." My hands were tingling, and every rainbow stripe was in evidence as I removed the wrapping paper.

Inside was a composition book—the kind with a black-and-white cover and pages sewn together with thick string. Someone had glued a magenta daisy over the white box for your name, and WIDE RULE had been edited to read WITCHES RULE.

"*'Rebecca Bishop's Book of Shadows,'*" I said, reading aloud from the words written in thick black ink on the daisy. "This is my mother's missing spell book—the one she used for the higher magics."

I cracked open the cover. After all our problems with Ashmole 782, I was braced for anything from mysterious illustrations to encoded script. Instead I found my mother's round, childish handwriting.

"*To summon a spirit recently dead and question it*" was the first spell in the book.

"Mom certainly believed in starting with a bang," I said, showing Matthew the words on the page. The notes beneath the spell recorded the dates when she and Emily had tried to work the magic, as well as the results. Their first three attempts had failed. On the fourth try, they succeeded.

Both of them were thirteen at the time.

"Christ," Matthew said. "They were babes. What business did they have with the dead?"

"Apparently they wanted to know if Bobby Woodruff liked Mary Bassett," I said, peering at the cramped script.

"Why didn't they just ask Bobby Woodruff?" Matthew wondered.

I flipped through the pages. Binding spells, banishing spells, protection spells, charms to summon the elemental powers—they were all in there, along with love magic and other coercive enchantments. My fingers stopped. Matthew sniffed.

Something thin and almost transparent was pressed onto a page inserted in the back of the book. Scrawled above it in a more mature version of the same round hand were the words:

Diana:

> *Happy Birthday!*
> *I kept this for you. It was our first indication that you were going to be a great witch.*
> *Maybe you'll need it one day.*
>   *Lots of love, Mom*

"It's my caul." I looked up at Matthew. "Do you think it's meaningful that I got it back on the same day the babies quickened?"

"No," Matthew said. "It's far more likely that the house gave it back to you tonight because you finally stopped running from what your mother and father knew since the very beginning."

"What's that?" I frowned.

"That you were going to possess an extraordinary combination of your parents' very different magical abilities," he replied.

The tenth knot burned on my wrist. I turned over my hand and looked at its writhing shape.

"That's why I can tie the tenth knot," I said, understanding for the first time where the power came from. "I can create because my father was a weaver, and I can destroy because my mother had the talent for higher, darker magics."

"A union of opposites," Matthew said. "Your parents were an alchemical wedding, too. One that produced a marvelous child."

I closed the spell book carefully. It would take me months—years, perhaps—to learn from my mother's mistakes and create spells of my own that would achieve the same ends. With one hand pressing my mother's spell book to my sternum and the other pressed against my abdomen, I leaned back and listened to the slow beating of Matthew's heart.

"Do not refuse me because I am dark and shadowed," I whispered, remembering a passage from an alchemical text I'd studied in Matthew's library. "That line from the *Aurora Consurgens* used to remind me of you, but now it makes me think of my parents, as well as my own magic and how hard I resisted it."

Matthew's thumb stroked my wrist, bringing the tenth knot to brilliant, colorful life.

"This reminds me of another part of the *Aurora Consurgens*," he murmured. *"As I am the end, so my lover is the beginning. I encompass the whole work of creation, and all knowledge is hidden in me."*

"What do you think it means?" I turned my head so I could see his expression.

He smiled, and his arms circled my waist, one hand now resting on the babies. They moved as if recognizing their father's touch.

"That I am a very lucky man," Matthew replied.

12

I woke up to Matthew's cool hands sliding under my pajama top, his lips soothing against my damp neck.

"Happy birthday," he murmured.

"My own private air conditioner," I said, snuggling against him. A vampire husband brought welcome relief in tropical conditions. "What a thoughtful present."

"There are more," he said, giving me a slow, wicked kiss.

"Fernando and Sarah?" I was almost past caring who might hear our lovemaking, but not quite.

"Outside. In the garden hammock. With the paper."

"We'll have to be quick, then." The local papers were short on news and long on advertisements. They took ten minutes to read—fifteen if you were shopping the back-to-school sales or wanted to know which of the three grocery chains had the best deal on bleach.

"I went out for the *New York Times* this morning," he said.

"Always prepared, aren't you?" I reached down and touched him. Matthew swore. In French. "You're just like Verin. Such a Boy Scout."

"Not always," he said, closing his eyes. "Not now, certainly."

"Awfully sure of yourself, too." My mouth slid along his in a teasing kiss. "The *New York Times*. What if I were tired? Cranky? Or hormonal? The Albany paper would have been more than enough to keep them busy then."

"I was relying on my presents to sweeten you up."

"Well, I don't know." A sinuous twist of my hand elicited another French curse. "Why don't I finish unwrapping this one? Then you can show me what else you've got."

By eleven o'clock on my birthday morning, the mercury had already climbed above ninety degrees. The August heat wave showed no signs of breaking.

Worried about Sarah's garden, I spliced together four hoses using a new binding spell and some duct tape so that I could reach all the flower beds.

My headphones were jammed into my ears, and I was listening to Fleetwood Mac. The house had fallen eerily silent, as if it were waiting for something to happen, and I found myself missing the beat of my parents' favorite band.

While dragging the hose across the lawn, my attention was momentarily caught by the large iron weather vane sprouting from the top of the hop barn. It hadn't been there yesterday. I wondered why the house was tinkering with the outbuildings. While I considered the question, two more weather vanes popped out of the ridgepole. They quivered for a moment like newly emerged plants, then whirled madly. When the motion stopped, they all pointed north. Hopefully, their position was an indication that rain was on the way. Until then, the hose was going to have to suffice.

I was giving the plants a good soaking when someone engulfed me in an embrace.

"Thank God! I've been so worried about you." The deep voice was muted by the sound of guitars and drums, but I recognized it nonetheless. I ripped the headphones from my ears and turned to face my best friend. His deep brown eyes were full of concern.

"Chris!" I flung my arms around his broad shoulders. "What are you doing here?" I searched his features for changes but found none. Still the same close-cropped curly hair, still the same walnut skin, still the same high cheekbones angled under straight brows, still the same wide mouth.

"I'm looking for you!" Chris replied. "What the hell is going on? You totally disappeared last November. You don't answer your phone or your e-mail. Then I see the fall teaching schedule and you're not on it! I had to get the chair of the history department drunk before he spilled that you were on medical leave. I thought you were dying—not pregnant."

Well, that was one less thing I'd have to tell him.

"I'm sorry, Chris. There was no cell-phone reception where I was. Or Internet."

"You could have called me from here," he said, not yet ready to let me off the hook. "I've left messages for your aunts, sent letters. Nobody responded."

I could feel Matthew's gaze, cold and demanding. I felt Fernando's attention, too.

"Who is this, Diana?" Matthew asked quietly, coming to my side.

"Chris Roberts. Who the hell are *you*?" Chris demanded.

"This is Matthew Clairmont, fellow of All Souls College, Oxford University." I hesitated. "My husband."

Chris's mouth dropped open.

"Chris!" Sarah waved from the back porch. "Come here and give me a hug!"

"Hi, Sarah!" Chris's hand rose in greeting. He turned and gave me an accusatory look. "You got married?"

"You're here for the weekend, right?" Sarah called.

"That depends, Sarah." Chris's shrewd glance moved from me to Matthew and back.

"On?" Matthew's brow rose in aristocratic disdain.

"On how long it takes me to figure out why Diana married somebody like you, Clairmont, and whether you deserve her. And don't waste your lord-of-the-manor act on me. I come from a long line of field hands. I am *not* impressed," Chris said, stalking toward the house. "Where's Em?"

Sarah froze, her face white. Fernando leaped up the porch steps to join her.

"Why don't we go inside?" he murmured, trying to steer her away from Chris.

"Can I have a word?" Matthew asked, putting his hand on Chris's arm.

"It's all right, Matthew. I had to tell Diana. I can tell Chris, too." Sarah's throat worked. "Emily had a heart attack. She died in May."

"God, Sarah. I'm so sorry." Chris enveloped her in a less bone-crushing version of the hug he'd given me. He rocked slightly on his feet, his eyes screwed tightly shut. Sarah moved with him, her body relaxed and open rather than tight and full of grief. My aunt had not yet gotten over Emily's death—like Fernando, she might never get over that fundamental loss—but there were small signs that she was beginning the slow process of learning to live again.

Chris's dark eyes opened and sought me out over Sarah's shoulder. They held anger and hurt, as well as sorrow and unanswered questions. *Why didn't you tell me? Where have you been? Why didn't you let me help?*

"I'd like to talk to Chris," I said softly. "Alone."

"You'll be most comfortable in the keeping room." Sarah drew away from Chris and wiped her eyes. The nod she gave me encouraged me to tell him our family's secret. Based on the tightness of his jaw, Matthew was not feeling as generous.

"Call if you need me." Matthew raised my hand to his lips. There was a warning squeeze, a tiny nip on the knuckle of my ring finger as if to remind me—and him—that we were husband and wife. Matthew reluctantly released me.

Chris and I passed through the house to the keeping room. Once we were inside, I slid the doors shut.

"You're married to Matthew Clairmont?" Chris exploded. "Since when?"

"About ten months. It all happened very quickly," I said apologetically.

"I'll say!" Chris lowered his voice. "I warned you about his reputation with women. Clairmont may be a great scientist, but he's also a notorious asshole! Besides, he's too old for you."

"He's only thirty-seven, Chris." Give or take fifteen hundred years. "And I should warn you, Matthew and Fernando are listening to every word we say." With vampires around, a closed door was no guarantee of privacy.

"How? Did your boyfriend—husband—bug the house?" Chris's tone was sharp.

"No. He's a vampire. They have exceptional hearing." Sometimes honesty really was the best policy.

A heavy pot crashed in the kitchen.

"A vampire." Chris's look suggested I had lost my mind. "Like on TV?"

"Not exactly," I said, proceeding with caution. Telling humans how the world really worked tended to unsettle them. I'd done it only once before—and it had been a huge mistake. My freshman roommate, Melanie, had passed out.

"A vampire," Chris repeated slowly, as if he were thinking it all through.

"You'd better sit down." I gestured toward the sofa. If he fell, I didn't want him to hit his head.

Ignoring my suggestion, Chris plopped himself in the wing chair instead. It was more comfortable, to be sure, but had been known to forcibly eject visitors it didn't like. I eyed it warily.

"Are you a vampire, too?" Chris demanded.

"No." I perched gingerly on the edge of my grandmother's rocking chair.

"Are you absolutely sure that Clairmont is? That's his child you're carrying, right?" Chris sat forward, as though a great deal depended on the answer.

"Children." I held two fingers in the air. "Twins."

Chris threw his hands in the air. "Well, no vampire ever knocked up a girl on *Buffy*. Not even Spike. And God knows he never practiced safe sex."

Bewitched had provided my mother's generation with their supernatural primer. For mine it was *Buffy the Vampire Slayer*. Whichever creatures had introduced Joss Whedon to our world had a lot to answer for. I sighed.

"I'm absolutely positive that Matthew is the father."

Chris's attention drifted to my neck.

"That's not where he bites me."

His eyes widened. "Where . . . ?" He shook his head. "No, don't tell me."

It was, I thought, a strange place to draw the line. Chris wasn't normally squeamish—or prudish. Still, he hadn't passed out. That was encouraging.

"You're taking this very well," I said, grateful for his equanimity.

"I'm a scientist. I'm trained to suspend disbelief and remain open-minded until something is disproved." Chris was now staring at the Blasted Tree. "Why is there a tree in the fireplace?"

"Good question. We don't really know. Maybe you have other questions I could answer, though." It was an awkward invitation, but I was still worried he might faint.

"A few." Once again Chris fixed his dark eyes on mine. He wasn't a witch, but it had been very difficult to lie to him for all these years. "You say Clairmont's a vampire, but you're not. What are *you*, Diana? I've known for some time that you aren't like other people."

I didn't know what to say. How do you explain to someone you love that you've failed to mention a defining characteristic of yourself?

"I'm your best friend—or I was until Clairmont came along. Surely you trust me enough to come out to me," Chris said. "No matter what it is, it won't change anything between us."

Beyond Chris's shoulder a green smudge trailed off toward the Blasted Tree. The green smudge became the indistinct form of Bridget Bishop, with her embroidered bodice and full skirts.

Be canny, daughter. The wind blows from the north, a sign of a battle to come. Who will stand with you, and who will stand against you?

I had plenty of enemies. I couldn't afford to lose a single friend.

"Maybe you don't trust me enough," Chris said softly when I didn't immediately respond.

"I'm a witch." My words were barely audible.

"Okay." Chris waited. "And?"

"And what?"

"That's it? That's what you've been afraid to tell me?"

"I'm not talking neo-pagan, Chris—though I am pagan, of course. I'm talking an abracadabra, spell-casting, potion-making witch." In this case Chris's love of prime-time TV might actually prove useful.

"Do you have a wand?"

"No. But I do have a firedrake. That's a kind of dragon."

"Cool." Chris grinned. "Very, very cool. Is that why you've stayed out of New Haven? Were you taking it to dragon obedience class or something?"

"Matthew and I had to get out of town quickly, that's all. I'm sorry I didn't tell you."

"Where were you?"

"In 1590."

"Did you get any research done?" Chris looked thoughtful. "I suppose that would cause all kinds of citation problems. What would you put in your footnotes? 'Personal conversation with William Shakespeare'?" He laughed.

"I never met Shakespeare. Matthew's friends didn't approve of him." I paused. "I did meet the queen."

"Even better," Chris said, nodding. "Equally impossible to footnote, however."

"You're supposed to be shocked!" This was not at all what I'd expected. "Don't you want proof?"

"I haven't been shocked by anything since the MacArthur Foundation called me. If that can happen, anything is possible." Chris shook his head. "Vampires and witches. Wow."

"There are daemons, too. But their eyes don't glow and they're not evil. Well, no more so than any other species."

"Other species?" Chris's tone sharpened with interest. "Are there were-wolves?"

"Absolutely not!" Matthew shouted in the distance.

"Touchy subject." I gave Chris a tentative smile. "So you're really fine with this?"

"Why wouldn't I be? The government spends millions searching for aliens in outer space, and it turns out you're right here. Think of all the grant money this could free up." Chris was always looking for a way to diminish the importance of the physics department.

"You can't tell anybody," I said hastily. "Not many humans know about us, and we need to keep it that way."

"We're bound to find out eventually," Chris said. "Besides, most people would be thrilled."

"You think? The dean of Yale College would be thrilled to know that they'd tenured a witch?" I raised my eyebrows. "My students' parents would be happy to discover that their beloved children are learning about the Scientific Revolution from a witch?"

"Well, maybe not the dean." Chris's voice dropped. "Matthew isn't going to bite me to keep me quiet?"

"No," I assured him.

Fernando inserted his foot between the keeping-room doors and nudged them open.

"I'd be happy to bite you instead, but only if you ask very nicely." Fernando put a tray on the table. "Sarah thought you might like coffee. Or something stronger. Call me if you need anything else. No need to shout." He gave Chris the kind of dazzling smile he'd bestowed on the coven's female membership at the Lughnasadh potluck.

"Saddling the wrong horse, Fernando," I warned as he departed.

"He's a vampire, too?" Chris whispered.

"Yep. Matthew's brother-in-law." I held up the whiskey bottle and the coffeepot. "Coffee? Whiskey?"

"Both," said Chris, reaching for a mug. He looked at me in alarm. "You haven't kept this witch business from your aunt, have you?"

"Sarah's a witch, too. So was Em." I poured a healthy slug of whiskey in his mug and topped it off with a bit of coffee. "This is the third or fourth pot of the day, so it's mostly decaf. Otherwise we have to scrape Sarah off the ceiling."

"Coffee makes her fly?" Chris took a sip, considered a moment, and added more whiskey.

"In a manner of speaking," I said, uncapping the water and taking a swig. The babies fluttered, and I gave my abdomen a gentle pat.

"I can't believe you're pregnant." For the first time, Chris sounded amazed.

"You've just learned that I spent most of last year in the sixteenth century, I have a pet dragon, and that you're surrounded by daemons, vampires, and witches, but it's my pregnancy that you find implausible?"

"Trust me, honey," Chris said, pulling out his best Alabama drawl. "It's way more implausible."

13

When the phone rang, it was pitch black outside. I shook myself from sleep, reaching across the bed to jostle Matthew awake. He wasn't there.

I rolled over and picked up his mobile from the bedside table. The name MIRIAM was displayed, along with the time. Three o'clock Monday morning. My heart thudded in alarm. Only an emergency would have induced her to call at such an hour.

"Miriam?" I said after pushing the answer button.

"Where is he?" Miriam's voice shook. "I need to speak with Matthew."

"I'll find him. He must be downstairs, or outside hunting." I threw off the covers. "Is something wrong?"

"Yes," Miriam said abruptly. Then she switched to another language, one I didn't understand. The cadence was unmistakable, though. Miriam Shephard was praying.

Matthew burst through the door, Fernando behind him.

"Here's Matthew." I hit the speaker button and handed him the phone. He was not going to have this conversation in private.

"What is it, Miriam?" Matthew said.

"There was a note. In the mailbox. A Web address was typed on it." There was a curse, a jagged sob, and Miriam's prayer resumed.

"Text me the address, Miriam," Matthew said calmly.

"It's him, Matthew. It's Benjamin," Miriam whispered. "And there was no stamp on the envelope. He must still be here. In Oxford."

I leaped out of bed, shivering in the predawn darkness.

"Text me the address," Matthew repeated.

A light came on in the hallway.

"What's going on?" Chris joined Fernando at the threshold, rubbing the sleep from his eyes.

"It's one of Matthew's colleagues from Oxford, Miriam Shephard. Something's happened at the lab," I told him.

"Oh," Chris said with a yawn. He shook his head to clear the cobwebs and frowned. "Not the Miriam Shephard who wrote the classic article about how inbreeding among zoo animals leads to a loss of heterozygosity?" I'd spent a lot of time around scientists, but it seldom helped me to understand what they were talking about.

"The same," Matthew murmured.

"I thought she was dead," Chris said.

"Not quite," said Miriam in her piercing soprano. "To whom am I speaking?"

"Chris—Christopher Roberts. Yale University," Chris stammered. He sounded like a graduate student introducing himself at his first conference.

"Oh. I liked your last piece in *Science*. Your research model is impressive, even though the conclusions are all wrong." Miriam sounded more like herself now that she was criticizing a fellow researcher. Matthew noticed the positive change, too.

"Keep her talking," Matthew encouraged Chris before issuing a quiet command to Fernando.

"Is that Miriam?" Sarah asked, shoving her arms through the sleeves of her bathrobe. "Don't vampires have clocks? It's three in the morning!"

"What's wrong with my conclusions?" Chris asked, his expression thunderous.

Fernando was back, and he handed Matthew his laptop. It was already on, the screen's glow illuminating the room. Sarah reached around the door frame and flicked the light switch, banishing the remaining darkness. Even so I could feel the shadows pressing down on the house.

Matthew perched on the edge of the bed, his laptop on his knee. Fernando tossed him another cell phone, and Matthew tethered it to the computer.

"Have you seen Benjamin's message?" Miriam sounded calmer than before, but fear kept her voice keen.

"I'm calling it up now," Matthew said.

"Don't use Sarah's Internet connection!" Her agitation was palpable. "He's monitoring traffic to the site. He might be able to locate you from your IP address."

"It's all right, Miriam," Matthew said, his voice soothing. "I'm using Fernando's mobile. And Baldwin's computer people made sure that no one can trace my location from it."

Now I understood why Baldwin had supplied us with new cell phones when we left Sept-Tours, changed all our phone plans, and canceled Sarah's Internet service.

An image of an empty room appeared on the screen. It was white-tiled and barren except for an old sink with exposed plumbing and an examination table. There was a drain in the floor. The date and time were in the lower left corner, the numbers on the clock whirring forward as each second passed.

"What's that lump?" Chris pointed to a pile of rags on the floor. It stirred.

"A woman," Miriam said. "She's been lying there since I got on the site ten minutes ago." As soon as Miriam said it, I could make out her thin arms and legs, the curve of her breast and belly. The scrap of cloth over her wasn't large enough to protect her from the cold. She shivered and whimpered.

"And Benjamin?" Matthew said, his eyes glued to the screen.

"He walked through the room and said something to her. Then he looked straight at the camera—and smiled."

"Did he say anything else?" Matthew asked.

"Yes. 'Hello, Miriam.'"

Chris leaned over Matthew's shoulder and touched the computer's track-pad. The image grew larger.

"There's blood on the floor. And she's chained to the wall." Chris stared at me. "Who's Benjamin?"

"My son." Matthew's glance flickered to Chris, then returned to the screen.

Chris crossed his arms over his chest and stared, unblinking, at the image.

Soft strains of music came out of the computer speakers. The woman shrank against the wall, her eyes wide.

"No," she moaned. "Not again. Please. No." She stared straight at the camera. "Help me."

My hands flashed with colors, and the knots on my wrists burned. I felt a tingle, dull but unmistakable.

"She's a witch. That woman is a witch." I touched the screen. When I drew my finger away, a thin green thread was attached to the tip.

The thread snapped.

"Can she hear us?" I asked Matthew.

"No," Matthew said grimly. "I don't believe so. Benjamin wants me to listen to him."

"No talking to our guests." There was no sign of Matthew's son, but I knew that cold voice. The woman instantly subsided, hugging her arms around her body.

Benjamin approached the camera until his face filled most of the screen. The woman was still visible over his shoulder. He'd staged this performance carefully.

"Another visitor has joined us—Matthew, no doubt. How clever of you to mask your location. And dear Miriam is still with us, I see." Benjamin smiled again. No wonder Miriam was shaken. It was a horrifying sight: those curved lips and the dead eyes I remembered from Prague. Even after more than four centuries, Benjamin was recognizable as the man whom Rabbi Loew had called Herr Fuchs.

"How do you like my laboratory?" Benjamin's arm swept the room. "Not as well equipped as yours, Matthew, but I don't need much. Experience is really the best teacher. All I require is a cooperative research subject. And warmbloods are so much more revealing than animals."

"Christ," Matthew murmured.

"I'd hoped the next time we talked it would be to discuss my latest successful experiment. But things haven't worked out quite as planned." Benjamin turned his head, and his voice became menacing. "Have they?"

The music grew louder, and the woman on the floor moaned and tried to block her ears.

"She used to love Bach," Benjamin reported with mock sadness. "The St. Matthew Passion in particular. I'm careful to play it whenever I take her. Now the witch becomes unaccountably distressed as soon as she hears the first strains." He hummed along with the next bars of music.

"Does he mean what I think he means?" Sarah asked uneasily.

"Benjamin is repeatedly raping that woman," Fernando said with barely controlled fury. It was the first time I'd seen the vampire beneath his easygoing façade.

"Why?" Chris asked. Before anyone could answer, Benjamin resumed.

"As soon as she shows signs of being pregnant, the music stops. It's the witch's reward for doing her job and pleasing me. Sometimes nature has other ideas, though."

The implications of Benjamin's words sank in. As in long-ago Jerusalem, this witch had to be a weaver. I covered my mouth as the bile rose.

The glint in Benjamin's eye intensified. He adjusted the angle of the camera and zoomed in on the blood that stained the woman's legs and the floor.

"Unfortunately, the witch miscarried." Benjamin's voice had the detachment of any scientist reporting his research findings. "It was the fourth month—the longest she's been able to sustain a pregnancy. So far. My son impregnated her last December, but that time she miscarried in the eighth week."

Matthew and I had conceived our first child in December, too. I'd miscarried early in that pregnancy, around the same time as Benjamin's witch. I started to shake at this new connection between me and the woman on the floor. Matthew's arm hooked around my hips, steadying me.

"I was so sure my ability to father a child was linked to the blood rage you gave me—a gift that I've shared with many of my own children. After the witch miscarried the first time, my sons and I tried impregnating daemons and humans without success. I concluded there must be some special reproductive affinity between vampires with blood rage and witches. But these failures mean I'll have to reexamine my hypothesis." Benjamin pulled a stool up to the camera and sat, oblivious to the growing agitation of the woman behind him. In the background the Bach continued to play.

"And there is another piece of information that I'll also have to factor into my deliberations: your marriage. Has your new wife replaced Eleanor in your affections? Mad Juliette? Poor Celia? That fascinating witch I met in Prague?" Benjamin snapped his fingers as if trying to remember something. "What was her name? Diana?"

Fernando hissed. Chris's skin broke out in raised bumps. He stared at Fernando and stepped away.

"I'm told your new wife is a witch, too. Why don't you ever share your ideas with me? You must know I'd understand." Benjamin leaned closer as if sharing a confidence. "We're both driven by the same things, after all: a lust for power, an unquenchable thirst for blood, a desire for revenge."

The music reached a crescendo, and the woman began to rock back and forth in an attempt to soothe herself.

"I can't help wondering how long you've known about the power in our blood. The witches surely knew. What other secret could the Book of Life possibly contain?" Benjamin paused as if waiting for an answer. "Not going to tell me, eh? Well, then. I have no choice but to go back to my own experiment. Don't worry. I'll figure out how to breed this witch eventually— or kill her trying. Then I'll look for a new witch. Maybe yours will suit."

Benjamin smiled. I drew away from Matthew, not wanting him to sense my fear. But his expression told me that he knew.

"Bye for now." Benjamin gave a jaunty wave. "Sometimes I let people watch me work, but I'm not in the mood for an audience today. I'll be sure to let you know if anything interesting develops. Meanwhile you might want to think about sharing what you know. It might save me from having to ask your wife."

With that, Benjamin switched off the lens and the sound. It left a black screen, with the clock still ticking down the seconds in the corner.

"What are we going to do?" Miriam asked.

"Rescue that woman," Matthew said, his fury evident, "for a start."

"Benjamin wants you to rush into the open and expose yourself," Fernando warned. "Your attack will have to be well planned and perfectly executed."

"Fernando's right," Miriam said. "You can't go after Benjamin until you're sure you can destroy him. Otherwise you put Diana at risk."

"That witch won't survive much longer!" Matthew exclaimed.

"If you are hasty and fail to bring Benjamin to heel, he will simply take another and the nightmare will begin again for some other unsuspecting creature," Fernando said, his hand clasped around Matthew's arm.

"You're right." Matthew dragged his eyes away from the screen. "Can you warn Amira, Miriam? She needs to know that Benjamin has one witch already and is likely to kidnap again."

"Amira isn't a weaver. She wouldn't be able to conceive Benjamin's child," I observed.

"I don't think Benjamin knows about weavers. Yet." Matthew rubbed at his jaw.

"What's a weaver?" Miriam and Chris said at the same moment. I opened my mouth to reply, but the slight shake of Matthew's head made me close it again.

"I'll tell you later, Miriam. Will you do what I asked?"

"Sure, Matthew," Miriam agreed.

"Call me later and check in." Matthew's worried glance settled on me.

"Stifle Diana with your excessive attention if you must, but I don't need a babysitter. Besides, I've got work to do." Miriam hung up.

A second later Chris delivered a powerful uppercut to Matthew's jaw. He followed it with a left hook. Matthew intercepted that blow with a raised palm.

"I took one punch, for Diana's sake." Matthew closed his fist around Chris's clenched hand. "My wife does, after all, bring out the protective instincts in people. But don't press your luck."

Chris didn't budge. Fernando sighed.

"Let it go, Roberts. You will not win a physical contest with a vampire." Fernando put his hand on Chris's shoulder, prepared to pull him away if necessary.

"If you let that bastard within fifty miles of Diana, you won't see another sunrise—vampire or no vampire. Are we clear on that?" Chris demanded, his attention locked on Matthew.

"Crystal," Matthew replied. Chris pulled his arm back, and Matthew released his fist.

"Nobody's getting any more sleep tonight. Not after this," Sarah said. "We need to talk. And lots of coffee—and don't you dare use decaf, Diana. But first I'm going outside to have a cigarette, no matter what Fernando says." Sarah marched out of the room. "See you in the kitchen," she shot over her shoulder.

"Keep that site online. When Benjamin is turning on the camera, he might do or say something that will give his location away." Matthew handed his laptop and the still-attached mobile to Fernando. There was still nothing but a black screen and that horrible clock marking the passage of time. Matthew angled his head toward the door, and Fernando followed Sarah.

"So let me get this straight. Matthew's Bad Seed is engaged in some down-home genetics research involving a hereditary condition, a kidnapped witch, and some half-baked ideas about eugenics." Chris folded his arms over his chest. There were a few details missing, but he had sized up the situation in no time at all. "You left some important plot twists out of the fairy tale you told me yesterday, Diana."

"She didn't know about Benjamin's scientific interests. None of us knew." Matthew stood.

"You must have known that the Bad Seed was as crazy as a shit-house rat. He is your son." Chris's eyes narrowed. "According to him you both share this blood-rage thing. That means you're both a danger to Diana."

"I knew he was unstable, yes. And his name is Benjamin." Matthew chose not to respond to the second half of Chris's remarks.

"Unstable? The man is a psychopath. He's trying to engineer a master race of vampire-witches. So why isn't the Bad—Benjamin locked up? That way he couldn't kidnap and rape his way onto the roster of scientific madmen alongside Sims, Verschuer, Mengele, and Stanley."

"Let's go to the kitchen." I urged them both in the direction of the stairs.

"After you," Matthew murmured, putting his hand on the small of my back. Relieved by his easy acquiescence, I began my descent.

There was a thud, a muffled curse.

Chris was pinned against the door, Matthew's hand wrapped around his windpipe.

"Based on the profanity that's come out of your mouth in the past twenty-four hours, I can only conclude that you think of Diana as one of the guys." Matthew gave me a warning look when I backed up to intervene. "She's not. She's my wife. I would appreciate it if you limited your vulgarity in her presence. Are we clear?"

"Crystal." Chris looked at him with loathing.

"I'm glad to hear it." Matthew was at my side in a flash, his hand once more on the dip in my spine where the shadowy firedrake had appeared. "Watch the stairs, *mon coeur*," he murmured.

When we reached the ground floor, I sneaked a backward glance at Chris. He was studying Matthew as though he were a strange new life-form—which I suppose he was. My heart sank. Matthew might have won the first few battles, but the war between my best friend and my husband was far from over.

By the time Sarah joined us in the kitchen, her hair exuded the scents of tobacco and the hop vine that was planted against the porch railings. I waved my hand in front of my nose—cigarette smoke was one of the few things that still triggered nausea this late in my pregnancy—and made coffee.

When it was ready, I poured the pot's steaming contents into mugs for Sarah, Chris, and Fernando. Matthew and I stuck to ordinary water. Chris was the first to break the silence.

"So, Matthew, you and Dr. Shephard have been studying vampire genetics for decades in an effort to understand blood rage."

"Matthew knew Darwin. He's been studying creature origins and evolution for more than a few decades." I wasn't going to tell Chris how much more, but I didn't want him to be blindsided by Matthew's age, as I had been.

"We have. My son has been working with us." Matthew gave me a quelling look.

"Yes, I saw that," Chris said, a muscle ticking in his cheek. "Not something I'd boast about, myself."

"Not Benjamin. My other son, Marcus Whitmore."

"Marcus Whitmore." Chris made an amused sound. "Covering all the bases, I see. You handle the evolutionary biology and neuroscience, Miriam Shephard is an expert on population genetics, and Marcus Whitmore is known for his study of functional morphology and efforts to debunk phenotypic plasticity. That's a hell of a research team you've assembled, Clairmont."

"I'm very fortunate," Matthew said mildly.

"Wait a minute." Chris looked at Matthew in amazement. "Evolutionary biology. Evolutionary physiology. Population genetics. Figuring out how blood rage is transmitted isn't your only research objective. You're trying to diagram evolutionary descent. You're working on the Tree of Life—and not just the human branches."

"Is that what the tree in the fireplace is called?" Sarah asked.

"I don't think so." Matthew patted her hand.

"Evolution. I'll be damned." Chris pushed away from the island. "So have you discovered the common ancestor for humans and you guys?" He waved in our direction.

"If by 'you guys' you mean creatures—daemons, vampires, and witches—then no." Matthew's brow arched.

"Okay. What are the crucial genetic differences separating us?"

"Vampires and witches have an extra chromosome pair," Matthew explained. "Daemons have a single extra chromosome."

"You've got a genetic map for these creature chromosomes?"

"Yes," Matthew said.

"Then you've probably been working on this little project since before 1990, just to keep up with the humans."

"That's right," Matthew said. "And I've been working since 1968 on how blood rage is inherited, if you must know."

"Of course. You adapted Donahue's use of family pedigrees to determine gene transmission between generations." Chris nodded. "Good call. How far along are you with sequencing? Have you located the blood-rage gene?"

Matthew stared at him without replying.

"Well?" Chris demanded.

"I had a teacher like you once," Matthew said coldly. "He drove me insane."

"And I have students like you. They don't last long in my lab." Chris leaned across the table. "I take it that not every vampire on the planet has your condition. Have you determined exactly how blood rage is inherited, and why some contract it and some don't?"

"Not entirely," Matthew admitted. "It's a bit more complicated with vampires, considering we have three parents."

"You need to pick up the pace, my friend. Diana is pregnant. With twins." Chris looked at me pointedly. "I assume you've drawn up full genetic profiles for the two of you and made predictions for inheritance patterns among your offspring, including but not limited to blood rage?"

"I've been in the sixteenth century for the best part of a year." Matthew really disliked being questioned. "I lacked the opportunity."

"High time we started, then," Chris remarked blandly.

"Matthew was working on something." I looked to Matthew for confirmation. "Remember? I found that paper covered with X's and O's."

"X's and O's? Lord God Almighty." This seemed to confirm Chris's worst fears. "You tell me you have three parents, but you remain married to a Mendelian inheritance model. I suppose that's what happens when you're as old as dirt and knew Darwin."

"I met Mendel once, too," Matthew said crisply, sounding like an irritated professor himself. "Besides, blood rage may be a Mendelian trait. We can't rule that out."

"Highly unlikely," Chris said. "And not just because of this three-parent problem—which I'll have to consider in more detail. It must create havoc in the data."

"Explain." Matthew tented his fingers in front of his face.

"I have to give an overview of non-Mendelian inheritance to a fellow of All Souls?" Chris's eyebrows rose. "Somebody needs to look at the appointment policies at Oxford University."

"Do you understand a word they're saying?" Sarah whispered.

"One in three," I said apologetically.

"I mean gene conversion. Infectious heredity. Genomic imprinting. Mosaicism." Chris ticked them off on his finger. "Ring any bells, Professor Clairmont, or would you like me to continue with the lecture I give to my undergraduates?"

"Isn't mosaicism a form of chimerism?" It was the only word I'd recognized.

Chris nodded at me approvingly.

"I'm a chimera—if that helps."

"Diana," Matthew growled.

"Chris is my best friend, Matthew," I said. "And if he's going to help you figure out how vampires and witches can reproduce—not to mention find a cure for the disease—he needs to know everything. That includes my genetic test results, by the way."

"That information can be deadly in the wrong hands," Matthew said.

"Matthew is right," Chris agreed.

"I'm so glad you think so." Matthew's words dripped acid.

"Don't patronize me, Clairmont. I know the dangers of human-subject research. I'm a black man from Alabama and grew up in the shadow of Tuskegee." Chris turned to me. "Don't hand over your genetic information to anybody outside this room—even if they're wearing a white coat. Especially if they're wearing a white coat, come to think of it."

"Thanks for your input, Christopher," Matthew said stiffly. "I'll be sure to pass your ideas on to the rest of my team."

"So what are we going to do about all this?" Fernando asked. "There may not have been any urgency before, but now . . ." He looked to Matthew for guidance.

"The Bad Seed's breeding program changes everything," Chris proclaimed before Matthew could speak. "First we have to figure out if blood rage really is what makes conception possible or if it's a combination of factors. And we need to know the likelihood of Diana's children contracting the disease. We'll need the witch and the vampire genetic maps for that."

"You'll need my DNA, too," I said quietly. "Not all witches can reproduce."

"Do you need to be a good witch? A bad witch?" Chris's silly jokes usually made me smile, but not tonight.

"You need to be a weaver," I replied. "You're going to need to sequence my genome in particular and compare it to that of other witches. And you'll need to do the same for Matthew and vampires who don't have blood rage. We have to understand blood rage well enough to cure it, or Benjamin and his children will continue to be a threat."

"Okay, then." Chris slapped his thighs. "We need a lab. And help. Plenty of data and computer time, too. I can put my people on this."

"Absolutely not." Matthew shot to his feet. "I have a lab, too. Miriam has been working on the problems of blood rage and the creature genomes for some time."

"Then she should come here immediately and bring her work with her. My students are good, Matthew. The best. They'll see things you and I have been conditioned not to see."

"Yes. Like vampires. And witches." Matthew ran his fingers through his hair. Chris looked alarmed at the transformation in his tidy appearance. "I don't like the idea of more humans knowing about us."

Matthew's words reminded me who *did* need to know about Benjamin's latest message. "Marcus. We need to tell Marcus."

Matthew dialed his number.

"Matthew? Is everything all right?" Marcus said as soon as he picked up the call.

"Not really. We have a situation." Matthew quickly told him about Benjamin and the witch he was keeping hostage. Then he told Marcus why.

"If I send you the Web address, will you have Nathaniel Wilson figure out how to monitor Benjamin's feed 24/7? And if he could find where the signal is originating from, that would save a lot of time," Matthew said.

"Consider it done," Marcus replied.

No sooner had Matthew disconnected than my own cell phone rang.

"Who now?" I said, glancing at the clock. The sun had barely risen.
"Hello?"

"Thank God you're awake," Vivian Harrison said, relieved.

"What's wrong?" My black thumb prickled.

"We've got trouble," she said grimly.

"What kind of trouble?" I asked. Sarah pressed her ear against the receiver next to mine. I tried to flap her away.

"I received a message from Sidonie von Borcke," Vivian said.

"Who is Sidonie von Borcke?" I'd never heard the name before.

"One of the Congregation's witches," Vivian and Sarah said in unison.

14

The coven failed the test." Vivian flung her satchel-size purse onto the kitchen island and poured herself a cup of coffee.

"Is she a witch, too?" Chris asked me in a whisper.

"I am," Vivian replied instead, noticing Chris for the first time.

"Oh." He looked at her appraisingly. "Can I take a cheek swab? It's painless."

"Maybe later." Vivian did a double take. "I'm sorry, but who are you?"

"This is Chris Roberts, Vivian, my colleague from Yale. He's a molecular biologist." I passed the sugar and gave Chris a pinch on the arm to keep him quiet. "Can we possibly talk in the family room? My head is killing me—and my feet are swelling up like balloons."

"Somebody complained to the Congregation about covenant violations in Madison County," Vivian told us when we were comfortably ensconced in the sofas and armchairs arranged in front of the TV.

"Do you know who it was?" Sarah asked.

"Cassie and Lydia." Vivian stared morosely into her coffee.

"The *cheerleaders* narked us out?" Sarah was dumbfounded.

"Figures," I said. They'd been inseparable since childhood, insufferable since adolescence, and indistinguishable since high school with their softly curling blond hair and blue eyes. Neither Cassie nor Lydia had let her witchy ancestry keep her in the shadows. Together they had co-captained the cheerleading squad and witches credited them with giving Madison its most successful football season in history by inserting victory spells into every chant and routine.

"And what are the charges—exactly?" Matthew had switched into lawyer mode.

"That Diana and Sarah have been consorting with vampires," Vivian muttered.

"Consorting?" Sarah's outrage was clear.

Vivian flung her hands up in the air. "I know, I know. It sounds positively lewd, but I assure you those were Sidonie's exact words. Happily, Sidonie is in Las Vegas and can't come in person to investigate. The Clark County covens are too heavily invested in real estate, and they're using spells to try to shore up the housing market."

"So what happens now?" I asked Vivian.

"I have to respond. In writing."

"Thank goodness. That means you can lie," I said, relieved.

"No way, Diana. She's too smart. I saw Sidonie question the SoHo coven two years ago when they opened up that haunted house on Spring Street, right where the Halloween parade lineup begins. It was masterful." Vivian shuddered. "She even got them to divulge how they suspended a bubbling cauldron over their parade float for six hours. After Sidonie's visit the coven was grounded for a full year—no flying, no apparating, and positively no exorcisms. They still haven't recovered."

"What kind of witch is she?" I asked.

"A powerful one," Vivian said with a snort. But that's not what I meant.

"Is her power elemental or based in the craft?"

"She's got a good grasp of spells, from what I hear," Sarah said.

"Sidonie can fly, and she's a respected seer, too," Vivian added.

Chris raised his hand.

"Yes, Chris?" Sarah sounded like a schoolmarm.

"Smart, powerful, flying—it doesn't matter. You can't let her find out about Diana's children, what with the Bad Seed's latest research project and this covenant you're all worried about."

"Bad Seed?" Vivian stared at Chris blankly.

"Matthew's son knocked up a witch. It seems that reproductive abilities run in the Clairmont family." Chris glared at Matthew. "And about this covenant you've all agreed to. I take it that witches aren't supposed to hang out with vampires?"

"Or with daemons. It makes humans uncomfortable," Matthew said.

"Uncomfortable?" Chris looked dubious. "So did blacks sitting on buses next to white people. Segregation isn't the answer."

"Humans notice creatures if we're in mixed groups," I said, hoping to placate Chris.

"We notice you, Diana, even when you're walking down Temple Street by yourself at ten o'clock in the morning," Chris said, shattering my last, fragile hope that I appeared to be just like everybody else.

"The Congregation was established to enforce the covenant, to keep us safe from human attention and interference," I said, sticking to my guns nonetheless. "In exchange we all stay out of human politics and religion."

"Think what you want, but forced segregation—or the covenant if you want to be fancy about it—is often about concerns for racial purity." Chris propped his legs on the coffee table. "Your covenant probably came into being because witches were having vampire babies. Making humans more 'comfortable' was just a convenient excuse."

Fernando and Matthew exchanged glances.

"I assumed that Diana's ability to conceive was unique—that this was the goddess at work, not part of some broader pattern." Vivian was aghast. "Scores of long-lived creatures with supernatural powers would be terrifying."

"Not if you want to engineer a super race. Then such a creature would be quite a genetic coup," Chris observed. "Do we happen to know of any megalomaniacs with an interest in vampire genetics? Oh, wait. We know two of them."

"I prefer to leave such things to God, Christopher." A dark vein pulsed in Matthew's forehead. "I have no interest in eugenics."

"I forgot. You're obsessed with species evolution—in other words, history and chemistry. Those are Diana's research interests. What a coincidence." Chris's eyes narrowed. "Based on what I've overheard, I have two questions, Professor Clairmont. Is it just vampires who are dying out, or are witches and daemons going extinct, too? And which of these so-called species cares the most about racial purity?"

Chris really *was* a genius. With every insightful question he was delving deeper into the mysteries bound up in the Book of Life, the de Clermont family's secrets, and the mysteries in my own—and Matthew's—blood.

"Chris is right," Matthew said with suspicious speed. "We can't risk the Congregation discovering Diana's pregnancy. If you have no objection, *mon coeur,* I think we should go to Fernando's house in Seville without delay. Sarah can come with us, of course. Then the coven's reputation won't be brought into disrepute."

"I said you can't let the Wicked Witch find out about Diana, not that she should run away," Chris said, disgusted. "Have you forgotten Benjamin?"

"Let's fight this war on one front at a time, Christopher." Matthew's expression must have matched his tone, because Chris immediately subsided.

"Okay. I'll go to Seville." I didn't want to, but I didn't want the Madison witches to suffer either.

"No, it's not okay," Sarah said, her voice rising. "The Congregation wants answers? Well, I want answers, too. You tell Sidonie von Borcke that I have been *consorting* with vampires since last October, ever since Satu Järvinen kidnapped and tortured my niece while Peter Knox stood by and did nothing. If that means I've violated the covenant, that's too damn bad. Without the de Clermonts, Diana would be dead—or worse."

"Those are serious allegations," Vivian said. "You're sure you want to make them?"

"Yes," Sarah said stubbornly. "Knox has already been banished from the Congregation. I want Satu's ass kicked off, too."

"They're looking for Knox's replacement now," Vivian reported. "It's rumored that Janet Gowdie is going to come out of retirement to fill the chair."

"Janet Gowdie is ninety if she's a day," Sarah said. "She can't possibly be up to the job."

"Knox insists that it be a witch known for her spell-casting abilities, as he was. No one—not even Janet Gowdie—ever bested him when it came to performing spells," Vivian said.

"Yet," said Sarah succinctly.

"There's something else, Sarah—and it might make you pause before you go after the witches of the Congregation." Vivian hesitated. "Sidonie has asked for a report on Diana. She says it's standard procedure to check on witches who haven't developed their magical talents to see if anything manifested later in life."

"If it's my power the Congregation is interested in, then Sidonie's request really has nothing to do with Sarah and me consorting with vampires," I said.

"Sidonie claims that she has a childhood assessment of Diana that indicated she was not expected to manifest any of the normal powers traditionally associated with witches," Vivian went on, looking miserable. "Peter Knox conducted it. Rebecca and Stephen agreed to his findings and signed off on it."

"Tell the Congregation that Rebecca and Stephen's assessment of their daughter's magical abilities was absolutely correct, down to the last detail." Sarah's eyes glittered with anger. "My niece has no normal powers."

"Well done, Sarah," Matthew said, his admiration of her careful truth evident. "That answer was worthy of my brother Godfrey."

"Thank you, Matthew," Sarah said with a little nod.

"Knox knows something—or suspects something—about me. He has since I was a child." I expected Matthew to argue. He didn't. "I thought we'd discovered what my parents were hiding: that I'm a weaver, like Dad. But now that I know about Mom's interest in higher magics, I wonder if that doesn't have something to do with Knox's interest as well."

"He's a dedicated practitioner of higher magics," Vivian mused. "And if you were able to devise new dark spells? I imagine that Knox would be willing to do almost anything to get his hands on them."

The house moaned, and the sound of a guitar filled the room with a recognizable melody. Of all the songs on my mother's favorite album, "Landslide" was the one that most tugged at my heart. Whenever I heard it, I remembered her holding me on her lap and humming.

"Mom loved this song," I said. "She knew that change was coming, and she was afraid of it, just like the woman in the song. But we can't afford fear anymore."

"What are you saying, Diana?" Vivian asked.

"The change my mom was expecting? It's here," I said simply.

"And even more change is on the way," Chris said. "You're not going to be able to keep the existence of creatures secret from humans for much longer. You're one autopsy, one genetic-counseling session, one home genetic-testing kit away from being outed."

"Nonsense," Matthew declared.

"Gospel. You have two choices. Do you want to be in control of the situation when it happens, Matthew, or do you want to get smacked upside the head with it?" Chris waited. "Based on our limited acquaintance, I'm guessing you'd prefer option A."

Matthew ran his fingers over his scalp and glared at Chris.

"I thought so." Chris tipped back his chair. "So. Given your predicament, what can Yale University do for you, Professor Clairmont?"

"No." Matthew shook his head. "You are not using research students and postgraduates to analyze creature DNA."

"It's scary as hell, I know," Chris continued in a gentler tone. "We'd all rather hide somewhere safe and let someone else make the tough decisions. But somebody is going to have to stand up and fight for what's right. Fernando tells me you're a pretty impressive warrior."

Matthew stared at Chris, unblinking.

"I'll stand with you, if that helps," Chris added, "provided you meet me halfway."

Matthew was not only an impressive warrior but an experienced one. He knew when he was beaten.

"You win, Chris," he said quietly.

"Good. Let's get started, then. I want to see the creature genetic maps. Then I want to sequence and reassemble the three creature genomes so they can be compared to the human genome." Chris ticked off one item after another. "I want to be sure that you've correctly identified the gene responsible for blood rage. And I want the gene that makes it possible for Diana to conceive your child isolated. I don't believe you've even started to look for that yet."

"Is there anything else I can help you with?" Matthew's brows rose.

"As a matter of fact, there is." Chris's chair thudded to the ground. "Tell Miriam Shephard I want her ass in Kline Biology Tower on Monday morning. It's on Science Hill. You can't miss it. My lab is on the fifth floor. I'd like her to explain how my conclusions in *Science* were wrong before she joins us for our first team meeting at eleven."

"I'll pass that message along." Matthew and Fernando glanced at each other, and Fernando shrugged as if to say, *His funeral*. "Just a reminder, Chris. The research you've outlined thus far will take years to complete. We won't be at Yale for very long. Diana and I will have to be back in Europe by October, if we want the twins born there. Diana shouldn't travel long distances after that."

"All the more reason to have as many people as possible working on the project." Chris stood up and put out his hand. "Deal?"

After a long pause, Matthew took it.

"Smart decision," Chris said, giving it a shake. "I hope you brought your checkbook, Clairmont. The Yale Center for Genome Analysis and the DNA Analysis Facility both charge steep fees, but they're fast and accurate." He looked at his watch. "My bag is already in the car. How long before you two can hit the road?"

"We'll be a few hours behind you," Matthew said.

Chris kissed Sarah on the cheek and gave me a hug. Then his finger rose in a gesture of warning. "Eleven A.M. on Monday, Matthew. Don't be late."

On that note he left.

"What have I done?" Matthew muttered when the front door slammed shut. He looked a bit shell-shocked.

"It will be fine, Matthew," Sarah said with surprising optimism. "I have a good feeling about all this."

A few hours later, we climbed into the car. I waved to Sarah and Fernando from the passenger seat, blinking back the tears. Sarah was smiling, but her arms were wrapped so tightly around herself that the knuckles were white. Fernando exchanged a few words with Matthew and clasped him briefly, hand to elbow, in the familiar de Clermont fashion.

Matthew slid behind the wheel. "All set?"

I nodded. His finger pressed the switch, and the engine turned over.

Keyboard and drums flooded out of the sound system, accompanied by piercing guitars. Matthew fumbled with the controls, trying to turn the music down. When that failed, he tried to turn it off. But no matter what he did, Fleetwood Mac warned us not to stop thinking about tomorrow. Finally he flung up his hands in defeat.

"The house is sending us off in style, I see." He shook his head and put the car in drive.

"Don't worry. It won't be able to keep the song going once we leave the property."

We drove down the long driveway toward the road, the bumps all but imperceptible thanks to the Range Rover's shock absorbers.

I twisted in the seat when Matthew flicked on the turn signal to leave the Bishop farm, but the last words of the song made me face forward again.

"Don't look back," I whispered.

Sol in Virgo

When the sun is in Virgo, send children to school.

This signe signifieth a change of place.

—Anonymous English Commonplace Book, c. 1590,
Gonçalves MS 4890, f. 9ʳ

15

M ore tea, Professor Bishop?"

"Hmm?" I looked up at the preppy young man with the expectant expression. "Oh. Yes. Of course. Thank you."

"Right away." He whisked the white porcelain teapot from the table.

I looked toward the door, but there was still no sign of Matthew. He was at Human Resources getting his identification badge while I waited for him in the rarefied atmosphere of the nearby New Haven Lawn Club. The hushed confines of the main building dampened the distinctive *plonk* of tennis balls and the screaming children enjoying the pool during the last week of summer vacation. Three brides-to-be and their mothers had been escorted through the room where I was sitting to view the facilities they would enjoy should they be married here.

This might be New Haven, but it was not my New Haven.

"Here you are, Professor." My attentive waiter was back, accompanied by the fresh scent of mint leaves. "Peppermint tea."

Living in New Haven with Matthew was going to require some adjustment. My little row house on the tree-lined, pedestrians-only stretch of Court Street was far more spartan than any of the residences we'd occupied over the last year, whether in the present or the past. It was furnished simply with flea-market finds, cheap pine furniture left over from my graduate-student days, and shelf upon shelf of books and journals. My bed didn't have a footboard or a headboard, never mind a canopy. But the mattress was wide and welcoming, and at the end of our long drive from Madison the two of us had collapsed into it with groans of relief.

We'd spent most of the weekend stocking the house with essentials like any normal New Haven couple: wine from the store on Whitney Avenue for Matthew, groceries for me, and enough electronics to outfit a computer lab. Matthew was horrified that I owned only a laptop. We left the computer store on Broadway with two of everything—one for him and one for me. Afterward we strolled the paths of the residential colleges while the carillon played in Harkness Tower. College and town were just beginning to swell with returning students who shouted greetings across the quad and shared complaints about reading lists and class schedules.

"It's good to be back," I had whispered, my hand hooked through his arm. It felt like we were embarking on a new adventure, just the two of us.

But today was different. I felt out of step and out of sorts.

"There you are." Matthew appeared at my elbow and gave me a lingering kiss. "I missed you."

I laughed. "We've been apart for an hour and a half."

"Exactly. Far too long." His attention wandered over the table, taking in the untouched pot of tea, my blank yellow legal pad, and the unopened copy of the latest *American Historical Review* that we'd rescued from my overstuffed department mailbox on our way to Science Hill. "How was your morning?"

"They've taken very good care of me."

"So they should." On our way into the grand brick building, Matthew had explained that Marcus was one of the founding members of the private club and that the facility was built on land he'd once owned.

"Can I get you something, Professor Clairmont?"

I pressed my lips together. A small crease appeared in the smooth skin between my husband's keen eyes.

"Thank you, Chip, but I believe we're ready to go."

It was not a moment too soon. I stood and gathered my things, slipping them into the large messenger bag at my feet.

"Can you put the charges on Dr. Whitmore's account?" Matthew murmured, pulling out my chair.

"Absolutely," Chip said. "No problem. Always a pleasure to welcome a member of Dr. Whitmore's family."

For once I beat Matthew outside.

"Where's the car?" I said, searching the parking lot.

"It's parked in the shade." Matthew lifted the messenger bag from my shoulder. "We're walking to the lab, not driving. Members are free to leave their cars here, and it's very close to the lab." He looked sympathetic. "This is strange for both of us, but the oddness will pass."

I took a deep breath and nodded. Matthew carried my bag, holding it by the short handle on top.

"It will be better once I'm in the library," I said, as much for my benefit as his. "Shall we get to work?"

Matthew held out his free hand. I took it, and his expression softened. "Lead the way," he said.

We crossed Whitney Avenue by the garden filled with dinosaur statuary, cut behind the Peabody, and approached the tall tower where Chris's labs were located. My steps slowed. Matthew looked up, and up some more.

"No. Please not there. It's worse than the Beinecke." His eyes were glued to the unappealing outlines of Kline Biology Tower, or KBT as it was known on campus. He'd likened the Beinecke, with its white marble walls carved into square hollows, to a giant ice-cube tray. "It reminds me of—"

"Your lab in Oxford was no great beauty either, as I recall," I said, cutting him off before he could give me another vivid analogy that would stay with me forever. "Let's go."

It was Matthew's turn to be reluctant now. He grumbled as we walked into the building, refused to put his blue-and-white Yale lanyard with its magnetized plastic ID card around his neck when the security guard asked him to, continued to complain in the elevator, and was glowering as we looked for the door to Chris's lab.

"It's going to be fine, Matthew. Chris's students will be thrilled to meet you," I assured him. Matthew was an internationally renowned scholar and a member of the Oxford University faculty. There were few institutions that impressed Yale, but that was one of them.

"The last time I was around students was when Hamish and I were fellows at All Souls." Matthew looked away in an effort to hide his nervousness. "I'm better suited to a research lab."

I pulled on his arm, forcing him to stop. Finally he met my eyes.

"You taught Jack all sorts of things. Annie, too," I reminded him, remembering how he'd been with the two children who had lived with us in Elizabethan London.

"That was different. They were . . ." Matthew trailed off, a shadow flitting through his eyes.

"Family?"

I waited for his response. He nodded reluctantly.

"Students want the same things Annie and Jack did: your attention, your honesty, and your faith in them. You're going to be brilliant at this. I promise."

"I'll settle for adequate," Matthew muttered. He scanned the hallway. "There's Christopher's lab. We should go. If I'm late, he's threatened to repossess my ID."

Chris pushed the door open, clearly frazzled. Matthew caught it and propped it open with his foot.

"Another minute, Clairmont, and I would have started without you. Hey, Diana," Chris said, kissing me on the cheek. "I didn't expect to see you here. Why aren't you at the Beinecke?"

"Special delivery." I motioned toward the messenger bag, and Matthew handed it over. "The page from Ashmole 782, remember?"

"Oh. Right." Chris didn't sound the least bit interested. He and Matthew were clearly focused on other questions.

"You two promised," I said.

"Right. Ashmole 782." Chris crossed his arms. "Where's Miriam?"

"I gave Miriam your invitation and will spare you her response. She will be here when—and if—she chooses." Matthew held up his ID card. Even the employment office couldn't take a bad picture of him. He looked like a model. "I'm official, or so they tell me."

"Good. Let's go." Chris took a white lab coat off the nearby rack and shrugged it over his shoulders. He held another out to Matthew.

Matthew looked at it dubiously. "I'm not wearing one of those."

"Suit yourself. No coat, no contact with the equipment. Up to you." Chris turned and marched off.

A woman approached him with a sheaf of papers. She was wearing a lab coat with the name CONNELLY embroidered on it and "Beaker" written above it in red marker.

"Thanks, Beaker." Chris looked them over. "Good. Nobody refused."

"What are those?" I asked.

"Nondisclosure forms. Chris said neither of you has to sign them." Beaker looked at Matthew and nodded in greeting. "We're honored to have you here, Professor Clairmont. I'm Joy Connelly, Chris's second-in-command. We're short a lab manager at the moment, so I'm filling in until Chris finds either Mother Teresa or Mussolini. Would you please swipe in so that we have a record of when you arrived? And you have to swipe out to leave. It keeps the records straight." She pointed to the reader by the door.

"Thank you, Dr. Connelly." Matthew obediently swiped his card. He was still not wearing a lab coat, though.

"Professor Bishop needs to swipe in, too. Lab protocol. And please call me Beaker. Everybody else does."

"Why?" Matthew asked while I fished my ID out of my bag. As usual, it had settled to the bottom.

"Chris finds nicknames easier to remember," Beaker said.

"He had seventeen Amys and twelve Jareds in his first undergraduate lecture," I added. "I don't think he'll ever recover."

"Happily, my memory is excellent, Dr. Connelly. So is your work on catalytic RNA, by the way." Matthew smiled. Dr. Connelly looked pleased.

"Beaker!" Chris bellowed.

"Coming!" Beaker called. "I sure hope he finds Mother Teresa soon," she muttered to me. "We don't need another Mussolini."

"Mother Teresa is dead," I whispered, running my card through the reader.

"I know. When Chris wrote the job description for the new lab manager, it listed 'Mother Teresa or Mussolini' under qualifications. We rewrote it, of course. Human Resources wouldn't have approved the posting otherwise."

"What did Chris call his last lab manager?" I was almost afraid to ask.

"Caligula." Beaker sighed. "We really miss her."

Matthew waited for us to enter before releasing the door. Beaker looked nonplussed by the courtesy. The door swooshed closed behind us.

A gaggle of white-coated researchers of all ages and descriptions waited for us inside, including senior researchers like Beaker, some exhausted-looking postdoctoral fellows, and a bevy of graduate students. Most sat on stools pulled up to the lab benches; a few lounged against sinks or cabinets. One sink bore a hand-lettered sign over it that said rather ominously THIS SINK RESERVED FOR HAZMAT. Tina, Chris's perpetually harried administrative assistant, was trying to extricate the filled-out nondisclosure forms from beneath a can of soda without disturbing the laptop that Chris was booting up. The hum of conversation stopped when we entered.

"Oh. My. God. That's—" A woman stared at Matthew and clapped a hand over her mouth. Matthew had been recognized.

"Hey, Professor Bishop!" A graduate student stood up, smoothing out his lab coat. He looked more nervous than Matthew. "Jonathan Garcia. Remember me? History of Chemistry? Two years ago?"

"Of course. How are you, Jonathan?" I felt several nudging looks as the attention in the room swung in my direction. There were daemons in Chris's lab. I looked around, trying to figure out who they were. Then I caught the cold stare of a vampire. He was standing by a locked cabinet with Beaker and another woman. Matthew had already noticed him.

"Richard," Matthew said with a cool nod. "I didn't know you'd left Berkeley."

"Last year." Richard's expression never wavered.

It had never occurred to me that there would already be creatures in Chris's lab. I'd visited him only once or twice, when he was working alone. My messenger bag suddenly felt heavy with secrets and possible disaster.

"There will be time for your reunion with Clairmont later, Shotgun," Chris said, hooking the laptop to a projector. There was a wave of appreciative laughter. "Lights please, Beaker."

The laughter quieted as the lights dimmed. Chris's research team leaned forward to see what he had projected on the whiteboard. Black-and-white bars marched across the top of the page, and the overflow was arranged underneath. Each bar—or ideogram, as Matthew had explained to me last night—represented a chromosome.

"This semester we have an all-new research project." Chris leaned against the whiteboard, his dark skin and white lab coat making him look like another ideogram on the display. "Here's our subject. Who wants to tell me what it is?"

"Is it alive or dead?" a cool female voice asked.

"Good question, Scully." Chris grinned.

"Why do you ask?" Matthew looked at the student sharply. Scully squirmed.

"Because," she explained, "if he's deceased—oh, the subject is male, by the way—the cause of death might have a genetic component."

The graduate students, eager to prove their worth, started tossing out rare and deadly genetic disorders faster than they could record them on their laptops.

"All right, all right." Chris held up his hand. "Our zoo has no more room for zebras. Back to basics, please."

Matthew's eyes danced with amusement. When I looked at him in confusion, he explained.

"Students tend to go for exotic explanations rather than the more obvious ones—like thinking a patient has SARS rather than a common cold. We call them 'zebras,' because they're hearing hoofbeats and concluding zebras rather than horses."

"Thanks." Between the nicknames and the wildlife, I was understandably disoriented.

"Stop trying to impress one another and look at the screen. What do you see?" Chris said, calling a halt to the escalating competition.

"It's male," said a weedy-looking young man in a bow tie, who was using a traditional laboratory notebook rather than a computer. Shotgun and Beaker rolled their eyes at each other and shook their heads.

"Scully already deduced that." Chris looked at them impatiently. He snapped his fingers. "Do *not* embarrass me in front of Oxford University, or you will all lift weights with me for the entire month of September."

Everybody groaned. Chris's level of physical fitness was legendary, as was his habit of wearing his old Harvard football jersey whenever Yale had a game. He was the only professor who was publicly, and routinely, booed in class.

"Whatever he is, he's not human," Jonathan said. "He has twenty-four chromosome pairs."

Chris looked down at his watch. "Four and a half minutes. Two minutes longer than I thought it would take, but much quicker than Professor Clairmont expected."

"Touché, Professor Roberts," Matthew said mildly. Chris's team slid glances in Matthew's direction, still trying to figure out what an Oxford professor was doing in a Yale research lab.

"Wait a minute. Rice has twenty-four chromosomes. We're studying *rice*?" asked a young woman I'd seen dining at Branford College.

"Of course we're not studying rice," Chris said with exasperation. "Since when did rice have a sex, Hazmat?" She must be the owner of the specially labeled sink.

"Chimps?" The young man who offered up this suggestion was handsome, in a studious sort of way, with his blue oxford shirt and wavy brown hair.

Chris circled one of the ideograms at the top of the display with a red Magic Marker. "Does that look like chromosome 2A for a chimp?"

"No," the young man replied, crestfallen. "The upper arm is too long. That looks like human chromosome 2."

"It is human chromosome 2." Chris erased his red mark and started to number the ideograms. When he got to the twenty-fourth, he circled it. "This is what we'll be focusing on this semester. Chromosome 24, known henceforward as CC so that the research team studying genetically modified rice over in Osborn doesn't get the heebie-jeebies. We have a lot of work to do. The DNA has been sequenced, but very few gene functions have been identified."

"How many base pairs?" Shotgun asked.

"Somewhere in the neighborhood of forty million," replied Chris.

"Thank God," Shotgun murmured, looking straight at Matthew. It sounded like an awful lot to me, but I was glad he was pleased.

"What does CC stand for?" asked a petite Asian woman.

"Before I answer that, I want to remind you that every person here has given Tina a signed nondisclosure agreement," Chris said.

"Are we working with something that will result in a patent?" A graduate student rubbed his hands together. "Excellent."

"We are working on a highly sensitive, highly confidential research project with far-reaching implications. What happens in this lab stays in this lab. No talking to your friends. No telling your parents. No boasting in the library. If you talk, you walk. Got it?"

Heads nodded.

"No personal laptops, no cell phones, no photographs. One lab terminal will have Internet access, but only Beaker, Shotgun, and Sherlock will have the access code," Chris continued, pointing to the senior researchers. "We'll be keeping lab notebooks the old-fashioned way, written in longhand on paper, and they will all be turned in to Beaker before you swipe out. For those who have forgotten how to use a pen, Bones will show you."

Bones, the weedy young man with the paper notebook, looked smug. A bit reluctantly the students parted with their cell phones, depositing them in a plastic bucket that Beaker carried around the room. Meanwhile Shotgun gathered up the laptops and locked them in a cabinet. Once the laboratory had been cleared of contraband electronics, Chris continued.

"When, in the fullness of time, we decide to go public with our findings—and yes, Professor Clairmont, they will one day be published, because that's what scientists do," Chris said, looking at Matthew sharply, "—none of you will have to worry about your careers ever again."

There were smiles all around.

"CC stands for 'creature chromosome.'"

The formerly smiling faces went blank.

"C-c-creature?" Bones asked.

"I told you there were aliens," said a man sitting next to Hazmat.

"He's not from outer space, Mulder," Chris said.

"Good name," I told Matthew, who looked bewildered. He didn't own a TV, after all. "I'll tell you why later."

"A werewolf?" Mulder said hopefully. Matthew scowled.

"No more guesses," Chris said hastily. "Okay, team. Hands up if you're a daemon."

Matthew's jaw dropped.

"What are you doing?" I whispered to Chris.

"Research," he replied, looking around the room. After a few moments of stunned silence, Chris snapped his fingers. "Come on. Don't be shy."

The Asian woman raised her hand. So did a young man who resembled a giraffe with his ginger-colored hair and long neck.

"Should have guessed it would be Game Boy and Xbox," Chris murmured. "Anyone else?"

"Daisy," the woman said, pointing to a dreamy-eyed creature wearing bright yellow and white clothes who was humming and staring out the window.

"Are you sure, Game Boy?" Chris sounded incredulous. "She's so . . . um, organized. And precise. She's nothing like you and Xbox."

"Daisy doesn't know it yet," Game Boy whispered, her forehead creased with concern, "so go easy on her. Finding out what you really are can freak you out."

"Perfectly understandable," Chris replied.

"What's a daemon?" Scully asked.

"A highly valued member of this research team who colors outside the lines." Chris's response was lightning quick. Shotgun pressed his lips together in amusement.

"Oh" was Scully's mild response.

"I must be a daemon, too, then," Bones claimed.

"Wannabe," Game Boy muttered.

Matthew's lips twitched.

"Wow. Daemons. I knew Yale was a better choice than Johns Hopkins," Mulder said. "Is this Xbox's DNA?"

Xbox looked at Matthew in silent entreaty. Daisy stopped humming and was now paying guarded attention to the conversation.

Matthew, Shotgun, and I were the grown-ups in this situation. Telling humans about creatures shouldn't be left to the students. I opened my mouth to reply, but Matthew put a hand on my shoulder.

"It's not your colleague's DNA," Matthew said. "It's mine."

"You're a daemon, too?" Mulder looked at Matthew with interest.

"No, I'm a vampire." Matthew stepped forward, joining Chris under the projector's light. "And before you ask, I can go outside during the day and my hair won't catch fire in the sunlight. I'm Catholic and have a crucifix. When I sleep, which is not often, I prefer a bed to a coffin. If you try to stake me, the wood will likely splinter before it enters my skin."

He bared his teeth. "No fangs either. And one last thing: I do not, nor have I ever, sparkled." Matthew's face darkened to emphasize the point.

I had been proud of Matthew on many previous occasions. I'd seen him stand up to a queen, a spoiled emperor, and his own awe-inspiring father. His courage—whether fighting with swords or struggling with his own daemons—was bone-deep. But nothing compared to how I felt watching him stand before a group of students and his scientific peers and own up to what he was.

"How old are you?" Mulder asked breathlessly. Like his namesake, Mulder was a true believer in all things wondrous and strange.

"Thirty-seven."

I heard exclamations of disappointment. Matthew took pity on them.

"Give or take about fifteen hundred years."

"Holy shit!" Scully blurted, looking as though her rational world had been turned inside out. "That's older than old. I just can't believe there's a vampire at Yale."

"You've obviously never been to the astronomy department," Game Boy said. "There are four vampires on the faculty there. And that new professor in economics—the woman they hired away from MIT—is definitely a vamp. Rumor has it there are a few in the chemistry department, but they keep to themselves."

"There are witches at Yale, too." My voice was quiet, and I avoided Shotgun's eyes. "We've lived alongside humans for millennia. Surely you'll want to study all three creature chromosomes, Professor Roberts?"

"I will." Chris's smile was slow and heartfelt. "Are you volunteering your DNA, Professor Bishop?"

"Let's take one creature chromosome at a time." Matthew gave Chris a warning look. He might be willing to let students pore over *his* genetic information, but Matthew remained unconvinced about letting them pry into mine.

Jonathan looked at me appraisingly. "So it's witches who sparkle?"

"It's really more of a glimmer," I said. "Not all witches have it. I'm one of the lucky ones, I guess." Saying the words felt freeing, and when nobody ran screaming from the room, I was flooded with a wave of relief and hope. I also had an insane urge to giggle.

"Lights, please," Chris said.

The lights came up gradually.

"You said we were working on several projects?" Beaker prompted.

"You'll be analyzing this, too." I reached into my messenger bag and drew out a large manila envelope. It was stiffened with cardboard inserts so that the contents wouldn't be bent and damaged. I untied the strings and pulled out the page from the Book of Life. The brightly colored illustration of the mystical union of Sol and Luna shone in the lab's fluorescent lights. Someone whistled. Shotgun straightened, his eyes fixed on the page.

"Hey, that's the chemical wedding of mercury and sulfur," Jonathan said. "I remember seeing something like that in class, Professor Bishop."

I gave my former student an approving nod.

"Shouldn't that be in the Beinecke?" Shotgun asked Matthew. "Or somewhere else that's safe?" The emphasis he placed on "safe" was so slight that I thought I might have imagined it. The expression on Matthew's face told me I hadn't.

"Surely it's safe here, Richard?" The prince-assassin was back in Matthew's smile. It made me uncomfortable to see Matthew's lethal personae among the flasks and test tubes.

"What are we supposed to do with it?" Mulder asked, openly curious.

"Analyze its DNA," I replied. "The illumination is on skin. I'd like to know how old the skin is—and the type of creature it came from."

"I just read about this kind of research," Jonathan said. "They're doing mtDNA analysis on medieval books. They hope it will help to date them and determine where they were made." Mitochondrial DNA recorded what an organism had inherited from all its maternal ancestors.

"Maybe you could pull those articles for your colleagues, in case they're not as well read as you are." Matthew looked pleased that Jonathan was up to date on the literature. "But we'll be extracting nuclear DNA as well as mtDNA."

"That's impossible," Shotgun protested. "The parchment has gone through a chemical process to turn skin into a writing surface. Both its age and the changes it underwent during manufacture would damage the DNA—if you could even extract enough to work with."

"It's difficult, but not impossible," Matthew corrected. "I've worked extensively with old, fragile, and damaged DNA. My methods should work with this sample, too."

There were excited looks around the room as the implications of the two research plans sank in. Both projects represented the kind of work that all scientists hoped to do, no matter what stage of their career they were in.

"You don't think cows or goats gave their hide for that page, do you, Dr. Bishop?" Beaker's uneasy voice quieted the room.

"No. I think it was a daemon, a human, a vampire, or a witch." I was pretty sure it wasn't human skin but couldn't rule it out entirely.

"Human?" Scully's eyes popped at the idea. The prospect of other creatures being flayed to make a book didn't seem to alarm her.

"Anthropodermic bibliopegy," Mulder whispered. "I thought it was a myth."

"Technically it's not anthropodermic bibliopegy," I said. "The book this came from isn't just bound in creature remains—it's completely constructed from it."

"Why?" Bones asked.

"Why not?" Daisy replied enigmatically. "Desperate times call for desperate measures."

"Let's not get ahead of ourselves," Matthew said, plucking the page from my fingers. "We're scientists. The whys come after the whats."

"I think that's enough for today," Chris said. "You all look like you need a break."

"I need a beer," Jonathan muttered.

"It's a bit early in the day, but I completely understand. Just remember—you talk, you walk," Chris said sternly. "That means no talking to each other outside these walls either. I don't want anyone to overhear."

"If someone did overhear us talking about witches and vampires, they'd just think we were playing D&D," Xbox said. Game Boy nodded.

"No. Talking," Chris repeated.

The door swooshed open. A tiny woman in a purple miniskirt, red boots, and a black T-shirt that read STAND BACK—I'M GOING TO TRY SCIENCE walked through.

Miriam Shephard had arrived.

"Who are you?" Chris demanded.

"Your worst nightmare—and new lab manager. Hi, Diana." Miriam pointed to the can of soda. "Whose is that?"

"Mine," Chris said.

"No food or drink in the lab. That goes double for you, Roberts," Miriam said, jabbing her finger in Chris's direction.

"Human Resources didn't tell me they were sending an applicant," Beaker said, confused.

"I'm not an applicant. I filled out the paperwork this morning, was hired, and got my dog tags." Miriam held up her ID card, which was, as mandated, attached to her lanyard.

"But I'm supposed to interview . . ." Chris began. "Who did you say you are?"

"Miriam Shephard. And HR waived the interview after I showed them this." Miriam pulled her cell phone out of her waistband. "I quote: 'Have your ass in my lab at nine A.M., and be prepared to explain my mistakes in two hours—no excuses.'" Miriam removed two sheets of paper from her messenger bag, which was stuffed with laptops and paper files. "Who is Tina?"

"I am." A smiling Tina stepped forward. "Hello, Dr. Shephard."

"Hello. I've got my hiring manifest or health-insurance waiver or something for you. And this is Roberts's formal reprimand for his inappropriate text message. File it." Miriam handed over the papers. She slung the bag from her shoulder and tossed it to Matthew. "I brought everything you asked for, Matthew."

The entire lab watched, openmouthed, as the bag full of computers sailed through the air. Matthew caught it without damaging a single laptop, and Chris looked at Miriam's throwing arm with naked admiration.

"Thank you, Miriam," Matthew murmured. "I trust you had an uneventful journey." His tone and choice of words were formal, but there was no disguising his relief at seeing her.

"I'm here, aren't I?" she said caustically. Miriam pulled another piece of paper out of the back pocket on her miniskirt. After examining it she looked up. "Which one of you is Beaker?"

"Here." Beaker walked toward Miriam, her hand extended. "Joy Connelly."

"Oh. Sorry. All I have is a ridiculous list of nicknames drawn from the dregs of popular culture, along with some acronyms." Miriam shook Beaker's hand, drew a pen out of her boot, and crossed something out. She scribbled something next to it. "Nice to meet you. I like your RNA work. Sound stuff. Very helpful. Let's go get coffee and figure out what needs to be done to whip this place into compliance."

"The closest decent coffee is a bit of a hike," Beaker said apologetically.

"Unacceptable." Miriam made another note on her paper. "We need a café in the basement as soon as possible. I toured the building on my way up here, and that space is wasted now."

"Should I come with you?" Chris asked, shifting on his feet.

"Not now," Miriam told him. "Surely you have something more important to do. I'll be back at one o'clock. That's when I want to see"—she paused and scrutinized her list—"Sherlock, Game Boy, and Scully."

"What about me, Miriam?" Shotgun asked.

"We'll catch up later, Richard. Nice to see a familiar face." She looked down at her list. "What does Roberts call you?"

"Shotgun." Richard's mouth twitched.

"I trust it's because of your speedy sequencing, not because you've taken to hunting like humans." Miriam's eyes narrowed. "Is what we're doing here going to be a problem, Richard?"

"Can't imagine why," Richard said with a small shrug. "The Congregation and its concerns are way above my pay grade."

"Good." Miriam surveyed her openly curious new charges. "Well? What are you waiting for? If you want something to do, you can always run some gels. Or unpack supply boxes. There are plenty of them stacked up in the corridor."

Everyone in the lab scattered.

"Thought so." She smiled at Chris. He looked nervous. "As for you, Roberts, I'll see you at two o'clock. We have your article to discuss. And your protocols to review. After that, you can take me to dinner. Somewhere nice, with steak and a good wine list."

Chris looked dazed but nodded.

"Could you give us a minute?" I asked Chris and Beaker. They moved off to the side, Beaker grinning from ear to ear and Chris pinching the bridge of his nose. Matthew joined us.

"You look surprisingly well for someone who's been to the sixteenth century and back, Matthew. And Diana's obviously *enceinte*," Miriam said, using the French word for "pregnant."

"Thanks. Are you at Marcus's place?" Matthew asked.

"That monstrosity on Orange Street? No chance. It's a convenient location, but it gives me the creeps." Miriam shivered. "Too much mahogany."

"You're welcome to stay with us on Court Street," I offered. "There's a spare bedroom on the third floor. You'd have privacy."

"Thanks, but I'm around the corner. At Gallowglass's condo," Miriam replied.

"What condo?" Matthew frowned.

"The one he bought on Wooster Square. Some converted church. It's very nice—a bit too Danish in decor, but far preferable to Marcus's dark-

and-gloomy period." Miriam looked at Matthew sharply. "Gallowglass did tell you he was coming with me?"

"No, he did not." Matthew ran his fingers through his hair.

I knew just how my husband felt: The de Clermonts had switched into overprotective mode. Only now they weren't protecting just me. They were protecting Matthew as well.

16

"Bad news, I'm afraid." Lucy Meriweather's lips twisted in a sympathetic grimace. She was one of the Beinecke librarians, and she'd helped me for years, both with my own research and on the occasions when I brought my students to the library to use the rare books there. "If you want to look at Manuscript 408, you'll have to go into a private room with a curator. And there's a limit of thirty minutes. They won't let you sit in the reading room with it."

"Thirty minutes? With a curator?" I was stunned by the restrictions, having spent the last ten months with Matthew, who never paid any attention to rules and regulations. "I'm a Yale professor. Why does a curator have to babysit me?"

"Those are the rules for everybody—even our own faculty. The whole thing *is* online," Lucy reminded me.

But a computer image, no matter how high the resolution, wasn't going to give me the information I needed. I'd last seen the Voynich manuscript—now Beinecke Library MS 408—in 1591, when Matthew had carried the book from Dr. Dee's library to the court of Emperor Rudolf in Prague, hoping that we could swap it for the Book of Life. Now I hoped it would shed light on what Edward Kelley might have done with the Book of Life's missing pages.

I'd been searching for clues to their whereabouts since we went to Madison. One missing page had an image of two scaly, long-tailed creatures bleeding into a round vessel. The other image was a splendid rendering of a tree, its branches bearing an impossible combination of flowers, fruit, and leaves and its trunk made up of writhing human shapes. I'd hoped that locating the two pages would be fairly straightforward in the age of Internet searches and digitized images. So far that had not been the case.

"Maybe if you could explain why you need to see the physical book . . ." Lucy trailed off.

But how could I tell Lucy I needed the book so I could use magic on it?

This was the Beinecke Library, for heaven's sake.

If anyone found out, it would ruin my career.

"I'll look at the Voynich tomorrow." Hopefully, I would have another plan by then, since I couldn't very well haul out my mother's book of shadows and devise new spells in front of a curator. Juggling my witch self and my scholar self was proving difficult. "Did the other books I requested arrive?"

"They did." Lucy's eyebrows lifted when she slid the collection of medieval magical texts across the desk, along with several early printed books. "Changing your research focus?"

In an effort to be prepared for any magical eventuality when finally it came time to recall Ashmole 782 and reunite it with its missing pages, I had called up books that might inspire my efforts to weave new higher-magic spells. Though my mother's spell book was a valuable resource, I knew from my own experience how far modern witches had fallen when compared to the witches of the past.

"Alchemy and magic aren't completely distinct," I told Lucy defensively. Sarah and Em had tried to get me to see that for years. At last I believed them.

Once I was settled in the reading room, the magical manuscripts were as intriguing as I'd hoped, with sigils that reminded me of weavers' knots and gramarye that was precise and potent. The early-modern books on witchcraft, most of which I knew only by title and reputation, were horrifying, however. Each one brimmed with hatred—for witches and anyone else who was different, rebellious, or refused to conform to societal expectations.

Hours later, still seething over Jean Bodin's vitriolic insistence that all foul opinions about witches and their evil deeds were warranted, I returned the books and manuscripts to Lucy and made an appointment for nine o'clock the next morning to view the Voynich manuscript with the head curator.

I tramped up the staircase to the main level of the library. Here, glass-encased books formed the Beinecke's spinal column, the core of knowledge and ideas around which the collection was built. Rows and rows of rare books were lined up on the shelves, bathed in light. It was a breathtaking sight, one that reminded me of my purpose as a historian: to rediscover the forgotten truths contained in those old, dusty volumes.

Matthew was waiting for me outside. He was lounging against the low wall overlooking the Beinecke's stark sculpture garden, his legs crossed at the ankles, thumbing through the messages on his phone. Sensing my presence, he looked up and smiled.

Not a creature alive could have resisted that smile or the look of concentration in those gray-green eyes.

"How was your day?" he asked after giving me a kiss. I'd asked him not to text me constantly, and he'd been unusually cooperative. As a result he genuinely didn't know.

"A bit frustrating. I suppose my research skills are bound to be rusty after so many months. Besides"—my voice dropped—"the books all look weird to me. They're so old and worn compared to how they looked in the sixteenth century."

Matthew put his head back and laughed. "I hadn't thought about that. Your surroundings have changed, too, since you last worked on alchemy at Baynard's Castle." He looked over his shoulder at the Beinecke. "I know the library is an architectural treasure, but I still think it looks like an ice-cube tray."

"So it does," I agreed with a smile. "I suppose if you'd built it, the Beinecke would look like a Norman keep or a Romanesque cloister."

"I was thinking of something Gothic—far more modern," Matthew teased. "Ready to go home?"

"More than ready," I said, wanting to leave Jean Bodin behind me.

He gestured at my book bag. "May I?"

Usually Matthew didn't ask. He was trying not to smother me, just as he was attempting to rein in his overprotectiveness. I rewarded him with a smile and handed it over without a word.

"Where's Roger?" I asked Lucy, looking down at my watch. I'd been granted exactly thirty minutes with the Voynich manuscript, and the curator was nowhere to be seen.

"Roger called in sick, just as he always does on the first day of classes. He hates the hysteria and all the freshmen asking for directions. You're stuck with me." Lucy picked up the box that held Beinecke MS 408.

"Sounds good." I tried to keep the excitement out of my voice. This might be exactly the break I needed.

Lucy led me to a small private room with windows overlooking the reading room, poor lighting, and a beat-up foam cradle. Security cameras mounted high on the walls would deter any reader from stealing or damaging one of the Beinecke's priceless books.

"I won't start the clock until you unwrap it." Lucy handed me the boxed manuscript. It was all she was carrying. There were no papers, reading materials, or even a cell phone to distract her from the job of monitoring me.

Though I normally flipped manuscripts open to look at the images, I wanted to take my time with the Voynich. I slid the manuscript's limp vellum binding—the early-modern equivalent of a paperback—through my fingers. Images flooded my mind, my witch's touch revealing that the present cover was put on the book several centuries after it was written and at least fifty years after I'd held it in Dee's library. I could see the bookbinder's face and seventeenth-century hairstyle when I touched the spine.

I carefully laid the Voynich in the waiting foam cradle and opened the book. I lowered my nose until it practically touched the first, stained page.

"What are you doing, Diana? Smelling it?" Lucy laughed softly.

"As a matter of fact, I am." If Lucy was going to cooperate with my strange requests this morning, I needed to be as honest as possible.

Openly curious, Lucy came around the table. She gave the Voynich a good sniff, too.

"Smells like an old manuscript to me. Lots of bookworm damage." She swung her reading glasses down and took an even closer look.

"Robert Hooke examined bookworms under his microscope in the seventeenth century. He called them 'the teeth of time.'" Looking at the first page of the Voynich, I could see why. It was riddled with holes in the upper right corner and the bottom margin, both of which were stained. "I think the bookworms must have been drawn to the oils that readers' fingers transferred to the parchment."

"What makes you say that?" Lucy asked. It was just the response I'd hoped for.

"The damage is worst where a reader would have touched to turn to the next folio." I rested my finger on the corner of the page, as if I were pointing to something.

That brief contact set off another explosion of faces, one morphing into another: Emperor Rudolf's avaricious expression; a series of unknown men dressed in clothing from different periods, two of them clerics; a woman taking careful notes; another woman packing up a box of books. And the daemon Edward Kelley, furtively tucking something into the Voynich's cover.

"There is a lot of damage on the bottom edge, too, where the manuscript would have rested against the body if you were carrying it." Ignorant of the slide show playing before my witch's third eye, Lucy peered down at the page. "The clothes of the time were probably pretty oily. Didn't most people wear wool?"

"Wool and silk." I hesitated, then decided to risk everything—my library card, my reputation, perhaps even my job. "Can I ask a favor, Lucy?"

She looked at me warily. "That depends."

"I want to rest my hand flat on the page. It will be only for a moment." I watched her carefully to gauge whether she was planning to call in the security guards for reinforcement.

"You can't touch the pages, Diana. You know that. If I let you, I would be fired."

I nodded. "I know. I'm sorry to put you in such a tough spot."

"Why do you need to touch it?" Lucy asked after a moment of silence, her curiosity aroused.

"I have a sixth sense when it comes to old books. Sometimes I can detect information about them that's not visible to the naked eye." That sounded weirder than I'd anticipated.

"Are you some kind of book witch?" Lucy's eyes narrowed.

"That's exactly what I am," I said with a laugh.

"I'd like to help you, Diana, but we're on camera—though there's no sound, thank God. Everything that happens in this room is taped, and someone is supposed to be watching the monitor whenever the room is occupied." She shook her head. "It's too risky."

"What if nobody could see what I was doing?"

"If you cut off the camera or put chewing gum on the lens—and yes, someone did try that—security will be here in five seconds," Lucy replied.

"I wasn't going to use chewing gum, but something like this." I pulled my familiar disguising spell around me. It would make any magic I worked all but invisible. Then I turned my right hand over and touched the tip of my ring finger to my thumb, pinching the green and yellow threads that filled the room into a tiny bundle. Together the two colors blended into the unnatural yellow-green that was good for disorientation and deception spells. I planned on tying them up in the fifth knot—since the security cameras definitely qualified as a challenge. The fifth knot's image burned at my right wrist in anticipation.

"Nice tats," Lucy commented, peering at my hands. "Why did you choose gray ink?"

Gray? When magic was in the air, my hands were every color of the rainbow. My disguising spell must be working.

"Because gray goes with everything." It was the first thing to cross my mind.

"Oh. Good thinking." She still looked puzzled.

I returned to my spell. It needed some black in it, as well as the yellow and green. I snagged the fine black threads that surrounded me on my left thumb and then slid them through a loop made by my right thumb and ring finger. The result looked like an unorthodox mudra—one of the hand positions in yoga.

"With knot of five, the spell will thrive," I murmured, envisioning the completed weaving with my third eye. The twist of yellow-green and black tied itself into an unbreakable knot with five crossings.

"Did you just bewitch the Voynich?" Lucy whispered with alarm.

"Of course not." After my experiences with bewitched manuscripts, I wouldn't do such a thing lightly. "I bewitched the air around it."

To show Lucy what I meant, I moved my hand over the first page, hovering about two inches above the surface. The spell made it appear that my fingers stopped at the bottom of the book.

"Um, Diana? Whatever you were trying to do didn't work. You're just touching the edge of the page like you're supposed to," Lucy said.

"Actually my hand is over here." I wiggled my fingers so that they peeked out over the top edge of the book. It was a bit like the old magician's trick where a woman was put in a box and the box was sawed in half. "Try it. Don't touch the page yet—just move your hand so that it covers the text."

I slid my hand out to give Lucy room. She followed my directions and slid her hand between the Voynich and the deception spell. Her hand appeared to stop when it reached the edge of the book, but if you looked carefully, you could see that her forearm was getting shorter. She withdrew quickly, as though she'd touched a hot pan. She turned to me and stared.

"You are a witch." Lucy swallowed, then smiled. "What a relief. I always suspected you were hiding something, and I was afraid it might be something unsavory—or even illegal." Like Chris, she didn't seem remotely surprised to discover that there really *were* witches.

"Will you let me break the rules?" I glanced down at the Voynich.

"Only if you tell me what you learn. This damned manuscript is the bane of our existence. We get ten requests a day to see it and turn down almost every one." Lucy returned to her seat and adopted a watchful position. "But be careful. If someone sees you, you'll lose your library privileges. And I don't think you would survive if you were banned from the Beinecke."

I took a deep breath and stared down at the open book. The key to activating my magic was curiosity. But if I wanted more than a dizzying display of faces, I would need to formulate a careful question before putting hand to parchment. I was more certain than ever that the Voynich held important clues about the Book of Life and its missing pages. But I was only going to get one chance to find out what they were.

"What did Edward Kelley place inside the Voynich, and what happened to it?" I whispered before looking down and gently resting my hand on the first folio of the manuscript.

One of the missing pages from the Book of Life appeared before my eyes: the illumination of the tree with its trunk full of writhing, human shapes. It was gray and ghostly, transparent enough that I could see through it to my hand and the writing on the Voynich's first folio.

A second shadowy page appeared atop the first: two dragons shedding their blood so that it fell into a vessel below.

A third insubstantial page layered over the previous two: the illumination of the alchemical wedding.

For a moment the layers of text and image remained stacked in a magical palimpsest atop the Voynich's stained parchment. Then, the alchemical wedding dissolved, followed by the picture of the two dragons. But the page with the tree remained.

Hopeful that the image had become real, I lifted my hand from the page and withdrew it. I gathered up the knot at the heart of the spell and jammed it over my pencil eraser, rendering it temporarily invisible and revealing Beinecke MS 408. My heart sank. There was no missing page from the Book of Life there.

"Not what you expected to see?" Lucy looked at me sympathetically.

"No. Something was here once—a few pages from another manuscript—but they're long gone." I pinched the bridge of my nose.

"Maybe the sale records mention them. We have boxes of paperwork on the Voynich's acquisition. Do you want to see them?" she asked.

The dates of book sales and the names of the people who bought and sold the books could be assembled into a genealogy that described a book's history and descent right down to the present. In this case it might also provide clues as to who might once have owned the pictures of the tree and the dragons that Kelley removed from the Book of Life.

"Absolutely!" I replied.

Lucy boxed up the Voynich and returned it to the locked hold. She returned shortly thereafter with a trolley loaded with folders, boxes, various notebooks, and a tube.

"Here's everything on the Voynich, in all its confusing glory. It's been picked through thousands of times by researchers, but nobody was looking for three missing manuscript pages." She headed toward our private room. "Come on. I'll help you sort through it all."

It took thirty minutes simply to organize the materials on the long table. Some of it would be no use at all: the tube and the scrapbook full of newspaper clippings, the old photostats, and lectures and articles written about the manuscript after the collector Wilfrid Voynich purchased it in 1912. That still left folders full of correspondence, handwritten notes, and a clutch of notebooks kept by Wilfrid's wife, Ethel.

"Here's a copy of the chemical analysis of the manuscript, a printout of the cataloging information, and a list of everyone granted access to the manuscript in the past three years." Lucy handed me a sheaf of papers. "You can keep them. Don't tell anyone I gave you that list of library patrons, though."

Matthew would have to go over the chemistry with me—it was all about the inks used in the manuscript, a subject that interested both of us. The list of people who'd seen the manuscript was surprisingly short. Hardly anyone got to look at it anymore. Those who had been granted access were mostly academics—a historian of science from the University of Southern California and another from Cal State Fullerton, a mathematician-cryptographer from Princeton, another from Australia. I'd had coffee with one of the visitors before leaving for Oxford: a writer of popular fiction who was interested in alchemy. One name jumped off the page, though.

Peter Knox had seen the Voynich this past May, before Emily died.

"That bastard." My fingers tingled, and the knots on my wrists burned in warning.

"Something wrong?" Lucy asked.

"There was a name on the list I didn't expect to see."

"Ah. A scholarly rival." She nodded sagely.

"I guess you could say that." But my difficulty with Knox was more than an argument over competing historical interpretations. This was war. And if I were going to win it, I would need to pull ahead of him for a change.

The problem was that I had little experience tracking down manuscripts and establishing their provenance. The papers I knew best had belonged to the chemist Robert Boyle. All seventy-four volumes of them had been presented to the Royal Society in 1769, and, like everything else in the Royal Society archives, they were meticulously cataloged, indexed, and cross-referenced.

"If I want to trace the Voynich's chain of ownership, where do I start?" I mused aloud, staring at the materials.

"The fastest way would be for one of us to start at the manuscript's origins and work forward while the other starts at the Beinecke's acquisition of it and works backward. With luck we'll meet at the middle." Lucy handed me a folder. "You're the historian. You take the old stuff."

I opened the folder, expecting to see something relating to Rudolf II. Instead I found a letter from a mathematician in Prague, Johannes Marcus Marci. It was written in Latin, dated 1665, and sent to someone in Rome addressed as *"Reverende et Eximie Domine in Christo Pater."* The recipient was a cleric then, perhaps one of the men I'd seen when I touched the corner of the Voynich's first page.

I quickly scanned the rest of the text, noting that the cleric was a Father Athanasius and that Marci's letter was accompanied by a mysterious book that needed deciphering. The Book of Life, perhaps?

Marci said that attempts had been made to contact Father Athanasius before, but the letters had been met with silence. Excited, I kept reading. When the third paragraph revealed the identity of Father Athanasius, however, my excitement turned to dismay.

"The Voynich manuscript once belonged to Athanasius Kircher?" If the missing pages had passed into Kircher's hands, they could be anywhere.

"I'm afraid so," Lucy replied. "I understand he was quite . . . er, wide-ranging in his interests."

"That's an understatement," I said. Athanasius Kircher's modest goal had been nothing less than universal knowledge. He had published forty books and was an internationally bestselling author as well as an inventor. Kircher's museum of rare and ancient objects was a famous stop on early European grand tours, his range of correspondents extensive, and his library vast. I didn't have the language skills to work through Kircher's oeuvre. More important, I lacked the time.

My phone vibrated in my pocket, making me jump.

"Excuse me, Lucy." I slid the phone out and checked the display. On it was a text message from Matthew.

Where are you? Gallowglass is waiting for you. We have a doctor's appointment in ninety minutes.

I cursed silently.

I'm just leaving the Beinecke, I typed back.

"My husband and I have a date, Lucy. I'm going to have to pick up with this again tomorrow," I said, closing the folder containing Marci's letter to Kircher.

"A reliable source told me you were on campus with someone tall, dark, and handsome." Lucy grinned.

"That's my husband, all right," I said. "Can I look through this stuff to-morrow?"

"Leave everything with me. Things are pretty slow around here at the moment. I'll see what I can piece together."

"Thanks for your help, Lucy. I'm under a tight—and nonnegotiable—deadline." I scooped up pencil, laptop, and pad of paper and rushed to meet Gallowglass. Matthew had seconded his nephew to act as my security de-tail. Gallowglass was also responsible for monitoring Benjamin's Internet feed, but so far the screen had remained blank.

"Hello, Auntie. You're looking bonny." He kissed me on the cheek.

"I'm sorry. I'm late."

"Of course you're late. You were with your books. I didn't expect you for another hour at least," Gallowglass said, dismissing my apology.

When we got to the lab, Matthew had the image of the alchemical wedding from Ashmole 782 in front of him and was so absorbed that he didn't even look up when the door pinged. Chris and Sherlock were standing at his shoulder, watching intently. Scully sat on a rolling stool nearby. Game Boy had a tiny instrument in her hand and was holding it dangerously close to the manuscript page.

"You get scruffier all the time, Gallowglass. When did you last comb your hair?" Miriam swiped a card through the reader at the door. It was marked VISITOR. Chris was taking security seriously.

"Yesterday." Gallowglass patted the back and sides of his head. "Why? Is a bird nesting in it?"

"One might well be." Miriam nodded in my direction. "Hi, Diana. Matthew will be with you soon."

"What's he doing?" I asked.

"Trying to teach a postgraduate student with no knowledge of biology or proper laboratory procedures how to remove DNA samples from parchment." Miriam looked at the group surrounding Matthew with disapproval. "I don't know why Roberts funds creatures who don't even know how to run agarose gels, but I'm just the lab manager."

Across the room Game Boy let out a frustrated expletive.

"Pull up a stool. This could be a while." Miriam rolled her eyes.

"Don't worry. It takes practice," Matthew told Game Boy, his voice soothing. "I'm nothing but thumbs with that computer game of yours. Try again."

Again? My mouth dried up. Making repeated stabs at the page from Ashmole 782 might damage the palimpsest. I started toward my husband, and Chris spotted me.

"Hey, Diana." He intercepted me with a hug. He looked at Gallowglass. "I'm Chris Roberts. Diana's friend."

"Gallowglass. Matthew's nephew." Gallowglass surveyed the room, and his nose wrinkled. "Something stinks."

"The grad students played a little joke on Matthew." Chris pointed to the computer terminal, which was festooned with wreaths of garlic bulbs. A crucifix designed for a car dashboard was attached to the mouse pad with a suction cup. Chris turned his attention to Gallowglass's neck with an intensity that was practically vampiric. "Do you wrestle?"

"Weeell, I have been known to do so for sport." Gallowglass looked down shyly, his cheeks dimpled.

"Not Greco-Roman by any chance?" Chris asked. "My partner injured his knee and will be in rehab for months. I'm looking for a temporary replacement."

"It must be Greek. I'm not sure about the Roman part."

"Where did you learn?" Chris asked.

"My grandfather taught me." Gallowglass scrunched up his face as his concentration deepened. "I think he wrestled a giant once. He was a fierce fighter."

"Is this a vampire grandfather?" Chris asked.

Gallowglass nodded.

"Vampire wrestling must be fun to watch." Chris grinned. "Like alligator wrestling, but without the tail."

"No wrestling. I'm serious, Chris." I wanted no responsibility, no matter how indirect, for causing bodily harm to a MacArthur genius.

"Spoilsport." Chris let out a piercing whistle. "Wolfman! Your wife is here."

Wolfman?

"I was aware of that, Christopher." Matthew's tone was frosty, but he gave me a warm smile that made my toes curl. "Hello, Diana. I'll be with you as soon as I'm finished with Janette."

"Game Boy's name is Janette?" Chris murmured. "Who knew?"

"I did. So did Matthew. Perhaps you could tell me why she's in my lab?" Miriam asked. "Janette's Ph.D. will be in computational bioinformatics. She belongs in a room full of terminals, not test tubes."

"I like the way her brain works," Chris said with a shrug. "She's a gamer and sees patterns in lab results that the rest of us miss. So she never did advanced work in biology. Who cares? I'm up to my eyeballs in biologists already."

Chris looked at Matthew and Game Boy working together and shook his head.

"What's wrong?" I asked.

"Matthew is wasted in a research laboratory. Your husband belongs in a classroom. He's a born teacher." Chris tapped Gallowglass on the arm. "Call me if you want to meet up in the gym. Diana has my number."

Chris went back to his work and I turned my attention to Matthew. I'd only seen flashes of this side of my husband, when he was interacting with Annie or Jack in London, but Chris was right. Matthew was using all the tools in a teacher's bag of tricks: modeling, positive reinforcement, patience, just the right amount of praise, and a touch of humor.

"Why can't we just swab the surface again?" Game Boy asked. "I know it came up with mouse DNA, but if we picked a fresh spot, it might be different."

"Maybe," Matthew said, "but there were a lot of mice in medieval libraries. Still, you should feel free to swab it again after you've taken this sample."

Game Boy sighed and steadied her hand.

"Deep breath, Janette." Matthew gave her an encouraging nod. "Take your time."

With great care Game Boy inserted a needle so fine it was almost invisible into the very edge of the parchment.

"There you go," Matthew said softly. "Slow and steady."

"I did it!" Game Boy shouted. You would have thought she'd split the atom. There were whoops of support, a high five, and a muttered "About time" from Miriam. But it was Matthew's response that mattered. Game Boy turned to him expectantly.

"Eureka," Matthew said, his hands spread wide. Game Boy grinned broadly. "Well done, Janette. We'll make a geneticist out of you yet."

"No way. I'd rather build a computer from spare parts than do that again." Game Boy stripped her gloves off quickly.

"Hello, darling. How was your day?" Matthew rose and kissed me on the cheek. One eyebrow lifted as he looked at Gallowglass, who silently conveyed that all was well.

"Let's see . . . I worked some magic in the Beinecke."

"Should I worry?" Matthew asked, clearly thinking of the havoc that witchwind and witchfire might cause.

"Nope," I said. "And I have a lead on one of the missing pages from Ashmole 782."

"That was quick. You can tell me about it on our way to the doctor's office," he said, swiping his card through the reader.

"By all means take your time with Diana. There's nothing pressing here.

One hundred and twenty-five vampire genes identified and only four hundred to go," Miriam called as we left. "Chris will be counting the minutes."

"Five hundred genes to go!" Chris shouted.

"Your gene prediction is way off," Miriam replied.

"A hundred bucks says it's not." Chris glanced up from a report.

"That the best you can do?" Miriam pursed her lips.

"I'll empty my piggy bank when I get home and let you know, Miriam,"
Chris said. Miriam's lips twitched.

"Let's go," said Matthew, "before they start arguing about something
else."

"Oh, they're not arguing," Gallowglass said, holding the door open for
us. "They're flirting."

My jaw dropped. "What makes you say that?"

"Chris likes to give people nicknames." Gallowglass turned to Matthew.
"Chris called you Wolfman. What does he call Miriam?"

Matthew thought for a moment. "Miriam."

"Exactly." Gallowglass grinned from ear to ear.

Matthew swore.

"Don't fret, Uncle. Miriam hasn't given any man a tumble since Bertrand was killed."

"Miriam . . . and a human?" Matthew sounded stunned.

"Nothing will come of it," Gallowglass said soothingly as the elevator
doors opened. "She will break Chris's heart, of course, but there's naught we
can do about it."

I was deeply grateful to Miriam. Now Matthew and Gallowglass had
someone to worry about besides me.

"Poor lad." Gallowglass sighed, pushing the button that closed the elevator doors. As we descended, he cracked his knuckles. "Perhaps I will wrestle
with him after all. A good thrashing always clears the mind."

A few days ago, I'd worried whether the vampires would survive being at
Yale once the students and faculty were around.

Now I wondered whether Yale would survive the vampires.

17

I stood in front of the refrigerator, staring at the images of our children with my hands curved around my belly. Where had the month of September gone?

The three-dimensional ultrasound pictures of Baby A and Baby B—Matthew and I had elected not to learn the sexes of our two children—were uncanny. Instead of the familiar ghostly silhouette I'd seen in friends' pregnancy scans, these revealed detailed images of faces with crinkled brows, thumbs rammed into mouths, perfectly bowed lips. My finger reached out, and I touched Baby B's nose.

Cool hands slid around me from behind, and a tall, muscular body provided a strong pillar for me to rest against. Matthew pressed lightly on a spot a few inches above my pubic bone.

"B's nose is just there in that picture," he said softly. His other hand rested a bit higher on the swell of my belly. "Baby A was here."

We stood silently as the chain that had always joined me to Matthew extended to accommodate these two bright, fragile links. For months I had *known* that Matthew's children—our children—were growing inside me. But I had not *felt* it. Everything was different now that I'd seen their faces, crumpled in concentration as they did the hard work of becoming.

"What are you thinking?" Matthew asked, curious about my extended silence.

"I'm not thinking. I'm feeling." And what I was feeling was impossible to describe.

His laugh was soft, as though he didn't want to disturb the babies' sleep.

"They're both all right," I assured myself. "Normal. Perfect."

"They are perfectly healthy. But none of our children will ever be normal. And thank God for that." He kissed me. "What's on your schedule for today?"

"More work at the library." My initial, magical lead that had promised to reveal the fate of at least one of the Book of Life's missing pages had turned into weeks of hard, scholarly slogging. Lucy and I had been working steadily to discover just how the Voynich manuscript came into Athanasius Kircher's hands and later into Yale's possession, hoping to catch a trace of the mysterious tree image that had remained superimposed on the Voynich for a few precious moments. We'd set up camp in the same small private room where I'd worked my spell so that we could talk without disturbing the growing number of students and faculty using the Beinecke's adjacent reading room. There we'd pored over library lists and indexes of Kircher's correspondence, and we'd written dozens of letters to various experts in the United States and abroad—with no concrete results.

"You're remembering what the doctor said about taking breaks?" Matthew asked. With the exception of the ultrasound, our trip to the doctor's office had been sobering. She had drummed into me the dangers of premature labor and preeclampsia, the necessity of staying hydrated, my body's additional need for rest.

"My blood pressure is fine." This, I understood, was one of the biggest risks: that through a combination of dehydration, fatigue, and stress, my blood pressure would suddenly spike.

"I know." Monitoring my blood pressure was my vampire husband's responsibility, and Matthew took it seriously. "But it won't remain that way if you push yourself."

"This is my twenty-fifth week of pregnancy, Matthew. It's almost October."

"I know that, too."

After October 1 the doctor was grounding me. If we remained in New Haven where we could continue working, the only way to get to the Bodleian Library would be by some combination of boat, plane, and automobile. Even now I was restricted to flights of no more than three hours.

"We can still get you to Oxford by plane." Matthew knew of my concerns. "It will have to stop in Montreal, and then Newfoundland, Iceland, and Ireland, but if you *must* get to London, we can manage it." His expression suggested that he and I might have different ideas about what circumstances would justify my crossing the Atlantic in this hopscotch fashion. "Of course, if you'd prefer we can go to Europe now."

"Let's not borrow trouble." I pulled away from him. "Tell me about your day."

"Chris and Miriam think they have a new approach to understanding the blood-rage gene," he said. "They're planning to trawl through my genome using one of Marcus's theories about noncoding DNA. Their current hypothesis is that it might contain triggers that control how and to what extent blood rage manifests in a given individual."

"This is Marcus's junk DNA—the ninety-eight percent of the genome that doesn't code proteins, right?" I took a bottle of water out of the fridge and popped the cap off to show my commitment to hydration.

"That's right. I'm still resistant to the notion, but the evidence they're pulling together is convincing." Matthew looked wry. "I really am an old Mendelian fossil, just as Chris said."

"Yes, but you're *my* Mendelian fossil," I said. Matthew laughed. "And if Marcus's hypothesis is correct, what will that mean in terms of finding a cure?"

His smile died. "It may mean that there is no cure—that blood rage is a hereditary genetic condition that develops in response to a multitude of factors. It can be far easier to cure a disease with a single, unequivocal cause, like a germ or a single gene mutation."

"Can the contents of my genome help?" There had been much discussion of the babies since I'd had my ultrasound, and speculation as to what effect a witch's blood—a weaver's in particular—might have on the blood-rage gene. I didn't want my children to end up as science experiments, especially after seeing Benjamin's horrific laboratory, but I had no objection to doing my bit for scientific progress.

"I don't want your DNA to be the subject of further scientific research." Matthew stalked to the window. "I should never have taken that sample from you back in Oxford."

I smothered a sigh. With every hard-won freedom Matthew granted me and each conscious effort he made not to smother me with overpossessiveness, his authoritarian traits had to find a new outlet. It was like watching someone try to dam up a raging river. And Matthew's inability to locate Benjamin and release his captive witch were only making it worse. Every lead Matthew received about Benjamin's current location turned into a dead end, just like my attempts to trace Ashmole 782's missing pages. Before I could try to reason with him, my phone rang. It was a distinctive ringtone—the opening bars of "Sympathy for the Devil"—which I had not yet managed to change. When the phone was programmed, someone had irrevocably attached it to one of my contacts.

"Your brother is calling." Matthew's tone was capable of freezing Old Faithful.

"What do you want, Baldwin?" There was no need for polite preamble.

"Your lack of faith wounds me, sister." Baldwin laughed. "I'm in New York. I thought I might come to New Haven and make sure that your accommodations are suitable."

Matthew's vampire hearing made my conversation with Baldwin completely audible. The oath he uttered in response to his brother's words was blistering.

"Matthew is with me. Gallowglass and Miriam are one block away. Mind your own business." I drew the phone from my ear, eager to disconnect.

"Diana." Baldwin's voice managed to extend to even my limited human hearing.

I returned the phone to my ear.

"There is another vampire working in Matthew's lab—Richard Bellingham is the name he goes by now."

"Yes." My eyes went to Matthew, who was standing in a deceptively relaxed position in front of the window—legs spread slightly, hands clasped behind his back. It was a stance of readiness.

"Be careful around him." Baldwin's voice flattened. "You don't want me to have to order Matthew to get rid of Bellingham. But I will do that, without hesitation, should I think he possesses information that could prove . . . difficult . . . for the family."

"He knows I'm a witch. And that I'm pregnant." It was evident that Baldwin knew a great deal about our life in New Haven already. There was no point in hiding the truth.

"Every vampire in that provincial town knows. And they travel to New York. Often." Baldwin paused. "In my family if you create a mess, you clean it up—or Matthew does. Those are your options."

"It's always such a pleasure to hear from you, *brother*."

Baldwin merely laughed.

"Is that all, *milord*?"

"It's '*sieur*.' Do you need me to refresh your memory of vampire law and etiquette?"

"No," I said, spitting out the word.

"Good. Tell Matthew to stop blocking my calls, and we won't have to repeat this conversation." The line went dead.

"That f—" I began.

Matthew wrenched the phone out of my hand and flung it across the room. It made a satisfying sound of breaking glass when it hit the mantel of the defunct fireplace. Then his hands were cradling my face as though the violent moment that came before had been a mirage.

"Now I'll have to get another phone." I looked into Matthew's stormy eyes. They were a reliable indication of his state of mind: clear gray when he was at ease, appearing green when his pupils enlarged with emotion and blotted out all but the bright rim around his iris. At the moment, the gray and green were battling for supremacy.

"Baldwin will no doubt have one here before the day is done." Matthew's attention fixed on the pulse at my throat.

"Let's hope your brother doesn't feel he needs to deliver it himself."

Matthew's eyes drifted to my lips. "He's not my brother. He's *your* brother."

"Hello the house!" Gallowglass's booming, cheerful voice rose up from the downstairs hall.

Matthew's kiss was hard and demanding. I gave him what he needed, deliberately softening my spine and my mouth so that he could feel, in this moment at least, that he was in charge.

"Oh. Sorry. Shall I come back?" Gallowglass said from the stairs. Then his nostrils flared as he detected my husband's overpowering clove scent. "Something wrong, Matthew?"

"Nothing that Baldwin's sudden and seemingly accidental death wouldn't fix," Matthew said darkly.

"Business as usual, then. I thought you might want me to walk Auntie to the library."

"Why?" Matthew asked.

"Miriam called. She's in a mood and wants you to 'get out of Diana's knickers and into my lab.'" Gallowglass consulted the palm of his hand. It was covered in writing. "Yep. That's exactly what she said."

"I'll get my bag," I murmured, pulling away from Matthew.

"Hello, Apple and Bean." Gallowglass stared, besotted, at the images on the fridge. He thought calling them Baby A and Baby B was beneath their dignity and so had bestowed nicknames upon them. "Bean has Granny's fingers. Did you notice, Matthew?"

Gallowglass kept the mood light and the banter flowing on our walk to campus. Matthew accompanied us to the Beinecke, as though he expected Baldwin to rise up out of the sidewalk before us with a new phone and another dire warning.

Leaving the de Clermonts behind, it was with relief that I opened the door into our research room.

"I've never seen such a tangled provenance!" Lucy exclaimed the moment I appeared. "So John Dee *did* own the Voynich?"

"That's right." I put down my pad of paper and my pencil. Other than my magic, they were the only items I carried. Happily, my power didn't set off the metal detectors. "Dee gave the Voynich to Emperor Rudolf in exchange for Ashmole 782." It was, in truth, a bit more complicated than that, as was often the case when Gallowglass and Matthew were involved in the transfer of property.

"The Bodleian Library manuscript that's missing three pages?" Lucy held her head in her hands and stared down at the notes, clippings, and correspondence littering the table.

"Edward Kelley removed those pages before Ashmole 782 was sent back to England. Kelley temporarily put them inside the Voynich for safekeeping. At some point he gave two of the pages away. But he kept one for himself—the page with the illumination of a tree on it." It really was impossibly tangled.

"So it must have been Kelley who gave the Voynich manuscript—along with the picture of the tree—to Emperor Rudolf's botanist, the Jacobus de Tepenecz whose signature is on the back of the first folio." Time had faded the ink, but Lucy had shown me photographs taken under ultraviolet light.

"Probably," I said.

"And after the botanist, an alchemist owned it?" She made some annotations on her Voynich timeline. It was looking a bit messy with our constant deletions and additions.

"Georg Baresch. I haven't been able to find out much about him." I studied my own notes. "Baresch was friends with de Tepenecz, and Marci acquired the Voynich from him."

"The Voynich manuscript's illustrations of strange flora would certainly intrigue a botanist—not to mention the illumination of a tree from Ashmole 782. But why would an alchemist be interested in them?" Lucy asked.

"Because some of the Voynich's illustrations resemble alchemical apparatus. The ingredients and processes needed to make the philosopher's stone were jealously guarded secrets, and alchemists often hid them in symbols: plants, animals, even people." The Book of Life contained the same potent blend of the real and the symbolic.

"And Athanasius Kircher was interested in words and symbols, too. That's why you think he would have been interested in the illumination of the tree as well as the Voynich," Lucy said slowly.

"Yes. It's why the missing letter that Georg Baresch claims he sent to Kircher in 1637 is so significant." I slid a folder in her direction. "The Kircher expert I know from Stanford is in Rome. She volunteered to go to the Pontifical Gregorian University archives, where the bulk of Kircher's correspondence is kept, and nose around. She sent me a transcription of the later letter from Baresch to Kircher written in 1639. It refers back to their exchange, but the Jesuits told her the original letter can't be found."

"When librarians say 'it's lost,' I always wonder if that's really true," she grumbled.

"Me, too." I thought wryly of my experiences with Ashmole 782.

Lucy opened the folder and groaned. "This is in Latin, Diana. You're going to have to tell me what it says."

"Baresch thought Kircher might be able to decipher the Voynich's secrets. Kircher had been working on Egyptian hieroglyphs. It made him an international celebrity, and people sent him mysterious texts and writings from far and wide," I explained. "To better hook Kircher's interest, Baresch forwarded partial transcripts of the Voynich to Rome in 1637 and again in 1639."

"There's no specific mention of a picture of a tree, though," Lucy said.

"No. But it's still possible that Baresch sent it to Kircher as an additional lure. It's of a much higher quality than the Voynich's pictures." I sat back in my chair. "I'm afraid that's as far as I've been able to get. What have you found out about the book sale where Wilfrid Voynich acquired the manuscript?"

Just as Lucy opened her mouth to reply, a librarian rapped on the door and entered.

"Your husband is on the phone, Professor Bishop." He looked at me in disapproval. "Please tell him that we aren't a hotel switchboard and don't usually take calls for our patrons."

"Sorry," I said, getting out of my chair. "I had an accident with my phone this morning. My husband is a bit . . . er, overprotective." I gestured apologetically at my rounded form.

The librarian looked slightly mollified and pointed to a phone on the wall that had a single flashing light. "Use that."

"How did Baldwin get here so fast?" I asked Matthew when we were connected. It was the only thing I could think of that would make Matthew call the library's main number. "Did he come by helicopter?"

"It's not Baldwin. We've discovered something strange about the picture of the chemical wedding from Ashmole 782."

"Strange how?"

"Come and see. I'd rather not talk about it on the phone."

"Be right there." I hung up and turned to Lucy. "I'm so sorry, Lucy, but I have to go. My husband wants me to help with a problem in his lab. Can we continue later?"

"Sure," she said.

I hesitated. "Would you like to come with me? You could meet Matthew—and see a page from Ashmole 782."

"One of the fugitive sheets?" Lucy was out of her chair in an instant. "Give me a minute and I'll meet you upstairs."

Rushing outside, we ran smack into my bodyguard.

"Slow down, Auntie. You don't want to joggle the babes." Gallowglass gripped my elbow until I was steady on my feet, then gazed down at my petite companion. "Are you all right, miss?"

"M-me?" Lucy stammered, craning her neck to make eye contact with the big Gael. "I'm fine."

"Just checking," Gallowglass said kindly. "I'm as big as a galleon under full sail. Running into me has bruised men far bigger than you."

"This is my husband's nephew, Gallowglass. Gallowglass, Lucy Meriweather. She's coming with us." After that hasty introduction, I dashed in the direction of Kline Biology Tower, my bag banging against my hip. After a few clumsy strides, Gallowglass took the bag and transferred it to his own arm.

"He carries your books?" Lucy whispered.

"And groceries," I whispered back. "He would carry me, too, if I let him." Gallowglass snorted.

"Hurry," I said, my worn sneakers squeaking on the polished floors of the building where Matthew and Chris worked.

At the doorway to Chris's lab, I swiped my ID card and the doors opened. Miriam was waiting for us inside, looking at her watch.

"Time!" she called. "I won. Again. That's ten dollars, Roberts."

Chris groaned. "I was sure Gallowglass would slow her down." The lab was quiet today, with only a handful of people working. I waved at Beaker. Scully was there, too, standing next to Mulder and a digital scale.

"Sorry to interrupt your research, but we wanted you to know straightaway what we discovered." Matthew glanced at Lucy.

"Matthew, this is Lucy Meriweather. I thought Lucy should see the page from Ashmole 782, since she's spending so much time searching for its lost siblings," I explained.

"A pleasure, Lucy. Come see what you're helping Diana to find." Matthew's expression went from wary to welcoming, and he gestured toward Mulder and Scully. "Miriam, can you log Lucy in as a guest?"

"Already done." Miriam tapped Chris on the shoulder. "Staring at that genetic map isn't getting you anywhere, Roberts. Take a break."

Chris flung down his pen. "We need more data."

"We're scientists. Of course we need more data." The air between Chris and Miriam hummed with tension. "Come and look at the pretty picture anyway."

"Oh, okay," Chris grumbled, giving Miriam a sheepish smile.

The illumination of the alchemical wedding rested on a wooden book stand. No matter how often I saw it, the image always amazed me—and not just because the personifications of sulfur and quicksilver looked like Matthew and me. So much detail surrounded the chemical couple: the rocky landscape, the wedding guests, the mythical and symbolic beasts who witnessed the ceremony, the phoenix who encompassed the scene within flaming wings. Next to the page was something that looked like a flat metal postal scale with a blank sheet of parchment in the tray.

"Scully will tell us what she discovered." Matthew gave the student the floor.

"This illuminated page is too heavy," Scully said, blinking her eyes behind a pair of thick lenses. "Heavier than a single page should be, I mean."

"Sarah and I both thought it felt heavy." I looked at Matthew. "Remember when the house first gave us the page in Madison?" I reminded him in a whisper.

He nodded. "Perhaps it's something a vampire can't perceive. Even now that I've seen Scully's evidence, the page feels entirely normal to me."

"I ordered some vellum online from a traditional parchment maker," Scully said. "It arrived this morning. I cut the sheet to the same size—nine inches by eleven and a half inches—and weighed it. You can have the leftovers, Professor Clairmont. We can all use some practice with that probe you've developed."

"Thank you, Scully. Good idea. And we'll run some core samples of the modern vellum for comparison's sake," Matthew said with a smile.

"As you can see," Scully resumed, "the new vellum weighed a little over an ounce and a half. When I weighed Professor Bishop's page the first time, it weighed thirteen ounces—as much as approximately nine sheets of ordinary vellum." Scully removed the fresh sheet of calfskin and put the page from Ashmole 782 in its place.

"The weight of the ink can't account for that discrepancy." Lucy put on her own glasses to take a closer look at the digital readout. "And the parchment used in Ashmole 782 looks like it's thinner, too."

"It's about half the thickness of the vellum. I measured it." Scully pushed her glasses back into place.

"But the Book of Life had more than a hundred pages—probably close to two hundred." I did some rapid calculations. "If a single page weighs thirteen ounces, the whole book would weigh close to a hundred and fifty pounds."

"That's not all. The page isn't always the same weight," Mulder said. He pointed to the scale's digital readout. "Look, Professor Clairmont. The weight's dropped again. Now it's down to seven ounces." He took up a clipboard and noted the time and weight on it.

"It's been fluctuating randomly all morning," Matthew said. "Thankfully, Scully had the good sense to leave the page on the scale. If she'd removed it immediately, we would have missed it."

"That wasn't deliberate." Scully flushed and lowered her voice. "I had to use the restroom. When I came back, the weight had risen to a full pound."

"What's your conclusion, Scully?" Chris asked in his teacher voice.

"I don't have one," she said, clearly frustrated. "Vellum can't lose weight and gain it again. It's dead. Nothing I'm observing is possible!"

"Welcome to the world of science, my friend," Chris said with a laugh. He turned to Scully's companion. "How about you, Mulder?"

"The page is clearly some sort of magical container. There are other pages inside it. Its weight changes because it's still somehow connected to the rest of the manuscript." Mulder slid a glance in my direction.

"I think you're right, Mulder," I said, smiling.

"We should leave it where it is and record its weight every fifteen minutes. Maybe there will be a pattern," Mulder suggested.

"Sounds like a plan." Chris looked at Mulder approvingly.

"So, Professor Bishop," Mulder said cautiously, "do you think there really are other pages inside this one?"

"If so, that would make Ashmole 782 a palimpsest," Lucy said, her imagination sparking. "A magical palimpsest."

My conclusion from today's events in the lab was that humans are much cleverer than we creatures give them credit for.

"It *is* a palimpsest," I confirmed. "But I never thought of Ashmole 782 as—what did you call it, Mulder?"

"A magical container," he repeated, looking pleased.

We already knew that Ashmole 782 was valuable because of its text and its genetic information. If Mulder was correct, there was no telling what else might be in it.

"Have the DNA results come back from the sample you took a few weeks ago, Matthew?" Maybe if we knew what creature the vellum came from, it would shed some light on the situation.

"Wait. You removed a piece of this manuscript and ran a chemical analysis on it?" Lucy looked horrified.

"Only a very small piece from the core of the page. We inserted a microscopic probe into the edge. You can't see the hole it made—not even with a magnifying glass," Matthew assured her.

"I've never heard of such a thing," Lucy said.

"That's because Professor Clairmont developed the technology, and he hasn't shared it with the rest of the class." Chris cast a disapproving look at Matthew. "But we're going to change that, aren't we, Matthew?"

"Apparently," said Matthew.

Miriam shrugged. "Give it up, Matthew. We've used it for years to remove DNA from all sorts of soft tissue samples. It's time somebody else had fun with it," she said.

"We'll leave the page to you, Scully." Chris inclined his head toward the other end of the lab in a clear request for a conversation.

"Can I touch it?" Lucy asked, her eyes glued to the page.

"Of course. It's survived all these years, after all," Matthew said. "Mulder, Scully, can you help Ms. Meriweather? Let us know when you're ready to leave, Lucy, and we'll get you back to work."

Based on Lucy's avid expression, we had plenty of time to talk.

"What is it?" I asked Chris. Now that we were away from his students, Chris looked as if he had bad news.

"If we're going to learn anything more about blood rage, we need more data," Chris said. "And before you say anything, Miriam, I'm not criticizing what you and Matthew have managed to figure out. It's as good as it could possibly be, given that most of your DNA samples come from the long dead—or the undead. But DNA deteriorates over time. And we need to develop the genetic maps for daemons and witches and sequence their genomes if we want to reach accurate conclusions about what makes you distinct."

"So we get more data," I said, relieved. "I thought this was serious."

"It is," Matthew said grimly. "One of the reasons the genetic maps for witches and daemons are less complete is that I had no good way to acquire DNA samples from living donors. Amira and Hamish were happy to volunteer theirs, of course, as were some of the regulars at Amira's yoga classes at the Old Lodge."

"But if you were to ask for samples from a broader cross section of creatures, you'd have to answer their questions about how the material was going to be used." Now I understood.

"We've got another problem," Chris said. "We simply don't have enough DNA from Matthew's bloodline to establish a pedigree that can tell us how blood rage is inherited. There are samples from Matthew, his mother, and Marcus Whitmore—that's all."

"Why not send Marcus to New Orleans?" Miriam asked Matthew.

"What's in New Orleans?" Chris asked sharply.

"Marcus's children," Gallowglass said.

"Whitmore has children?" Chris looked at Matthew incredulously. "How many?"

"A fair few," Gallowglass said, cocking his head to the side. "Grandchildren, too. And Mad Myra's got more than her fair share of blood rage, doesn't she? You'd be wanting her DNA, for sure."

Chris thumped a lab bench, the rack of empty test tubes rattling like bones.

"Goddamn it, Matthew! You told me you had no other living offspring. I've been wasting my time with results based on three family samples while your grandchildren and great-grandchildren are running up and down Bourbon Street?"

"I didn't want to bother Marcus," Matthew said shortly. "He has other concerns."

"Like what? Another psychotic brother? There's been nothing on the Bad Seed's video feed for weeks, but that's not going to continue indefinitely. When Benjamin pops up again, we'll need more than predictive modeling and hunches to outsmart him!" Chris exclaimed.

"Calm down, Chris," Miriam said, putting a hand on his arm. "The vampire genome already includes better data than either the witch or the daemon genome."

"But it's still shaky in places," Chris argued, "especially now that we're looking at the junk DNA. I need more witch, daemon, and vampire DNA—stat."

"Game Boy, Xbox, and Daisy all volunteered to be swabbed," Miriam said. "It violates modern research protocols, but I don't think it's an insurmountable problem provided you're transparent about it later, Chris."

"Xbox mentioned a club on Crown Street where the daemons hang out." Chris wiped at his tired eyes. "I'll go down and recruit some volunteers."

"You can't go there. You'll stick out as a human—and a professor," Miriam said firmly. "I'll do it. I'm far scarier."

"Only after dark." Chris shot her a slow smile.

"Good idea, Miriam," I said hastily. I wanted no further information about what Miriam was like when the sun went down.

"You can swab me," Gallowglass said. "I'm not Matthew's bloodline, but it could help. And there are plenty of other vampires in New Haven. Give Eva Jäeger a ring."

"Baldwin's Eva?" Matthew was stunned. "I haven't seen Eva since she discovered Baldwin's role in the German stock market crash of 1911 and left him."

"I don't think either of them would appreciate your being so indiscreet, Matthew," Gallowglass chided.

"Let me guess: She's the new hire in the economics department," I said. "Wonderful. Baldwin's ex. That's just what we need."

"And have you run into more of these New Haven vampires?" Matthew demanded.

"A few," Gallowglass said vaguely.

As Matthew opened his mouth to inquire further, Lucy interrupted us.

"The page from Ashmole 782 changed its weight three times while I was standing there." She shook her head in amazement. "If I hadn't seen it my-self, I wouldn't have believed it. I'm sorry to break this up, but I have to get back to the Beinecke."

"I'll go with you, Lucy," I said. "You still haven't told me what you've learned about the Voynich."

"After all this science, it's not very exciting," she said apologetically.

"It is to me." I kissed Matthew. "See you at home."

"I should be there by late afternoon." He hooked me into his arm and pressed his mouth against my ear. His next words were low so that the other vampires would have to strain to hear them. "Don't stay too long at the li-brary. Remember what the doctor said."

"I remember, Matthew," I promised him. "Bye, Chris."

"See you soon." Chris gave me a hug and released me quickly. He looked down at my protruding stomach reproachfully. "One of your kids just el-bowed me."

"Or kneed you." I laughed, smoothing a hand over the bump. "They're both pretty active these days."

Matthew's gaze rested on me: proud, tender, a shade worried. It felt like falling into a pile of freshly fallen snow—crisp and soft at the same time. If we had been at home, he would have pulled me into his arms so that he, too, could feel the kicks, or knelt before me to watch the bulges of feet and hands and elbows.

I smiled at him shyly. Miriam cleared her throat.

"Take care, Gallowglass," Matthew murmured. It was no casual farewell, but an order.

His nephew nodded. "As if your wife were my own."

We returned to the Beinecke at a statelier pace, chatting about the Voynich and Ashmole 782. Lucy was even more caught up in the mystery now. Gallowglass insisted we pick up something to eat, so we stopped at the pizza place on Wall Street. I waved to a fellow historian who was sitting in one of the scarred booths with stacks of index cards and an enormous soft drink, but she was so absorbed in her work she barely acknowledged me.

Leaving Gallowglass at his post outside the Beinecke, we went to the staff room with our late lunch. Everybody else had already eaten, so we had the place to ourselves. In between bites Lucy gave me an overview of her findings.

"Wilfrid Voynich bought Yale's mysterious manuscript from the Jesuits in 1912," she said, munching on a cucumber from her healthy salad. "They were quietly liquidating their collections at the Villa Mondragone outside Rome."

"Mondragone?" I shook my head, thinking of Corra.

"Yep. It got its name from the heraldic device of Pope Gregory XIII— the guy who reformed the calendar. But you probably know more about that than I do."

I nodded. Crossing Europe in the late sixteenth century had required familiarity with Gregory's reforms if I had wanted to know what day it was.

"More than three hundred volumes from the Jesuit College in Rome were moved to the Villa Mondragone sometime in the late nineteenth century. I'm still a bit fuzzy on the details, but there was some sort of confiscation of church property during Italian unification." Lucy stabbed an anemic cherry tomato with her fork. "The books sent to Villa Mondragone were reportedly the most treasured volumes in the Jesuit library."

"Hmm. I wonder if I could get a list." I'd owe my friend from Stanford even more, but it might lead to one of the missing pages.

"It's worth a shot. Voynich wasn't the only interested collector, of course. The Villa Mondragone sale was one of the greatest private book auctions of the twentieth century. Voynich almost lost the manuscript to two other buyers."

"Do you know who they were?" I asked.

"Not yet, but I'm working on it. One was from Prague. That's all I've been able to discover."

"Prague?" I felt faint.

"You don't look well," Lucy said. "You should go home and rest. I'll keep working on it and see you tomorrow," she added, closing up her empty Styrofoam container.

"Auntie. You're early," Gallowglass said when I exited the building.

"Ran into a research snag." I sighed. "The whole day has been a few bits of progress sandwiched between two thick slices of frustration. Hopefully, Matthew and Chris will make further discoveries in the lab, because we're running out of time. Or perhaps I should say *I'm* running out of time."

"It will all work out in the end," Gallowglass said with a sage nod. "It always does."

We cut across the green and through the gap between the courthouse and City Hall. On Court Street we crossed the railroad tracks and headed toward my house.

"When did you buy your condo on Wooster Square, Gallowglass?" I asked, finally getting around to one of many questions about the de Clermonts and their relationship to New Haven.

"After you came here as a teacher," Gallowglass said. "I wanted to be sure you were all right in your new job, and Marcus was always telling stories about a robbery at his house or that his car had been vandalized."

"I take it Marcus wasn't living in his house at the time," I said, raising an eyebrow.

"Lord no. He hasn't been in New Haven for decades."

"Well, we're perfectly safe here." I looked down the pedestrians-only length of Court Street, a tree-lined, residential enclave in the heart of the city. As usual, it was deserted, except for a black cat and some potted plants.

"Perhaps," Gallowglass said dubiously.

We had just reached the stairs leading to the front door when a dark car pulled up to the intersection of Court and Olive Streets where we had been only moments before. The car idled while a lanky young man with sandy blond hair unfolded from the passenger seat. He was all legs and arms, with surprisingly broad shoulders for someone so slender. I thought he must be an undergraduate, because he wore one of the standard Yale student uniforms:

dark jeans and a black T-shirt. Sunglasses shielded his eyes, and he bent over and spoke to the driver.

"Good God." Gallowglass looked as though he'd seen a ghost. "It can't be."

I studied the undergraduate without recognition. "Do you know him?"

The young man's eyes met mine. Mirrored lenses could not block the effects of a vampire's cold stare. He took the glasses off and gave me a lopsided smile.

"You're a hard woman to find, Mistress Roydon."

18

That voice. When I'd last heard it, it was higher, without the low rumble at the back of his throat.

Those eyes. Golden brown shot through with gold and leafy green. They still looked older than his years.

His smile. The left corner had always lifted higher than the right.

"Jack?" I choked on the name as my heart constricted.

A hundred pounds of white dog pawed out of the backseat of the car, hopping over the gearshift and through the open door, long hair flying and pink tongue lolling out of his mouth. Jack grabbed him by the collar.

"Stay, Lobero." Jack ruffled the hair atop the dog's shaggy head, revealing glimpses of black button eyes. The dog gazed at him adoringly, thumped his tail, and sat panting to await further instruction.

"Hello, Gallowglass." Jack walked slowly toward us.

"Jackie." Gallowglass's voice was thick with emotion. "I thought you were dead."

"I was. Then I wasn't." Jack looked down at me, unsure of his welcome. Leaving no room for doubt, I flung my arms around him.

"Oh, Jack." Jack smelled of coal fires and foggy mornings rather than warm bread, as he had when he was a child. After a moment of hesitation, he enfolded me within long, lean arms. He was older and taller, but he still felt fragile, as though his mature appearance were nothing more than a shell.

"I missed you," Jack whispered.

"Diana!" Matthew was still more than two blocks away, but he'd spotted the car blocking the entrance into Court Street, as well as the strange man who held me. From his perspective I must have looked trapped, even with Gallowglass standing nearby. Instinct took over, and Matthew ran, his body a blur.

Lobero raised an alarm with a booming bark. Komondors were a lot like vampires: bred to protect those they loved, loyal to family, large enough to take down wolves and bears, and ready to die rather than yield to another creature.

Jack sensed the threat, without seeing its source. He transformed before my eyes into a creature from nightmares, teeth bared and eyes glassy and black. He grabbed me and held me tight, shielding me from whatever loomed behind. But he was restricting the flow of air into my lungs as well.

"No! Not you, too," I gasped, wasting the last of my breath. Now there was no way for me to warn Matthew that someone had given our bright, vulnerable boy blood rage.

Before Matthew could hurtle over the car's hood, a man climbed out of the driver's seat and grabbed him. He must be a vampire, too, I thought dizzily, if he had the strength to stop Matthew.

"Stop, Matthew. It's Jack." The man's deep, rumbling voice and distinctive London accent conjured up unwelcome memories of a single drop of blood falling into a vampire's waiting mouth.

Andrew Hubbard. The vampire king of London was in New Haven. Stars flickered at the edges of my vision.

Matthew snarled and twisted. Hubbard's spine met the metal frame of the car with a bone-crushing thud.

"It's Jack," Hubbard repeated, gripping Matthew by the neck and forcing him to listen.

This time the message got through. Matthew's eyes widened, and he looked in our direction.

"Jack?" Matthew's voice was hoarse.

"Master Roydon?" Without turning, Jack cocked his head to the side as Matthew's voice penetrated the black haze of the blood rage. His grip loosened.

I drew in a lungful of air, struggling to push back the star-filled darkness. My hand went instinctively to my belly, where I felt a reassuring poke, then another. Lobero sniffed at my feet and hands as if trying to figure out my relationship to his master, then sat before me and growled at Matthew.

"Is this another dream?" There was a trace of the lost child he had once been in his bass voice, and Jack squeezed his eyes shut rather than risk waking up.

"It's no dream, Jack," Gallowglass said softly. "Step away from Mistress Roydon now. Matthew poses no danger to his mate."

"Oh, God. I touched her." Jack sounded horrified. Slowly he turned and held up his hands in surrender, willing to accept whatever punishment Matthew saw fit to mete out. Jack's eyes, which had been returning to normal, darkened again. But he wasn't angry. So why was the blood rage resurfacing?

"Hush," I said, gently lowering his arm. "You've touched me a thousand times. Matthew doesn't care."

"I wasn't . . . this . . . before." Jack's voice was taut with self-loathing.

Matthew drew closer slowly so as not to startle Jack. Andrew Hubbard slammed the car door and followed him. The centuries had done little to change the London vampire famous for his priestly ways and his brood of adopted creatures of all species and ages. He looked the same: clean-shaven, pale of face, and blond of hair. Only Hubbard's slate-colored eyes and somber clothing provided notes of contrast to his otherwise pallid appearance. And his body was still tall and thin, with slightly stooped, broad shoulders.

As the two vampires approached, the dog's growl turned more menacing and his lips peeled back from his teeth.

"Come, Lobero," Matthew commanded. He crouched down and waited patiently while the dog considered his options.

"He's a one-man dog," Hubbard warned. "The only creature he'll listen to is Jack."

Lobero's wet nose pushed into my hand, and then he sniffed his master. The dog's muzzle lifted to take in the other scents before he moved toward Matthew and Hubbard. Lobero recognized Father Hubbard, but Matthew received a more thorough evaluation. When he was through, Lobero's tail shifted from left to right. It wasn't exactly a wag, but the dog had instinctively acknowledged the alpha in this pack.

"Good boy." Matthew stood and pointed to his heel. Lobero obediently swung around and followed as Matthew joined Jack, Gallowglass, and me.

"All right, *mon coeur*?" Matthew murmured.

"Of course," I said, still a bit short of breath.

"And you, Jack?" Matthew rested a hand on Jack's shoulder. It was not the typical de Clermont embrace. This was a father greeting his son after a long separation—a father who feared that his child had been through hell.

"I'm better now." Jack could always be relied upon to tell the truth when asked a direct question. "I overreact when I'm surprised."

"So do I." Matthew's grip on him tightened a fraction. "I'm sorry. You had your back turned, and I wasn't expecting ever to see you again."

"It's been . . . difficult. To stay away." The faint vibration in Jack's voice suggested it had been more than difficult.

"I can imagine. Why don't we go inside and you can tell us your tale?" This was not a casual invitation; Matthew was asking Jack to bare his soul. Jack looked worried at the prospect.

"What you say is your choice, Jack," Matthew assured him. "Tell us nothing, tell us everything, but let's go inside while you do it. Your latest Lobero is no quieter than your first. He'll have the neighbors calling the police if he keeps barking."

Jack nodded.

Matthew's head cocked to the side. The gesture made him look a bit like Jack. He smiled. "Where has our little boy gone? I don't have to crouch down anymore to meet your eyes."

The remaining tension left Jack's body with Matthew's gentle teasing. He grinned shyly and scratched Lobero's ears.

"Father Hubbard will come with us. Could you take the car, Gallow-glass, and park it somewhere where it's not blocking the road?" Matthew asked.

Gallowglass held out his hand, and Hubbard put the keys into it.

"There's a briefcase in the trunk," Hubbard said. "Bring it back with you."

Gallowglass nodded, his lips pressed into a thin line. He gave Hubbard a blistering look before stalking toward the car.

"He never has liked me." Hubbard straightened the lapels on his austere black jacket, which he wore over a black shirt. Even after more than six hundred years, the vampire remained a cleric at heart. He nodded to me, acknowledging my presence for the first time. "Mistress Roydon."

"My name is Bishop." I wanted to remind him of the last time we'd seen each other and the agreement that he'd made—and broken, based on the evidence before me.

"Dr. Bishop, then." Hubbard's strange, multicolored eyes narrowed.

"You didn't keep your promise," I hissed. Jack's agitated stare settled on my neck.

"What promise?" Jack demanded from behind me.

Damn. Jack had always had excellent hearing but I'd forgotten he was now gifted with preternatural senses, too.

"I swore that I'd take care of you and Annie for Mistress Roydon," Hubbard said.

"Father Hubbard kept his word, mistress," Jack said quietly. "I wouldn't be here otherwise."

"And we're grateful to him." Matthew looked anything but. He tossed me the keys to the house. Gallowglass still had my bag, and without its contents I had no way to open the door.

Hubbard caught them instead and turned the key in the lock.

"Take Lobero upstairs and get him some water, Jack. The kitchen's on the first floor." Matthew plucked the keys from Hubbard's grasp as he went past and put them in a bowl on the hall table.

Jack called to Lobero and obediently started up the worn, painted treads.

"You're a dead man, Hubbard—and so is the one who made Jack a vampire." Matthew's voice was no more than a hollow murmur. Jack heard it nonetheless.

"You can't kill him, Master Roydon." Jack stood at the top of the stairs, his fingers wrapped tightly around Lobero's collar. "Father Hubbard is your grandson. He's my maker, too."

Jack turned away, and we heard the cabinet doors open, then water running from an open tap. The sounds were oddly homely considering that a conversational bomb had just gone off.

"My grandson?" Matthew looked at Hubbard in shock. "But that means . . ."

"Benjamin Fox is my sire." Andrew Hubbard's origins had always been shrouded in obscurity. London legends said that he had been a priest when the Black Death first visited England in 1349. After Hubbard's parishioners all succumbed to the illness, Hubbard had dug his own grave and climbed into it. Some mysterious vampire had brought Hubbard back from the brink of death—but no one seemed to know who.

"As far as your son was concerned, I was only a tool—someone he made to further his aims in England. Benjamin hoped I would have blood rage," Hubbard continued. "He also hoped I would help him organize an army to stand against the de Clermonts and their allies. But he was disappointed on both counts, and I've managed to keep him away from me and my flock. Until now."

"What's happened?" Matthew asked brusquely.

"Benjamin wants Jack. I can't let him have the boy again," was Hubbard's equally abrupt reply.

"Again?" That madman had been with Jack. I turned blindly toward the stairs, but Matthew caught me by the wrists and trapped me against his chest.

"Wait," he commanded.

Gallowglass came through the door with a large black briefcase and my book bag. He surveyed the scene and dropped what he was carrying.

"What's happened now?" he asked, looking from Matthew to Hubbard.

"Father Hubbard made Jack a vampire," I said as neutrally as I could. Jack was listening after all.

Gallowglass slammed Hubbard against the wall. "You bastard. I could smell your scent all over him. I thought—"

It was Gallowglass's turn to be tossed against something—in his case it was the floor. Hubbard pressed one polished black shoe against the big Gael's sternum. I was astonished that someone who looked so skeletal could be so strong.

"Thought what, Gallowglass?" Hubbard's tone was menacing. "That I'd violated a child?"

Upstairs, Jack's rising agitation soured the air. He'd learned from an early age how quickly ordinary quarrels could turn violent. As a boy he'd found even a hint of disagreement between Matthew and me distressing.

"Corra!" I cried, instinctively wanting her support.

By the time my firedrake swooped down from our bedroom and landed on the newel post, Matthew had averted any potential bloodshed by picking up Gallowglass and Hubbard by the scruffs of their necks, prying them apart, and shaking them until their teeth rattled.

Corra gave an irritated bleat and fixed a malevolent stare on Father Hubbard, suspecting quite rightly that he was to blame for her interrupted nap.

"I'll be damned." Jack's fair head peeked over the railing. "Didn't I tell you Corra would survive the timewalking, Father H?" He gave a hoot of delight and pounded on the painted wood. Jack's behavior reminded me so strongly of the joyous boy he had once been that I had to fight back the tears.

Corra let out an answering cry of welcome, followed by a stream of fire and song that filled the entrance with happiness. She took flight, zooming up and latching her wings around Jack. Then she tucked her head atop his and began to croon, her tail encircling his ribs so that the spade-shaped tip could gently pat his back. Lobero padded over to his master and gave Corra a suspicious sniff. She must have smelled like family, and therefore a creature to be included among his many responsibilities. He dropped down at Jack's side, head on his paws but eyes still watchful.

"Your tongue is even longer than Lobero's," Jack said, trying not to giggle as Corra tickled his neck. "I can't believe she remembers me."

"Of course she remembers you! How could she forget someone who spoiled her with currant buns?" I said with a smile.

By the time we were settled in the living room overlooking Court Street, the blood rage had receded from Jack's veins. Aware of his low position in the house's pecking order, he waited until everyone else took a chair before choosing his own seat. He was ready to join the dog on the floor when Matthew patted the sofa cushion.

"Sit with me, Jack." Matthew's invitation held a note of command. Jack sat, pulling at the knees of his jeans.

"You look to be about twenty," Matthew observed, hoping to draw him into conversation.

"Twenty, maybe twenty-one," Jack said. "Leonard and I—You remember Leonard?" Matthew nodded. "We figured it out because of my memories of the Armada. Nothing specific, you understand, just the fear of the Spanish invasion in the streets, the lighting of the beacons, and the victory celebrations. I must have been at least five in 1588 to remember that."

I did some rapid calculations. That meant Jack was made a vampire in 1603. "The plague."

The disease had swept through London with a vengeance that year. I noticed a mottled patch on his neck, just under his ear. It looked like a bruise, but it must be a mark left by a plague sore. For it to have remained visible even after Jack became a vampire suggested that he had been moments from death when Hubbard transformed him.

"Aye," Jack said, looking down at his hands. He turned them this way and that. "Annie died from it ten years earlier, soon after Master Marlowe was killed in Deptford."

I'd wondered what had happened to our Annie. I had imagined her a prosperous seamstress with her own business. I'd hoped she would have married a good man and had children. But she'd died while still a teenager, her life snuffed out before it truly began.

"That was a dreadful year, 1593, Mistress Roydon. The dead were everywhere. By the time Father Hubbard and I learned she was sick, it was too late," Jack said, his expression bereft.

"You're old enough to call me Diana," I said gently.

Jack plucked at his jeans without replying. "Father Hubbard took me in when you . . . left," he continued. "Sir Walter was in trouble, and Lord Northumberland was too busy at court to look after me." Jack smiled at Hubbard with obvious affection. "Those were good times, running about London with the gang."

"I was on very intimate terms with the sheriff during your so-called good times," Hubbard said drily. "You and Leonard got into more mischief than any two boys who ever lived."

"Nah," Jack said, grinning. "The only really serious trouble was when we snuck into the Tower to take Sir Walter his books and stayed on to pass a letter from him to Lady Raleigh."

"You did—" Matthew shuddered and shook his head. "Christ, Jack. You never could distinguish between a petty crime and a hanging offense."

"I can now," Jack said cheerfully. Then his expression became nervous once more. Lobero's head rose, and he rested his muzzle on Jack's knee.

"Don't be mad at Father Hubbard. He only did what I asked, Master Roydon. Leonard explained creatures to me long before I became one, so I knew what you and Gallowglass and Davy were. Things made better sense after that." Jack paused. "I should have had the courage to face death and accept it, but I couldn't go to my grave without seeing you again. My life felt . . . unfinished."

"And how does it feel now?" Matthew asked.

"Long. Lonely. And hard—harder than I ever imagined." Jack twisted Lobero's hair, rolling the strands until they formed a tight rope. He cleared his throat. "But it was all worth it for today," he continued softly. "Every bit of it."

Matthew's long arm reached for Jack's shoulder. He squeezed it, then quickly let go again. For a moment I saw desolation and grief on my husband's face before he donned his composed mask once more. It was the vampire version of a disguising spell.

"Father Hubbard told me his blood might make me ill, Master Roydon." Jack shrugged. "But I was already sick. What difference would it make to change one illness for another?"

No difference at all, I thought, except that one killed you and the other could make you a killer.

"Andrew was right to tell you," Matthew said. Father Hubbard looked surprised by this admission. "I don't imagine your grandsire gave him the same consideration." Matthew was careful to use the terms that Hubbard and Jack used to describe their relationship to Benjamin.

"No. He wouldn't have done. My grandsire doesn't believe that he owes anyone an explanation for any of his actions." Jack shot to his feet and traveled aimlessly around the room, Lobero following. He examined the moldings around the door, running his fingers along the wood. "You have the sickness in your blood, too, Master Roydon. I remember it from Greenwich. But it doesn't control you, like it does my grandsire. And me."

"It did once." Matthew looked at Gallowglass and gave him a slight nod.

"I remember when Matthew was as wild as the devil and nigh invincible with a sword in his hand. Even the bravest men ran in terror." Gallowglass leaned forward, hands clasped and knees spread wide.

"My grandsire told me about Master—Matthew's past." Jack shuddered. "He said that Matthew's talent for killing was in me, too, and I had to be true to it or you would never recognize me as your blood."

I'd seen Benjamin's unspeakable cruelty on camera, how he twisted hopes and fears into a weapon to destroy a creature's sense of self. That he'd done so with Jack's feelings for Matthew made me blind with fury. I clenched my hands into fists, tightening the cords in my fingers until the magic threatened to burst through my skin.

"Benjamin doesn't know me as well as he thinks." Anger was building in Matthew, too, his spicy scent growing sharper. "I would recognize you as mine before the entire world, and proudly—even if you weren't my blood."

Hubbard looked uneasy. His attention shifted from Matthew to Jack.

"You would make me your blood-sworn son?" Jack slowly turned to Matthew. "Like Philippe did with Mistress Roydon—I mean, Diana?"

Matthew's eyes widened slightly as he nodded, trying to absorb the fact that Philippe had known of Matthew's grandchildren when Matthew had not. A look of betrayal crossed his face.

"Philippe visited me whenever he came to London," Jack explained, oblivious to the changes in Matthew. "He told me to listen for his blood vow, because it was loud and I would probably hear Mistress Roydon before I saw her. And you were right, Mis—Diana. Matthew's father really was as big as the emperor's bear."

"If you met my father, then I'm sure you heard plenty of tales about my bad behavior." The muscle in Matthew's jaw had started ticking as betrayal turned to bitterness, his pupils growing larger by the second as his rage continued to gain ground.

"No," Jack said, confusion wrinkling his brow. "Philippe spoke only of his admiration and said you would teach me to ignore what my blood was telling me to do."

Matthew jerked as though he'd been hit.

"Philippe always made me feel closer to you and Mistress Roydon. Calmer, too." Jack looked nervous again. "But it has been a long time since I saw Philippe."

"He was captured in the war," Matthew explained, "and died as a result of what he suffered."

It was a careful half-truth.

"Father Hubbard told me. I'm glad Philippe didn't live to see—" This time the shudder traveled through Jack from the marrow of his bones to the surface of his skin. His eyes went full black without warning, filled with horror and dread.

Jack's present suffering was far worse than what Matthew had to endure. With Matthew it was only bitter fury that brought the blood rage to the surface. With Jack a wider range of emotions triggered it.

"It's all right." Matthew was with him in an instant, one hand clamped around his neck and the other resting on his cheek. Lobero pawed at Matthew's foot as if to say, *Do something.*

"Don't touch me when I'm like this," Jack snarled, pushing at Matthew's chest. But he might as well have tried to move a mountain. "You'll make it worse."

"You think you can order me about, pup?" Matthew's eyebrow arched. "Whatever you think is so terrible, just say it. You'll feel better once you do."

With Matthew's encouragement Jack's confession tumbled from some dark place inside where he stored up everything that was evil and terrifying.

"Benjamin found me a few years ago. He said he'd been waiting for me. My grandsire promised to take me to you, but only after I'd proved that I was really one of Matthew de Clermont's blood."

Gallowglass swore. Jack's eyes darted to him, and a snarl broke free.

"Keep your eyes on me, Jack." Matthew's tone made it clear that any resistance would be met with a swift and harsh reprisal. My husband was performing an impossible balancing act, one that required unconditional love along with a steady assertion of dominance. Pack dynamics were always fraught. With blood rage they could turn deadly in an instant.

Jack dragged his attention from Gallowglass, and his shoulders lowered a fraction.

"Then what happened?" Matthew prompted.

"I killed. Again and again. The more I killed, the more I wanted to kill. The blood did more than feed me—it fed the blood rage, too."

"It was clever of you to understand that so quickly," Matthew said approvingly.

"Sometimes I came to my senses long enough to realize that what I was doing was wrong. I tried to save the warmbloods then, but I couldn't stop drinking," Jack confessed. "I managed to turn two of my prey into vampires. Benjamin was pleased with me then."

"Only two?" A shadow flitted across Matthew's features.

"Benjamin wanted me to save more, but it took too much control. No matter what I did, most of them died." Jack's inky eyes filled with blood tears, the pupils taking on a red sheen.

"Where did these deaths occur?" Matthew sounded only mildly curious, but my sixth sense told me the question was crucial to understanding what had happened to Jack.

"Everywhere. I had to keep moving. There was so much blood. I had to get away from the police, and the newspapers. . . ." Jack shuddered.

VAMPIRE ON THE LOOSE IN LONDON. I remembered the vivid headline and all the clippings of the "vampire murders" that Matthew had collected from around the world. I bowed my head, not wanting Jack to realize I knew that he was the murderer whom European authorities were seeking.

"But it's the ones that lived who suffered the most," Jack continued, his voice deadening further with every word. "My grandsire took my children from me and said he would make sure they were raised properly."

"Benjamin used you." Matthew looked deep into his eyes, trying to make a connection. Jack shook his head.

"When I made those children, I broke my vow to Father Hubbard. He said the world didn't need more vampires—there were plenty already—and if I was lonely, I could take care of creatures whose families didn't want them anymore. All Father Hubbard asked was that I not make children, but I failed him again and again. After that, I couldn't go back to London—not with so much blood on my hands. And I couldn't stay with my grandsire. When I told Benjamin I wanted to leave, he went into a terrible rage and killed one of my children in retaliation. His sons held me down and forced me to watch." Jack bit back a harsh sound. "And my daughter. My daughter. They—"

He retched. He clamped a hand over his mouth, but it was too late to keep the blood from escaping as he vomited. It streamed over his chin, soaking into his dark shirt. Lobero leaped up, barking sharply and pawing at his back.

Unable to stay away a moment longer, I rushed to Jack's side.

"Diana!" Gallowglass cried. "You must not—"

"Don't tell me what to do. Get me a towel!" I snapped.

Jack fell to his hands and knees, his landing softened by Matthew's strong arms. I knelt beside him as he continued to purge his stomach of its contents. Gallowglass handed me a towel. I used it to mop Jack's face and hands, which were covered with blood. The towel was soon sodden and icy cold from my frantic efforts to stanch the flow, the contact with so much vampire blood making my hands numb and clumsy.

"The force of the vomiting must have broken some blood vessels in his stomach and throat," Matthew said. "Andrew, can you get a pitcher of water? Put plenty of ice in it."

Hubbard went to the kitchen and was back in moments.

"Here," he said, thrusting the pitcher at Matthew.

"Raise his head, Diana," Matthew instructed. "Keep hold of him, Andrew. His body is screaming for blood, and he'll fight against taking water."

"What can I do?" Gallowglass said, his voice gruff.

"Wipe off Lobero's paws before he tracks blood all over the house. Jack won't need any reminders of what's happened." Matthew gripped Jack's chin. "Jack!"

Jack's glassy black eyes swiveled toward Matthew.

"Drink this," Matthew commanded, raising Jack's chin a few inches. Jack spluttered and snapped in an attempt to throw him off. But Hubbard kept Jack immobilized long enough to empty the pitcher.

Jack hiccupped, and Hubbard loosened his hold.

"Well done, Jackie," Gallowglass said.

I smoothed Jack's hair away from his forehead as he bent forward again, clutching at his visibly heaving stomach.

"I got blood on you," he whispered. My shirt was streaked with it.

"So you did," I said. "It's not the first time a vampire's bled on me, Jack."

"Try to rest now," Matthew told him. "You're exhausted."

"I don't want to sleep." Jack swallowed hard as the gorge rose again in his throat.

"Shh." I rubbed his neck. "I can promise there will be no nightmares."

"How can you be sure?" Jack asked.

"Magic." I traced the pattern of the fifth knot on his forehead and lowered my voice to a whisper. "Mirror shimmers, monsters shake, banish nightmares until he wakes."

Jack's eyes slowly closed. After a few minutes, he was curled on his side, sleeping peacefully.

I wove another spell—one that was meant just for him. It required no words, for no one would ever use it but me. The threads surrounding Jack were a furious snarl of red, black, and yellow. I pulled on the healing green threads that surrounded me, as well as the white threads that helped break curses and establish new beginnings. I twisted them together and tied them around Jack's wrist, fixing the braid with a secure, six-crossed knot.

"There's a guest room upstairs," I said. "We'll put Jack to bed there. Corra and Lobero will let us know if he stirs."

"Would that be all right?" Matthew asked Hubbard.

"When it comes to Jack, you don't need my permission," Hubbard replied.

"Yes I do. You're his father," Matthew said.

"I'm only his sire," Hubbard said softly. "You're Jack's father, Matthew. You always have been."

19

Matthew carried Jack up to the third floor, cradling his body as if he were a baby. Lobero and Corra accompanied us, both beasts aware of the job they had to do. While Matthew stripped off Jack's blood-soaked shirt, I rummaged in our bedroom closet for something he could wear instead. Jack was easily six feet tall, but he had a much rangier frame than Matthew. I found an oversize Yale men's crew team shirt that I sometimes slept in, hoping it would do. Matthew slipped Jack's seemingly boneless arms into it and pulled it over his lolling head. My spell had knocked him out cold.

Together we settled him on the bed, neither of us speaking unless it was absolutely necessary. I drew the sheet up around Jack's shoulders while Lobero watched my every move from the floor. Corra perched on the lamp, attentive and unblinking, her weight bending the shade to an alarming degree.

I touched Jack's sandy hair and the dark mark on his neck, then pressed my hand over his heart. Even though he was asleep, I could feel the parts of him warring for control: mind, body, soul. Though Hubbard had ensured that Jack would be twenty-one forever, he had a weariness that made him seem like a man three times that age.

Jack had been through so much. Too much, thanks to Benjamin. I wanted that madman obliterated from the face of the earth. The fingers on my left hand splayed wide, my wrist stinging where the knot circled my pulse. Magic was nothing more than desire made real, and the power in my veins responded to my unspoken wishes for revenge.

"Jack was our responsibility, and we weren't there for him." My voice was low and fierce. "And Annie . . ."

"We're here for Jack now." Matthew's eyes held the same sorrow and anger that I knew were in my own. "There's nothing we can do for Annie, except pray that her soul found rest."

I nodded, controlling my emotions with difficulty.

"Take a shower, *ma lionne*. Hubbard's touch and Jack's blood . . ."

Matthew couldn't abide it when my skin carried the scent of another creature. "I'll stay with him while you do. Then you and I will go downstairs and talk to . . . my grandson." His final words were slow and deliberate, as though he were getting his tongue used to them.

I squeezed his hand, kissed Jack lightly on the forehead, and reluctantly headed into the bathroom in a futile effort to wash myself clean of the evening's events.

Thirty minutes later we found Gallowglass and Hubbard sitting opposite each other at the simple pine dining table. They glared. They stared. They growled. I was glad Jack wasn't awake to witness it.

Matthew dropped my hand and walked the few steps to the kitchen. He pulled out a bottle of sparkling water for me and three bottles of wine. After distributing them he went back for a corkscrew and four glasses.

"You may be my cousin, but I still don't like you, Hubbard." Gallowglass's growl subsided into an inhuman sound that was far more disturbing.

"It's mutual." Hubbard hoisted his black briefcase onto the table and left it within easy reach.

Matthew worked the corkscrew into his bottle, watching his nephew and Hubbard jockey for position without comment. He poured himself a glass of wine and drank it down in two gulps.

"You're not fit to be a parent," Gallowglass said, eyes narrowing.

"Who is?" Hubbard shot back.

"Enough." Matthew didn't raise his voice, but there was a timbre in it that lifted the hairs on my neck and instantly silenced Gallowglass and Hubbard. "Has the blood rage always affected Jack this way, Andrew, or has it worsened since he met Benjamin?"

Hubbard sat back in his chair with a sardonic smile. "That's where you want to start, is it?"

"How about *you* start by explaining why you made Jack a vampire when you knew it could give him blood rage!" My anger had burned straight through any courtesy I might once have extended to him.

"I gave him a choice, Diana," Hubbard retorted, "not to mention a chance."

"Jack was dying of plague!" I cried. "He wasn't capable of making a clear decision. You were the grown-up. Jack was a child."

"Jack was full on twenty years—a man, not the boy you left with Lord Northumberland. And he'd been through hell waiting in vain for your return!" Hubbard said.

Afraid we might wake Jack, I lowered my voice. "I left you with plenty of money to keep both Jack and Annie out of harm's way. Neither of them should have wanted for anything."

"You think a warm bed and food in his belly could mend Jack's broken heart?" Hubbard's otherworldly eyes were cold. "He looked for you every day for *twelve years.* That's twelve years of going to the docks to meet the ships from Europe in hopes that you would be aboard; twelve years interviewing every foreigner he could find in London to inquire if you had been seen in Amsterdam, or Lübeck, or Prague; and twelve years walking up to anyone he suspected of being a witch to show that person a picture he'd drawn of the famous sorceress Diana Roydon. It's a miracle the plague took his life and not the queen's justices!"

I blanched.

"You had a choice, too," Hubbard reminded me. "So if you want to cast blame for Jack's becoming a vampire, blame yourself or blame Matthew. He was your responsibility. You made him mine."

"That wasn't our bargain, and you know it!" The words slipped out of my mouth before I could stop them. I froze, a look of horror on my face. This was another secret I'd kept from Matthew, one that I'd thought was safely behind me.

Gallowglass's breath hissed in surprise. Matthew's icy gaze splintered against my skin. Then the room fell utterly silent.

"I need to speak to my wife and my grandson, Gallowglass. Alone," Matthew said. The emphasis he placed on "my wife" and "my grandson" was subtle but unmistakable.

Gallowglass stood, his face set in lines of disapproval. "I'll be upstairs with Jack."

Matthew shook his head. "Go home and wait for Miriam. I'll call when Andrew and Jack are ready to join you."

"Jack will stay here," I said, my voice rising again, "with us. Where he belongs."

The forbidding look Matthew directed my way silenced me immediately, even though the twenty-first century was no place for a Renaissance prince and a year ago I would have protested his high-handedness. Now I knew that my husband was hanging on to his control by a very slender thread.

"I'm not staying under the same roof as a de Clermont. Especially not him," Hubbard said, pointing in Gallowglass's direction.

"You forget, Andrew," Matthew said, "*you* are a de Clermont. So is Jack."

"I was never a de Clermont," Hubbard said viciously.

"Once you drank Benjamin's blood, you were never anything else." Matthew's voice was clipped. "In this family you do what I say."

"Family?" Hubbard scoffed. "You were part of Philippe's pack, and now you answer to Baldwin. You don't have a family of your own."

"Apparently I do." Matthew's mouth twisted with regret. "Time to go, Gallowglass."

"Very well, Matthew. I'll let you send me off—this time—but I'll not go far. And if my instincts tell me there's trouble, I'm coming back and to hell with vampire custom and law." Gallowglass got up and kissed me on the cheek. "Holler if you need me, Auntie."

Matthew waited until the front door closed before he turned on Hubbard. "Exactly what deal did you strike with my mate?" he demanded.

"It's my fault, Matthew. I went to Hubbard—" I began, wanting to confess and get it over with.

The table reverberated under the force of Matthew's blow. "Answer me, Andrew."

"I agreed to protect anyone who belonged to her, even you," Hubbard said shortly. In this respect he was a de Clermont to the bone—volunteering nothing, only giving away what he must.

"And in exchange?" Matthew asked sharply. "You wouldn't make such a vow without getting something equally precious in return."

"Your *mate* gave me one drop of blood—one single drop," Hubbard said, his tone resentful. I'd tricked him, abiding to the letter of his request rather than its spirit. Apparently Andrew Hubbard held grudges.

"Did you know then that I was your grandfather?" Matthew asked. I couldn't imagine why this was important.

"Yes," Andrew said, looking slightly green.

Matthew hauled him across the table so that they were nose to nose. "And what did you learn from that one drop of blood?"

"Her true name—Diana Bishop. Nothing more, I swear. The witch used her magic to make sure of it." On Hubbard's tongue the word "witch" sounded filthy and obscene.

"Never take advantage of my wife's protective instincts again, Andrew. If you do, I'll have your head." Matthew's grip tightened. "Given your prurience, there isn't a vampire alive who would fault me for doing so."

"I don't care what the two of you get up to behind closed doors—though others will, since your mate is obviously pregnant and there isn't a hint of another man's scent on her." Hubbard pursed his lips in disapproval.

At last I understood Matthew's earlier question. By knowingly taking my blood and seeking out my thoughts and memories, Andrew Hubbard had done the vampire equivalent of watching his grandparents have sex. Had I not found a way to slow its flow so he got only the drop he asked for and nothing more, Hubbard would have seen into our private lives and might have learned Matthew's secrets as well as my own. My eyes closed tight against the realization of the damage that would have resulted.

A distracting murmur came from Andrew's briefcase. It reminded me of the noise I sometimes heard during a lecture, when a student's phone went off unexpectedly.

"You left your phone on speaker," I said, my attention drawn to the low chatter. "Someone is leaving a message."

Matthew and Andrew both frowned.

"I don't hear anything," Matthew said.

"And I don't own a mobile phone," Hubbard added.

"Where is it coming from, then?" I asked, looking around. "Did someone turn on the radio?"

"The only thing in my briefcase is this." Hubbard released its two brass clasps and withdrew something.

The chattering grew louder as a jolt of power entered my body. Every sense I had was heightened, and the threads that bound the world chimed in sudden agitation, coiling and twisting in the space between me and the sheet of vellum that Andrew Hubbard held in his fingers. My blood responded to the faint vestiges of magic that clung to this solitary page from the Book of Life, and my wrists burned as a faint, familiar scent of must and age filled the room.

Hubbard turned the page so that it faced me, but I already knew what I would see there: two alchemical dragons locked together, the blood from their wounds falling into a basin from which naked, pale figures rose. It depicted the stage in the alchemical process after the chemical marriage of the moon queen and the sun king: *conceptio,* when a new and powerful substance sprang forth from the union of opposites—male and female, light and dark, sun and moon.

After spending weeks in the Beinecke looking for Ashmole 782's missing pages, I'd unexpectedly encountered one of them in my own dining room.

"Edward Kelley sent it to me the autumn after you left. He told me not to let it out of my sight." Hubbard slid the page toward me.

We had only caught a glimpse of this illumination in Rudolf's palace. Later Matthew and I had speculated that what we thought were two dragons might actually be a firedrake and an ouroboros. One of the alchemical dragons was indeed a firedrake, with two legs and wings, and the other was a snake with its tail in its mouth. The ouroboros at my wrist writhed in recognition, its colors shining with possibility. The image was mesmerizing, and now that I had time to study it properly, small things struck me: the dragons' rapt expressions as they gazed into each other's eyes, the look of wonder on their progeny's faces as they emerged from the basin where they'd been born, the striking balance between two such powerful creatures.

"Jack made sure Edward's picture was safe no matter what. Plague, fire, war—the boy never let anything touch it. He claimed it belonged to you, Mistress Roydon," Hubbard said, interrupting my reveries.

"To me?" I touched the corner of the vellum, and one of the twins gave a strong kick. "No. It belongs to all of us."

"And yet you have some kind of special connection to it. You're the only one who has ever heard it speak," Andrew said. "Long ago, a witch in my care said he thought it came from the witches' first spell book. But an old vampire passing through London said it was a page from the Book of Life. I pray to God that neither tale is true."

"What do you know about the Book of Life?" Matthew's voice was a peal of thunder.

"I know that Benjamin wants it," Hubbard said. "He told Jack as much. But that wasn't the first time my sire mentioned the book. Benjamin looked for it in Oxford long ago—before he made me a vampire."

That meant Benjamin had been looking for the Book of Life since before the middle of the fourteenth century—far longer than Matthew had been interested in it.

"My sire thought he might find it in the library of an Oxford sorcerer. Benjamin took the witch a gift in exchange for the book: a brass head that supposedly spoke oracles." Hubbard's face filled with sadness. "It is always a pity to see such a wise man taken in by superstition. *'Do not turn to idols or make for yourselves any gods of cast metal,'* sayeth the Lord."

Gerbert of Aurillac had reputedly owned just such a miraculous device. I had thought Peter Knox was the member of the Congregation who was most interested in Ashmole 782. Was it possible that Gerbert had been in league with Benjamin all these years and it was he who sought out Peter Knox's help?

"The witch in Oxford took the brass head but wouldn't relinquish the book," Hubbard continued. "Decades later my sire still cursed him for his duplicity. I never did discover the witch's name."

"I believe it was Roger Bacon—an alchemist and a philosopher as well as a witch." Matthew looked at me. Bacon once owned the Book of Life, and had called it the "true secret of secrets."

"Alchemy is one of the witches' many vanities," Hubbard said with disdain. His expression turned anxious. "My children tell me Benjamin has been back in England."

"He has. Benjamin has been watching my lab in Oxford." Matthew made no mention of the fact that the Book of Life was currently a few blocks away from that very laboratory. Hubbard might be his grandson, but that didn't mean Matthew trusted him.

"If Benjamin is in England, how will we keep him away from Jack?" I asked Matthew urgently.

"Jack will return to London. My sire is no more welcome there than you are, Matthew." Hubbard stood. "So long as he is with me, Jack will be safe."

"No one is safe from Benjamin. Jack is not going back to London." The note of command was back in Matthew's voice. "Nor are you, Andrew. Not yet."

"We've done very well without your interference," Hubbard retorted. "It's a bit late for you to decide you want to lord it over your children like some ancient Roman father."

"The paterfamilias. A fascinating tradition." Matthew settled back in his chair, his wineglass cupped in his hand. He looked no longer like a prince but a king. "Imagine giving one man the power of life and death over his wife, his children, his servants, anyone he adopted into his family, and even his close relatives who lacked a strong father of their own. It reminds me a bit of what you tried to accomplish in London."

Matthew sipped at his wine. Hubbard looked more uncomfortable with each passing moment.

"My children obey me willingly," Hubbard said stiffly. "They honor me, as godly children should."

"Such an idealist," Matthew said, softly mocking. "You know who came up with the paterfamilias, of course."

"The Romans, as I said," Hubbard replied sharply. "I am educated, Matthew, in spite of your doubts on this score."

"No, it was Philippe." Matthew's eyes gleamed with amusement. "Philippe thought Roman society could benefit from a healthy dose of vampire family discipline, and a reminder of the father's importance."

"Philippe de Clermont was guilty of the sin of pride. God is the only true Father. You are a Christian, Matthew. Surely you agree." Hubbard's expression held the fervency of a true believer.

"Perhaps," Matthew said, as though he were seriously considering his grandson's argument. "But until God calls us to Him, I will have to suffice. Like it or not, Andrew, in the eyes of other vampires I am your paterfamilias, the head of your clan, your alpha—call it what you like. And all your children—including Jack and all the other strays you've adopted be they daemon, vampire, or witch—are *mine* under vampire law."

"No." Hubbard shook his head. "I never wanted any part of the de Clermont family."

"What you want doesn't matter. Not anymore." Matthew put down his wine and took my hand in his.

"To command my loyalty, you would have to recognize my sire—Benjamin—as your son. And you will *never* do that," Hubbard said savagely. "As head of the de Clermonts, Baldwin takes the family's honor and position seriously. He won't permit you to branch out on your own given the scourge in your blood."

Before Matthew could respond to Andrew's challenge, Corra uttered a warning squawk. Realizing that Jack must have awoken, I rose from my seat to go to him. Unfamiliar rooms had terrified him as a child.

"Stay here," Matthew said, his grip on my hand tightening.

"He needs me!" I protested.

"Jack needs a strong hand and consistent boundaries," Matthew said softly. "He knows you love him. But he can't handle such strong feelings at the moment."

"I trust him." My voice quavered with anger and hurt.

"I don't," Matthew said sharply. "It's not just anger that sets off the blood rage in him. Love and loyalty do, too."

"Don't ask me to ignore him." I wanted Matthew to stop acting the role of paterfamilias long enough to behave like a true father.

"I'm sorry, Diana." A shadow settled in Matthew's eyes, one that I thought was gone forever. "I have to put Jack's needs first."

"What needs?" Jack stood in the door. He yawned, tufts of hair standing up in apparent alarm. Lobero pushed past his master and went straight to Matthew, looking for acknowledgment of a job well done.

"You need to hunt. The moon is bright, alas, but not even I can control the heavens." Matthew's lie flowed from his tongue like honey. He ruffled Lobero's ears. "We're all going—you, me, your father, even Gallowglass. Lobero can come, too."

Jack's nose wrinkled. "Not hungry."

"Don't feed, then. But you're hunting nevertheless. Be ready at midnight. I'll pick you up."

"Pick me up?" Jack looked from me to Hubbard. "I thought we would stay here."

"You'll be just around the corner with Gallowglass and Miriam. Andrew will be there with you," Matthew assured him. "This house isn't large enough for a witch and three vampires. We're nocturnal creatures, and Diana and the babies need their sleep."

Jack looked at my belly wistfully. "I always wanted a baby brother."

"You may well get two sisters instead," Matthew said, chuckling.

My hand lowered automatically over my belly as one of the twins gave another strong kick. They had been unusually active ever since Jack showed up.

"Are they moving?" Jack asked me, his face eager. "Can I touch them?"

I looked at Matthew. Jack's glance slid in the same direction.

"Let me show you how." Matthew's tone was easy, though his eyes were sharp. He took Jack's hand and pressed it into the side of my belly.

"I don't feel anything," Jack said, frowning with concentration.

A particularly strong kick, followed by a sharp elbow, thudded against the wall of my uterus.

"Whoa!" Jack's face was inches from mine, his eyes full of wonder. "Do they kick like that all day?"

"It feels like it." I wanted to smooth down the mess of Jack's hair. I wanted to take him into my arms and promise him that no one was ever going to hurt him again. But I could offer him neither of these comforts.

Sensing the maternal turn my mood had taken, Matthew lifted Jack's hand away. Jack's face fell, experiencing it as rejection. Furious with Matthew, I reached to jerk Jack's hand back. Before I could, Matthew put his hand at my waist and pulled me against his side. It was an unmistakable gesture of possession.

Jack's eyes went black.

Hubbard pitched forward to intervene, and Matthew froze him in place with a look.

In the space of five heartbeats, Jack's eyes returned to normal. When they were brown and green once more, Matthew gave him an approving smile.

"Your instinct to protect Diana is entirely appropriate," Matthew told him. "Believing you have to shield her from me is not."

"I'm sorry, Matthew," Jack whispered. "It won't happen again."

"I accept your apology. Sadly, it *will* happen again. Learning to control your illness isn't going to be easy—or quick." Matthew's tone turned brisk. "Kiss Diana good night, Jack, and get settled at Gallowglass's house. It's a former church around the corner. You'll feel right at home."

"Hear that, Father H?" Jack grinned. "Wonder if it has bats in its belfry, like yours."

"I no longer have a bat problem," Hubbard said sourly.

"Father H still lives in a church in the city," Jack explained, suddenly animated. "It's not the same one you visited. That old heap burned down. Most of this one did, too, come to think of it."

I laughed. Jack had always loved telling stories and had a talent for it, too.

"Now just the tower remains. Father H did it up so nicely you hardly notice it's just a pile of rubbish." Jack grinned at Hubbard and gave me a perfunctory kiss on the cheek, his mood swinging from blood rage to happiness in a remarkably short period of time. He sped down the stairs. "Come on, Lobero. Let's go wrestle with Gallowglass."

"Midnight," Matthew called after him. "Be ready. And be nice to Miriam, Jack. If you don't, she'll make you wish you'd never been reborn."

"Don't worry, I'm used to dealing with difficult females!" Jack replied. Lobero barked with excitement and orbited Jack's legs to encourage him outside.

"Keep the picture, Mistress Roydon. If both Matthew and Benjamin covet it, then I wish to be as far away from it as possible," Andrew said.

"How generous, Andrew." Matthew's hand shot out and closed around Hubbard's throat. "Stay in New Haven until I give you leave to go."

Their eyes clashed, slate and gray-green. Andrew was the first to look away.

"Come on, Father H!" Jack bellowed. "I want to see Gallowglass's church, and Lobero needs a walk."

"Midnight, Andrew." Matthew's words were perfectly cordial, but there was a warning in them.

The door closed, and the sound of Lobero's barking faded. When it had faded completely, I turned on Matthew.

"How could you—"

The sight of Matthew, his head buried in his hands, brought me to an abrupt stop. My anger, which had been blazing, slowly fizzled. He looked up, his face ravaged with guilt and sorrow.

"Jack . . . Benjamin . . ." Matthew shuddered. "God help me, what have I done?"

20

Matthew sat in the broken-down easy chair opposite the bed where Diana was sleeping, plowing through another inconclusive set of test results so that he and Chris could reevaluate their research strategy at tomorrow's meeting. Given the late hour, he was taken by surprise when his phone's screen lit up.

Moving carefully so as not to wake his wife, Matthew padded silently out of the room and down the stairs to the kitchen, where he could speak without being overheard.

"You need to come," Gallowglass said, his voice gruff and low. "Now."

Matthew's flesh prickled, and his eyes rose to the ceiling as though he could see through the plaster and floorboards into the bedroom. His first instinct was always to protect her, even though it was clear that the danger was elsewhere.

"Leave Auntie at home," Gallowglass said flatly, as though he could witness Matthew's actions. "Miriam's on her way." The phone went dead.

Matthew stared down at the display for a moment, its bright colors bringing a note of false cheer to the early-morning hours before they faded to black.

The front door creaked open.

Matthew was at the top of the stairs by the time Miriam walked through it. He studied her closely. There was not a drop of blood on her, thank God. Even so, Miriam's eyes were wide and her face bore a haunted expression. Very little frightened his longtime friend and colleague, but she was clearly terrified. Matthew swore.

"What's wrong?" Diana descended from the third floor, her coppery hair seeming to capture all the available light in the house. "Is it Jack?"

Matthew nodded. Gallowglass wouldn't have called otherwise.

"I'll only be a minute," Diana said, reversing her direction to get dressed.

"No, Diana," Miriam said quietly.

Diana froze, her hand on the banister. She twisted her body around and met Miriam's eyes.

"Is he d-dead?" she whispered numbly. Matthew was at her side in the space of a human heartbeat.

"No, *mon coeur*. He's not dead." Matthew knew this was Diana's worst nightmare: that someone she loved would be taken from her before the two of them could say a proper farewell. But whatever was taking place in the house on Wooster Square might somehow be worse.

"Stay with Miriam." Matthew pressed a kiss against her stiff lips. "I'll be home soon."

"He's been doing so well," Diana said. Jack had been in New Haven for a week, and his blood rage had diminished in both frequency and intensity. Matthew's strict boundaries and consistent expectations had already made a difference.

"We knew there would be setbacks," Matthew said, tucking a silky strand of hair behind Diana's ear. "I know you won't sleep, but try to rest at least." He was worried she'd do nothing but pace and stare out the window until he returned with news.

"You can read these while you wait." Miriam drew a thick stack of articles out of her bag. She was making an effort to sound brisk and matter-of-fact, her bittersweet scent of galbanum and pomegranate stronger now. "This is everything you asked for, and I added some other articles you might be interested in: all of Matthew's studies on wolves, as well as some classic pieces on wolf parenting and pack behavior. It's basically Dr. Spock for the modern vampire parent."

Matthew turned to Diana in amazement. Once again, his wife had surprised him. Her cheeks reddened, and she took the articles from Miriam.

"I need to understand how this vampire family stuff works. Go. Tell Jack I love him." Diana's voice broke. "If you can."

Matthew squeezed her hand without replying. He would make no promises on that score. Jack had to understand that his access to Diana depended on his behavior—and Matthew's approval.

"Prepare yourself," Miriam murmured when he passed her. "And I don't care if Benjamin is your son. If you don't kill him after seeing this, I will."

*   *   *

In spite of the late hour, Gallowglass's house was not the only one in the neighborhood that was still illuminated. New Haven was a college town, after all. Most of Wooster Square's night owls sought a strange companionship, working in full view with curtains and blinds open. What distinguished the vampire's house was that the drapes were tightly closed and only cracks of golden light around the edges of the windows betrayed the fact that someone was still awake.

Inside the house pools of lamplight cast a warm glow over a few personal belongings. Otherwise it was sparsely decorated with Danish Modern furniture made from blond wood accented with occasional antiques and splashes of bold color. One of Gallowglass's most treasured possessions—a tattered eighteenth-century Red Ensign that he and Davy Hancock had stripped from their beloved cargo ship the *Earl of Pembroke* before it was refitted and renamed *Endeavour*—was balled up on the floor.

Matthew sniffed. The house was filled with the bitter, acrid scent that Diana had likened to a coal fire, and faint strains of Bach filled the air. The St. Matthew Passion—the same music that Benjamin played in his laboratory to torture his captive witch. Matthew's stomach twisted into a heavy knot.

He rounded the corner of the living room. What he saw brought him to an immediate stop. Stark murals in shades of black and gray covered every inch of the canvas-hued walls. Jack stood atop a makeshift scaffold constructed from pieces of furniture, wielding a soft artist's pencil. The floor was littered with pencil stubs and the paper peelings that Jack had torn away to reveal fresh charcoal.

Matthew's eyes swept the walls from floor to ceiling. Detailed landscapes, studies of animals and plants that were almost microscopic in their precision, and sensitive portraits were linked together with breathtaking swaths of line and form that defied painterly logic. The overall effect was beautiful yet disturbing, as if Sir Anthony van Dyck had painted Picasso's *Guernica*.

"Christ." Matthew's right hand automatically made the sign of the cross.

"Jack ran out of paper two hours ago," Gallowglass said grimly, pointing to the easels in the front window. Each now bore a single sheet, but the drifts of paper surrounding their tripod supports suggested that these were merely a selection from a larger series of drawings.

"Matthew." Chris came from the kitchen, sipping a cup of black coffee, the aroma of the roasted beans blending with Jack's bitter scent.

"This is no place for a warmblood, Chris," Matthew said, keeping a wary eye on Jack.

"I promised Miriam I'd stay." Chris settled into a worn plantation chair and placed his coffee mug on the wide arms. When he moved, the woven seat underneath him creaked like a ship under sail. "So Jack's another one of your grandchildren?"

"Not now, Chris. Where's Andrew?" Matthew said, continuing to observe Jack at work.

"He's upstairs getting more pencils." Chris had a sip of coffee, his dark eyes taking in the details of what Jack was sketching now: a naked woman, her head thrown back in agony. "I wish like hell he would go back to drawing daffodils."

Matthew wiped his hand across his mouth, hoping to remove the sourness that rose up from his stomach. Thank God that Diana hadn't come with him. Jack would never be able to look her in the eyes again if he knew she'd seen this.

Moments later Hubbard returned to the living room. He put a box of fresh supplies on the stepladder where Jack balanced. Utterly absorbed in his work, Jack didn't react to Hubbard's presence any more than he had to Matthew's arrival.

"You should have called me sooner." Matthew kept his voice deliberately calm. In spite of his efforts, Jack turned glassy, unseeing eyes toward him as his blood rage responded to the tension in the air.

"Jack's done this before," Hubbard said. "He's drawn on his bedroom walls and on the walls in the church undercroft. But he's never made so many images so quickly. And never . . . him." He looked up.

Benjamin's eyes, nose, and mouth dominated one wall, looking down on Jack with an expression that was equal parts avarice and malice. His features were unmistakable in their cruelty, and somehow more ominous for not being contained within the outlines of a human face.

Jack had moved a few feet along from Benjamin's portrait and was now working on the last empty stretch of wall. The pictures around the room followed a rough sequence of events leading from Jack's time in London before Hubbard had made him a vampire all the way to the present day.

The easels in the window were the starting point for Jack's troubling image cycle.

Matthew examined them. Each held what artists called a study—a single element of a larger scene that helped them to understand particular problems of composition or perspective. The first was a drawing of a man's hand, skin cracked and coarsened through poverty and manual labor. The image of a cruel mouth with missing teeth occupied another easel. The third showed the crisscrossing laces on a man's breeches, along with a finger hooked and ready to pull them free. The last was of a knife, pressing against a boy's prominent hip bone until the tip slid into the skin.

Matthew put the solitary images together in his mind—hand, mouth, breeches, knife—while the St. Matthew Passion thundered in the background. He swore at the abusive scene that instantly sprang to mind.

"One of Jack's earliest memories," Hubbard said.

Matthew was reminded of his first encounter with Jack, when he would have taken the boy's ear if not for Diana's intervention. He had been yet another creature to offer Jack violence instead of compassion.

"If not for his art and music, Jack would have destroyed himself. We have often thanked God for Philippe's gift." Andrew gestured toward the cello propped up in the corner.

Matthew had recognized the instrument's distinctive scroll the moment he clapped eyes on it. He and Signor Montagnana, the instrument's Venetian maker, had dubbed the cello "the Duchess of Marlborough" for its generous, yet still elegant, curves. Matthew had learned to play on Duchess back when lutes fell out of favor and were replaced by violins, violas, and cellos. Duchess had mysteriously disappeared while he was in New Orleans disciplining Marcus's brood of children. When Matthew returned, he had asked Philippe what had happened to the instrument. His father had shrugged and muttered something about Napoleon and the English that had made no sense at all.

"Does Jack always listen to Bach when he draws?" Matthew murmured.

"He prefers Beethoven. Jack started listening to Bach after . . . you know." Hubbard's mouth twisted.

"Perhaps his drawings can help us find Benjamin," Gallowglass said.

Matthew's eyes darted over the many faces and places that might provide vital clues.

"Chris already took pictures," Gallowglass assured him.

"And a video," Chris added, "once he got to . . . er, him." Chris, too, avoided saying Benjamin's name and simply waved to where Jack was still sketching and crooning something under his breath.

Matthew held his hand up for silence.

"All the king's horses and all the king's men / Couldn't put Jack back together again.'" He shuddered and dropped what little remained of his pencil. Andrew handed him a replacement, and Jack began another detailed study of a male hand, this one reaching out in a gesture of entreaty.

"Thanks be to God. He's nearing the end of his frenzy." Some of the tension in Hubbard's shoulders dissipated. "Soon Jack will be back in his right mind."

Wanting to take advantage of the moment, Matthew moved silently to the cello. He gripped it by the neck and picked the bow off the floor where Jack had carelessly dropped it.

Matthew sat on the edge of a wooden chair, holding his ear near the instrument while he plucked and worked the bow over the strings, still able to hear the cello's round tones over the Bach that blared from the speakers on a nearby bookcase.

"Shut that noise off," he told Gallowglass, making a final adjustment to the tuning pegs before he began to play. For a few measures, the cello's music clashed with the choir and orchestra. Then Bach's great choral work fell silent. Into the void, Matthew poured music that was an intermediary step between the histrionic strains of the Passion and something that he hoped would help Jack regain his emotional bearing.

Matthew had chosen the piece carefully: the Lacrimosa from Johann Christian Bach's Requiem. Even so, Jack startled at the change in musical accompaniment, his hand stilling against the wall. As the music washed through him, his breathing became slower and more regular. When he resumed sketching, it was to draw the outlines of Westminster Abbey instead of another creature in pain.

While he played, Matthew bent his head in supplication. Had a choir been present, as the composer intended, they would have been singing the Latin mass for the dead. Since he was alone, Matthew made the cello's mournful tones imitate the absent human voices.

Lacrimosa dies illa, Matthew's cello sang. *"Tearful will be that day, / On which from the ash arises / The guilty man who is to be judged."*

Spare him therefore, God, Matthew prayed as he played the next line of music, putting his faith and anguish into every stroke of the bow.

When he reached the end of the Lacrimosa, Matthew took up the strains of Beethoven's Cello Sonata no. 1 in F Major. Beethoven had written the piece for piano as well as for cello, but Matthew hoped Jack was familiar enough with the music to fill in the missing notes.

The strokes of Jack's charcoal pencil slowed further, becoming gentler with each passing measure. Matthew recognized the torch of the Statue of Liberty, the steeple of the Center Church in New Haven.

Jack's temporary madness might be slowing to a close as he moved toward the present day, but Matthew knew he was not free of it yet.

One image was missing.

To help nudge Jack along, Matthew turned to one of his favorite pieces of music: Fauré's inspiring, hopeful Requiem. Long before he'd met Diana, one of his great joys had been to go to New College and listen to the choir perform the piece. It was not until the strains of the last section, In Paradisum, that the image Matthew had been waiting for took shape under Jack's hand. By that point Jack was sketching in time to the stately music, his body swaying to the cello's peaceful song.

"May the ranks of angels receive you, and with Lazarus, / Once a poor man, may you have eternal rest." Matthew knew these verses by heart, for they accompanied the corpse from church to grave—a place of peace that was too often denied to a creature like him. Matthew had sung these same words over Philippe's body, wept through them when Hugh had died, punished himself with them when Eleanor and Celia had perished, and repeated them for fifteen centuries as he mourned Blanca and Lucas, his warmblooded wife and child.

Tonight, however, the familiar words led Jack—and Matthew with him—to a place of second chances. Matthew watched, riveted, as Jack brought Diana's familiar, lovely face to life against the wall's creamy surface. Her eyes were wide and full of joy, her lips parted in astonishment and lifting into the beginning of a smile. Matthew had missed the precious moments when Diana first recognized Jack. He witnessed them now.

Seeing her portrait confirmed what Matthew already suspected: that it was Diana who had the power to bring Jack's life full circle. Matthew might make Jack feel safe the way a father should, but it was Diana who made him feel loved.

Matthew continued to move the bow against the strings, his fingers pressing and plucking to draw the music out. At last Jack stopped, the pencil dropping from his nerveless hands and clattering to the floor.

"You are one hell of an artist, Jack," Chris said, leaning forward in his seat to better view Diana's image.

Jack's shoulders slumped in exhaustion, and he looked around for Chris. Though they were hazy with exhaustion, there was no sign of blood rage in his eyes. They were once again brown and green.

"Matthew." Jack jumped off the top of the scaffold, soaring through the air and landing with the silence of a cat.

"Good morning, Jack." Matthew put the cello aside.

"The music—was it you?" Jack asked with a confused frown.

"I thought you might benefit from something less Baroque," Matthew said, rising to his feet. "The seventeenth century can be a bit florid for vampires. It's best taken in small doses." His glance flickered to the wall, and Jack drew a shaking hand across his forehead as he realized what he'd done.

"I'm sorry," he said, stricken. "I'll paint over it, Gallowglass. Today. I promise."

"No!" Matthew, Gallowglass, Hubbard, and Chris said in unison.

"But the walls," Jack protested. "I've ruined them."

"No more so than da Vinci or Michelangelo did," Gallowglass said mildly. "Or Matthew, come to think of it, with his doodles on the emperor's palace in Prague." Humor illuminated Jack's eyes for a moment before the light dimmed once more.

"A running deer is one thing. But nobody could possibly want to see these pictures—not even me," Jack said, staring at a particularly gruesome drawing of a decaying corpse floating faceup in the river.

"Art and music must come from the heart," Matthew said, gripping his great-grandson by the shoulder. "Even the darkest places need to be brought into the light of day, or else they'll grow until they swallow a man whole."

Jack's expression was bleak. "What if they already have?"

"You wouldn't have tried to save that woman if you were dark through and through." Matthew pointed to a desolate figure looking up at an outstretched hand. The hand matched Jack's, right down to the scar at the base of the thumb.

"But I didn't save her. She was too frightened to let me help her. Afraid of me!" Jack tried to jerk away, his elbow cracking with the strain, but Matthew refused to let him go.

"It was *her* darkness that stopped her—*her* fear—not yours," Matthew insisted.

"I don't believe you," Jack said, stubbornly holding on to the notion that his blood rage made him guilty, no matter what. Matthew got a small taste of what Philippe and Ysabeau had endured with his own steadfast refusals to accept absolution.

"That's because you've got two wolves fighting inside you. We all do." Chris joined Matthew.

"What do you mean?" Jack asked, his expression wary.

"It's an old Cherokee legend—one that my grandmother, Nana Bets, learned from her grandmother."

"You don't look like a Cherokee," Jack said, eyes narrowing.

"You'd be surprised by what's in my blood. I'm mostly French and African, with a little bit of English, Scottish, Spanish, and Native American thrown into the mix. I'm a lot like you, really. Phenotype can be misleading," Chris said with a smile. Jack looked confused, and Matthew made a mental note to buy him a basic biology textbook.

"Uh-huh," Jack said skeptically, and Chris laughed. "And the wolves?"

"According to my grandmother's people, two wolves live inside every creature: one evil and the other good. They spend all their time trying to destroy each other."

It was, Matthew thought, as good a description of blood rage as he was ever likely to hear from someone not afflicted with the disease.

"My bad wolf is winning." Jack looked sad.

"He doesn't have to," Chris promised. "Nana Bets said the wolf who wins is the wolf you feed. The evil wolf feeds on anger, guilt, sorrow, lies, and regret. The good wolf needs a diet of love and honesty, spiced up with big spoonfuls of compassion and faith. So if you want the good wolf to win, you're going to have to starve the other one."

"What if I can't stop feeding the bad wolf?" Jack looked worried. "What if I fail?"

"You won't fail," Matthew said firmly.

"We won't let you," Chris said, nodding in agreement. "There are five of us in this room. Your big bad wolf doesn't stand a chance."

"Five?" Jack whispered, looking around at Matthew and Gallowglass, Hubbard and Chris. "You're all going to help me?"

"Every last one of us," Chris promised, taking Jack's hand. When Chris jerked his head at him, Matthew obediently rested his own hand on top.

"All for one and all that jazz." Chris turned to Gallowglass. "What are you waiting for? Get over here and join us."

"Bah. The Musketeers were all tossers," Gallowglass said, scowling as he stalked toward them. In spite of his dismissive words, Matthew's nephew laid his huge paw atop theirs. "Don't be telling Baldwin about this, young Jack, or I'll give your evil wolf a double helping of dinner."

"What about you, Andrew?" Chris called across the room.

"I believe the saying is '*Un pour tous, tous pour un,*' not 'All for one and all that jazz.'"

Matthew winced. The words were right enough, but Hubbard's Cockney accent made them practically unintelligible. Philippe should have delivered a French tutor along with the cello.

Hubbard's gaunt hand was the last to join the pile. Matthew saw his thumb move top to bottom, then right to left, as the priest bestowed his blessing on their strange pact. They were an unlikely band, Matthew thought: three creatures related by blood, a fourth bound by loyalty, and a fifth who had joined them for no apparent reason other than that he was a good man.

He hoped that, together, they would be enough to help Jack heal.

In the aftermath of his furious activity, Jack had wanted to talk. He sat with Matthew and Hubbard in the living room, surrounded by his past, and shifted the burden of some of his harrowing experiences onto Matthew's shoulders. On the subject of Benjamin, however, he was mute. Matthew wasn't surprised. How could words convey the horror Jack had endured at Benjamin's hands?

"Come on, Jackie," Gallowglass interrupted, holding up Lobero's leash. "Mop needs a walk."

"I'd like a bit of fresh air, too." Andrew unfolded from a strange red chair that looked like a piece of modern sculpture but that Matthew had discovered was surprisingly comfortable.

As the front door closed, Chris sauntered into the living room with a fresh cup of coffee. Matthew didn't know how the man survived with so much caffeine in his veins.

"I talked to your son tonight—your other son, Marcus." Chris took up his usual seat in the plantation chair. "Nice guy. Smart, too. You must be proud of him."

"I am," Matthew said warily. "Why did Marcus call?"

"We called him." Chris sipped at his coffee. "Miriam thought he should see the video. Once he had, Marcus agreed we should take some more blood from Jack. We took two samples."

"You *what?*" Matthew was aghast.

"Hubbard gave me permission. He is Jack's next of kin," Chris replied calmly.

"You think I'm worried about informed consent?" Matthew was barely able to keep his temper in check. "Drawing blood from a vampire in the grip of blood rage—you could have been killed."

"It was a perfect opportunity to monitor the changes that take place in a vampire's body chemistry at the onset of blood rage," Chris said. "We'll need that information if we want to have a shot at coming up with a medicine that might lessen the symptoms."

Matthew frowned. "Lessen the symptoms? We're looking for a cure."

Chris reached down and picked up a folder. He offered it to Matthew. "The latest findings."

Both Hubbard and Jack had been swabbed and given blood samples. They'd been rushed through processing, and their genome report was due any day. Matthew took the folder with nerveless fingers, afraid of what he might find inside it.

"I'm sorry, Matthew," Chris said with heartfelt regret.

Matthew's eyes raced over the results, flipping the pages.

"Marcus identified them. No one else would have. We weren't looking in the right place," Chris said.

Matthew couldn't absorb what he was seeing. It changed . . . everything.

"Jack has more of the triggers in his noncoding DNA than you do." Chris paused. "I have to ask, Matthew. Are you sure you can trust Jack around Diana?"

Before Matthew could respond, the front door opened. There was none of the usual chatter that accompanied Jack's appearance, or Gallowglass's cheerful whistling, or Andrew's pious sermonizing. The only sound was Lobero's low whine.

Matthew's nostrils flared, and he leaped to his feet, the test results scattering around him. Then he was gone, moving to the doorway in a flash.

"What the hell?" Chris said behind him.

"We met someone while we were out walking," Gallowglass said, leading a reluctant Lobero into the house.

M ove," Baldwin commanded, holding Jack by the scruff of his neck. Matthew had seen that hand tear another vampire's head clean off.

Jack hadn't witnessed that brutal episode, but he knew he was at Baldwin's mercy just the same. The boy was white-skinned and wide-eyed, with
enormous black pupils. Not surprisingly, he obeyed Baldwin without hesitation.

Lobero knew it, too. Gallowglass still held the leash, but the dog circled
the Gael's feet with eyes fixed on his master.

"It's okay, Mop," Jack assured his dog in a whisper, but Lobero was having none of it.

"Trouble, Matthew?" Chris was so close that Matthew could feel his
breath.

"There's always trouble," Matthew said grimly.

"Go home," Jack urged Chris. "Take Mop, too, and—" Jack stopped
with a wince. Blood suffused the skin on his neck where Baldwin's fingertips were leaving a dark bruise.

"They're staying," Baldwin hissed.

Jack had made a strategic error. Baldwin delighted in destroying what
other people loved. Some experience in his past must have shaped the impulse, but Matthew had never discovered what it was. Baldwin would never
let Chris or Mop go now. Not until he got what he came for.

"And you don't give orders. You take them." Baldwin was careful to keep
the boy between him and Matthew as he pushed him toward the living
room. It was a devastatingly simple and effective tactic, one that brought
back painful memories.

Jack is not Eleanor, Matthew told himself. Jack was a vampire, too. But
he was Matthew's blood, and Baldwin could use him to bring Matthew to
heel.

"That stunt you pulled in the square will be the last time you challenge me, mongrel." Baldwin's shirt showed teeth marks at the shoulder, and there were beads of blood around the torn fabric.

Christ. Jack had bitten Baldwin.

"But I'm not yours." Jack sounded desperate. "Tell him that I belong to you, Matthew!"

"And who do you think Matthew belongs to?" Baldwin whispered in his ear, quietly menacing.

"Diana," Jack snarled, turning on his captor.

"Diana?" Baldwin's laugh was mocking, and the blow he gave Jack would have flattened a warmblood twice his size and weight. Jack's knees met the hard wooden floors. "Get in here, Matthew. And shut that dog up."

"Disavow Jack before the de Clermont sire and I'll see you to hell personally," Hubbard hissed, grabbing at Matthew's sleeve as he went past.

Matthew looked at him coldly, and Hubbard dropped his arm.

"Let him go. He's my blood," Matthew said, stalking into the room. "Then go back to Manhattan where you belong, Baldwin."

"Oh," Chris said in a tone that suggested he finally saw the light. "Of course. You live on Central Park, don't you?"

Baldwin didn't reply. In fact, he owned most of that stretch of Fifth Avenue and liked to keep a close eye on his investments. Recently he had been developing his hunting ground in the Meatpacking District, filling it with nightclubs to complement the butcher shops, but as a rule he preferred not to reside where he fed.

"No wonder you're such an entitled bastard," Chris said. "Well, buddy, you're in New Haven now. We play by different rules here."

"Rules?" Baldwin drawled. "In New Haven?"

"Yeah. All for one and all that jazz." It was Chris's call to arms.

Matthew was so close that he could feel Chris's muscles bunch and was prepared when the small knife went past his ear. The thin blade was so insignificant that it would barely have damaged a human's skin, never mind Baldwin's tough hide. Matthew reached up and pinched it between his fingertips before it could reach its target. Chris scowled at him reproachfully, and Matthew shook his head.

"Don't." Matthew might have let Chris get in a solid punch, but Baldwin had narrower views when it came to the privileges that should be afforded to warmbloods. He turned to Baldwin. "Leave. Jack is my blood and my problem."

"And miss all the fun?" Baldwin bent Jack's head to the side. Jack looked up at Baldwin, his expression black and deadly. "Quite a resemblance, Matthew."

"I like to think so," Matthew said coolly, giving Jack a tight smile. He took Lobero's lead from Gallowglass. The dog quieted immediately. "Baldwin might be thirsty. Offer him a drink, Gallowglass."

Maybe that would sweeten Baldwin's mood long enough to get Jack safely away. Matthew could send him to Marcus's house with Hubbard. It was a better alternative than Diana's house on Court Street. If his wife got wind of Baldwin's presence, she'd be on Wooster Square with a firedrake and a lightning bolt.

"I've got a full larder," Gallowglass said. "Coffee, wine, water, blood. I'm sure I could scare up some hemlock and honey if you'd prefer that, Uncle."

"What I require only the boy can provide." Without warning or preamble, Baldwin's teeth ripped into Jack's neck. His bite was savage, deliberately so.

This was vampire justice—swift, unbending, remorseless. For minor infractions the sire's punishment would consist only of this public show of submission. Through that blood the sire received a thin trickle of his progeny's innermost thoughts and memories. The ritual stripped a vampire's soul bare, making him shamefully vulnerable. Acquiring another creature's secrets, by whatever means, sustained a vampire in much the same way the hunt did, nourishing that part of his soul that forever sought to possess more.

If the offenses were more significant, the ritual of submission would be followed by death. Killing another vampire was physically taxing, emotionally draining, and spiritually devastating. It was why most vampire sires appointed one of their kin to do it for them. Though Philippe and Hugh had polished the de Clermonts' façade to a high sheen over the centuries, it was Matthew who had performed all of the house's dirty maintenance.

There were hundreds of ways to kill a vampire, and Matthew knew them all. You could drink a vampire dry as he had Philippe. You could weaken a vampire physically by releasing his blood slowly and putting him in the dreaded state of suspension known as thrall. Unable to fight back, the vampire could be tortured into a confession or mercifully allowed to die. There was beheading and evisceration, though some preferred the more old-fashioned method of punching through the rib cage and wrenching out the heart. You could sever the carotid and the aorta, a method that Gerbert's lovely assassin, Juliette, had tried and failed to use on him.

Matthew prayed that taking Jack's blood and his memories would suffice for Baldwin tonight.

Too late, he remembered that Jack's memories held tales best left untold.

Too late, he caught the scent of honeysuckle and summer storms.

Too late, he saw Diana release Corra.

Diana's firedrake rose up from her mistress's shoulders and into the air. Corra swooped down on Baldwin with a shriek, talons extended and wings aflame. Baldwin grabbed the firedrake by the foot with his free hand, wresting her body away. Corra hurtled into the wall, her wing crumpling at the impact. Diana bent double, grabbing at her own arm in sudden pain, but it didn't shake her resolve.

"Take your hands. Off. My. Son." Diana's skin was gleaming, the subtle nimbus that was always visible without her disguising spell now appearing as a distinctive, prismatic light. Rainbows of color shot under her skin—not just the hands but up her arms, along the tendons of her neck, twisting and spiraling as though the cords in her fingers had extended through her whole body.

When Lobero lunged at the end of his lead, trying to get to Corra, Matthew let the dog go. Lobero crouched over the firedrake, licking at her face and nudging her with his nose as she struggled to get up and go to Diana's aid.

But Diana didn't need help—not from Matthew, not from Lobero, not even from Corra. His wife straightened, splayed out her left hand with the palm facing down, and directed her fingers at the floor. The wooden planks shattered and split, re-forming into thick canes that rose up and wound themselves around Baldwin's feet, keeping him in place. Lethally long, sharp thorns sprang out of the shoots, digging through his clothes and into flesh.

Diana fixed her gaze on Baldwin, reached out with her right hand, and pulled. Jack's wrist jerked out and to the side as if he were tethered to her. The rest of him followed, and in moments he was lying in a heap on the floor, out of Baldwin's reach.

Matthew adopted a similar pose to Lobero's, standing over Jack's body to shield him.

"Enough, Baldwin." Matthew's hand sliced through the air.

"I'm sorry, Matthew," Jack whispered, remaining on the floor. "He came out of nowhere and went straight for Gallowglass. When I'm surprised—" He stopped with a shudder, his knees drawing close to his chest. "I didn't know who he was."

Miriam came into the room. After studying the scene, she took charge. She pointed Gallowglass and Hubbard in Jack's direction and cast a worried look at Diana, who stood unmoving and unblinking, as though she had taken root in the living room.

"Is Jack okay?" Chris asked, his voice strained.

"He'll be fine. Every vampire alive has been bitten by their sire at least once," Miriam said, trying to put his mind at rest. Chris didn't seem comforted by this revelation about creature family life.

Matthew helped Jack up. The bite mark on his neck was shallow and would heal quickly, but at the moment it looked gruesome. Matthew touched it briefly, hoping to reassure Jack that he would, as Miriam promised, be fine.

"Can you see to Corra?" Matthew asked Miriam as he handed Jack off to Gallowglass and Hubbard.

Miriam nodded.

Matthew was already crossing the room, his hands wrapping around Baldwin's throat.

"I want your word that if Diana lets you go, you will not touch her for what happened here tonight." Matthew's fingers tightened. "If not, I will kill you, Baldwin. Make no mistake about that."

"We're not finished here, Matthew," Baldwin warned.

"I know." Matthew locked his eyes on his brother until the man nodded.

Then he turned to Diana. The colors pulsing beneath her skin reminded him of the shining ball of energy she had gifted him in Madison before either of them knew she was a weaver. The colors were brightest at her fingertips, as though her magic were waiting there, ready to be released. Matthew knew how unpredictable his own blood rage could be when it was that close to the surface, and he treated his wife with caution.

"Diana?" Matthew smoothed the hair back from her face, searching her blue-and-gold irises for signs of recognition. Instead he saw infinity, her eyes fixed on some invisible vista. He changed tack, trying to bring her back to the here and now.

"Jack is with Gallowglass and Andrew, *ma lionne.* Baldwin will not harm him tonight." Matthew's words were carefully chosen. "You should take him back home."

Chris started, ready to voice a protest.

"Perhaps Chris will go with you," Matthew continued smoothly. "Corra and Lobero, too."

"Corra," Diana croaked. Her eyes flickered, but not even concern for her firedrake could break her mesmerized stare. Matthew wondered what she saw that the rest of them did not and why it held such a powerful attraction for her. He felt a disturbing pang of jealousy.

"Miriam is with Corra." Matthew found himself unable to look away from the navy depths of her eyes.

"Baldwin . . . hurt her." Diana sounded confused, as though she had forgotten that vampires were not like other creatures. She rubbed absently at her arm.

Just when Matthew thought whatever it was that held her might give way to reason, Diana's anger caught again. He could smell it—taste it.

"He hurt Jack." Diana's fingers opened wide in a sudden spasm. No longer concerned with the wisdom of getting between a weaver and her power, Matthew caught them before they could work magic.

"Baldwin will let you take Jack home. In return you have to release Baldwin. We can't have the two of you at war. The family wouldn't survive it." Based on what he'd seen tonight, Diana was as single-minded as Baldwin when it came to destroying the obstacles in her way.

Matthew lifted her hands and brushed the knuckles with his lips. "Remember when we talked about our children in London? We spoke then about what they would need."

That got Diana's attention. *At last.* Her eyes focused on him.

"Love," she whispered. "A grown-up to take responsibility for them. A soft place to land."

"That's right." Matthew smiled. "Jack needs you. Release Baldwin from your spell."

Diana's magic gave way in a shudder that passed through her from feet to head. She flicked her fingers in Baldwin's direction. The thorns withdrew from his skin. The canes loosened, retracting back into the splintered floorboards surrounding the vampire. Soon he was free and Gallowglass's house was returned to its normal, disenchanted state.

While her spell slowly unraveled, Diana went to Jack and cupped his face. The skin on his neck was already starting to knit together, but it would take several days to heal completely. Her generous mouth became a thin line.

"Don't worry," Jack told her, covering the wound self-consciously.

"Come on, Jackie. Diana and I will take you to Court Street. You must be famished." Gallowglass clapped his hand on Jack's shoulder. Jack was exhausted but tried to look less wan for Diana's sake.

"Corra," Diana said, beckoning to her firedrake. Corra limped toward her, gaining strength as she drew closer to her mistress. When the weaver and the firedrake were nearly touching, Corra faded into invisibility as she and Diana became one.

"Let Chris help you home," Matthew said, careful to keep his broad frame between his wife and the disturbing images on the walls. She was, thankfully, too tired to do more than glance at them.

Matthew was pleased to see that Miriam had rounded up everyone in the house except Baldwin. They were huddled in the entrance—Chris, Andrew, Lobero, and Miriam—waiting for Diana, Gallowglass, and Jack. The more creatures there to support the boy, the better.

Watching them go took every ounce of control Matthew had. He forced himself to wave encouragingly at Diana when she turned for one more glimpse of him. Once they disappeared between the houses on Court Street, he returned to Baldwin.

His brother was staring up at the last section of the murals, his shirt dotted with dark stains where Jack's teeth and Diana's briars had pierced the skin.

"Jack is the vampire murderer. I saw it in his thoughts, and now I see it here on the walls. We've been looking for him for more than a year. How has he evaded the Congregation all this time?" Baldwin asked.

"He was with Benjamin. Then he was on the run." Matthew deliberately avoided looking at the horrifying images that surrounded Benjamin's disembodied features. They were, he supposed, no more hideous than other brutal acts that vampires had perpetrated over the years. What made them so unbearable was that Jack had done them.

"Jack has to be stopped." Baldwin's tone was matter-of-fact.

"God forgive me." Matthew lowered his head.

"Philippe was right. Your Christianity really does make you perfect for your job." Baldwin snorted. "What other faith promises to wash away your sins if only you confess them?"

Sadly, Baldwin had never grasped the concept of atonement. His view of Matthew's faith was purely transactional—you went to church, confessed, and walked out a clean man. But salvation was more complicated. Philippe had come to understand that in the end, although he had long found Matthew's constant search for forgiveness irritating and irrational.

"You know very well there's no place for him among the de Clermonts— not if his disease is as serious as these pictures suggest." Baldwin saw in Jack what Benjamin had seen: a dangerous weapon, one that could be shaped and twisted to make it as deadly as possible. Unlike Benjamin, Baldwin had a conscience. He would not use the weapon that had come so unexpectedly into his hand, but neither would he allow it to be used by another.

Matthew's head remained bowed, weighted down with memories and regret. Baldwin's next words were expected, but Matthew felt them as a blow nevertheless.

"Kill him," commanded the head of the de Clermont family.

When Matthew returned home to the brightly painted red door with the white trim and the black pediment, it opened wide.

Diana had been waiting. She had changed into something that would ward off the chill and was bundled into one of his old cardigans, lessening the scent of the others she'd come into contact with that night. Even so, Matthew's kiss of greeting was rough and possessive, and he only reluctantly drew away.

"What's wrong?" Diana's fingers went to Philippe's arrowhead. It had become a reliable signal that her anxiety was climbing. The smudges of color on their tips told the same tale, growing more visible with every passing moment.

Matthew looked heavenward, hoping to find some guidance. What he saw instead was a sky totally devoid of stars. The reasonable, human part of him knew that this was due to the city's bright lights and tonight's full moon. But the vampire within was instinctively alarmed. There was nothing to orient him in such a place, no markers to guide his way.

"Come." Matthew picked up Diana's coat from the chair in the front hall, took his wife's hand, and led her down the steps.

"Where are we going?" she said, struggling to keep up.

"To a place where I can see the stars," Matthew replied.

22

Matthew headed north and west and out of the city with Diana beside him. He drove uncharacteristically fast, and in less than fifteen minutes they were on a quiet lane tucked into the shadow of the peaks known locally as the Sleeping Giant. Matthew pulled in to an otherwise dark driveway and shut off the car's ignition. A porch light came on, and an elderly man peered into the darkness.

"That you, Mr. Clairmont?" The man's voice was faint and thready but there was still a sharp intelligence in his eyes.

"It is, Mr. Phelps," Matthew said with a nod. He circled the car and helped Diana down. "My wife and I are going up to the cottage."

"Nice to meet you, ma'am," Mr. Phelps said, touching his forehead with his hand. "Mr. Gallowglass called to warn me you might be stopping by to check on things. He said not to worry if I heard somebody out here."

"I'm sorry we woke you," Diana said.

"I'm an old man, Mrs. Clairmont. I don't get much shut-eye these days. I figure I'll sleep when I'm dead," Mr. Phelps said with a wheezing laugh. "You'll find everything you need up on the mountain."

"Thank you for watching over the place," Matthew said.

"It's a family tradition," Mr. Phelps replied. "You'll find Mr. Whitmore's Ranger by the shed, if you don't want to use my old Gator. I don't imagine your wife will want to walk all that way. The park gates are closed, but you know how to get in. Have a nice night."

Mr. Phelps went back inside, the screen hitting the door frame with a snap of aluminum and mesh.

Matthew took Diana by the elbow and steered her toward what looked like a cross between a golf cart with unusually rugged tires and a dune buggy. He let go of her only long enough to round the vehicle and climb in.

The gate into the park was so well hidden it was all but invisible, and the dirt trail that served as a road was unlit and unmarked, but Matthew found both with ease. He navigated a few sharp turns, climbing steadily as they traveled up the side of the mountain, passing through the edges of heavy forest until they reached an open field with a small wooden house tucked under the trees. The lights were on inside, making it as golden and inviting as a cottage in a fairy tale.

Matthew stopped Marcus's Ranger and engaged the brake. He took a deep breath to drink in the night scents of mountain pine and dew-touched grass. Below, the valley looked bleak. He wondered if it was his mood or the silvered moonlight that rendered it so unwelcoming.

"The ground is uneven. I don't want you to fall." Matthew held out his hand, giving Diana the choice whether to take it or not.

After a concerned look, she put her hand in his. Matthew scanned the horizon, unable to stop searching for new threats. Then his attention turned skyward.

"The moon is bright tonight," he mused. "Even here it's hard to see the stars."

"That's because it's Mabon," Diana said quietly.

"Mabon?" Matthew looked startled.

She nodded. "One year ago you walked into the Bodleian Library and straight into my heart. As soon as that wicked mouth of yours smiled, the moment your eyes lightened with recognition even though we'd never met before, I knew that my life would never be the same."

Diana's words gave Matthew a momentary reprieve from the relentless agitation that Baldwin's order and Chris's news had set off in him, and for a brief moment the world was poised between absence and desire, between blood and fear, between the warmth of summer and the icy depths of winter.

"What's wrong?" Diana searched his face. "Is it Jack? The blood rage? Baldwin?"

"Yes. No. In a way." Matthew drove his hands through his hair and whirled around to avoid her keen gaze. "Baldwin knows that Jack killed those warmbloods in Europe. He knows that Jack is the vampire murderer."

"Surely this isn't the first time a vampire's thirst for blood has resulted in unexpected deaths," Diana said, trying to defuse the situation.

"This time it's different." There was no easy way to say it. "Baldwin ordered me to kill Jack."

"No. I forbid it." Diana's words echoed, and a wind kicked up from the east. She whirled around, and Matthew caught her. She struggled in his grip, sending a gray-and-brown twist of air howling around his feet.

"Don't walk away from me." He wasn't sure he could control himself if she did. "You must listen to reason."

"No." Still she tried to avoid him. "You can't give up on him. Jack won't always have blood rage. You're going to find a cure."

"Blood rage has no cure." Matthew would have given his life to change that fact.

"What?" Diana's shock was evident.

"We've been running the new DNA samples. For the first time, we're able to chart a multigenerational pedigree that extends beyond Marcus. Chris and Miriam traced the blood-rage gene from Ysabeau through me and Andrew down to Jack." Matthew had Diana's complete attention now.

"Blood rage is a developmental anomaly," he continued. "There's a genetic component, but the blood-rage gene appears to be triggered by something in our noncoding DNA. Jack and I have that something. *Maman*, Marcus, and Andrew don't."

"I don't understand," Diana whispered.

"During my rebirth something already in my noncoding, human DNA reacted to the new genetic information flooding my system," Matthew said patiently. "We know that vampire genes are brutal—they push aside what's human in order to dominate the newly modified cells. But they don't replace everything. If they did, my genome and Ysabeau's would be identical. Instead I am her child—a combination of the genetic ingredients I inherited from my human parents as well as what I inherited from her."

"So you had blood rage *before* Ysabeau made you a vampire?" Diana was understandably confused.

"No. But I possessed the triggers the blood-rage gene needed to express itself," Matthew said. "Marcus has identified specific noncoding DNA that he believes plays a role."

"In what he calls junk DNA?" Diana asked.

Matthew nodded.

"Then a cure is still possible," she insisted. "In a few years—"

"No, *mon coeur*." He couldn't allow her hopes to rise. "The more we understand the blood-rage gene and learn about the noncoding genes, the better the treatment might become, but this is not a disease we can cure. Our only hope is to prevent it and, God willing, lessen its symptoms."

"Until you do, you can teach Jack how to control it." Diana's face remained set in stubborn lines. "There's no need to kill him."

"Jack's symptoms are far worse than mine. The genetic factors that appear to trigger the disease are present at much higher levels in him." Matthew blinked back the blood tears that he could feel forming. "He won't suffer. I promise you."

"But *you* will. You say I pay a price for dealing with matters of life and death? So do you. Jack will be gone, but you will live on, hating yourself," Diana said. "Think of what Philippe's death has cost you."

Matthew could think of little else. He had killed other creatures since his father's death, but only to settle his own scores. Until tonight the last de Clermont sire to command him to kill had been Philippe. And the death Philippe had ordered was his own.

"Jack is suffering, Diana. This would mean an end to it." Matthew used the same words Philippe had to convince his wife to admit the inevitable.

"For him maybe. Not for us." Diana's hand strayed to the round swell of her belly. "The twins could have blood rage. Will you kill them, too?"

She waited for him to deny it, to tell her that she was insane to even think of such a thing. But he didn't.

"When the Congregation discovers what Jack has done—and it's only a matter of time before they do—they will kill him. And they won't care how frightened he is or how much pain they cause. Baldwin will try to kill Jack before it comes to that, to keep the Congregation out of the family business. If he tries to run, Jack could fall into Benjamin's hands. If he does, Benjamin will exact a terrible revenge for Jack's betrayal. Death would be a blessing then." Matthew's face and voice were impassive, but the agony that flashed through Diana's eyes would haunt him forever.

"Then Jack will disappear. He'll go far away, where nobody can find him."

Matthew smothered his impatience. He'd known that Diana was stubborn when he first met her. It was one of the reasons he loved her—even though at times it drove him to distraction. "A lone vampire cannot survive. Like wolves, we have to be part of a pack or we go mad. Think of Benjamin, Diana, and what happened when I abandoned him."

"We'll go with him," she said, grasping at straws in her efforts to save Jack.

"That would only make it easier for Benjamin or the Congregation to hunt him down."

"Then you must establish a scion immediately, as Marcus suggested," Diana said. "Jack will have a whole family to protect him."

"If I do, I'll have to acknowledge Benjamin. That would expose not only Jack's blood rage but my own. It would put Ysabeau and Marcus in terrible danger—the twins, too. And it's not just them who will suffer if we stand against the Congregation without Baldwin's support." Matthew drew a ragged breath. "If you're at my side—my consort—the Congregation will demand your submission as well as mine."

"Submission?" Diana said faintly.

"This is war, Diana. That's what happens to women who fight. You heard my mother's tale. Do you think your fate would be any different at the vampires' hands?"

She shook her head.

"You must believe me: We are far better off remaining in Baldwin's family than striking out on our own," he insisted.

"You're wrong. The twins and I will never be entirely safe under Baldwin's rule. Neither will Jack. Standing our ground is the only possible way forward. Every other road just leads back into the past," Diana said. "And we know from experience that the past is never more than a temporary reprieve."

"You don't understand the forces that would gather against us if I do this. Everything my children and grandchildren have done or will ever do is laid at my doorstep under vampire law. The vampire murders? I committed them. Benjamin's evil deeds? I am guilty of them." Matthew had to make Diana see what this decision might cost.

"They can't blame you for what Benjamin and Jack did," Diana protested.

"But they can." Matthew cradled her hands between his. "I made Benjamin. If I hadn't, none of these crimes would have taken place. It was my job, as Benjamin's sire and Jack's grandsire, to curb them if possible or to kill them if not."

"That's barbaric." Diana tugged at her hands. He could feel the power burning under her skin.

"No, that's vampire honor. Vampires can survive among warmbloods because of three systems of belief: law, honor, and justice. You saw vampire justice at work tonight," Matthew said. "It's swift—and brutal. If I stand as sire of my own scion, I'll have to mete it out, too."

"Rather you than Baldwin," Diana retorted. "If he's in charge, I'll always wonder if this is the day he will grow tired of protecting me and the twins and order our deaths."

His wife had a point. But it put Matthew in an impossible situation. To save Jack, Matthew would have to disobey Baldwin. If he disobeyed Baldwin, he would have no choice but to become the sire of his own scion. That would require convincing a pack of rebellious vampires to accept his leadership and risk their own extermination by exposing the blood rage in their ranks. It would be a bloody, violent, and complicated process.

"Please, Matthew," Diana whispered. "I beg you: Do not follow Baldwin's order."

Matthew examined his wife's face. He took into account the pain and desperation he saw in her eyes. It was impossible to say no.

"Very well," Matthew replied reluctantly. "I'll go to New Orleans—on one condition."

Diana's relief was evident. "Anything. Name it."

"You don't come with me." Matthew kept his voice even, though the mere mention of being away from his mate was enough to send the blood rage surging through his veins.

"Don't you dare order me to stay here!" Diana said, her own anger flaring.

"You can't be anywhere near me while I do this." Centuries of practice made it possible for Matthew to keep his own feelings in check, in spite of his wife's agitation. "I don't want to go anywhere without you. Christ, I can barely let you out of my sight. But having you in New Orleans while I battle my own grandchildren would put you in terrible danger. And it wouldn't be Baldwin or the Congregation who would be putting your safety at risk. It would be me."

"You would never hurt me." Diana had clung to this belief from the beginning of their relationship. It was time to tell her the truth.

"Eleanor thought that—once. Then I killed her in a moment of madness and jealousy. Jack's not the only vampire in this family whose blood rage is set off by love and loyalty." Matthew met his wife's eyes. "So is mine."

"And you and Eleanor were merely lovers. We're mates." Diana's expression revealed her dawning understanding. "All along you've said I shouldn't trust you. You swore you would kill me yourself before you let anyone else touch me."

"I told you the truth." Matthew's fingertips traced the line of Diana's cheekbone, sweeping up to catch the tear that threatened to fall from the corner of her eye.

"But not the whole truth. Why didn't you tell me that our mating bond was going to make your blood rage worse?" Diana cried.

"I thought I could find a cure. Until then, I thought I could manage my feelings," Matthew replied. "But you have become as vital to me as breath and blood. My heart no longer knows where I end and you begin. I knew that you were a powerful witch from the moment I saw you, but how could I have imagined that you would have so much power over me?"

Diana answered him not with words but with a kiss that was startling in its intensity. Matthew's response matched it. When they drew apart they were both shaken. Diana touched her lips with trembling fingers. Matthew rested his head atop hers, his heart—her heart—thudding with emotion.

"Founding a new scion will require my complete attention, as well as complete control," Matthew said when at last he was able to speak. "If I succeed—"

"You must," Diana said firmly. "You will."

"Very well, *ma lionne*. *When* I succeed, there will still be times when I'll have to handle matters on my own," Matthew explained. "It isn't that I distrust you, but I cannot trust myself."

"Like you've handled Jack," Diana said. Matthew nodded.

"Being apart from you will be a living hell, but being distracted would be unspeakably dangerous. As for my control . . . well, I think we know just how little I have when you are around." He brushed her lips with another kiss, this one seductive. Diana's cheeks reddened.

"What will I do while you're in New Orleans?" Diana asked. "There must be some way I can help you."

"Find that missing page from Ashmole 782," Matthew replied. "We'll need the Book of Life for leverage—no matter what happens between me and Marcus's children." The fact that the search would keep Diana from being directly involved in the disaster should this harebrained scheme fail was an added benefit. "Phoebe will help you look for the third illumination. Go to Sept-Tours. Wait there for me."

"How will I know you're all right?" Diana asked. The reality of their impending separation was beginning to sink in.

"I'll find a way. But no phone calls. No e-mails. We can't leave a trail of evidence for the Congregation to follow if Baldwin—or one of my own blood—turns me in," Matthew said. "You have to remain in his good graces, at least until you are recognized as a de Clermont."

"But that's months away!" Diana's expression turned desperate. "What if the children are born early?"

"Marthe and Sarah will deliver them," he said gently. "There's no telling how long this will take, Diana." *It could be years,* Matthew thought.

"How will I make the children understand why their father isn't with them?" she asked, somehow hearing his unspoken words.

"You will tell the twins I had to stay away because I loved them—and their mother—with all my heart." Matthew's voice broke. He pulled her into his arms, holding her as though that might delay her inevitable departure.

"Matthew?" The familiar voice came out of the darkness.

"Marcus?" Diana had not heard his approach, though Matthew had picked up first his scent and then the soft sound of his son's footsteps as he climbed the mountain.

"Hello, Diana." Marcus stepped out of the shadows and into a patch of moonlight.

She frowned with concern. "Is something wrong at Sept-Tours?"

"Everything in France is fine. I thought Matthew needed me here," Marcus said.

"And Phoebe?" Diana asked.

"With Alain and Marthe." Marcus sounded tired. "I couldn't help but overhear your plans. There will be no turning back once we put them in motion. Are you sure about forming a scion, Matthew?"

"No," Matthew said, unable to lie. "But Diana is." He looked at his wife. "Chris and Gallowglass are waiting for you down the path. Go now, *mon coeur.*"

"This minute?" For a moment Diana looked frightened at the enormity of what they were about to do.

"It will never be any easier. You're going to have to walk away from me.

Don't look back. And for God's sake don't run." Matthew would never be able to control himself if she did.

"But—" Diana pressed her lips together. She nodded and dashed the back of her hand against her cheek, brushing away sudden tears.

Matthew put more than a thousand years of longing into one last kiss.

"I'll never—" Diana began.

"Hush." He silenced her with another touch of his lips. "No nevers for us, remember?"

Matthew set her away from him. It was only a few inches, but it might have been a thousand leagues. As soon as he did, his blood howled. He turned her so she could see the two faint circles of light from their friends' flashlights.

"Don't make this harder on him," Marcus told Diana softly. "Go now. Slowly."

For a few seconds, Matthew wasn't sure she would be able to do it. He could see the gold and silver threads hanging from her fingertips, sparking and shimmering as if trying to fuse together something that had been suddenly, horribly broken. She took a tentative step. Then another. Matthew saw the muscles in her back trembling as she struggled to keep her composure. Her head dropped. Then she squared her shoulders and slowly walked in the opposite direction.

"I knew from the goddamn beginning you were going to break her heart," Chris called to Matthew when she reached him. He drew Diana into his arms.

But it was Matthew's heart that was breaking, taking with it his composure, his sanity, and his last traces of humanity.

Marcus watched him without blinking as Gallowglass and Chris led Diana away. When they disappeared from sight, Matthew leaped forward. Marcus caught him.

"Are you going to make it without her?" Marcus asked his father. He had been away from Phoebe for less than twelve hours and already he was uneasy at their separation.

"I have to," Matthew said, though at the moment he couldn't imagine how.

"Does Diana know what being apart will do to you?" Marcus still had nightmares about Ysabeau and how much she had suffered during Philippe's capture and death. It had been like watching someone go through the worst withdrawal imaginable—the shaking, the irrational behavior, the physical pain. And his grandparents were among the fortunate few vampires who, though mated, could be separated for periods of time. Matthew's blood rage made that impossible. Even before Matthew and Diana were fully mated, Ysabeau had warned Marcus that his father was not to be trusted if something were to happen to Diana.

"Does she know?" Marcus repeated.

"Not entirely. She knows what will happen to me if I stay here and obey my brother, though." Matthew shook off his son's arm. "You don't have to go along with this—with me. You still have a choice. Baldwin will take you in, so long as you beg for his forgiveness."

"I made my choice in 1781, remember?" Marcus's eyes were silver in the moonlight. "Tonight you've proved it was the right one."

"There are no guarantees this will work," Matthew warned. "Baldwin might refuse to sanction the scion. The Congregation could get wind of what we're doing before we're through. God knows your own children have reason to oppose it."

"They're not going to make it easy for you, but my children will do what I tell them to do. Eventually. Besides," Marcus said, "you're under my protection now."

Matthew looked at him in surprise.

"The safety of you, your mate, and those twins she's carrying is now the Knights of Lazarus's top priority," Marcus explained. "Baldwin can threaten all he wants, but I have more than a thousand vampires, daemons, and yes, even witches, under my command."

"They'll never obey you," Matthew said, "not when they find out what you're asking them to fight for."

"How do you think I recruited them in the first place?" Marcus shook his head. "Do you really think you're the only two creatures on the planet who have reason to dislike the covenant's restrictions?"

But Matthew was too distracted to respond. He already felt the first, restless impulse to go after Diana. Soon he wouldn't be able to sit still for more than a few moments before his instincts demanded he go to her. And it would only get worse from there.

"Come on." Marcus put his arm across his father's shoulders. "Jack and Andrew are waiting for us. I suppose the damn dog will have to come to New Orleans, too."

Still Matthew didn't respond. He was listening for Diana's voice, her distinctive step, the rhythm of her heartbeat.

There was only silence, and stars too faint to show him the way home.

Sol in Libra

When the sun passeth through Libra, it is
a good time for journeys. Beware of open
enemies, war, and opposition.

—Anonymous English Commonplace Book, c. 1590,
Gonçalves MS 4890, f. 9ʳ

23

"Let me in, Miriam, before I break down the damn door." Gallowglass wasn't in the mood for games.

Miriam flung the door open. "Matthew may be gone, but don't try anything funny. I'm still watching you."

That was no surprise to Gallowglass. Jason had once told him that learning how to be a vampire under Miriam's guidance had convinced him that there was indeed an all-knowing, all-seeing, and vengeful deity. Contrary to biblical teachings, however, She was female and sarcastic.

"Did Matthew and the others get off safely?" Diana asked quietly from the top of the stairs. She was ghostly pale, and a small suitcase sat at her feet. Gallowglass cursed and leaped up the steps.

"They did," he said, grabbing the case before she did something daft and tried to carry it herself. Gallowglass found it more mysterious with every passing hour that Diana didn't simply topple over given the burden of the twins.

"Why did you pack a suitcase?" Chris asked. "What's going on?"

"Auntie is going on a journey." Gallowglass still thought leaving New Haven was a bad idea, but Diana had informed him that she was going—with him or without him.

"Where?" Chris demanded. Gallowglass shrugged.

"Promise me you'll keep working on the DNA samples from Ashmole 782 as well as the blood-rage problem, Chris," Diana said as she descended the stairs.

"You know I don't leave research problems unfinished." Chris turned on Miriam. "Did you know that Diana was leaving?"

"How could I not? She made enough noise getting her suitcase out of the closet and calling the pilot." Miriam grabbed Chris's coffee. She took a sip and grimaced. "Too sweet."

"Get your coat, Auntie." Gallowglass didn't know what Diana had planned—she said she would tell him once they were in the air—but he doubted they were headed for a Caribbean island with swaying palms and warm breezes.

For once Diana didn't protest at his hovering.

"Lock the door when you leave, Chris. And make sure the coffeepot is unplugged." She stood on her toes and kissed her friend on the cheek. "Take care of Miriam. Don't let her walk across New Haven Green at night, even if she is a vampire."

"Here," Miriam said, handing over a large manila envelope. "As requested."

Diana peeked inside. "Are you sure you don't need them?"

"We have plenty of samples," she replied.

Chris looked deep into Diana's eyes. "Call if you need me. No matter why, no matter when, no matter where—I'll be on the next flight."

"Thank you," she whispered, "I'll be fine. Gallowglass is with me."

To his surprise, the words brought Gallowglass no joy.

How could they, when they were uttered with such resignation?

The de Clermont jet lifted off from the New Haven airport. Gallowglass stared out the window, tapping his phone against his leg. The plane banked, and he sniffed the air. North by northeast.

Diana was sitting next to him, eyes closed and lips white. One hand was resting lightly on Apple and Bean as though she were comforting them. There was a trace of moisture on her cheeks.

"Don't cry. I cannot bear it," Gallowglass said gruffly.

"I'm sorry. I can't seem to help it." Diana turned in her seat so that she faced the opposite side of the cabin. Her shoulders trembled.

"Hell, Auntie. Looking the other way does no good." Gallowglass unclipped his seat belt and crouched by her leather recliner. He patted Diana on the knee. She grasped his hand. The power pulsed under her skin. It had abated somewhat since the astonishing moment when she'd wrapped the sire of the de Clermont family in a briar patch, but it was still all too visible. Gallowglass had even seen it through the disguising spell Diana wore until she boarded the jet.

"How was Marcus with Jack?" she asked, her eyes still closed.

"Marcus greeted him as an uncle should and distracted him with tales of his children and their antics. Lord knows they're an entertaining bunch,"

Gallowglass said under his breath. But this wasn't what Diana really wanted to know.

"Matthew was bearing up as well as could be expected," he continued more gently. There had been a moment when it appeared Matthew was going to strangle Hubbard, but Gallowglass wasn't going to worry about something that was, on the face of it, an excellent notion.

"I'm glad you and Chris called Marcus," Diana whispered.

"That was Miriam's idea," Gallowglass admitted. Miriam had been protecting Matthew for centuries, just as he had been looking after Diana. "As soon as she saw the test results Miriam knew that Matthew would need his son at his side."

"Poor Phoebe," Diana said, a note of worry creeping into her voice. "Marcus couldn't have had time to give her much of an explanation."

"Don't fret about Phoebe." Gallowglass had spent two months with the girl and had taken her measure. "She's got a strong spine and a stout heart, just like you."

Gallowglass insisted Diana sleep. The aircraft's cabin was outfitted with seats that converted to beds. He made sure Diana had drifted off before he marched into the cockpit and demanded to know their destination.

"Europe," the pilot told him.

"What do you mean 'Europe'?" That could be anywhere from Amsterdam to the Auvergne to Oxford.

"Madame de Clermont hasn't chosen her final destination. She told me to head to Europe. So I'm headed for Europe."

"She must be going to Sept-Tours. Go to Gander, then," Gallowglass instructed.

"That was my plan, sir," the pilot said drily. "Do you want to fly her?"

"Yes. No." What Gallowglass wanted was to hit something. "Hell, man. You do your job and I'll do mine."

There were times Gallowglass wished with all his heart he'd fallen in battle to someone other than Hugh de Clermont.

After landing safely at the airport in Gander, Gallowglass helped Diana down the stairs so that she could do as the doctor had ordered and stretch her legs.

"You're not dressed for Newfoundland," he observed, settling a worn leather jacket over her shoulders. "The wind will shred that pitiful excuse for a coat to ribbons."

"Thank you, Gallowglass," Diana said, shivering.

"What's your final destination, Auntie?" he asked after their second lap of the tiny airstrip.

"Does it matter?" Diana's voice had gone from resigned to weary to something worse.

Hopeless.

"No, Auntie. It's Nar-SAR-s'wauk—not NUR-sar-squawk," Gallowglass explained, tucking one of the down-filled blankets around Diana's shoulder. Narsarsuaq, on the southern tip of Greenland, was colder even than Gander. Diana had insisted on taking a brisk walk anyway.

"How do you know?" she asked peevishly, her lips slightly blue.

"I just know." Gallowglass motioned to the flight attendant, who brought him a steaming mug of tea. He poured a dollop of whiskey into it.

"No caffeine. Or alcohol," Diana said, waving the tea away.

"My own mam drank whiskey every day of her pregnancy—and look how hale and hearty I turned out," Gallowglass said, holding the mug in her direction. His voice turned wheedling. "Come on, now. A wee nip won't do you any harm. Besides, it can't be as bad for Apple and Bean as frostbite."

"They're fine," Diana said sharply.

"Oh, aye. Finer than frog's hair." Gallowglass extended his hand farther and hoped that the tea's aroma would persuade her to indulge. "It's Scottish Breakfast tea. One of your favorites."

"Get thee behind me, Satan," Diana grumbled, taking the mug. "And your mam couldn't have been drinking whiskey while she carried you. There's no evidence of whiskey distillation in Scotland or Ireland before the fifteenth century. You're older than that."

Gallowglass smothered a sigh of relief at her historical nitpicking.

Diana drew out a phone.

"Who are you calling, Auntie?" Gallowglass asked warily.

"Hamish."

When Matthew's best friend picked up the call, his words were exactly what Gallowglass expected them to be.

"Diana? What's wrong? Where are you?"

"I can't remember where my house is," she said in lieu of explanation.

"Your house?" Hamish sounded confused.

"My house," Diana repeated patiently. "The one Matthew gave me in London. You made me sign off on the maintenance bills when we were at Sept-Tours."

London? Being a vampire was no help at all in his present situation, Gallowglass realized. It would be far better to have been born a witch. Perhaps then he could have divined how this woman's mind worked.

"It's in Mayfair, on a little street near the Connaught. Why?"

"I need the key. And the address." Diana paused for a moment, mulling something over before she spoke. "I'll need a driver, too, to get around the city. Daemons like the Underground, and vampires own all the major cab companies."

Of course they owned the cab companies. Who else had the time to memorize the three hundred twenty routes, twenty-five thousand streets, and twenty thousand landmarks within six miles of Charing Cross that were required in order to get a license?

"A driver?" Hamish sputtered.

"Yes. And does that fancy Coutts account I have come with a bank card—one with a high spending limit?"

Gallowglass swore. She looked at him frostily.

"Yes." Hamish's wariness increased.

"Good. I need to buy some books. Everything Athanasius Kircher ever wrote. First or second editions. Do you think you could send out a few inquiries before the weekend?" Diana studiously avoided Gallowglass's piercing gaze.

"Athanasius who?" Hamish asked. Gallowglass could hear a pen scratching on paper.

"Kircher." She spelled it out for him, letter by letter. "You'll have to go to the rare-book dealers. There must be copies floating around London. I don't care how much they cost."

"You sound like Granny," Gallowglass muttered. That alone was reason for concern.

"If you can't get me copies by the end of next week, I suppose I'll have to go to the British Library. But fall term has started, and the rare-book room is bound to be full of witches. I'm sure it would be better if I stayed at home."

"Could I talk to Matthew?" Hamish said a trifle breathlessly.

"He's not here."

"You're alone?" He sounded shocked.

"Of course not. Gallowglass is with me," Diana replied.

"And Gallowglass knows about your plan to sit in the public reading rooms of the British Library and read these books by—what's his name? Athanasius Kircher? Have you gone completely mad? The whole Congregation is looking for you!" Hamish's voice rose steadily with each sentence.

"I am aware of the Congregation's interest, Hamish. That's why I asked you to buy the books," Diana said mildly.

"Where is Matthew?" Hamish demanded.

"I don't know." Diana crossed her fingers when she told the lie.

There was a long silence.

"I'll meet you at the airport. Let me know when you're an hour away," Hamish said.

"That's not necessary," she said.

"One hour before you land, call me." Hamish paused. "And Diana? I don't know what the hell is going on, but of one thing I'm sure: Matthew loves you. More than his own life."

"I know," Diana whispered before she hung up.

Now she'd gone from hopeless to dead-sounding.

The plane turned south and east. The vampire at the controls had overheard the conversation and acted accordingly.

"What is that oaf doing?" Gallowglass growled, shooting to his feet and upsetting the tea tray so that the shortbread biscuits scattered all over the floor. "You cannot head directly for London!" he shouted into the cockpit. "That's a four-hour flight, and she's not to be in the air for more than three."

"Where to, then?" came the pilot's muffled reply as the plane changed course.

"Put in at Stornoway. It's a straight shot, and less than three hours. From there it will be an easy jump to London," Gallowglass replied.

That settled it. Marcus's ride with Matthew, Jack, Hubbard, and Lobero, no matter how hellish, couldn't possibly compare to this.

* * *

"It's beautiful." Diana held her hair away from her face. It was dawn, and the sun was just rising over the Minch. Gallowglass filled his lungs with the familiar air of home and set about remembering a sight he had often dreamed of: Diana Bishop standing here, on the land of his ancestors.

"Aye." He turned and marched toward the jet. It was waiting on the taxiway, lights on and ready to depart.

"I'll be there in a minute." Diana scanned the horizon. Autumn had painted the hills with umber and golden strokes among the green. The wind carried the witch's red hair out in a streak that glowed like embers.

Gallowglass wondered what had captured her attention. There was nothing to see but a misguided gray heron, his long, bright yellow legs too insubstantial to hold up the rest of his body.

"Come, Auntie. You'll freeze to death out here." Ever since he'd parted with his leather jacket, Gallowglass had worn nothing more than his habitual uniform of T-shirt and torn jeans. He no longer felt the cold, but he remembered how the early-morning air in this part of the world could cut to the bone.

The heron stared at Diana for a moment. He ducked his head up and down, stretching his wings and crying out. The bird took flight, soaring away toward the sea.

"Diana?"

She turned blue-gold eyes in Gallowglass's direction. His hackles rose. There was something otherworldly in her gaze that made him recall his childhood, and a dark room where his grandfather cast runes and uttered prophecies.

Even after the plane took to the skies, Diana remained fixed on some unseen, distant view. Gallowglass stared out the window and prayed for a strong tailwind.

"Will we ever stop running, do you think?" Her voice startled him.

Gallowglass didn't know the answer and couldn't bear to lie to her. He remained silent.

Diana buried her face in her hands.

"There, there." He rocked her against his chest. "You mustn't think the worst, Auntie. It's not like you."

"I'm just so tired, Gallowglass."

"With good reason. Between past and present, you've had a hell of a year." Gallowglass tucked her head under his chin. She might be Matthew's lion, but even lions had to close their eyes and rest occasionally.

"Is that Corra?" Diana's fingers traced the outlines of the firedrake on his forearm. Gallowglass shivered. "Where does her tail go?"

She lifted his sleeve before he could stop her. Her eyes widened.

"You weren't meant to see that," Gallowglass said. He released her and tugged the soft fabric back into place.

"Show me."

"Auntie, I think it's best—"

"Show me," Diana repeated. "Please."

He grasped the hem of his shirt and pulled it over his head. His tattoos told a complicated tale, but only a few chapters would be of interest to Matthew's wife. Diana's hand went to her mouth.

"Oh, Gallowglass."

A siren sat on a rock above his heart, her arm extended so that her hand reached over to his left bicep. She held a clutch of cords. The cords snaked down his arm, falling and twisting to become Corra's sinuous tail, which swirled around his elbow until it met with the firedrake's body.

The siren had Diana's face.

"You're a hard woman to find, but you're an even harder one to forget." Gallowglass pulled his shirt back over his head.

"How long?" Diana's eyes were blue with regret and sympathy.

"Four months." He didn't tell her that it was the latest in a series of similar images that had been inked over his heart.

"That's not what I meant," Diana said softly.

"Oh." Gallowglass stared between his knees at the carpeted floor. "Four hundred years. More or less."

"I'm so sor—"

"I won't have you feeling sorry for something you couldn't prevent," Gallowglass said, silencing her with a slash of his hand. "I knew you could never be mine. It didn't matter."

"Before I was Matthew's, I was yours," Diana said simply.

"Only because I was watching you grow into Matthew's wife," he said roughly. "Granddad always did have an unholy ability to give us jobs we could neither refuse nor perform without losing some piece of our souls." Gallowglass took a deep breath.

"Until I saw the newspaper story about Lady Pembroke's laboratory book," he continued, "a small part of me hoped fate might have another surprise up her sleeve. I wondered if you might come back different, or without Matthew, or without loving him as much as he loves you."

Diana listened without saying a word.

"So I went to Sept-Tours to wait for you, like I promised Granddad I would. Emily and Sarah were always going on about the changes your time-walking might have wrought. Miniatures and telescopes are one thing. But there was only ever one man for you, Diana. And God knows there was only ever one woman for Matthew."

"It's strange to hear you say my name," Diana said softly.

"So long as I call you Auntie, I never forget who really owns your heart," Gallowglass said gruffly.

"Philippe shouldn't have expected you to watch over me. It was cruel," she said.

"No crueler than what Philippe expected from you," Gallowglass replied. "And far less so than what Granddad demanded of himself."

Seeing her confusion, Gallowglass continued.

"Philippe always put his own needs last," Gallowglass said. "Vampires are creatures ruled by their desire, with instincts for self-preservation that are much stronger than any warmblood's. But Philippe was never like the rest of us. It broke his heart every time Granny got restless and went away. Then I didn't understand why Ysabeau felt it necessary to leave. Now that I've heard her tale, I think Philippe's love frightened her. It was so deep and selfless that Granny simply couldn't trust it—not after what her sire put her through. Part of her was always braced for Philippe to turn on her, to demand something for himself that she couldn't give."

Diana looked thoughtful.

"Whenever I see Matthew struggle to give you the freedom you need—to let you do something without him that you think is minor but that is an agony of worrying and waiting for him—it reminds me of Philippe," Gallowglass said, drawing his tale to a close.

"What are we going to do now?" She didn't mean when they got to London, but he pretended she did.

"Now we wait for Matthew," Gallowglass said flatly. "You wanted him to establish a family. He's off doing it."

Under the surface of her skin, Diana's magic pulsed again in iridescent agitation. It reminded Gallowglass of long nights watching the aurora borealis from the sandy stretch of coastline beneath the cliffs where his father and grandfather had once lived.

"Don't worry. Matthew won't be able to stay away for long. It's one thing to wander in the darkness because you know no different, but it's quite another to enjoy the light only to have it taken from you," Gallowglass said.

"You sound so sure," she whispered.

"I am. Marcus's children are a handful, but he'll make them heel." Gallowglass lowered his voice. "I assume there's a good reason you chose London?"

Her glance flickered.

"I thought so. You're not just looking for the last missing page. You're going after Ashmole 782. And I'm not talking nonsense," Gallowglass said, raising his hand when Diana opened her mouth to protest. "You'll be wanting people around you, then. People you can trust unto death, like Granny and Sarah and Fernando." He drew out his phone.

"Sarah already knows I'm on my way to Europe. I told her I'd let her know where I was once I was settled." Diana frowned at the phone. "And Ysabeau is still Gerbert's prisoner. She's not in touch with the outside world."

"Oh, Granny has her ways," Gallowglass said serenely, his fingers racing across the keys. "I'll just send her a message and tell her where we're headed. Then I'll tell Fernando. You can't do this alone, Auntie. Not what you've got planned."

"You're taking this very well, Gallowglass," Diana said gratefully. "Matthew would be trying to talk me out of it."

"That's what you get for falling in love with the wrong man," he said under his breath, slipping the phone back into his pocket.

Ysabeau de Clermont picked up her sleek red phone and looked at the illuminated display. She noted the time—7:37 A.M. Then she read the waiting message. It began with three repetitions of a single word:

Mayday
Mayday
Mayday

She'd been expecting Gallowglass to get in touch ever since Phoebe had notified her that Marcus had departed in the middle of the night, mysteriously and suddenly, to go off and join Matthew.

Ysabeau and Gallowglass had decided early on that they needed a way to notify each other when things went "pear-shaped," to use her grandson's expression. Their system had changed over the years, from beacons and secret messages written in onion juice to codes and ciphers, then to objects sent through the mail without explanation. Now they used the phone.

At first Ysabeau had been dubious about owning one of these cellular contraptions, but given recent events she was glad to have it restored to her. Gerbert had confiscated it shortly after her arrival in Aurillac, in the vain hope that being without it would make her more malleable.

Gerbert had returned the phone to Ysabeau several weeks ago. She had been taken hostage to satisfy the witches and to make a public show of the Congregation's power and influence. Gerbert was under no illusion that his prisoner would part with a scrap of information that would help them find Matthew. He was, however, grateful that Ysabeau was willing to play along with the charade. Since arriving at Gerbert's home, she had been a model prisoner. He claimed that having her phone back was a reward for good behavior, but she knew it was largely due to the fact that Gerbert could not figure out how to silence the many alarms that sounded throughout the day.

Ysabeau liked these reminders of events that had altered her world: just before midday, when Philippe and his men had burst into her prison and she felt the first glimmers of hope; two hours before sunrise, when Philippe had first admitted that he loved her; three in the afternoon, the hour she had found Matthew's broken body in the half-built church in Saint-Lucien; 1:23 P.M., when Matthew drew the last drops of blood from Philippe's pain-ravaged body. Other alarms marked the hour of Hugh's death and Godfrey's, the hour when Louisa had first exhibited signs of blood rage, the hour when Marcus had demonstrated definitively that the same disease had not touched him. The rest of her daily alarms were reserved for significant historical events, such as the births of kings and queens whom Ysabeau had called friends, wars that she had fought in and won, and battles that she had unaccountably lost in spite of her careful plans.

The alarms rang day and night, each one a different, carefully chosen song. Gerbert had particularly objected to the alarm that blasted "Chant de Guerre pour l'Armée du Rhin" at 5:30 P.M.—the precise moment when the revolutionary mob swept through the gates of the Bastille in 1789. But these tunes served as aide-mémoire, conjuring up faces and places that might otherwise have faded away over time.

Ysabeau read the rest of Gallowglass's message. To anyone else it would have appeared nothing more than a garbled combination of shipping forecast, aeronautical distress signal, and horoscope, with its references to shadows, the moon, Gemini, Libra, and a series of longitude and latitude coordinates. Ysabeau reread the message twice: once to make sure she had correctly ascertained its meaning and a second time to memorize Gallowglass's instructions. Then she typed her reply.

Je Viens

"I am afraid it is time for me to go, Gerbert," Ysabeau said without a trace of regret. She looked across the faux-Gothic horror of a room to where her jailer sat before a computer at the foot of an ornate carved table. At the opposite end, a heavy Bible rested on a raised stand flanked by thick white candles, as though Gerbert's work space were an altar. Ysabeau's lip curled at the pretension, which was matched by the room's heavy nineteenth-century woodwork, pews converted to settees, and garish green-and-blue silk wallpaper ornamented with chivalric shields. The only authentic items in the room were the enormous stone fireplace and the monumental chess set before it.

Gerbert peered at his computer screen and hit a key on the keyboard. He groaned.

"Jean-Luc will come from Saint-Lucien and help if you are still having trouble with your computer," Ysabeau said.

Gerbert had hired the nice young man to set up a home computer network after Ysabeau had shared two morsels of Sept-Tours gossip gleaned from conversations around the dinner table: Nathaniel Wilson's belief that future wars would be fought on the Internet and Marcus's plan to handle a majority of the Knights of Lazarus's banking through online channels.

Baldwin and Hamish had overruled her grandson's extraordinary idea, but Gerbert didn't need to know that.

While installing the components of Gerbert's hastily purchased system, Jean-Luc had needed to call back to the office several times for advice. Marcus's dear friend Nathaniel had set up the small business in Saint-Lucien to bring the villagers into the modern age, and though he was now in Australia, he was happy to help his former employee whenever his greater experience was required. On this occasion Nathaniel had walked Jean-Luc through the various security configurations that Gerbert requested.

Nathaniel added a few modifications of his own, too.

The end result was that Ysabeau and Nathaniel knew more about Gerbert of Aurillac than she had dreamed was possible, or indeed had ever wanted, to know. It was astonishing how much a person's online shopping habits revealed about his character and activities.

Ysabeau had made sure Jean-Luc signed Gerbert up for various social-media services to keep the vampire occupied and out of her way. She could not imagine why these companies all chose shades of blue for their logos. Blue had always struck her as such a serene, soothing color, yet all social media offered was endless agitation and posturing. It was worse than the court of Versailles. Come to think of it, Ysabeau reflected, Louis-Dieudonné had quite liked blue as well.

Gerbert's only complaint about his new virtual existence was that he had been unable to secure "Pontifex Maximus" as a user name. Ysabeau told him that it was probably for the best, since it might constitute a violation of the covenant in the eyes of some creatures.

Sadly for Gerbert—though happily for Ysabeau—an addiction to the Internet and an understanding of how best to use it did not always go hand in hand. Because of the sites he frequented, Gerbert was plagued by computer viruses. He also tended to pick overly complex passwords and lose track of which sites he'd visited and how he had found them. This led to many phone calls with Jean-Luc, who unfailingly bailed Gerbert out of his difficulties and thereby kept up to date on how to access all Gerbert's online information.

With Gerbert thus engaged, Ysabeau was free to wander around his castle, going through his belongings and copying down the surprising entries in the vampire's many address books.

Life as Gerbert's hostage had been most illuminating.

"It is time for me to go," Ysabeau repeated when Gerbert finally tore his eyes away from the screen. "There is no reason to keep me here any longer. The Congregation won. I have just received word from the family that Matthew and Diana are no longer together. I imagine that the strain was too much for her, poor girl. You must be very pleased."

"I hadn't heard. And you?" Gerbert's expression was suspicious. "Are you pleased?"

"Of course. I have always despised witches." Gerbert had no need to know how completely Ysabeau's feelings had changed.

"Hmm." He still looked wary. "Has Matthew's witch gone to Madison? Surely Diana Bishop will want to be with her aunt if she has left your son."

"I am sure she longs for home," Ysabeau said vaguely. "It is typical, after heartbreak, to seek out what is familiar."

Ysabeau thought it was a promising sign, therefore, that Diana had chosen to return to the place where she and Matthew had enjoyed a life together. As for heartbreak, there were many ways to ease the pain and loneliness that went along with being mated to the sire of a great vampire clan—which Matthew would soon be. Ysabeau looked forward to sharing them with her daughter-in-law, who was made of sterner stuff than most vampires would have expected.

"Do you need to clear my departure with someone? Domenico? Satu, perhaps?" Ysabeau asked solicitously.

"They dance to my tune, Ysabeau," Gerbert said with a scowl.

It was pathetically easy to manipulate Gerbert if his ego was involved. And it was always involved. Ysabeau hid her satisfied smile.

"If I release you, you will go back to Sept-Tours and stay there?" Gerbert asked.

"Of course," she said promptly.

"Ysabeau," he growled.

"I have not left de Clermont territory since shortly after the war," she said with a touch of impatience. "Unless the Congregation decides to take me prisoner again, I will remain in de Clermont territory. Only Philippe himself could persuade me to do otherwise."

"Happily, not even Philippe de Clermont is capable of ordering us about from the grave," Gerbert said, "though I am sure he would dearly love to do so."

You would be surprised, you toad, Ysabeau thought.

"Very well, then. You are free to go." Gerbert sighed. "But do try to remember we are at war, Ysabeau. To keep up appearances."

"Oh, I would never forget we are at war, Gerbert." Unable to maintain her countenance for another moment, and afraid she might find a creative use for the iron poker that was propped up by the fireplace, Ysabeau went to find Marthe.

Her trusted companion was downstairs in the meticulous kitchen, sitting by the fireplace with a battered copy of *Tinker Tailor Soldier Spy* and a steaming cup of mulled wine. Gerbert's butcher stood at the nearby chopping block, dismembering a rabbit for his master's breakfast. The Delft tile on the walls provided an oddly cheerful note.

"We are going home, Marthe," Ysabeau said.

"Finally." Marthe got to her feet with a groan. "I hate Aurillac. The air here is bad. *Adiu siatz,* Theo."

"*Adiu siatz,* Marthe," Theo grunted, whacking the unfortunate rabbit.

Gerbert met them at the front door to bid them farewell. He kissed Ysabeau on both cheeks, his actions supervised by a dead boar that Philippe had killed, the head of which had been preserved and mounted on a plaque over the fire. "Shall I have Enzo drive you?"

"I think we will walk." It would give her and Marthe the opportunity to make plans. After so many weeks conducting espionage under Gerbert's roof, it was going to be difficult to let go of her excessive caution.

"It's eighty miles," Gerbert pointed out.

"We shall stop in Allanche for lunch. A large herd of deer once roamed the woods there." They would not make it so far, for Ysabeau had already sent Alain a message to meet them outside Murat. Alain would drive them from there to Clermont-Ferrand, where they would board one of Baldwin's infernal flying machines and proceed to London. Marthe abhorred air travel, which she believed was unnatural, but they could not allow Diana to arrive at a cold house. Ysabeau slipped Jean-Luc's card into Gerbert's hand. "Until next time."

Arm in arm, Ysabeau and Marthe walked out into the crisp dawn. The towers of Château des Anges Déchus grew smaller and smaller behind them until they disappeared from sight.

"I must set a new alarm, Marthe. Seven thirty-seven A.M. Do not let me forget. "Marche Henri IV' would be most appropriate for it, I think," Ysabeau whispered as their feet moved quickly north toward the dormant peaks of the ancient volcanoes and onward to their future.

T his cannot be my house, Leonard." The palatial brick mansion's expansive five-windowed frontage and towering four stories in one of London's toniest neighborhoods made it inconceivable. I felt a pang of regret, though. The tall windows were trimmed in white to stand out against the warm brick, their old glass winking in the midday sunshine. Inside, I imagined that the house would be flooded with light. It would be warm, too, for there were not the usual two chimneys but three. And there was enough polished brass on the front door to start a marching band. It would be a glorious bit of history to call home.

"This is where I was told to go, Mistress . . . er, Mrs. . . . . um, Diana." Leonard Shoreditch, Jack's erstwhile friend and another of Hubbard's disreputable gang of lost boys, had been waiting—with Hamish—in the private arrivals area at London City Airport in the Docklands. Leonard now parked the Mercedes and craned his neck over the seat, awaiting further instructions.

"I promise you it's your house, Auntie. If you don't like it, we'll swap it for a new one. But let's discuss future real-estate transactions inside, please—not sitting in the street where any creature might see us. Get the luggage, lad." Gallowglass clambered out of the front passenger seat and slammed the door behind him. He was still angry not to have been the one to drive us to Mayfair. But I'd been ferried around London by Gallowglass before and preferred to take my chances with Leonard.

I gave the mansion another dubious look.

"Don't worry, Diana. Clairmont House isn't half so grand inside as it is out. There is the staircase, of course. And some of the plasterwork is ornate," Hamish said as he opened the car door. "Come to think of it, the whole house *is* rather grand."

Leonard rooted around in the car trunk and removed my small suitcase and the large, hand-lettered sign he'd been holding when he met us. Leonard had wanted to do things properly, he said, and the sign bore the name CLAIRMONT in blocky capitals. When Hamish had told him we needed to

be discreet, Leonard had drawn a line through the name and scrawled ROY-
DON underneath it in even darker characters using a felt-tip marker.

"How did you know to call Leonard?" I asked Hamish as he helped me
out of the car. When last seen in 1591, Leonard had been in the company of
another boy with the strangely fitting name of Amen Corner. As I recalled,
Matthew had thrown a dagger at the two simply for delivering a message
from Father Hubbard. I couldn't imagine that my husband had stayed in
touch with either young man.

"Gallowglass texted me his number. He said we should keep our affairs
in the family as much as possible." Hamish turned curious eyes on me. "I
wasn't aware Matthew owned a private car-hire business."

"The company belongs to Matthew's grandson." I'd spent most of the
journey from the airport staring at the promotional leaflets in the pocket
behind the driver's seat, which advertised the services of Hubbards of
Houndsditch, Ltd., "proudly meeting London's most discriminating trans-
portation needs since 1917."

Before I could explain further, a small, aged woman with ample hips
and a familiar scowl pulled open the arched blue door. I stared in shock.

"You're looking bonny, Marthe." Gallowglass stooped and kissed her.
Then he turned and frowned down the short flight of stairs that rose from
the sidewalk. "Why are you still out on the curb, Auntie?"

"Why is Marthe here?" My throat was dry and the question came out in
a croak.

"Is that Diana?" Ysabeau's bell-like voice cut through the quiet murmur
of city sounds. "Marthe and I are here to help, of course."

Gallowglass whistled. "Being held against your will agreed with you,
Granny. You haven't looked so lively since Victoria was crowned."

"Flatterer." Ysabeau patted her grandson on the cheek. Then she looked
at me and gasped. "Diana is as white as snow, Marthe. Get her inside, Gallowglass. At once."

"You heard her, Auntie," he said, sweeping me off my feet and onto the
top step.

Ysabeau and Marthe propelled me through the airy entrance with its
gleaming black-and-white marble floor and a curved staircase so splendid it
made my eyes widen. The four flights of stairs were topped with a domed
skylight that let in the sunshine and picked out the details in the moldings.

From there I was ushered into a tranquil reception room. Long drapes in gray figured silk hung at the windows, their color a pleasing contrast to the creamy walls. The upholstery pulled in shades of slate blue, terra-cotta, cream, and black to accent the gray, and the faint fragrance of cinnamon and cloves clung to all of it. Matthew's taste was everywhere, too: in a small orrery, its brass wires gleaming; a piece of Japanese porcelain; the warmly colored rug.

"Hello, Diana. I thought you might need tea." Phoebe Taylor arrived, accompanied by the scent of lilacs and the gentle clatter of silver and porcelain.

"Why aren't you at Sept-Tours?" I asked, equally astonished to see her.

"Ysabeau told me I was needed here." Phoebe's neat black heels clicked against the polished wood. She eyed Leonard as she put the tea tray down on a graceful table that was polished to such a high sheen that I could see her reflection in it. "I'm so sorry, but I don't believe we've met. Would you like some tea?"

"Leonard Shoreditch, ma-madam, at your service," Leonard said, stammering slightly. He bent in a stiff bow. "And thank you. I would dearly love some tea. White. Four sugars."

Phoebe poured steaming liquid into a cup and put only three cubes of sugar in it before she handed it off to Leonard. Marthe snorted and sat down in a straight-backed chair next to the tea table, obviously intent on supervising Phoebe—and Leonard—like a hawk.

"That will rot your teeth, Leonard," I said, unable to stop the maternal intervention.

"Vampires don't worry much about tooth decay, Mistress . . . er, Mrs. . . . um, Diana." Leonard's hand shook alarmingly, making the tiny cup and saucer with its red Japanese-style decoration clatter. Phoebe blanched.

"That's Chelsea porcelain, and quite early, too. Everything in the house should be in display cases at the V&A Museum." Phoebe handed me an identical cup and saucer with a beautiful silver spoon balanced on the edge. "If anything is broken, I'll never forgive myself. They're irreplaceable."

If Phoebe were going to marry Marcus as she planned, she would have to get used to being surrounded by museum-quality objects.

I took a sip of the scalding hot, sweet, milky tea and sighed with pleasure.

Silence fell. I took another sip and looked around the room. Gallowglass was stuffed into a Queen Anne corner chair, his muscular legs splayed wide. Ysabeau was enthroned in the most ornate chair in the room: high-backed, its frame covered in silver leaf, and upholstered in damask. Hamish shared a mahogany settee with Phoebe. Leonard nervously perched on one of the side chairs that flanked the tea table.

They were all waiting. Since Matthew wasn't present, our friends and family were looking to me for guidance. The burden of responsibility settled on my shoulders. It was uncomfortable, just as Matthew had predicted.

"When did the Congregation set you free, Ysabeau?" I asked, my mouth still dry in spite of the tea.

"Gerbert and I came to an agreement shortly after you arrived in Scotland," she replied breezily, though her smile told me there was more to the story.

"Does Marcus know you're here, Phoebe?" Something told me he had no idea.

"My resignation from Sotheby's takes effect on Monday. He knew I had to clear out my desk." Phoebe's words were carefully chosen, but the underlying response to my question was clearly no. Marcus was still under the impression that his fiancée was in a heavily fortified castle in France, not an airy town house in London.

"Resignation?" I was surprised.

"If I want to go back to work at Sotheby's, I'll have centuries to do so." Phoebe looked around her. "Though properly cataloging the de Clermont family's possessions could take me several lifetimes."

"Then you are still set on becoming a vampire?" I asked.

Phoebe nodded. I should sit down with her and try to talk her out of it. Matthew would have her blood on his hands if anything went wrong. And something always went wrong in this family.

"Who's gonna make her a vamp?" Leonard whispered to Gallowglass. "Father H?"

"I think Father Hubbard has enough children. Don't you, Leonard?" Come to think of it, I needed to know that number as soon as possible— and how many were witches and daemons.

"I suppose so, Mistress . . . er, Mrs. . . . er—"

"The proper form of address for *Sieur* Matthew's mate is '*Madame*.' From now on, you will use that title when speaking to Diana," Ysabeau said briskly. "It simplifies matters."

Marthe and Gallowglass turned in Ysabeau's direction, their faces registering surprise.

"*Sieur* Matthew," I repeated softly. Until now Matthew had been "*Milord*" to his family. But Philippe had been called "*Sieur*" in 1590. "*Everyone here calls me either 'sire' or 'Father,'*" Philippe had told me when I asked how he should be addressed. At the time I'd thought the title was nothing more than an antiquated French honorific. Now I knew better. To call Matthew "*Sieur*"—the vampire sire—marked him head of a vampire clan.

As far as Ysabeau was concerned, Matthew's new scion was a fait accompli.

"*Madame* what?" Leonard asked, confused.

"Just *Madame*," Ysabeau replied serenely. "You may call me Madame Ysabeau. When Phoebe marries Milord Marcus, she will be Madame de Clermont. Until then you may call her Miss Phoebe."

"Oh." Leonard's look of intense concentration indicated he was chewing on these morsels of vampire etiquette.

Silence fell again. Ysabeau stood.

"Marthe put you in the Forest Room, Diana. It is next to Matthew's bedchamber," she said. "If you are finished with the tea, I will take you upstairs. You should rest for a few hours before you tell us what you require."

"Thank you, Ysabeau." I put the cup and saucer on the small round table at my elbow. I wasn't finished with my tea, but its heat had quickly dissipated through the fragile porcelain. As for what I required, where to start?

Together Ysabeau and I crossed the foyer, climbed the graceful staircase up to the first floor, and kept going.

"You will have your privacy on the second floor," Ysabeau explained. "There are only two bedrooms on that level, as well as Matthew's study and a small sitting room. Now that the house is yours, you may arrange things as you like, of course."

"Where are the rest of you sleeping?" I asked as Ysabeau turned onto the second-floor landing.

"Phoebe and I have rooms on the floor above you. Marthe prefers to sleep on the lower ground floor, in the housekeeper's rooms. If you feel crowded, Phoebe and I can move into Marcus's home. It is near St. James's Palace, and once belonged to Matthew."

"I can't imagine that will be necessary," I said, thinking of the size of the house.

"We'll see. Your bedchamber." Ysabeau pushed open a wide, paneled door with a gleaming brass knob. I gasped.

Everything in the room was in shades of green, silver, pale gray, and white. The walls were papered with hand-painted depictions of branches and leaves against a pale gray background. Silver accents gave the effect of moonlight, the mirrored moon in the center of the ceiling's plasterwork appearing to be the source of the light. A ghostly female face looked down from the mirror with a serene smile. Four depictions of Nyx, the personification of night, anchored the four quadrants of the room's ceiling, her veil billowing out in a smoky black drapery that was painted so realistically it looked like actual fabric. Silver stars were entangled in the veiling, catching the light from the windows and the mirror's reflection.

"It is extraordinary, I agree," Ysabeau said, pleased by my reaction. "Matthew wanted to create the effect of being outside in the forest, under a moonlit sky. Once this bedchamber was decorated, he said it was too beautiful to use and moved to the room next door."

Ysabeau went to the windows and drew the curtains open. The bright light revealed an ancient four-poster canopied bed set into a recess in the wall, which slightly minimized its considerable size. The bed hangings were silk and bore the same design as the wallpaper. Another large-scale mirror topped the fireplace, trapping images of trees on the wallpaper and sending them back into the room. The shining surface reflected the room's furniture, too: the small dressing table between the large windows, the chaise by the fire, the gleaming flowers and leaves inlaid into the low walnut chest of drawers. The room's decoration and furnishings must have cost Matthew a fortune.

My eyes fell on a vast canvas of a sorceress sitting on the ground and sketching magical symbols. It hung on the wall opposite the bed, between the tall windows. A veiled woman had interrupted the sorceress's work, her outstretched hand suggesting that she wanted the witch's help. It was an odd choice of subject for a vampire's house.

"Whose room was this, Ysabeau?"

"I think Matthew made it for you—only he did not realize it at the time." Ysabeau twitched open another pair of curtains.

"Has another woman slept here?" There was no way I could rest in a room that Juliette Durand had once occupied.

"Matthew took his lovers elsewhere," Ysabeau answered, equally blunt. When she saw my expression, she softened her tone. "He has many houses. Most of them mean nothing to him. Some do. This is one of them. He would not have given you a gift he didn't value himself."

"I never believed that being separated from him would be so hard." My voice was muted.

"Being the consort in a vampire family is never easy," Ysabeau said with a sad smile. "And sometimes being apart is the only way to stay together. Matthew had no choice but to leave you this time."

"Did Philippe ever banish you from his side?" I studied my composed mother-in-law with open curiosity.

"Of course. Mostly Philippe sent me away when I was an unwelcome distraction. On other occasions to keep me from being implicated if disaster struck—and in his family it struck more often than not." She smiled. "My husband always commanded me to go when he knew I would not be able to resist meddling and was worried for my safety."

"So Matthew learned how to be overprotective from Philippe?" I asked, thinking of all the times he had stepped into harm's way to keep me from it.

"Matthew had mastered the art of fussing over the woman he loved long before he became a vampire," Ysabeau replied softly. "You know that."

"And did you always obey Philippe's orders?"

"No more than you obey Matthew." Ysabeau's voice dropped conspiratorially. "And you will quickly discover that you are never so free to make your own decisions as when Matthew is off being patriarchal with someone else. Like me, you might even come to look forward to these moments apart."

"I doubt it." I pressed a fist into the small of my back in an effort to work out the kinks. It was something Matthew usually did. "I should tell you what happened in New Haven."

"You must never explain Matthew's actions to anyone," Ysabeau said sharply. "Vampires don't tell tales for a reason. Knowledge is power in our world."

"You're Matthew's mother. Surely I'm not supposed to keep secrets from you." I sifted through the events of the past few days. "Matthew discovered the identity of one of Benjamin's children—and met a great-grandson he didn't know he had." Of all the strange twists and turns our lives had taken, meeting up with Jack and his father had to be the most significant, not least because we were now in Father Hubbard's city. "His name is Jack Blackfriars, and he lived in our household in 1591."

"So my son knows at last about Andrew Hubbard," Ysabeau said, her face devoid of emotion.

"You *knew?*" I cried.

Ysabeau's smile would have terrified me—once. "And do you still think I deserve your complete honesty, daughter?"

Matthew had warned me that I wasn't equipped to lead a pack of vampires.

"You are a sire's consort, Diana. You must learn to tell others only what they need to know, and nothing more," she instructed.

Here was my first lesson learned, but there were sure to be more.

"Will you teach me, Ysabeau?"

"Yes." Her one-word response was more trustworthy than any lengthy vow. "First you must be careful, Diana. Even though you are Matthew's mate and his consort, you are a de Clermont and must remain so until this matter of a scion is settled. Your status in Philippe's family will protect Matthew."

"Matthew said the Congregation will try to kill him—and Jack, too—once they find out about Benjamin and the blood rage," I said.

"They will try. We will not let them. But for now you must rest." Ysabeau pulled back the bed's silk coverlet and plumped the pillows.

I circled the enormous bed, wrapping my hand around one of the posts that supported the canopy. The carving under my fingers felt familiar. *I've slept in this bed before,* I realized. This was not another woman's bed. It was mine. It had been in our house in the Blackfriars in 1590 and had somehow survived all these centuries to end up in a chamber that Matthew had dedicated to moonlight and enchantment.

After a whispered word of thanks to Ysabeau, I rested my head on the soft pillows and drifted off into troubled sleep.

*   *   *

I slept for nearly twenty-four hours, and it might have been longer but for a loud car alarm that pulled me out of my dreams and plunged me into an unfamiliar, green-tinged darkness. It was only then that other sounds penetrated my consciousness: the bustle of traffic on the street outside my windows, a door closing somewhere in the house, a quickly hushed conversation in the hallway.

Hoping that a pounding flow of hot water would ease my stiff muscles and clear my head, I explored the warren of small rooms beyond a white door. I found not only a shower but also my suitcase resting on a folding stand designed for much grander pieces of luggage. From it I pulled out the two pages from Ashmole 782 and my laptop. The rest of my packing had left a great deal to be desired. Except for some underwear, several tank tops, yoga tights that no longer fit me, a pair of mismatched shoes, and black maternity pants, there was nothing else in the bag. Happily, Matthew's closet held plenty of pressed shirts. I slid one made of gray broadcloth over my arms and shoulders and avoided the closed door that surely led to his bedroom.

I padded downstairs in bare feet, my computer and the large envelope with the pages from the Book of Life in my arms. The grand first-floor rooms were empty—an echoing ballroom with enough crystal and gold paint to renovate Versailles, a smaller music room with a piano and other instruments, a formal salon that looked to have been decorated by Ysabeau, an equally formal dining room with an endless stretch of mahogany table and seating for twenty-four, a library full of eighteenth-century books, and a games room with green-felted card tables that looked as if it had been plucked from a Jane Austen novel.

Longing for a homier atmosphere, I descended to the ground floor. No one was in the sitting room, so I poked around in office spaces, parlors, and morning rooms until I found a more intimate dining room than the one upstairs. It was located at the rear of the house, its bowed window looking out over a small private garden. The walls were painted to resemble brick, lending the space a warm, inviting air. Another mahogany table—this one round rather than rectangular—was encircled by only eight chairs. On its surface was an assortment of carefully arranged old books.

Phoebe entered the room and put a tray bearing tea and toast on a small sideboard. "Marthe told me you would be up at any moment. She said that this was what you would need first thing and that if you were still hungry, you could go down to the kitchen for eggs and sausage. We don't eat up here as a rule. By the time the food makes it up the stairs, it's stone cold."

"What is all this?" I gestured at the table.

"The books you requested from Hamish," Phoebe explained, straightening a volume that was slightly off kilter. "We're still waiting for a few items. You're a historian, so I put them in chronological order. I hope that's all right."

"But I only asked for them on Thursday," I said, bewildered. It was now Sunday morning. How could she have managed such a feat? One of the sheets of paper bore a title and date—*Arca Noë* 1675—in a neat, feminine hand, along with a price and the name and address of a book dealer.

"Ysabeau knows every dealer in London." Phoebe's mouth lifted into a mischievous smile, changing her face from attractive to beautiful. "And no wonder. The phrase 'the price isn't important' will galvanize any auction house, no matter the lateness of the hour, even on the weekend."

I picked up another volume—Kircher's *Obeliscus Pamphilius*—and opened the cover. Matthew's sprawling signature was on the flyleaf.

"I had a rummage through the libraries here and at Pickering Place first. There didn't seem much point in purchasing something that was already in your possession," Phoebe explained. "Matthew has wide-ranging tastes when it comes to books. There's a first edition of *Paradise Lost* at Pickering Place and a first edition of *Poor Richard's Almanack* signed by Franklin upstairs."

"Pickering Place?" Unable to stop myself, I traced the letters of Matthew's signature with my finger.

"Marcus's house over by St. James's Palace. It was a gift from Matthew, I understand. He lived there before he built Clairmont House," Phoebe said. Her lips pursed. "Marcus may be fascinated by politics, but I don't think it's appropriate for the Magna Carta and one of the original copies of the Declaration of Independence to remain in private hands. I'm sure you agree."

My finger rose from the page. Matthew's likeness hovered for a moment above the blank spot where his signature had been. Phoebe's eyes widened.

"I'm sorry," I said, releasing the ink back onto the paper. It swirled back onto the surface, re-forming into my husband's signature. "I shouldn't practice magic in front of warmbloods."

"But you didn't say any words or write down a charm." Phoebe looked confused.

"Some witches don't need to recite spells to make magic." Remembering Ysabeau's words, I kept my explanation as brief as possible.

"Oh." She nodded. "I still have a great deal to learn about creatures."

"Me, too." I smiled warmly at her, and Phoebe gave me a tentative smile in return.

"I assume you're interested in Kircher's imagery?" Phoebe asked, carefully opening another of the thick tomes. It was his book on magnetism, *Magnes sive De Arte Magnetica.* The engraved title page showed a tall tree, its wide branches bearing the fruits of knowledge. These were chained together to suggest their common bond. In the center God's divine eye looked out from the eternal world of archetypes and truth. A ribbon wove among the tree's branches and fruits. It bore a Latin motto: *Omnia nodis arcanis connexa quiescunt.* Translating mottoes was a tricky business, since their meanings were deliberately enigmatic, but most scholars agreed that it referred to the hidden magnetic influences that Kircher believed gave unity to the world: *"All things are at rest, connected by secret knots."*

"'They all wait silently, connected by secret knots,'" Phoebe murmured. "Who are 'they'? And what are they waiting for?"

With no detailed knowledge of Kircher's ideas about magnetism, Phoebe had read an entirely different meaning in the inscription.

"And why are these four disks larger?" she continued, pointing to the center of the page. Three of the disks were arranged in a triangular fashion around one containing an unblinking eye.

"I'm not sure," I confessed, reading the Latin descriptions that accompanied the images. "The eye represents the world of archetypes."

"Oh. The origin of all things." Phoebe looked at the image more closely.

"What did you say?" My own third eye opened, suddenly interested in what Phoebe Taylor had to say.

"Archetypes are original patterns. See, here are the sublunar world, the heavens, and man," she said, tapping in succession each of the three disks surrounding the archetypal eye. "Each one of them is linked to the world of archetypes—their point of origin—as well as to one another. The motto suggests we should see the chains as knots, though. I'm not sure if that's relevant."

"Oh, I think it's relevant," I said under my breath, more certain than ever that Athanasius Kircher and the Villa Mondragone sale were crucial links in the series of events that led from Edward Kelley in Prague to the final missing page. Somehow, Father Athanasius must have learned about the world of creatures. Either that or he was one himself.

"The Tree of Life is a powerful archetype in its own right, of course," Phoebe mused, "one that also describes the relationships between parts of the created world. There's a reason genealogists use family trees to show lines of descent."

Having an art historian in the family was going to be an unexpected boon—from both a research standpoint and a conversational one. Finally I had someone to talk to about arcane imagery.

"And you already know how important trees of knowledge are in scientific imagery. Not all of them are this representational, though," Phoebe said with regret. "Most are just simple branching diagrams, like Darwin's Tree of Life from *On the Origin of Species.* It was the only image in the whole book. Too bad Darwin didn't think to hire a proper artist like Kircher did—someone who could produce something truly splendid."

The knotted threads that had been waiting silently all around me began to chime. There was something I was missing. Some powerful connection that was nearly within my grasp, if only . . .

"Where is everybody?" Hamish poked his head into the room.

"Good morning, Hamish," Phoebe said with a warm smile. "Leonard has gone to pick up Sarah and Fernando. Everybody else is here somewhere."

"Hullo, Hamish." Gallowglass waved from the garden window. "Feeling better after your sleep, Auntie?"

"Much, thank you." But my attention was fixed on Hamish.

"He hasn't called," Hamish said gently in response to my silent question.

I wasn't surprised. Nevertheless, I stared down at my new books to hide my disappointment.

"Good morning, Diana. Hello, Hamish." Ysabeau sailed into the room and offered her cheek to the daemon. He kissed it obediently. "Has Phoebe located the books you need, Diana, or should she keep looking?"

"Phoebe has done an amazing job—and quickly, too. I'm afraid I still need help, though."

"Well, that is what we are here for." Ysabeau beckoned her grandson inside and gave me a steadying look. "Your tea has gone cold. Marthe will bring more, and then you will tell us what must be done."

After Marthe dutifully appeared (this time with something minty and decaffeinated rather than the strong black brew that Phoebe had poured) and Gallowglass joined us, I brought out the two pages from Ashmole 782. Hamish whistled.

"These are two illuminations removed from the Book of Life in the sixteenth century—the manuscript known today as Ashmole 782. One has yet to be found: an image of a tree. It looks a little like this." I showed them the frontispiece from Kircher's book on magnestism. "We have to find it before anyone else does, and that includes Knox, Benjamin, and the Congregation."

"Why do they all want the Book of Life so badly?" Phoebe's shrewd, olive-colored eyes were guileless. I wondered how long they would stay that way after she became a de Clermont and a vampire.

"None of us really know," I admitted. "Is it a grimoire? A story of our origins? A record of some kind? I've held it in my hands twice: once in its damaged state at the Bodleian in Oxford and once in Emperor Rudolf's cabinet of curiosities when it was whole and complete. I'm still not sure why so many creatures are seeking the book. All I can say with certainty is that the Book of Life is full of power—power and secrets."

"No wonder the witches and vampires are so keen to acquire it," Hamish said drily.

"The daemons as well, Hamish," I said. "Just ask Nathaniel's mother, Agatha Wilson. She wants it, too."

"Wherever did you find this second page?" He touched the picture of the dragons.

"Someone brought it to New Haven."

"Who?" Hamish asked.

"Andrew Hubbard." After Ysabeau's warnings I wasn't sure how much to reveal. But Hamish was our lawyer. I couldn't keep secrets from him. "He's a vampire."

"Oh, I'm well aware of who—and what—Andrew Hubbard is. I'm a daemon and work in the City, after all," Hamish said with a laugh. "But I'm surprised Matthew let him get near. He despises the man."

I could have explained how much things had changed, and why, but the tale of Jack Blackfriars was Matthew's to tell.

"What does the missing picture of the tree have to do with Athanasius Kircher?" Phoebe asked, bringing our attention back to the matter at hand.

"While I was in New Haven, my colleague Lucy Meriweather helped me track down what might have happened to the Book of Life. One of Rudolf's mysterious manuscripts ended up in Kircher's hands. We thought that the illumination of the tree might have been included with it." I gestured at the frontispiece to *Magnes sive De Arte Magnetica*. "I'm more certain than ever that Kircher had at least seen the image, based solely on that illustration."

"Can't you just look through Kircher's books and papers?" Hamish asked.

"I can," I replied with a smile, "provided the books and papers can still be located. Kircher's personal collection was sent to an old papal residence for safekeeping—Villa Mondragone in Italy. In the early twentieth century, the Jesuits began to discreetly sell off some of the books to raise revenue. Lucy and I think they sold the page then."

"In that case there should be records of the sale," Phoebe said thoughtfully. "Have you contacted the Jesuits?"

"Yes." I nodded. "They have no records of it—or if they do, they aren't sharing them. Lucy wrote to the major auction houses, too."

"Well, she wouldn't have got very far. Sales information is confidential," Phoebe said.

"So we were told." I hesitated just long enough for Phoebe to offer what I was afraid to ask for.

"I'll e-mail Sylvia today and tell her that I won't be able to clear out my desk tomorrow as planned," Phoebe said. "I can't hold Sotheby's off indefinitely, but there are other resources I can check and people who might talk to me if approached in the right way."

Before I could respond, the doorbell rang. After a momentary pause, it rang again. And again. The fourth time the ringing went on and on as though the visitor had jammed a finger into the button and left it there.

"Diana!" shouted a familiar voice. The ringing was replaced by pounding.

"Sarah!" I cried, rising to my feet.

A fresh October breeze swept into the house, carrying with it the scents of brimstone and saffron. I rushed into the hall. Sarah was there, her face white and her hair floating around her shoulders in a mad tangle of red. Fernando stood behind her, carrying two suitcases as though their collective weight were no more than a first-class letter.

Sarah's red-rimmed eyes met mine, and she dropped Tabitha's cat carrier on the marble floor with a thud. She held her arms wide, and I moved into them. Em had always offered me comfort when I felt alone and frightened as a child, but right now Sarah was exactly who I needed.

"It will be all right, honey," she whispered, holding me tight.

"I just spoke to Father H, and he said I'm to follow your instructions to the letter, Mistress . . . Madame," Leonard Shoreditch said cheerfully, pushing past Sarah and me on his way into the house. He gave me a jaunty salute.

"Did Andrew say anything else?" I asked, drawing away from my aunt. Perhaps Hubbard had shared news of Jack—or Matthew.

"Let's see." Leonard pulled on the end of his long nose. "Father H said to make sure you know where London begins and ends, and if there's trouble, go straight to St. Paul's and help will be along presently."

Hearty slaps indicated that Fernando and Gallowglass had been reunited.

"No problems?" Gallowglass murmured.

"None, except that I had to persuade Sarah not to disable the smoke detector in the first-class lavatory so she could sneak a cigarette," Fernando said mildly. "Next time she needs to fly internationally, send a de Clermont plane. We'll wait."

"Thank you for getting her here so quickly, Fernando," I said with a grateful smile. "You must be wishing you'd never met me and Sarah. All the Bishops seem to do is get you more entangled with the de Clermonts and their problems."

"On the contrary," he said softly, "you are freeing me from them." To my astonishment, Fernando dropped the bags and knelt before me.

"Get up. Please." I tried to lift him.

"The last time I fell to my knees before a woman, I had lost one of Isabella of Castile's ships. Two of her guards forced me to do so at sword point, so that I might beg for her forgiveness," Fernando said with a sardonic lift to his mouth. "As I'm doing so voluntarily on this occasion, I will get up when I am through."

Marthe appeared, taken aback by the sight of Fernando in such an abject position.

"I am without kith or kin. My maker is gone. My mate is gone. I have no children of my own." Fernando bit into his wrist and clenched his fist. The blood welled up from the wound, streaming over his arm and splashing onto the black-and-white floor. "I dedicate my blood and body to the service and honor of your family."

"Blimey," Leonard breathed. "That's not how Father H does it." I had seen Andrew Hubbard induct a creature into his flock, and though the two ceremonies weren't identical, they were similar in tone and intent.

Once again everyone in the house waited for my response. There were probably rules and precedents to follow, but at that moment I neither knew nor cared what they were. I took Fernando's bloody hand in mine.

"Thank you for putting your trust in Matthew," I said simply.

"I have always trusted him," Fernando said, looking up at me with sharp eyes. "Now it is time for Matthew to trust himself."

25

I found it." Phoebe put a printed e-mail before me on the Georgian writing desk's tooled-leather surface. The fact that she hadn't first knocked politely on the door to the sitting room told me that something exciting had happened.

"Already?" I regarded her in amazement.

"I told my former supervisor that I was looking for an item for the de Clermont family—a picture of a tree drawn by Athanasius Kircher." Phoebe glanced around the room, her connoisseur's eye caught by the black-and-gold chinoiserie chest on a stand, the faux bamboo carvings on a chair, the colorful silk cushions splashed across the chaise longue by the window. She peered at the walls, muttering the name Jean Pillement and words like "impossible" and "priceless" and "museum."

"But the illustrations in the Book of Life weren't drawn by Kircher." Frowning, I picked up the e-mail. "And it's not a picture. It's a page torn out of a manuscript."

"Attribution and provenance are crucial to a good sale," Phoebe explained. "The temptation to link the picture to Kircher would have been irresistible. And if the edges of the parchment were cleaned up and the text was invisible, it would have commanded a higher price as a stand-alone drawing or painting."

I scanned the message. It began with a tart reference to Phoebe's resignation and future marital state. But it was the next lines that caught my attention:

I do find record of the sale and purchase of "an allegory of the Tree of Life believed to have once been displayed in the museum of Athanasius Kircher, SJ, in Rome." Could this be the image the de Clermonts are seeking?

"Who bought it?" I whispered, hardly daring to breathe.

"Sylvia wouldn't tell me," Phoebe said, pointing to the final lines of the e-mail. "The sale was recent, and the details are confidential. She revealed the purchase price: sixteen hundred and fifty pounds."

"That's all?" I exclaimed. Most of the books Phoebe had purchased for me cost far more than that.

"The possible Kircher provenance wasn't firm enough to convince potential buyers to spend more," she said.

"Is there really no way to discover the buyer's identity?" I began to imagine how I might use magic to find out more.

"Sotheby's can't afford to tell their clients' secrets." Phoebe shook her head. "Imagine how Ysabeau would react if her privacy was violated."

"Did you call me, Phoebe?" My mother-in-law was standing in the arched doorway before the seed of my plan could put out its first shoots.

"Phoebe's discovered that a recent sale at Sotheby's describes a picture very like the one I'm looking for," I explained to Ysabeau. "They won't tell us who bought it."

"I know where the sales records are kept," Phoebe said. "When I go to Sotheby's to hand in my keys, I could take a look."

"No, Phoebe. It's too risky. If you can tell me exactly where they are, I may be able to figure out a way to get access to them." Some combination of my magic and Hubbard's gang of thieves and lost boys could manage it. But my mother-in-law had her own ideas.

"Ysabeau de Clermont calling for Lord Sutton." The clear voice echoed against the room's high ceilings.

Phoebe looked shocked. "You can't just call the director of Sotheby's and expect him to do your bidding."

Apparently Ysabeau could—and did.

"Charles. It's been too long." Ysabeau draped herself over a chair and let her pearls fall through her fingers. "You've been so busy, I've had to rely on Matthew for news. And the refinancing he helped you arrange—did it achieve what you had hoped?"

Ysabeau made soft, encouraging sounds of interest and expressions of appreciation at his cleverness. If I had to describe her behavior, I would be tempted to call it kittenish—provided the kitten were a baby Bengal tiger.

"Oh, I am so glad, Charles. Matthew felt sure it would work." Ysabeau ran a delicate finger over her lips. "I was wondering if you could help with a little situation. Marcus is getting married, you see—to one of your employees. They met when Marcus picked up those miniatures you were so kind as to procure for me in January."

Lord Sutton's precise reply was inaudible, but the warm hum of contentment in his voice was unmistakable.

"The art of matchmaking." Ysabeau's laugh was crystalline. "How witty you are, Charles. Marcus has his heart set on buying Phoebe a special gift, something he remembers seeing long ago—a picture of a family tree."

My eyes widened. "Psst!" I waved. "It's not a family tree. It's—"

Ysabeau's hand made a dismissive gesture as the murmurs on the other end of the line turned eager.

"I believe Sylvia was able to track the item down to a recent sale. But of course she is too discreet to tell me who bought it." Ysabeau nodded through the apologetic response for a few moments. Then the kitten pounced. "You will contact the owner for me, Charles. I cannot bear to see my grandson disappointed at such a happy time."

Lord Sutton was reduced to utter silence.

"The de Clermonts are fortunate to have such a long and happy relationship with Sotheby's. Matthew's tower would have collapsed under the weight of his books if not for meeting Samuel Baker."

"Good Lord." Phoebe's jaw dropped.

"And you managed to clear out most of Matthew's house in Amsterdam. I never liked that fellow or his pictures. You know the one I mean. What was his name? The one whose paintings all look unfinished?"

"Frans Hals," Phoebe whispered, eyes round.

"Frans Hals." Ysabeau nodded approvingly at her future granddaughter-in-law. "Now you and I must convince him to let go of the portrait of that gloomy minister he has hanging over the fireplace in the upstairs parlor."

Phoebe squeaked. I suspected that a trip to Amsterdam would be included in one of her upcoming cataloging adventures.

Lord Sutton made some assurances, but Ysabeau was having none of it.

"I trust you completely, Charles," she interrupted—though it was clear to everyone, Lord Sutton in particular, that she did not. "We can discuss this over coffee tomorrow."

It was Lord Sutton's turn to squeak. A rapid stream of explanations and justifications followed.

"You don't need to come to France. I'm in London. Quite close to your offices on Bond Street, as a matter of fact." Ysabeau tapped her cheek with her finger. "Eleven o'clock? Good. Give my regards to Henrietta. Until tomorrow."

She hung up. "What?" she demanded, looking at Phoebe and me in turn.

"You just manhandled Lord Sutton!" Phoebe exclaimed. "I thought you said diplomacy was required."

"Diplomacy, yes. Elaborate schemes, no. Simple is often best." Ysabeau smiled her tiger smile. "Charles owes Matthew a great deal. In time, Phoebe, you will have many creatures in your debt, too. Then you will see how easy it is to achieve your desires." Ysabeau eyed me sharply. "You look pale, Diana. Aren't you happy that you will soon have all three missing pages from the Book of Life?"

"Yes," I said.

"Then what is the problem?" Ysabeau's eyebrow lifted.

The problem? Once I had the three missing pages, there would be nothing standing between me and the need to steal a manuscript from the Bodleian Library. I was about to become a book thief.

"Nothing," I said faintly.

Back at the desk in the aptly named Chinese Room, I looked again at Kircher's engravings, trying not to think what might happen should Phoebe and Ysabeau find the last missing page. Unable to concentrate on my efforts to locate every engraving of a tree in Kircher's substantial body of work, I rose and went to the window. The street below was quiet, with only the occasional parent leading a child down the sidewalk or a tourist holding a map.

Matthew could always jostle me out of my worries with a snatch of song, or a joke, or (even better) a kiss. Needing to feel closer to him, I prowled down the vacant second-floor hallway until I reached his study. My hand hovered over the knob. After a moment of indecision, I twisted it and went inside.

The aroma of cinnamon and cloves washed over me. Matthew could not have been here in the past twelve months, yet his absence—and my pregnancy—had made me more sensitive to his scent.

Whichever decorator had designed my opulent bedchamber and the confection of a sitting room where I'd spent the morning had not been allowed in here. This room was masculine and unfussy, its walls lined with bookshelves and windows. Splendid globes—one celestial, the other terrestrial—sat in wooden stands, ready to be consulted should a question of astronomy or geography present itself. Natural curiosities were scattered here and there on small tables. I trod a clockwise path around the room as though weaving a spell to bring Matthew back, stopping occasionally to examine a book or to give the celestial globe a spin. The oddest chair I'd ever seen required a longer pause. Its high, deeply curved back had a leather-covered book stand mounted on it, and the seat was shaped rather like a saddle. The only way to occupy the chair would be to sit astride it, as Gallowglass did whenever he turned a chair at the dining-room table. Someone sitting astride the seat and facing the book stand would have the contraption at the perfect height for holding a book or some writing equipment. I tried out the theory by swinging my leg over the padded seat. It was surprisingly comfortable, and I imagined Matthew sitting here, reading for hours in the ample light from the windows.

I dismounted the chair and turned. What I saw hanging over the fireplace made me gasp: a life-size double portrait of Philippe and Ysabeau.

Matthew's mother and father wore splendid clothes from the middle of the eighteenth century, that happy period of fashion when women's gowns did not yet resemble birdcages and men had abandoned the long curls and high heels of the previous century. My fingers itched to touch the surface of the painting, convinced that they would be met with silks and lace rather than canvas.

What was most striking about the portrait was not the vividness of their features (though it would be impossible not to recognize Ysabeau) but the way the artist had captured the relationship between Philippe and his wife.

Philippe de Clermont faced the viewer in a cream-and-blue silk suit, his broad shoulders square to the canvas and his right hand extended toward Ysabeau as if he were about to introduce her. A smile played at his lips, the hint of softness accentuating the stern lines of his face and the long sword that hung from his belt. Philippe's eyes, however, did not meet mine as his position suggested they should. Instead they were directed in a sidelong glance at Ysabeau. Nothing, it seemed, could drag his attention away from the woman he loved. Ysabeau was painted in three-quarter profile, one hand resting lightly in her husband's fingers and the other holding up the folds of her cream-and-gold silk dress as though she were stepping forward to be closer to Philippe. Instead of looking up at her husband, however, Ysabeau stared boldly at the viewer, her lips parted as if surprised to be interrupted in such a private moment.

I heard footsteps behind me and felt the tingling touch of a witch's glance.

"Is that Matthew's father?" Sarah asked, standing at my shoulder and looking up at the grand canvas.

"Yes. It's an amazing likeness," I said with a nod.

"I figured as much, given how perfectly the artist captured Ysabeau." Sarah's attention turned to me. "You don't look well, Diana."

"That's not surprising, is it?" I said. "Matthew is out there, trying to stitch together a family. It may get him killed, and I asked him do it."

"Not even you could make Matthew do something he didn't want to do," Sarah said bluntly.

"You don't know what happened in New Haven, Sarah. Matthew discovered he had a grandson he didn't know about—Benjamin's son—and a great-grandson, too."

"Fernando told me all about Andrew Hubbard, and Jack, and the blood rage," Sarah replied. "He told me that Baldwin ordered Matthew to kill the boy, too—but you wouldn't let him do it."

I looked up at Philippe, wishing that I understood why he had appointed Matthew the official de Clermont family executioner. "Jack was like a child to us, Sarah. And if Matthew killed Jack, what would stop him from killing the twins if they, too, turn out to have blood rage?"

"Baldwin would never ask Matthew to kill his own flesh and blood," Sarah said.

"Yes," I said sadly. "He would."

"Then it sounds as though Matthew is doing what he has to do," she said firmly. "You need to do your job, too."

"I am," I said, sounding defensive. "My job is to find the missing pages from the Book of Life and then put it back together so that we can use it as leverage—with Baldwin, with Benjamin, even the Congregation."

"You have to take care of the twins, too," Sarah pointed out. "Mooning around up here on your own isn't going to do you—or them—any good."

"Don't you dare play the baby card with me," I said, coldly furious. "I'm trying very hard not to hate my own children—not to mention Jack—right now." It wasn't fair, nor was it logical, but I was blaming them for our separation, even though I had been the one to insist upon it.

"I hated you for a while." Sarah's tone was matter-of-fact. "If not for you, Rebecca would still be alive. Or so I told myself."

Her words came as no surprise. Children always know what grown-ups are thinking. Em had never made me feel that it was my fault that my parents were dead. Of course, she'd known what they were planning—and why. But Sarah was a different story.

"Then I got over it," Sarah continued quietly. "You will, too. One day you'll see the twins and you'll realize that Matthew is right there, staring out at you from an eight-year-old's eyes."

"My life doesn't make sense without Matthew," I said.

"He can't be your whole world, Diana."

"He already is," I whispered. "And if he succeeds in breaking free of the de Clermonts, he's going to need me to be at his side like Ysabeau was for Philippe. I'll never be able to fill her shoes."

"Bullshit." Sarah jammed her hands onto her hips. "And if you think Matthew wants you to be like his mother, you're crazy."

"You have a lot to learn about vampires." Somehow the line didn't sound as convincing when a witch delivered it.

"Oh. Now I see the problem." Sarah's eyes narrowed. "Em said you'd come back to us different—whole. But you're still trying to be something you're not." She pointed an accusatory finger at me. "You've gone all vampire again."

"Stop it, Sarah."

"If Matthew had wanted a vampire bride, he could have his pick. Hell, he could have turned you into a vampire last October in Madison," she said. "You'd willingly given him most of your blood."

"Matthew wouldn't change me," I said.

"I know. He promised me as much the morning before you left." Sarah looked daggers at me. "Matthew doesn't mind that you're a witch. Why do you?" When I didn't reply, she grabbed my hand.

"Where are we going?" I asked as my aunt dragged me down the stairs.

"Out." Sarah stopped in front of the gaggle of vampires standing in the front hall. "Diana needs to remember who she is. You're coming, too, Gallowglass."

"Ooo-kaaay," Gallowglass said uneasily, drawing out the two syllables. "Are we going far?"

"How the hell do I know?" Sarah retorted. "This is my first time in London. We're going to Diana's old house—the one she and Matthew shared in Elizabethan times."

"My house is gone—it burned down in the Great Fire," I said, trying to escape.

"We're going anyway."

"Oh, Christ." Gallowglass threw a set of car keys at Leonard. "Get the car, Lenny. We're going for a Sunday drive."

Leonard grinned. "Right."

"Why is that boy always hanging around?" Sarah asked, watching as the gangly vampire bolted toward the back of the house.

"He belongs to Andrew," I explained.

"In other words he belongs to you," she said with a nod. My jaw dropped. "Oh, yes. I know all about vampires and their crazy ways." Apparently, Fernando didn't have the same reluctance as Matthew and Ysabeau did to tell vampire tales.

Leonard pulled up to the front door with a squeal of tires. He was out of the car and had the rear door opened in a blink. "Where to, madame?"

I did a double take. It was the first time Leonard hadn't stumbled over my name.

"Diana's house, Lenny," Sarah answered. "Her real house, not this over-decorated dust-bunny sanctuary."

"I'm sorry, but it's not there anymore, miss," Leonard said, as though the Great Fire of London had been his fault. Knowing Leonard, this was entirely possible.

"Don't vampires have any imagination?" Sarah asked tartly. "Take me where the house *used* to be."

"Oh." Leonard looked at Gallowglass, wide-eyed.

Gallowglass shrugged. "You heard the lady," my nephew said.

We rocketed across London, heading east. When we passed Temple Bar and moved onto Fleet Street, Leonard turned south toward the river.

"This isn't the way," I said.

"One-way streets, madame," he said. "Things have changed a bit since you were last here." He made a sharp left in front of the Blackfriars Station. I put my hand on the door handle to get out and heard a click as the child-proof locks engaged.

"Stay in the car, Auntie," Gallowglass said.

Leonard jerked the steering wheel to the left once more, and we jostled over pavement and rough road surfaces.

"Blackfriars Lane," I said reading the sign that zipped past. I jiggled the door handle. "Let me out."

The car stopped abruptly, blocking the entrance to a loading dock.

"Your house, madame," Leonard said, sounding like a tour guide and waving at the red-and-cream brick office building that loomed above us. He released the door locks. "It's safe to walk about. Please mind the uneven pavement. Don't want to have to explain to Father H how you broke your leg, do I?"

I stepped out onto the stone sidewalk. It was firmer footing than the usual mud and muck of Water Lane, as we'd called the street in the past. Automatically I headed in the general direction of St. Paul's Cathedral. I felt a hand on my elbow, holding me back.

"You know how Uncle feels about you wandering around town unaccompanied." Gallowglass bowed, and for a moment I saw him in doublet and hose. "At your service, Madame Roydon."

"Where exactly are we?" Sarah asked, scanning the nearby alleys. "This doesn't look like a residential area."

"The Blackfriars. Once upon a time, hundreds of people lived here." It took me only a few steps to reach a narrow cobbled street that used to lead to the inner precincts of the old Blackfriars Priory. I frowned and pointed. "Wasn't the Cardinal's Hat in there?" It was one of Kit Marlowe's watering holes.

"Good memory, Auntie. They call it Playhouse Yard now."

Our house had backed up to that part of the former monastery. Gallowglass and Sarah followed me into the cul-de-sac. Once it had been filled to bursting with merchants, craftsmen, housewives, apprentices, and children— not to mention carts, dogs, and chickens. Today it was deserted.

"Slow down," Sarah said peevishly, struggling to keep up.

It didn't matter how much the old neighborhood had changed. My heart had provided the necessary directions, and my feet followed, swift and sure. In 1591 I would have been surrounded by the ramshackle tenement and entertainment complex that had sprung up within the former priory. Now there were office buildings, a small residence serving well-heeled business executives, more office buildings, and the headquarters of London's apothecaries. I crossed Playhouse Yard and slipped between two buildings.

"Where is she going now?" Sarah asked Gallowglass, her irritation mounting.

"Unless I miss my guess, Auntie's looking for the back way to Baynard's Castle."

At the foot of a narrow thoroughfare called Church Entry, I stopped to get my bearings. If only I could orient myself properly, I could find my way to Mary's house. Where had the Fields' printing shop been? I shut my eyes to avoid the distraction of the incongruous modern buildings.

"Just there," I pointed. "That's where the Fields' shop was. The apothecary lived a few houses along the lane. This way led down to the docks." I kept turning, my arms tracing the line of buildings I saw in my mind. "The door to Monsieur Vallin's silver shop stood here. You could see our back garden from this spot. And here was the old gate that I took to get to Baynard's Castle." I stood for a moment, soaking in the familiar feeling of my former home and wishing I could open my eyes and find myself in the Countess of Pembroke's solar. Mary would have understood my current predicament perfectly and been generous with advice on matters dynastic and political.

"Holy shit," Sarah gasped.

My eyes flew open. A transparent wooden door was a few yards away, set into a crumbling, equally transparent stone wall. Mesmerized, I tried to take a step toward it but was prevented from doing so by the blue and amber threads that swirled tightly around my legs.

"Don't move!" Sarah sounded panicked.

"Why?" I could see her through a scrim of Elizabethan shop fronts.

"You've cast a counterclock. It rewinds images from past times, like a movie," Sarah said, peering at me through the windows of Master Prior's pastry shop.

"Magic," Gallowglass moaned. "Just what we need."

An elderly woman in a neat navy blue cardigan and a pale blue shirt-waist dress who was very much of the here and now came out of the nearby apartment building.

"You'll find this part of London can be a bit tricky, magically speaking," she called out in that authoritative, cheerful tone that only British women of a certain age and social status could produce. "You'll want to take some precautions if you plan on doing any more spell casting."

As the woman approached, I was struck by a sense of déjà vu. She re-minded me of one of the witches I'd known in 1591—an earthwitch called Marjorie Cooper, who had helped me to weave my first spell.

"I'm Linda Crosby." She smiled, and the resemblance to Marjorie be-came more pronounced. "Welcome home, Diana Bishop. We've been ex-pecting you."

I stared at her, dumbfounded.

"I'm Diana's aunt," Sarah said, wading into the silence. "Sarah Bishop."

"Pleasure," Linda said warmly, shaking Sarah's hand. Both witches stared down at my feet. During our brief introductions, time's blue and amber bindings had loosened somewhat, fading away one by one as they were absorbed back into the fabric of the Blackfriars. Monsieur Vallin's front door was still all too evident, however.

"I'd give it a few more minutes. You are a timewalker, after all," Linda said, perching on one of the curved benches that surrounded a circular brick planter. It occupied the same spot as had the wellhead in the Cardi-nal's Hat yard.

"Are you one of Hubbard's family?" Sarah asked, reaching into her pocket. Out came her forbidden cigarettes. She offered one to Linda.

"I'm a witch," Linda said, taking the cigarette. "And I live in the City of London. So, yes—I am a member of Father Hubbard's family. Proudly so."

Gallowglass lit the witches' cigarettes and then his own. The three puffed away like chimneys, careful to direct the smoke so it didn't waft toward me.

"I haven't met Hubbard yet," Sarah confessed. "Most of the vampires I know don't think much of him."

"Really?" Linda asked with interest. "How very odd. Father Hubbard is a beloved figure here. He protects everybody's interests, be they daemon, vampire, or witch. So many creatures have wanted to move into his territory that it's led to a housing crisis. He can't buy property fast enough to satisfy the demand."

"He's still a wanker," Gallowglass muttered.

"Language!" Linda said, shocked.

"How many witches are there in the city?" Sarah asked.

"Three dozen," Linda responded. "We limit the numbers, of course, or it would be madness in the Square Mile."

"The Madison coven is the same size," Sarah said approvingly. "Makes it easier to hold the meetings, that's for sure."

"We gather once a month in Father Hubbard's crypt. He lives in what's left of the Greyfriars Priory, just over there." Linda aimed her cigarette at a point north of Playhouse Yard. "These days most of the creatures in the City proper are vampires—financiers and hedge-fund managers and such. They don't like to hire out their meeting rooms to witches. No offense, sir."

"None taken," Gallowglass said mildly.

"The Greyfriars? Has Lady Agnes moved on?" I asked, surprised. The ghost's antics had been the talk of the town when I lived here.

"Oh, no. Lady Agnes is still there. With Father Hubbard's help, we were able to broker an agreement between her and Queen Isabella. They seem to be on friendly terms now—which is more than I can say for the ghost of Elizabeth Barton. Ever since that novel about Cromwell came out, she's been impossible." Linda eyed my belly speculatively. "At our Mabon tea this year, Elizabeth Barton said you're having twins."

"I am." Even the ghosts of London knew my business.

"It's so difficult to tell which of Elizabeth's prophecies are to be taken seriously when every one of them is accompanied by shrieking. It's all so . . . vulgar." Linda pursed her lips in disapproval, and Sarah nodded sympathetically.

"Um, I hate to break this up, but I think my spell for the counterclock thingy expired." Not only could I see my own ankle (provided I lifted my leg up—otherwise the babies were in the way), but Monsieur Vallin's door had utterly vanished.

"Expired?" Linda laughed. "You make it sound as though your magic has a sell-by date."

"I certainly didn't tell it to stop," I grumbled. Then again, I had never told it to start either.

"It stopped because you didn't wind it up tight enough," Sarah said. "If you don't give a counterclock a good crank, it runs down."

"And we do recommend that you not stand on top of the counterclock once you cast it," Linda said, sounding a bit like my middle-school gym teacher. "You want to address the spell without blinking, then step away from it at the last minute."

"My mistake," I murmured. "Can I move now?"

Linda surveyed Playhouse Yard with a crinkled brow. "Yes, I do believe it's perfectly safe now," she proclaimed.

I groaned and rubbed at my back. Standing still for so long had made it ache, and my feet felt like they were going to explode. I propped one of them upon the bench where Sarah and Linda were sitting and bent to loosen the ties on my sneakers.

"What's that?" I said, peering through the bench's slats. I reached down and retrieved a scroll of paper tied up with a red ribbon. The fingers on my right hand tingled when I touched it, and the pentacle at my wrist swirled with color.

"It's tradition for people to leave requests for magic in the yard. There's always been a concentration of power associated with this spot." Linda's voice softened. "A great witch lived here once, you see. Legend says she'll return one day, to remind us of all we once were and could be again. We haven't forgotten her and trust that she will not forget us."

The Blackfriars was haunted by my past self. Part of me had died when we left London. It was the part that had once been able to juggle being Matthew's wife, Annie and Jack's mother, Mary Sidney's alchemical assistant, and a weaver-in-training. And another part of me had joined it in the grave when I walked away from Matthew on the mountain outside New Haven. I buried my head in my hands.

"I've made a mess of things," I whispered.

"No, you dove into the deep end and got in over your head," Sarah replied. "This is what Em and I worried about when you and Matthew first got involved. You both moved so fast, and we knew that neither of you had thought about what this relationship was going to require."

"We knew we would face plenty of opposition."

"Oh, you two had the star-crossed-lovers part down—and I understand how romantic it can be to feel it's just the two of you against the world." Sarah chuckled. "Em and I were star-crossed lovers, after all. In upstate New York in the 1970s, nothing was more star-crossed than two women falling in love."

Her tone grew serious. "But the sun always rises the next morning. Fairy tales don't tell you much about what happens to star-crossed lovers in the bright light of day, but somehow you have to figure out how to be happy."

"We were happy here," I said quietly. "Weren't we, Gallowglass?"

"Aye, Auntie, you were—even with Matthew's spymaster breathing down his neck and the whole country on the lookout for witches." Gallowglass shook his head. "How you managed it, I've never understood."

"You managed it because neither of you were trying to be something you weren't. Matthew wasn't trying to be civilized, and you weren't trying to be human," Sarah said. "You weren't trying to be Rebecca's perfect daughter, or Matthew's perfect wife, or a tenured professor at Yale either."

She took my hands in hers, scroll and all, and turned them so the palms faced up. My weaver's cords stood out bright against the pale flesh.

"You're a witch, Diana. A weaver. Don't deny your power. Use it." Sarah looked pointedly at my left hand. "All of it."

My phone pinged in the pocket of my jacket. I scrambled for it, hoping against hope it was some kind of message from Matthew. He'd promised to let me know how he was doing. The display indicated there was a text waiting from him. I opened it eagerly.

The message contained no words that the Congregation could use against us, only a picture of Jack. He was sitting on a porch, his face split into a wide grin as he listened to someone—a man, though his back was to the camera and I could see nothing more than the black hair curling around his collar— tell a story as only a southerner could. Marcus stood behind Jack, one hand draped casually over his shoulder. Like Jack, he was grinning.

They looked like two ordinary young men enjoying a laugh over the weekend. Jack fit perfectly into Marcus's family, as though he belonged.

"Who's that with Marcus?" Sarah said, looking over my shoulder.

"Jack." I touched his face. "I'm not sure who the other man is."

"That's Ransome." Gallowglass sniffed. "Marcus's eldest, and he puts Lucifer to shame. Not the best role model for young Jack, but I reckon Matthew knows best."

"Look at the lad," Linda said fondly, standing so she could get a look at the picture, too. "I've never seen Jack look so happy—except when he was telling stories about Diana, of course."

St. Paul's bells rang the hour. I pushed the button on my phone, dimming the display. I would look at the picture again later, in private.

"See, honey. Matthew is doing just fine," Sarah said, her voice soothing.

But without seeing his eyes, gauging the set of his shoulders, hearing the tone of his voice, I couldn't be sure.

"Matthew's doing his job," I reminded myself, standing up. "I need to get back to mine."

"Does that mean you're ready to do whatever it takes to keep your family together like you did in 1591—even if higher magics are involved?" Sarah's eyebrow shot up in open query.

"Yes." I sounded more convinced than I felt.

"Higher magics? How deliciously dark." Linda beamed. "Can I help?"

"No," I said quickly.

"Possibly," Sarah said at the same time.

"Well, if you need us, give a ring. Leonard knows how to reach me," Linda said. "The London coven is at your disposal. And if you were to come to one of our meetings, it would be quite a boost to morale."

"We'll see," I said vaguely, not wanting to make a promise I couldn't keep. "The situation is complicated, and I wouldn't want to get anyone into trouble."

"Vampires are always trouble," Linda said with a primly disapproving look, "holding grudges and going off half-cocked on some vendetta or other. It's really very trying. Still, we are all one big family, as Father Hubbard reminds us."

"One big family." I looked at our old neighborhood. "Maybe Father Hubbard was on the right track all along."

"Well, we think so. Do consider coming to our next meeting. Doris makes a divine Battenberg cake."

Sarah and Linda swapped telephone numbers just in case, and Gallowglass went to Apothecaries' Hall and let out an earsplitting whistle to call Leonard around with the car. I took the opportunity to snap a picture of Playhouse Yard and sent it to Matthew without a comment or a caption.

Magic was nothing more than desire made real, after all.

The October breeze came off the Thames and carried my unspoken wishes into the sky, where they wove a spell to bring Matthew safely back to me.

26

A slice of Battenberg cake with a moist pink-and-yellow checkerboard interior and canary-colored icing sat before me at our secluded table at the Wolseley, along with still more contraband black tea. I lifted the lid on the teapot and drank in its malty aroma, sighing happily. I'd been craving tea and cake ever since our unexpected meeting with Linda Crosby at the Blackfriars.

Hamish, who was a breakfast regular there, had commandeered a large table at the bustling Piccadilly restaurant for the entire morning and proceeded to treat the space—and the staff—as though they were his office. Thus far he'd taken a dozen phone calls, made several lunch engagements (three of them for the same day next week, I noted with alarm), and read every London daily in its entirety. He had also, bless him, wheedled my cake out of the pastry chef hours before it was normally served, citing my condition as justification. The speed with which the request was met was either an additional indication of Hamish's importance or a sign that the young man who wielded the whisks and rolling pins understood the special relationship between pregnant women and sugar.

"This is taking forever," Sarah grumbled. She'd bolted down a soft-boiled egg with toast batons, consumed an ocean of black coffee, and had been dividing her attention between her wristwatch and the door ever since.

"When it comes to extortion, Granny doesn't like to rush." Gallowglass smiled affably at the ladies at a nearby table, who were casting admiring glances at his muscular, tattooed arms.

"If they don't arrive soon, I'll be walking back to Westminster under my own steam thanks to all the caffeine." Hamish waved down the manager. "Another cappuccino, Adam. Better make it a decaf."

"Of course, sir. More toast and jam?"

"Please," Hamish said, handing Adam the empty toast rack. "Strawberry. You know I can't resist the strawberry."

"And why is it again that we couldn't wait for Granny and Phoebe at the house?" Gallowglass shifted nervously on his tiny seat. The chair was not designed for a man of his size, but rather for MPs, socialites, morning-television personalities, and other such insubstantial persons.

"Diana's neighbors are wealthy and paranoid. There hasn't been any activity at the house for nearly a year. Suddenly there are people around at all hours and Allens of Mayfair is making daily deliveries." Hamish made room on the table for his fresh cappuccino. "We don't want them thinking you're an international drug cartel and calling the police. West End Central station is full of witches, especially the CID. And don't forget: You're not under Hubbard's protection outside the City limits."

"Hmph. You're not worried about the coppers. You just didn't want to miss anything." Gallowglass wagged a finger at him. "I'm on to you, Hamish."

"Here's Fernando," Sarah said in a tone suggesting that deliverance had come at last.

Fernando tried to hold open the door for Ysabeau, but Adam beat him to it. My mother-in-law looked like a youthful film star, and every male head in the room turned as she entered with Phoebe in her wake. Fernando hung back, his dark coat the perfect backdrop for Ysabeau's off-white and taupe ensemble.

"No wonder Ysabeau prefers to stay at home," I said. She stood out like a beacon on a foggy day.

"Philippe always said it was easier to withstand a siege than to cross a room at Ysabeau's side. He had to fend off her admirers with more than a stick, I can tell you." Gallowglass rose as his grandmother approached. "Hello, Granny. Did they give in to your demands?"

Ysabeau offered her cheek to be kissed. "Of course."

"In part," Phoebe said hastily.

"Was there trouble?" Gallowglass asked Fernando.

"None worth mentioning." Fernando pulled out a chair. Ysabeau slid onto it gracefully, crossing her slim ankles.

"Charles was most accommodating when you consider how many company policies I expected him to violate," she said, refusing the menu Adam offered her with a little moue of distaste. "Champagne, please."

"The hideous painting you took off his hands will more than compensate for it," Fernando said, installing Phoebe into her place at the table. "Whatever made you buy it, Ysabeau?"

"It is not hideous, though abstract expressionism is an acquired taste," she admitted. "The painting is raw, mysterious—sensual. I will give it to the Louvre and force Parisians to expand their minds. Mark my words: This time next year, Clyfford Still will be at the top of every museum's wish list."

"Expect a call from Coutts," Phoebe murmured to Hamish. "She wouldn't haggle."

"There is no need to worry. Both Sotheby's and Coutts know I am good for it." Ysabeau extracted a slip of paper from her sleek leather bag and extended it to me. "Voilà."

"T. J. Weston, Esquire." I looked up from the slip. "This is who bought the page from Ashmole 782?"

"Possibly." Phoebe's reply was terse. "The file contained nothing but a sales slip—he paid cash—and six pieces of misdirected correspondence. Not a single address we have for Weston is valid."

"It shouldn't be that hard to locate him. How many T. J. Westons can there be?" I wondered.

"More than three hundred," Phoebe replied. "I checked the national directory. And don't assume that T. J. Weston is a man. We don't know the buyer's sex or nationality. One of the addresses is in Denmark."

"Do not be so negative, Phoebe. We will make calls. Use Hamish's connections. And Leonard is outside. He will drive us where we need to go." Ysabeau looked unconcerned.

"My connections?" Hamish buried his head in his hands and groaned. "This could take weeks. I might as well live at the Wolseley, given all the coffees I'm going to have with people."

"It won't take weeks, and you don't need to worry about your caffeine intake." I put the paper in my pocket, slung my messenger bag over my shoulder, and hoisted myself to my feet, almost upsetting the table in the process.

"Lord bless us, Auntie. You get bigger by the hour."

"Thank you for noticing, Gallowglass." I'd managed to wedge myself between a coatrack, the wall, and my chair. He leaped up to extricate me.

"How can you be so sure?" Sarah asked me, looking as doubtful as Phoebe.

Wordlessly I held up my hands. They were multicolored and shining.

"Ah. Let us get Diana home," Ysabeau said. "I do not think the proprietor would appreciate having a dragon in his restaurant any more than I did having one in my house."

"Put your hands in your pockets," Sarah hissed. They really were rather bright.

I was not yet at the waddling stage of pregnancy, but it was still a challenge to make my way through the close tables, especially with my hands jammed into my raincoat.

"Please clear the way for my daughter-in-law," Ysabeau said imperiously, taking my elbow and tugging me along. Men stood, pulled their chairs in, and fawned as she passed.

"My husband's stepmother," I whispered to one outraged woman who was gripping her fork like a weapon. She was appropriately disturbed by the notion that I had married a boy of twelve and gotten pregnant by him, for Ysabeau was far too young to have children older than that. "Second marriage. Younger wife. You know how it is."

"So much for blending in," Hamish muttered. "Every creature in WI will know that Ysabeau de Clermont is in town after this. Can't you control her, Gallowglass?"

"Control Granny?" Gallowglass roared with laughter and slapped Hamish on the back.

"This is a nightmare," Hamish said as more heads turned. He reached the front door. "See you tomorrow, Adam."

"Your usual table for one, sir?" Adam asked, offering Hamish his umbrella.

"Yes. Thank God."

Hamish stepped into a waiting car and headed back to his office in the City. Leonard tucked me into the rear of the Mercedes with Phoebe, and Ysabeau and Fernando took the passenger seat. Gallowglass lit a cigarette and ambled along the sidewalk, emitting more smoke than a Mississippi steamboat. We lost sight of him outside the Coach and Horses, where Gallowglass indicated through a series of silent gestures that he was going in for a drink.

"Coward," Fernando said, shaking his head.

*　*　*

"Now what?" Sarah asked after we were back at Clairmont House in the cozy morning room. Though the front parlor was comfortable and welcoming, this snug spot was my favorite room in the house. It contained a ragtag assemblage of furniture, including a stool that I was certain had been in our house in the Blackfriars, which made the room feel as if it had been lived in rather than decorated.

"Now we find T. J. Weston, Esquire, whoever she or he may be." I propped up my feet on the age-blackened Elizabethan stool with a groan, letting the warmth from the crackling fire seep into my aching bones.

"It will be like finding a needle in a haystack," Phoebe said, allowing herself the small discourtesy of a sigh.

"Not if Diana uses her magic it won't," Sarah said confidently.

"Magic?" Ysabeau's head swung around, and her eyes sparkled.

"I thought you didn't approve of witches?" My mother-in-law had made her feelings on this matter known from the very beginning of my relationship with Matthew.

"Ysabeau might not like witches, but she's got nothing except admiration for magic," Fernando said.

"You draw a mighty fine line, Ysabeau," Sarah said with a shake of her head.

"What kind of magic?" Gallowglass had returned, unnoticed, and was standing in the hall, his hair and coat dripping with moisture. He rather resembled Lobero after a long run in the emperor's Stag Moat.

"A candle spell can work when you're searching for a lost object," Sarah said thoughtfully. She was something of an expert on candle spells, since Em had been famous for leaving her things all around the house—and Madison.

"I remember a witch who used some earth and a knotted piece of linen," Ysabeau said. Sarah and I turned to her, mouths open in astonishment. She drew herself straight and regarded us with hauteur. "You need not look so surprised. I have known a great many witches over the years."

Fernando ignored Ysabeau and spoke to Phoebe instead. "You said one of the addresses for T. J. Weston was in Denmark. What about the others?"

"All from the UK: four in England and one in Northern Ireland," Phoebe said. "In England the addresses were all in the south—Devon, Cornwall, Essex, Wiltshire."

"Do you really need to meddle with magic, Auntie?" Gallowglass looked concerned. "Surely there's a way for Nathaniel to use his computers and find this person. Did you write the addresses down, Phoebe?"

"Of course." She produced a crumpled Boots receipt covered with handwriting. Gallowglass looked at it dubiously. "I couldn't very well take a notebook into the file room. It would have been suspicious."

"Very clever," Ysabeau assured her. "I will send the addresses on to Nathaniel so he can get to work on them."

"I still think magic would be faster—so long as I can figure out what spell to use," I said. "I'll need something visual. I'm better with visuals than with candles."

"What about a map?" Gallowglass suggested. "Matthew must have a map or two in his library upstairs. If not, I could go around to Hatchards and see what they've got." He had only just returned, but Gallowglass was clearly eager to be outdoors in the frigid downpour. It was, I supposed, as close to the weather in the middle of the Atlantic as he was likely to find.

"A map might work—if it were big enough," I said. "We'll be no better off if the spell is only able to pinpoint that T. J. Weston's location is in Wiltshire." I wondered if it would be possible for Leonard to drive me around the county with a box of candles.

"There's a lovely map shop just by Shoreditch," Leonard said proudly, as though he were personally responsible for its location. "They make big maps what hang on walls. I'll give them a ring."

"What will you need besides the map?" Sarah asked. "A compass?"

"It's too bad I don't have the mathematical instrument Emperor Rudolf gave me," I said. "It was always whirring around as though it were trying to find something." At first I'd thought its movements indicated that somebody was searching for Matthew and me. Over time I'd wondered if the compendium swung into action whenever someone was searching for the Book of Life.

Phoebe and Ysabeau exchanged a look.

"Excuse me." Phoebe slipped out of the room.

"That brass gadget that Annie and Jack called a witch's clock?" Gallowglass chuckled. "I doubt that would be much help, Auntie. It couldn't even keep proper time, and Master Habermel's latitude charts were a bit . . . er, fanciful." Habermel had been utterly defeated by my request to include a reference to the New World and had simply picked a coordinate that for all I knew would have put me in Tierra del Fuego.

"Divination is the way to go," Sarah said. "We'll put candles on the four cardinal points of north, east, south, and west, then sit you in the center with a bowl of water and see what develops."

"If I'm going to divine by water, I'll need more space than this." The breakfast room would fill up with witchwater at an alarming speed.

"We could use the garden," Ysabeau suggested. "Or the ballroom upstairs. I never did think the Trojan War was a suitable subject for the frescoes, so it would be no great loss if they were damaged."

"We might want to tune up your third eye before you start, too," Sarah said, looking critically at my forehead as though it were a radio.

Phoebe returned with a small box. She handed it to Ysabeau.

"Perhaps we should see if this can help first." Ysabeau drew Master Habermel's compendium from the cardboard container. "Alain packed up some of your things from Sept-Tours. He thought they would make you feel more at home here."

The compendium was a beautiful instrument, expertly fashioned from brass, gilded and silvered to make it shine, and loaded with everything from a storage slot for paper and pencil to a compass, latitude tables, and a small clock. At the moment the instrument appeared to be going haywire, for the dials on the face of the compendium were spinning around. We could hear the steady whir of the gears.

Sarah peered at the instrument. "Definitely enchanted."

"It's going to wear itself out." Gallowglass extended a thick finger, ready to give the hands on the clock a poke to slow them down.

"No touching," Sarah said sharply. "You can never anticipate how a bewitched object will respond to unwanted interference."

"Did you ever put it near the picture of the chemical wedding, Auntie?" Gallowglass asked. "If you're right, and Master Habermel's toy acts up when someone is looking for the Book of Life, then maybe seeing the page will quiet it."

"Good idea. The picture of the chemical wedding is in the Chinese Room along with the picture of the dragons." I lumbered to my feet. "I left them on the card table."

Ysabeau was gone before I could straighten up. She was back quickly, holding the two pages as though they were glass and might shatter at any moment. As soon as I laid them on the table, the hand on the compendium dial began to swing slowly from left to right instead of revolving around its central pin. When I picked the pages up, the compendium began to spin again—though slower than it had before.

"I do not think the compendium registers when someone is looking for the Book of Life," Fernando said. "The instrument itself seems to be searching for the book. Now that it senses some of the pages are nearby, it is narrowing its focus."

"How strange." I put the pages back on the table and watched in fascination as the hand slowed and resumed its pendulum swing.

"Can you use it to find the last missing page?" Ysabeau said, staring at the compendium with equal fascination.

"Only if I drive all over England, Wales, and Scotland with it." I wondered how long it would take me to damage the delicate, priceless instrument, holding it on my lap while Gallowglass or Leonard sped up the M40.

"Or you could devise a locator spell. With a map and that contraption, you might be able to triangulate the missing page's position," Sarah said thoughtfully, tapping her lips with her finger.

"What kind of locator spell do you have in mind?" This went well beyond bell, book, and candle or writing a charm on a moonwort pod.

"We'd have to try a few and see—test them to figure out which is best," Sarah mused. "Then you'd need to perform it under the right conditions, with plenty of magical support so the spell doesn't get bent out of shape."

"Where are you going to find magical support in Mayfair?" Fernando asked.

"Linda Crosby," my aunt and I said at the same time.

Sarah and I spent more than a week testing and retesting spells in the basement of the house in Mayfair as well as the tiny kitchen of Linda's flat in the Blackfriars. After nearly drowning Tabitha and having the fire brigade show up twice in Playhouse Yard, I had finally managed to cobble together some knots and a handful of magically significant items into a locator spell that might—just might—work.

The London coven met in a portion of the medieval Greyfriars crypt that had survived a series of disasters over its long history, from the dissolu-

tion of the monasteries to the Blitz. Atop the crypt stood Andrew Hubbard's house: the church's former bell tower. It was twelve stories tall and
had only one large room on each of its floors. Outside the tower he had
planted a pleasant garden in the one corner of the old churchyard that had
resisted urban renewal.

"What a strange house," Ysabeau murmured.

"Andrew is a very strange vampire," I replied with a shiver.

"Father H likes lofty spaces, that's all. He says they make him feel closer
to God." Leonard rapped on the door again.

"I just felt a ghost go by," Sarah said, drawing her coat more closely
around her. There was no mistaking the cold sensation.

"I don't feel anything," Leonard said with a vampire's cavalier disregard
for something as corporeal as warmth. His rapping turned to pounding.
"Come on, sunshine!"

"Patience, Leonard. We are not all twenty-year-old vampires!" Linda
Crosby said crossly once she'd wrestled the door open. "There are a prodi-
gious number of stairs to climb."

Happily, we had only to descend one floor from the main entrance level
to reach the room that Hubbard had set aside for the use of the City of London's official coven.

"Welcome to our gathering!" Linda said as she led us down the staircase.

Halfway down, I stopped with a gasp.

"Is that . . . you?" Sarah stared at the walls in amazement.

The walls were covered with images of me—weaving my first spell, calling forth a rowan tree, watching Corra as she flew along the Thames, standing beside the witches who had taken me under their wing when I was first
learning about my magic. There was Goody Alsop, the coven's elder, with
her fine features and stooped shoulders; the midwife Susanna Norman; and
the three remaining witches Catherine Streeter, Elizabeth Jackson, and
Marjorie Cooper.

As for the artist, that was clear without a signature. Jack had painted
these images, smearing the walls with wet plaster and adding the lines and
color so that they became a permanent part of the building. Smoke-stained,
mottled with damp, and cracked with age, they had somehow retained their
beauty.

"We are fortunate to have such a room to work in," Linda said, beaming.

"Your journey has long been a source of inspiration for London's witches. Come and meet your sisters."

The three witches waiting at the bottom of the stairs studied me with interest, their glances snapping and crackling against my skin. They might not have the power of the Garlickhythe gathering in 1591, but these witches were not devoid of talent.

"Here is our Diana Bishop, come back to us once more," Linda said. "She has brought her aunt with her, Sarah Bishop, and her mother-in-law, who I trust needs no introduction."

"None at all," said the most elderly of the four witches. "We've all heard cautionary tales about Mélisande de Clermont."

Linda had warned me the coven had some doubts about tonight's proceedings. She had handpicked the witches who would help us: firewitch Sybil Bonewits, waterwitch Tamsin Soothtell, and windwitch Cassandra Kyteler. Linda's powers relied heavily on the element of earth. So, too, did Sarah's.

"Times change," Ysabeau said crisply. "If you would like me to leave . . ."

"Nonsense." Linda shot a warning glance at her fellow witch. "Diana asked for you to be here when she cast her spell. We will all muddle through somehow. Won't we, Cassandra?"

The elderly witch gave a curt nod.

"Make way for the maps if you please, ladies!" Leonard said, his arms full of tubes. He dumped them on a rickety table encrusted with wax and beat a fast retreat up the stairs. "Call me if you need anything." The door to the crypt slammed shut behind him.

Linda directed the placement of the maps, for after much fiddling we had found that the best results came from using a huge map of the British Isles surrounded by individual county maps. The map of Great Britain alone took up a section of floor that was around six feet by four feet.

"This looks like a bad elementary-school geography project," Sarah muttered as she straightened a map of Dorset.

"It may not be pretty, but it works," I replied, drawing Master Habermel's compendium from my bag. Fernando had devised a protective sleeve for it using one of Gallowglass's clean socks. It was miraculously undamaged. I got out my phone, too, and took a few shots of the murals on the wall. They made me feel closer to Jack—and to Matthew.

"Where should I put the pages from the Book of Life?" Ysabeau had been given custody of the precious sheets of vellum.

"Give the picture of the chemical wedding to Sarah. You hold on to the one with the two dragons," I said.

"Me?" Ysabeau's eyes widened. It had been a controversial decision, but I had prevailed against Sarah and Linda in the end.

"I hope you don't mind. The chemical-wedding picture came to me from my parents. The dragons belonged to Andrew Hubbard. I thought we could balance the spell by keeping them in witch and vampire hands." All my instincts told me this was the right decision.

"Of c-course." Ysabeau's tongue slipped on the familiar words.

"It will be all right. I promise." I gave her arm a squeeze. "Sarah will be standing opposite, and Linda and Tamsin will be on either side."

"You should be worrying about the spell. Ysabeau can take care of herself." Sarah handed me a pot of red ink and a quill pen made from a white feather with striking brown and gray markings.

"It's time, ladies," Linda said with a brisk clap. She distributed brown candles to the other members of the London coven. Brown was a propitious color for finding lost objects. It had the added benefit of grounding the spell—which I was sorely in need of, given my inexperience. Each witch took her place outside the ring of county maps, and they all lit their candles with whispered spells. The flames were unnaturally large and bright—true witch's candles.

Linda escorted Ysabeau to her place just below the south coast of England. Sarah stood across from her, as promised, above the north coast of Scotland. Linda walked clockwise three times around the carefully arranged witches, maps, and vampire, sprinkling salt to cast a protective circle.

Once everyone was in her proper place, I took the stopper out of the bottle of red ink. The distinctive scent of dragon's-blood resin filled the air. There were other ingredients in the ink, too, including more than a few drops of my own blood. Ysabeau's nostrils flared at the coppery tang. I dipped the quill pen into the ink and pressed the chiseled silver nib onto a narrow slip of parchment. It had taken me two days to find someone willing to make me a pen using a feather from a barn owl—far longer than it would have in Elizabethan London.

Letter by letter, working from the outside of the parchment to the center, I wrote the name of the person I sought.

T, N, J, O, W, T, E, S

T J WESTON

I folded the parchment carefully to hide the name. Now it was my turn to walk outside the sacred circle and work another binding. After slipping Master Habermel's compendium into the pocket of my sweater along with the parchment rectangle, I began a circular perambulation from the place between the firewitch and the waterwitch. I passed by Tamsin and Ysabeau, Linda and Cassandra, Sarah and Sybil.

When I arrived back at the place where I began, a shimmering line ran outside the salt, illuminating the witches' astonished faces. I turned my left hand palm up. For a moment there was a flicker of color on my index finger, but it was gone before I could determine what it had been. Even without the missing hue, my hand gleamed with gold, silver, black, and white lines of power that pulsed under the skin. The streaks twisted and twined into the orobouros-shaped tenth knot that surrounded the prominent blue veins at my wrist.

I stepped through a narrow gap in the shimmering line and drew the circle closed. The power roared through it, keening and crying out for release. Corra wanted out, too. She was restless, shifting and stretching inside me.

"Patience, Corra," I said, stepping carefully over the salt and onto the map of England. Each step took me closer to the spot that represented London. At last my feet rested on the City. Corra released her wings with a snap of skin and bone and a cry of frustration.

"Fly, Corra!" I commanded.

Free at last, Corra shot around the room, sparks streaming from her wings and tongues of flame escaping from her mouth. As she gained altitude and found air currents that would help to carry her where she wanted to go, the beating of her wings slowed. Corra caught sight of her portrait and cooed in approval, reaching out to pat the wall with her tail.

I pulled the compendium from my pocket and held it in my right hand. The folded slip of parchment went into my left. My arms stretched wide, and I waited while the threads that bound the world and filled the Greyfriars crypt snaked and slithered over me, seeking out the cords that had been absorbed into my hands. When they met, the cords lengthened and expanded, filling my whole body with power. They knotted around my joints, created a protective web around my womb and heart, and traveled along veins and the pathways forged by nerves and sinews.

I recited my spell:

> *Missing pages*
> *Lost and found*
> *Where is Weston*
> *On this ground?*

Then I blew on the slip of parchment, and Weston's name caught light, the red ink bursting into flame. I cupped the fiery words in my palm where they continued to burn bright. Overhead, Corra circled above the map watchfully, her keen eyes alert.

The compendium's gears whirred, and the hands on the main dial moved. A roaring filled my ears as a bright thread of gold shot out from the compendium. It spun outward until it met up with the two pages from the Book of Life. Another thread came from the compendium's gilded dial. It slithered off to a map at Linda's feet.

Corra swept down and pounced on the spot, crying out with triumph as though she had caught some unsuspecting prey. A town's name illuminated, a bright burst of flame leaving the charred outlines of letters.

The spell complete, the roaring diminished. Power receded from my body, loosening the knotted cords. But they did not recoil back into my hands. They stayed where they were, running through me as if they had formed a new bodily system.

When the power had retreated, I swayed slightly. Ysabeau started forward.

"No!" Sarah cried. "Don't break the circle, Ysabeau."

My mother-in-law clearly thought this was madness. Without Matthew here she was prepared to be overprotective in his stead. But Sarah was right: Nobody could break the circle but me. Feet dragging, I returned to the same spot where I'd started weaving my spell. Sybil and Tamsin smiled encouragingly as the fingers on my left hand flicked and furled, releasing the circle's hold. All that remained to do then was to trudge around the circle counterclockwise, unmaking the magic.

Linda was much quicker, briskly walking her own path in reverse. The moment she was through, both Ysabeau and Sarah rushed to my side. The London witches raced to the map that revealed Weston's location.

"*Dieu,* I have not seen magic like that for centuries. Matthew told me true when he said you were a formidable witch," Ysabeau said with admiration.

"Very nice spell casting, honey." Sarah was proud of me. "Not a single wobble of doubt or moment of hesitation."

"Did it work?" I certainly hoped so. Another spell of that magnitude would require weeks of rest first. I joined the witches at the map. "Oxfordshire?"

"Yes," Linda said doubtfully. "But I fear we may not have asked a specific enough question."

There, on the map, was the blackened outline of a very English-sounding village called Chipping Weston.

"The initials were on the paper, but I forgot to include them in the words of the spell." My heart sank.

"It is far too soon to admit defeat." Ysabeau already had her phone out and was dialing. "Phoebe? Does a T. J. Weston live in Chipping Weston?"

The possibility that T. J. Weston could live in a town called Weston had not occurred to any of us. We waited for Phoebe's reply.

Ysabeau's face relaxed in sudden relief. "Thank you. We will be home soon. Tell Marthe that Diana will need a compress for her head and cold cloths for her feet."

Both were aching, and my legs were more swollen with each passing minute. I looked at Ysabeau gratefully.

"Phoebe tells me there is a T. J. Weston in Chipping Weston," Ysabeau reported. "He lives in the Manor House."

"Oh, well done. Well done, Diana." Linda beamed at me. The other London witches clapped, as though I had just performed a particularly difficult piano solo without flubbing a note.

"This is not a night we will soon forget," Tamsin said, her voice shaking with emotion, "for tonight a weaver came back to London, bringing the past and future together so that old worlds might die and new be born."

"That's Mother Shipton's prophecy," I said, recognizing the words.

"Ursula Shipton was born Ursula Soothtell. Her aunt, Alice Soothtell, was my ancestor," Tamsin said. "She was a weaver, like you."

"*You* are related to Ursula Shipton!" Sarah exclaimed.

"I am," Tamsin replied. "The women in my family have kept the knowledge of weavers alive, even though we have had only one other weaver born into the family in more than five hundred years. But Ursula prophesied that the power was not lost forever. She foresaw the years of darkness, when witches would forget weavers and all they represent: hope, rebirth, change. Ursula saw this night, too."

"How so?" I thought of the few lines of Mother Shipton's prophecy that I knew. None of them seemed relevant to tonight's events.

"'*And those that live will ever fear / The dragon's tail for many year, / But time erases memory. / You think it strange. But it will be,*'" Tamsin recited. She nodded, and the other witches joined in, speaking in one voice.

> *And before the race is built anew,*
> *A silver serpent comes to view*
> *And spews out men of like unknown*
> *To mingle with the earth now grown*
> *Cold from its heat, and these men can*
> *Enlighten the minds of future man.*

"The dragon and the serpent?" I shivered.

"They foretell the advent of a new golden age for creatures," Linda said. "It has been too long in coming, but we all are pleased to have lived to see it."

It was too much responsibility. First the twins, then Matthew's scion, and now the future of the species? My hand covered the bump where our children grew. I felt pulled in too many directions, the parts of me that were witch battling with the parts that were scholar, wife, and now mother.

I looked at the walls. In 1591 every part of me had fit together. In 1591 I had been myself.

"Do not worry," Sybil said gently. "You will be whole once more. Your vampire will help you."

"We will all help you," Cassandra said.

27

"Stop here," Gallowglass ordered. Leonard stepped on the Mercedes' brakes, and they engaged immediately and silently in front of the Old Lodge's gatehouse. Since no one was prepared to wait in London for news of the third page except for Hamish, who was busy saving the euro from collapse, my full entourage had come along, Fernando following in one of Matthew's inexhaustible supply of Range Rovers.

"No. Not here. Go on to the house," I told Leonard. The gatehouse would remind me too much of Matthew. As we passed down the drive, the Old Lodge's familiar outlines emerged from the Oxfordshire fog. It was strange to see it again without the surrounding fields filled with sheep and piles of hay, and only one chimney sending a thin plume of smoke into the sky. I rested my forehead against the car's cold window and let the black-and-white half-timbering and the diamond-shaped panes of glass remind me of other, happier times.

I sat back in the deep leather seat and reached for my phone. There was no new message from Matthew. I consoled myself with looking once more at the two pictures he'd already sent: Jack with Marcus and Jack sitting on his own with a sketch pad propped on his knee, utterly absorbed in what he was doing. This last picture had arrived after I sent Matthew my shot of the Greyfriars frescoes. Thanks to the magic of photography, I had captured the ghost of Queen Isabella as well, her face arranged in a look of haughty disdain.

Sarah's glance fell on me. She and Gallowglass had insisted we rest for a few hours here before traveling on to Chipping Weston. I had protested. Weaving spells always left me feeling hollow afterward, and I'd assured them that my paleness and lack of appetite were due entirely to magic. Sarah and Gallowglass had ignored me.

"Here, madame?" Leonard slowed in front of the clipped yew hedge that stood between the gravel driveway and the moat. In 1590 we'd simply ridden right into the house's central courtyard, but now neither automobile could make it over the narrow stone bridge.

Instead, we traveled around to the small courtyard at the rear of the house that had been used for deliveries and tradesmen when I lived here before. A small Fiat was parked there, along with a battered lorry that was clearly used for chores around the estate. Amira Chavan, Matthew's friend and tenant, was waiting for us.

"It is good to see you again, Diana," Amira said, her tingling glance familiar. "Where is Matthew?"

"Away on business," I said shortly, climbing out of the car. Amira gasped and hurried forward.

"You're pregnant," she said in the tone one would use to announce the discovery of life on Mars.

"Seven months," I said, arching my back. "I could use one of your yoga classes." Amira led extraordinary classes here at the Old Lodge—classes that catered to a mixed clientele of daemons, witches, and vampires.

"No tying yourself into a pretzel." Gallowglass took my elbow gently. "Come inside, Auntie, and rest a spell. You can put your feet up on the table while Fernando makes us all something to eat."

"I'm not lifting a pan—not with Amira here." Fernando kissed Amira on the cheek. "No incidents that I should worry about, *shona?*"

"I haven't seen or sensed anything." Amira smiled at Fernando with fondness. "It has been too long since we've seen each other."

"Make Diana some akuri on toast and I will forgive you," Fernando said with an answering grin. "The scent alone will transport me to heaven."

After a round of introductions, I found myself in the tiny room where we had taken our family meals in 1590. There was no map on the wall, but a fire burned cheerily, dispelling some of the dampness.

Amira put plates of scrambled eggs and toast before us, along with bowls of rice and lentils. Everything was fragrant with chilies, mustard seed, lime, and coriander. Fernando hovered over the dishes, inhaling the aromatic steam.

"Your kanda poha reminds me of that little stall we visited on our way to Gharapuri to see the caves, the one that had the chai made with coconut milk." He inhaled deeply.

"It should," Amira said, sticking a spoon in the lentils. "He was using my grandmother's recipe. And I ground the rice the traditional way, in an iron mortar and pestle, so it is very good for Diana's pregnancy."

In spite of my insistence that I was not hungry, there was something downright alchemical in the effect that cumin and lime had on my appetite. Soon I was looking down at an empty plate.

"That's more like it," Gallowglass said with satisfaction. "Now, why don't you lie on the settle and close your eyes. If you're not comfortable there, you can always rest on the bed in Pierre's old office, or your own bed, come to think of it."

The settle was oaken, heavily carved, and designed to discourage loafing. It had been in the formal parlor during my previous life in the house and had simply drifted a few rooms to provide a seat underneath the window. The stack of papers on the end of it suggested that this was where Amira sat in the mornings to catch up on the news.

I was beginning to understand how Matthew treated his houses. He lived in them, left them, and returned decades or centuries later without touching the contents other than to slightly rearrange the furniture. It meant he owned a series of museums, rather than proper homes. I thought of the memories that awaited me in the rest of the house—the great hall where I'd met George Chapman and Widow Beaton, the formal parlor where Walter Raleigh had discussed our predicament under the watchful eyes of Henry VIII and Elizabeth I, and the bedchamber where Matthew and I had first set foot in the sixteenth century.

"The settle will be fine," I said hastily. If Gallowglass would surrender his leather jacket and Fernando his long woolen coat, the carved roses on the backrest wouldn't jab into my side too sharply. To make my desire real, the pile of coats by the fireplace arranged themselves into a makeshift mattress. Surrounded by scents of bitter orange, sea spray, lilac, tobacco, and narcissus, I felt my eyes grow heavy and I drifted into sleep.

"No one has caught so much as a glimpse of him," Amira said, her low voice waking me from my nap.

"Still, you shouldn't be teaching classes so long as Benjamin poses a risk to your safety." Fernando sounded uncharacteristically firm. "What if he were to walk through the front door?"

"Benjamin would find himself facing two dozen furious daemons, vampires, and witches, that's what," Amira replied. "Matthew told me to stop, Fernando, but the work that I'm doing seems more important now than ever."

"It is." I swung my legs off the settle and sat up, rubbing the sleep from my eyes. According to the clock, forty-five minutes had passed. It was impossible to gauge the passage of time from the changing light, since we were still entombed in fog.

Sarah called to Marthe, who brought tea. It was mint and rose hips, with none of the caffeine that would have made me more alert, but it was blessedly hot. I'd forgotten how cold sixteenth-century homes could be.

Gallowglass made a spot for me close to the fire. It saddened me to think of all that concern directed at me. He was so worthy of being loved; I didn't want him to be alone. Something in my expression must have revealed what was on my mind.

"No pity, Auntie. The winds do not always blow as the ship desires," he murmured, tucking me into my chair.

"The winds do what I tell them to do."

"And I plot my own course. If you don't stop clucking over me, I'll tell Matthew what you're up to and you can deal with two royally pissed-off vampires instead of one."

It was a prudent time to change the subject.

"Matthew is establishing his own family, Amira," I said, turning to our host. "It will have all kinds of creatures in it. Who knows, we might even let in humans. We'll need all the yoga we can get if he succeeds." I paused as my right hand began to tingle and pulse with color. I studied it for a moment in silence, then came to a decision. I wished the stiff leather portfolio that Phoebe had bought to protect the pages from the Book of Life was here at the table and not across the room. Despite the nap, I was still exhausted.

The portfolio appeared on a nearby table.

"Abracadabra," Fernando murmured.

"Since you live at Matthew's house, it only seems right to explain why we've all descended on you," I said to Amira. "You've probably heard stories about the witches' first grimoire?"

Amira nodded. I handed her the two pages we'd already gathered.

"These come from that book—the same book the vampires call the

Book of Life. We think another page is in the possession of someone named T. J. Weston, living in Chipping Weston. Now that we're all fed and watered, Phoebe and I are going to see if he or she is amenable to selling it."

Ysabeau and Phoebe appeared right on cue. Phoebe was as white as a sheet. Ysabeau looked mildly bored.

"What's wrong, Phoebe?" I asked.

"There's a Holbein. In the bathroom." She pressed her hands against her cheeks. "A small oil painting of Thomas More's daughter, Margaret. It shouldn't be hung over a toilet!"

I was beginning to understand why Matthew found my constant objections to the way his family treated their library books tiresome.

"Stop being so prudish," Ysabeau said with mild irritation. "Margaret was not the kind of woman to be bothered by a bit of exposed flesh."

"You think—That is—" Phoebe sputtered. "It's not the decorum of the situation that troubles me, but the fact that Margaret More might tumble into the loo at any moment!"

"I understand, Phoebe." I tried to sound sympathetic. "Would it help to know that there are other, far larger and more important works by Holbein in the parlor?"

"And upstairs. The whole sainted family is in one of the attics." Ysabeau pointed heavenward. "Thomas More was an arrogant young man, and he did not grow more humble with age. Matthew did not seem to mind, but Thomas and Philippe nearly came to blows on several occasions. If his daughter drowns in the lavatory, it will serve him right."

Amira began to giggle. After a shocked look, Fernando joined in. Soon we were all laughing, even Phoebe.

"What is all this noise? What has happened now?" Marthe eyed us suspiciously from the door.

"Phoebe is adjusting to being a de Clermont," I said, wiping at my eyes.

"Bonne chance," Marthe said. This only made us laugh harder.

It was a welcome reminder that, different though we might be, we were a family of sorts—no stranger or more idiosyncratic than thousands that had come before us.

"And these pages you've brought—are they from Matthew's collections as well?" Amira said, picking up the conversation where we'd abandoned it.

"No. One of them was given to my parents, and the other was in the hands of Matthew's grandson, Andrew Hubbard."

"Hmm. So much fear." Amira's eyes lost focus. She was a witch with significant insight and empathic powers.

"Amira?" I looked at her closely.

"Blood and fear." She shuddered, not seeming to hear me. "It's in the parchment itself, not just the words."

"Should I stop her?" I asked Sarah. In most situations it was best to let a witch's second sight play itself out, but Amira had slipped too quickly into her vision of another time and place. A witch might wander so far into a thicket of images and feelings that she couldn't find her way out of them.

"Absolutely not," Sarah said. "There are two of us to help her if she gets lost."

"A young woman—a mother. She was killed in front of her children," Amira murmured. My stomach flipped. "Their father was already dead. When the witches brought her husband's body to her, they dropped it at her feet and made her look at what they had done to him. It was she who first cursed the book. So much knowledge, lost forever." Amira's eyes drifted closed. When they opened again, they were shining with unshed tears. "This parchment was made from the skin that stretched over her ribs."

I knew that the Book of Life had dead creatures in it, but I never imagined I would know anything more about them than whatever their DNA was capable of revealing. I bolted for the door, stomach heaving. Corra flapped her wings in agitation, turning this way and that to stabilize her position, but there was little room for her to maneuver thanks to the growing presence of the twins.

"Shh. That will not be your fate. I promise you," Ysabeau said, catching me in her arms. She was cool and solid, her strength evident in spite of her graceful build.

"Am I doing the right thing to try to mend this broken book?" I asked once the roiling in my guts had stopped. "And to do it without Matthew?"

"Right or wrong, it must be done." Ysabeau smoothed back my hair, which had tumbled forward, obscuring my face. "Call him, Diana. He would not want you to suffer like this."

"No." I shook my head. "Matthew has his job to do. I have mine."

"Let us finish it then," Ysabeau said.

*　*　*

Chipping Weston was the type of picturesque English village where novelists liked to set murder mysteries. It looked like a postcard or a film set, but it was home to several hundred people who lived in thatched houses spread out over a handful of narrow lanes. The village green had retained its stocks for punishing its citizens found guilty of some wrongdoing, and there were two pubs so that even if you had a falling-out with half your neighbors, you'd still have a place to go where you could have your evening pint.

The Manor House was not difficult to find.

"The gates are open." Gallowglass cracked his knuckles.

"What is your plan, Gallowglass? Running at the front door and battering it down with your bare hands?" I climbed out of Leonard's car. "Come on, Phoebe. Let's go ring the bell."

Gallowglass was behind us as we walked straight through the open front gates and skirted the round stone planter that I suspected had been a fountain before it was filled in with soil. Standing in the middle were two box trees clipped to resemble dachshunds.

"How extraordinary," Phoebe murmured, eyeing the green sculptures.

The door to the manor was set in the middle of a bank of low windows. There was no bell, but an iron knocker—also shaped like a dachshund—had been inexpertly affixed to the stout Elizabethan panels. Before Phoebe could give me a lecture about the preservation of old houses, I lifted the dog and rapped sharply.

Silence.

I rapped again, putting a bit more weight into it.

"We are standing in plain view of the road," Gallowglass growled. "That's the sorriest excuse for a wall I've ever seen. A child could step over it."

"Not everybody can have a moat," I said. "I hardly think Benjamin has ever heard of Chipping Weston, never mind followed us here."

Gallowglass was unconvinced and continued to look around like an anxious owl.

I was about to rap again when the door was flung open. A man wearing goggles and a parachute slung around his shoulders like a cape stood in the entrance. Dogs swarmed around his feet, wriggling and barking.

"Whenever have you been?" The stranger engulfed me in a hug while I tried to sort out what his strange question meant. The dogs leaped and frolicked, excited to meet me now that their master had signaled his approval. He let me go and lifted his goggles, his nudging stare feeling like a buss of welcome.

"You're a daemon," I said unnecessarily.

"And you're a witch." With one green eye and one blue, he studied Gallowglass. "And he's a vampire. Not the same one you had with you before, but still big enough to replace the lightbulbs."

"I don't do lightbulbs," Gallowglass said.

"Wait. I know you," I said, sifting through the faces in my memory. This was one of the daemons I'd seen in the Bodleian last year when I'd first encountered Ashmole 782. He liked lattes and taking apart microfilm readers. He always wore earbuds, even when they weren't attached to anything. "Timothy?"

"The same." Timothy turned his eyes to me and cocked his fingers and thumbs so they looked like six-shooters. He was, I noticed, still wearing mismatched cowboy boots, but this time one was green and the other blue—to match his eyes, one presumed. He clicked his tongue against his teeth. "Told you, babe: You're the one."

"Are you T. J. Weston?" Phoebe asked, trying to make her voice heard above the din of yelping, wriggling dogs.

Timothy stuffed his fingers in his ears and mouthed, "I can't hear you."

"Oy!" Gallowglass shouted. "Shut your gobs, little yappers."

The barking stopped instantly. The dogs sat, jaws open and tongues lolling, and looked at Gallowglass adoringly. Timothy removed a finger from one of his ears.

"Nice," the daemon said with a low whistle of appreciation. The dogs immediately started barking again.

Gallowglass bundled us all inside, muttering darkly about sight lines and defensive positions and possible hearing damage to Apple and Bean. Peace was achieved once he got down on the floor in front of the fireplace and let the dogs scramble all over him, licking and burrowing as if their pack's alpha had been returned to them after a long absence.

"What are their names?" Phoebe inquired, trying to count the number of tails in the squirming mound.

"Hansel and Gretel, obviously." Timothy looked at Phoebe as though she were hopeless.

"And the other four?" Phoebe asked.

"Oscar. Molly. Rusty. And Puddles." Timothy pointed to each dog in turn.

"He likes to play outside in the rain?"

"No," Timothy replied. "She likes to piddle on the floor. Her name was Penelope, but everybody in the village calls her Puddles now."

A graceful segue from this subject to the Book of Life was impossible, so I plunged forward. "Did you buy a page from an illuminated manuscript that has a tree on it?"

"Yep." Timothy blinked.

"Would you be willing to sell it to me?" There was no point in being coy.

"Nope."

"We're prepared to pay handsomely for it." Phoebe might not like the de Clermonts' casual indifference to where pictures were hung, but she was beginning to see the benefits of their purchasing power.

"It's not for sale." Timothy ruffled the ears of one of the dogs who then returned to Gallowglass and began to gnaw on the toe of his boot.

"Can I see it?" Perhaps Timothy would let me borrow it, I thought.

"Sure." Timothy divested himself of the parachute and strode out of the room. We scrambled to keep up.

He led us through several rooms that had clearly been designed for different purposes from the ones they were now used for. A dining room had a battered drum kit set up in the center with DEREK AND THE DERANGERS painted on the bass-drum head, and another room looked like an electronics graveyard except for the chintz sofas and beribboned wallpaper.

"It's in there. Somewhere," Timothy said, gesturing at the next room.

"Holy Mother of God," Gallowglass said, astonished.

"There" was the former library. "Somewhere" covered a multitude of possible hiding places, including unopened shipping crates and mail, cardboard cartons full of sheet music going back to the 1920s, and stacks and stacks of old newspapers. There was a large collection of clock faces of all sizes, descriptions, and vintages, too.

And there were manuscripts. Thousands of manuscripts.

"I think it's in a blue folder," Timothy said, scratching his chin. He had obviously started shaving at some point earlier in the day but only partially completed the task, leaving two grizzled patches.

"How long have you been buying old books?" I asked, picking up the first one that came to hand. It was an eighteenth-century student science notebook, German, and of no particular value except to a scholar of Enlightenment education.

"Since I was thirteen. That's when my gran died and left me this place. My mom left when I was five, and my dad, Derek, died of an accidental overdose when I turned nine, so it was just me and Gran after that." Timothy looked around the room fondly. "I've been restoring it ever since. Do you want to see my paint chips for the gallery upstairs?"

"Maybe later," I said.

"Okay." His face fell.

"Why do manuscripts interest you?" When trying to get answers from daemons and undergraduates, it was best to ask genuinely open-ended questions.

"They're like the house—they remind me of something I shouldn't forget," Timothy said, as though that explained everything.

"With any luck one of them will remind him where he put the page from your book," Gallowglass said under his breath. "If not, it's going to take us weeks to go through all this rubbish."

We didn't have weeks. I wanted Ashmole 782 out of the Bodleian and stitched back together so that Matthew could come home. Without the Book of Life, we were vulnerable to the Congregation, Benjamin, and whatever private ambitions Knox and Gerbert might harbor. Once it was safely in our possession, they would all have to deal with us on our terms—scion or no scion. I pushed up my sleeves.

"Would it be all right with you, Timothy, if I used magic in your library?" It seemed polite to ask.

"Will it be loud?" Timothy asked. "The dogs don't like noise."

"No," I said, considering my options. "I think it will be completely silent."

"Oh, well, that's okay, then," he said, relieved. He put his goggles back on for additional security.

"More magic, Auntie?" Gallowglass's eyebrows lowered. "You've been using an awful lot of it lately."

"Wait until tomorrow," I murmured. If I got all three missing pages, I was going to the Bodleian. Then it was gloves-off time.

A flurry of papers rose from the floor.

"You've started already?" Gallowglass said, alarmed.

"No," I said.

"Then what's causing the ruckus?" Gallowglass moved toward the agitated pile.

A tail wagged from between a leather-bound folio and a box of pens.

"Puddles!" Timothy said.

The dog emerged, tail first, pulling a blue folder.

"Good doggy," Gallowglass crooned. He crouched down and held out his hand. "Bring it to me."

Puddles stood with the missing page from Ashmole 782 gripped in her teeth, looking very pleased with herself. She did not, however, take it to Gallowglass.

"She wants you to chase her," Timothy explained.

Gallowglass scowled. "I'm not chasing that dog."

In the end we all chased her. Puddles was the fastest, cleverest dachshund who'd ever lived, darting under furniture and feinting left and then right before dashing away again. Gallowglass was speedy, but he was not small. Puddles slipped through his fingers again and again, her glee evident.

Finally Puddles' need to pant meant that she had to drop the now slightly moist blue folder in front of her paws. Gallowglass took the opportunity to reach in and secure it.

"What a good girl!" Timothy picked up the squirming dog. "You're going to win the Great Dachshund Games this summer. No question." A slip of paper was attached to one of Puddles' claws. "Hey. There's my council tax bill."

Gallowglass handed me the folder.

"Phoebe should do the honors," I said. "If not for her, we wouldn't be here." I passed the folder on to her.

Phoebe cracked it open. The image inside was so vivid that it might have been painted yesterday, and its striking colors and the details of trunk and leaf only increased the sense of vibrancy that came from the page. There was power in it. That much was unmistakable.

"It's beautiful." Phoebe lifted her eyes. "Is this the page you've been looking for?"

"Aye," Gallowglass said. "That's it, all right."

Phoebe placed the page in my waiting hands. As soon as the parchment touched them, they brightened, shooting little sparks of color into the room. Filaments of power erupted from my fingertips, connecting to the parchment with an almost audible snap of electricity.

"There's a lot of energy on that page. Not all of it good," Timothy said, backing away. "It needs to go back into that book you discovered in the Bodleian."

"I know you don't want to sell the page," I said, "but could I borrow it? Just for a day?" I could go straight to the Bodleian, recall Ashmole 782, and have the page back tomorrow afternoon—provided the Book of Life let me remove it again, once I'd returned it to the binding.

"Nope." Timothy shook his head.

"You won't let me buy it. You won't let me borrow it," I said, exasperation mounting. "Do you have some sentimental attachment to it?"

"Of course I do. I mean, he's my ancestor, isn't he?"

Every eye in the room went to the illustration of the tree in my hands. Even Puddles looked at it with renewed interest, sniffing the air with her long, delicate nose.

"How do you know that?" I whispered.

"I see things—microchips, crossword puzzles, you, the guy whose skin made that parchment. I knew who you were from the moment you walked into Duke Humfrey's." Timothy looked sad. "I told you as much. But you didn't listen to me and left with the big vampire. You're the one."

"The one for what?" My throat closed. Daemon visions were bizarre and surreal, but they could be shockingly accurate.

"The one who will learn how it all began—the blood, the death, the fear. And the one who can put a stop to it, once and for all." Timothy sighed. "You can't buy my grandfather, and you can't borrow him. But if I give him to you, for safekeeping, you'll make his death mean something?"

"I can't promise you that, Timothy." There was no way I could swear to something so enormous and imprecise. "We don't know what the book will reveal. And I certainly can't guarantee that anything will change."

"Can you make sure his name won't be forgotten, once you learn what it is?" Timothy asked. "Names are important, you know."

A sense of the uncanny washed over me. Ysabeau had told me the same thing shortly after I met her. I saw Edward Kelley in my mind's eye. *"You will find your name in it, too,"* he had cried when Emperor Rudolf made him hand over the Book of Life. The hackles on my neck rose.

"I won't forget his name," I promised.

"Sometimes that's enough," Timothy said.

28

It was several hours past midnight, and any hope I had of sleep was gone. The fog had lifted slightly, and the brightness of the full moon pierced through the gray wisps that still clung to the trunks of trees and the low places in the park where the deer slept. One or two members of the herd were still out, picking over the grass in search of the last remaining fodder. A hard frost was coming; I could sense it. I was attuned to the rhythms of the earth and sky in ways that I had not been before I lived in a time when the day was organized around the height of the sun instead of the dial of a clock, and the season of the year determined everything from what you ate to the physic that you took.

I was in our bedchamber again, the one where Matthew and I had spent our first night in the sixteenth century. Only a few things had changed: the electricity that powered the lamps, the Victorian bellpull that hung by the fire to call the servants to tend to it or bring tea (though why this was necessary in a vampire household, I could not fathom), the closet that had been carved out of an adjoining room.

Our return to the Old Lodge after meeting Timothy Weston had been unexpectedly tense. Gallowglass had flatly refused to take me to Oxford after we located the final page of the Book of Life, though it was not yet the supper hour and Duke Humfrey's was open until seven o'clock during term time. When Leonard offered to drive, Gallowglass threatened to kill him in disturbingly detailed and graphic terms. Fernando and Gallowglass had departed, ostensibly to talk, and Gallowglass had returned with a rapidly healing split lip, a slightly bruised eye, and a mumbled apology to Leonard.

"You aren't going," Fernando said when I headed for the door. "I'll take you tomorrow, but not tonight. Gallowglass is right: You look like death."

"Stop coddling me," I said through gritted teeth, my hands still shooting out intermittent sparks.

"I'll coddle you until your mate—and my sire—returns," Fernando said. "The only creature on this earth who could make me take you to Oxford is Matthew. Feel free to call him." He held out his phone.

That had been the end of the discussion. I'd accepted Fernando's ultimatum with poor grace, though my head was pounding and I'd worked more magic in the past week than I had my whole life previous.

"So long as you have these three pages, no other creature can possess the book," Amira said, trying to comfort me. But it seemed like a poor consolation when the book was so close.

Not even the sight of the three pages, lined up on the long table in the great hall, had improved my mood. I'd been anticipating and dreading this moment since we left Madison, but now that it was here, it felt strangely anticlimactic.

Phoebe had arranged the images carefully, making sure they didn't touch. We'd learned the hard way that they seemed to have a magnetic affinity. When I'd arrived home and bundled them together in preparation for going to the Bodleian, a soft keening had come from the pages, followed by a chattering that everybody heard—even Phoebe.

"You can't just march into the Bodleian with these three pages and stuff them back into an enchanted book," Sarah said. "It's crazy. There are bound to be witches in the room. They'll come running."

"And who knows how the Book of Life will respond?" Ysabeau poked at the illustration of the tree with her finger. "What if it shrieks? Ghosts might be released. Or Diana might set off a rain of fire." After her experiences in London, Ysabeau had been doing some reading. She was now prepared to discuss a wide variety of topics, including spectral apparitions and the number of occult phenomena that had been observed in the British Isles over the past two years.

"You're going to have to steal it," Sarah said.

"I'm a tenured professor at Yale, Sarah! I can't! My life as a scholar—"

"Is probably over," Sarah said, finishing my sentence.

"Come now, Sarah," Fernando chided. "That is a bit extreme, even for you. Surely there is a way for Diana to check out Ashmole 782 and return it at some future date."

I tried to explain that you didn't borrow books from the Bodleian, but to no avail. With Ysabeau and Sarah in charge of logistics and Fernando and Gallowglass in charge of security, I was relegated to a position where

I could only advise, counsel, and warn. They were more high-handed than Matthew.

And so here I was at four o'clock in the morning, staring out the window and waiting for the sun to rise.

"What should I do?" I murmured, my forehead pressed against the cold, diamond-shaped panes.

As soon as I asked the question, my skin flared with awareness, as though I'd stuck a finger into an electrical socket. A shimmering figure dressed in white came from the forest, accompanied by a white deer. The otherworldly animal walked sedately at the woman's side, unafraid of the huntress who held a bow and a quiver of arrows in her hand. *The goddess.*

She stopped and looked up at my window. "Why so sad, daughter?" her silvery voice whispered. "Have you lost what you most desire?"

I had learned not to answer her questions. She smiled at my reluctance.

"Dare to join me under this full moon. Perhaps you will find it once more." The goddess rested her fingers on the deer's antlers and waited.

I slipped outside undetected. My feet crunched across the gravel paths of the knot gardens, then left dark impressions in the frost-touched grass. Soon, I stood in front of the goddess.

"Why are you here?" I asked.

"To help you." The goddess's eyes were silver and black in the moonlight. "You will have to give something up if you want to possess the Book of Life—something precious to you."

"I've given enough." My voice trembled. "My parents, then my first child, then my aunt. Not even my life is my own anymore. It belongs to you."

"And I do not abandon those who serve me." The goddess withdrew an arrow from her quiver. It was long and silver, with owl-feather fletches. She offered it to me. "Take it."

"No." I shook my head. "Not without knowing the price."

"No one refuses me." The goddess put the arrow shaft into her bow, aimed. It was then I noticed that her weapon lacked its pointed tip. Her hand drew back, the silver string pulled taut.

There was no time to react before the goddess released the shaft. It shot straight toward my breast. I felt a searing pain, a yank of the chain around my neck, and a tingling feeling of warmth between my left shoulder blade and my spine. The golden links that had held Philippe's arrowhead slithered down my body and landed at my feet. I felt the fabric that covered my chest for the telltale wetness of blood, but there was nothing except a small hole to indicate where the shaft had passed through.

"You cannot outrun my arrow. No creature can. It is part of you now," she said. "Even those born to strength should carry weapons."

I searched the ground around my feet, looking for Philippe's jewel. When I straightened, I could feel its point pressing into my ribs. I stared at the goddess in astonishment.

"My arrow never misses its target," the goddess said. "When you have need of it, do not hesitate. And aim true."

"They've been moved *where*?" This could not be happening. Not when we were so close to finding answers.

"The Radcliffe Science Library." Sean was apologetic, but his patience was wearing thin. "It's not the end of the world, Diana."

"But . . . that is . . ." I trailed off, the completed call slip for Ashmole 782 dangling from my fingers.

"Don't you read your e-mails? We've been sending out notices about the move for months," Sean said. "I'm happy to take the request and put it in the system, since you've been away and apparently out of reach of the Internet. But none of the Ashmole manuscripts are here, and you can't call them up to this reading room unless you have a bona fide intellectual reason that's related to the manuscripts and maps that are still here."

Of all the exigencies we had planned for this morning—and they were many and varied—the Bodleian Library's decision to move rare books and manuscripts from Duke Humfrey's to the Radcliffe Science Library had not been among them. We'd left Sarah and Amira at home with Leonard in case we needed magical backup. Gallowglass and Fernando were both outside, loafing around the statue of Mary Herbert's son William and being photographed by female visitors. Ysabeau had gained entrance to the library after enticing the head of development with a gift to rival the annual budget of Liechtenstein. She was now on a private tour of the facility. Phoebe, who had attended Christ Church and was therefore the only member of my book posse in possession of a library card, had accompanied me into Duke

Humfrey's and was now waiting patiently in a seat overlooking Exeter College's gardens.

"How aggravating." No matter how many rare books and precious manuscripts they'd relocated, I was absolutely sure Ashmole 782 was still here. My father had not bound the Book of Life to its call number after all, but to the library. In 1850 the Radcliffe Science Library didn't exist.

I looked at my watch. It was only ten-thirty. A swarm of children on a school trip were released into the quadrangle, their high-pitched voices echoing against the stone walls. How long would it take me to manufacture an excuse that would satisfy Sean? Phoebe and I needed to regroup. I tried to reach the spot on my lower back where the tip of the goddess's arrow was lodged. The shaft kept my posture ramrod straight, and if I slouched the slightest bit, I felt a warning prickle.

"And don't think it's going to be easy to come up with a good rationale for looking at your manuscript here," Sean warned, reading my mind. Humans never failed to activate their usually dormant sixth sense at the most inopportune moments. "Your friend has been sending requests of all sorts for weeks, and no matter how many times he asks to see manuscripts here, the requests keep getting redirected to Parks Road."

"Tweed jacket? Corduroy pants?" If Peter Knox was in Duke Humfrey's, I was going to throttle him.

"No. The guy who sits by the card catalogs." Sean jerked his thumb in the direction of the Selden End.

I backed carefully out of Sean's office across from the old call desk and felt the numbing sensation of a vampire's stare. *Gerbert?*

"Mistress Roydon."

Not Gerbert.

Benjamin's arm was draped over Phoebe's shoulders, and there were spots of red on the collar of her white blouse. For the first time since I'd met her, Phoebe looked terrified.

"Herr Fuchs." I spoke slightly louder than usual. Hopefully, Ysabeau or Gallowglass would hear his name over the din that the children were causing. I forced my feet to move toward him at an even pace.

"What a surprise to see you here—and looking so . . . fertile." Benjamin's eyes drifted slowly over my breasts to where the twins lay curled in my belly. One of them was kicking furiously, as though to make a break for freedom. Corra, too, twisted and snarled inside me.

No fire or flame. The oath I'd taken when I got my first reader's card floated through my mind.

"I expected Matthew. Instead I get his mate. And my brother's, too." Benjamin's nose went to the pulse under Phoebe's ear. His teeth grazed her flesh. She bit her lip to keep from crying out. "What a good boy Marcus is, always standing by his father. I wonder if he'll stand by you, pet, once I've made you mine."

"Let her go, Benjamin." Once the words were out of my mouth, the logical part of my brain registered their pointlessness. There was no chance that Benjamin was going to let Phoebe go.

"Don't worry. You won't be left out." His fingers stroked the place on Phoebe's neck where her pulse hammered. "I've got big plans for you, too, Mistress Roydon. You're a good breeder. I can see that."

Where was Ysabeau?

The arrow burned against my spine, inviting me to use its power. But how could I target Benjamin without running the risk of harming Phoebe? He had placed Phoebe slightly in front of him, like a shield.

"This one dreams of being a vampire." Benjamin's mouth lowered, brushed against Phoebe's neck. She whimpered. "I could make those dreams come true. With any luck I could send you back to Marcus with blood so strong you could bring him to his knees."

Philippe's voice rang in my mind: *Think—and stay alive.* That was the job he had given me. But my thoughts ran in disorganized circles. Snatches of spells and half-remembered warnings from Goody Alsop chased Benjamin's threats. I needed to concentrate.

Phoebe's eyes begged me to do *something.*

"Use your pitiful power, witch. I may not know what's in the Book of Life—yet—but I've learned that witches are no match for vampires."

I hesitated. Benjamin smiled. I stood at the crossroads between the life I'd always thought I wanted—scholarly, intellectual, free from the complicated messiness of magic—and the life I now had. If I worked magic here, in the Bodleian Library, there would be no turning back.

"Something wrong?" he drawled.

My back continued to burn, the pain spreading into my shoulder. I lifted my hands and separated them as though they held a bow, then aimed my left index finger at Benjamin to create a line of sight.

My hand was no longer colorless. A blaze of purple, thick and vivid, ran all the way down to the palm. I groaned inwardly. Of course my magic would decide to change *now*. Think. *What was the magical significance of purple?*

I felt the sensation of a rough string scraping against my cheek. I twisted my lips and directed a puff of air toward it. *No distractions. Think. Stay alive.*

When my focus returned to my hands, there was a bow in them—a real, tangible bow made of wood ornamented with silver and gold. I felt a strange tingle from the wood, one I recognized. *Rowan.* And there was an arrow between my fingers, too: silver-shafted and tipped with Philippe's golden arrowhead. Would it find its target as the goddess had promised? Benjamin twisted Phoebe so that she was directly in front of him.

"Take your best shot, witch. You'll kill Marcus's warmblood, but I'll still have everything I came for."

The image of Juliette's fiery death came to mind. I closed my eyes.

I hesitated, unable to shoot. The bow and arrow dissolved between my fingers. I'd done exactly what the goddess had instructed me not to do.

I heard the pages of the books lying open on nearby desks ruffle in a sudden breeze. The hair on the back of my neck rose. *Witchwind.*

There must be another witch in the library. I opened my eyes to see who it was.

It was a vampire.

Ysabeau stood before Benjamin, one hand wrapped around his throat and the other pushing Phoebe in my direction.

"Ysabeau." Benjamin looked at her sourly.

"Expecting someone else? Matthew, perhaps?" Blood welled from a small puncture wound on him that was filled with Ysabeau's finger. That pressure was enough to keep Benjamin where he was. Nausea swept over me in a wave. "He is otherwise engaged. Phoebe, dearest, you must take Diana down to Gallowglass and Fernando. At once." Without looking away from her prey, Ysabeau pointed in my direction with her free hand.

"Let's go," Phoebe murmured, pulling at my arm.

Ysabeau removed her finger from Benjamin's neck with an audible pop. His hand clamped over the spot.

"We're not finished, Ysabeau. Tell Matthew I'll be in touch. Soon."

"Oh, I will." Ysabeau gave him a terrifyingly toothy smile. She took two steps backward, took my other elbow, and jerked me around to face the exit.

"Diana?" Benjamin called.

I stopped but didn't turn around.

"I hope your children are both girls."

"Nobody speaks until we're in the car." Gallowglass let out a piercing whistle. "Disguising spell, Auntie."

I could feel that it had slipped out of shape but couldn't muster the energy to do much about it. The nausea I'd felt upstairs was getting worse.

Leonard squealed up to the gates of Hertford College.

"I hesitated. Just like with Juliette." Then it had almost cost Matthew his life. Today it was Phoebe who had paid for my fear.

"Mind your head," Gallowglass said, inserting me into the passenger seat.

"Thank God we used Matthew's bloody great car," Leonard muttered to Fernando as he slid in the front. "Back home?"

"Yes," I said.

"No," Ysabeau said at the same moment, appearing on the other side of the car. "To the airport. We are going to Sept-Tours. Call Baldwin, Gallowglass."

"I am *not* going to Sept-Tours," I said. Live under Baldwin's thumb? Never.

"What about Sarah?" Fernando asked from the front seat.

"Tell Amira to drive Sarah to London and meet us there." Ysabeau tapped Leonard on the shoulder. "If you do not put your foot on the gas pedal immediately, I cannot be held accountable for my actions."

"We're all in. Go!" Gallowglass closed the door of the cargo space just as Leonard squealed into reverse, narrowly missing a distinguished don on a bicycle.

"Bloody hell. I've not got the temperament for crime," Gallowglass said, huffing slightly. "Show us the book, Auntie."

"Diana does not have the book." Ysabeau's words caused Fernando to stop mid-conversation and look back at us.

"Then what is the rush?" Gallowglass demanded.

"We met Matthew's son." Phoebe sat forward and began to speak loudly in the direction of Fernando's cell phone. "Benjamin knows that Diana is pregnant, Sarah. You are not safe, nor is Amira. Leave. At once."

"Benjamin?" Sarah's voice was unmistakably horrified.

A large hand jerked Phoebe back. It twisted her head to the side.

"He bit you." Gallowglass's face whitened. He grabbed me and inspected every inch of my face and neck. "Christ. Why didn't you call for help?"

Thanks to Leonard's complete disregard for traffic restrictions or speed limits, we were nearly to the M40.

"He had Phoebe." I shrank into the seat, trying to stabilize my roiling stomach by clamping both arms over the twins.

"Where was Granny?" Gallowglass asked.

"Granny was listening to a horrible woman in a magenta blouse tell me about the library's building works while sixty children screamed in the quadrangle." Ysabeau glared at Gallowglass. "Where were *you*?"

"Both of you stop it. We were all exactly where we planned to be." As usual, Phoebe's voice was the only reasonable one. "And we all got out alive. Let's not lose sight of the big picture."

Leonard sped onto the M40, headed for Heathrow.

I held a cold hand to my forehead. "I'm so sorry, Phoebe." I pressed my lips together as the car swayed. "I couldn't think."

"Perfectly understandable," Phoebe said briskly. "May I please speak to Miriam?"

"Miriam?" Fernando asked.

"Yes. I know that I am not infected with blood rage, because I didn't ingest any of Benjamin's blood. But he did bite me, and she may wish to have a sample of my blood to see if his saliva has affected me."

We all stared at her, openmouthed.

"Later," Gallowglass said curtly. "We'll worry about science and that godforsaken manuscript later."

The countryside rushed by in a blur. I rested my forehead against the glass and wished with all my heart that Matthew was with me, that the day had ended differently, that Benjamin didn't know I was pregnant with twins.

His final words—and the prospect of the future they painted—taunted me as we drew closer to the airport.

I hope your children are both girls.

* * *

"Diana!" Ysabeau's voice interrupted my troubled sleep. "Matthew or Baldwin. Choose." Her tone was fierce. "One of them has to be told."

"Not Matthew." I winced and sat straighter. That damned arrow was still jabbing my shoulder. "He'll come running, and there's no reason for it. Phoebe is right. We're all alive."

Ysabeau swore like a sailor and pulled out her red phone. Before anyone could stop her, she was speaking to Baldwin in rapid French. I caught only half of it, but based on her awed response, Phoebe obviously understood more.

"Oh, Christ." Gallowglass shook his shaggy head.

"Baldwin wishes to speak with you." Ysabeau extended the phone in my direction.

"I understand you've seen Benjamin." Baldwin was as cool and composed as Phoebe.

"I did."

"He threatened the twins?"

"He did."

"I'm your brother, Diana, not your enemy," Baldwin said. "Ysabeau was right to call me."

"If you say so," I said. *"Sieur."*

"Do you know where Matthew is?" he demanded.

"No." I didn't know—not exactly. "Do you?"

"I presume he is off somewhere burying Jack Blackfriars."

The silence that followed Baldwin's words was lengthy.

"You are an utter bastard, Baldwin de Clermont." My voice shook.

"Jack was a necessary casualty of a dangerous and deadly war—one that you started, by the way." Baldwin sighed. "Come home, sister. That's an order. Lick your wounds and wait for him. It's what we've all learned to do when Matthew goes off to assuage his guilty conscience."

He hung up on me before I could manage a reply.

"I. Hate. Him." I spit out each word.

"So do I," Ysabeau said, taking back her phone.

"Baldwin is jealous of Matthew, that's all," Phoebe said. This time her reasonableness was irritating, and I felt the power rush through my body.

"I don't feel right." My anxiety spiked. "Is something wrong? Is someone following us?"

Gallowglass forced my head around. "You look hectic. How far are we from London?"

"London?" Leonard exclaimed. "You said Heathrow." He wrenched the wheel to head in a different direction off the roundabout.

My stomach proceeded on our previous route. I retched, trying to hold down the vomit. But it wasn't possible.

"Diana?" Ysabeau said, holding back my hair and wiping at my mouth with her silk scarf. "What is it?"

"I must have eaten something that didn't agree with me," I said, suppressing another urge to vomit. "I've felt funny for the last few days."

"Funny how?" Gallowglass's voice was urgent. "Do you have a headache, Diana? Are you having trouble breathing? Does your shoulder pain you?"

I nodded, the bile rising.

"You said she was anxious, Phoebe?"

"Of course Diana was anxious," Ysabeau retorted. She dumped the contents of her purse onto the seat and held it under my chin. I couldn't imagine throwing up into a Chanel bag, but at this point anything was possible. "She was preparing to do battle with Benjamin!"

"Anxiety is a symptom of some condition I can't pronounce. Diana had leaflets about it in New Haven. You hold on, Auntie!" Gallowglass sounded frantic.

I wondered dimly why he sounded so alarmed before I vomited again, right into Ysabeau's purse.

"Hamish? We need a doctor. A vampire doctor. Something's wrong with Diana."

Sol in Scorpio

When the sun is in the signe of Scorpio, expect
death, feare, and poison. During this dangerous time,
beware of serpents and all other venomous creatures.
Scorpio rules over conception and childbirth,
and children born under this sign are
blessed with many gifts.

—Anonymous English Commonplace Book, c. 1590,
Gonçalves MS 4890, f. 9^r

"Where is Matthew? He should be here," Fernando murmured, turning away from the view of Diana sitting in the small, sunny room where she spent most of her time since being put on a strict regime of bed rest.

Diana was still brooding over what happened in the Bodleian. She had not forgiven herself for allowing Benjamin to threaten Phoebe or for letting the opportunity to kill Matthew's son slip through her fingers. But Fernando feared that this would not be the last time her nerves would fail in the face of the enemy.

"Diana's fine." Gallowglass was propped up against the wall in the hallway opposite the door, his arms crossed. "The doctor said so this morning. Besides, Matthew can't return until he gets his new family sorted out."

Gallowglass had been their only link to Matthew for weeks. Fernando swore. He pounced, pressing his mouth tightly against Gallowglass's ear and his hand against his windpipe.

"You haven't told Matthew," Fernando said, lowering his voice so that no one else in the house could hear. "He has a right to know what's happened here, Gallowglass: the magic, finding that page from the Book of Life, Benjamin's appearance, Diana's condition—all of it."

"If Matthew wanted to know what was happening to his wife, he would be here and not bringing a pack of recalcitrant children to heel," Gallowglass choked out, grasping Fernando's wrist.

"And you believe this because *you* would have stayed?" Fernando released him. "You are more lost than the moon in winter. It does not matter where Matthew is. Diana belongs to him. She will never be yours."

"I know that." Gallowglass's blue eyes did not waver.

"Matthew may kill you for this." There was not a touch of histrionics in Fernando's pronouncement.

"There are worse things than my being killed," Gallowglass said evenly. "The doctor said no stress or the babes could die. So could Diana. Not even

Matthew will harm them while I have breath in my body. That's my job—
and I do it well."

"When I next see Philippe de Clermont—and he is no doubt toasting
his feet before the devil's fire—he will answer to me for asking this of you."
Fernando knew that Philippe enjoyed making other people's decisions. He
should have made a different one in this case.

"I would have done it regardless." Gallowglass stepped away. "I don't
seem to have a choice."

"You always have a choice. And you deserve a chance to be happy." There
had to be a woman out there for Gallowglass, Fernando thought—one who
would make him forget Diana Bishop.

"Do I?" Gallowglass's expression turned wistful.

"Yes. Diana has a right to be happy, too." Fernando's words were deliberately blunt. "They've been apart long enough. It's time Matthew came
home."

"Not unless his blood rage is under control. Being away from Diana so
long will have made him unstable enough. If Matthew finds out the pregnancy is putting her life in peril, God only knows what he'll do." Gallowglass matched blunt with blunt. "Baldwin is right. The greatest danger we
face is not Benjamin, and it isn't the Congregation—it's Matthew. Better
fifty enemies outside the door than one within it."

"So Matthew is your enemy now?" Fernando spoke in a whisper. "And
you think he's the one who has lost his senses?"

Gallowglass made no reply.

"If you know what is good for you, Gallowglass, you will walk out of
this house the minute Matthew returns. Wherever you go—and the ends of
the earth may not be far enough to keep you from his wrath—I advise you
to spend time on your knees begging God for His protection."

The Domino Club on Royal Street hadn't changed much since Matthew
had first walked through its doors almost two centuries ago. The three-story
façade, gray walls, and crisp black-and-white–painted trim was the same,
the height of the arched windows at street level suggesting an openness to
the outside world that was belied by the closing of their heavy shutters.
When the shutters were flung wide at five o'clock, the general public would

be welcomed to a beautiful polished bar and to enjoy music provided by a variety of local performers.

But Matthew was not interested in tonight's entertainment. His eyes were fixed on an ornate iron railing wrapped around the second-floor balcony that provided a sheltering overhang for the pedestrians below. That floor and the one above were restricted to members. A significant portion of the Domino Club's membership roster had signed up when it was founded in 1839—two years before the Boston Club, officially the oldest gentlemen's club in New Orleans, opened its doors. The rest had been carefully selected according to their looks, breeding, and ability to lose large sums of money at the gambling tables.

Ransome Fayrweather, Marcus's eldest son and the club's owner, would be on the second floor in his office overlooking the corner. Matthew pushed open the black door and entered the cool, dark bar. The place smelled of bourbon and pheromones, the most familiar cocktail in the city. The heels of his shoes made a soft *snick* against the checkered marble floor.

It was four o'clock, and only Ransome and his staff were on the premises.

"Mr. Clairmont?" The vampire behind the bar looked as though he'd seen a ghost and took a step toward the cash register. One glance from Matthew and he froze.

"I'm here to see Ransome." Matthew stalked toward the stairs. No one stopped him.

Ransome's door was closed, and Matthew opened it without knocking.

A man sat with his back to the door and his feet propped up on the windowsill. He was wearing a black suit, and his hair was the same rich brown as the wood of the mahogany chair in which he sat.

"Well, well. Grandpa's home," Ransome said in a treacle-dipped drawl. He didn't turn to look at his visitor, and a worn ebony-and-ivory domino kept moving between his pale fingers. "What brings you to Royal Street?"

"I understand you wish to settle accounts." Matthew took a seat opposite, leaving the heavy desk between him and his grandson.

Ransome slowly turned. The man's eyes were cold chips of green glass in an otherwise handsome and relaxed face. Then his heavy lids dropped, hiding all that sharpness and suggesting a sensual somnolence that Matthew knew was nothing more than a front.

"As you're aware, I'm here to bring you to heel. Your brothers and sister have all agreed to support me and the new scion." Matthew sat back in his chair. "You're the last holdout, Ransome."

All of Marcus's other children had submitted quickly. When Matthew told them they carried the genetic marker for blood rage, they had been first stunned and then furious. After that had come fear. They were schooled enough in vampire law to know that their bloodline made them vulnerable, that if any other vampire found out about their condition, they could face immediate death. Marcus's children needed Matthew as much as he needed them. Without him, they would not survive.

"I have a better memory than they do," Ransome said. He opened his desk drawer and pulled out an old ledger.

With every day away from Diana, Matthew's temper shortened and his propensity for violence increased. It was vital to have Ransome on his side. And yet, at this moment, he wanted to throttle this grandson. The whole business of confessing and seeking atonement had taken much longer than he'd anticipated—and it was keeping him far from where he should be.

"I had no choice but to kill them, Ransome." It took an effort for Matthew to keep his voice even. "Even now Baldwin would rather I kill Jack than risk having him expose our secret. But Marcus convinced me I had other options."

"Marcus told you that last time. Yet you still culled us, one by one. What's changed?" Ransome asked.

"I have."

"Never try to con a con, Matthew," Ransome said in the same lazy drawl. "You've still got that look in your eye that warns creatures not to cross you. Had you lost it, your corpse would be laid out in my foyer. The barkeep was told to shoot you on sight."

"To give him credit, he did reach for the shotgun by the register." Matthew's attention never drifted from Ransome's face. "Tell him to pull the knife from his belt next time."

"I'll be sure to pass on that tip." Ransome's domino paused momentarily, caught between his middle and ring fingers. "What happened to Juliette Durand?"

The muscle in Matthew's jaw ticked. The last time he came to town, Juliette Durand had been with him. When the two left New Orleans, Marcus's boisterous family was significantly smaller. Juliette was Gerbert's creature and had been eager to prove her usefulness at a time when Matthew was growing tired of being the de Clermont family's problem solver. She had disposed of more vampires in New Orleans than Matthew had.

"My wife killed her." Matthew didn't elaborate.

"Sounds like you found yourself a good woman," Ransome said, snapping open the ledger before him. He took the cap off a nearby pen, the tip of which looked as if it had been chewed by a wild animal. "Care to play a game of chance with me, Matthew?"

Matthew's cool eyes met Ransome's brighter green gaze. Matthew's pupils were growing larger by the second. Ransome's lip curled in a scornful smile.

"Afraid?" Ransome asked. "Of me? I'm flattered."

"Whether I play the game or not depends on the stakes."

"My sworn allegiance if you win," Ransome replied, his smile foxy.

"And if I lose?" Matthew's drawl was not treacle-coated but was just as disarming.

"That's where the chance comes in." Ransome sent the domino spinning into the air.

Matthew caught it. "I'll take your wager."

"You don't know what the game is yet," Ransome said.

Matthew stared at him impassively.

Ransome's lips tipped up at the corners. "If you weren't such a bastard, I might grow to like you," he observed.

"Likewise," Matthew said crisply. "The game?"

Ransome drew the ledger closer. "If you can name every sister, brother, niece, nephew, and child of mine you killed in New Orleans all those years ago—as well as any other vampires you killed in the city along the way—I will throw myself in with the rest."

Matthew studied his grandson.

"Wish you'd asked for the terms sooner?" Ransome grinned.

"Malachi Smith. Crispin Jones. Suzette Boudrot. Claude Le Breton." Matthew paused as Ransome searched the ledger's entries for the names.

"You should have kept them in chronological order instead of alphabetical. That's how I remember them."

Ransome looked up in surprise. Matthew's smile was small and wolfish, the kind to make any fox run for the hills.

Matthew continued to recite names long after the downstairs bar opened for business. He finished just in time to see the first gamblers arrive at nine o'clock. Ransome had consumed a fifth of bourbon by then. Matthew was still sipping his first glass of 1775 Château Lafite, which he had given to Marcus in 1789 when the Constitution went into effect. Ransome had been storing it for his father since the Domino Club opened.

"I believe that settles matters, Ransome." Matthew stood and placed the domino on the desk.

Ransome looked dazed. "How can you possibly remember all of them?"

"How could I ever forget?" Matthew drank down the last of his wine. "You have potential, Ransome. I look forward to doing business with you in future. Thank you for the wine."

"Son of a bitch," Ransome muttered under his breath as the sire of his clan departed.

Matthew was weary to the bone and ready to murder something when he returned to the Garden District. He'd walked there from the French Quarter, hoping to burn off some excess emotion. The endless list of names had stirred up too many memories, none of them pleasant. Guilt had followed in their wake.

He took out his phone, hoping that Diana had sent him a photograph. The images she sent thus far were his lifeline. Though Matthew had been furious to discover from them that his wife was in London rather than Sept-Tours, there had been moments over the past weeks when the glimpses into her life there were all that kept him sane.

"Hello, Matthew." To his surprise, Fernando sat on the wide front steps of Marcus's house, waiting for him. Chris Roberts was perched nearby.

"Diana?" It was part howl, part accusation, and entirely terrifying. Behind Fernando the door opened.

"Fernando? Chris?" Marcus looked startled. "What are you doing here?"

"Waiting for Matthew," Fernando replied.

"Come inside. All of you." Marcus beckoned them forward. "Miss Davenport is watching." His neighbors were old, idle, and nosy.

Matthew, however, was beyond the reach of reason. He'd been nearly there several times, but the unexpected sight of Fernando and Chris had sent him over. Now that Marcus knew that his father had blood rage, he understood why Matthew always went away—alone—to recover when he got into this state.

"Who is with her?" Matthew's voice was like a musket firing: first a raspy sound of warning, then a loud report.

"Ysabeau, I expect," Marcus said. "Phoebe. And Sarah. And of course Gallowglass."

"Don't forget Leonard," Jack said, appearing behind Marcus. "He's my best friend, Matthew. Leonard would never let anything happen to Diana."

"You see, Matthew? Diana is just fine." Marcus had already heard from Ransome that Matthew had come from Royal Street, having achieved his goal of family solidarity. Marcus couldn't imagine what had put Matthew in such a foul mood, given his success.

Matthew's arm moved quickly and with enough power to pulverize a human's bones. Instead of choosing a soft target, however, he smashed his hand into one of the white Ionic pillars supporting the upper gallery of the house. Jack put a restraining hand on his other arm.

"If this keeps up, I'm going to have to move back to the Marigny," Marcus said mildly, eyeing a cannonball-size depression near the front door.

"Let me go," Matthew said. Jack's hand dropped to his side, and Matthew shot up the steps and stalked down the long hall to the back of the house. A door slammed in the distance.

"Well, that went better than I expected." Fernando stood.

"He's been worse since my mo—" Jack bit his lip and avoided Marcus's gaze.

"You must be Jack," Fernando said. He bowed, as though Jack were royalty and not a penniless orphan with a deadly disease. "It is an honor to meet you. *Madame* your mother speaks of you often, and with great pride."

"She's not my mother," Jack said, lightning quick. "It was a mistake."

"That was no mistake," Fernando said. "Blood may speak loudly, but I always prefer the tales told by the heart."

"Did you say '*madame*'?" Marcus's lungs felt tight, and his voice sounded strange. He hadn't let himself hope that Fernando would do such a selfless thing, and yet . . .

"Yes, *milord.*" Fernando bowed again.

"Why is he bowing to you?" Jack whispered to Marcus. "And who is '*milord*'?"

"Marcus is '*milord,*' because he is one of Matthew's children," Fernando explained. "And I bow to you both, because that is how family members who are not of the blood treat those who are—with respect and gratitude."

"Thank God. You've joined us." The air left Marcus's lungs in a whoosh of relief.

"I sure as hell hope there's enough bourbon in this house to wash down all the bullshit," Chris said. " '*Milord*' my ass. And I'm not bowing to anybody."

"Duly noted," Marcus said. "What brings you both to New Orleans?"

"Miriam sent me," Chris said. "I've got test results for Matthew, and she didn't want to send them electronically. Plus, Fernando didn't know how to find Matthew. Good thing Jack and I stayed in touch." He smiled at the young man. Jack grinned back.

"As for me, I am here to save your father from himself," Fernando bowed again, this time with a trace of mockery. "With your permission, *milord.*"

"Be my guest," Marcus said, stepping inside. "But if you call me '*milord*' or bow to me one more time, I'll put you in the bayou. And Chris will help me."

"I'll show you where Matthew is," Jack said, already eager to rejoin his idol.

"What about me? We need to catch up," Chris said, grabbing his arm. "Have you been sketching, Jack?"

"My sketchbook is upstairs. . . ." Jack cast a worried look toward the back garden. "Matthew isn't feeling well. He never leaves me when I'm like this. I should—"

Fernando rested his hands on the young man's tense shoulders. "You remind me of Matthew, back when he was a young vampire." It hurt Fernando's heart to see it, but it was true.

"I do?" Jack sounded awed.

"You do. Same compassion. Same courage, too." Fernando looked at Jack thoughtfully. "And you share Matthew's hope that if you shoulder the burdens of others, they will love you in spite of the sickness in your veins."

Jack looked at his feet.

"Did Matthew tell you that his brother Hugh was my mate?" Fernando asked.

"No," Jack murmured.

"Long ago Hugh told Matthew something very important. I am here to remind him of it." Fernando waited for Jack to meet his eyes.

"What?" Jack asked, unable to hide his curiosity.

"If you truly love someone, you will cherish what they despise most about themselves." Fernando's voice dropped. "Next time Matthew forgets that, you remind him. And if you forget, I'll remind you. Once. After that, I'm telling Diana that you are wallowing in self-hatred. And your mother is not nearly as forgiving as I am."

Fernando found Matthew in the narrow back garden, under the cover of a small gazebo. The rain that had been threatening all evening had finally started to fall. He was oddly preoccupied with his phone. Every minute or so, his thumb moved, followed by a fixed stare, then another movement of the thumb.

"You're as bad as Diana, staring at her phone all the time without ever sending a message." Fernando's laughter stopped abruptly. "It's you. You've been in touch with her all along."

"Just pictures. No words. I don't trust myself—or the Congregation—with words." Matthew's thumb moved.

Fernando had heard Diana say to Sarah, "Still no word from Matthew." Literally speaking, the witch had not lied, which had prevented the family from knowing her secret. And as long as Diana sent only pictures, there would be little way for Matthew to know how badly things had gone wrong in Oxford.

Matthew's breath was ragged. He steadied it with visible effort. His thumb moved.

"Do that one more time and I'll break it. And I'm not talking about the phone."

The sound that came out of Matthew's mouth was more bark than laugh, as if the human part of him had given up the fight and let the wolf win.

"What do you think Hugh would have done with a cell phone?" Matthew cradled his in both hands as though it were his last precious link to the world outside his own troubled mind.

"Not much. Hugh wouldn't remember to charge it, for a start. I loved your brother with all my heart, Matthew, but he was hopeless when it came to daily life."

This time Matthew's answering chuckle sounded less like a sound a wild animal might make.

"I take it that patriarchy has been more difficult than you anticipated?" Fernando didn't envy Matthew for having to assert his leadership over this pack.

"Not really. Marcus's children still hate me, and rightfully so." Matthew's fingers closed on the phone, his eyes straying to the screen like an addict's. "I just saw the last of them. Ransome made me account for every vampire death I was responsible for in New Orleans—even the ones that had nothing to do with purging the blood rage from the city."

"That must have taken some time," Fernando murmured.

"Five hours. Ransome was surprised I remembered them all by name," Matthew said.

Fernando was not.

"Now all of Marcus's children have agreed to support me and be included in the scion, but I wouldn't want to test their devotion," Matthew continued. "Mine is a family built on fear—fear of Benjamin, of the Congregation, of other vampires, even of me. It's not based on love or respect."

"Fear is easy to root. Love and respect take more time," Fernando told him.

The silence stretched, became leaden.

"Do you not want to ask me about your wife?"

"No." Matthew stared at an ax buried in a thick stump. There were piles of split logs all around it. He rose and picked up a fresh log. "Not until I'm well enough to go to her and see for myself. I couldn't bear it, Fernando. Not being able to hold her—to watch our children grow inside her—to know she is safe, it's been—"

Fernando waited until the ax thunked into the wood before he prompted Matthew to continue.

"It's been what, *Mateus?*"

Matthew pulled the ax free. He swung again.

Had Fernando not been a vampire, he wouldn't have heard the response.

"It's been like having my heart ripped out." Matthew's axhead cleaved the wood with a mighty crack. "Every single minute of every single day."

Fernando gave Matthew forty-eight hours to recover from the ordeal with Ransome. Confessions of past sins were never easy, and Matthew was particularly prone to brooding.

Fernando took advantage of that time to introduce himself to Marcus's children and grandchildren. He made sure they understood the family rules and who would punish those who disobeyed them, for Fernando had appointed himself Matthew's enforcer—and executioner. The New Orleans branch of the Bishop-Clairmont family was rather subdued afterward, and Fernando decided Matthew could now go home. Fernando was increasingly concerned about Diana. Ysabeau said her medical condition was unchanged, but Sarah was still worried. Something was not right, she told Fernando, and she suspected that only Matthew would be able to fix it.

Fernando found Matthew in the garden as he often was, eyes black and hackles raised. He was still in the grip of blood rage. Sadly, there was no more wood for him to chop in Orleans Parish.

"Here." Fernando dropped a bag at Matthew's feet.

Inside the bag Matthew found his small ax and chisel, T-handled augers of various sizes, a frame saw, and two of his precious planes. Alain had neatly wrapped the planes in oiled cloth to protect them during their travels. Matthew stared at his well-used tools, then at his hands.

"Those hands haven't always done bloody work," Fernando reminded him. "I remember when they healed, created, made music."

Matthew looked at him, mute.

"Will you make them on straight legs or with a curved base so they can be rocked?" Fernando asked conversationally.

Matthew frowned. "Make what?"

"The cradles. For the twins." Fernando let his words sink in. "I think oak is best—stout and strong—but Marcus tells me that cherry is traditional in America. Perhaps Diana would prefer that."

Matthew picked up his chisel. The worn handle filled his palm. "Rowan. I'll make them out of rowan for protection."

Fernando squeezed Matthew's shoulder with approval and departed.

Matthew dropped the chisel back into the bag. He took out his phone, hesitated, and snapped a photograph. Then he waited.

Diana's response was swift and made his bones hollow with longing. His wife was in the bath. He recognized the curves of the copper tub in the Mayfair house. But these were not the curves that interested him.

His wife—his clever, wicked wife—had propped the phone on her breastbone and taken a picture down the length of her naked body. All that was visible was the mound of her belly, the skin stretched impossibly tight, and the tips of her toes resting on the curled edge of the tub.

If he concentrated, Matthew could imagine her scent rising from the warm water, feel the silk of her hair between his fingers, trace the long, strong lines of her thigh and shoulder. Christ, he missed her.

"Fernando said you needed lumber." Marcus was standing before him, frowning.

Matthew dragged his eyes away from the phone. What he needed, only Diana could provide.

"Fernando also said if anyone woke him in the next forty-eight hours, there would be hell to pay," Marcus said, looking at the stacks of split logs. They certainly wouldn't lack firewood this winter. "You know how Ransome loves a challenge—not to mention a brush with the devil—so you can imagine his response."

"Do tell," Matthew said with a dry chuckle. He hadn't laughed in some time, so the sound was rusty and raw.

"Ransome has already been on the phone to the Krewe of Muses. I expect the Ninth Ward Marching Band will be here by suppertime. Vampire or no, they'll rouse Fernando for sure." Marcus looked down at his father's leather tool bag. "Are you finally going to teach Jack to carve?" The boy had been begging Matthew for lessons since he arrived.

Matthew shook his head. "I thought he might like to help me make cradles instead."

Matthew and Jack worked on the cradles for almost a week. Every cut of wood, every finely hewn dovetail that joined the pieces together, every swipe of the plane helped to reduce Matthew's blood rage. Working on a present for Diana made him feel connected to her again, and he began to talk about the children and his hopes.

Jack was a good pupil, and his skills as an artist proved handy when it came to carving decorative designs into the cradles. While they worked, Jack asked Matthew about his childhood and how he'd met Diana at the Bodleian. No one else would have gotten away with asking such direct, personal questions, but the rules were always slightly different where Jack was concerned.

When they were finished, the cradles were works of art. Matthew and Jack wrapped them carefully in soft blankets to protect them on the journey back to London.

It was only after the cradles were finished and ready to go that Fernando told Matthew about Diana's condition.

Matthew's response was entirely expected. First he went still and silent. Then he swung into action.

"Get the pilot on the phone. I'm not waiting until tomorrow. I want to be in London by morning," Matthew said, his tone clipped and precise. "Marcus!"

"What's wrong?" Marcus said.

"Diana isn't well." Matthew scowled ferociously at Fernando. "I should have been told."

"I thought you had been." Fernando didn't need to say anything else. Matthew knew who had kept this from him. Fernando suspected that Matthew knew why as well.

Matthew's usually mobile face turned to stone, and his normally expressive eyes were blank.

"What happened?" Marcus said. He told Jack where to find his medical bag and called for Ransome.

"Diana found the missing page from Ashmole 782." Fernando took Matthew by the shoulders. "There's more. She saw Benjamin at the Bodleian Library. He knows about the pregnancy. He attacked Phoebe."

"Phoebe?" Marcus was distraught. "Is she all right?"

"Benjamin?" Jack inhaled sharply.

"Phoebe is fine. And Benjamin is nowhere to be found," Fernando reassured them. "As for Diana, Hamish called Edward Garrett and Jane Sharp. They're overseeing her case."

"They're among the finest doctors in the city, Matthew," Marcus said. "Diana couldn't be in better care."

"She will be," Matthew said, picking up a cradle and heading out the door. "She'll be in mine."

30

"You shouldn't have any problem with it now," I told the young witch sitting before me. She had come at the suggestion of Linda Crosby to see if I could figure out why her protection spell was no longer effective.

Working out of Clairmont House, I had become London's chief magical diagnostician, listening to accounts of failed exorcisms, spells gone bad, and elemental magic on the loose, and then helping the witches find solutions. As soon as Amanda cast her spell for me, I could see the problem: When she recited the words, the blue and green threads around her got tangled up with a single strand of red that pulled on the six-crossed knots at the core of the spell. The gramarye had become convoluted, the spell's intentions murky, and now instead of protecting Amanda it was the magical equivalent of an angry Chihuahua, snarling and snapping at everything that came close.

"Hello, Amanda," Sarah said, sticking her head in to see how we were faring. "Did you get what you needed?"

"Diana was brilliant, thanks," Amanda said.

"Wonderful. Let me show you out," Sarah said.

I leaned back on the cushions, sad to see Amanda go. Since the doctors from Harley Street had me on bed rest, my visitors were few.

The good news was that I didn't have preeclampsia—at least not as it usually develops in warmbloods. I had no protein in my urine, and my blood pressure was actually below normal. Nevertheless, swelling, nausea, and shoulder pain were not symptoms the jovial Dr. Garrett or his aptly named colleague, Dr. Sharp, wished to ignore—especially not after Ysabeau explained that I was Matthew Clairmont's mate.

The bad news was that they put me on modified bed rest nonetheless, and so I would remain until the twins were born—which Dr. Sharp hoped would not be for another four weeks at least, although her worried look suggested that this was an optimistic projection. I was allowed to do some gentle stretching under Amira's supervision and take two ten-minute walks around the garden per day. Stairs, standing, lifting were positively forbidden.

My phone buzzed on the side table. I picked it up, hoping for a text from Matthew.

A picture of the front door of Clairmont House was waiting for me.

It was then that I noticed how quiet it was, the only sound the ticking of the house's many clocks.

The creak of the front-door hinges and the soft scrape of wood against marble broke the silence. Without thinking I shot to my feet, teetering on legs that had grown weaker during my enforced inactivity.

And then Matthew was there.

All that either of us could do for the first long moments was to drink in the sight of the other. Matthew's hair was tousled and slightly wavy from the damp London air, and he was wearing a gray sweater and black jeans. Fine lines around his eyes showed the stress he'd been under.

He stalked toward me. I wanted to jump up and run at him, but something in his expression kept me glued to the spot.

When at last Matthew reached me, he cradled my neck with his fingertips and searched my eyes. His thumb brushed across my lips, bringing the blood to the surface. I saw the small changes in him: the firm set of his jaw, the unusual tightness of his mouth, the hooded expression caused by the lowering of his eyelids.

My lips parted as his thumb made another pass over my tingling mouth.

"I missed you, *mon coeur,*" Matthew said, his voice rough. He leaned down with the same deliberation as he had crossed the room, and he kissed me.

My head spun. He was *here.* My hands gripped his sweater as though that could keep him from disappearing. A raspy catch in the back of his throat that was almost a growl kept me quiet when I prepared to rise up and meet him in his embrace. Matthew's free hand roamed over my back, my hip, and settled on my belly. One of the babies gave a sharp, reproachful kick. He smiled against my mouth, the thumb that had first stroked my lip now featherlight on my pulse. Then he registered the books, flowers, and fruit.

"I'm absolutely fine. I was a bit nauseated and had a pain in my shoulder, that's all," I said quickly. His medical education would send his mind racing toward all sorts of terrible diagnoses. "My blood pressure is fine, and so are the babies."

"Fernando told me. I'm sorry I wasn't here," he murmured, his fingers rubbing my tense neck muscles. For the first time since New Haven, I let myself relax.

"I missed you, too." My heart was too full to let me say more.

But Matthew didn't want more words. The next thing I knew I was airborne, cradled in his arms with my feet dangling.

Upstairs, Matthew put me in the leafy surrounds of the bed we'd slept in so many lifetimes ago in the Blackfriars. Silently he undressed me, examining every inch of exposed flesh as though he had been given an unexpected glimpse of something rare and precious. He was utterly silent as he did so, letting his eyes and the gentleness of his touch speak for him.

Over the course of the next few hours, Matthew reclaimed me, his fingers erasing every trace of the other creatures I'd been in contact with since he departed. At some point he let me undress him, his body responding to mine with gratifying speed. Dr. Sharp had been absolutely clear on the risks associated with any contraction of my uterine muscles, however. There would be no release of sexual tension for me, but just because I had to deny my body's needs, that didn't mean Matthew did, too. When I reached for him, however, he stilled my hand and kissed me deeply.

Together, Matthew said without a word. *Together, or not at all.*

"Don't tell me you can't find him, Fernando," Matthew said, not even trying to sound reasonable. He was in the kitchen of Clairmont House, scrambling eggs and making toast. Diana was upstairs resting, unaware of the conference taking place on the lower ground floor.

"I still think we should ask Jack," Fernando said. "He could help us narrow down the options, at least."

"No. I don't want him involved." Matthew turned to Marcus. "Is Phoebe all right?"

"It was too close for comfort, Matthew," Marcus said grimly. "I know you don't approve of Phoebe's becoming a vampire, but—"

"You have my blessing," Matthew interrupted. "Just choose someone who will do it properly."

"Thank you. I already have." Marcus hesitated. "Jack has been asking to see Diana."

"Send him over this evening." Matthew flipped the eggs onto a plate. "Tell him to bring the cradles. Around seven. We'll be expecting him."

"I'll tell him," Marcus said. "Anything else?"

"Yes," Matthew said. "Someone must be feeding Benjamin information. Since you can't find Benjamin, you can look for him—or her."

"And then?" Fernando asked.

"Bring them to me," Matthew replied as he left the room.

We remained locked alone in the house for three days, twined together, talking little, never separated for more than the few moments when Matthew went downstairs to make me something to eat or to accept a meal dropped off by the Connaught's staff. The hotel had apparently worked out a food-for-wine scheme with Matthew. Several cases of 1961 Château Latour left the house in exchange for exquisite morsels of food, such as hard-boiled quail eggs in a nest of seaweed and delicate ravioli filled with tender cèpes that the chef assured Matthew had been flown in from France only that morning.

On the second day, Matthew and I trusted ourselves to talk, and similarly tiny mouthfuls of words were offered up and digested alongside the delicacies from a few streets away. He reported on Jack's efforts at self-governance in the thick of Marcus's sprawling brood. Matthew spoke with great admiration of Marcus's deft handling of his children and grandchildren, all of whom had names worthy of characters in a nineteenth-century penny dreadful. And, reluctantly, Matthew told me of his struggles not only with his blood rage but with his desire to be at my side.

"I would have gone mad without the pictures," he confessed, spooned up against my back with his long, cold nose buried in my neck. "The images of where we'd lived, or the flowers in the garden, or your toes on the edge of the bath kept my sanity from slipping entirely."

I shared my own tale with a slowness worthy of a vampire, gauging Matthew's reactions so that I could take a break when necessary and let him absorb what I'd experienced in London and Oxford. There was finding Timothy and the missing page, as well as meeting up with Amira and being back at the Old Lodge. I showed Matthew my purple finger and shared the goddess's proclamation that to possess the Book of Life I would have to give up something I cherished. And I spared no details from my account of meeting Benjamin—not my own failures as a witch, nor what he'd done to Phoebe, not even his final, parting threat.

"If I hadn't hesitated, Benjamin would be dead." I'd been over the event hundreds of times and still didn't understand why my nerve had failed. "First Juliette and now—"

"You cannot blame yourself for choosing not to kill someone," Matthew said, pressing a finger to my lips. "Death is a difficult business."

"Do you think Benjamin is still here, in England?" I asked.

"Not here," Matthew assured me, rolling me to face him. "Never again where you are."

Never is a long time. Philippe's admonishment came back to me clearly.

I pushed the worry away and pulled my husband closer.

"Benjamin has utterly vanished," Andrew Hubbard told Matthew. "That's what he does."

"That's not entirely true. Addie claims she saw him in Munich," Marcus said. "She alerted her fellow knights."

While Matthew was in the sixteenth century, Marcus had admitted women into the brotherhood. He began with Miriam, and she helped him name the rest. Matthew wasn't sure if this was madness or genius at work, but if it helped him locate Benjamin, he was prepared to remain agnostic. Matthew blamed Marcus's progressive ideas on his onetime neighbor Catherine Macaulay, who had occupied an important place in his son's life when he was first made a vampire and filled his ears with her bluestocking ideas.

"We could ask Baldwin," Fernando said. "He is in Berlin, after all."

"Not yet," Matthew said.

"Does Diana know you're looking for Benjamin?" Marcus asked.

"No," Matthew said as he headed back to his wife with a plate of food from the Connaught.

"Not yet," Andrew Hubbard muttered.

That evening it was difficult to determine who was more overjoyed at our reunion: Jack or Lobero. The pair got twisted in a tangle of legs and feet, but

Jack finally managed to extricate himself from the beast, who nevertheless beat him to my chaise longue in the Chinese Room and leaped onto the cushion with a triumphant bark.

"Down, Lobero. You'll make the thing collapse." Jack stooped and kissed me respectfully on the cheek. "Grandmother."

"Don't you dare!" I warned, taking his hand in mine. "Save your grandmotherly endearments for Ysabeau."

"I told you she wouldn't like it," Matthew said with a grin. He snapped his fingers at Lobero and pointed to the floor. The dog slid his forelegs off the chaise, leaving his backside planted firmly against me. It took another snap of the fingers for him to slide off entirely.

"Madame Ysabeau said she has standards to maintain, and I will have to do two extremely wicked things before she will let me call her Grandmother," Jack said.

"And yet you're still calling her Madame Ysabeau?" I looked at him in amazement. "What's keeping you? You've been back in London for days."

Jack looked down, his lips curved at the prospect of more delicious mischief to come. "Well, I've been on my best behavior, *madame.*"

"Madame?" I groaned and threw a pillow at him. "That's worse than calling me 'Grandmother.'"

Jack let the pillow hit him square in the face.

"Fernando's right," Matthew said. "Your heart knows what to call Diana, even if your thick head and vampire propriety are telling you different. Now, help me bring in your mother's present."

Under Lobero's careful supervision, Matthew and Jack carried in first one, then another cloth-wrapped bundle. They were tall and seemingly rectangular in shape, rather like small bookcases. Matthew had sent me a picture of a stack of wood and some tools. The two must have worked on the items together. I smiled at the sudden image of them, dark head and light bowed over a common project.

As Matthew and Jack gradually unwrapped the two objects, it became clear that they were not bookcases but cradles: two beautiful, identically carved and painted, wooden cradles. Their curved bases hung inside sturdy wooden stands that sat on level feet. This way the cradles could be rocked gently in the air or removed from their supports and put on the floor to be nudged with a foot. My eyes filled.

"We made them out of rowan wood. Ransome couldn't figure out where the hell we were going to find Scottish wood in Louisiana, but he obviously doesn't know Matthew." Jack ran his fingers along one of the smooth edges.

"The cradles are rowan, but the stand is made from oak—strong American white oak." Matthew regarded me with a touch of anxiety. "Do you like them?"

"I love them." I looked up at my husband, hoping my expression would tell him just how much. It must have, for he cupped the side of my face tenderly and his own expression was happier than I'd seen since we returned to the present.

"Matthew designed them. He said it's how cradles used to be made, so you could get them up off the floor and out of the way of the chickens," Jack explained.

"And the carving?" A tree had been incised into the wood at the foot of each cradle, its roots and branches intertwined. Carefully applied silver and gold paint highlighted the leaves and bark.

"That was Jack's idea," Matthew said, putting his hand on the younger man's shoulder. "He remembered the design on your spell box and thought the symbol was fitting for a baby's bed."

"Every part of the cradles has meaning," Jack said. "The rowan is a magical tree, you know, and white oak symbolizes strength and immortality. The finials on the four corners are shaped like acorns—that's for luck—and the rowanberries carved on the supports are supposed to protect them. Corra's on the cradles, too. Dragons guard rowan trees to keep humans from eating their fruit."

I looked more closely and saw that a firedrake's curving tail provided the arc for the cradles' rockers.

"These will be the two safest babies in all the world, then," I said, "not to mention the luckiest, sleeping in such beautiful beds."

His gifts having been given and gratefully received, Jack sat on the floor with Lobero and told animated tales about life in New Orleans. Matthew relaxed in one of the japanned easy chairs, watching the minutes tick by with Jack showing no sign of blood rage.

The clocks were striking ten when Jack left for Pickering Place, which he described as crowded but of good cheer.

"Is Gallowglass there?" I hadn't seen him since Matthew returned.

"He left right after we arrived back in London. Said he had somewhere to go and would be back when he was able." Jack shrugged.

Something must have flickered in my eyes, for Matthew was instantly watchful. He said nothing, however, until he'd seen Jack and Lobero downstairs and safely on their way.

"It's probably for the best," Matthew said when he returned. He arranged himself in the chaise longue behind me so that he could serve as my backrest. I settled into him with a sigh of contentment as he circled his arms around me.

"That all of our family and friends are at Marcus's house?" I snorted. "Of course you think that's for the best."

"No. That Gallowglass has decided to go away for a little while." Matthew pressed his lips against my hair. I stiffened.

"Matthew . . ." I needed to tell him about Gallowglass.

"I know, *mon coeur*. I've suspected it for some time, but when I saw him with you in New Haven, I was sure." Matthew rocked one of the cradles with a gentle push of his finger.

"Since when?" I asked.

"Maybe from the beginning. Certainly from the night Rudolf touched you in Prague," Matthew replied. The emperor had behaved so badly on Walpurgisnacht, the same night we'd seen the Book of Life whole and complete for the last time. "Even then it came as no surprise, simply a confirmation of something I already, on some level, understood."

"Gallowglass didn't do anything improper," I said quickly.

"I know that, too. Gallowglass is Hugh's son and incapable of dishonor." Matthew's throat moved as he cleared the emotion from his voice. "Perhaps once the babies are born, he will be able to move on with his life. I would like him to be happy."

"Me, too," I whispered, wondering how many knots and threads it would take to help Gallowglass find his mate.

"Where has Gallowglass gone?" Matthew glowered at Fernando, though they both knew that his nephew's sudden disappearance wasn't Fernando's fault.

"Wherever it is, he's better off there than here waiting for you and Diana to welcome your children into the world," Fernando said.

"Diana doesn't agree." Matthew flipped through his e-mail. He'd taken to reading it downstairs, so that Diana didn't know about the intelligence he was gathering on Benjamin. "She's asking for him."

"Philippe was wrong to make Gallowglass watch over her." Fernando downed a cup of wine.

"You think so? It's what I would have done," Matthew said.

"Think, Matthew," Dr. Garrett said impatiently. "Your children have vampire blood in them—though how that is possible, I will leave between you and God. That means they have some vampire immunity at least. Wouldn't you rather your wife give birth at home, as women have done for centuries?"

Now that Matthew was back, he expected to play a significant role in determining how the twins would be brought into the world. As far as he was concerned, I should deliver in the hospital. My preference was to give birth at Clairmont House, with Marcus in attendance.

"Marcus hasn't practiced obstetrics for years," Matthew grumbled.

"Hell, man, you taught him anatomy. You taught *me* anatomy, come to think of it!" Dr. Garrett was clearly at the end of his rope. "Do you think the uterus has suddenly wandered off to a new location? Talk sense into him, Jane."

"Edward is right," Dr. Sharp said. "The four of us have dozens of medical degrees between us and more than two millennia of combined experience. Marthe has very likely delivered more babies than anyone now living, and Diana's aunt is a certified midwife. I suspect we'll manage."

I suspected she was right. So did Matthew, in the end. Having been overruled about the twins' delivery, he was eager to get out of the room when Fernando arrived. The two disappeared downstairs. They often closeted themselves together, talking family business.

"What did Matthew say when you told him you'd sworn your allegiance to the Bishop-Clairmont family?" I asked Fernando when he came upstairs later to say hello.

"He told me I was mad," Fernando replied with a twinkle in his eye. "I told Matthew that I expect to be made a godfather to your eldest child in return."

"I'm sure that can be arranged," I said, though I was beginning to worry at the number of godparents the children were going to have.

"I hope you're keeping track of all the promises you've made," I remarked to Matthew later that afternoon.

"I am," he said. "Chris wants the smartest and Fernando the eldest. Hamish wants the best-looking. Marcus wants a girl. Jack wants a brother. Gallowglass expressed an interest in being godfather to any blond babies before we left New Haven." Matthew ticked them off on his fingers.

"I'm having twins, not a litter of puppies," I said, staggered by the number of interested parties. "Besides, we're not royals. And I'm pagan! The twins don't need so many godparents."

"Do you want me to pick the godmothers, too?" Matthew's eyebrow rose.

"Miriam," I said hastily, before he could suggest any of his terrifying female relatives. "Phoebe, of course. Marthe. Sophie. Amira. I'd like to ask Vivian Harrison, too."

"See. Once you get started, they mount up quickly," Matthew said with a smile.

That left us with six godparents per child. We were going to be drowning in silver baby cups and teddy bears, if the piles of tiny clothes, booties, and blankets Ysabeau and Sarah had already purchased were any indication.

Two of the twins' potential godparents joined us for dinner most evenings. Marcus and Phoebe were so obviously in love that it was impossible not to feel romantic in their presence. The air between them thrummed with tension. Phoebe, for her part, was as unflappable and self-possessed as ever. She didn't hesitate to lecture Matthew on the state of the frescoes in the ballroom and how shocked Angelica Kauffmann would be to find her work neglected in such a fashion. Nor did Phoebe plan on allowing the de Clermont family treasures to be kept from the eyes of the public indefinitely.

"There are ways to share them anonymously, and for a fixed period of time," she told Matthew.

"Expect to see the picture of Margaret More from the Old Lodge's upstairs loo on display at the National Portrait Gallery very soon." I squeezed Matthew's hand encouragingly.

"Why didn't someone warn me it would be so difficult to have historians in the family?" he asked Marcus, looking a trifle dazed. "And how did we end up with two?"

"Good taste," Marcus said, giving Phoebe a smoldering glance.

"Indeed." Matthew's mouth twitched at the obvious double entendre.

When it was just the four of us like this, Matthew and Marcus would talk for hours about the new scion—though Marcus preferred to call it "Matthew's clan" for reasons that had as much to do with his Scottish grandfather as with his dislike of applying botanical and zoological terms to vampire families.

"Members of the Bishop-Clairmont scion—or clan if you insist—will have to be especially careful when they mate or marry," Matthew said one evening over dinner. "The eyes of every vampire will be on us."

Marcus did a double take. "Bishop-Clairmont?"

"Of course," Matthew said with a frown. "What did you expect us to be called? Diana doesn't use my name, and our children will bear both. It's only right that a family composed of witches and vampires has a name that reflects that."

I was touched by his thoughtfulness. Matthew could be such a patriarchal, overprotective creature, but he had not forgotten my family's traditions.

"Why, Matthew de Clermont," Marcus said with a slow smile. "That's downright progressive for an old fossil like you."

"Hmph." Matthew sipped at his wine.

Marcus's phone buzzed, and he looked at his display. "Hamish is here. I'll go down and let him in."

Muted conversation floated up the stairs. Matthew rose. "Stay with Diana, Phoebe."

Phoebe and I exchanged worried looks.

"It will be so much more convenient when I'm a vampire, too," she said, trying in vain to hear what was being said downstairs. "At least then we'll know what's going on."

"Then they'll just take a walk," I said. "I need to devise a spell—one that will magnify the sound waves. Something using air and a bit of water, perhaps."

"Shh." Phoebe tilted her head and made an impatient sound. "Now they've lowered their voices. How maddening."

When Matthew and Marcus reappeared with Hamish in tow, their faces told me that something was seriously wrong.

"There's been another message from Benjamin." Matthew crouched before me, his eyes level with mine. "I don't want to keep this from you, Diana, but you must stay calm."

"Just tell me," I said, my heart in my throat.

"The witch that Benjamin captured is dead. Her child died with her." Matthew's eyes searched mine, which filled with tears. And not only for the young witch but for myself, and my own failure. *If I hadn't hesitated, Benjamin's witch might still be alive.*

"Why can't we have the time we need to sort things out and deal with this huge mess we seem to have made? And why do people have to keep dying while we do it?" I cried.

"There was no way to prevent this," Matthew said, stroking my hair away from my forehead. "Not this time."

"What about next time?" I demanded.

The men were grim and silent.

"Oh. Of course." I drew in a sharp lungful of air, and my fingers tingled. Corra burst out from my ribs with an agitated squawk and launched herself upward to perch on the chandelier. "You'll stop him. Because next time he's coming for me."

I felt a pop, a trickle of liquid.

Matthew looked down to my rounded belly in shock.

The babies were on their way.

31

"Don't you dare tell me not to push." I was red-faced and sweating, and all I wanted was to get these babies out of me as quickly as possible.

"Do. Not. Push," Marthe repeated. She and Sarah had me walking around in an effort to ease the aching in my back and legs. The contractions were still around five minutes apart, but the pain was becoming excruciating, radiating from my spine around to my belly.

"I want to lie down." After weeks of resisting bed rest, now I just wanted to crawl back into the bed, with its rubber-covered mattress and sterilized sheets. The irony was not lost on me, nor on anyone else in the room.

"You're not lying down," Sarah said.

"Oh, God. Here comes another one." I stopped in my tracks and gripped their hands. The contraction lasted a long time. I had just straightened up and started breathing normally when another one hit. "I want Matthew!"

"I'm right here," Matthew said, taking Marthe's place. He nodded to Sarah. "That was fast."

"The book said the contractions are supposed to get gradually closer together." I sounded like a peevish schoolmarm.

"Babies don't read books, honey," Sarah said. "They have their own ideas about these things."

"And when they're of a mind to be born, babies make no bones about it," Dr. Sharp said, entering the room with a smile. Dr. Garrett had been called away to another delivery at the last minute, so Dr. Sharp had taken charge of my medical team. She pressed the stethoscope against my belly, moved it, and pressed again. "You're doing marvelously, Diana. So are the twins. No sign of distress. I'd recommend we try to deliver vaginally."

"I want to lie down," I said through gritted teeth as another band of steel shot out from my spine and threatened to cut me in two. "Where's Marcus?"

"He's just across the hall," Matthew said. I dimly remembered ejecting Marcus from the room when the contractions intensified.

"If I need a cesarean, can Marcus be here in time?" I demanded.

"You called?" Marcus said, entering the room in scrubs. His genial grin and unruffled demeanor calmed me instantly. Now that he'd returned, I couldn't remember why I'd kicked him out of the room.

"Who moved the damn bed?" I puffed my way through another contraction. The bed seemed to be in the same place, but this was clearly an illusion for it was taking forever for me to reach it.

"Matthew did," Sarah said breezily.

"I did no such thing," Matthew protested.

"In labor we blame absolutely everything on the husband. It keeps the mother from developing homicidal fantasies and reminds the men they aren't the center of attention," Sarah explained.

I laughed, thereby missing the rising wave of pain that accompanied the next fierce contraction.

"Fu—Sh—Godda—" I pressed my lips firmly together.

"You are *not* getting through tonight's main event without swearing, Diana," Marcus said.

"I don't want a string of profanity to be the first words the babies hear." Now I recalled the reason for Marcus's expulsion: He'd suggested I was being too prim in the midst of my agony.

"Matthew can sing—and he's loud. I'm sure he could drown you out."

"God—blasted—it hurts," I said, doubling over. "Move the fucking bed if you want to be helpful, but stop arguing with me, you asshole!"

My reply was met with shocked silence.

"Atta girl," Marcus said. "I knew you had it in you. Let's have a look."

Matthew helped me onto the bed, which had been stripped of its priceless silk coverlet and most of its curtains. The two cradles stood in front of the fire, waiting for the twins. I stared at them while Marcus conducted his examination.

Thus far this had been the most physically intrusive four hours of my life. I'd had more things jabbed into me and more stuff taken out of me than I thought possible. It was oddly dehumanizing, considering that I was responsible for bringing new life into the world.

"Still a little while to go," Marcus said, "but things are speeding up nicely."

"Easy for you to say." I would have hit him, but he was positioned between my thighs and the babies were in the way.

"This is your last chance for an epidural," Marcus said. "If you say no, and we have to do a C-section, we'll have to knock you out completely."

"There's no need for you to be heroic, *ma lionne*," Matthew said.

"I'm not being heroic," I told him for the fourth or fifth time. "We have no idea what an epidural might do to the babies." I stopped, my face scrunched in an attempt to block the pain.

"You have to keep breathing, honey," Sarah pushed her way to my side. "You heard her, Matthew. She isn't taking the epidural, and there's no point in arguing with her about it. Now, about the pain. Laughter helps, Diana. So does focusing on something else."

"Pleasure helps, too," Marthe said, adjusting my feet on the mattress in such a way that my back immediately relaxed.

"Pleasure?" I said, confused. Marthe nodded. I looked at her in horror. "You can't mean *that*."

"She does," Sarah said. "It can make a huge difference."

"No. How can you even suggest such a thing?" I couldn't think of a less erotically charged moment. Walking now seemed like a very good idea, and I swung my legs over the edge of the bed. That was as far as I got before another contraction seized me. When it was over, Matthew and I were alone.

"Don't even think about it," I said when he put his arms around me.

"I understand 'no' in two dozen languages." His steadiness was annoying.

"Don't you want to yell at me or *something*?" I asked.

Matthew took a moment to consider. "Yes."

"Oh." I'd expected a song and dance about the sanctity of pregnant women and how he would put up with anything for me. I giggled.

"Lie on your left side and I'll rub your back." Matthew pulled me down next to him.

"That's the only thing you're going to rub," I warned.

"So I understand," he said with more aggravating control. "Lie down. Now."

"That sounds more like you. I was beginning to think they'd given *you* the epidural by mistake." I turned and fitted my body into his.

"Witch," he said, nipping me on the shoulder.

It was a good thing I was lying down when the next contraction hit.

"We don't want you to push, because there's no telling how long this will take and the babies aren't ready to be born yet. It's been four hours and eighteen minutes since the contractions started. There could be another day of this ahead of you. You need to rest. That's one reason I wanted you to have the nerve blocker." Matthew used his thumbs to massage the small of my back.

"It's only been four hours and eighteen minutes?" My voice was faint.

"Nineteen minutes now, but yes." Matthew held me while my body was racked with another fierce contraction. When I was able to think straight, I groaned softly and pressed back into Matthew's hand.

"Your thumb is in an absolutely divine spot." I sighed with relief.

"And this spot?" Matthew's thumb traveled lower and closer to my spine.

"Heaven," I said, able to breathe through the next contraction a bit better.

"Your blood pressure is still normal, and the back rub seems to be helping. Let's do it properly." Matthew called for Marcus to bring in the oddly shaped, leather-padded chair with the reading stand from his library and had him set it up by the window, a pillow resting on the support that was designed to hold a book. Matthew helped me sit astride it, facing the pillow.

My belly swelled out and made contact with the back of the chair.

"What on earth is this chair really for?"

"Watching cockfights and playing all-night card games," Matthew said. "You'll find it's much easier on your lower back if you can lean forward a bit and rest your head on the pillow."

It was. Matthew began a thorough massage that started at my hips and moved up until he was loosening the muscles at the base of my skull. I had three more contractions while he was working, and though they were prolonged, Matthew's cool hands and strong fingers seemed to soften some of the pain.

"How many pregnant women have you helped this way?" I asked, mildly curious about where he had acquired this skill. Matthew's hands stilled.

"Only you." His soothing motions continued.

I turned my head and found him looking at me, though his fingers never stopped moving.

"Ysabeau said I'm the only one to sleep in this bedroom."

"Nobody I met seemed worthy of it. But I could envision you in this room—with me, of course—shortly after we met."

"Why do you love me so much, Matthew?" I couldn't see the attraction, especially not when I was rotund, facedown, and gasping with pain. His response was swift.

"To every question I have ever had, or ever will have, you are the answer." He pulled my hair away from my neck and kissed me on the soft flesh beneath the ear. "Do you feel like getting up for a bit?"

A sudden, sharper pain that coursed through my lower extremities kept me from responding. I gasped instead.

"That sounds like ten centimeters' dilation to me," Matthew murmured. "Marcus?"

"Good news, Diana," Marcus said cheerfully as he walked into the room. "You get to push now!"

Push I did. For what seemed like days.

I tried it the modern way first: lying down, with Matthew clasping my hand, a look of adoration on his face.

That didn't work well.

"It's not necessarily a sign of trouble," Dr. Sharp told us, looking at Matthew and me from her vantage point between my thighs. "Twins can take longer to get moving during this stage of labor. Right, Marthe?"

"She needs a stool," Marthe said with a frown.

"I brought mine," Dr. Sharp said. "It's in the hall." She jerked her head in that direction.

And so the babies that were conceived in the sixteenth century opted to eschew modern medical convention and be born the old-fashioned way: on a simple wooden chair with a horseshoe-shaped seat.

Instead of having a half dozen strangers share the birth experience, I was surrounded by the ones I loved: Matthew behind me, holding me up physically and emotionally; Jane and Marthe at my feet, congratulating me on having babies so considerate as to present themselves to the world headfirst; Marcus offering a gentle suggestion every now and then; Sarah at my side, telling me when to breathe and when to push; Ysabeau standing by the door, relaying messages to Phoebe, who waited in the hall and sent a constant stream of texts to Pickering Place, where Fernando, Jack, and Andrew were waiting for news.

It was excruciating.

It took forever.

When at 11:55 P.M. the first indignant cry was heard at long last, I started to weep and laugh. A fierce protective feeling took root where my child had been only moments before, filling me with purpose.

"Is it okay?" I asked, looking down.

"She is perfect," Marthe said, beaming at me proudly.

"She?" Matthew sounded dazed.

"It is a girl. Phoebe, tell them *Madame* has given birth to a girl," Ysabeau said with excitement.

Jane held the tiny creature up. She was blue and wrinkled and smeared with gruesome-looking substances that I'd read about but was inadequately prepared to see on my own child. Her hair was jet-black, and there was plenty of it.

"Why is she blue? What's wrong with her? Is she dying?" I felt my anxiety climb.

"She'll turn as red as a beet in no time," Marcus said, looking down at his new sister. He held out a pair of scissors and a clamp to Matthew. "And there's certainly nothing wrong with her lungs. I think you should do the honors."

Matthew stood, motionless.

"If you faint, Matthew Clairmont, I will never let you forget it," Sarah said testily. "Get your ass over there and cut the cord."

"You do it, Sarah." Matthew's hands trembled on my shoulders.

"No. I want Matthew to do it," I said. If he didn't, he was going to regret it later.

My words got Matthew moving, and he was soon on his knees next to Dr. Sharp. In spite of his initial reluctance, once he was presented with a baby and the proper medical equipment, his movements were practiced and sure. After the cord was clamped and cut, Dr. Sharp quickly swaddled our daughter in a waiting blanket. Then she presented this bundle to Matthew.

He stood, dumbstruck, cradling the tiny body in his large hands. There was something miraculous in the juxtaposition of a father's strength with his daughter's vulnerability. She stopped crying for a moment, yawned, and resumed yelling at the cold indignity of her current situation.

"Hello, little stranger," Matthew whispered. He looked at me in awe. "She's beautiful."

"Lord, just listen to her," Marcus said. "A solid eight on the Apgar test, don't you think, Jane?"

"I agree. Why don't you weigh and measure her while we clean up a bit and get ready for the next one?"

Suddenly aware that my job was only half done, Matthew handed the baby into Marcus's care. He then gave me a long look, a deep kiss, and a nod.

"Ready, *ma lionne?*"

"As I'll ever be," I said, seized by another sharp pain.

Twenty minutes later, at 12:15 A.M., our son was born. He was larger than his sister, in both length and weight, but blessed with a similarly robust lung capacity. This, I was told, was a very good thing, though I did wonder if we would still feel that way in twelve hours. Unlike our firstborn, our son had reddish blond hair.

Matthew asked Sarah to cut the cord, since he was wholly absorbed in murmuring a stream of pleasant nonsense into my ear about how beautiful I was and how strong I'd been, all the while holding me upright.

It was after the second baby was born that I started to shake from head to foot.

"What's. Wrong?" I asked through chattering teeth.

Matthew had me out of the birthing stool and onto the bed in a blink.

"Get the babies over here," he ordered.

Marthe plopped one baby on me, and Sarah deposited the other. The babies' limbs were all hitched up and their faces puce with irritation. As soon as I felt the weight of my son and daughter on my chest, the shaking stopped.

"That's the one downside to a birthing stool when there are twins," Dr. Sharp said, beaming. "Mums can get a bit shaky from the sudden emptiness, and we don't get a chance to let you bond with the first child before the second one needs your attention."

Marthe pushed Matthew aside and wrapped both babies in blankets without ever seeming to disturb their position, a bit of vampire legerdemain that I was sure was beyond the capacity of most midwives, no matter how experienced. While Marthe tended to the babies, Sarah gently massaged my stomach until the afterbirth came free with a final, constrictive cramp.

Matthew held the babies for a few moments while Sarah gently cleaned me. A shower, she told me, could wait until I felt like getting up—which I was sure would be approximately never.

She and Marthe removed the sheets and replaced them with new ones, all without my being required to stir. In no time I was propped up against the bed's downy pillows, surrounded by fresh linen. Matthew put the babies back into my arms. The room was empty.

"I don't know how you women survive it," he said, pressing his lips against my forehead.

"Being turned inside out?" I looked at one tiny face, then the other. "I don't know either." My voice dropped. "I wish Mom and Dad were here. Philippe, too."

"If he were, Philippe would be shouting in the streets and waking the neighbors," Matthew said.

"I want to name him Philip, after your father," I said softly. At my words our son cracked one eye open. "Is that okay with you?"

"Only if we name our daughter Rebecca," Matthew said, his hand cupping her dark head. She screwed up her face tighter.

"I'm not sure she approves," I said, marveling that someone so tiny could be so opinionated.

"Rebecca will have plenty of other names to choose from if she continues to object," Matthew said. "Almost as many names as godparents, come to think of it."

"We're going to need a spreadsheet to figure that mess out," I said, hitching Philip higher in my arms. "He is definitely the heavy one."

"They're both a very good size. And Philip is eighteen inches long." Matthew looked at his son with pride.

"He's going to be tall, like his father." I settled more deeply into the pillows.

"And a redhead like his mother and grandmother," Matthew said. He rounded the bed, gave the fire a poke, then lay next to me, propped up on one elbow.

"We've spent all this time searching for ancient secrets and long-lost books of magic, but they're the true chemical wedding," I said, watching while Matthew put his finger in Philip's tiny hand. The baby gripped it with surprising strength.

"You're right." Matthew turned his son's hand this way and that. "A little bit of you, a little bit of me. Part vampire, part witch."

"And all ours," I said firmly, sealing his mouth with a kiss.

                                    *   *   *

"I have a daughter and a son," Matthew told Baldwin. "Rebecca and Philip. Both are healthy and well."

"And their mother?" Baldwin asked.

"Diana got through it beautifully." Matthew's hands shook whenever he thought of what she'd been through.

"Congratulations, Matthew." Baldwin didn't sound happy.

"What is it?" Matthew frowned.

"The Congregation already knows about the birth."

"How?" Matthew demanded. Someone must be watching the house—either a vampire with very sharp eyes, or a witch with strong second sight.

"Who knows?" Baldwin said wearily. "They're willing to hold in abeyance the charges against you and Diana in exchange for an opportunity to examine the babies."

"Never." Matthew's anger caught light.

"The Congregation only wants to know what the twins are," Baldwin said shortly.

"Mine. Philip and Rebecca are mine," Matthew replied.

"No one seems to be disputing that—impossible though it supposedly is," Baldwin said.

"This is Gerbert's doing." Every instinct told him that the vampire was a crucial link between Benjamin and the search for the Book of Life. He had been manipulating Congregation politics for years, and in all likelihood pulled Knox, Satu, and Domenico into his schemes.

"Perhaps. Not every vampire in London is Hubbard's creature," Baldwin said. "Verin still intends to go to the Congregation on the sixth of December."

"The babies' birth doesn't change anything," Matthew said, though he knew that it did.

"Take care of my sister, Matthew," Baldwin said quietly. Matthew thought he detected a note of real worry in his brother's tone.

"Always," Matthew replied.

The grandmothers were the babies' first visitors. Sarah's grin stretched from ear to ear, and Ysabeau's face was shining with happiness. When we shared the babies' first names, they both were touched at the thought that the legacy of the children's absent grandparents would be carried into the future.

"Leave it to you two to have twins that aren't even born on the same day," Sarah said, swapping Rebecca for Philip, who had been staring at his grandmother with a fascinated frown. "See if you can get her to open her eyes, Ysabeau."

Ysabeau blew gently on Rebecca's face. Her eyes popped wide, and she began to scream, waving her mittened hands at her grandmother. "There. Now we can see you properly, my beauty."

"They're different signs of the zodiac, too," Sarah said, swaying gently with Philip in her arms. Unlike his sister, Philip was content to lie still and quietly observe his surroundings, his dark eyes wide.

"Who are?" I was feeling drowsy, and Sarah's chatter was too complicated for me to follow.

"The babies. Rebecca is a Scorpio, and Philip is a Sagittarius. The serpent and the archer," Sarah replied.

The de Clermonts and the Bishops. The tenth knot and the goddess. The arrow's owl-feather fletches tickled my shoulder, and the firedrake's tail tightened around my aching hips. A premonitory finger drew up my spine, leaving my nerves tingling.

Matthew frowned. "Something wrong, *mon coeur?*"

"No. Just a strange feeling." The urge to protect that had taken root in the aftermath of the babies' birth grew stronger. I didn't want Rebecca and Philip tied to some larger weaving, the design of which could never be understood by someone as small and insignificant as their mother. They were my children—our children—and I would make sure that they were allowed to find their own path, not follow the one that destiny and fate handed them.

"Hello, Father. Are you watching?"

Matthew stared at his computer screen, his phone tucked between his shoulder and his ear. This time Benjamin had called to deliver the message. He wanted to hear Matthew's reactions to what he was seeing on the screen.

"I understand that congratulations are in order." Benjamin's voice was pinched with fatigue. The body of a dead witch lay on an operating table behind him, cut open in a vain attempt to save the child she'd been carrying. "A girl. A boy, too."

"What do you want?" The question was expressed calmly, but Matthew was seething inside. Why could no one find his godforsaken son?

"Your wife and daughter, of course." Benjamin's eyes hardened. "Your witch is fertile. Why is that, Matthew?"

Matthew remained silent.

"I'll find out what makes that witch so special." Benjamin leaned forward and smiled. "You know I will. If you tell me what I want to know now, I won't have to extract it from her later."

"You will never touch her." Matthew's voice—and his control—broke. Upstairs a baby cried.

"Oh, but I will," Benjamin promised softly. "Over and over again, until Diana Bishop gives me what I want."

I couldn't have slept for more than thirty or forty minutes before Rebecca's furious cries woke me. When my bleary eyes focused, I saw that Matthew was walking her in front of the fireplace, murmuring endearments and words of comfort.

"I know. The world can be a harsh place, little one. It will be easier to bear in time. Can you hear the logs crackle? See the lights play on the wall? That's fire, Rebecca. You may have it in your veins, like your mother. Shh. It's just a shadow. Nothing but a shadow." Matthew cuddled the baby closer, crooning a French lullaby.

> *Chut! Plus de bruit,*
> *C'est la ronde de nuit,*
> *En diligence, faisons silence.*
> *Marchons sans bruit,*
> *C'est la ronde de nuit.*

Matthew de Clermont was in love. I smiled at his adoring expression.

"Dr. Sharp said they'd be hungry," I told him from the bed, rubbing the sleep out of my eyes. My lip caught in my teeth. She had also explained that premature babies could be difficult to feed because the muscles they needed in order to suckle hadn't developed sufficiently.

"Shall I get Marthe?" Matthew asked above Rebecca's insistent cries. He knew that I was nervous about breast-feeding.

"Let's try it on our own," I said. Matthew positioned a pillow in my lap and handed me Rebecca. Then he woke Philip, who was sleeping soundly. Both Sarah and Marthe had drummed into me the importance of nursing both children at the same time, or else I would no sooner feed one than the other would be hungry.

"Philip is going to be the troublemaker," Matthew said contentedly, lifting him from the cradle. Philip frowned at his father, his huge eyes blinking.

"How can you tell?" I shifted Rebecca slightly to make room for Philip.

"He's too quiet," Matthew said with a grin.

It took several tries before Philip latched on. Rebecca, however, was impossible.

"She won't stop crying long enough to suck," I said in frustration.

Matthew put his finger in her mouth, and she obediently closed it around the tip. "Let's switch them. Maybe the scent of the colostrum—and her brother—will convince Rebecca to give it a try."

We made the necessary adjustments. Philip screamed like a banshee when Matthew moved him, and he hiccupped and huffed a bit on the other breast just to make sure we understood that such interruptions would not be tolerated in the future. There were a few snuffling moments of indecision while Rebecca rooted around to see what the fuss was about before she cautiously took my breast. After her first suck, her eyes popped wide.

"Ah. Now she understands. Didn't I tell you, little one?" Matthew murmured. *"Maman* is the answer for everything."

Sol in Sagittarius

Sagittarius governs faith, religion, writings, bookes, and the interpretation of dreames. Those born under the signe of the archer shall work great wonders and receive much honour and joye. While Sagittarius rules the heavens, consult with lawyers about thy business. It is a good season for making oaths and striking bargains.

Anonymous English Commonplace Book, c. 1590,
Gonçalves Manuscript 4890, f. 9ᵛ

T he twins are ten days old. Don't you think they're a bit young to be made members of a chivalric order?" I yawned and walked up and down the second-floor hallway with Rebecca, who was resentful of being removed from her cozy fireside cradle.

"All new members of the de Clermont family become knights as soon as possible," Matthew said, passing me with Philip. "It's tradition."

"Yes, but most new de Clermonts are grown women and men! And we have to do this at Sept-Tours?" My thought processes had slowed to a crawl. As he had promised, Matthew took care of the children during the night, but so long as I was breast-feeding, I was still awakened every few hours.

"There or Jerusalem," Matthew said.

"Not Jerusalem. In December? Are you mad?" Ysabeau appeared on the landing, silent as a ghost. "The pilgrims are twelve deep. Besides, the babies should be christened at home, in the church their father built, not in London. Both ceremonies can take place on the same day."

"Clairmont House is our home at the moment, *Maman*." Matthew scowled. He was growing weary of the grandmothers and their constant interference. "And Andrew has volunteered to christen them here, if need be."

Philip, who had already exhibited an uncanny sensitivity to his father's mercurial moods, arranged his features in a perfect imitation of Matthew's frown and waved one arm in the air as if calling for a sword so they could vanquish their enemies together.

"Sept-Tours it is, then," I said. While Andrew Hubbard was no longer a constant thorn in my side, I was not eager for him to take on the role of the children's spiritual adviser.

"If you're sure," Matthew said.

"Will Baldwin be invited?" I knew Matthew had told him about the twins. Baldwin had sent me a lavish bouquet of flowers and two teething rings made of silver and horn for Rebecca and Philip. Teething rings were a common gift for newborns, of course, but in this case I felt sure it was a none-too-subtle reminder of the vampire blood in their veins.

"Probably. But let's not worry about that now. Why don't you take a walk with Ysabeau and Sarah—get out of the house for a little while. There's plenty of milk if the babies get fussy," Matthew suggested.

I did as Matthew suggested, though I had the uncomfortable feeling that the babies and I were being positioned on a vast de Clermont chessboard by creatures who had been playing the game for centuries.

That feeling grew stronger with each passing day as we prepared to go to France. There were too many hushed conversations for my peace of mind. But my hands were full with the twins, and I had no time for family politics at the moment.

"Of course I invited Baldwin," Marcus said. "He has to be there."

"And Gallowglass?" Matthew asked. He had sent his nephew pictures of the twins, along with their full and rather imposing monikers. Matthew had hoped that Gallowglass might respond when he found out that he was Philip's godfather and that the baby bore one of his names, but he had been disappointed.

"Give him time," Marcus said.

But time had not been on Matthew's side lately, and he had no expectation it would cooperate now.

"There's been no further word from Benjamin," Fernando reported. "He's gone silent. Again."

"Where the hell is he?" Matthew drove his fingers through his hair.

"We're doing our best, Matthew. Even as a warmblood, Benjamin was devious to a fault."

"Fine. If we can't locate Benjamin, then let's turn our attention to Knox," Matthew said. "He'll be easier to smoke out than Gerbert—and the two of them are providing information to Benjamin. I'm sure of it. I want proof."

He wouldn't rest until every creature who posed a danger to Diana or the twins was found and destroyed.

"Ready to go?" Marcus chucked Rebecca under the chin, and her mouth made a perfect O of happiness. She adored her older brother.

"Where's Jack?" I said, frazzled. No sooner did I get one child situated than another wandered off. A simple leave-taking had become a logistical nightmare roughly equivalent to sending a battalion off to war.

"Going for a walk with the beast. Speaking of which, where is Corra?" Fernando asked.

"Safely tucked away." In fact, Corra and I were having a difficult time of it. She had been restless and moody since the twins' birth and didn't appreciate getting wedged back into me for a journey to France. I wasn't happy with the arrangement myself. Being in sole possession of my body again was glorious.

A series of loud barks and the sudden appearance of the world's largest floor sweeper heralded Jack's return.

"Come on, Jack. Don't keep us waiting," Marcus called. Jack trotted up to his side, and Marcus held out a set of keys. "Think you can manage to get Sarah, Marthe, and your grandmother to France?"

"Course I can," Jack said, grabbing at the key ring. He hit the buttons on the key fob, and they unlocked another large vehicle, this one outfitted with a dog bed rather than infant seats.

"How exciting to be setting off for home." Ysabeau slipped her arm through Jack's elbow. "I am reminded of the time Philippe asked me to take sixteen wagons from Constantinople to Antioch. The roads were terrible, and there were bandits all along the route. It was a most difficult journey, full of dangers and the threat of death. I had a splendid time."

"As I recall, you lost most of the wagons," Matthew said with a dark look. "The horses, too."

"Not to mention a fair amount of other people's money," Fernando recalled.

"Only ten wagons were lost. The other six arrived in perfect condition. As for the money, it was merely reinvested," Ysabeau said, her voice dripping with hauteur. "Pay no attention, Jack. I will tell you about my adventures as we drive. It will keep your mind off the traffic."

Phoebe and Marcus set out in one of his trademark blue sports cars—this one British and looking as though James Bond should be driving it. I was beginning to appreciate the value of two-seat automobiles and thought longingly of spending the next nine hours with only Matthew for company.

Given the speed at which Marcus and Phoebe traveled and the fact they wouldn't have to stop en route for bathroom breaks, diaper changes, and meals, it was not surprising that the couple was waiting for us when we arrived at Sept-Tours, standing at the top of the torchlit stairs along with Alain and Victoire, welcoming us home.

"Milord Marcus tells me we will have a full house for the ceremonies, Madame Ysabeau," Alain said, greeting his mistress. His wife, Victoire, danced with excitement when she spied the baby carriers and rushed over to lend a hand.

"It will be like the old days, Alain. We will set up cots in the barn for the men. Those who are vampires will not mind the cold, and the rest will get used to it." Ysabeau sounded unconcerned as she handed Marthe her gloves and turned to help with the babies. They were swaddled within an inch of their lives to protect them from the freezing temperatures. "Are not Milord Philip and Milady Rebecca the most beautiful creatures you have ever seen, Victoire?"

Victoire was incapable of more than oohs and aahs, but Ysabeau seemed to find her response sufficient.

"Shall I help with the babies' luggage?" Alain asked, surveying the contents of the overstuffed cargo space.

"That would be wonderful, Alain." Matthew directed him to the bags, totes, portable playpens, and stacks of disposable diapers.

Matthew took a baby carrier in each hand and, with much input from Marthe, Sarah, Ysabeau, and Victoire on the icy state of the stairs, climbed to the front door. Inside, the magnitude of where he was, and why, struck him. Matthew was bringing the latest in a long line of de Clermonts back to their ancestral home. It didn't matter if our family was only a lowly scion of that distinguished lineage. This was, and would always be, a place steeped in tradition for our children.

"Welcome home." I kissed him.

He kissed me back, then gave me one of his dazzling, slow smiles. "Thank you, *mon coeur*."

Returning to Sept-Tours had been the right decision. Hopefully, no mishaps would darken our otherwise pleasant homecoming.

In the days leading up to the christening, it seemed as though my wishes would be granted.

Sept-Tours was so busy with the preparations for the twins' christening that I kept expecting Philippe to burst into the room, singing and telling jokes. But it was Marcus who was the life of the household now, roaming all over the place as if he owned it—which I suppose he technically did—and jollying everybody into a more festive mood. For the first time, I could see why Marcus reminded Fernando of Matthew's father.

When Marcus ordered that all the furniture in the great hall be replaced with long tables and benches capable of seating the expected hordes, I had a dizzying sense of déjà vu as Sept-Tours was transformed back to its medieval self. Only Matthew's rooms remained unchanged. Marcus had declared them off-limits, since the guests of honor were sleeping there. I retreated to Matthew's tower at regular intervals to feed, bathe, and change the babies— and to rest from the constant crush of people employed to clean, sort, and move furniture.

"Thank you, Marthe," I said upon my return from a brisk walk in the garden. She had happily left the crowded kitchen in favor of nanny duty and another of her beloved murder mysteries.

I gave my sleeping son a gentle pat on the back and picked Rebecca up from the cradle. My lips compressed into a thin line at her low weight relative to her brother's.

"She is hungry." Marthe's dark eyes met mine.

"I know." Rebecca was always hungry and never satisfied. My thoughts danced away from the implications. "Matthew said it's too early for concern." I buried my nose in Rebecca's neck and breathed in her sweet baby smell.

"What does Matthew know?" Marthe snorted. "You are her mother."

"He wouldn't like it," I warned.

"Matthew would like it less if she dies," Marthe said bluntly.

Still I hesitated. If I followed Marthe's broad hints without consulting him, Matthew would be furious. But if I asked Matthew for his input, he would tell me that Rebecca was in no immediate danger. That might be true, but she certainly wasn't brimming over with health and wellness. Her frustrated cries broke my heart.

"Is Matthew still hunting?" If I were going to do this, it had to be when Matthew wasn't around to fret.

"So far as I know."

"Shh, it's all right. Mommy's going to fix it," I murmured, sitting down by the fire and undoing my shirt with one hand. I put Rebecca to my right breast, and she latched on immediately, sucking with all her might. Milk dribbled out of the corner of her mouth, and her whimper turned into an outright wail. She had been easier to feed before my milk came in, as though colostrum were more tolerable to her system.

That was when I'd first started to worry.

"Here." Marthe held out a sharp, thin knife.

"I don't need it." I swung Rebecca onto my shoulder and patted her back. She let out a gassy belch, and a stream of white liquid followed.

"She cannot digest the milk properly," Marthe said.

"Let's see how she handles this, then." I rested Rebecca's head on my forearm, flicked my fingertips toward the soft, scarred skin at my left elbow where I'd tempted her father to take my blood, and waited while red, life-giving fluid swelled from the veins.

Rebecca was instantly alert.

"Is this what you want?" I curled my arm, pressing her mouth to my skin. I felt the same sense of suction that I did when she nursed at my breast, except that now the child wasn't fussy—she was ravenous.

Freely flowing venous blood was bound to be noticed in a house full of vampires. Ysabeau was there in moments. Fernando was nearly as quick. Then Matthew appeared like a tornado, his hair disheveled from the wind.

"Everyone. Out." He pointed to the stairs. Without waiting to see if they obeyed him, he dropped to his knees before me. "What are you doing?"

"I'm feeding your daughter." Tears stung my eyes.

Rebecca's contented swallowing was audible in the quiet room.

"Everybody's been wondering for months what the children would be. Well, here's one mystery solved: Rebecca needs blood to thrive." I inserted my pinkie gently between her mouth and my skin to break the suction and slow the flow of blood.

"And Philip?" Matthew asked, his face frozen.

"He seems satisfied with my milk," I said. "Maybe, in time, Rebecca will take to a more varied diet. But for now she needs blood, and she's going to get it."

"There are good reasons we don't turn children into vampires," Matthew said.

"We have not *turned* Rebecca into anything. She came to us this way.

And she's not a vampire. She's a vampitch. Or a wimpire." I wasn't trying to be ridiculous, though the names invited laughter.

"Others will want to know what kind of creature they're dealing with," Matthew said.

"Well, they're going to have to wait," I snapped. "It's too soon to tell, and I won't have people forcing Rebecca into a narrow box for their own convenience."

"And when her teeth come in? What then?" Matthew asked, his voice rising. "Have you forgotten Jack?"

Ah. So it was the blood rage, more than whether they were vampire or witch, that was worrying Matthew. I passed the soundly sleeping Rebecca to him and buttoned my shirt. When I was finished, he had her tucked tightly against his heart, her head cradled between his chin and shoulder. His eyes were closed, as if to block out what he had seen.

"If Rebecca or Philip has blood rage, then we will deal with it—together, as a family," I said, brushing the hair from where it had tumbled over his forehead. "Try not to worry so much."

"Deal with it? How? You can't reason with a two-year-old in a killing rage," Matthew said.

"Then I'll spellbind her." It wasn't something we'd discussed, but I'd do it without hesitation. "Just as I'd spellbind Jack, if that was the only way to protect him."

"You will not do to our children what your parents did to you, Diana. You would never forgive yourself."

The arrow resting along my spine pricked my shoulder, and the tenth knot writhed on my wrist as the cords within me snapped to attention. This time there was no hesitation.

"To save my family, I'll do what I must."

"It's done," Matthew said, putting down his phone.

It was the sixth of December, one year and one day since Philippe had marked Diana with his blood vow. On Isola della Stella, a small island in the Venetian lagoon, a sworn testament of her status as a de Clermont sat on the desk of a Congregation functionary waiting to be entered into the family pedigree.

"So Aunt Verin came through in the end," Marcus said.

"Perhaps she has been in touch with Gallowglass." Fernando hadn't given up hope that Hugh's son would return in time for the christening.

"Baldwin did it." Matthew sat back in his chair and wiped his hands over his face.

Alain appeared with an apology for the interruption, a stack of mail, and a glass of wine. He cast a worried glance at the three vampires huddled around the kitchen fire and left without comment.

Fernando and Marcus looked at each other, their consternation evident.

"Baldwin? But if Baldwin did it . . ." Marcus trailed off.

"He's more worried about Diana's safety than the de Clermonts' reputation," Matthew finished. "The question is, what does he know that we don't?"

The seventh of December was our anniversary, and Sarah and Ysabeau baby-sat the twins to give Matthew and me a few hours on our own. I prepared bottles of milk for Philip, mixed blood and a bit of milk for Rebecca, and brought the pair down to the family library. There Ysabeau and Sarah had constructed a wonderland of blankets, toys, and mobiles to entertain them and were looking forward to the evening with their grandchildren.

When I suggested we would simply have a quiet dinner in Matthew's tower so as to be within calling distance if there was a problem, Ysabeau handed me a set of keys.

"Dinner is waiting for you at Les Revenants," she said.

"Les Revenants?" It was not a place I'd heard of before.

"Philippe built the castle to house Crusaders coming home from the Holy Land," Matthew explained. "It belongs to *Maman.*"

"It's your house now. I'm giving it to you," Ysabeau said. "Happy anniversary."

"You can't give us a house. It's too much, Ysabeau," I protested.

"Les Revenants is better suited to a family than this place is. It is really quite cozy." Ysabeau's expression was touched with wistfulness. "And Philippe and I were happy there."

"Are you sure?" Matthew asked his mother.

"Yes. And you will like it, Diana," Ysabeau said with a lift of her eyebrows. "All the rooms have doors."

"How could anyone describe this as cozy?" I asked when we arrived at the house outside Limousin.

Les Revenants was smaller than Sept-Tours, but not by much. There were only four towers, Matthew pointed out, one on each corner of the square keep. But the moat that surrounded it was large enough to qualify as a lake, and the splendid stable complex and beautiful interior courtyard rather took away from any claims that this was more modest than the official de Clermont residence. Inside, however, there was an intimate feeling to the place, in spite of its large public rooms on the ground floor. Though the castle had been built in the twelfth century, it had been thoroughly renovated and was now fully updated with modern conveniences such as bathrooms, electricity, and even heat in some of the rooms. Despite all that, I was just winding myself up to reject the gift and any idea that we would ever live here when my clever husband showed me the library.

The Gothic Revival room with its beamed ceiling, carved woodwork, large fireplace, and decorative heraldic shields was tucked into the southwest corner of the main building. A large bank of windows overlooked the inner courtyard while another, smaller window framed the Limousin countryside. Bookcases lined the only two straight walls, rising to the ceiling. A curved walnut staircase led up to a gallery that gave access to the higher shelves. It reminded me a bit of Duke Humfrey's Reading Room, with its dark woodwork and hushed lighting.

"What is all this stuff?" The walnut shelves were filled with boxes and books arranged higgledy-piggledy.

"Philippe's personal papers," Matthew said. "*Maman* moved them here after the war. Anything having to do with official de Clermont family business or the Knights of Lazarus is still at Sept-Tours, of course."

This had to be the most extensive personal archive in the world. I sat with a thunk, suddenly sympathetic to Phoebe's plight among all the family's artistic treasures, and I covered my mouth with my hand.

"I suppose you'll want to sort through them, Dr. Bishop," Matthew said, planting a kiss on my head.

"Of course I do! They could tell us about the Book of Life and the early days of the Congregation. There may be letters here that refer to Benjamin and to the witch's child in Jerusalem." My mind reeled with the possibilities.

Matthew looked doubtful. "I think you're more likely to find Philippe's designs for siege engines and instructions about the care and feeding of horses than anything about Benjamin."

Every historical instinct told me that Matthew was grossly underestimating the significance of what was here. Two hours after he'd shown me into the room, I was still there, poking among the boxes while Matthew drank wine and humored me by translating texts when they were in ciphers or a language I didn't know. Poor Alain and Victoire ended up serving the romantic anniversary dinner they'd prepared for us on the library table rather than down in the dining room.

We moved into Les Revenants the next morning, along with the children, and with no further complaints from me about its size, heating bills, or the number of stairs I would be required to climb to take a bath. The last worry was moot in any event, since Philippe had installed a screw-drive elevator in the tall tower after a visit to Russia in 1811. Happily, the elevator had been electrified in 1896 and no longer required the strength of a vampire to turn the crank.

Only Marthe accompanied us to Les Revenants, though Alain and Victoire would have preferred to join us in Limousin and leave Marcus's house party in other, younger, hands. Marthe cooked and helped Matthew and me get used to the logistical demands of caring for two infants. As Sept-Tours filled up with knights, Fernando and Sarah would join us here— Jack, too, if he found the crush of strangers overwhelming—but for now we were on our own.

Though we rattled around Les Revenants, it gave us a chance to finally be a family. Rebecca was putting on weight now that we knew how to nourish her tiny body properly. And Philip weathered every change of routine and location with his usual thoughtful expression, staring at the light moving against the stone walls or listening with quiet contentment to the sound of me shuffling papers in the library.

Marthe watched over the children whenever we asked her to, giving Matthew and me a chance to reconnect after our weeks of separation and the stresses and joys of the twins' birth. During those precious moments on our own, we walked hand in hand along the moat and talked about our plans for the house, including where I would plant my witch's garden to take best advantage of the sunshine and the perfect spot for Matthew to build the twins a tree house.

No matter how wonderful it was to be alone, however, we spent every moment we could with the new lives we had created. We sat before the fire in our bedroom and watched Rebecca and Philip inch and squirm closer, staring at each other with rapt expressions as their hands clasped. The two were always happiest when they were touching, as though the months they'd spent together in my womb had accustomed them to constant contact. They would soon be too large to do so, but for now we put them to sleep in the same cradle. No matter how we arranged them, they always ended up with their tiny arms wrapped tightly around each other and their faces pressed together.

Every day Matthew and I worked in the library, looking for clues about Benjamin's present whereabouts, the mysterious witch in Jerusalem and her equally mysterious child, and the Book of Life. Philip and Rebecca were soon familiar with the smell of paper and parchment. Their heads turned to follow the sound of Matthew's voice reading aloud from documents written in Greek, Latin, Occitan, Old French, ancient German dialects, Old English, and Philippe's unique patois.

Philippe's linguistic idiosyncrasy was echoed in whatever organizational scheme he had used for storing his personal files and books. Concerted efforts to locate Crusade-era documents, for example, yielded a remarkable letter from Bishop Adhémar justifying the spiritual motives for the First Crusade, bizarrely accompanied by a 1930s shopping list that enumerated the items Philippe wanted Alain to send from Paris: new shoes from Berluti, a copy of *La Cuisine en Dix Minutes,* and the third volume of *The Science of Life* by H. G. Wells, Julian Huxley, and G. P. Wells.

Our time together as a family felt miraculous. There were opportunities for laughter and song, for marveling in the tiny perfection of our children, for confessing how anxious we had both been about the pregnancy and its possible complications.

Though our feelings for each other had never faltered, we reaffirmed them in those quiet, perfect days at Les Revenants even as we braced for the challenges the next weeks would bring.

* * *

"These are the knights who have agreed to attend." Marcus handed Matthew the guest list. His father's eyes raced down the page.

"Giles. Russell. Excellent." Matthew flipped the page over. "Addie. Verin. Miriam." He looked up. "Whenever did you make Chris a knight?"

"While we were in New Orleans. It seemed right," Marcus said a touch sheepishly.

"Well done, Marcus. Given who will be in attendance at the children's christening, I wouldn't imagine anyone from the Congregation would dare to cause trouble," Fernando said with a smile. "I think you can relax, Matthew. Diana should be able to enjoy the day as you'd hoped."

Matthew didn't feel relaxed, however.

"I wish we'd found Knox." Matthew gazed out the kitchen window at the snow. Like Benjamin, Knox had disappeared without a trace. What this suggested was too terrifying to put into words.

"Shall I question Gerbert?" Fernando asked. They had discussed the possible repercussions if they acted in a way to suggest that Gerbert was a traitor. It could bring the vampires in the southern half of France into open conflict for the first time in more than a millennium.

"Not yet," Matthew said, reluctant to add to their troubles. "I'll keep looking through Philippe's papers. There must be some clue there as to where Benjamin is hiding."

"Jesus, Mary, and Joseph. There cannot be anything more we need to pack for a thirty-minute drive to my mother's house." For the past week, Matthew had been making sacrilegious references to the Holy Family and their December journeys, but it was all the more striking today, when the twins were to be christened. Something was bothering him, but he refused to tell me what it was.

"I want to be sure Philip and Rebecca are completely comfortable, given the number of strangers they'll be meeting," I said, bouncing Philip up and down in an attempt to get him to burp now rather than spit up halfway through the trip.

"Maybe the cradle can stay?" Matthew said hopefully.

"We have plenty of room to take it with us, and they're going to need at least one nap. Besides, I've been reliably informed that this is the largest motorized vehicle in Limousin, with the exception of Claude Raynard's hay wagon." The local populace had bestowed upon Matthew the nickname Gaston Lagaffe after the lovably inept comic book character, and had gently teased him about his *grande guimbarde* ever since he ran to the store for bread and got the Range Rover wedged between a tiny Citroën and an even more minuscule Renault.

Matthew slammed the rear hatch shut without comment.

"Stop glowering, Matthew," Sarah said, joining us in front of the house. "Your children are going to grow up thinking you're a bear."

"Don't you look beautiful," I commented. Sarah was dressed to the nines in a deep green tailored suit and a luscious cream silk blouse that set off her red hair. She looked both glamorous and festive.

"Agatha made it for me. She knows her stuff," Sarah said, turning around so we could admire her further. "Oh, before I forget: Ysabeau called. Matthew should ignore all the cars parked along the drive and come straight up to the door. They've saved a place for you in the courtyard."

"Cars? Parked along the drive?" I looked at Matthew in shock.

"Marcus thought it might be a good idea to have some of the knights present," he said smoothly.

"Why?" My stomach somersaulted as my instincts warned me that all was not as it seemed.

"In case the Congregation decides to take exception to the event," Matthew said. His eyes met mine, cool and tranquil as a summer sea.

In spite of Ysabeau's warning, nothing could possibly have prepared me for the enthusiastic welcome we received. Marcus had transformed Sept-Tours into Camelot, with flags and banners twisting in the stiff December breeze, their bright colors standing out against both the snow and the dark local basalt. Atop the square keep, the de Clermont family's black-and-silver standard with the ouroboros on it had been topped by a large square flag bearing the great seal of the Knights of Lazarus. The two pieces of silk flapped on the same pole, extending the height of the already tall tower by nearly thirty feet.

"Well, if the Congregation didn't know something was happening before, they do now," I said, looking at the spectacle.

"There didn't seem much point in trying to be inconspicuous," Matthew said. "We shall start as we intend to go on. And that means we aren't going to hide the children from the truth—or the rest of the world."

I nodded and took his hand in mine.

When Matthew pulled in to the courtyard, it was filled with well-wishers. He carefully navigated the car among the throngs, occasionally stopping by an old friend who wanted to shake his hand and congratulate us on our good fortune. He slammed on the brakes hard, however, when he saw Chris Roberts standing with a large grin on his face and a silver tankard in his hand.

"Hey!" Chris banged on the window with the tankard. "I want to see my goddaughter. Now."

"Hello, Chris! I didn't realize you were coming," Sarah said, lowering the window and giving him a kiss.

"I'm a knight. I have to be here." Chris's grin grew.

"So I've been told," Sarah said. There had been other warmblooded members before Chris—Walter Raleigh and Henry Percy to name just two—but I had never thought to count my best friend among them.

"Yep. I'm going to make my students call me *Sir* Christopher next semester," Chris said.

"Better that than *St.* Christopher," said a piercing soprano voice. Miriam grinned, her hands on her hips. The pose showed off the T-shirt she was wearing under a demure navy blazer. It, too, was navy and had SCIENCE: RUINING EVERYTHING SINCE 1543 spelled out across the chest along with a unicorn, an Aristotelian depiction of the heavens, and the outline of God and Adam from Michelangelo's Sistine Chapel. A red bar sinister obliterated each image.

"Hello, Miriam!" I waved.

"Park the car so we can see the sprogs," she demanded.

Matthew obliged, but when a crowd started to form, he said that the babies needed to be out of the cold and beat a hasty retreat into the kitchen, armed with a diaper bag and using Philip as a shield.

"How many people are here?" I asked Fernando. We had passed dozens of parked cars.

"At least a hundred," he replied. "I haven't stopped to count."

Based on the feverish preparations in the kitchen, there were more than a few warmbloods in attendance. I saw a stuffed goose go into the oven and a pig come out of it, ready to be basted with wine and herbs. My mouth watered at the aromas.

Shortly before eleven in the morning, the church bells in Saint-Lucien pealed. By that time Sarah and I had changed the twins into matching white gowns made of silk and lace and little caps sewn by Marthe and Victoire. They looked every inch sixteenth-century babies. We bundled them into blankets and made our way downstairs.

It was then that the ceremonies took an unexpected turn. Sarah climbed into one of the family's ATVs with Ysabeau, and Marcus directed us to the Range Rover. Once we were strapped in, Marcus drove us not to the church but to the goddess's temple on the mountain.

My eyes filled at the sight of the well-wishers gathered beneath the oak and cypress. Only some of the faces were familiar to me, but Matthew recognized far more. I spotted Sophie and Margaret, with Nathaniel by their side. Agatha Wilson was there, too, looking at me vaguely as though she recognized but wasn't able to place me. Amira and Hamish stood together, both looking slightly overwhelmed by all the ceremony. But it was the dozens of unfamiliar vampires present who surprised me most. Their stares were cold and curious, but not malicious.

"What is this about?" I asked Matthew when he opened my door.

"I thought we should divide the ceremony into two parts: a pagan naming ceremony here, and a Christian baptism at the church," he explained. "That way Emily could be a part of the babies' day."

Matthew's thoughtfulness—and his efforts to remember Em—rendered me temporarily mute. I knew he was always hatching plans and conducting business while I slept. I hadn't imagined his nocturnal work included overseeing the arrangements for the christening.

"Is it all right, *mon coeur*?" he asked, anxious at my silence. "I wanted it to be a surprise."

"It's perfect," I said when I was able. "And it will mean so much to Sarah."

The guests formed a circle around the ancient altar dedicated to the goddess. Sarah, Matthew, and I took our places within it. My aunt had anticipated that I wouldn't remember a single word of any baby-naming ritual that I had ever witnessed or taken part in, and she was prepared to officiate. The ceremony was a simple but important moment in a young witch's life, since it was a formal welcome into the community. But there was more to it than that, as Sarah knew.

"Welcome, friends and family of Diana and Matthew," Sarah began, her cheeks pink with cold and excitement. "We are gathered here today to bestow upon their children the names that they will take with them as they go into the world. Among witches to call something by name is to recognize its power. By naming these children, we honor the goddess who entrusted them to our care and express gratitude for the gifts she has given them."

Matthew and I had used a formula to come up with the babies' names—and I had vetoed the vampire tradition of five first names in favor of an elemental foursome. With a hyphenated last name, that seemed ample. Each of the babies' first names came from a grandparent. Their second name honored a de Clermont tradition of bestowing the names of archangels on Matthew and members of his family. We took their third name from yet another grandparent. For the fourth and final name, we selected someone who had been important to their conception and birth.

No one knew the babies' full names until now—except for Matthew, Sarah, and me.

Sarah directed Matthew to hold Rebecca up so that her face was turned to the sky.

"Rebecca Arielle Emily Marthe," Sarah said, her voice ringing through the clearing, "we welcome you into the world and into our hearts. Go forth with the knowledge that all here will recognize you by this honorable name and hold your life sacred."

Rebecca Arielle Emily Marthe, the trees and the wind whispered back. I was not the only one to hear it. Amira's eyes widened, and Margaret Wilson cooed and waved her arms in joy.

Matthew lowered Rebecca, his expression full of love as he looked down on the daughter who resembled him so much. Rebecca reached up and touched his nose with her delicate finger in return, a gesture of connection that filled my heart to bursting.

When it was my turn, I lifted Philip to the sky, offering him to the goddess and the elements of fire, air, earth, and water.

"Philip Michael Addison Sorley," Sarah said, "we also welcome you into the world and into our hearts. Go forth knowing that all present will recognize you by this honorable name and hold your life sacred."

The vampires exchanged glances when they heard Philip's last given name and searched the crowd for Gallowglass. We had chosen Addison because it was my father's middle name, but Sorley belonged to the absent Gael. I wished he had been able to hear it echo through the trees.

"May Rebecca and Philip bear their names proudly, grow into their promise in the fullness of time, and trust that they will be cherished and protected by all those who have borne witness to the love their parents have for them. Blessed be," Sarah said, her eyes shining with unshed tears.

It was impossible to find a dry eye in the clearing or to know who was the most moved by the ceremony. Even my normally vocal daughter was awed by the occasion and sucked pensively on her lower lip.

From the clearing we decamped to the church. The vampires walked, beating everybody down the hill. The rest of us used a combination of ATVs and cars with four-wheel drive, which led to much self-congratulation on Matthew's part as to the wisdom of his automotive preferences.

At the church the crowd of witnesses swelled to include people from the village, and, as on the day of our marriage, the priest was waiting for us at the door with the godparents.

"Does every Catholic religious ceremony take place in the open air?" I asked, tucking Philip's blanket more firmly around him.

"A fair few of them," Fernando replied. "It never made any sense to me, but I am an infidel, after all."

"Shh," Marcus warned, eyeing the priest with concern. "Père Antoine is admirably ecumenical and agreed to pass lightly over the usual exorcisms, but let's not push him. Now, does anyone know the words of the ceremony?"

"I do," Jack said.

"Me, too," Miriam said.

"Good. Jack will take Philip, and Miriam will hold Rebecca. You two can do the talking. The rest of us will look attentive and nod when it seems appropriate," Marcus said, his bonhomie unwavering. He gave the priest a thumbs-up. *"Nous sommes prêts, Père Antoine!"*

Matthew took my arm and steered me inside.

"Are they going to be okay?" I whispered. The godparents included only one lonely Catholic, accompanied by a converso, a Baptist, two Presbyterians, one Anglican, three witches, a daemon, and three vampires of uncertain religious persuasion.

"This is a house of prayer, and I beseeched God to watch over them," Matthew murmured as we took our places near the altar. "Hopefully, He is listening."

But neither we—nor God—needed to worry. Jack and Miriam answered all the priest's questions about their faith and the state of the children's souls in perfect Latin. Philip chortled when the priest blew on his face to expel any evil spirits and objected strenuously when salt was put in his tiny mouth. Rebecca seemed more interested in Miriam's long curls, one of which was clenched in her fist.

As for the rest of the godparents, they were a formidable group. Fernando, Marcus, Chris, Marthe, and Sarah (in place of Vivian Harrison, who could not be there) served with Miriam as godparents for Rebecca. Jack, along with Hamish, Phoebe, Sophie, Amira, and Ysabeau (who stood up for her absent grandson Gallowglass) promised to guide and care for Philip. Even for a nonbeliever such as myself, the ancient words spoken by the priest made me feel that these children were going to be looked after and cared for, no matter what might happen.

The ceremony drew to a close, and Matthew visibly relaxed. Père Antoine asked Matthew and me to come forward and take Rebecca and Philip from their godparents. When we faced the congregation for the first time, there was one spontaneous cheer, then another.

"And there's an end to the covenant!" an unfamiliar vampire said in a loud voice. "About bloody time, too."

"Hear, hear, Russell," several murmured in reply.

The bells rang out overhead. My smile turned to laughter as we were caught up in the happiness of the moment.

As usual, that was when everything started to go wrong.

The south door opened, letting in a gust of cold air. A man stood silhouetted against the light. I squinted, trying to make out his features. Throughout the church, vampires seemed to vanish only to reappear in the nave, barring the new arrival from coming any farther inside.

I drew closer to Matthew, holding Rebecca tight. The bells fell silent, though the air still reverberated with their final echoes.

"Congratulations, sister." Baldwin's deep voice filled the space. "I've come to welcome your children into the de Clermont family."

Matthew drew himself up to his full height. Without a backward look, he handed Philip to Jack and marched down the aisle to his brother.

"Our children are not de Clermonts," Matthew said coldly. He reached into his jacket and thrust a folded document at Baldwin. "They belong to me."

33

The creatures gathered for the christening let out a collective gasp. Ysabeau signaled to Père Antoine, who quickly shepherded the villagers from the church. Then she and Fernando took up watchful positions on either side of Jack and me.

"Surely you don't expect me to acknowledge a corrupt, diseased branch of this family and give it my blessing and respect?" Baldwin crumpled the document in his fist.

Jack's eyes blackened at the insult.

"Matthew entrusted Philip to you. You are responsible for your godson," Ysabeau reminded Jack. "Do not let Baldwin's words provoke you to ignore your sire's wishes."

Jack drew a deep, shaky breath and nodded. Philip cooed for Jack's attention, and when he received it, he rewarded his godfather with a frown of concern. When Jack looked up again, his eyes were green and brown once again.

"This hardly seems like friendly behavior to me, Uncle Baldwin," Marcus said calmly. "Let's wait and discuss family business after the feast."

"No, Marcus. We'll discuss it now and get it over with," Matthew said, countermanding his son.

In another time and place, Henry VIII's courtiers had delivered the news of his fifth wife's infidelity in church so that the king would think twice before killing the messenger. Matthew apparently believed it might keep Baldwin from killing him, too.

When Matthew suddenly appeared behind his brother, having only a moment before been in front, I realized that his decision to remain here was actually intended to protect Baldwin. Matthew, like Henry, would not shed blood on holy ground.

That did not mean, however, that Matthew was going to be entirely merciful. He had his brother in an unbreakable hold, with one long arm wrapped around Baldwin's neck so that Matthew was grasping his own bicep. His right hand drove into Baldwin's shoulder blade with enough force to snap it in two, his expression devoid of emotion and his eyes balanced evenly between gray and black.

"And that is why you never let Matthew Clairmont come up behind you," one vampire murmured to another.

"Soon it will hurt like hell, too," his friend replied. "Unless Baldwin blacks out first."

Wordlessly I passed Rebecca to Miriam. My hands were itching with power, and I hid them in the pockets of my coat. The arrow's silver shaft felt heavy against my spine, and Corra was on high alert, her wings ready to spring open. After New Haven my familiar didn't trust Baldwin any more than I did.

Baldwin almost succeeded in overcoming Matthew—or at least I thought he had. Before I could cry out in warning, it became evident that Baldwin's seeming advantage was only a clever trick by Matthew to lull him into changing his position. When he did, Matthew used Baldwin's own weight and a quick, bone-cracking kick to his brother's leg to drop him to his knees. Baldwin let out a strangled grunt.

It was a vivid reminder that though Baldwin might be the bigger man, Matthew was the killer.

"Now, *sieur*." Matthew's arm lifted slightly so that his brother hung by his chin, putting more pressure on his neck. "It would please me if you would reconsider my respectful request to establish a de Clermont scion."

"Never," Baldwin gurgled out. His lips were turning blue from lack of oxygen.

"My wife tells me that the word 'never' is not to be used where the Bishop-Clairmonts are concerned." Matthew's arm tightened, and Baldwin's eyes began to roll back into his head. "I'm not going to let you pass out, by the way, nor am I going to kill you. If you're unconscious or dead, you can't agree to my request. So if you're determined to keep saying no, you can look forward to many hours of this."

"Let. Me. Go." Baldwin struggled to get each word out. Deliberately Matthew let him take a short, gasping breath. It was enough to keep the vampire going but not to permit him to recover.

"Let *me* go, Baldwin. After all these years, I want to be something more than the de Clermont family's black sheep," Matthew murmured.

"No," Baldwin said thickly.

Matthew adjusted his arm so that his brother could get out more than a word or two at a time, though this still didn't remove the bluish cast from his lips. Matthew took the wise precaution of driving the heel of his shoe into his brother's ankle in case Baldwin planned on using the extra oxygen to fight back. Baldwin howled.

"Take Rebecca and Philip back to Sept-Tours," I told Miriam, pushing up my sleeves. I didn't want them to see their father like this. Nor did I want them to see their mother use magic against a member of their family. The wind picked up around my feet, swirling the dust in the church into miniature tornadoes. The flames in the candelabrum danced, ready to do my bidding, and the water in the baptismal font began to bubble.

"Release me and mine, Baldwin," Matthew said. "You don't want us anyway."

"Might . . . need . . . you. My . . . killer . . . after . . . all," Baldwin replied.

The church erupted into shocked exclamations and whispered exchanges as this de Clermont secret was openly mentioned, though I was sure that some present knew the role Matthew had played in the family.

"Do your own dirty work for a change," Matthew said. "God knows you're as capable of murder as I am."

"You. Different. Twins. Have blood rage. Too?" Baldwin bit out.

The assembled guests fell silent.

"Blood rage?" A vampire's voice cut through the quiet, his Irish accent slight but noticeable. "What is he talking about, Matthew?"

The vampires in the church traded worried glances as the murmur of conversation resumed. Blood rage was clearly more than they had bargained for when they'd accepted Marcus's invitation. Fighting the Congregation and protecting vampire-witch children was one thing. A disease that might transform you into a bloodthirsty monster was quite another.

"Baldwin told you true, Giles. My blood is tainted," Matthew said. His eyes locked with mine, the pupils slightly enlarged. *Leave while you can,* they silently urged.

But this time Matthew would not be alone. I pushed my way past Ysabeau and Fernando and headed for my husband's side.

"That means Marcus . . ." Giles trailed off. His eyes narrowed. "We cannot allow the Knights of Lazarus to be led by someone with blood rage. It is impossible."

"Don't be such a bloody lobcock," the vampire next to Giles said in a crisp British accent. "Matthew's already been grand master, and we were none the wiser. In fact, if memory serves, Matthew was an uncommonly good commander of the brotherhood in more than one tricky situation. I believe that Marcus, though a rebel and a traitor, shows promise as well." The vampire smiled, but his nod toward Marcus was respectful.

"Thank you, Russell," Marcus said. "Coming from you, that's a compliment."

"Terribly sorry about the brotherhood slip, Miriam," Russell said with a wink. "And I'm no physician, but I do believe that Matthew is about to render Baldwin unconscious."

Matthew adjusted his arm slightly, and Baldwin's eyeballs returned to their normal position.

"My father's blood rage is under control. There's no reason for us to act out of fear and superstition," Marcus said, addressing everyone in the church. "The Knights of Lazarus were founded to protect the vulnerable. Every member of the order swore an oath to defend his or her fellow knights to the death. I needn't remind anyone here that Matthew is a knight. From this moment, so, too, are his children."

The need for an infant investiture for Rebecca and Philip made sense now.

"So what do you say, Uncle?" Marcus strode down the aisle to stand before Baldwin and Matthew. "Are you still a knight, or have you become a coward in your old age?"

Baldwin turned purple—and not from lack of oxygen.

"Careful, Marcus," Matthew warned. "I will have to let him go eventually."

"Knight." Baldwin looked at Marcus with loathing.

"Then start behaving like one and treat my father with the respect he's earned." Marcus looked around the church. "Matthew and Diana want to establish a scion, and the Knights of Lazarus will support them when they do. Anybody who disagrees is welcome to formally challenge my leadership. Otherwise the matter is not up for discussion."

The church was absolutely silent.

Matthew's lips lifted into a smile. "Thank you."

"Don't thank me yet," Marcus said. "We've still got the Congregation to contend with."

"An unpleasant task, to be sure, but not an unmanageable one," Russell said drily. "Let Baldwin go, Matthew. Your brother has never been very fast, and Oliver is at your left elbow. He's been longing to teach Baldwin a lesson ever since your brother broke his daughter's heart."

Several of the guests chuckled and the winds of opinion began to blow in our favor.

Slowly Matthew did as Russell suggested. He made no attempt to get away from his brother or to shield me. Baldwin remained on his knees for a few moments, then climbed to his feet. As soon as he did, Matthew knelt before him.

"I place my trust in you, *sieur*," Matthew said, bowing his head. "I ask for your trust in return. Neither I nor mine will dishonor the de Clermont family."

"You know I cannot, Matthew," Baldwin said. "A vampire with blood rage is never in control, not absolutely." His eyes flickered to Jack, but it was Benjamin he was thinking of—and Matthew.

"And if a vampire could be?" I demanded.

"Diana, this is no time for wishful thinking. I know that you and Matthew have been hoping for a cure, but—"

"If I gave you my word, as Philippe's blood-sworn daughter, that any of Matthew's kin with blood rage can be brought under control, would you recognize him as the head of his family?" I was inches away from Baldwin, and my power was humming. My suspicion that my disguising spell had burned away was borne out by the curious looks I received.

"You can't promise that," Baldwin said.

"Diana, don't—" Matthew began, but I cut him off with a look.

"I can and I do. We don't have to wait for science to come up with a solution when a magical one already exists. If any member of Matthew's family acts on their blood rage, I will spellbind them," I said. "Agreed?"

Matthew stared at me in shock. And with good reason. This time last year I was still clinging to the belief that science was superior to magic.

"No," Baldwin said with a shake of his head. "Your word is not good enough. You would have to prove it. Then we would all have to wait and see if your magic is as good as you think it is, witch."

"Very well," I said promptly. "Our probation starts now."

Baldwin's eyes narrowed. Matthew looked up at his brother.

"Queen checks king," Matthew said softly.

"Don't get ahead of yourself, brother." Baldwin hoisted Matthew to his feet. "Our game is far from over."

"It was left in Père Antoine's office," Fernando said hours after the last revelers had gone to their beds. "No one saw who brought it."

Matthew looked down at the preserved stillborn fetus. A girl.

"He's even more insane than I thought." Baldwin looked pale, and not just because of what had happened in the church.

Matthew read the note again.

"*Congratulations on your children's birth,*" it said. "*I wanted you to have my daughter, since I will soon possess yours.*" The note was signed simply "*Your son.*"

"Someone is reporting your every move to Benjamin," Baldwin said.

"The question is who." Fernando put his hand on Matthew's arm. "We won't let him take Rebecca—or Diana."

The prospect was so chilling that Matthew could only nod.

In spite of Fernando's assurances, Matthew would not know another moment's peace until Benjamin was dead.

After the drama of the christening, the rest of the winter holiday was a quiet family affair. Our guests departed, except for the extended Wilson family, who remained at Sept-Tours to enjoy what Agatha Wilson described as "very merry mayhem." Chris and Miriam returned to Yale, still committed to reaching a better understanding of blood rage and its possible treatment. Baldwin took off for Venice at the earliest opportunity to try to manage the Congregation's response to any news trickling in from France.

Matthew flung himself into Christmas preparations, determined to banish any lingering sourness after the christening. He went off into the woods on the other side of the moat and came back with a tall fir tree for the great hall, which he draped with tiny white lights that shone like fireflies.

Remembering Philippe and his decorations for Yule, we cut moons and stars out of silver and gold paper. With the combination of a flying spell and a binding charm, I swirled them into the air and let them settle onto the branches, where they winked and sparkled in the firelight.

Matthew went to Saint-Lucien for mass on Christmas Eve. He and Jack were the only vampires in attendance, which pleased Père Antoine. After the christening he was understandably reluctant to have too many creatures in his pews.

The children were fed and sleeping soundly when Matthew returned, stomping the snow from his shoes. I was sitting by the fire in the great hall with a bottle of Matthew's favorite wine and two glasses. Marcus had assured me that a single glass every now and again wouldn't affect the babies, provided I waited a couple of hours before I nursed.

"Peace, perfect peace," Matthew said, cocking his head for signs that the babies were stirring.

"Silent night, holy night," I agreed with a grin, leaning over to switch off the baby monitor. Like blood-pressure cuffs and power tools, such equipment was optional in a vampire household.

While I fiddled with the controls, Matthew tackled me. Weeks of separation and standing up to Baldwin had brought out his playful side.

"Your nose is freezing," I said, giggling as he drew its tip along the warm skin of my neck. I gasped. "Your hands, too."

"Why do you think I took a warmblood for a wife?" Matthew's icy fingers rummaged around underneath my sweater.

"Wouldn't a hot-water bottle have been less trouble?" I teased. His fingers found what they sought, and I arched into his touch.

"Perhaps." Matthew kissed me. "But not nearly so much fun."

The wine forgotten, we marked the hours until midnight in heartbeats rather than minutes. When the bells of the nearby churches in Dournazac and Châlus rang to celebrate the birth of a child in long-ago and faraway Bethlehem, Matthew paused to listen to the solemn yet still-exuberant sound.

"What are you thinking?" I asked as the bells died away.

"I was remembering how the village celebrated Saturnalia when I was a child. There were not many Christians, apart from my parents and a few other families. On the last day of the festival—the twenty-third of

December—Philippe went to every house, pagan and Christian, and asked the children what they wished for the New Year." Matthew's smile was wistful. "When we woke up the next morning, we discovered that our wishes had been granted."

"That sounds like your father," I observed. "What did you wish for?"

"More food, usually," Matthew said with a laugh. "My mother said the only way to account for the amount I ate was hollow legs. Once I asked for a sword. Every boy in the village idolized Hugh and Baldwin. We all wanted to be like them. As I recall, the sword I received was made of wood and broke the first time I swung it."

"And now?" I whispered, kissing his eyes, his cheeks, his mouth.

"Now I want nothing more than to grow old with you," Matthew said.

The family came to us on Christmas Day, saving us from having to bundle up Rebecca and Philip yet again. From the changes to their routine, the twins were aware that this was no ordinary day. They demanded to be part of things, and I finally took them to the kitchen with me to keep them quiet. There I constructed a magical mobile out of flying fruit to occupy them while I helped Marthe put the finishing touches on a meal that would make both vampires and warmbloods happy.

Matthew was a nuisance, too, picking at the dish of nuts I'd whipped up from Em's recipe. At this point if any of them lasted till dinner, it was going to be a Christmas miracle.

"Just one more," he wheedled, sliding his hands around my waist.

"You've eaten half a pound of them already. Leave some for Marcus and Jack." I wasn't sure if vampires got sugar highs, but I wasn't eager to find out. "Still liking your Christmas present?"

I'd been trying to figure out what to get the man who had everything ever since the children were born, but when Matthew told me his wish was to grow old with me, I knew exactly what to do for his present.

"I love it." He touched his temples, where a few silver strands showed in the black.

"You always said I was going to give you gray hairs." I grinned.

"And I thought it was impossible. That was before I learned that *impossible n'est pas Diana*," he said, paraphrasing Ysabeau. Matthew grabbed a handful of nuts and went to the babies before I could react. "Hello, beauty."

Rebecca cooed in response. She and Philip shared a complex vocabulary of coos, grunts, and other soft sounds that Matthew and I were trying to master.

"That's definitely one of her happy noises," I said, putting a pan of cookies in the oven. Rebecca adored her father, especially when he sang. Philip was less sure that singing was a good idea.

"And are you happy, too, little man?" Matthew picked Philip up from his bouncy seat, narrowly missing the flying banana I'd tossed into the mobile at the last minute. It was like a bright yellow comet, streaking through the other orbiting fruit. "What a lucky boy you are to have a mother who will make magic for you."

Philip, like most babies his age, was all eyes as he watched the orange and the lime circle the grapefruit I'd suspended in midair.

"He won't always think that having a witch for a mommy is so wonderful." I went to the fridge and searched for the vegetables I needed for the gratin. When I closed the door, I discovered Matthew waiting for me behind it. I jumped in surprise.

"You have to start making a noise or giving me some other clue to warn me that you're moving," I complained, pressing my hand against my hammering heart.

Matthew's compressed lips told me that he was annoyed.

"Do you see that woman, Philip?" He pointed to me, and Philip directed his wiggling head my way. "She is a brilliant scholar and a powerful witch, though she doesn't like to admit it. And you have the great good fortune to call her *Maman*. That means you are one of the few creatures who will ever learn this family's most cherished secret." Matthew drew Philip close to him and murmured something in his ear.

When Matthew finished and drew away, Philip looked up at his father— and smiled. This was the first time either of the babies had done so, but I had seen this particular expression of happiness before. It was slow and genuine and lit his entire face from within.

Philip might have my hair, but he had Matthew's smile.

"Exactly right." Matthew nodded at his son with approval and returned Philip to his bouncy chair. Rebecca looked at Matthew with a frown, slightly irritated at having been left out of the boys' discussion. Matthew obligingly whispered in her ear as well, then blew a raspberry on her belly.

Rebecca's eyes and mouth were round, as though her father's words had impressed her—though I suspected that the raspberry might have something to do with it, too.

"What nonsense have you told them?" I asked, attacking a potato with a peeler. Matthew removed the two from my fingers.

"It wasn't nonsense," he said calmly. Three seconds later the potato was entirely without skin. He took another from the bowl.

"Tell me."

"Come closer," he said, beckoning to me with the peeler. I took a few steps in his direction. He beckoned again. "Closer."

When I was standing right next to him, Matthew bent his face toward mine.

"The secret is that I may be the head of the Bishop-Clairmont family, but you are its heart," he whispered. "And the three of us are in perfect agreement: The heart is more important."

Matthew had already passed over the box containing letters between Philippe and Godfrey several times.

It was only out of desperation that he riffled through the pages.

"My most reverend sire and father," Godfrey's letter began.

> *The most dangerous among The Sixteen have been executed*
> *in Paris, as you ordered. As Matthew was unavailable for the*
> *job, Mayenne was happy to oblige, and thanks you for your*
> *assistance with the matter of the Gonzaga family. Now that he*
> *feels secure, the duke has decided to play both sides, negotiating*
> *with Henri of Navarre and Philip of Spain at the same time.*
> *But cleverness is not wisdom, as you are wont to say.*

So far the letter contained nothing more than references to Philippe's political machinations.

"As for the other matter," Godfrey continued,

> *I have found Benjamin Ben-Gabriel as the Jews call him, or*
> *Benjamin Fuchs as the emperor knows him, or Benjamin the*
> *Blessed as he prefers. He is in the east as you feared, moving*

between the emperor's court, the Báthory, the Drăculeşti, and His Imperial Majesty in Constantinople. There are worrying tales of Benjamin's relationship with Countess Erzsébet, which, if circulated more widely, will result in Congregation inquiries detrimental to the family and those we hold dear.

Matthew's term on the Congregation is near an end, as he will have served his half century. If you will not involve him in business that so directly concerns him and his bloodline, then I beg you to see to it yourself or to send some trusted person to Hungary with all speed.

In addition to the tales of excess and murder with Countess Erzsébet, the Jews of Prague similarly speak of the terror Benjamin caused in their district, when he threatened their beloved rabbi and a witch from Chelm. Now there are impossible tales of an enchanted creature made of clay who roams the streets protecting the Jews from those who would feast on their blood. The Jews say Benjamin seeks another witch as well, an Englishwoman who they claim was last seen with Ysabeau's son. But this cannot be true, for Matthew is in England and would never lower himself to associate with a witch.

Matthew's breath hissed from between tight lips.

Perhaps they confuse the English witch with the English daemon Edward Kelley, whom Benjamin visited in the emperor's palace in May. According to your friend Joris Hoefnagel, Kelley was placed in Benjamin's custody a few weeks later after he was accused of murdering one of the emperor's servants. Benjamin took him to a castle in Křivoklát, where Kelley tried to escape and nearly died.

There is one more piece of intelligence I must share with you, Father, though I hesitate to do so, for it may be nothing more than the stuff of fantasy and fear. According to my informants, Gerbert was in Hungary with the countess and Benjamin. The witches of Pozsony have complained formally to the

*Congregation about women who have been taken and tortured
by these three infamous creatures. One witch escaped and before
death took her was able only to say these words: "They search
within us for the Book of Life."*

Matthew remembered the horrifying image of Diana's parents, split
open from throat to groin.

*These dark matters put the family in too much danger.
Gerbert cannot be allowed to fascinate Benjamin with the power
that witches have, as he has been. Matthew's son must be kept
away from Erzsébet Báthory, lest your mate's secret be
discovered. And we must not let the witches pursue the Book of
Life any further. You will know how best to achieve these ends,
whether by seeing to them yourself or by summoning the
brotherhood.*

*I remain your humble servant and entrust your soul to God
in the hope that He will see us safe together so we might speak
more of these matters than present circumstances make wise.*

Your loving son, Godfrey

From the Confrérie, Paris, this 20th day of December 1591

Matthew folded the letter carefully.

At last he had some idea where to look. He would go to Central Europe
and search for Benjamin himself.

But first he had to tell Diana what he'd learned. He had kept the news
of Benjamin from her as long as he could.

The babies' first Christmas was as loving and festive as anyone could wish.
With eight vampires, two witches, one human vampire-in-waiting, and
three dogs in attendance, it was also lively.

Matthew showed off the half dozen strands of gray hair that had resulted from my Christmas spell and explained happily that every year I'd
give him more. I had asked for a six-slice toaster, which I had received,
along with a beautiful antique pen inlaid with silver and mother-of-pearl.

Ysabeau criticized these gifts as insufficiently romantic for a couple so recently wed, but I didn't need more jewelry, had no interest in traveling, and wasn't interested in clothes. A toaster suited me to the ground.

Phoebe had encouraged the entire family to think of gifts that were handmade or hand-me-down, which struck us all as both meaningful and practical. Jack modeled the sweater Marthe had knit for him and the cuff links from his grandmother that had once belonged to Philippe. Phoebe wore a pair of glittering emeralds in her ears that I'd assumed had come from Marcus until she blushed furiously and explained that Marcus had given her something handmade, which she had left at Sept-Tours for safety's sake. Given her color, I decided not to inquire further. Sarah and Ysabeau were pleased with the photo albums we'd presented that documented the twins' first month of life.

Then the ponies arrived.

"Philip and Rebecca must ride, of course," Ysabeau said as though this were self-evident. She supervised as her groom, Georges, led two small horses off the trailer. "This way they can grow accustomed to the horses before you put them in the saddle." I suspected she and I might have different ideas on how soon that blessed day might occur.

"They are Paso Finos," Ysabeau continued. "I thought an Andalusian like yours might be too much for a beginner. Phoebe said we are supposed to give hand-it-overs, but I have never been a slave to principle."

Georges led a third animal from the trailer: Rakasa.

"Diana's been asking for a pony since she could talk. Now she's finally got one," Sarah said. When Rakasa decided to investigate her pockets for anything interesting such as apples or peppermints, Sarah jumped away. "Horses have big teeth, don't they?"

"Perhaps Diana will have better luck teaching her manners than I did," Ysabeau said.

"Here, give her to me," Jack said, taking the horse's lead rope. Rakasa followed him, docile as a lamb.

"I thought you were a city boy," Sarah called after him.

"My first job—well, my first honest job—was taking care of gentlemen's horses at the Cardinal's Hat," Jack said. "You forget, Granny Sarah, cities used to be full of horses. Pigs, too. And their sh—"

"Where there's livestock, there's that," Marcus said before Jack could finish. The young Paso Fino he was holding had already proved his point. "You've got the other one, sweetheart?"

Phoebe nodded, completely at ease with her equine charge. She and Marcus followed Jack to the stables.

"The little mare, Rosita, has established herself as head of the herd," Ysabeau said. "I would have brought Balthasar, too, but as Rosita brings out his amorous side I've left him at Sept-Tours—for now." The idea that Matthew's enormous stallion would try to act upon his intentions with a horse as small as Rosita was inconceivable.

We were sitting in the library after dinner, surrounded by the remains of Philippe de Clermont's long life, a fire crackling in the stone fireplace, when Jack stood and went to Matthew's side.

"This is for you. Well, for all of us, really. *Grand-mère* said that all families of worth have them." Jack handed Matthew a piece of paper. "If you like it, Fernando and I will have it made into a standard for the tower here at Les Revenants."

Matthew stared down at the paper.

"If you don't like it—" Jack reached to reclaim his gift.

Matthew's arm shot out and he caught Jack by the wrist.

"I think it's perfect." Matthew looked up at the boy who would always be like our firstborn child, though I had nothing to do with his warm-blooded birth and Matthew was not responsible for his rebirth. "Show it to your mother. See what she thinks."

Expecting a monogram or a heraldic shield, I was stunned to see the image Jack had devised to symbolize our family. It was an entirely new orobouros, made not of a single snake with a tail in its mouth but two creatures locked forever in a circle with no beginning and no ending. One was the de Clermont serpent. The other was a firedrake, her two legs tucked against her body and her wings extended. A crown rested on the firedrake's head.

"*Grand-mère* said the firedrake should wear a crown because you're a true de Clermont and outrank the rest of us," Jack explained matter-of-factly. He picked nervously at the pocket of his jeans. "I can take the crown off. And make the wings smaller."

"Matthew's right. It's already perfect." I reached for his hand and pulled him down so I could give him a kiss. "Thank you, Jack."

Everyone admired the official emblem of the Bishop-Clairmont family, and Ysabeau explained that new silver and china would have to be ordered, as well as a flag.

"What a lovely day," I said, one arm around Matthew and the other waving farewell to our family as they departed, my left thumb prickling in sudden warning.

"I don't care how reasonable your plan is. Diana's not going to let you go to Hungary and Poland without her," Fernando said. "Have you forgotten what happened to you when you left her to go to New Orleans?"

Fernando, Marcus, and Matthew had spent most of the hours between midnight and dawn arguing over what to do about Godfrey's letter.

"Diana must go to Oxford. Only she can find the Book of Life," Matthew said. "If something goes wrong and I can't find Benjamin, I'll need that manuscript to lure him into the open."

"And when you do find him?" Marcus said sharply.

"Your job is to take care of Diana and my children," Matthew said, equally sharp. "Leave Benjamin to me."

I watched the heavens for auguries and plucked at every thread that seemed out of place to try to foresee and rectify whatever evil my thumb warned me was abroad.

But the trouble did not gallop over the hill like an apocalyptic horseman, or cruise into the driveway, or even call on the phone.

The trouble was already in the house—and had been for some time.

I found Matthew in the library late one afternoon a few days after Christmas, several folded sheets of paper before him. My hands turned every color in the rainbow, and my heart sank.

"What's that?" I asked.

"A letter from Godfrey." He slid it in my direction. I glanced at it, but it was written in Old French.

"Read it to me," I said, sitting down next to him.

The truth was far worse than I had allowed myself to imagine. Based on the letter Benjamin's killing spree had lasted centuries. He'd preyed on witches, and very probably weavers in particular. Gerbert was almost certainly involved. And that one phrase—*"They search within us for the Book of Life"*—turned my blood to fire and ice.

"We have to stop him, Matthew. If he finds out we've had a daughter . . ." I trailed off. Benjamin's final words to me in the Bodleian haunted me. When I thought of what he might try to do to Rebecca, the power snapped through my veins like the lash of a whip.

"He already knows." Matthew met my eyes, and I gasped at the rage I saw there.

"Since when?"

"Sometime before the christening," Matthew said. "I'm going to look for him, Diana."

"How will you find him?" I asked.

"Not by using computers or by trying to find his IP address. He's too clever for that. I'll find him the way I know best: tracking him, scenting him, cornering him," Matthew said. "Once I do that, I'll tear him limb from limb. If I fail—"

"You can't," I said flatly.

"I may." Matthew's eyes met mine. He needed me to hear him, not reassure him.

"Okay," I said with a calmness I didn't feel, "what happens if you fail?"

"You'll need the Book of Life. It's the only thing that may lure Benjamin out of hiding so he can be destroyed—once and for all."

"The only thing besides me," I said.

Matthew's darkening eyes said that using me as bait to catch Benjamin was not an option.

"I'll leave for Oxford tomorrow. The library is closed for the Christmas vacation. There won't be any staff around except for security," I said.

To my surprise, Matthew nodded. He was going to let me help.

"Will you be all right on your own?" I didn't want to fuss over him, but I needed to know. Matthew had already suffered through one separation. He nodded.

"What shall we do about the children?" Matthew asked.

"They need to stay here, with Sarah and Ysabeau and with enough of my milk and blood to feed them until I return. I'll take Fernando with me—no one else. If someone is watching us and reporting back to Benjamin, then we need to do what we can to make it look as though we're still here and everything is normal."

"Someone is watching us. There's no doubt about it." Matthew pushed his fingers through his hair. "The only question is whether that someone belongs to Benjamin or to Gerbert. That wily bastard's role in this may have been bigger than we thought."

"If he and your son have been in league all this time, there's no telling how much they know," I said.

"Then our only hope is to possess information they don't yet have. Get the book. Bring it back here and see if you can fix it by reinserting the pages Kelley removed," Matthew said. "Meanwhile I'll find Benjamin and do what I should have done long ago."

"When will you leave?" I asked.

"Tomorrow. After you go, so I can make sure that you aren't being followed," he said, rising to his feet.

I watched in silence as the parts of Matthew I knew and loved—the poet and the scientist, the warrior and the spy, the Renaissance prince and the father—fell away until only the darkest, most forbidding part of him remained. He was only the assassin now.

But he was still the man I loved.

Matthew took me by the shoulders and waited until I met his eyes. "Be safe."

His words were emphatic, and I felt the force of them. He cupped my face in his hands, searching every inch as though trying to memorize it.

"I meant what I said on Christmas Day. The family will survive if I don't come back. There are others who can serve as its head. But you are its heart."

I opened my mouth to protest, and Matthew pressed his fingers against my lips, staying my words.

"There is no point in arguing with me. I know this from experience," he said. "Before you I was nothing but dust and shadows. You brought me to life. And I cannot survive without you."

Sol in Capricorn

The tenth house of the zodiack is Capricorn.
It signifieth mothers, grandmothers, and ancestors of the
female sex. It is the sign of resurrection and rebirth. In
this month, plant seedes for the future.

—Anonymous English Commonplace Book, c. 1590,

Gonçalves MS 4890, f. 9ᵛ

34

Andrew Hubbard and Linda Crosby were waiting for us at the Old Lodge. In spite of my efforts to persuade my aunt to stay at Les Revenants, she insisted on coming with Fernando and me.

"You're not doing this alone, Diana," Sarah said in a tone that didn't invite argument. "I don't care that you're a weaver or that you have Corra for help. Magic on this scale requires three witches. And not just any witches. You need spell casters."

Linda Crosby turned up with the official London grimoire—an ancient tome that smelled darkly of belladonna and wolfsbane. We exchanged hellos while Fernando caught Andrew up on how Jack and Lobero were faring.

"Are you sure you want to get involved with this?" I asked Linda.

"Absolutely. The London coven hasn't been involved in anything half so exciting since we were called in to help foil the 1971 attempt to steal the crown jewels." Linda rubbed her hands together.

Andrew had, through his contacts with the London underworld of grave diggers, tube engineers, and pipe fitters, obtained detailed schematics of the warren of tunnels and shelving that constituted the book-storage facilities for the Bodleian Library. He unrolled these on the long refectory table in the great hall.

"There are no students or library staff on-site at the moment because of the Christmas holiday," Andrew said. "But there are builders everywhere." He pointed to the schematics. "They're converting the former underground book storage into work space for readers."

"First they moved the rare books to the Radcliffe Science Library and now this." I peered at the maps. "When do the work crews finish for the day?"

"They don't," Andrew said. "They've been working around the clock to minimize disruptions during the academic term."

"What if we go to the reading room and you put in a request just as though it were an ordinary day at the Bodleian?" Linda suggested. "You know, fill out the slip, stuff it in the Lamson tube, and hope for the best. We could stand by the conveyor belt and wait for it. Maybe the library knows how to fulfill your request, even without staff." Linda sniffed when she saw my amazed look at her knowledge of the Bodleian's procedures. "I went to St. Hilda's, my girl."

"The pneumatic-tube system was shut down last July. The conveyor belt was dismantled this August." Andrew held up his hands. "Do not harm the messenger, ladies. I am not Bodley's librarian."

"If Stephen's spell is good enough, it won't care about the equipment—just that Diana has requested something she truly needs," Sarah said.

"The only way to know for sure is to go to the Bodleian, avoid the workers, and find a way into the Old Library." I sighed.

Andrew nodded. "My Stan is on the excavation crew. Been digging his whole life. If you can wait until nightfall, he'll let you in. He'll get in trouble, of course, but it won't be the first time, and there's not a prison built that can hold him."

"Good man, Stanley Cripplegate," Linda said with a satisfied nod. "Always such a help in the autumn when you need the daffodil bulbs planted."

Stanley Cripplegate was a tiny whippet of a man with a pronounced underbite and the sinewy outlines of someone who had been malnourished since birth. Vampire blood had given him longevity and strength, but there was only so much it could do to lengthen bones. He distributed bright yellow safety helmets to the four of us.

"Aren't we going to be . . . er, conspicuous in this getup?" Sarah asked.

"Being as you're ladies, you're already conspicuous," Stan said darkly. He whistled. "Oy! Dickie!"

"Quiet," I hissed. This was turning out to be the loudest, most conspicuous book heist in history.

"S'all right. Dickie and me, we go way back." Stan turned to his colleague. "Take these ladies and gents up to the first floor, Dickie."

Dickie deposited us, helmets and all, in the Arts End of Duke Humfrey's Reading Room between the bust of King Charles I and the bust of Sir Thomas Bodley.

"Is it me, or are they watching us?" Linda said, scowling at the unfortunate monarch, hands on her hips.

King Charles blinked.

"Witches have been on the security detail since the middle of the nine-teenth century. Stan warned us not to do anything we oughtn't around the pictures, statues, and gargoyles." Dickie shuddered. "I don't mind most of them. They're company on dark nights, but that one's a right creepy old bugger."

"You should have met his father," Fernando commented. He swept his hat off and bowed to the blinking monarch. "Your Majesty."

It was every library patron's nightmare—that you were secretly being observed whenever you took a forbidden cough drop out of your pocket. In the Bodleian's case, it turned out the readers had good reason to worry. The nerve center for a magical security system was hidden behind the eyeballs of Thomas Bodley and King Charles.

"Sorry, Charlie." I tossed my yellow helmet in the air, and it sailed over to land on the king's head. I flicked my fingers, and the brim tilted down over his eyes. "No witnesses for tonight's events." Fernando handed me his helmet.

"Use mine for the founder. Please."

Once I'd obscured Sir Thomas's sight, I began to pluck and tweak the threads that bound the statues to the rest of the library. The spell's knots weren't complicated—just thrice- and four-crossed bindings—but there were so many of them, all piled on top of one another like a severely over-taxed electrical panel. Finally I discovered the main knot through which all the other knots were threaded and carefully untied it. The uncanny feeling of being observed vanished.

"That's better," Linda murmured. "Now what?"

"I promised to call Matthew once we were inside," I said, drawing out my phone. "Give me a minute."

I pushed past the lattice barricade and walked down the silent, echoing main avenue of Duke Humfrey's Library. Matthew picked up on the first ring.

"All right, *mon coeur*?" His voice thrummed with tension, and I briefly filled him in on our progress so far.

"How were Rebecca and Philip after I left?" I asked when my tale was told.

"Fidgety."

"And you?" My voice softened.

"More fidgety."

"Where are you?" I asked. Matthew had waited until after I left for England, then started driving north and east toward Central Europe.

"I just left Germany." He wasn't going to give me any more details in case I encountered an inquisitive witch.

"Be careful. Remember what the goddess said." Her warning that I would have to give something up if I wanted to possess Ashmole 782 still haunted me.

"I will." Matthew paused. "There's something I want you to remember, too."

"What?"

"Hearts cannot be broken, Diana. And only love makes us truly immortal. Don't forget, *ma lionne*. No matter what happens." He disconnected the line.

His words sent a shiver of fear up my spine, setting the goddess's silver arrow rattling. I repeated the words of the charm I'd woven to keep him safe and felt the familiar tug of the chain that bound us together.

"All is well?" Fernando asked quietly.

"As expected." I slipped the phone back into my pocket. "Let's get started."

We had agreed that the first thing we would try was simply to replicate the steps by which Ashmole 782 had come into my hands the first time. With Sarah, Linda, and Fernando looking on, I filled out the boxes on the call slip. I signed it, put my reader's-card number in the appropriate blank, and carried it over to the spot in the Arts End where the pneumatic tube was located.

"The capsule is here," I said, removing the hollow receptacle. "Maybe Andrew was wrong and the delivery system is still working." When I opened it, the capsule was full of dust. I coughed.

"And maybe it doesn't matter one way or the other," Sarah said with a touch of impatience. "Load it up and let her rip."

I put the call slip into the capsule, closed it securely, and placed it back in the compartment.

"What next?" Sarah said a few minutes later.

The capsule was right where I'd left it.

"Let's give it a good whack." Linda slapped the end of the compartment, causing the wooden supports it was attached to—and which held up the gallery above—to shake alarmingly. With an audible whoosh, the capsule disappeared.

"Nice work, Linda," Sarah said with obvious admiration.

"Is that a witch's trick?" Fernando asked, his lips twitching.

"No, but it always improves the Radio 4 signal on my stereo," Linda said brightly.

Two hours later we were all still waiting by the conveyor belt for a manuscript that showed absolutely no sign of arriving.

Sarah sighed. "Plan B."

Without a word Fernando unbuttoned his dark coat and slipped it from his shoulders. A pillowcase was sewn into the back lining. Inside, sandwiched between two pieces of cardboard, were the three pages that Edward Kelley had removed from the Book of Life.

"Here you are," he said, handing over the priceless parcel.

"Where do you want to do it?" Sarah asked.

"The only place that's large enough is there," I said, pointing to the spot between the splendid stained-glass window and the guard's station. "No—don't touch that!" My voice came out in a whispered shriek.

"Why not?" Fernando asked, his hands wrapped around the wooden uprights of a rolling stepladder that blocked our way.

"It's the world's oldest stepladder. It's nearly as ancient as the library." I pressed the manuscript pages to my heart. "Nobody touches it. Ever."

"Move the damn ladder, Fernando," Sarah instructed. "I'm sure Ysabeau has a replacement for it if it gets damaged. Push that chair out of the way while you're at it."

A few nail-biting moments later, I was ripping into a box of salt that Linda had carried up in a Marks & Spencer shopping bag. I whispered prayers to the goddess, asking for her help finding this lost object while I outlined a triangle with the white crystals. When that was done, I doled out the pages from the Book of Life, and Sarah, Linda, and I each stood at one of the points of the triangle. We directed the illustrations into the center, and I repeated the spell I'd written earlier:

Missing pages
Lost then found, show
Me where the book is bound.

"I still think we need a mirror," Sarah whispered after an hour of expectant silence had passed. "How's the library going to show us anything if we don't give her a place to project an apparition?"

"Should Diana have said '*show us* where the book is bound,' not '*show me*'?" Linda looked to Sarah. "There are three of us."

I stepped out of the triangle and put the illustration of the chemical wedding on the guard's desk. "It's not working. I don't feel *anything*. Not the book, not any power, not magic. It's like the whole library has gone dead."

"Well, it's not surprising the library is feeling poorly." Linda clucked in sympathy. "Poor thing. All these people poking at its entrails all day."

"There's nothing for it, honey," Sarah said. "On to Plan C."

"Maybe I should try to revise the spell first." Anything was better than Plan C. It violated the last remaining shreds of the library oath I'd taken when a student, and it posed a very real danger to the building, the books, and the nearby colleges.

But it was more than that. I was hesitating now for some of the same reasons I had hesitated when facing Benjamin in this very place. If I used my full powers here, in the Bodleian, the last remaining links to my life as a scholar would dissolve.

"There's nothing to be afraid of," Sarah said. "Corra will be fine."

"She's a firedrake, Sarah," I retorted. "She can't fly without causing sparks. Look at this place."

"A tinderbox," Linda agreed. "Still, I cannot see another way."

"There has to be one," I said, poking my index finger into my third eye in hopes of waking it up.

"Come on, Diana. Stop thinking about your precious library card. It's time to kick some magical ass."

"I need some air first." I turned and headed downstairs. Fresh air would steady my nerves and help me think. I pounded down the wooden treads that had been laid over the stone and pushed through the glass doors and into the Old Schools Quadrangle, gulping in the cold, dust-free December air, Fernando following at my heels.

"Hello, Auntie."

Gallowglass emerged from the shadows.

His mere presence told me that something terrible had happened.

His next quiet words confirmed it.

"Benjamin has Matthew."

"He can't. I just talked to him." The silver chain within me swayed.

"That was five hours ago," Fernando said, checking his watch. "When you spoke, did Matthew say where he was?"

"Only that he was leaving Germany," I whispered numbly. Stan and Dickie approached, frowns on their faces.

"Gallowglass," Stan said with a nod.

"Stan," Gallowglass replied.

"Problem?" Stan asked.

"Matthew's gone off the grid," Gallowglass explained. "Benjamin's got him."

"Ah." Stan looked worried. "Benjamin always was a bastard. I don't imagine he's improved over the years."

I thought of my Matthew in the hands of that monster.

I remembered what Benjamin had said about his hope that I would bear a girl.

I saw my daughter's tiny, fragile finger touch the tip of Matthew's nose.

"There is no way forward that doesn't have him in it," I said.

Anger burned through my veins, followed by a crashing wave of power— fire, air, earth, and water—that swept everything else before it. I felt a strange absence, a hollowness that told me I had lost something vital.

For a moment I wondered if it were Matthew. But I could still feel the chain that bound us. What was essential to my well-being was still there.

Then I realized it was not something essential I'd lost but something *habitual,* a burden carried so long that I had become inured to its heaviness.

Now that long-cherished thing was gone—just as the goddess had foretold.

I whirled around, blindly seeking the library entrance in the darkness.

"Where are you going, Auntie?" Gallowglass said, holding the door closed so that I couldn't pass. "Did you not hear me? We must go after Matthew. There's no time to lose."

The thick panels of glass turned to glittering sand, and the brass hinges and handles clanged against the stone threshold. I stepped over the debris and half ran, half flew up the stairs to Duke Humfrey's.

"Auntie!" Gallowglass shouted. "Have you lost your mind?"

"No!" I shouted back. "And if I use my magic, I won't lose Matthew either."

"Lose Matthew?" Sarah said as I slid my way into Duke Humfrey's, accompanied by Gallowglass and Fernando.

"The goddess. She told me I would have to give something up if I wanted Ashmole 782," I explained. "But it wasn't Matthew."

The feeling of absence had been replaced by a blooming sensation of released power that banished any remaining worries.

"Corra, fly!" I spread my arms wide, and my firedrake screeched into the room, zooming around the galleries and down the long aisle that connected the Arts End and the Selden End.

"What was it, then?" Linda asked, watching Corra's tail pat Thomas Bodley's helmet.

"Fear."

My mother had warned me of its power, but I had misunderstood, as children often do. I'd thought it was the fear of others that I needed to guard against, but it was my own terror. Because of that misunderstanding, I'd let the fear take root inside me until it clouded my thoughts and affected how I saw the world.

Fear had also choked out any desire to work magic. It had been my crutch and my cloak, keeping me from exercising my power. Fear had sheltered me from the curiosity of others and provided an oubliette where I could forget who I really was: a witch. I'd thought I'd left fear behind me months ago when I learned I was a weaver, but I had been clinging to its last vestiges without knowing it.

No more.

Corra dropped down on a current of air, extending her talons forward and beating her wings to slow herself. I grabbed the pages from the Book of Life and held them up to her nose. She sniffed.

The firedrake's roar of outrage filled the room, rattling the stained glass.

Though she had spoken to me seldom since our first encounter in Goody Alsop's house, preferring to communicate in sounds and gestures, Corra chose to speak now.

"Death lies heavy on those pages. Weaving and bloodcraft, too." She shook her head as if to rid her nostrils of the scent.

"Did she say bloodcraft?" Sarah's curiosity was evident.

"We'll ask the beastie questions later," Gallowglass said, his voice grim.

"These pages come from a book. It's somewhere in this library. I need to find it." I focused on Corra rather than the background chatter. "My only hope of getting Matthew back may be inside it."

"And if I bring you this terrible book, what then?" Corra blinked, her eyes silver and black. I was reminded of the goddess, and of Jack's rage-filled gaze.

"You want to leave me," I said with sudden understanding. Corra was a prisoner just as I had been a prisoner, spellbound with no means to escape.

"Like your fear, I cannot go unless you set me free," Corra said. "I am your familiar. With my help you have learned how to spin what was, weave what is, and knot what must be. You have no more need of me."

But Corra had been with me for months and, like my fear, I had grown used to relying on her. "What if I can't find Matthew without your help?"

"My power will never leave you." Corra's scales were brilliantly iridescent, even in the library's darkness. I thought of the shadow of the firedrake on my lower back and nodded. Like the goddess's arrow and my weaver's cords, Corra's affinity for fire and water would always be within me.

"Where will you go?" I asked.

"To ancient, forgotten places. There I will await those who will come when their weavers release them. You brought the magic back, as it was foretold. Now I will no longer be the last of my kind, but the first." Corra's exhale steamed in the air between us.

"Bring me the book, then go with my blessing." I looked deep into her eyes and saw her yearning to be her own creature. "Thank you, Corra. I may have brought the magic back, but you gave it wings."

"And now it is time for you to use them," Corra said. With three beats of her own spangled, webbed appendages, she climbed to the rafters.

"Why is Corra flying around up here?" Sarah hissed. "Send her down the conveyor-belt shaft and into the library's underground storage rooms. That's where the book is."

"Stop trying to shape the magic, Sarah." Goody Alsop had taught me the dangers of thinking you were smarter than your own power. "Corra knows what she's doing."

"I hope so," Gallowglass said, "for Matthew's sake."

Corra sang out notes of water and fire, and a low, hushed chattering filled the air.

"The Book of Life. Do you hear it?" I asked, looking around for the source of the sound. It wasn't the pages on the guard's desk, though they were starting to murmur, too.

My aunt shook her head.

Corra circled the oldest part of Duke Humfrey's. The murmurs grew louder with every beat of her wings.

"I hear it," Linda said, excited. "A hum of conversation. It's coming from that direction."

Fernando hopped over the lattice barrier into the main aisle of Duke Humfrey's. I followed after him.

"The Book of Life can't be up here," Sarah protested. "Someone would have noticed."

"Not if it's hiding in plain sight," I said, pulling priceless books off a nearby shelf, opening them to examine their contents, then sliding each back into place only to grasp another. The voices still cried out, calling to me, begging me to find them.

"Auntie? I think Corra found your book." Gallowglass pointed.

Corra was perched on the barred cage of the book hold, where the manuscripts were locked away and stored for patrons to use the following day. Her head was inclined as though she were listening to the still-chattering voices. She cooed and clucked in response, her head bobbing up and down.

Fernando had followed the sound to the same place and was standing behind the call desk where Sean spent his days. He was looking up at one of the shelves. There, next to an Oxford University telephone directory, sat a gray cardboard box so ordinary in appearance that it was begging not to be noticed—though it was pretty eye-catching at the moment, with light seeping out from the joins at the corners. Someone had clipped a curling note to it: *"Boxed. Return to stacks after inspection."*

"It can't be." But every instinct told me it was.

I held up my hand, and the box tipped backward and landed in my palm. I lowered it carefully to the desk. When I took my hands from it, the lid blew off, landing several feet away. Inside, the metal clasps were straining to hold the book closed.

Gently, aware of the many creatures within it, I lifted Ashmole 782 out of its protective carton and laid it down on the wooden surface. I rested my hand flat on the cover. The chattering ceased.

Choose, the many voices said as one.

"I choose you," I whispered to the book, releasing the clasps on Ashmole 782. Their metal was warm and comforting to the touch. *My father,* I thought.

Linda thrust the pages that belonged in the Book of Life in my direction. Slowly, deliberately, I opened the book.

I turned the rough paper that had been inserted into the binding to protect the contents and the parchment page that bore both Elias Ashmole's handwritten title as well as my father's pencil addition. The first of Ashmole 782's alchemical illustrations—a female baby with black hair—stared at me from the next page.

When I first saw this image of the philosophical child, I had been struck by how it deviated from standard alchemical imagery. Now I couldn't help noticing that the baby resembled my own daughter, her tiny hands clutching a silver rose in one hand and a golden rose in the other as though proclaiming to the world that she was the child of a witch and a vampire.

But the alchemical child had never been intended to serve as the first illumination in the Book of Life. She was supposed to follow the chemical wedding. After centuries of separation, it was time to replace the three pages Edward Kelley had removed from this precious book.

The page stubs were just visible in the valley of the Book of Life's spine. I fitted the illustration of the chemical wedding into the gap, pressing the edge to its stub. Page and stub knit themselves together before my eyes, their severed threads joining up once more.

Lines of text raced across the page.

I took up the illumination of the orobouros and the firedrake shedding their blood to create new life and put it in its place.

A strange keening rose from the book. Corra chattered in warning.

Without hesitation and without fear, I slid the final page into Ashmole 782. The Book of Life was once more whole and complete.

A bloodcurdling howl tore what remained of the night in two. A wind rose at my feet, climbing up my body and lifting the hair away from my face and shoulders like strands of fire.

The force of the air turned the pages of the book, flipping them faster and faster. I tried to stop their progress, pressing my fingers against the vellum so that I could read the words that were emerging from the heart of the palimpsest as the alchemical illustrations faded. But there were too many to comprehend. Chris's student was right. The Book of Life wasn't simply a text.

It was a vast repository of knowledge: creature names and their stories, births and deaths, curses and spells, miracles wrought by magic and blood.

It was the story of us—weavers and the vampires who carried blood rage in their veins and the extraordinary children who were born to them.

It told me not only of my predecessors going back countless generations. It told me how such a miraculous creation was possible.

I struggled to absorb the tale the Book of Life told as the pages turned.

> *Here begins the lineage of the ancient tribe known as the Bright Born. Their father was Eternity and their mother Change, and Spirit nurtured them in her womb. . . .*

My mind raced, trying to identify the alchemical text that was so similar.

> *. . . for when the three became one, their power was boundless as the night. . . .*

> *And it came to pass that the absence of children was a burden to the Athanatoi. They sought the daughters. . . .*

Whose daughters? I tried to stop the pages, but it was impossible.

> *. . . discovered that the mystery of bloodcraft was known to the Wise Ones.*

What was bloodcraft?

On and on went the words, racing, twining, twisting. Words split in two, formed other words, mutating and reproducing at a furious pace.

There were names, faces, and places torn from nightmares and woven into the sweetest of dreams.

> *Their love began with absence and desire, two hearts becom-*
> *ing one. . . .*

I heard a whisper of longing, a cry of pleasure, as the pages continued to turn.

> *. . . when fear overcame them, the city was bathed in the*
> *blood of the Bright Born.*

A howl of terror rose from the page, followed by a child's frightened whimper.

> *. . . the witches discovered who among them had lain with the*
> *Athanatoi. . . .*

I pressed my hands against my ears, wanting to block out the drumbeat litany of names and more names.

> *Lost . . .*
> *Forgotten . . .*
> *Feared . . .*
> *Outcast . . .*
> *Forbidden . . .*

As the pages flew before my eyes, I could see the intricate weaving that had made the book, the ties that bound each page to lineages whose roots lay in the distant past.

When the last page turned, it was blank.

Then new words began to appear there as though an unseen hand were still writing, her job not yet complete.

> *And thus the Bright Born became the Children of the Night.*

Who will end their wandering? the unseen hand wrote.

Who will carry the blood of the lion and the wolf?
    Seek the bearer of the tenth knot, for the last shall once more be the first.

My mind was dizzy with half-remembered words spoken by Louisa de Clermont and Bridget Bishop, snatches of alchemical poetry from the *Aurora Consurgens,* and the steady flood of information from the Book of Life.

A new page grew out of the spine of the book, extending itself like Corra's wing, unfurling like a leaf on the bough of a tree. Sarah gasped.

An illumination, the colors shining with silver, gold, and precious stones crushed into the pigment, bloomed from the page.

"Jack's emblem!" Sarah cried.

It was the tenth knot, fashioned from a firedrake and an orobouros eternally bound. The landscape that surrounded them was fertile with flowers and greenery so lush that it might have been paradise.

The page turned, and more words flowed forth from their hidden source.

Here continues the lineage of the most ancient Bright Born.

The unseen hand paused, as if dipping a pen in fresh ink.

Rebecca Arielle Emily Marthe Bishop-Clairmont, daughter of Diana Bishop, last of her line, and Matthew Gabriel Philippe Bertrand Sébastien de Clermont, first of his line. Born under the rule of the serpent.
    Philip Michael Addison Sorley Bishop-Clairmont, son of the same Diana and Matthew. Born under the protection of the archer.

Before the ink could possibly be dry, the pages flipped madly back to the beginning.

While we watched, a new branch sprouted from the trunk of the tree at the center of the first image. Leaves, flowers, and fruit burst forth along its length.

The Book of Life clapped shut, the clasps engaging. The chattering ceased, leaving the library silent. I felt power surge within me, rising to unprecedented levels.

"Wait," I said, scrambling to open the book again so that I could study the new image more closely. The Book of Life resisted me at first, but it sprang open once I wrestled with it.

It was empty. Blank. Panic swept through me.

"Where did it all go?" I turned the pages. "I need the book to get Matthew back!" I looked up at Sarah. "What did I do wrong?"

"Oh, Christ." Gallowglass was white as snow. "Her eyes."

I twisted to glance over my shoulder, expecting to see some spectral librarian glaring at me.

"There's nothing behind you, honey. And the book hasn't gone far." Sarah swallowed hard. "It's inside you."

I was the Book of Life.

35

"Y̶ou are so pathetically predictable." Benjamin's voice penetrated the dull fog that had settled over Matthew's brain. "I can only pray that your wife is equally easy to manipulate."

A searing pain shot through his arm, and Matthew cried out, unable to stop himself. The reaction only encouraged Benjamin. Matthew pressed his lips together, determined not to give his son further satisfaction.

A hammer struck iron—a familiar, homely sound he remembered from his childhood. Matthew felt the ring of the metal as a vibration in the marrow of his bones.

"There. That should hold you." Cold fingers gripped his chin. "Open your eyes, Father. If I have to open them for you, I don't think you will like it."

Matthew forced his lids open. Benjamin's inscrutable face was inches away. His son made a soft, regretful sound.

"Too bad. I'd hoped you would resist me. Still, this is only the first act." Benjamin twisted Matthew's head down.

A long, red-hot iron spike was driven through Matthew's right forearm and into the wooden chair beneath him. As it cooled, the stench of burning flesh and bone lessened somewhat. He did not have to see the other arm to know that it had undergone a similar treatment.

"Smile. We don't want the family back home to miss a minute of our reunion." Benjamin grabbed him by the hair and wrenched his head up. Matthew heard the whirring of a camera.

"A few warnings: First, that spike has been positioned carefully between the ulna and the radius. The hot metal will have fused to the surrounding bones just enough that if you struggle, they will splinter. I'm led to believe it's quite painful." Benjamin kicked the chair leg, and Matthew's jaw clamped shut as a terrible pain shot down into his hand. "See? Second, I have no interest in killing you. There is nothing you can do, say, or threaten that will make me deliver you into death's gentler hands. I want to banquet on your agony and savor it."

Matthew knew that Benjamin was expecting him to ask a particular question, but his thick tongue would not obey his brain's commands. Still he persisted. Everything depended on it.

"Where. Is. Diana?"

"Peter tells me she is in Oxford. Knox may not be the most powerful witch to have ever lived, but he has ways of tracking her location. I would let you talk to him directly, but that would spoil the unfolding drama for our viewers back home. By the way, they can't hear you. Yet. I'm saving that for when you break down and beg." Benjamin had carefully positioned himself so his back was to the camera. That way, his lips couldn't be read. But Matthew's face was visible.

"Diana. Not. Here?" Matthew formed each syllable carefully. He needed whoever might be watching to know that his wife was still free.

"The Diana you saw was a mirage, Matthew," Benjamin chortled. "Knox cast a spell, projecting an image of her into that empty room upstairs. Had you watched for a bit longer, you would have seen it loop back to the beginning, like a film."

Matthew had known it was an illusion. The image of Diana was blond, for Knox had not seen his wife since they'd returned from the past. Even had the hair color been right, Matthew would have known that it was not really Diana, for no spark of animation or warmth drew him to her. Matthew had entered Benjamin's compound knowing he would be taken. It was the only way to force Benjamin to make his next move and bring his twisted game to a close.

"If only you had been immune to love, you might have been a great man. Instead you are ruled by that worthless emotion." Benjamin leaned closer, and Matthew could smell the scent of blood on his lips. "It is your great weakness, Father."

Matthew's hand clenched reflexively at the insult, and his forearm paid the price, the ulna cracking like arid clay beneath a baking sun.

"That was foolish, wasn't it? You accomplished nothing. Your body is already suffering enormous stress, your mind filled with anxieties about your wife and children. It will take you twice as long to heal under these conditions." Benjamin forced Matthew's jaws open, studying his gums and tongue. "You're thirsty. Hungry, too. I have a child downstairs—a girl, three or four. When you're ready to feed on her, let me know. I'm trying to determine if the blood of virgins is more restorative than the blood of whores. So far the data is inconclusive." Benjamin made a note on a medical chart attached to a clipboard.

"Never."

"Never is a long time. Philippe taught me that," Benjamin said. "We'll see how you feel later. No matter what you decide, your responses will help me answer another research question: How long does it take to starve the piety out of a vampire so that he stops believing that God will save him?"

A very long time, Matthew thought.

"Your vital signs are still surprisingly strong, considering all the drugs I've pumped into your system. I like the disorientation and sluggishness they provoke. Most prey experience acute anxiety when their reactions and instincts are dulled. I see some evidence of that here, but not enough for my purposes. I'll have to up the dose." Benjamin threw the clipboard onto a small metal cabinet on wheels. It looked to be from World War II. Matthew noticed the metal chair next to the cabinet. The coat on it looked familiar.

His nostrils flared.

Peter Knox. He wasn't in the room now, but he was nearby. Benjamin was not lying about that.

"I'd like to get to know you better, Father. Observation can only help me to discover surface truths. Even ordinary vampires keep so many secrets. And you, my sire, are anything but ordinary." Benjamin advanced on him. He tore open Matthew's shirt, exposing his neck and shoulders. "Over the years I've learned how to maximize the information I glean from a creature's blood. It's all about the pace, you see. One must not rush. Or be too greedy."

"No." Matthew had expected that Benjamin would violate his mind, but it was impossible not to react instinctively against the intrusion. He scrambled against the chair. One forearm snapped. Then the other.

"If you break the same bones over and over, they never heal. Think about that, Matthew, before you try to escape from me again. It's futile. And I can drive spikes between your tibia and fibula to prove it."

Benjamin's sharp nail scored Matthew's skin. The blood welled to the surface, cold and wet.

"Before we are done, Matthew, I will know everything about you and your witch. Given enough time—and vampires have plenty of that—I will be able to witness every touch you've bestowed upon her. I will know what brings her pleasure as well as pain. I will know the power she wields and the secrets of her body. Her vulnerabilities will be as open to me as if her soul were a book." Benjamin stroked Matthew's skin, gradually increasing the circulation to his neck. "I could smell her fear in the Bodleian, of course, but now I want to understand it. So afraid, yet so remarkably brave. It will be thrilling to break her."

Hearts cannot be broken, Matthew reminded himself. He managed to croak out a single word. "Why?"

"Why?" Benjamin's voice crackled with fury. "Because you didn't have the courage to kill me outright. Instead, you destroyed me one day, one drop of blood at a time. Rather than confess to Philippe that you had failed him and revealed the de Clermonts' secret plans for Outremer, you made me a vampire and flung me out into the streets of a city crowded with warmbloods. Do you remember what it's like to feel a hunger for blood that cuts you in two with longing and desire? Do you remember how strong the blood rage is when you are first changed?"

Matthew did remember. And he had hoped—no. God help him, Matthew had *prayed* that Benjamin would be cursed with blood rage.

"You cared more for Philippe's good opinion than you cared for your own child." Benjamin's voice shook with rage, his eyes black as night. "Since the moment I was made a vampire, I have lived to destroy you and Philippe and all of the de Clermonts. My revenge gave me purpose, and time has been my friend. I've waited. I've planned. I've made my own children and taught them how to survive as I learned to survive: by raping and killing. It was the only path you left for me to follow."

Matthew's eyes closed in an attempt to blot out not only Benjamin's face but also the knowledge of his failures as a son and a father. But Benjamin would not allow it.

"Open your eyes," his son snarled. "Soon, you will have no more secrets from me."

Matthew's eyes flew open in alarm.

"As I learn about your mate, I will discover so much about you as well," Benjamin continued. "There is no better way to know a man than to understand his woman. I learned that from Philippe, as well."

The gears in Matthew's brain clinked and clunked. Some awful truth was fighting to make itself known.

"Was Philippe able to tell you about the time he and I spent together during the war? It didn't go according to my plans. Philippe spoiled so many of them when he visited the witch in the camp—an old Gypsy woman," Benjamin explained. "Someone tipped him off to my presence, and as usual Philippe took matters into his own hands. The witch stole most of his thoughts, scrambled the rest like eggs, and then hanged herself. It was a setback, to be sure. He had always had such an orderly mind. I had been looking forward to exploring it, in all its complex beauty."

Matthew's roar of protest came out as a croak, but the screaming in his head went on and on. This he had not expected.

It had been Benjamin—his son—who had tortured Philippe during the war and not some Nazi functionary.

Benjamin struck Matthew across the face, breaking his cheekbone.

"Quiet. I am telling you a bedtime story." Benjamin's fingers pressed into the broken bones of Matthew's face, playing them like an instrument whose only music was pain. "By the time the commander at Auschwitz released Philippe into my custody, it was too late. After the witch there was only one coherent thing left in that once-brilliant mind: Ysabeau. She can be surprisingly sensual, I discovered, for someone so cold."

As much as Matthew wanted to stop his ears against the words, there was no way to do so.

"Philippe hated his own weakness, but he could not let her go," Benjamin continued. "Even in the midst of his madness, weeping like a baby, he thought of Ysabeau—all the while knowing I was sharing in his pleasure." Benjamin smiled, displaying his sharp teeth. "But that's enough family talk for now. Prepare yourself, Matthew. This is going to hurt."

O n the plane home, Gallowglass had warned Marcus that something un-expected had happened to me at the Bodleian.

"You will find Diana . . . altered," Gallowglass said carefully into the phone.

Altered. It was an apt description for a creature who was composed of knots, cords, chains, wings, seals, weapons, and now, words and a tree. I didn't know what that made me, but it was a far cry from what I had been before.

Even though he'd been warned of the change, Marcus was visibly shocked when I climbed out of the car at Sept-Tours. Phoebe accepted my metamorphosis with greater equanimity, as she did most things.

"No questions, Marcus," Hamish said, taking my elbow. He'd seen on the plane what questions did to me. No disguising spell could hide the way my eyes went milky white and displayed letters and symbols at even the hint of a query, more letters appearing on my forearms and the backs of my hands.

I expressed silent thanks that my children would never know me any different and would therefore think it normal to have a palimpsest for a mother.

"No questions," Marcus quickly agreed.

"The children are in Matthew's study with Marthe. They have been rest-less for the past hour, as if they knew you were coming," Phoebe said, fol-lowing me into the house.

"I'll see Becca and Philip first." In my eagerness I flew up the stairs rather than walking. There seemed little point in doing anything else.

My time with the children was soul shaking. On the one hand, they made me feel closer to Matthew. But with my husband in danger, I couldn't help noticing how much the shape of Philip's blue eyes resembled that of his father's. There was a similarly stubborn cast to his chin, too, young and im-mature though it was. And Becca's coloring—her hair as dark as a raven's wing, eyes that were not the usual baby blue but already a brilliant gray-green, milky skin—was eerily like Matthew's. I cuddled them close, whispering promises into their ears about what their father would do with them when he returned home.

When I had spent as much time with them as I dared, I returned downstairs, slowly and on foot this time, and demanded to see the video feed from Benjamin.

"Ysabeau is in the family library, watching it now." Miriam's palpable worry made my blood run colder than anything had since Gallowglass materialized at the Bodleian.

I steeled myself for the sight, but Ysabeau slammed the laptop shut as soon as I entered the room.

"I told you not to bring her here, Miriam."

"Diana has a right to know," Miriam said.

"Miriam is right, Granny." Gallowglass gave his grandmother a quick kiss in greeting. "Besides, Auntie won't obey your orders any more than you obeyed Baldwin when he tried to keep you from Philippe until his wounds healed." He pried the laptop from Ysabeau's fingers and opened the lid.

What I saw made me utter a strangled sound of horror. Were it not for Matthew's distinctive gray-green eyes and black hair, I might not have known him.

"Diana." Baldwin strode into the room, his expression carefully schooled to show no reaction to my appearance. But he was a soldier, and he understood that pretending something hadn't happened didn't make it go away. He reached out with surprising gentleness and touched my hairline. "Does it hurt?"

"No." When my body had absorbed the Book of Life, a tree had appeared on it as well. Its trunk covered the back of my neck, perfectly aligned with the column of my spine. Its roots spread across my shoulders. The tree's branches fanned out under my hair, covering my scalp. The tips of the branches peeked out along my hairline, behind my ears, and around the edges of my face. Like the tree on my spell box, the roots and branches were strangely intertwined along the sides of my neck in a pattern resembling Celtic knotwork.

"Why are you here?" I asked. We hadn't heard from Baldwin since the christening.

"Baldwin was the first to see Benjamin's message," Gallowglass explained. "He contacted me straightaway, then shared the news with Marcus."

"Nathaniel had beaten me to it. He traced Matthew's last cell communication—a call made to you—to a location inside Poland," Baldwin said.

"Addie saw Matthew in Dresden, en route to Berlin," Miriam reported. "He asked her for information about Benjamin. While he was with her, Matthew got a text. He left immediately."

"Verin joined Addie there. They've picked up Matthew's trail. One of Marcus's knights spotted him leaving what we used to call Breslau." Baldwin glanced at Ysabeau. "He was traveling southeast. Matthew must have wandered into a trap."

"He was going north until then. Why did he change direction?" Marcus frowned.

"Matthew may have gone to Hungary," I said, trying to envision all this on the map. "We found a letter from Godfrey that mentioned Benjamin's connections there."

Marcus's phone rang.

"What do you have?" Marcus listened for a moment, then went to one of the other laptops dotting the surface of the library table. Once the screen illuminated, he keyed in a Web address. Close-up shots from the video feed appeared, the images enhanced to provide greater clarity. One was of a clipboard. Another, a corner of fabric draped over a chair. The third, a window. Marcus put down his cell phone and turned on the speaker.

"Explain, Nathaniel," he ordered, sounding more like Nathaniel's commanding officer than his friend.

"The room is pretty barren—there's not much in the way of clues that might help us get a better fix on Matthew's location. These items seemed to have the most potential."

"Can you zoom in on the clipboard?"

On the other side of the world, Nathaniel manipulated the image.

"That's the kind we used for medical charts. They were on every hospital ward, hanging on the bed rails." Marcus tilted his head. "It's an intake form. Benjamin's done what any doctor would—taken Matthew's height, weight, blood pressure, pulse." Marcus paused. "And he's indicated the medications Matthew is on."

"Matthew's not on any medications," I said.

"He is now," Marcus said shortly.

"But vampires can only feel the effects of drugs if . . ." I trailed off.

"If they ingest them through a warmblood. Benjamin has been feeding him—or force-feeding him—spiked blood." Marcus braced his arms against the table and swore. "And the drugs in question are not exactly palliative for a vampire."

"What is he on?" My mind felt numb, and the only parts of me that seemed to be alive were the cords running through my body like roots, like branches.

"A cocktail of ketamine, opiates, cocaine, and psilocybin." Marcus's tone was flat and impassive, but his right eyelid twitched.

"Psilocybin?" I asked. The others I was at least familiar with.

"A hallucinogen derived from mushrooms."

"That combination will make Matthew insane," Hamish said.

"Killing Matthew would be too quick for Benjamin's purposes," Ysabeau said. "What about this fabric?" She pointed to the screen.

"I think it's a blanket. It's mostly out of the picture frame, but I included it anyway," Nathaniel said.

"There are no landmarks outside," Baldwin observed. "All you can see is snow and trees. It could be a thousand places in Central Europe at this time of year."

In the central frame, Matthew's head turned slightly.

"Something's happening," I said, pulling the laptop toward me.

Benjamin led a girl into the room. She couldn't have been more than four and had on a long white nightgown with lace at the collar and cuffs. The cloth was stained with blood.

The girl wore a dazed expression, her thumb in her mouth.

"Phoebe, take Diana to the other room." Baldwin's order was immediate.

"No. I'm staying here. Matthew won't feed on her. He won't." I shook my head.

"He's out of his mind with pain, blood loss, and drugs," Marcus said gently. "Matthew's not responsible for his actions."

"My husband will not feed on a child," I said with absolute conviction.

Benjamin arranged the toddler on Matthew's knee and stroked the girl's neck. The skin was torn, and blood had caked around the wound.

Matthew's nostrils flared in instinctive recognition that sustenance was nearby. He turned his head from the girl deliberately.

Baldwin's eyes never left the screen. He watched his brother first warily, then with amazement. As the seconds ticked by, his expression became one of respect.

"Look at that control," Hamish murmured. "Every instinct in him must be screaming for blood and survival."

"Still think Matthew doesn't have what it takes to lead his own family?" I asked Baldwin.

Benjamin's back was turned to us, so we couldn't see his reaction, but the vampire's frustration was evident in the violent blow he slammed across Matthew's face. No wonder my husband's features didn't look familiar. Then Benjamin roughly grabbed the child and held her so that her neck was directly under Matthew's nose. The video feed had no sound, but the child's face twisted as she screamed in terror.

Matthew's lips moved, and the child's head turned, her sobs quieting slightly. Next to me Ysabeau began to sing.

"*Der Mond ist aufgegangen, / Die goldnen Sternlein prangen / Am Himmel hell und klar.*'" Ysabeau sang the words in time to the movement of Matthew's mouth.

"Don't, Ysabeau," Baldwin bit out.

"What is that song?" I asked, reaching to touch my husband's face. Even in his torment, he remained shockingly expressionless.

"It's a German hymn. Some of the verses have become a popular lullaby. Philippe used to sing it after . . . he came home." Baldwin's face was ravaged for a moment with grief and guilt.

"It is a song about God's final judgment," Ysabeau said.

Benjamin's hands moved. When they stilled, the child's body hung limply, head bent back at an impossible angle. Though he hadn't killed the child, Matthew hadn't been able to save her either. Hers was another death Matthew would carry with him forever. Rage burned in my veins, clear and bright.

"Enough. This ends. Tonight." I grabbed a set of keys that someone had thrown on the table. I didn't care which car they belonged to, though I hoped it was Marcus's—and therefore fast. "Tell Verin I'm on my way."

"No!" Ysabeau's anguished cry stopped me in my tracks. "The window. Can you enlarge that part of the picture for me, Nathaniel?"

"There's nothing out there but snow and trees," Hamish said, frowning.

"The wall next to the window. Focus there." Ysabeau pointed to the grimy wall on the screen as though Nathaniel could somehow see her. Even though he couldn't, Nathaniel obligingly zoomed in.

As a clearer picture emerged, I couldn't imagine what Ysabeau thought she saw. The wall was stained with damp and had not been painted for some time. It might once have been white, like the tiles, but it was grayish now. The image on the screen continued to resolve and sharpen as Nathaniel worked. Some of the grimy smudges turned out to be a series of numbers marching down the wall.

"My clever child," Ysabeau said, her eyes running red with blood and grief. She stood, her limbs trembling. "That monster. I will tear him to pieces."

"What is it, Ysabeau?" I asked.

"The clue was in the song. Matthew knows we are watching him," Ysabeau said.

"What is it, *Grand-mère*?" Marcus repeated, peering at the image. "Is it the numbers?"

"One number. Philippe's number." Ysabeau pointed to the last in the series.

"His number?" Sarah asked.

"It was given to him at Auschwitz-Birkenau. After the Nazis captured Philippe trying to liberate Ravensbrück, they sent him there," Ysabeau said.

These were names out of nightmares, places that would forever be synonymous with the savagery of mankind.

"The Nazis tattooed it on Philippe—over and over again." The fury built in Ysabeau's voice, making it ring like a warning bell. "It is how they discovered he was different."

"What are you saying?" I couldn't believe it, and yet . . .

"It was Benjamin who tortured Philippe," Ysabeau said.

Philippe's image swam before me—the hollow eye socket where Benjamin had blinded him, the horrible scars on his face. I remembered the shaky handwriting on the letter he'd left for me, his body too damaged to control a pen's movement.

And the same creature who had done that to Philippe now had my husband.

"Get out of my way." I tried to push past Baldwin as I raced for the door. But Baldwin held me tight.

"You aren't going to wander into the same trap that he did, Diana," Baldwin said. "That's exactly what Benjamin wants."

"I'm going to Auschwitz. Matthew is not going to die there, where so many died before," I said, twisting in Baldwin's grip.

"Matthew isn't at Auschwitz. Philippe was moved from there to Majdanek on the outskirts of Lublin soon after he was captured. It's where we found my father. I went over every inch of the camp searching for other survivors. There was no room like that in it."

"Then Philippe was taken somewhere else before being sent to Majdanek— to another labor camp. One run by Benjamin. It was he who tortured Philippe. I am certain of it," Ysabeau insisted.

"How could Benjamin be in charge of a camp?" I'd never heard of such a thing. Nazi concentration camps were run by the SS.

"There were tens of thousands of them, all over Germany and Poland— labor camps, brothels, research facilities, farms," Baldwin explained. "If Ysabeau is right, Matthew could be anywhere."

Ysabeau turned on Baldwin. "You are free to stay here and wonder where your brother is, but I am going to Poland with Diana. We will find Matthew ourselves."

"Nobody is going anywhere." Marcus slammed his hand on the table. "Not without a plan. Where exactly was Majdanek?"

"I'll pull up a map." Phoebe reached for the computer.

I stilled her hand. There was something disturbingly familiar about that blanket. . . . It was tweed, a heathery brown with a distinctive weave.

"Is that a button?" I looked more closely. "That's not a blanket. It's a jacket." I stared at it some more. "Peter Knox wore a jacket like that. I remember the fabric from Oxford."

"Vampires won't be able to free Matthew if Benjamin has witches like Knox with him, too!" Sarah exclaimed.

"This is like 1944 all over again," Ysabeau said quietly. "Benjamin is playing with Matthew—and with us."

"If so, then Matthew's capture was not his goal." Baldwin crossed his arms and narrowed his eyes at the screen. "The trap Benjamin set was meant to snare another."

"He wants Auntie," Gallowglass said. "Benjamin wants to know why she can bear a vampire's child."

Benjamin wants me to bear his child, I thought.

"Well, he's not going to experiment on Diana to find out," Marcus said emphatically. "Matthew would rather die where he is than let that happen."

"There's no need for experiments. I already know why weavers can have children with blood-rage vampires." The answer was running up my arms in letters and symbols from languages long dead or never spoken except by witches performing spells. The cords in my body were twisting and turning into brightly hued helices of yellow and white, red and black, green and silver.

"So the answer was in the Book of Life," Sarah said, "just as the vampires thought it would be."

"And it all began with a discovery of witches." I pressed my lips together to avoid revealing any more. "Marcus is right. If we go after Benjamin without a plan and the support of other creatures, he will win. And Matthew will die."

"I'm sending you a road map of southern and eastern Poland now," Nathaniel said over the speaker. Another window opened on the screen. "Here is Auschwitz." A purple flag appeared. "And here is Majdanek." A red flag marked a location on the outskirts of a city so far to the east it was practically in Ukraine. There were miles and miles of Polish ground in between.

"Where do we start?" I asked. "At Auschwitz and move east?"

"No. Benjamin will not be far from Lublin," Ysabeau insisted. "The witches we interrogated when Philippe was found said the creature who tortured him had long-standing ties to that region. We assumed they were talking about a local Nazi recruit."

"What else did the witches say?" I asked.

"Only that Philippe's captor had tortured the witches of Chelm before turning his attentions to my husband," Ysabeau said. "They called him 'the Devil.'"

Chelm. Within seconds I found the city. Chelm was just to the east of Lublin. My witch's sixth sense told me that Benjamin would be there—or very close.

"That's where we should start looking," I said, touching the city on the map as though somehow Matthew could feel my fingers. On the video feed, I saw that he had been left alone with a dead child. His lips were still moving, still singing . . . to a girl who would never hear anything again.

"Why are you so sure?" Hamish asked.

"Because a witch I met in sixteenth-century Prague was born there. The witch was a weaver—like me." As I spoke, names and family lineages emerged on my hands and arms, the marks as black as any tattoo. They appeared for only a moment before fading into invisibility, but I knew what they signaled: Abraham ben Elijah was probably not the first—nor the last—weaver in the city. Chelm was where Benjamin had made his mad attempts to breed a child.

On the screen, Matthew looked down at his right hand. It was spasming, the index finger tapping irregularly on the arm of the chair.

"It looks as though the nerves in his hand have been damaged," Marcus said, watching his father's fingers twitch.

"That's not involuntary movement." Gallowglass bent until his chin practically rested on the keyboard. "That's Morse code."

"What is he saying?" I was frantic at the thought that we might already have missed part of the message.

"D. Four. D. Five. C. Four." Gallowglass spelled out each letter in turn. "Christ. Matthew's making no sense at all. D. X—"

"C4," Hamish said, his voice rising. "DXC4." He whooped in excitement. "Matthew didn't walk into a trap. He sprang it deliberately."

"I don't understand," I said.

"D4 and D5 are the first two moves of the Queen's Gambit—it's one of the classic openings in chess." Hamish went to the fire, where a heavy chess set waited on a table. He moved two pawns, one white and then one black. "White's next move forces Black to either put his key pieces in jeopardy and gain greater freedom or play it safe and limit his maneuverability." Hamish moved another white pawn next to the first.

"But when Matthew is White, he never initiates the Queen's Gambit, and when he's Black, he declines it. Matthew always plays it safe and protects his queen," Baldwin said, crossing his arms over his chest. "He defends her at all costs."

"I know. That's why he loses. But not this time." Hamish picked up the black pawn and knocked over the white pawn that was diagonal to it in the center of the board. "DXC4. Queen's Gambit accepted."

"I thought Diana was the white queen," Sarah said, studying the board. "But you're making it sound like Matthew is playing Black."

"He is," Hamish said. "I think he's telling us the child was Benjamin's white pawn—the player he sacrificed, believing that it would give him an advantage over Matthew. Over us."

"Does it?" I asked.

"That depends on what we do next," Hamish said. "In chess, Black would either continue to attack pawns to gain an advantage in the endgame or get more aggressive and move in his knights."

"Which would Matthew do?" Marcus asked.

"I don't know," Hamish said. "Like Baldwin said, Matthew never accepts the Queen's Gambit."

"It doesn't matter. He wasn't trying to dictate our next move. He was telling us not to protect his queen." Baldwin swung his head around and addressed me directly. "Are you ready for what comes next?"

"Yes."

"You hesitated once before," Baldwin said. "Marcus told me what happened the last time you faced Benjamin in the library. This time, Matthew's life depends on you."

"It won't happen again." I met his gaze, and Baldwin nodded.

"Will you be able to track Matthew, Ysabeau?" Baldwin asked.

"Better than Verin," she replied.

"Then we will leave at once," Baldwin said. "Call your knights to arms, Marcus. Tell them to meet me in Warsaw."

"Kuźma is there," Marcus said. "He will marshal the knights until I arrive."

"You cannot go, Marcus," Gallowglass said. "You must stay here, with the babes."

"No!" Marcus said. "He's my father. I can scent him just as easily as Ysabeau. We'll need every advantage."

"You aren't going, Marcus. Neither is Diana." Baldwin braced his arms on the table and fixed his eyes on Marcus and me. "Everything until now has been a skirmish—a preamble to this moment. Benjamin has had almost a thousand years to plan his revenge. We have hours. We all must be where we are most needed—not where our hearts lead us."

"My *husband* needs me," I said tightly.

"Your husband needs to be found. Others can do that, just as others can fight," Baldwin replied. "Marcus must stay here, because Sept-Tours has the legal status of sanctuary only if the grand master is within its walls."

"And we saw how much good that did us against Gerbert and Knox," Sarah said bitterly.

"One person died." Baldwin's voice was as cold and clear as an icicle. "It was regrettable, and a tragic loss, but if Marcus had not been here, Gerbert and Domenico would have overrun the place with their children and you would all be dead."

"You don't know that," Marcus said.

"I do. Domenico boasted of their plans. You will stay here, Marcus, and protect Sarah and the children so that Diana can do her job."

"My job?" My brows lifted.

"You, sister, are going to Venice."

A heavy iron key flew through the air. I put my hand up, and it landed in my palm. The key was heavy and ornate, with an exquisite bow wrought in the shape of the de Clermont orobouros, a long stem, and a chunky bit with complicated star-shaped wards. I owned a house there, I dimly recalled. Perhaps this was the key to it?

Every vampire in the room was staring at my hand in shock. I turned it this way and that, but there didn't seem to be anything odd about it other than the normal rainbow colors, marked wrist, and odd bits of lettering. It was Gallowglass who regained his tongue first.

"You cannot send Auntie in there," he said, giving Baldwin a combative shove. "What are you thinking, man?"

"That she is a de Clermont—and that I am more useful tracking Matthew with Ysabeau and Verin than I am sitting in a council chamber arguing about the terms of the covenant." Baldwin turned glittering eyes on me. He shrugged. "Maybe Diana can change their mind."

"Wait." Now it was my turn to look amazed. "You can't—"

"Want you to sit in the de Clermont seat at the Congregation's table?" Baldwin's lip curved. "Oh, but I do, sister."

"I'm not a vampire!"

"Nothing says you have to be. The only way that Father would agree to the covenant was if there were always a de Clermont among the Congregation members. The council cannot meet without one of us present. But I've gone over the original treaty. It does not stipulate that the family's representative must be a vampire." Baldwin shook his head. "If I didn't know better, I would think that Philippe foresaw this day and planned it all."

"What do you expect Auntie to do?" Gallowglass demanded. "She may be a weaver, but she's no miracle worker."

"Diana needs to remind the Congregation that this is not the first time complaints have been made about a vampire in Chelm," Baldwin said.

"The Congregation has known about Benjamin and done *nothing*?" I couldn't believe it.

"They didn't know it was Benjamin, but they knew that something was wrong there," Baldwin replied. "Not even the witches cared enough to investigate. Knox may not be the only witch cooperating with Benjamin."

"If so, we'll not get far in Chelm without the Congregation's support," Hamish said.

"And if the witches there have been Benjamin's victims, a group of vampires will need the Chelm coven's blessing if we want to succeed, as well as the Congregation's support," Baldwin added.

"That means persuading Satu Järvinen to side with us," Sarah pointed out, "not to mention Gerbert and Domenico."

"It is impossible, Baldwin. There is too much bad blood between the de Clermonts and the witches," Ysabeau agreed. "They will never help us save Matthew."

"*Impossible n'est pas français,*" I reminded her. "I'll handle Satu. By the time I join you, Baldwin, you'll have the full support of the Congregation's witches. The daemons', too. I make no promises about Gerbert and Domenico."

"That's a tall order," Gallowglass warned.

"I want my husband back." I turned to Baldwin. "What now?"

"We'll go straight to Matthew's house in Venice. The Congregation has demanded that you and Matthew appear before them. If they see the two of us arrive, they'll assume I've done their bidding," Baldwin said.

"Will she be in any danger there?" Marcus asked.

"The Congregation wants a formal proceeding. We will be watched—closely—but no one will want to start a war. Not before the meeting is over, at any rate. I will go with Diana as far as Isola della Stella where the Congregation headquarters, Celestina, is located. After that, she can take two attendants with her into the cloister. Gallowglass? Fernando?" Baldwin turned to his nephew and his brother's mate.

"With pleasure," Fernando replied. "I haven't been to a Congregation meeting since Hugh was alive."

"Of course I'm going to Venice," Gallowglass growled. "If you think Auntie's going without me, you're daft."

"I thought as much. Remember: They can't start the meeting without you, Diana. The council chamber's door won't unlock without the de Clermont key," Baldwin explained.

"Oh. So that's why the key is enchanted," I said.

"Enchanted?" Baldwin asked.

"Yes. A protection spell was forged into the key when it was made." The witches who had done it were skilled, too. Over the centuries the spell's gramarye had hardly weakened at all.

"The Congregation moved into Isola della Stella in 1454. The keys were made then and have been handed down ever since," Baldwin said.

"Ah. That explains it. The spell was cast to ensure that you don't duplicate the key. If you tried, it would destroy itself." I turned the key over in my palm. "Clever."

"Are you sure about this, Diana?" Baldwin studied me closely. "There's no shame in admitting you're not ready to confront Gerbert and Satu again. We can come up with another plan."

I turned and met Baldwin's gaze without flinching.

"I'm sure."

"Good." He reached for a sheet of paper that was waiting on the table. A de Clermont ouroboros was pressed into a disk of black wax at the bottom, next to Baldwin's decisive signature. He handed it to me. "You can present this to the librarian when you arrive."

It was his formal recognition of the Bishop-Clairmont scion.

"I didn't need to see Matthew with that girl to know he was ready to lead his own family," Baldwin said in answer to my amazed expression.

"When?" I asked, unable to say more.

"The moment he let you intervene between us in the church—and didn't succumb to his blood rage," Baldwin replied. "I'll find him, Diana. And I'll bring him home."

"Thank you." I hesitated, then said the word that was not only on my tongue but in my heart. "Brother."

37

The sea and sky were leaden and the wind fierce when the de Clermont plane touched down at the Venice airport.

"Fine Venetian weather, I see." Gallowglass buffered me from the blasts as we descended the airplane stairs behind Baldwin and Fernando.

"At least it's not raining," Baldwin said, scanning the tarmac.

Of the many things I'd been warned about, the fact that the house might have an inch or two of water in the ground floor was the least of my concerns. Vampires could have a maddening sense of what was truly important.

"Can we please go?" I said, marching toward the waiting car.

"It won't make it five o'clock any sooner," Baldwin observed as he followed me. "They refuse to change the meeting time. It's tr—"

"Tradition. I know." I climbed into the waiting car.

The car took us only as far as an airport dock, where Gallowglass helped me into a small, fast boat. It had the de Clermont crest on its gleaming helm and tinted windows on the cabin. Soon we were at another dock, this one floating in front of a fifteenth-century palazzo on the curve of the Grand Canal.

Ca' Chiaromonte was an appropriate dwelling for someone like Matthew who had played a pivotal role in Venetian business and political life for centuries. Its three floors, Gothic façade, and sparkling windows screamed wealth and status. Had I been here for any other reason than to save Matthew, I would have reveled in its beauty, but today the place felt as gloomy as the weather outside. A stout, dark-haired man with a prominent nose, round glasses with thick lenses, and a long-suffering expression was there to greet us.

"*Benvegnùa, madame,*" he said with a bow. "It is an honor to welcome you to your home. And it is always a pleasure to see you again, Ser Baldovino."

"You're a terrible liar, Santoro. We need coffee. And something stronger for Gallowglass." Baldwin handed the man his gloves and coat and guided me toward the palazzo's open door. It was tucked inside a small portico that was, as predicted, a few inches underwater despite the sandbags that had been arranged in piles by the door. Inside, a floor of terra-cotta and white tiles stretched into the distance, with another door at the far end. The dark wood paneling was illuminated by candles set into sconces with mirrored backs to magnify the light. I peeled off the hood on my heavy raincoat, unwound my scarf, and surveyed my surroundings.

"*D'accordo,* Ser Baldovino." Santoro sounded about as sincere as Ysabeau. "And for you, Madame Chiaromonte? Milord Matteo has good taste in wine. A glass of Barolo, perhaps?"

I shook my head.

"It's Ser Matteo now," Baldwin said from the end of the corridor. Santoro's jaw dropped. "Don't tell me you're surprised, you old goat. You've been encouraging Matthew to rebel for centuries." Baldwin stomped up the stairs.

I fumbled with the buttons on my sodden coat. It wasn't raining at the moment, but the air was thick with moisture. Venice, I had discovered, was mostly water, valiantly (if vainly) held together with bricks and mortar. While I did so, I stole a look at the rich furniture in the hall. Fernando saw my wandering attention."

"Venetians understand two languages, Diana: wealth and power. The de Clermonts speak both—fluently," he said. "Besides, the city would have collapsed into the sea long ago if not for Matthew and Baldwin, and the Venetians know it. Neither of them have reason to hide here." Fernando took my coat and handed it to Santoro. "Come, let me show you upstairs."

The bedroom that had been prepared for me was decorated in reds and golds, and the fire in the tiled fireplace was lit, but the flames and bright colors could not warm me. Five minutes after the door closed behind Fernando, I found my way back downstairs.

I sank onto a padded bench in one of the lanternlike bay windows that jutted over the Grand Canal. A fire crackled in one of the house's cavernous fireplaces. A familiar motto—WHAT NOURISHES ME DESTROYS ME—was carved into the wooden mantel. It reminded me of Matthew, of our time in London, of past deeds that even now threatened my family.

"Please, Auntie. You must rest," Gallowglass murmured with concern once he'd discovered me there. "It's hours until the Congregation will hear your case."

But I refused to move. Instead, I sat among the leaded windows, each one capturing a fractured glimpse of the city outside, and listened to the bells mark the slow passing of the hours.

"It's time." Baldwin put his hand on my shoulder.

I stood and turned to face him. I was wearing the brightly embroidered Elizabethan jacket I'd worn home from the past along with a thick black turtleneck and wool trousers. I was dressed for Chelm so I could be ready to leave the moment the proceedings were over.

"You have the key?" Baldwin asked.

I slid it out of my pocket. Fortunately, the coat had been designed to hold an Elizabethan housewife's many accoutrements. Even so, the key to the Congregation chamber was so large it was a tight fit.

"Let's go, then," Baldwin said.

We found Gallowglass downstairs with Fernando. Both were draped in black cloaks, and Gallowglass settled a matching black velvet garment over my shoulders. It was ancient and heavy. My fingers traced Matthew's insignia on the folds of fabric that covered my right arm.

The fierce wind had not abated, and I gripped the bottom of my hood to keep it from blowing open. Fernando and Gallowglass swept into the launch, which lifted and fell with the swell of the waves in the canal.

Baldwin kept a firm grip on my elbow as we walked over the slippery surface. I hopped aboard the launch just as the deck tipped precipitously toward the landing, aided by the sudden application of Gallowglass's boot to a metal cleat on the side of the boat. I ducked into the cabin, and Gallowglass clambered aboard behind me.

We sped through the mouth of the Grand Canal, zipping across the stretch of water in front of San Marco and ducking into a smaller canal that cut through the Castello district and returned us to the lagoon north of the city. We passed by San Michele, with its high walls and cypress trees shielding the gravestones. My fingers twisted, spinning the black and blue cords within me as I murmured a few words to remember the dead.

As we crossed the lagoon, we passed some inhabited islands, like Murano and Burano, and others occupied only by ruins and dormant fruit trees. When the stark walls protecting the Isola della Stella came into view, my flesh tingled. Baldwin explained that the Venetians thought the place was cursed. It was no wonder. There was power here, both elemental magic and the residue left by centuries of spells cast to keep the place secure and turn away curious human eyes.

"The island is going to sense that I shouldn't be entering through a vampire's door," I told Baldwin. I could hear the spirits the witches had bound to the place as they swept around the perimeter making security checks. Whoever warded Isola della Stella and Celestina was far more sophisticated than the witch who had installed the magical surveillance system I'd dismantled at the Bodleian.

"Move quickly, then. Congregation rules forbid expulsion of anyone who reaches the cloister that lies at the center of Celestina. If you have the key, you have the right to enter with two companions. It's always been this way," Baldwin said calmly.

Santoro cut the engines, and the boat moved smoothly into the protected landing. As we passed under the archway, I saw the faint outlines of the de Clermont ouroboros on the keystone. Time and salt air had softened the chiseled insignia, and to a casual viewer it would have looked like nothing more than a shadow.

Inside, the steps that led to the high marble landing were thick with algae. A vampire might risk the climb, but not a witch. Before I could figure out a solution, Gallowglass had sprung from the boat and was on the landing. Santoro tossed a length of rope to him, and Gallowglass tied the boat to a bollard with practiced speed. Baldwin turned to issue his last-minute instructions.

"Once you reach the council chamber, take your seat without engaging in conversation. It's become common practice for the members to chat endlessly before we convene, but this is no ordinary meeting. The de Clermont representative is always the presiding member. Call the creatures to order as quickly as you can."

"Right." This was the part of the day I relished least. "Does it matter where I sit?"

"Your seat is opposite the door—between Gerbert and Domenico." With that, Baldwin gave me a kiss on the cheek. "*Buona fortuna,* Diana."

"Bring him home, Baldwin." I clutched at his sleeve for a moment. It was the last sign of weakness I could afford.

"I will. Benjamin expected his father to look for him, and he believes you will run after him," Baldwin said. "He will not be expecting me."

High above, bells tolled.

"We must go," Fernando said.

"Take care of my sister," Baldwin told him.

"I am taking care of my sire's mate," Fernando replied, "so you need not worry. I will guard her with my life."

Fernando grasped me around the waist and lifted me up, while Gallow-glass reached down and snagged me by the arm. In two seconds I was standing on the landing, Fernando beside me. Baldwin hopped from the launch to a smaller speedboat. With a salute he maneuvered his new vessel to the mouth of the slip. He would wait there until the bells rang five o'clock, signaling the beginning of the meeting.

The door that stood between the Congregation and me was heavy and black with age and moisture. The lock was uncannily shiny in comparison and looked as though it had been recently polished. I suspected that magic kept it gleaming, and a brush of my fingers confirmed my suspicion. But this was just a benign protection spell to prevent the elements from damaging the metal. Based on what I'd seen from the windows of Ca' Chiaromonte, an enterprising Venetian witch could make a fortune enchanting the plaster and bricks in the city to stop them from crumbling.

The key felt warm as my hand closed around it. I drew it from my pocket, slipped the end of the stem and the bit into the lock, and turned. The mechanism inside the lock activated quickly and without complaint.

I grasped the heavy ring and pulled the door open. Beyond, there was a dark corridor with a veined-marble floor. I could see no more than a yard ahead of me in the darkness.

"Let me show you the way," Fernando said, taking my arm.

After the gloom of the corridor, I was temporarily blinded when we reached the dim light of the cloister. When my eyes focused, I saw rounded archways that were supported by graceful double columns. In the center of the space was a marble wellhead—a reminder that the cloister had been constructed long before modern conveniences like electricity and running water. In the days when travel was difficult and dangerous, the Congregation had met for months on end, living on the island until their business was finished.

The low murmur of conversation stopped. I pulled the hooded cloak around me, hoping to hide whatever markings of power might be visible on my skin. The thick folds also masked the tote bag slung over my shoulder. Quickly I surveyed the crowd. Satu stood alone. She avoided my eyes, but I was aware of her discomfort at seeing me again. More than that, the witch felt . . . wrong somehow, and my stomach flipped in a minor version of the revulsion I felt when another witch lied to me. Satu was wearing a disguising spell, but it did no good. I knew what she was hiding.

The other creatures present huddled into groups according to species. Agatha Wilson was standing with her two fellow daemons. Domenico and Gerbert were together, exchanging surprised looks. The Congregation's remaining two witches were both women. One was stern-looking, with a tight braided bun woven from brown hair threaded with gray. She wore the ugliest dress I had ever seen, accented by an ornate choker. A small portrait miniature adorned the center of the gold-and-enameled necklace—an ancestor, no doubt. The other witch was pleasantly round-faced, with pink cheeks and white hair. Her skin was remarkably unlined, which made it impossible to determine her age. Something about this witch tugged at me, too, but I couldn't figure out what it was. The flesh on my arms prickled, warning me that the Book of Life held an answer to my unspoken questions, but I couldn't take the time to decipher it now.

"I am pleased to see that the de Clermonts have bowed to the Congregation's request to see this witch." Gerbert appeared before me. I had not seen him since La Pierre. "We meet again, Diana Bishop."

"Gerbert." I met his gaze unflinchingly, though it made my flesh shrink. His lips curled.

"I see you are the same proud creature you were before." Gerbert turned to Gallowglass. "To see such a noble lineage as the de Clermonts brought to confusion and ruin by a girl!"

"They used to say something similar about Granny," Gallowglass shot back. "If we can survive Ysabeau we can survive this 'girl.'"

"You may think differently once you learn the extent of the witch's offenses," Gerbert replied.

"Where is Baldwin?" Domenico joined us, a scowl on his face.

Gears whirred and clanged overhead.

"Saved by the bell," Gallowglass said. "Stand aside, Domenico."

"A change of de Clermont representative at this late hour, and without notification, is most irregular, Gallowglass," Gerbert said.

"What are you waiting for, Gallowglass? Unlock the door," Domenico commanded.

"It's not me who holds the key," Gallowglass said, his voice soft. "Come, Auntie. You have a meeting to attend."

"What do you mean, you don't have the key?" Gerbert asked, his voice so sharp the sound cut through the enchanted carillon playing overhead. "You are the only de Clermont present."

"Not so. Baldwin recognized Diana Bishop as a blood-sworn daughter of Philippe de Clermont weeks ago." Gallowglass gave Gerbert a mocking smile.

Across the cloister, one of the witches gasped and whispered to her neighbor.

"That's impossible," Domenico said. "Philippe de Clermont has been dead for more than half a century. How—"

"Diana Bishop is a timewalker." Gerbert looked at me in loathing. Across the courtyard the white-haired witch's dimples grew deeper. "I should have guessed. This is all part of some vast enchantment she has been working. I warned you that this witch must be stopped. Now we will pay the price for your failure to act appropriately." He pointed an accusing finger at Satu.

The first toll of the hours sounded.

"Time to go," I said briskly. "We wouldn't want to be late and disrupt the Congregation's traditions." Their failure to agree to an earlier meeting time still rankled.

As I approached the door, the weight of the key filled my palm. There were nine locks, and every one had a key in it, save one. I slipped the metal bit into the remaining keyhole and twisted it with a flick of my wrist. The locking mechanisms whirred and clicked. Then the door swung open.

"After you." I stepped aside so the others could file by. My first Congregation meeting was about to begin.

The council chamber was magnificent, decorated with brilliant frescoes and mosaics that were illuminated from the light of torches and hundreds of candles. The vaulted ceiling seemed miles above, and a gallery circled the room three or four stories up. That lofty space was where the Congregation's records were kept. Thousands of years of records, based on a quick visual inventory of the shelves. In addition to books and manuscripts, there were earlier writing technologies, including scrolls and glass frames of the kind that held papyrus fragments. Banks of shallow drawers suggested there might even be clay tablets up there.

My eyes dropped to survey the meeting room, dominated by a large oval table surrounded by high-backed chairs. Like the locks, and the keys that opened them, each chair was inscribed with a symbol. Mine was right where Baldwin had promised it would be: on the far side of the room, opposite the door.

A young human woman stood inside, presenting each Congregation member who entered with a leather folio. At first I thought it must contain the meeting's agenda. Then I noticed that each folio was a different thickness, as though items had been requested from the shelves above according to the members' specific instructions.

I was the last to enter the room, and the door clanged shut behind me.

"Madame de Clermont," the woman said, her dark eyes brimming with intelligence. "I am Rima Jaén, the Congregation's librarian. Here are the documents *Sieur* Baldwin requested for the meeting. If there is anything more you require, you have only to let me know."

"Thank you," I said, taking the materials from her.

She hesitated. "Pardon my presumption, madame, but have we met? You seem so familiar. I know you are a scholar. Have you ever visited the Gonçalves archive in Seville?"

"No, I have never worked there," I said, adding, "but I believe I know the owner."

"Señor Gonçalves nominated me for this job after I was made redundant," Rima said. "The Congregation's former librarian retired quite unexpectedly in July, after suffering a heart attack. The librarians are, by tradition, human. *Sieur* Baldwin took on the task of replacing him."

The librarian's heart attack—and Rima's appointment—had come a few weeks after Baldwin found out about my blood vow. I strongly suspected that my new brother had engineered the whole business. The de Clermonts' king became more interesting by the hour.

"You are keeping us waiting, Professor Bishop," Gerbert said testily, though based on the hum of conversation among the delegates he was the only creature who minded.

"Allow Professor Bishop a chance to get her bearings. It is her first meeting," said the dimpled witch in a broad Scots accent. "Are you able to remember yours, Gerbert, or is that happy day lost in the mists of time?"

"Give that witch a chance and she'll spellbind us all," Gerbert said. "Do not underestimate her, Janet. Knox's assessment of her childhood power and potential was grossly misleading, I fear."

"Thank you kindly, but I don't believe it's I who needs the warning," Janet said with a twinkle in her gray eyes.

I took the folio from Rima and passed her the folded document that gave the Bishop-Clairmont family official standing in the vampire world.

"Can you file that, please?" I asked.

"Happily, Madame de Clermont," Rima said. "The Congregation librarian is also its secretary. I'll take whatever actions the document requires while you are meeting."

Having handed off the papers that formally established the Bishop-Clairmont scion, I circumnavigated the table, the black cloak billowing around my feet.

"Nice tats," Agatha whispered as I walked by, pointing to her own hairline. "Great cape, too."

I smiled at her without comment and kept going. When I reached my chair, I wrestled with the damp cloak, not wanting to relinquish the tote bag while I did so. Finally I managed to get it off and hung it over the back of my chair.

"There are hooks by the door," Gerbert said.

I turned to face him. His eyes widened. My jacket had long sleeves to hide the Book of Life's text, but my eyes were fully on view. And I'd deliberately pulled my hair back into a long red braid that revealed the tips of the branches that covered my scalp.

"My power is unsettled at the moment, and some people are made uncomfortable by my appearance," I said. "I prefer to keep my cloak nearby. Or I can use a disguising spell like Satu. But hiding in plain sight is as much a lie as any spoken form of deceit."

I looked at each creature of the Congregation in turn, daring any of them to react to the letters and symbols that I knew were passing across my eyes.

Satu glanced away, but not quickly enough to mask her frightened look. The sudden movement stretched her poor excuse for a disguising spell. I searched for the spell's signature, but there was none. Satu's disguising spell had not been cast. She herself had woven it—and not very skillfully.

I know your secret, sister, I said silently.

And I have long suspected yours, Satu replied, her voice as bitter as wormwood.

Oh, I've picked up a few more along the way, I said.

After my slow survey of the room, only Agatha risked asking a question. "What happened to you?" she whispered.

"I chose my path." I dropped the tote bag on the table and lowered myself into the chair. The bag was bound to me so tightly that even at this short distance I could feel the tug.

"What's that?" Domenico asked suspiciously.

"A Bodleian Library tote bag." I had taken it from the library shop when we retrieved the Book of Life, making sure to leave a twenty-pound note under the pencil cup near the till. Fittingly, the canvas bag had the library oath emblazoned upon it in red and black letters.

Domenico opened his mouth to ask another question, but I silenced him with a look. I had waited long enough for today's meeting to begin. Domenico could ask me questions after Matthew was free.

"I call this meeting to order. I am Diana Bishop, Philippe de Clermont's blood-sworn daughter, and I represent the de Clermonts." I turned to Domenico. He crossed his arms and refused to speak. I continued.

"This is Domenico Michele, and Gerbert of Aurillac is to my left. I know Agatha Wilson from Oxford, and Satu Järvinen and I spent some time together in France." My back smarted with the memory of her fire. "I'm afraid the rest of you will have to introduce yourselves."

"I am Osamu Watanabe," said the young male daemon sitting next to Agatha. "You look like a manga character. Can I draw you later?"

"Sure," I said, hoping that the character in question didn't turn out to be evil.

"Tatiana Alkaev," said a platinum blond daemon with the dreamy blue eyes. All she needed was a sleigh pulled by white horses and she would be the perfect heroine in a Russian fairy tale. "You're full of answers, but I have no questions at this time."

"Excellent." I turned to the witch with the forbidding expression and the execrable taste in clothing. "And you?"

"I am Sidonie von Borcke," she said, putting on a pair of reading glasses and opening her leather folio with a snap. "And I have no knowledge of this so-called blood vow."

"It's in the librarian's report. Second page, at the bottom, in the addendum, third line," Osamu said helpfully. Sidonie glared at him. "I seem to recall that it begins 'Additions to vampire pedigrees (alphabetical): Almasi, Bettingcourt, de Clermont, Díaz—"

"Yes, I see it now, Mr. Watanabe," Sidonie snapped.

"I believe it's my turn to be introduced, dear Sidonie." The white-haired witch smiled beneficently. "I am Janet Gowdie, and meeting you is a long-awaited pleasure. I knew your father and mother. They were a great credit to our people, and I still feel their loss keenly."

"Thank you," I said, moved by the woman's simple tribute.

"We were told the de Clermonts had a motion for us to consider?" Janet gently steered the meeting back on track.

I gave her a grateful look. "The de Clermonts formally request the assistance of the Congregation in tracking down a member of the Bishop-Clairmont scion, Benjamin Fox or Fuchs. Mr. Fox contracted blood rage from his father, my husband, Matthew Clairmont, and has been kidnapping and raping witches for centuries in an attempt to impregnate them, mostly in the area surrounding the Polish city of Chelm. Some of you may remember complaints made by the Chelm coven, which the Congregation ignored. To date, Benjamin's desire to create a witch-vampire child has been thwarted, in large part because he does not know what the witches discovered long ago—namely, that vampires with blood rage can reproduce biologically, but only with a particular kind of witch called a weaver."

The room was completely quiet. I took a deep breath and continued.

"My husband, in an attempt to draw Benjamin into the open, went into Poland where he disappeared. We believe Benjamin has captured him and is holding him in a facility that served as a Nazi labor camp or research laboratory during the Second World War. The Knights of Lazarus have pledged to get my husband back, but the de Clermonts will need witches and daemons to come to our aid as well. Benjamin must be stopped."

I looked around the room once more. Every person in it save Janet Gowdie was slack-jawed with amazement.

"Discussion? Or should we move straight to the vote?" I asked, eager to forstall a long debate.

After a long silence, the Congregation chamber was filled with an indignant clamor as the representatives began to shout questions at me and accusations at each other.

"Discussion it is," I said.

38

"You must eat something," Gallowglass insisted, pressing a sandwich into my hand.

"I have to go back in there. The second vote will take place soon." I pushed the sandwich away. Baldwin had, among his many other instructions, reminded me about the Congregation's elaborate voting procedures: three votes on any motion, with discussion in between. It was normal for the votes to swing wildly from one position to the other as Congregation members considered—or pretended to consider—opposing views.

I lost the first vote, eight opposed and one—me—in favor. Some voted against me on procedural grounds, since Matthew and I had violated the covenant and the Congregation had already voted to uphold that ancient pact. Others voted it down because the scourge of blood rage threatened the health and safety of all warmbloods—daemon, human, and witch. Newspaper reports of the vampire murders were produced and read aloud. Tatiana objected to rescuing the witches of Chelm, who, she tearfully claimed, had cast a spell on her vacationing grandmother that made her break out in boils. No amount of explaining could convince Tatiana that she was actually thinking of Cheboksary, even though Rima procured aerial photographs to prove that Chelm was not a beachfront spot on the Volga.

"Is there word from Baldwin or Verin?" I asked. Isola della Stella suffered from poor cell-phone reception, and within the walls of Celestina the only way to catch a signal was by standing in the exposed center of the cloister in a steady downpour.

"None." Gallowglass put a mug of tea in my hand and closed my fingers around it. "Drink."

Worry for Matthew and impatience with the Congregation's Byzantine rules and regulations made my stomach flip. I handed the mug back to Gallowglass, untouched.

"Don't take the Congregation's decision to heart, Auntie. My father always said that the first vote was all about posturing and that more often than not the second vote reversed the first."

I picked up the Bodleian tote bag, nodded, and returned to the council chamber. The hostile looks I received from Gerbert and Domenico once I was inside made me wonder if Hugh had been an optimist when it came to Congregation politics.

"Blood rage!" Gerbert hissed, grabbing at my arm. "How did the de Clermonts keep this from us?"

"I don't know, Gerbert," I replied, shaking off his grip. "Ysabeau lived under your roof for weeks and you never discovered it."

"It's half past ten." Sidonie von Borcke strode into the room. "We adjourn at midnight. Let's conclude this sordid business and move on to more important matters—like our investigation of the Bishop family's covenant violations."

There was nothing more pressing than ridding the world of Benjamin but I bit my tongue and took my chair, resting the tote bag on the table in front of me. Domenico reached for it, still curious about its contents.

"Don't." I looked at him. Apparently my eyes spoke volumes, for he withdrew his hand quickly.

"So, Sidonie, am I to understand you're calling the question?" I asked her abruptly. In spite of her calls for a quick resolution, she was proving to be a major impediment to the deliberations, drawing out every exchange with irrelevant detail until I was ready to scream.

"Not at all," she huffed. "I merely wish us to consider the matter with proper efficiency."

"I remain opposed to intervening in what is clearly a family problem," Gerbert said. "Madame de Clermont's proposal seeks to open this unfortunate matter to greater scrutiny. Already the Knights of Lazarus are on the scene and looking for her husband. It is best to let matters take their course."

"And the blood rage?" It was the first time Satu had said anything with the exception of her "no" when called upon in the first vote.

"Blood rage is a matter for the vampires to handle. We will discipline the de Clermont family for their serious lapse in judgment and take appropriate measures to locate and exterminate all who might be infected." Gerbert tented his fingers and looked around the table. "You can all rest easy on that score."

"I agree with Gerbert. Furthermore, no scion can be established under a diseased sire," Domenico said. "It's unthinkable. Matthew Clairmont must be put to death, and all his children with him." The vampire's eyes gleamed.

Osamu raised his hand and waited to be recognized.

"Yes, Mr. Watanabe?" I nodded in his direction.

"What's a weaver?" he asked. "And what do they have in common with vampires who have blood rage?"

"What makes you think they have anything in common?" Sidonie snapped.

"It's only logical that blood-rage vampires and weaving witches have something in common. How could Diana and Matthew have had children otherwise?" Agatha looked at me expectantly. Before I could answer, Gerbert stood and loomed over me.

"Is that what Matthew discovered in the Book of Life?" he demanded. "Did you unearth a spell that joins the two species?"

"Sit down, Gerbert." Janet had been knitting steadily for hours, looking up every now and again to make a judicious comment or smile benignly.

"The witch must answer!" Gerbert exclaimed. "What spell is at work here, and how did you perform it?"

"The answer is in the Book of Life." I dragged the tote bag toward me and drew out the volume that had been hidden for so long in the Bodleian Library.

There were gasps of astonishment around the table.

"This is a trick," Sidonie pronounced. She rose and made her way around the table. "If that is the witches' lost book of spells, I demand to examine it."

"It's the vampire's lost history," Domenico growled as she went past his chair.

"Here." I handed the Book of Life to Sidonie.

The witch tried to spring the clasps, pushing and tugging at the metal fittings, but the book refused to cooperate with her. I held out my hands and the book flew across the space between us, eager to be back where it belonged. Sidonie and Gerbert exchanged a long look.

"You open it, Diana," Agatha said, her eyes round. I thought back to what she'd said in Oxford all those months ago—that Ashmole 782 belonged to the daemons as well as the witches and vampires. Somehow, she had already divined a sense of the contents.

I placed the Book of Life on the table while the Congregation gathered around me. The clasps opened immediately at my touch. Whispers and sighs filled the air, followed by the eldritch traces left by the spirits of the creatures who were bound to the pages.

"Magic isn't permitted on Isola della Stella," Domenico protested, an edge of panic in his voice. "Tell her, Gerbert!"

"If I were working magic, Domenico, you'd know it," I retorted.

Domenico paled as the wraiths grew more coherent, taking on elongated human form with hollow, dark eyes.

I flipped the book open. Everybody bent forward for a closer look.

"There's nothing there," Gerbert said, his face twisted with fury. "The book is blank. What have you done to our book of origins?"

"This book smells . . . odd," Domenico said, giving the air a suspicious sniff. "Like dead animals."

"No, it smells of dead creatures." I ruffled the pages so that the scent rose in the air. "Daemons. Vampires. Witches. They're all in there."

"You mean . . ." Tatiana looked horrified.

"That's right." I nodded. "That's parchment made from creature skin. The leaves are sewn together with creature hair, too."

"But where is the text?" Gerbert asked, his voice rising. "The Book of Life is supposed to hold the key to many mysteries. It's our sacred text—the vampire's history."

"Here is your sacred text." I pushed up my sleeves. Letters and symbols swirled and ran just under my skin, coming to the surface like bubbles on a pond, only to dissolve. I had no idea what my eyes were doing, but I suspected they were full of characters, too. Satu backed away from me.

"You bewitched it," Gerbert snarled.

"The Book of Life was bewitched long ago," I said. "All I did was open it."

"And it chose you." Osamu reached out a finger to touch the letters on my arm. A few of them gathered around the point where his skin met mine before they danced away again.

"Why did the book choose Diana Bishop?" Domenico asked.

"Because I'm a weaver—a maker of spells—and there are precious few of us left." I sought out Satu once more. Her lips were pressed together, and her eyes begged me to remain silent. "We had too much creative power, and our fellow witches killed us."

"The same power that makes it possible for you to create new spells gives you the ability to create new life," Agatha said, her excitement evident.

"It's a special blessing the goddess bestows on female weavers," I replied. "Not all weavers are women, of course. My father was a weaver, too."

"It's impossible," Domenico snarled. "This is more of the witch's treachery. I've never heard of a weaver, and the ancient scourge of blood rage has mutated into an even more dangerous form. As for children born to witches and vampires, we cannot allow such an evil to take root. They would be monsters, beyond reason or control."

"I must take issue with you on that point, Domenico," Janet said.

"On what grounds?" he said with a touch of impatience.

"On the grounds that I am such a creature and am neither evil nor monstrous."

For the first time since my arrival, the attention of the room was directed elsewhere.

"My grandmother was the child of a weaver and a vampire." Janet's gray eyes latched on to mine. "Everyone in the Highlands called him Nickie-Ben."

"Benjamin," I breathed.

"Aye." Janet nodded. "Young witches were told to be careful on moonless nights, lest Nickie-Ben catch them. My great-granny, Isobel Gowdie, didn't listen. They had a mad love affair. The legends say he bit her on the shoulder. When Nickie-Ben went away, he left something behind without knowing it: a daughter. I am named after her."

I looked down at my arms. In a kind of magical Scrabble, letters rose and arranged themselves into a name: *JANET GOWDIE, DAUGHTER OF ISOBEL GOWDIE AND BENJAMIN FOX.* Janet's grandmother had been one of the Bright Born.

"When was your grandmother conceived?" An account of a Bright Born's life might tell me something about my own children's futures.

"In 1662," Janet said. "Granny Janet died in 1912, bless her, at the age of two hundred and fifty. She kept her beauty right until the end, but then, unlike me, Granny Janet was more vampire than witch. She was proud to have inspired the legends of the *baobhan sith,* having lured many a man to her bed only to cause each of them death and ruin. And it was fearful to behold Granny Janet's temper when she was crossed."

"But that would make you . . ." My eyes were round.

"I'll be one hundred and seventy next year," Janet said. She murmured a few words and her white hair was revealed to be a dusky black. Another murmured spell showed her skin was a luminous, pearly white.

Janet Gowdie looked no more than thirty. My children's lives began to take shape in my imagination.

"And your mother?" I asked.

"My mam lived for a full two hundred years. With each passing generation, our lives get shorter."

"How do you hide what you are from the humans?" Osamu asked.

"Same way the vampires do, I suppose. A bit of luck. A bit of help from our fellow witches. A bit of human willingness to turn away from the truth," Janet replied.

"This is utter nonsense," Sidonie said hotly. "You are a famous witch, Janet. Your spell-casting ability is renowned. And you come from a distinguished line of witches. Why you would want to sully your family's reputation with this story is beyond me."

"And there it is," I said, my voice soft.

"There what is?" Sidonie sounded like a testy schoolmarm.

"The disgust. The fear. The dislike of anybody who doesn't conform to your simpleminded expectations of the world and how it should work."

"Listen to me, Diana Bishop—"

But I was through listening to Sidonie or anybody else who used the covenant as a shield to hide their own inner darkness.

"No. You listen to me," I said. "My parents were witches. I'm the bloodsworn daughter of a vampire. My husband, and the father of my children, is a vampire. Janet, too, is descended from a witch and a vampire. When will you stop pretending that there's some pure-blooded witch ideal in the world?"

Sidonie stiffened. "There *is* such an ideal. It is how our power has been maintained."

"No. It's how our power has *died*," I retorted. "If we keep abiding by the covenant, in a few generations we won't have any power left. The whole purpose of that agreement was to keep the species from mixing and reproducing."

"More nonsense!" Sidonie cried. "The covenant's purpose is first and foremost to keep us safe."

"Wrong. The covenant was drawn up to prevent the birth of children like Janet: powerful, long-lived, neither witch nor vampire nor daemon but something in between," I said. "It's what all creatures have feared. It's what Benjamin wants to control. We cannot let him."

"In between?" Janet arched her brows. They were, now that I was seeing her clearly, as black as night. "Is that the answer, then?"

"Answer to what?" Domenico demanded.

But I was not ready to share that secret from the Book of Life. Not until Miriam and Chris had found the scientific evidence to back up what the manuscript had revealed to me. Once again I was saved from answering by the ringing of Celestina's bells.

"It is nearly midnight. We must adjourn—for now," Agatha Wilson said, her eyes shining. "I call the question. Will the Congregation support the de Clermonts in their efforts to rid the world of Benjamin Fox?"

Everyone returned to their seats and we went around the table one by one, casting our votes.

This time the vote was more encouraging: four in favor and five opposed. I had made progress in the second vote, earning the support of Agatha, Osamu, and Janet, but not enough to guarantee the outcome when the third, and final, vote was taken tomorrow. Especially not when my old enemies, Gerbert, Domenico, and Satu, were among the holdouts.

"The meeting will resume tomorrow afternoon at five o'clock." Aware of every minute that Matthew was spending in Benjamin's custody, I had argued once more for an earlier meeting time. And once more, my request had been denied.

Wearily I gathered up my leather folio—which I'd never opened—and the Book of Life. The past seven hours had been grueling. I couldn't stop thinking about Matthew and what he was enduring while the Congregation hemmed and hawed. And I was worried about the children, too, who were without both of their parents. I waited for the room to empty. Janet Gowdie and Gerbert were the last to leave.

"Gerbert?" I called.

He stopped on his way out the door, his back to me.

"I haven't forgotten what happened in May," I said, the power burning brightly in my hands. "One day you will answer to me for Emily Mather's death."

Gerbert's head swung around. "Peter said you and Matthew were hiding something. I should have listened to him."

"Didn't Benjamin already tip you off about what the witches dis-covered?" I asked.

But Gerbert hadn't lived so long to be caught so easily. His lip curled.

"Until next evening," he said, giving Janet and me a small, formal bow.

"We should call him Nickie-Bertie," Janet commented. "He and Benja-min would make a right pair of devils."

"They would indeed," I replied uneasily.

"Are you free tomorrow for lunch?" Janet Gowdie asked as we walked out of the meeting chamber and into the cloister, her musical Scots voice reminding me of Gallowglass.

"Me?" Even after all that had happened tonight, I was surprised she would be seen with a de Clermont.

"Neither of us fits into one of the Congregation's tiny boxes, Diana," Janet said, her smooth skin dimpling with amusement.

Gallowglass and Fernando were waiting for me under the cloister's ar-cade. Gallowglass frowned to see me in a witch's company.

"All right, Auntie?" he asked, worried. "We should go. It's getting late."

"I just want to have a quick word with Janet before we leave." I searched Janet's face, looking for a sign that she might be trying to win my friendship for some nefarious purpose, but all I saw was concern. "Why are you help-ing me?" I asked bluntly.

"I promised Philippe I would," Janet said. She dropped her knitting bag at her feet and drew up the sleeve of her shirt. "You are not the only one whose skin tells a tale, Diana Bishop."

Tattooed on her arm was a number. Gallowglass swore. I gasped. "Were you at Auschwitz with Philippe?" My heart was in my mouth.

"No. I was at Ravensbrück," she said. "I was working in France for the SOE—the Special Operations Executive—when I was captured. Philippe was trying to liberate the camp. He managed to get a few of us out before the Nazis caught him."

"Do you know where Philippe was held after Auschwitz?" I asked, my tone urgent.

"No, though we did look for him. Was it Nickie-Ben who had him?" Janet's eyes were dark with sympathy.

"Yes," I replied. "We think he was somewhere near Chelm."

"Benjamin had witches working for him then, too. I remember wondering at the time why everything within fifty miles of Chelm was lost in a dense fog. We couldn't find our way through it, no matter how we tried." Janet's eyes filled. "I am sorry we failed Philippe. We will do better this time. 'Tis a matter of Bishop-Clairmont family honor. And I am Matthew de Clermont's kin, after all."

"Tatiana will be the easiest to sway," I said.

"Not Tatiana," Janet said with a shake of her head. "She is infatuated with Domenico. Her sweater does more than enhance her figure. It also hides Domenico's bites. We must persuade Satu instead."

"Satu Järvinen will never help me," I said, thinking of the time we'd spent together at La Pierre.

"Oh, I think she will," Janet said. "Once we explain that we'll offer her up to Benjamin in exchange for Matthew if she doesn't. Satu is a weaver like you, after all. Perhaps Finnish weavers are more fertile than those from Chelm."

Satu was staying at a small establishment on a quiet *campo* on the opposite side of the Grand Canal from Ca' Chiaromonte. It looked perfectly ordinary from the outside, with brightly painted flower boxes and stickers on the windows indicating its rating relative to other area establishments (four stars) and the credit cards it accepted (all of them).

Inside, however, the veneer of normalcy proved thin.

The proprietress, Laura Malipiero, sat behind a desk in the front lobby swathed in purple and black velvet, shuffling a tarot deck. Her hair was wild and curly, with streaks of white through the black. A garland of black paper bats was draped over the mailboxes, and the scent of sage and dragon's-blood incense hung in the air.

"We're full," she said, not looking up from her cards. A cigarette was clasped in the corner of her mouth. It was purple and black, just like her outfit. At first I didn't think it was lit. Signorina Malipiero was sitting under a sign that read VIETATO FUMARE, after all. But then the witch took a deep drag on it. There was indeed no smoke, though the tip glowed.

"They say she's the richest witch in Venice. She made her fortune selling enchanted cigarettes." Janet eyed her with disapproval. She had donned her disguising spell again and to the casual observer looked to be a frail nonagenarian rather than a slender thirty-something.

"I'm sorry, sisters, but the Regata delle Befane is this week, and there isn't a room to be had in this part of Venice." Signorina Malipiero's attention remained on her cards.

I'd seen notices all over town announcing the annual Epiphany gondola race to see who could get from San Tomà to the Rialto the fastest. There were two races, of course: the official regatta in the morning and the far more exciting and dangerous one at midnight that involved not just brute strength but magic, too.

"We aren't interested in a room, Signorina Malipiero. I'm Janet Gowdie, and this is Diana Bishop. We're here to see Satu Järvinen on Congregation business—if she's not practicing for the gondola race, that is."

The Venetian witch looked up in shock, her dark eyes huge and her cigarette dangling.

"Room 17, is it? No need to trouble yourself. We can show ourselves up." Janet beamed at the stunned witch and bundled me off in the direction of the stairs.

"You, Janet Gowdie, are a bulldozer," I said breathlessly as she hustled me down the corridor. "Not to mention a mind reader." It was such a useful magical talent.

"What a lovely thing to say, Diana." Janet knocked on the door. *"Cameriera!"*

There was no answer. And after yesterday's marathon Congregation meeting, I was tired of waiting. I wrapped my fingers around the doorknob and murmured an opening spell. The door swung open. Satu Järvinen was waiting for us inside, both hands up, ready to work magic.

I snared the threads that surrounded her and pulled them tight, binding her arms to her sides. Satu gasped.

"What do you know about weavers?" I demanded.

"Not as much as you do," Satu replied.

"Is this why you treated me so badly at La Pierre?" I asked.

Satu's expression was steely. Her actions then had been taken in the interest of self-preservation. She felt no remorse. "I won't let you expose me. They'll kill us all if they find out what weavers can do," Satu said.

"They'll kill me anyway for loving Matthew. What do I have to lose?"

"Your children," Satu spit.

That, it turned out, was going too far.

"You are unfit to possess a witch's gifts. I bind thee, Satu Järvinen, delivering you into the hands of the goddess without power or craft." With the index finger of my left hand, I pulled the threads one more inch and knotted them tight. My finger flared darkly purple. It was, I had discovered, the color of justice.

Satu's power left her in a *whoosh*, sucking the air out of the room.

"You can't spellbind me!" she cried. "It's forbidden!"

"Report me to the Congregation," I said. "But before you do, know this: Nobody will be able to break the knot that binds you—except me. And what use will you be to the Congregation in this state? If you want to keep your seat, you'll have to keep your silence—and hope that Sidonie von Borcke doesn't notice."

"You will pay for this, Diana Bishop!" Satu promised.

"I already have," I said. "Or have you forgotten what you did to me in the name of sisterly solidarity?"

I advanced on her slowly. "Being spellbound is nothing compared to what Benjamin will do to you if he discovers that you are a weaver. You'll have no way to defend yourself and will be entirely at his mercy. I've seen what Benjamin does to the witches he tries to impregnate. Not even you deserve that."

Satu's eyes flickered with fear.

"Vote for the de Clermont motion this afternoon." I released Satu's arms, but not the binding spell that limited her power. "For your own sake, if not for Matthew."

Satu tried and failed to use her magic against me.

"Your power is gone. I wasn't lying, sister." I turned and stalked away. At the doorway I stopped and turned. "And don't ever threaten my children again. If you do, you'll be begging me to throw you down a hole and forget about you."

Gerbert tried to delay the final vote on procedural grounds, arguing that the current constitution of the governing council did not meet the criteria set out in foundational documents dating from the Crusader period. These stipulated the presence of three vampires, three witches, and three daemons.

Janet stopped me from strangling the creature by quickly explaining that since she and I were both part vampire and part witch, the Congregation was equally balanced. While she argued percentages, I examined Gerbert's so-called foundational documents and discovered words such as "unalienable" that were decidedly eighteenth-century in their tone. Presented with a list of the linguistic anachronisms in this supposedly Crusader document, Gerbert scowled at Domenico and said these were obviously later transcriptions of lost originals.

No one believed him.

Janet and I won the vote: six to three. Satu voted as we told her to do, her attitude subdued and defeated. Even Tatiana joined our ranks thanks to Osamu, who had devoted his morning to mapping the precise location of not only Chelm but every Russian city beginning with *Ch* just to prove that the Polish city's witches had nothing to do with her grandmother's skin affliction. When the two entered the council chamber hand in hand, I figured she might have switched not only sides but boyfriends.

Once the vote was tallied and recorded, we didn't linger to celebrate. Instead Gallowglass, Janet, Fernando, and I took off in the de Clermont launch, headed across the lagoon for the airport.

As planned, I sent a three-letter text to Hamish with the results of the vote: **QGA**. It stood for Queen's Gambit Accepted, a code to indicate that the Congregation had been persuaded to support Matthew's rescue. We did not know if anyone was monitoring our communications, but we'd decided to be cautious.

His response was immediate.

Well done. Standing by for your arrival.

I checked in with Marcus, who reported that the twins were always hungry and had completely monopolized Phoebe's attention. As for Jack, Marcus said he was as well as could be expected.

After my exchange with Marcus, I sent a text to Ysabeau.

Worried about the bishop pair.

It was another chess reference. We had dubbed Gerbert, onetime bishop of Rome, and his sidekick Domenico the "bishop pair" because they always seemed to be working together. After their latest defeat, they were bound to retaliate. Gerbert might already have warned Knox that I had won the vote and we were on our way.

Ysabeau took longer to reply than Marcus had.

The bishop pair cannot checkmate our king unless the queen and her rook allow it.

There was a long pause, then another message.

And I will die first.

39

The air bit through my thick cloak, making me withdraw from the blast of wind that threatened to split me in two. I had never experienced cold like this and wondered how anyone survived a winter in Chelm.

"There." Baldwin pointed to a low huddle of buildings in the valley below.

"Benjamin has at least a dozen of his children with him." Verin stood at my elbow, a pair of binoculars in her fingers. She offered them to me, in case my warmblooded eyes weren't strong enough to see where my husband was being kept, but I refused them.

I knew exactly where Matthew was. The closer I got to him, the more agitated my power became, leaping to the surface of my skin in an attempt to escape. That, and my witch's third eye, more than made up for any warmblooded deficiencies.

"We'll wait until twilight to strike. That's when a detail of Benjamin's children go out to hunt." Baldwin looked grim. "They've been preying on Chelm and Lublin, bringing back the homeless and the weak for their father to feed on."

"Wait?" I'd done nothing but for three days. "I'm not going to wait another moment!"

"He is still alive, Diana." Ysabeau's response should have brought me comfort, but it only made the ice around my heart thicken at the thought of what Matthew would continue to suffer for the next six hours as we waited for darkness to fall.

"We can't attack the compound when it's at full strength," Baldwin said. "We must be strategic about this, Diana—not emotional."

Think—and stay alive. Reluctantly, I turned away from dreams of Matthew's quick release to focus on the challenges before us. "Janet said Knox put wards around the main building."

Baldwin nodded. "We were waiting for you to disarm them."

"How will the knights get into position without Benjamin knowing?" I asked.

"Tonight the Knights of Lazarus will use the tunnels to enter Benjamin's compound from below." Fernando's expression was calculating. "Twenty, maybe thirty, should be enough."

"Chelm is built on chalk, you see, and the ground beneath it is honeycombed with tunnels," Hamish explained, unrolling a small, crudely drawn map. "The Nazis destroyed some of them, but Benjamin kept these open. They connect his compound and the town and provide a way for him and his children to prey on the city without ever appearing aboveground."

"No wonder Benjamin was so hard to track down," Gallowglass murmured, looking at the underground maze.

"Where are the knights now?" I had yet to see the massing of troops I'd been told were in Chelm.

"Standing by," Hamish replied.

"Fernando will decide when to send them into the tunnels. As Marcus's marshal, the decision is his," Baldwin said, acknowledging Fernando with a nod.

"Actually, it's mine," Marcus said, appearing suddenly against the snow.

"Marcus!" I pushed my hood back, terror gripping me. "What's happened to Rebecca and Philip? Where are they?"

"Nothing has happened. The twins are at Sept-Tours with Sarah, Phoebe, and three dozen knights—all of them handpicked for their loyalty to the de Clermonts and their dislike of Gerbert and the Congregation. Miriam and Chris are there, too." Marcus took my hands in his. "I couldn't sit in France waiting for news. Not when I could be helping to free my father. And Matthew might need my help after that, too."

Marcus was right. Matthew would need a doctor—a doctor who understood vampires and how to heal them.

"And Jack?" It was all I could squeeze out, though Marcus's words had helped my heart rate return to something approaching normal.

"He's fine, too," Marcus said firmly. "Jack had one bad episode last night when I told him he couldn't come along, but Marthe turns out to be something of a hellcat when provoked. She threatened to keep Jack from seeing Philip, and that sobered him right up. He never lets the child out of his sight. Jack says it's his job to protect his godson, no matter what." Marcus turned to Fernando. "Walk me through your plan."

Fernando went over the operation in detail: where the knights would be positioned, when they would move on the compound, the roles that Gallowglass, Baldwin, Hamish, and now Marcus would play.

Even though it all sounded flawless, I was still worried.

"What is it, Diana?" Marcus asked, sensing my concern.

"So much of our strategy relies on the element of surprise," I said. "What if Gerbert has already tipped off Knox and Benjamin? Or Domenico? Even Satu might have decided she was safer from Benjamin if she could gain Knox's trust."

"Don't worry, Auntie," Gallowglass assured me, his blue eyes taking on a stormy cast. "Gerbert, Domenico, and Satu are all sitting on Isola della Stella. The Knights of Lazarus have them surrounded. There's no way for them to get off the island."

Gallowglass's words did little to lessen my concern. The only thing that could help was freeing Matthew and putting an end to Benjamin's machinations—for good.

"Ready to examine the wards?" Baldwin asked, knowing that giving me something to do would help keep my anxiety in check.

After swapping my highly visible black cloak for a pale gray parka that blended into the snow, Baldwin and Gallowglass took me within shouting distance of Benjamin's compound. In silence I took stock of the wards that protected the place. There were a few alarm spells, a trigger spell that I suspected would unleash some kind of elemental conflagration or storm, and a handful of diversions that were designed to do nothing more than delay an attacker until a proper defense could be mounted. Knox had used spells that were complicated, but they were old and worn, too. It wouldn't take much to pick apart the knots and leave the place unguarded.

"I'll need two hours and Janet," I whispered to Baldwin as we withdrew.

Together Janet and I freed the compound from its invisible barbed-wire perimeter. There was one alarm spell we had to leave in place, however. It was linked directly back to Knox, and I feared that even tinkering with the knots would alert him to our presence.

"He's a clever bugger," Janet said, wiping a tired hand across her eyes.

"Too clever for his own good. His spells were lazy," I said. "Too many crossings, not enough threads."

"When this is all over, we are going to have several evenings by the fireside where you explain what you just said," Janet warned.

"When this is over, and Matthew is home, I'll happily sit by the fireside for the rest of my life," I replied.

Gallowglass's hovering presence reminded me that time was passing.

"Time to go," I said briskly, nodding toward the silent Gael.

Gallowglass insisted we eat something and took us to a café in Chelm. There I managed to swallow down some tea and two bites of hot-milk cake while the warmth from the clanging radiator thawed my extremities.

As the minutes ticked by, the regular metallic sounds from the café's heating system began to sound like warning bells. Finally Gallowglass announced that the hour had come when we were to meet up with Marcus's army.

He took us to a prewar house on the outskirts of town. Its owner had been happy to hand over the keys and head to warmer climes in exchange for a hefty cash vacation fund and the promise that he would find his leaking roof fixed when he returned.

The vampire knights who were assembled in the cellar were mostly unfamiliar to me, though I did recognize a few faces from the twins' christening. As I looked at them, rugged of line and quietly ready for whatever awaited them below, I was struck by the fact that these were warriors who had fought in modern world wars and revolutions, as well as medieval Crusades. They were some of the finest soldiers who had ever lived, and like all soldiers they were prepared to sacrifice their lives for something greater than themselves.

Fernando gave his final orders while Gallowglass opened a makeshift door. Beyond it was a small ledge and a rickety ladder that led down into darkness.

"Godspeed," Gallowglass whispered as the first of the vampires dropped out of sight and landed silently on the ground below.

We waited while the knights chosen to destroy Benjamin's hunting party did their work. Still nervous that someone might alert him to our presence and that he might respond by taking Matthew's life, I stared fixedly at the earth between my feet.

It was excruciating. There was no way to receive any progress reports. For all we knew, Marcus's knights could have met with unexpected resistance. Benjamin might have sent out more of his children to hunt. He might have sent out none.

"This is the hell of war," said Gallowglass. "It's not the fighting or even the dying that destroys you. It's the wondering."

No more than an hour later—though it felt like days—Giles pushed open the door. His shirt was stained with gore. There was no way to determine how much of it belonged to him and what might be traces of Benjamin's now-dead children. He beckoned us forward.

"Clear," he told Gallowglass. "But be careful. The tunnels echo, so watch your step."

Gallowglass handed Janet down and then me, making no use of the waiting ladder with its rusted metal treads that might give us away. It was so dark in the tunnel that I couldn't see the faces of the vampires who caught us, but I could smell the battle on them.

We hurried along the tunnel with as much speed as our need for silence allowed. Given the darkness, I was glad to have a vampire on each arm to steer me around the bends and would have fallen several times without the assistance of their keen eyes and quick reflexes.

Baldwin and Fernando were waiting for us at the intersection of three tunnels. Two blood-spattered mounds covered with tarps and a powdery white substance that gave off a faint glow marked where Benjamin's children had met their death.

"We covered the heads and bodies with quicklime to mask the scent," Fernando said. "It won't eliminate it completely, but it should buy us some time."

"How many?" Gallowglass asked.

"Nine," Baldwin replied. One of his hands was completely clean and bore a sword, the other was caked with substances I preferred not to identify. The contrast made my stomach heave.

"How many are still inside?" Janet murmured.

"At least another nine, probably more." Baldwin didn't look worried at the prospect. "If they're anything like this lot, you can expect them to be cocksure and clever."

"Dirty fighters, too," Fernando said.

"As expected," Gallowglass said, his tone easy and relaxed. "We'll be waiting for your signal to move into the compound. Good luck, Auntie."

Baldwin whisked me away before I could say a word of farewell to Gallowglass and Fernando. Perhaps it was better that way, since the single glance I cast over my shoulder captured faces that were etched with exhaustion.

The tunnel that Baldwin took us through led to the gates outside Benjamin's compound where Ysabeau and Hamish were waiting. With all the wards down save the one on the gate that led directly to Knox, the only risk was that a vampire's keen eyes would spot us.

Janet reduced that possibility with an all-encompassing disguising spell that concealed not only me but everybody within twenty feet.

"Where's Marcus?" I had expected to see him here.

Hamish pointed.

Marcus was already inside the perimeter, propped in the crook of a tree, a rifle aimed at a window. He must have breached the compound's stone walls by swinging from tree limb to tree limb. With no wards to worry about, provided he didn't use the gate, Marcus had taken advantage of the pause in the action and would now provide cover for us as we went through the gate and entered the front door.

"Sharpshooter," commented Baldwin.

"Marcus learned to handle a gun as a warmblood. He hunted squirrels when he was a child," added Ysabeau. "Smaller and faster than vampires, I'm told."

Marcus never acknowledged our presence, but he knew we were there. Janet and I set to work on the final knots that bound the alarm spell to Knox. She cast an anchoring spell, the kind witches used to shore up the foundations of their houses and keep their children from wandering away, and as I unbound the ward, I redirected its energy toward her. Our hope was that the spell wouldn't even notice that the heavy object it now guarded was a granite boulder and not a massive iron gate.

It worked.

We would have been inside the house in moments if not for the inconvenient interruption of one of Benjamin's sons, who came out to catch a cigarette only to discover the front gate standing open. His eyes widened.

A small hole appeared in his forehead.

One eye disappeared. Then another.

Benjamin's son clutched at his throat. Blood welled between his fingers, and he emitted a strange whistling sound.

"Hello, *salaud*. I'm your grandmother." Ysabeau thrust a dagger into the man's heart.

The simultaneous loss of blood from so many places made it easy for Baldwin to grab the man's head and twist it, breaking his neck and killing the vampire instantly. With another wrench his head came off his shoulders.

It had taken about forty-five seconds from the time Marcus fired his first shot to the moment Baldwin put the vampire's head facedown in the snow.

Then the dogs started to bark.

"Merde," Ysabeau whispered.

"Now. Go." Baldwin took my arm, and Ysabeau took charge of Janet. Marcus tossed his rifle to Hamish, who caught it easily. He let forth a piercing whistle.

"Shoot anything that comes out of that door," Marcus ordered. "I'm going after the dogs."

Unsure whether the whistle was meant to call the fierce-sounding canines or the waiting Knights of Lazarus, I hurried along into the compound's main building. It was no warmer inside than out. An emaciated rat scurried down the hall, which was lined with identical doors.

"Knox knows we're here," I said. There was no need for quiet or a disguising spell now.

"So does Benjamin," Ysabeau said grimly.

As planned, we parted ways. Ysabeau went in search of Matthew. Baldwin, Janet, and I were after Benjamin and Knox. With luck we would find them all in the same place and converge upon them, supported by the Knights of Lazarus once they breached the lower levels of the compound and made their way upstairs.

A soft cry drew us to one of the closed doors. Baldwin flung it open.

It was the room we'd seen on the video feed: the grimy tiles, drain in the floor, windows overlooking the snow, numbers written with a grease pencil on the walls, even the chair with a tweed coat lying over the back.

Matthew was sitting in another chair, his eyes black and his mouth open in a soundless scream. His ribs had been spread open with a metal device, exposing his slow-beating heart, the regular sound of which had brought me such comfort whenever he drew me close.

Baldwin rushed toward him, cursing Benjamin.

"It's not Matthew," I said.

Ysabeau's shriek in the distance told me she had stumbled onto a similar scene.

"It's not Matthew," I repeated, louder this time. I went to the next door and twisted the knob.

There was Matthew, sitting in the same chair. His hands—his beautiful, strong hands that touched me with such love and tenderness—had been severed at the wrists and were sitting in a surgical basin in his lap.

No matter which door we opened, we found Matthew in some horrific tableau of pain and torment. And every illusory scene had been staged especially for me.

After my hopes had been raised and dashed a dozen times, I blew all the doors in the house off their hinges with a single word. I didn't bother looking inside any of the open rooms. Apparitions could be quite convincing, and Knox's were very good indeed. But they were not flesh and blood. They were not my Matthew, and I was not deceived by them even though those I had seen would remain with me forever.

"Matthew will be with Benjamin. Find him." I walked away without waiting for Baldwin or Janet to agree. "Where are you, Mr. Knox?"

"Dr. Bishop." Knox was waiting for me when I rounded the corner. "Come. Have a drink with me. You won't be leaving this place, and it may be your last chance to enjoy the comforts of a warm room—until you conceive Benjamin's child, that is."

Behind me I slammed down an impenetrable wall of fire and water so that no one could follow.

Then I threw up another behind Knox, boxing us into a small section of the corridor.

"Nicely done. Your spell-casting talents have emerged, I see," said Knox.

"You will find me . . . altered," I said, using Gallowglass's phrase. The magic was waiting inside me, begging to fly. But I kept it under control, and the power obeyed me. I felt it there, still and watchful.

"Where have you been?" Knox asked.

"Lots of places. London. Prague. France." I felt the tingle of magic in my fingertips. "You've been to France, too."

"I went looking for your husband and his son. I found a letter, you see.

In Prague." Knox's eyes gleamed. "Imagine my surprise, stumbling upon Emily Mather—never a terribly impressive witch—binding your mother's spirit inside a stone circle."

Knox was trying to distract me.

"It reminded me of the stone circle I cast in Nigeria to bind your parents. Perhaps that was Emily's intention."

Words crawled beneath my skin, answering the silent questions his words engendered.

"I should never have let Satu do the honors where you were concerned, my dear. I've always suspected that you were different," Knox said. "Had I opened you up last October, as I did your mother and father all those years ago, you could have been spared so much heartache."

But there had been more in the past fourteen months than heartache. There had been unexpected joy, too. I clung to that now, anchoring myself to it as firmly as if Janet were working her magic.

"You're very quiet, Dr. Bishop. Have you nothing to say?"

"Not really. I prefer actions to words these days. They save time."

At last I released the magic spooled tightly within me. The net I'd made to capture Knox was black and purple, woven through with strands of white, silver, and gold. It spread out in wings from my shoulder blades, reminding me of the absent Corra, whose power, as she promised, was still mine.

"With knot of one, the spell's begun." My netlike wings spread wider.

"Very impressive bit of illusory work, Dr. Bishop." Knox's tone was patronizing. "A simple banishing spell will—"

"With knot of two, the spell be true." The silver and gold threads in my net gleamed bright, balancing the dark and light powers that marked the crossroads of the higher magics.

"It's too bad Emily didn't have your skill," Knox said. "She might have gotten more out of your mother's bound spirit than the gibberish I found when I stole her thoughts at Sept-Tours."

"With knot of three, the spell is free." The giant wings beat once, sending a soft eddy of air through the magical box I'd constructed. They gently separated from my body, rising higher until they hovered over Knox. He cast a look upward, then resumed.

"Your mother babbled to Emily about chaos and creativity and repeated the words of that charlatan Ursula Shipton's prophecy: *Old worlds die and new be born.* That's all I got out of Rebecca in Nigeria, too. Being with your father weakened her abilities. She needed a husband who could challenge her."

"With knot of four, the power is stored." A dark, potent spiral slowly unwound at the spot where the two wings were joined.

"Shall we open you up and see if you are more like your mother or your father?" Knox's hand made a lazy gesture, and I felt his magic cut a searing path across my chest.

"With knot of five, this spell will thrive." The purple threads in the net tightened around the spiral. "With knot of six, this spell I fix." The gold threads gleamed. A casual brush of my hand sealed the wound in my chest.

"Benjamin was quite interested in what I told him about your mother and father. He has plans for you, Diana. You will carry Benjamin's children, and they will become like the witches of old: powerful, wise, long-lived. There will be no more hiding in the shadows for us then. We will rule over the other warmbloods, as we should."

"With knot of seven, the spell will waken." A low keening filled the air, reminiscent of the sound the Book of Life made in the Bodleian. Then it had been a cry of terror and pain. Now it sounded like a call for vengeance.

For the first time, Knox looked worried.

"You cannot escape from Benjamin, any more than Emily could escape from me at Sept-Tours. She tried, of course, but I prevailed. All I wanted was the witch's spell book. Benjamin said Matthew once had it." Knox's eyes took on a fevered glint. "When I possess it, I will have the upper hand over the vampires, too. Even Gerbert will bow to me then."

"With knot of eight, the spell will wait." I pulled the net into the twisted shape that signified infinity. As I manipulated the threads, my father's shadowy form appeared.

"Stephen." Knox licked his lips. "This is an illusion, too."

My father ignored him, crossing his arms and looking at me sharply. "You ready to finish this, peanut?"

"I am, Dad."

"You don't have the power to finish me," Knox snarled. "Emily discovered that when she tried to keep me from having knowledge of the lost book of spells. I took her thoughts and stopped her heart. Had she only cooperated—"

"With knot of nine, the spell is mine."

The keening rose into a shriek as all the chaos contained in the Book of Life and all the creative energy that bound the creatures together in one place burst from the web I'd made and engulfed Peter Knox. My father's hands were among those that reached out of the dark void to grasp him while he struggled, keeping him in a whirling vortex of power that would eat him alive.

Knox cried out in terror as the spell drained his life away. He unraveled before my eyes as the spirits of all the weavers who had come before me, including my father, deliberately unpicked the threads that made up this damaged creature, reducing Knox to a lifeless shell.

One day I would pay a price for what I'd done to a fellow witch. But I had avenged Emily, whose life had been taken for no other reason than a dream of power.

I had avenged my mother and father, who loved their daughter enough to die for her.

I drew the goddess's arrow from my spine. A bow crafted from rowan and trimmed with silver and gold appeared in my left hand.

Vengeance had been mine. Now it was time for the goddess's justice.

I turned to my father, a question in my eyes.

"He's upstairs. Third floor. Sixth door on the left." My father smiled. "Whatever price the goddess exacted from you, Matthew is worth it. Just as you were."

"He's worth everything," I said, lowering the magical walls I'd built and leaving the dead behind so I could find the living.

Magic, like any resource, is not infinite in its supply. The spell I'd used to eliminate Knox had drained me of a significant amount of power. But I'd taken the risk knowing that without Knox, Benjamin had only physical strength and cruelty in his arsenal.

I had love and nothing more to lose.

Even without the goddess's arrow, we were evenly matched.

The house had far fewer rooms in it now that Knox's illusions were gone. Instead of an unending array of identical doors, the house now showed its true character: filthy, rife with the scents of death and fear, a place of horror.

My feet raced up the stairs. I couldn't spare an ounce of magic now. I had no idea where any of the others were. But I did know where to find Matthew. I pushed open the door.

"There you are. We've been expecting you." Benjamin was standing behind a chair.

This time the creature in it was undeniably the man I loved. His eyes were black and filled with blood rage and pain, but they flickered in recognition.

"Queen's Gambit complete," I told him.

Relieved, Matthew's eyes drifted closed.

"I hope you know better than to shoot that arrow," Benjamin said. "In case you're not as well versed in anatomy as you are in chemistry, I've made sure that Matthew will die instantly if my hand isn't here to support this."

This was a large iron spike Benjamin had driven into Matthew's neck.

"You remember when Ysabeau poked her finger into me at the Bodleian? It created a seal. That's what I've done here." Benjamin wiggled the spike a bit, and Matthew howled. A few drops of blood appeared. "My father doesn't have much blood left in him. I've fed him nothing but shards of glass for two days and he's been slowly bleeding out internally."

It was then I noticed the pile of dead children in the corner.

"Earlier meals," Benjamin said in response to my glance. "It was a challenge to come up with ways to torment Matthew, since I wanted to make sure he still had eyes to see me take you, and ears to hear your screams. But I found a way."

"You are a monster, Benjamin."

"Matthew made me one. Now, don't waste any more of your energy. Ysabeau and Baldwin are bound to be here soon. This is the very room where I kept Philippe, and I left a trail of bread crumbs to make sure my grandmother finds it. Baldwin will be so surprised to hear who it was that killed his father, don't you think? I saw it all in Matthew's thoughts. As for you . . . well, you cannot imagine the things Matthew would like to do to you in the privacy of his bed. Some of them made me blush, and I'm not exactly prudish."

I felt Ysabeau's presence behind me. A rain of photographs fell upon the floor. Pictures of Philippe. Here. In agony. I shot a look of fury at Benjamin.

"I would like nothing more than to shred you to pieces with my bare hands, but I would not deprive Philippe's daughter of the pleasure." Ysabeau's voice was cold and serrated. It rasped against my ears almost painfully.

"Oh, she'll have pleasure with me, Ysabeau. I assure you of that." Benjamin whispered something in Matthew's ear, and I saw Matthew's hand twitch as if he wanted to strike his son but his broken bones and shredded muscles made that impossible. "Here's Baldwin. It's been a long time, Uncle. I have something to tell you—a secret Matthew has been keeping. He keeps so many, I know, but this is a juicy one, I promise." Benjamin paused for effect. "Philippe did not die because of me. It was Matthew who killed him."

Baldwin stared at him impassively.

"Do you want to take a shot at him before my children send you to hell to see your father?" Benjamin asked.

"Your children won't be sending me anywhere. And if you think I am surprised by this supposed secret, you are even more delusional than I feared," Baldwin said. "I know Matthew's work when I see it. He's almost too good at what he does."

"Drop that." Benjamin's voice cracked like a whip as his cold, unfathomable eyes settled on my left hand.

While the two of them were having their discussion, I'd taken the opportunity to lift the bow.

"Drop it now or he dies." Benjamin withdrew the spike slightly, and the blood flowed.

I dropped the bow with a clatter.

"Smart girl," he said, thrusting the spike home again. Matthew moaned. "I liked you even before I learned you were a weaver. So that's what makes you special? Matthew has been shamefully reluctant to determine the limits of your power, but never fear. I'll make sure we know exactly how far your abilities extend."

Yes, I was a smart girl. Smarter than Benjamin knew. And I understood the limits of my power better than anyone else ever would. As for the goddess's bow, I didn't need it. What I needed in order to destroy Benjamin was still in my other hand.

I lifted my pinkie slightly so that it brushed Ysabeau's thigh in warning. "With knot of ten, it begins again."

My words came out like a breath, insubstantial and easy to ignore, just as the tenth knot was seemingly a simple loop. As they traveled into the room, my spell took on the weight and power of a living thing. I extended my left arm straight as though it still held the goddess's bow. My left index finger burned a bright purple.

My right hand drew back in a lightning-quick move, fingers curled loosely around the white fletchings on the golden arrow's shaft. I stood squarely at the crossroads between life and death.

And I did not hesitate.

"Justice," I said, and unfurled my fingers.

Benjamin's eyes widened.

The arrow sprang from my hand through the center of the spell, picking up momentum as it flew. It hit Benjamin's chest with audible force, cleaving him wide open and bursting his heart. A blinding wave of power engulfed the room. Silver and gold threads shot everywhere, accompanied by strands of purple and green. *The sun king. The moon queen. Justice. The goddess.*

With an otherworldly cry of frustrated anguish, Benjamin loosened his fingers, and the blood-covered spike began to slip.

Working quickly, I twisted the threads surrounding Matthew into a single rope that caught the end of the spike. I pulled it taut, keeping it in place as Benjamin's blood poured forth and he dropped heavily to the floor.

The few bare lightbulbs in the room flickered, then went out. I'd had to draw on every bit of energy in the place to kill Knox and then Benjamin. All that was left now was the power of the goddess: the shimmering rope hanging in the middle of the room, the words moving underneath my skin, the power snapping at the ends of my fingers.

It was over.

Benjamin was dead and could no longer torment anyone.

And Matthew, though broken, was alive.

After Benjamin fell, everything seemed to happen at once. Ysabeau pulled the vampire's dead body away. Baldwin was at Matthew's side, calling for Marcus and checking on his injuries. Verin and Gallowglass and Hamish burst into the room. Fernando followed soon thereafter.

I stood in front of Matthew and cradled his head against my heart, sheltering him from further harm. With one hand I held up the iron implement that was keeping him alive. Matthew let out an exhausted sigh and shifted slightly against me.

"It's all right now. I'm here. You're safe," I murmured, trying to bring him what little comfort I could. "You're alive."

"Couldn't die." Matthew's voice was so faint it didn't even qualify as a whisper. "Not without saying goodbye."

Back in Madison, I'd made Matthew promise not to leave me without a proper farewell. My eyes filled as I thought of all he'd been through to honor his word.

"You kept your promise," I said. "Rest now."

"We need to move him, Diana." Marcus's calm voice couldn't disguise his urgency. He put his hand around the spike, ready to take my place.

"Don't let Diana watch." Matthew's voice was raw and guttural. His skeletal hand twitched on the arm of the chair in protest, but it was not able to do more. "I beg you."

With nearly every inch of Matthew's body injured, there were precious few places I could touch him that wouldn't compound his pain. I located a few centimeters of undamaged flesh gleaming in the glow cast by the Book of Life and dropped a kiss as soft as down on the tip of his nose.

Unsure if he could hear me, and knowing that his eyes were swollen shut, I let my breath wash over him, bathing him in my scent. Matthew's nostrils flared a fraction, signaling that he had registered my proximity. Even that little movement made him wince, and I had to steel myself not to cry out at what Benjamin had done to him.

"You can't hide from me, my love," I said instead. "I see you, Matthew. And you will always be perfect in my eyes."

His breath came out in a ragged gasp, his lungs unable to expand fully because of the pressure from broken ribs. With a herculean effort, Matthew cracked one eye open. It was filmed over with blood, the pupil shot wide and enormous from blood rage and trauma.

"It's dark." Matthew's voice took on a frantic edge, as though he feared that the darkness signaled his death. "Why is it so dark?"

"It's all right. Look." I blew on my fingertip, and a blue-gold star appeared on the tip of my finger. "See. This will light our way."

It was a risk, and I knew it. He might not be able to see the small ball of fire, and then his panic would only increase. Matthew peered at my finger and flinched slightly as the light came into focus. His pupil tightened a tiny amount in response, which I took as a good sign.

His next breath was less ragged as his anxiety subsided.

"He needs blood," Baldwin said, keeping his voice level and low.

I tried to push my sleeve up without lowering my gleaming finger, which Matthew was staring at fixedly.

"Not yours," Ysabeau said, stilling my efforts. "Mine."

Matthew's agitation rose again. It was like watching Jack struggle to rein in his emotions.

"Not here," he said. "Not with Diana watching."

"Not here," Gallowglass agreed, giving my husband back some small measure of control.

"Let his brothers and his son take care of him, Diana." Baldwin lowered my hand.

And so I let Gallowglass, Fernando, Baldwin, and Hamish lace their arms together into a sling while Marcus held the iron spike in place.

"My blood is strong, Diana," Ysabeau promised, gripping my hand tightly. "It will heal him."

I nodded. But I had told Matthew the truth earlier: In my eyes he would always be perfect. His outward wounds didn't matter to me. It was the wounds to his heart, mind, and soul that had me worried, for no amount of vampire blood could heal those.

"Love and time," I murmured, as though trying to figure out the components of a spell, watching from a distance as the men settled an unconscious Matthew into the cargo hold of one of the cars that were waiting for us. "That's what he needs."

Janet came up and put a comforting hand on my shoulder.

"Matthew Clairmont is an ancient vampire," she observed, "and he has you. So I'm thinking love and time will do the trick."

Sol in Aquarius

When the sun passeth through the water-bearer's
sign, it betokens great fortune, faithful friends, and the
aide of princes. Therefore, do not feare changes that
take place when Aquarius ruleth the earth.

—Anonymous English Commonplace Book, c. 1590,
Gonçalves MS 4890, f. 10ʳ

Matthew said only one word on the flight: "Home."

We arrived in France six days after the events in Chelm. Matthew still couldn't walk. He wasn't able to use his hands. Nothing remained in his stomach for more than thirty minutes. Ysabeau's blood, as promised, was slowly mending the crushed bones, damaged tissues, and injuries to Matthew's internal organs. After first falling unconscious due to a combination of drugs, pain, and exhaustion, he now refused to close his eyes to rest.

And he hardly ever spoke. When he did, it was usually to refuse something.

"No," he said when we turned toward Sept-Tours. "Our home."

Faced with a range of options, I told Marcus to take us to Les Revenants. It was a strangely fitting name given its present owner, for Matthew had returned home more ghost than man after what Benjamin had done to him.

No one had dreamed that Matthew would prefer Les Revenants to Sept-Tours, and the house was cold and lifeless when we arrived. He sat in the foyer with Marcus while his brother and I raced around lighting fires and making up a bed for him. Baldwin and I were discussing which room would be best for Matthew given his present physical limitations when the convoy of cars from Sept-Tours filled the courtyard. Not even the vampires could beat Sarah to the door, she was so eager to see us. My aunt knelt in front of Matthew. Her face was soft with compassion and concern.

"You look like hell," she said.

"Feel worse." Matthew's once-beautiful voice was harsh and grating, but I treasured every terse word.

"When Marcus says it's okay, I'd like to put a salve on your skin that will help you heal," Sarah said, touching the raw skin on his forearm.

The cry of a furious, hungry baby split the air.

"Becca." My heart leaped at the prospect of seeing the twins again. But Matthew did not seem to share my happiness.

"No." Matthew's eyes were wild, and he shook from head to toe. "No. Not now. Not like this."

Since Benjamin had taken control of Matthew's mind and body, I insisted that now Matthew was free he should be allowed to set the terms of his own daily existence and even his medical treatment. But this I would not allow. I scooped Rebecca out of Ysabeau's arms, kissed her smooth cheek, and dropped the baby into the crook of Matthew's elbow.

The moment Becca saw Matthew's face, she stopped crying.

The moment Matthew had his daughter in his arms, he stopped shaking, just as I had the night she was born. My eyes filled at his terrified, awestruck expression.

"Good thinking," Sarah murmured. She gave me the once-over. "You look like hell, too."

"Mum," Jack said, kissing me on the cheek. He tried to give me Philip, but the baby squirmed away from me, his face twisting and turning.

"What is it, little man?" I touched Philip's face with a fingertip. My hands flashed with power, and the letters that now waited under the surface of my skin rose up, arranging themselves into stories that had yet to be told. I nodded and gave the baby a kiss on the forehead, feeling the tingle on my lips that confirmed what the Book of Life had already revealed to me. My son had power—lots of power. "Take him to Matthew, Jack."

Jack knew full well the horrors Benjamin was capable of committing. He steeled himself to see evidence of them before he turned. I saw Matthew through Jack's eyes: his hero, home from battle, gaunt and wounded. Jack cleared his throat, and the growling sound had me concerned.

"Don't leave Philip out of the reunion, Dad." Jack wedged Philip securely into the crook of Matthew's other arm.

Matthew's eyes flickered with surprise at the greeting. It was such a small word—*Dad*—but Jack had never called Matthew anything except Master Roydon and Matthew. Though Andrew Hubbard had insisted that Matthew was Jack's true father, and Jack had been quick to call me "Mother," he had been strangely reluctant to bestow a similar honor on the man he worshipped.

"Philip gets cross when Becca gets all the attention." Jack's voice was roughened with suppressed rage, and he made his next words deliberately playful and light. "Granny Sarah has all kinds of advice on how to treat younger brothers and sisters. Most of it involves ice cream and trips to the zoo." Jack's banter didn't fool Matthew.

"Look at me." Matthew's voice was weak and raspy, but there was no mistaking that this was an order.

Jack met his eyes.

"Benjamin is dead," Matthew said.

"I know." Jack looked away, shifting restlessly from one foot to the other.

"Benjamin can't hurt you. Not anymore."

"He hurt you. And he would have hurt my mother." Jack looked at me, and his eyes filled with darkness.

Fearing that the blood rage would engulf him, I took a step in Jack's direction. I stopped before taking another, forcing myself to let Matthew handle it.

"Eyes on me, Jack."

Matthew's skin was gray with effort. He had uttered more words since Jack's arrival than he had in a full week, and they were sapping his strength. Jack's wandering attention returned to the head of his clan.

"Take Rebecca. Give her to Diana. Then come back."

Jack did as asked, while the rest of us watched warily in case either he or Matthew lost control.

With Becca safely in my arms, I kissed her and told her in a whisper what a good girl she was not to fuss at being taken from her father.

Becca frowned, indicating she was playing this game under protest.

Back at Matthew's side, Jack reached for Philip.

"No. I'll keep him." Matthew's eyes were getting ominously dark, too. "Take Ysabeau home, Jack. Everybody else go, too."

"But, *Matthieu*," Ysabeau protested. Fernando whispered something in her ear. Reluctantly she nodded. "Come, Jack. On the way to Sept-Tours, I will tell you a story about the time Baldwin attempted to banish me from Jerusalem. Many men died."

After delivering that thinly veiled warning, Ysabeau swept Jack from the room.

"Thank you, *Maman*," Matthew murmured. He was still supporting Philip's weight, and his arms shook alarmingly.

"Call if you need me," Marcus whispered as he headed out the door.

As soon as it was just the four of us in the house, I took Philip from Matthew's lap and plunked both babies in the cradle by the fireplace.

"Too heavy," Matthew said wearily as I tried to lift him from the chair. "Stay here."

"You will not stay here." I studied the situation and decided on a solution. I marshaled the air to support my hastily woven levitation spell. "Stand back, I'm going to try magic." Matthew made a faint sound that might have been an attempt at laughter.

"Don't. The floor's okay," he said, his words slurring with exhaustion.

"The bed's better," I replied firmly as we skimmed over the floor to the elevator.

During our first week at Les Revenants, Matthew permitted Ysabeau to come and feed him. He regained some of his strength and a bit more mobility. He still couldn't walk, but he could stand provided he had assistance, his arms hanging limply at his sides.

"You're making such quick progress," I said brightly, as though everything in the world were rosy.

Inside my head it was very dark indeed. And I was screaming in anger, fear, and frustration as the man I loved struggled to find his way through the shadows of the past that had overtaken him in Chelm.

Sol in Pisces

When the sun is in Pisces, expect weariness and sadness.

Those who can banish feare will experience forgiveness

and understanding. You will be called to work in

faraway places.

—*Anonymous English Commonplace Book, c. 1590,*
Gonçalves MS 4890, f. 10r

"I want some of my books," Matthew said with deceptive casualness. He rattled off a list of titles. "Hamish will know where to find them." His friend had gone back to London briefly, then returned to France. Hamish had been ensconced in Matthew's rooms at Sept-Tours ever since. He spent his days trying to keep clueless bureaucrats from ruining the world economy and his nights depleting Baldwin's wine cellar.

Hamish arrived at Les Revenants with the books, and Matthew asked him to sit and have a glass of Champagne. Hamish seemed to understand that this attempt at normalcy was a turning point in Matthew's recovery.

"Why not? Man cannot live on claret alone." With a subtle glance at me, Hamish indicated that he would take care of Matthew.

Hamish was still there three hours later—and the two of them were playing chess. My knees weakened at the unexpected sight of Matthew sitting on the white side of the board, considering his options. Since Matthew's hands were still useless—the hand was a terribly complicated bit of anatomical engineering, it turned out—Hamish moved the pieces according to Matthew's encoded commands.

"E4," Matthew said.

"The Central Variation? How daring of you." Hamish moved one of the white pawns.

"You accepted the Queen's Gambit," Matthew said mildly. "What did you expect?"

"I expect you to mix things up. Once upon a time, you refused to put your queen at risk. Now you do it every game." Hamish frowned. "It's a poor strategy."

"The queen did just fine last time," I whispered in Matthew's ear, and he smiled.

When Hamish left, Matthew asked me to read to him. It was now a ritual for us to sit in front of the fire, the snow falling past the windows and one of Matthew's beloved books in my hand: Abelard, Marlowe, Darwin, Thoreau, Shelley, Rilke. Often Matthew's lips moved along with the words as I uttered them, proving to me—and, more important, to him—that his mind was as sharp and whole as ever.

"*I am the daughter of Earth and Water, / And the nursling of the Sky,*'" I read from his battered copy of *Prometheus Unbound*.

"'*I pass through the pores of the ocean and shores,*'" Matthew whispered. "'*I change, but I cannot die.*'"

After Hamish's visit our society at Les Revenants gradually expanded. Jack was invited to join Matthew and to bring his cello with him. He played Beethoven for hours on end, and not only did the music have positive effects on my husband, it unfailingly put my daughter to sleep as well.

Matthew was improving, but he still had a long way to go. When he rested fitfully, I dozed at his side and hoped that the babies wouldn't stir. He let me help him bathe and dress, though he hated himself—and me—for it. Whenever I thought I couldn't endure another moment of watching him struggle, I focused on some patch of skin that had knit itself back together. Like the shadows of Chelm, the scars would never fully disappear.

When Sarah came to see him, her worry was palpable. But Matthew was not the cause of her concern.

"How much magic are you using to stay upright?" Accustomed to living with bat-eared vampires, she had waited until I walked her to the car before she asked.

"I'm fine," I said, opening the car door for her.

"That wasn't my question. I can see you're fine. That's what worries me," Sarah said. "Why aren't you at death's door?"

"It doesn't matter," I said, dismissing her question.

"It will when you collapse," Sarah retorted. "You can't possibly keep this up."

"You forget, Sarah: The Bishop-Clairmont family specializes in the impossible." I closed the car door to muffle her ongoing protests.

I should have known that my aunt would not be silenced so easily. Baldwin showed up twenty-four hours after her departure—uninvited and unannounced.

"This is a bad habit of yours," I said, thinking back to the moment he'd returned to Sept-Tours and stripped the sheets from our bed. "Surprise us again and I'll put enough wards on this house to repel the Four Horsemen of the Apocalypse."

"They haven't been spotted in Limousin since Hugh died." Baldwin kissed me on each cheek, taking time in between to make a slow assessment of my scent.

"Matthew isn't receiving visitors today," I said, drawing away. "He had a difficult night."

"I'm not here to see Matthew." Baldwin fixed eagle eyes on me. "I'm here to warn you that if you don't start taking care of yourself, I will put myself in charge here."

"You have no—"

"Oh, but I do. You are my sister. Your husband is not able to look after your welfare at the moment. Look after it yourself or accept the consequences." Baldwin's voice was implacable.

The two of us faced off in silence for a few moments. He sighed when I refused to break my stare.

"It's really quite simple, Diana. If you collapse—and based on your scent, I'd say you have a week at most before that happens—Matthew's instincts will demand that he try to protect his mate. That will distract him from his primary job, which is to heal."

Baldwin had a point.

"The best way to handle a vampire mate—especially one with blood rage like Matthew—is to give him no reason to think you need any protection. Take care of yourself—first and always," Baldwin said. "Seeing you healthy and happy will do Matthew more good, mentally and physically, than his maker's blood or Jack's music. Do we understand each other?"

"Yes."

"I'm so glad." Baldwin's mouth lifted into a smile. "Answer your e-mail while you're at it. I send you messages. You don't answer. It's aggravating."

I nodded, afraid that if I opened my mouth, detailed instructions on just what he could do with his e-mail might pop out.

Baldwin stuck his head into the great hall to check on Matthew. He pronounced him utterly useless because he could not engage in wrestling, warfare, or other brotherly pursuits. Then, mercifully, he left.

Dutifully I opened my laptop.

Hundreds of messages awaited, most from the Congregation demanding explanations and Baldwin giving me orders.

I lowered the lid on my computer and returned to Matthew and my children.

*   *   *

A few nights after Baldwin's visit, I woke to the sensation of a cold finger jerking against my spine as it traced the trunk of the tree on my neck.

The finger moved in barely controlled fits and starts to my shoulders, where it found the outline left by the goddess's arrow and the star left by Satu Järvinen.

Slowly the finger traveled down to the dragon that encircled my hips. *Matthew's hands were working again.*

"I needed the first thing I touched to be you," he said, realizing he'd awakened me.

I was barely able to breathe, and any response on my part was out of the question. But my unspoken words wanted to be set free nevertheless. The magic rose within me, letters forming phrases under my skin.

"The price of power." Matthew's hand circled my forearm, his thumb stroking the words as they appeared. The movement was rough and irregular at first, but it grew smoother and steadier with every pass over my skin. He had observed the changes in me since I'd become the Book of Life but never mentioned them until now.

"So much to say," he murmured, his lips brushing my neck. His fingers delved, parted my flesh, touched my core.

I gasped. It had been so long, but his touch was still familiar. Matthew's fingers went unerringly to the places that brought me the most pleasure.

"But you don't need words to tell me what you feel," Matthew said. "I see you, even when you hide from the rest of the world. I hear you, even when you're silent."

It was a pure definition of love. Like magic, the letters amassing on my forearms disappeared as Matthew stripped my soul bare and guided my body to a place where words were indeed unnecessary. I trembled through my release, and though Matthew's touch became light as a feather, his fingers never stopped moving.

"Again," he said, when my pulse quickened once more.

"It's not possible," I said. Then he did something that made me gasp.

"Impossible n'est pas français," Matthew replied, giving me a nip on the ear. "And next time your brother comes to call, tell him not to worry. I'm perfectly able to take care of my wife."

Sol in Aries

The signe of the ram signifies dominion and wisdom.

While the sun resides in Aries, you will see growth in all

your works. It is a time for new beginnings.

—*Anonymous English Commonplace Book, c. 1590,*
Gonçalves MS 4890, f. 7

"Answer your fucking e-mail!"

Apparently Baldwin was having a bad day. Like Matthew, I was beginning to appreciate the ways that modern technology allowed us to keep the other vampires in the family at arm's length.

"I've put them off as long as I can." Baldwin glowered at me from the computer screen, the city of Berlin visible through the huge windows behind him. "You are going to Venice, Diana."

"No I'm not." We had been having some version of this conversation for weeks.

"Yes you are." Matthew leaned over my shoulder. He was walking now, slowly but just as silently as ever. "Diana will meet with the Congregation, Baldwin. But speak to her like that again and I'll cut your tongue out."

"Two weeks," Baldwin said, completely unfazed by his brother's threat. "They've agreed to give her two more weeks."

"It's too soon." The physical effects of Benjamin's torture were fading, but it had left Matthew's control over his blood rage as thin as a knife's edge and his temper just as sharp.

"She'll be there." He closed the lid on the laptop, effectively shutting out his brother and his final demands.

"It's too soon," I repeated.

"Yes, it is—far too soon for me to travel to Venice and face Gerbert and Satu." Matthew's hands were heavy on my shoulders. "If we want the covenant formally set aside—and we do—one of us must make the case to the Congregation."

"What about the children?" I was grasping at straws.

"The three of us will miss you, but we will manage. If I look sufficiently inept in front of Ysabeau and Sarah, I won't have to change a single diaper while you're gone." Matthew's fingers increased in pressure, as did the sense of responsibility resting on my shoulders. "You must do this. For me. For us. For every member of our family who has been harmed because of the covenant: Emily, Rebecca, Stephen, even Philippe. And for our children, so that they can grow up in love instead of fear."

There was no way I could refuse to go to Venice after that.

The Bishop-Clairmont family swung into action, eager to help ready our case for the Congregation. It was a collaborative, multispecies effort that began with honing our argument down to its essential core. Hard as it was to strip away the insults and injuries, large and small, that we had suffered, success depended on being able to make our request not seem like a personal vendetta.

In the end it was breathtakingly simple—at least it was after Hamish took charge. All we needed to do, he said, was establish beyond a doubt that the covenant had been drawn up because of a fear of miscegenation and the desire to keep bloodlines artificially pure to preserve the power balance among creatures.

Like most simple arguments, ours required hours of mind-numbing work. We all contributed our talents to the project. Phoebe, who was a gifted researcher, searched the archives at Sept-Tours for documents that touched on the covenant's inception and the Congregation's first meetings and debates. She called Rima, who was thrilled to be asked to do something other than filing, and had her search for supporting documents in the Congregation library on Isola della Stella.

These documents helped us piece together a coherent picture of what the founders of the Congregation had truly feared: that relationships between creatures would result in children who were neither daemon nor vampire nor witch but same terrifying combination, muddying the ancient, supposedly pure creature bloodlines. Such a concern was warranted given a twelfth-century understanding of biology and the value that was placed on inheritance and lineage at that time. And Philippe de Clermont had had the political acumen to suspect that the children of such unions would be powerful enough to rule the world if they so desired.

What was more difficult, not to mention more dangerous, was demonstrating that this fear had actually contributed to the decline of the otherworldly creatures. Centuries of inbreeding meant that vampires found it difficult to make new vampires, witches were less powerful, and daemons were increasingly prone to madness. To make this part of our case, the Bishop-Clairmonts needed to expose both the blood rage and the weavers in our family.

I wrote up a history of weavers using information from the Book of Life. I explained that the weavers' creative power was difficult to control and made them vulnerable to the animosity of their fellow witches. Over time witches grew complacent and had less use for new spells and charms. The old ones worked fine, and the weavers went from being treasured members of their communities to hunted outcasts. Sarah and I sat down together and drew up an account of my parents' lives in painful detail to drive this point home—my father's desperate attempts to hide his talents, Knox's efforts to discover them, and their terrible deaths.

Matthew and Ysabeau recorded a similarly difficult tale, one of madness and the destructive power of anger. Fernando and Gallowglass scoured Philippe's private papers for evidence of how he had kept his mate safe from extermination and their joint decision to protect Matthew in spite of his showing signs of the illness. Both Philippe and Ysabeau believed that careful upbringing and hard-won control would be a counterweight to whatever illness was present in his blood—a classic example of nurture over nature. And Matthew confessed that his own failures with Benjamin demonstrated just how dangerous blood rage could be if left to develop on its own.

Janet arrived at Les Revenants with the Gowdie grimoire and a copy of her great-grandmother Isobel's trial transcript. The trial records described her amorous relationship with the devil known as Nickie-Ben in great detail, including his nefarious bite. The grimoire proved that Isobel was a weaver of spells, as she proudly identified her unique magical creations and the prices that she'd demanded for sharing them with her sisters in the Highlands. Isobel also identified her lover as Benjamin Fox—Matthew's son. Benjamin had actually signed his name into the family record found in the front of the book.

"It's still not sufficient," Matthew worried, looking over the papers. "We still can't explain *why* weavers and blood-rage vampires like you and I can conceive children."

I could explain it. The Book of Life had shared that secret with me. But I didn't want to say anything until Miriam and Chris delivered the scientific evidence.

I was beginning to think I would have to make our case to the Congregation without their help when a car pulled into the courtyard.

Matthew frowned. "Who could that be?" he asked, putting down his pen and going to the window. "Miriam and Chris are here. Something must be wrong at the Yale lab."

Once the pair were inside and Matthew had received assurances that the research team he'd left in New Haven was thriving, Chris handed me a thick envelope.

"You were right," he said. "Nice work, Professor Bishop."

I hugged the packet to my chest, unspeakably relieved. Then I handed it to Matthew.

He tore into the envelope, his eyes racing over the lines of text and the black-and-white ideograms that accompanied them. He looked up, his lips parted in astonishment.

"I was surprised, too," Miriam admitted. "As long as we approached daemons, vampires, and witches as separate species distantly related to humans but distinct from one another, the truth was going to elude us."

"Then Diana told us the Book of Life was about what joined us together, not what separated us," Chris continued. "She asked us to compare her genome to both the daemon genome and the genomes of other witches."

"It was all there in the creature chromosome," Miriam said, "hiding in plain sight."

"I don't understand," Sarah said, looking blank.

"Diana was able to conceive Matthew's child because they both have daemon blood in them," Chris explained. "It's too early to know for sure, but our hypothesis is that weavers are descended from ancient witch-daemon unions. Blood-rage vampires like Matthew are produced when a vampire with the blood-rage gene creates another vampire from a human with some daemon DNA."

"We didn't find much of a daemonic presence in Ysabeau's genetic sample, or Marcus's either," Miriam added. "That explains why they never manifested the disease like Matthew or Benjamin did."

"But Stephen Proctor's mother was human," Sarah said. "She was a total pain in the ass—sorry, Diana—but definitely not daemonic."

"It doesn't have to be an immediate relationship," Miriam said. "There just has to be enough daemon DNA in the mix to trigger the weaver and blood-rage genes. It could have been one of Stephen's distant ancestors. As Chris said, these findings are pretty raw. We'll need decades to understand them completely."

"One more thing: Baby Margaret is a weaver, too." Chris pointed to the paper in Matthew's hands. "Page thirty. There's no question about it."

"I wonder if that's why Em was so adamant that Margaret shouldn't fall into Knox's hands," Sarah mused. "Maybe she discovered the truth somehow."

"This will shake the Congregation to its foundations," I said.

"It does more than that. The science makes the covenant completely irrelevant," Matthew said. "We're not separate species."

"So we're just different races?" I asked. "That makes our miscegenation argument even stronger."

"You need to catch up on your reading, Professor Bishop," Chris said with a smile. "Racial identity has no biological basis—at least none accepted by most scientists." Matthew had told me something like that long ago in Oxford.

"But that means—" I stopped.

"You aren't monsters after all. There are no such thing as daemons, vampires, and witches. Not biologically. You're just humans with a difference." Chris grinned. "Tell the Congregation to stick that in their pipe and smoke it."

I didn't use exactly those words in my cover statement to the enormous dossier that we sent to Venice in advance of the Congregation meeting, but what I did say amounted to the same thing.

The days of the covenant were done.

And if the Congregation wanted to continue to function, it was going to have to find something better to do with its time than police the boundaries between daemon, vampire, witch, and human.

When I went to the library the morning before my departure for Venice, however, I found that something had been left out of the file.

While we were doing our research, it had been impossible to ignore the sticky traces of Gerbert's fingers. He seemed to lurk in the margins of every document and every piece of evidence. It was hard to pin much on him directly, but the circumstantial evidence was clear: Gerbert of Aurillac had known for some time about the special abilities of weavers. He'd even held one in thrall: the witch Meridiana, who had cursed him as she died. And he had been feeding Benjamin Fuchs information about the de Clermonts for centuries. Philippe had found him out and confronted him about it just before he left on his final mission to Nazi Germany.

"Why didn't the information about Gerbert go to Venice?" I demanded of Matthew when at last I found him in the kitchen making my tea. Ysabeau was with him, playing with Philip and Becca.

"Because it's better if the rest of the Congregation doesn't know about Gerbert's involvement," Matthew said.

"Better for whom?" I asked sharply. "I want that creature exposed and punished."

"But the Congregation's punishments are so very unsatisfactory," Ysabeau said, her eyes gleaming. "Too much talking. Not enough pain. If it is punishment you want, let me do it." Her fingernails rapped against the counter, and I shivered.

"You've done enough, *Maman*," Matthew said, giving her a forbidding glance.

"Oh, that." Ysabeau waved her hand dismissively. "Gerbert has been a very naughty boy. But he will cooperate with Diana tomorrow because of it. You will find Gerbert of Aurillac entirely supportive, daughter."

I sat down on the kitchen stool with a thunk.

"While Ysabeau was being held in Gerbert's house, she and Nathaniel did a bit of snooping," Matthew explained. "They've been monitoring his e-mail and Internet usage ever since."

"Did you know that nothing you see on the Internet ever dies, Diana? It lives on and on, just like a vampire." Ysabeau looked genuinely fascinated by the comparison.

"And?" I still had no idea where this was leading.

"Gerbert isn't just fond of witches," Ysabeau said. "He's had a string of daemon lovers, too. One of them is still living on the Via della Scala in Rome, in a palatial and drafty set of apartments that he bought for her in the seventeenth century."

"Wait. Seventeenth century?" I tried to think straight, though it was difficult with Ysabeau looking like Tabitha after she'd devoured a mouse.

"Not only did Gerbert 'consort' with daemons, he turned one into a vampire. Such a thing is strictly forbidden—not by the covenant but by vampire law. For good reason, it turns out now that we know what triggers blood rage," Matthew said. "Not even Philippe knew about her—though he did know about some of Gerbert's other daemon lovers."

"And we're blackmailing him over it?" I said.

"'Blackmail' is such an ugly word," Ysabeau said. "I prefer to think that Gallowglass was exceptionally persuasive when he dropped by Les Anges Déchus last night to wish Gerbert safe journey."

"I don't want some covert de Clermont operation against Gerbert. I want the world to know what a snake he is," I said. "I want to beat him fair and square in open battle."

"Don't worry. The whole world will know. One day. One war at a time, *ma lionne.*" Matthew softened the commanding edge of his remark with a kiss and a cup of tea.

"Philippe preferred hunting to warfare." Ysabeau dropped her voice, as though she didn't want Becca and Philip to overhear her next words. "You see, when you hunt, you get to play with your prey before you destroy it. That is what we are doing with Gerbert."

"Oh." There was, admittedly, something appealing about that prospect.

"I felt sure you would understand. You are named after the goddess of the chase, after all. Happy hunting in Venice, my dear," Ysabeau said, patting me on the hand.

Sol in Taurus

The Bull governeth money, credit, debts, and gifts. While the sun is in Taurus, deal with unfinished business. Settle your affaires, lest they trouble you later. Should you receive an unexpected reward, invest it for the future.

—Anonymous English Commonplace Book, c. 1590,
Gonçalves Manuscript 4890, f. 7ʳ

Venice looked very different to my eyes in May than it had in January, and not solely because the sky was blue and the lagoon tranquil.

When Matthew had been in Benjamin's clutches, the city felt cold and unwelcoming. It was a place I wanted to leave as quickly as possible. When I did, I never expected to return.

But the goddess's justice would not be complete until the covenant was overturned.

And so I found myself back at Ca' Chiaromonte, sitting on a bench in the back garden rather than a bench overlooking the Grand Canal, waiting once more for the Congregation's meeting to begin.

This time Janet Gowdie waited with me. Together we went over our case one last time, imagining what arguments would be made against it while Matthew's precious pet turtles slipped and slid across the gravel paths in pursuit of a mosquito snack.

"Time to go," Marcus announced just before the bells began to ring four o'clock. He and Fernando would accompany us to Isola della Stella. Janet and I had tried to assure the rest of the family that we would be fine on our own, but Matthew wouldn't hear of it.

The Congregation's membership was the same as it had been at the January meeting. Agatha, Tatiana, and Osamu gave me encouraging smiles, though the reception that I received from Sidonie von Borcke and the vampires was decidedly frosty. Satu slipped into the cloister at the last moment as if she hoped not to be noticed. Gone was the self-assured witch who had kidnapped me from the garden at Sept-Tours. Sidonie's appraising stare suggested that Satu's transformation had not gone unnoticed, and I suspected that a change in the witches' representatives would soon be made.

I strolled across the cloister to join the two vampires.

"Domenico. Gerbert," I said, nodding at each in turn.

"Witch," Gerbert sneered.

"And a de Clermont, too." I angled my body so that my lips were close to Gerbert's ear. "Don't get too complacent, Gerbert. The goddess may have saved you for last, but make no mistake: Your day of judgment is coming." I drew away and was gratified to see a spark of fear in his eyes.

When I slid the de Clermont key in the meeting chamber lock, I was overcome by a sense of déjà vu. The doors swung open and the uncanny feeling increased. My eyes locked on the the ouroboros—the tenth knot— carved onto the back of the de Clermont seat and the silver and gold threads in the room snapped with power.

All witches are taught to believe in signs. Happily, the meaning of this one was clear without any need for further magic or complicated interpretation: *This is your seat. Here is where you belong.*

"I call this meeting to order," I said, rapping on the table once I'd reached my assigned place.

My left finger bore a thick ribbon of violet. The goddess's arrow had disappeared after I'd used it to kill Benjamin, but the vivid purple mark— the color of justice—remained.

I studied the room—the wide table, the records of my people and my children's ancestors, the nine creatures gathered to make a decision that would change the lives of thousands like them all around the world. High above I felt the spirits of those who had come before, their glances freezing and nudging and tingling.

"Give us justice," they said with one voice, *"and remember our names."*

"We won," I reported to the members of the de Clermont and Bishop-Clairmont families who had assembled in the salon to greet us when we returned from Venice. "The covenant has been repealed."

There were cheers, and hugs, and congratulations. Baldwin raised his wineglass in my direction, in a less effusive demonstration of approval.

My eyes sought out Matthew.

"No surprise," he said. The silence that followed was heavy with words that, though unspoken, I heard nonetheless. He bent to pick up his daughter. "See, Rebecca? Your mother fixed everything once again."

Becca had discovered the pure pleasure of chewing on her own fingers. I was very glad the vampire equivalent of milk teeth had not come in yet. Matthew removed her hand from her mouth and waved it in my direction, distracting his daughter from the tantrum she was planning. *"Bonjour, Maman."*

Jack was bouncing Philip on his knee. The baby looked both intrigued and concerned. "Nice work, Mum."

"I had plenty of help." My throat thickened as I looked not only at Jack and Philip but at Sarah and Agatha, whose heads were bent close together as they gossiped about the Congregation meeting, Fernando, who was amusing Sophie and Nathaniel with tales of Gerbert's stiff demeanor and Domenico's fury, and Phoebe and Marcus, who were enjoying a lingering reunion kiss. Baldwin stood with Matthew and Becca. I approached them.

"This belongs to you, brother." The de Clermont key rested heavy in the palm of my outstretched hand.

"Keep it." Baldwin closed my fingers around the cool metal.

The conversation in the salon died away.

"What did you say?" I whispered.

"I told you to keep it," Baldwin repeated.

"You can't mean—"

"But I do. Everyone in the de Clermont family has a job. You know that." Baldwin's golden-brown eyes gleamed. "As of today, overseeing the Congregation is yours."

"I can't. I'm a professor!" I protested.

"Set the Congregation's meeting schedule around your classes. As long as you answer your e-mail," Baldwin said with mock severity, "you should have no problem juggling your responsibilities. I've neglected the family's affairs long enough. Besides, I'm a warrior, not a politician."

I looked to Matthew in mute appeal, but he had no intention of rescuing me from this particular plight. His expression was filled with pride, not protectiveness.

"What about your sisters?" I said, my mind racing. "Surely Verin will object."

"It was Verin's suggestion," Baldwin said. "And after all, you are my sister, too."

"That settles it, then. Diana will serve on the Congregation until she tires of the job." Ysabeau kissed me on one cheek, then the other. "Just think of how much it will upset Gerbert when he discovers what Baldwin has done."

Still feeling dazed, I slid the key back into my pocket.

"It has turned into a beautiful day," Ysabeau said, looking out into the spring sunlight. "Let us take a walk in the garden before dinner. Alain and Marthe have prepared a feast—without Fernando's help. Marthe is in an extremely good mood because of it."

Laughter and chatter followed our family out the door. Matthew handed Becca off to Sarah.

"Don't be long, you two," Sarah said.

Once we were alone, Matthew kissed me with a sharp hunger that gradually became something deeper and less desperate. It was a reminder that his blood rage was still not fully in check and my being away had taken a toll.

"Was everything all right in Venice, *mon coeur*?" he inquired when he had regained his equilibrium.

"I'll tell you all about it later," I said. "Though I should warn you: Gerbert is up to no good. He tried to thwart me at every turn."

"What did you expect?" Matthew left my side to join the rest of the family. "Don't worry about Gerbert. We'll figure out what game he's playing, never fear."

Something unexpected caught my eye. I stopped in my tracks.

"Diana?" Matthew looked back at me and frowned. "Are you coming?"

"In a minute," I promised.

He regarded me strangely but stepped outside.

I knew you would be the first to see me. Philippe's voice was a whisper of sound, and I could still see Ysabeau's horrid furniture through him. None of that mattered. He was perfect—whole, smiling, his eyes sparkling with amusement and affection.

"Why me?" I asked.

You have the Book of Life now. You no longer need my help. Philippe's gaze met mine.

"The covenant—" I started.

I heard. I hear most things. Philippe's grin widened. *I am proud that it was one of my children that destroyed it. You have done well.*

"Is seeing you my reward?" I said, fighting back the tears.

One of them, Philippe said. *In time you will have the others.*

"Emily." The moment I said her name, Philippe's form began to fade. "No! Don't go. I won't ask questions. Just tell her I love her."

She knows that. So does your mother. Philippe winked. *I am utterly surrounded by witches. Do not tell Ysabeau. She would not like it.*

I laughed.

And there is my *reward for years of good behavior. Now, I want no more tears, do you understand?* His finger rose. *I am heartily sick of them.*

"What do you want instead?" I wiped at my eyes.

More laughter. More dancing. His expression was mischievous. *And more grandchildren.*

"I had to ask," I said with another laugh.

But the future will not be all laughter, I fear. Philippe's expression sobered. *Your work is not done, daughter. The goddess asked me to give this back to you.* He held out the same gold-and-silver arrow that I had shot into Benjamin's heart.

"I don't want it." I backed away, my hand raised to ward off this unwanted gift.

I didn't want it either, and yet someone must see that justice is done. His arm extended farther.

"Diana?" Matthew called from outside.

I would not be hearing my husband's voice if not for the goddess's arrow.

"Coming!" I called back.

Philippe's eyes filled with sympathy and understanding. I touched the golden point hesitantly. The moment my flesh made contact with it, the arrow vanished and I felt its heavy weight at my back once more.

From the first moment we met, I knew you were the one, Philippe said. His words were a strange echo of what Timothy Weston had told me at the Bodleian last year, and again at his house.

With a final grin, his ghost began to dissipate.

"Wait!" I cried. "The one what?"

The one who could bear my burdens and not break, Philippe's voice whispered in my ear. I felt a subtle press of lips on my cheek. *You will not carry them alone. Remember that, daughter.*

I bit back a sob at his departure.

"Diana?" Matthew called again, this time from the doorway. "What's happened? You look like you've seen a ghost."

I had, but this was not the time to tell Matthew about it. I felt like weeping, but Philippe wanted joy, not sorrow.

"Dance with me," I said, before a single tear could fall.

Matthew folded me into his arms. His feet moved across the floor, sweeping us out of the salon and into the great hall. He asked no questions, even though the answers were in my eyes.

I trod on his toe. "Sorry."

"You're trying to lead again," he murmured. He pressed a kiss to my lips, then whirled me around. "At the moment your job is to follow."

"I forgot," I said with a laugh.

"I'll have to remind you more often, then." Matthew swung me tight to his body. His kiss was rough enough to be a warning and sweet enough to be a promise.

Philippe was right, I thought as we walked out into the garden.

Whether leading or following, I would never be alone in a world that had Matthew in it.

Sol in Gemini

The signe of Gemini dealeth with the partnership between a husband and wife, and all matters that dependeth likewise upon faith. A man born in this sign hath a good and honest heart and a fine wit that will lead him to learn many things. He will be quick to anger, but soon to reconcile. He is bold of speech even before the prince. He is a great dissimulator, a spreader abroad of clever fantasies and lies. He shall be much entangled with troubles by reason of his wife, but he shall prevail against their enemies.

—Anonymous English Commonplace Book, c. 1590,
Gonçalves Manuscript 4890, f. 8ʳ

I'm sorry to disturb you, Professor Bishop."

I looked up from my manuscript. The Royal Society's reading room was flooded with summer sunshine. It raked through the tall, multipaned windows and spilled across the generous reading surfaces.

"One of the fellows asked me to give this to you." The librarian handed me an envelope with the Royal Society's insignia on it. Someone had written my name across the front in a dark, distinctive scrawl. I nodded in thanks.

Philippe's ancient silver coin—the one he sent to make sure that someone returned home or obeyed his commands—was inside. I'd found a new use for it, one that was helping Matthew manage his blood rage while I returned to a more active life. My husband's condition was steadily improving after his ordeal with Benjamin but his mood was still volatile and his anger quick to catch. A full recovery would take time. If Matthew felt his need for me rising to dangerous levels, all he had to do was send me this coin, and I would join him right away.

I returned the bound manuscripts I'd been consulting to the attendant on the desk and thanked him for their help. It was the end of my first full week back in the archives—a trial run to see how my magic responded to repeated contact with so many ancient texts and brilliant, though dead, intellects. Matthew was not the only one struggling for control, and I'd had a few tricky moments when it seemed it might be impossible for me to return to the work I loved, but each additional day made that goal more achievable.

Since facing the Congregation in April, I had come to understand myself as a complicated weaving and not just a walking palimpsest. My body was a tapestry of witch, daemon, and vampire. Some of the threads that made me were pure power, as symbolized by Corra's shadowy form. Some were drawn from the skill that my weaver's cords represented. The rest were spun from the knowledge contained in the Book of Life. Every knotted strand gave me the strength to use the goddess's arrow for justice rather than the pursuit of vengeance or power.

Matthew was waiting for me in the foyer when I descended the grand staircase from the library to the main floor. His gaze cooled my skin and heated my blood, just as it always had. I dropped the coin into his waiting palm.

"All right, *mon coeur?*" he asked after kissing me in greeting.

"Perfectly all right." I tugged on the lapel of his black jacket, a small sign of possessiveness. Matthew had dressed the part of the distinguished professor today with his steel gray trousers, crisp white shirt, and fine wool jacket. I'd picked out his tie. Hamish had given it to him this past Christmas, and the green-and-gray Liberty print picked up the changeable colors of his eyes. "How did it go?"

"Interesting discussion. Chris was brilliant, of course," Matthew said, modestly giving my friend center stage.

Chris, Matthew, Miriam, and Marcus had been presenting research findings that expanded the limits of what was considered "human." They showed how the evolution of *Homo sapiens* included DNA from other creatures, like Neanderthals, previously thought to have been a different species. Matthew had been sitting on most of the evidence for years. Chris said Matthew was as bad as Isaac Newton when it came to sharing his research with others.

"Marcus and Miriam performed their usual charmer-and-curmudgeon routine," Matthew said, releasing me at last.

"And what was the fellows' reaction to this bit of news?" I unpinned Matthew's name tag and slipped it into his pocket. PROFESSOR MATTHEW CLAIRMONT, it read, FRS, ALL SOULS (OXON), YALE UNIVERSITY (USA). Matthew had accepted a one-year visiting research appointment in Chris's lab. They'd received a huge grant to study noncoding DNA. It would lay the groundwork for the revelations they would one day make about other hominid creatures who were not extinct like the Neanderthals but were hiding in plain sight among humans. In the fall we would be off to New Haven again.

"They were surprised," Matthew said. "Once they heard Chris's paper, however, their surprise turned to envy. He really was impressive."

"Where is Chris now?" I said, looking over my shoulder for my friend as Matthew steered me toward the exit.

"He and Miriam left for Pickering Place," Matthew said. "Marcus wanted to collect Phoebe before they all go to some oyster bar near Trafalgar Square."

"Do you want to join them?" I asked.

"No." Matthew's hand settled on my waist. "I'm taking you out to dinner, remember?"

Leonard was waiting for us at the curb. "Afternoon, *sieur*. Madame."

"'Professor Clairmont' will do, Leonard," Matthew said mildly as he handed me into the back of the car.

"Righty-ho," Leonard said with a cheerful grin. "Clairmont House?"

"Please," Matthew said, getting into the car with me.

It was a beautiful June day, and it probably would have taken us less time to walk from the Mall to Mayfair than it did to drive, but Matthew insisted we take the car for safety's sake. We had seen no evidence that any of Benjamin's children had survived the battle in Chelm, nor had Gerbert or Domenico given us reason for concern since their stinging defeat in Venice, but Matthew didn't want to take chances.

"Hello, Marthe!" I called into the house as we came in the door. "How is everything?"

"*Bien*," she said. "*Milord* Philip and *Milady* Rebecca are just waking from their nap."

"I asked Linda Crosby to come over a bit later and lend a hand," Matthew said.

"Already here!" Linda followed us through the door, carrying not one but two Marks & Spencer bags. She handed one to Marthe. "I've brought the next book in the series about that lovely detective and her beau— Gemma and Duncan. And here's the knitting pattern I told you about."

Linda and Marthe had become fast friends, in large part because they had nearly identical interests in murder mysteries, needlecraft, cooking, gardening, and gossip. The two of them had made a compelling and utterly self-serving case that the children should always be attended to by family members or, failing that, both a vampire and a witch working as babysitters. Linda argued that this was a wise precaution because we didn't yet understand the babies' talents and tendencies—though Rebecca's preference for blood and inability to sleep suggested she was more vampire than witch, just as Philip seemed more witch than vampire given the stuffed elephant I sometimes saw swooping over his cradle.

"We can still stay home tonight," I suggested. Matthew's plans involved an evening gown, a tuxedo, and the goddess only knew what else.

"No." Matthew was still overly fond of the word. "I am taking my wife out to dinner." His tone indicated this was no longer a topic for discussion.

Jack pelted down the stairs. "Hi, Mum! I put your mail upstairs. Dad's too. Gotta run. Dinner with Father H tonight."

"Be back by breakfast, please," Matthew said as Jack shot through the open door.

"No worries, Dad. After dinner, I'll be out with Ransome," Jack said as the door banged closed behind him. The New Orleans branch of the Bishop-Clairmont clan had arrived in London two days ago to take in the sights and visit with Marcus.

"Knowing that he's out with Ransome does not alleviate my concerns." Matthew sighed. "I'm going to see the children and get dressed. Are you coming?"

"I'll be right behind you. I just want to stick my head in the ballroom first and see how the caterers are getting along with the preparations for your birthday party."

Matthew groaned.

"Stop being such an old grouch," I said.

Together Matthew and I climbed the stairs. The second floor, which was usually cold and silent, hummed with activity. Matthew followed me to the tall, wide doors. Caterers had set up tables all around the edges of the room, leaving a large space for dancing. In the corner, musicians were practicing tunes for tomorrow night.

"I was born in November, not June," Matthew muttered, his frown deepening. "On All Souls Day. And why did we have to invite so many people?"

"You can grumble and nitpick all you want. It won't change the fact that tomorrow is the anniversary of the day you were reborn a vampire and your family wanted to celebrate it with you." I examined one of the floral arrangements. Matthew had picked the odd selection of plants, which included willow branches and honeysuckle, as well as the wide selection of music from different eras that the band was expected to play during the dancing. "If you don't want so many guests, you should think twice before you make any more children."

"But I like making children with you." Matthew's hand slid around my hip until it came to rest on my abdomen.

"Then you can expect an annual repeat of this event," I said, giving him a kiss. "And more tables with each passing year."

"Speaking of children," Matthew said, cocking his head and listening to some sound inaudible to a warmblood, "your daughter is hungry."

"*Your* daughter is *always* hungry," I said, putting a gentle palm to his cheek.

Matthew's former bedroom had been converted to a nursery and was now the twins' special kingdom—complete with a zoo full of stuffed animals, enough equipment to outfit a baby army, and two tyrants to rule over it.

Philip turned his head to the door when we entered, his look triumphant as he stood and gripped the side of his cradle. He had been peering down into his sister's bed. Rebecca had hauled herself to a seated position and was staring at Philip with interest, as if trying to figure out how he'd managed to grow so quickly.

"Good God. He's standing." Matthew sounded stunned. "But he's not even seven months old."

I glanced at the baby's strong arms and legs and wondered why his father was surprised.

"What have you been up to?" I said, pulling Philip from the cradle and giving him a hug.

A stream of unintelligible sounds came from the baby's mouth, and the letters under my skin surfaced to lend Philip assistance as he answered my question.

"Really? You've had a very lively day, then," I said, handing him to Matthew.

"I believe you are going to be as much of a handful as your namesake," Matthew said fondly, his finger caught in Philip's fierce grip.

We got the children changed and fed, talking more about what I'd discovered in Robert Boyle's papers that day and what new insights the presentations at the Royal Society had afforded Matthew into the problems of understanding the creature genomes.

"Give me a minute. I need to check my e-mail." I received more of it than ever now that Baldwin had appointed me the official de Clermont representative so that he could devote more time to making money and bullying his family.

"Hasn't the Congregation bothered you enough this week?" Matthew asked, his grouchiness returning. I'd spent too many evenings working on policy statements about equality and openness and trying to untangle convoluted daemon logic.

"There is no end in sight, I'm afraid," I said, taking Philip with me into the Chinese Room, which was now my home office. I switched on my computer and held him on my knee while I scrolled through the messages.

"There's a picture from Sarah and Agatha," I called out. The two women were on a beach somewhere in Australia. "Come and see."

"They look happy," Matthew said, looking over my shoulder with Rebecca in his arms. Rebecca made sounds of delight at the sight of her grandmother.

"It's hard to believe it's been more than a year since Em's death," I said. "It's good to see Sarah smiling again."

"Any news from Gallowglass?" Matthew asked. Gallowglass had left for parts unknown and hadn't responded to our invitation to Matthew's party.

"Not so far," I said. "Maybe Fernando knows where he is." I would ask him tomorrow.

"And what does Baldwin allow?" Matthew said, looking at the list of senders and seeing his brother's name.

"He arrives tomorrow." I was pleased that Baldwin was going to be there to wish Matthew well on his birthday. It lent additional weight to the occasion and would quiet any false rumors that Baldwin didn't fully support his brother or the new Bishop-Clairmont scion. "Verin and Ernst will be with him. And I should warn you: Freyja is coming, too."

I hadn't yet met Matthew's middle sister. I was, however, looking forward to it after Janet Gowdie regaled me with tales of her past exploits.

"Christ, not Freyja, too." Matthew groaned. "I need a drink. Do you want anything?"

"I'll have some wine," I said absently, continuing to scroll down through the list of messages from Baldwin, Rima Jaén in Venice, other members of the Congregation, and my department chair at Yale. I was busier than I'd ever been. Happier, too.

When I joined Matthew in his study, he was not fixing our drinks. Instead he was standing in front of the fireplace, Rebecca balanced on his hip, staring up at the wall above the mantel with a curious expression on his face. Following his stare, I could see why.

The portrait of Ysabeau and Philippe that usually hung there was gone. A small tag was pinned to the wall. SIR JOSHUA REYNOLDS'S PORTRAIT OF AN UNKNOWN MARRIED COUPLE TEMPORARILY REMOVED FOR THE EXHIBITION *SIR JOSHUA REYNOLDS AND HIS WORLD* AT THE ROYAL GREENWICH PICTURE GALLERY.

"Phoebe Taylor strikes again," I murmured. She was not yet a vampire but was already well known in vampire circles for her ability to identify the art in their possession that would provide considerable tax relief should they be willing to give the works to the nation. Baldwin adored her.

But the sudden disappearance of his parents was not the real reason Matthew was transfixed.

In place of the Reynolds was another canvas: a portrait of Matthew and me. It was clearly Jack's work, with his trademark combination of seventeenth-century attention to detail and modern sensitivity to color and line. This was confirmed by the small card propped on the mantelpiece with *"Happy birthday, Dad"* scrawled on it.

"I thought he was painting your portrait. It was supposed to be a surprise," I said, thinking of our son's whispered requests that I occupy Matthew's attention while he sketched.

"Jack told me he was painting *your* portrait," Matthew said.

Instead Jack had painted the two of us together, in the formal drawing room by one of the house's grand windows. I was sitting in an Elizabethan chair, a relic from our house in Blackfriars. Matthew stood behind me, his eyes clear and bright as they looked at the viewer. My eyes met the viewer's too, touched by an otherworldliness that suggested I was not an ordinary human.

Matthew reached over my shoulder to clasp my raised left hand, our fingers woven tight. My head was angled slightly toward him, and his was angled slightly down, as though we had been interrupted in midconversation.

The pose exposed my left wrist and the ouroboros that circled my pulse. It sent a message of strength and solidarity, this symbol of the Bishop-Clairmonts. Our family had begun with the surprising love that developed between Matthew and me. It grew because our bond was strong enough to withstand the hatred and fear of others. And it would endure because we had discovered, like the witches so many centuries ago, that a willingness to change was the secret of survival.

More than that, the ouroboros symbolized our partnership. Matthew and I were an alchemical marriage of vampire and witch, death and life, sun and moon. That combination of opposites created something finer and more precious than either of us could ever have been separately.

We were the tenth knot.

Unbreakable.

Without beginning or end.

Acknowledgments

My heartfelt thanks . . .

. . . to my gentle readers for their feedback: Fran, Jill, Karen, Lisa, and Olive.

. . . to Wolf Gruner, Steve Kay, Jake Soll, and Susanna Wang, all of whom were generous with their expertise and kind with their criticisms.

. . . to Lucy Marks, who gathered expert opinions on how much a sheet of vellum might weigh.

. . . to Hedgebrook, for their radical (and much needed) hospitality when I needed it most.

. . . to Sam Stoloff and Rich Green, for championing the All Souls Trilogy from beginning to end.

. . . to Carole DeSanti and the rest of the All Souls team at Viking and Penguin for supporting this book, and the previous two, during every step of the publication process.

. . . to the foreign publishers who brought the story of Diana and Matthew to readers around the world.

. . . to Lisa Halttunen for editing and preparing the manuscript for the publisher.

. . . to my assistants, Jill Hough and Emma Divine, for making my life possible.

. . . to my friends for their steadfastness.

. . . to my family for making life worth living: my parents, Olive and Jack, Karen, John, Lexie, Jake, Lisa.

. . . to my readers for letting the Bishops and de Clermonts into your hearts and lives.